A *Pocket Guide* to the popular **Lord of the Rings movies**, Hollywood's live action version of J.R.R. Tolkien's 1954-55 book *The Lord of the Rings*, released in 2001, 2002 and 2003.

This *Pocket Guide* includes an account of the *Lord of the Rings* productions, with chapters on the cast, crew, music, visual effects, critical reception, and a scene-by-scene analysis of the three movies.

Burger King toy figures from the Lord of the Rings movies.

© New Line Productions, Inc. The Lord of the Rings, and the names of the characters, events, items and places therein, are trademarks of The Saul Zaentz Company d/b/a Tolkien Enterprises under license to New Line Productions, Inc. All Rights Reserved.

THE LORD OF THE RINGS MOVIES

POCKET GUIDE

JEREMY MARK ROBINSON

CRESCENT MOON

Crescent Moon Publishing
P.O. Box 393
Maidstone
Kent
ME14 5XU, U.K.

First published 2011.
© Jeremy Mark Robinson 2011.

Printed and bound in the U.S.A.
Set in Helvetica Neue Condensed 9 on 11pt.
Designed by Radiance Graphics.

The right of Jeremy Mark Robinson to be identified as the author of this book has been asserted generally in accordance with sections 77 and 78 of the Copyright, Designs and Patents Act 1988.

All rights reserved. No part of this book may be reprinted or reproduced, stored in a retrieval system, or transmitted, in any form or by any means, electronic, mechanical, photocopying, recording or otherwise, without permission from the publisher.

British Library Cataloguing in Publication data available for this title.

ISBN-13 9781861712790

CONTENTS

Acknowledgements 6
Abbreviations 7
Illustrations 9
Introduction 11

1 Adaptions of J.R.R. Tolkien's Works 13
2 Adapting *The Lord of the Rings* For the 2001-2003 Films 16
3 The Movie Studio and the Deal 35
4 Casting and Personnel 49
5 Peter Jackson 64
6 The Making of the *Lord of the Rings* Movies 66
7 The Look and Style of the *Lord of the Rings* Films 89
8 Visual Effects 100
9 Music 107
10 Differences Between the Book and the Films 111
11 Selling the 2001-2003 *Lord of the Rings* Movies 147
12 Recipe For a Sword and Sorcery Movie 162
13 *The Fellowship of the Ring* Film (2001) 166
14 *The Fellowship of the Ring,* Scene By Scene 176
15 The Film of *The Two Towers* (2002) 242
16 *The Two Towers*, Scene By Scene 257
17 *The Return of the King* Film (2003) 333
18 *The Return of the King,* Scene By Scene 345
19 Further Criticisms of the *Lord of the Rings* Movies 419

Best and Worst Moments in the *Lord of the Rings* Movies 424
Availability 425
Bibliography 426
Filmography 429

ACKNOWLEDGEMENTS

To the authors and publishers quoted, including Allen & Unwin, Unwin Hyman, HarperCollins, Ballantine Books, Macmillan, Virgin, Tolkien Society, Mitchell Beazley, Pavilion, Wallflower Press, Courage Books, Junction Books, Abacus, and Oxford University Press.

Picture credits:
New Line Productions, Inc. The Lord of the Rings, and the names of the characters, events, items and places therein, are trademarks of The Saul Zaentz Company d/b/a Tolkien Enterprises under license to New Line Productions, Inc.

Getty Images. Hulton Archive. X-Box.

Every effort has been made to contact copyright owners of the illustrations. No copyright infringement is intended. We welcome enquiries about any copyright issues for future editions of this book.

ABBREVIATIONS

FR	*The Fellowship of the Ring*
HME	*The History of Middle-earth*
L	*The Letters of J.R.R. Tolkien*
LR	*The Lord of the Rings*
MC	*The Monster and the Critics and Other Essays*
RK	*The Return of the King*
S	*The Silmarllion*
TL	*Tree and Leaf*
TT	*The Two Towers*
Sib	*Peter Jackson* by Brian Sibley

FA	First Age
SA	Second Age
TA	Third Age

Some of the people behind the Lord of the Rings movies: the studio (top left); the producer (top right); the star (above left); writers and director (above right); and some cast and crew photos (right and below).

© New Line Productions, Inc. The Lord of the Rings, and the names of the characters, events, items and places therein, are trademarks of The Saul Zaentz Company d/b/a Tolkien Enterprises under license to New Line Productions, Inc.

It's fairy tale time in Hollywood: elves, hobbits, dwarves, wizards, kings, princesses, warriors, wraiths, Satan-size demons and magic rings.

© New Line Productions, Inc. The Lord of the Rings, and the names of the characters, events, items and places therein, are trademarks of The Saul Zaentz Company d/b/a Tolkien Enterprises under license to New Line Productions, Inc.

INTRODUCTION
♠

For me, J.R.R. Tolkien is an astonishing writer, but not the most brilliant as a stylist (Rainer Maria Rilke, Francesco Petrarch and D.H. Lawrence beat him there), not the greatest writer of letters and diaries (John Cowper Powys, André Gide and Henry Miller trump him there), or the creator of the most intriguing and compelling characters (William Shakespeare and Thomas Hardy effortlessly top him there), or the most accomplished creator of battles and action (Homer and Mary Renault surpass him there), or a writer with the most profound things to say about being alive (Sir Thomas Browne and Chuang-tzu outshine Tolkien there), or the most fascinating writer in terms of his personal life (Arthur Rimbaud and Lord Byron beat him in that respect). And most any poet is a more enchanting poet than Tolkien.

Tolkien's Middle-earth writings are among the high watermarks in fantasy and heroic romance, yes, but for me the *Earthsea* books of Ursula Le Guin, for instance, are more profound in terms of philosophical and spiritual statements, and far better written as prose and poetry.

But there is something compelling about John Ronald Reuel Tolkien and his fictions – principally, his three most well-known works, *The Hobbit* (1937), *The Lord of the Rings* (1954-55) and *The Silmarillion* (1977), which this study concentrates on much more than his lesser-known books (such as *Leaf By Niggle*, or *The Adventures of Tom Bombadil*). One thing is certain, Tolkien's books have become a cultural phenomenon in the contemporary era, with the 2001-2003 Hollywood film versions of *The Lord of the Rings* further enhancing Tolkien's global reach.

Philip Toynbee declared, in 1961, that Tolkien's 'childish books had passed into a merciful oblivion', a wonderful statement, just a teeeeeensy bit inaccurate. In 1997, *The Lord of the Rings* was voted the top book of the 20th century by readers in a British bookstore's poll (Waterstone's bookstore). 104 out of 105 stores and 25,000 readers put *The Lord of the Rings* at the top (*1984* by George Orwell was second).

The results of the poll angered many lit'ry critics in Blighty. Howard Jacobson, Mark Lawson, Bob Inglis, Germaine Greer and Susan Jeffreys were among those irritated by *Lord of the Rings'* success among readers. The *Daily Telegraph* readers' poll came up with the same results. The Folio Society also ran a poll (of 50,000 members), and Middle-earth was top again (*Pride and Prejudice* was second and *David Copperfield* was third).

Around 100 million copies of *The Lord of the Rings* had been sold by the end of the twentieth century, and 60 million copies of *The Hobbit,* with sales of around 3 million per year of the two books combined. Readers just love reading Tolkien's books. It's that simple. You can't force people to buy books or go see movies; there's isn't a magic formula (or ruling ring) to hypnotize readers and consumers (if there was, it'd be worth billions). And the Tolkien phenomenon began with *readers*. Back in 1937, 1954 and 1955, the publishers Allen & Unwin did their bit, of course, with reviews, blurbs, advertizing and so on, promoting *The Hobbit* and *The Lord of the Rings,* but it was readers who first started the phenomenon that has become truly global.

This is a much shortened edition of my 2008 book on Tolkien. That book was long (812) and dense: this *Pocket Guide* aims to deliver a more concise account of the *Lord of the Rings* productions. For a pocket guide to J.R.R. Tolkien and his works, please see the companion volume.

Some of the spelling I use is deliberately eccentric. Amounts in British pounds (£) have been converted to U.S. dollars ($) at the rate of 1:1.6. The book is intended to be dipped into, rather than read straight through.

NOTES: INTRODUCTION

1. In A. Becker, 45.
2. And also correcting the text.

Jeremy Mark Robinson
Kent, England, 2010

CHAPTER 1

ADAPTIONS OF
J.R.R. TOLKIEN'S WORKS

ADAPTING TOLKIEN

The decision to sell the film rights to *The Lord of the Rings* came down to 'cash or kudos', as John Ronald Reuel Tolkien succinctly put it. Commentators have noted that Tolkien sold the film rights for a small amount, but when he sold the rights, in 1967, maybe he thought he wouldn't be around to see the results anyway (he was 75). The deal meant that Tolkien's estate wouldn't have any influence over any adaptions of *The Lord of the Rings*. Whoever held the rights (United Artists, Saul Zaentz) had them in perpetuity.

The Tolkien estate (and Christopher Tolkien in particular) was still a key influence on how Tolkien's work was perceived in later years, following Tolkien's death in 1973. Adaptors of Tolkien's fiction wouldn't want to alienate the Tolkien estate, because some Tolkien fans still regarded the family and estate as the true keepers of the flame.

The Tolkien estate, or at least members of Tolkien's family, tended to be opposed to the idea of any film adaption, the Hollywood adaption included. As Michael White commented, 'the Tolkien family are certain to dislike the [2001] film more than anyone' (247). But they will benefit from it – and not only financially. Tolkien's books will be read by millions more readers because of the success of the early 2000s films.

Tolkien had welcomed the idea of an animated movie of *The Lord of the Rings* at one time – at least that 'vulgarization' was preferable in comparison to the 'sillification' of the BBC radio version of 1957.

The audience of the *Lord of the Rings* films read books, and had read *The Lord of the Rings*. Nearly all of the negative responses to any *Lord of the Rings* films for Tolkien fans derive from comparisons with the book.

Tolkien knew all about translating material – he spent quite a bit of his academic career doing just that, rendering work from Anglo-Saxon or Old German into English. And in some of his Middle-earth writings, he went the other way, translating from modern English into Old English. But translating fiction into another medium was a different matter. Tolkien asserted that the canons of narrative art in any medium cannot be wholly different; the failure of poor films is often precisely in exaggeration, and in the intrusion of unwarranted matter owing to not perceiving where the core of the original lies.

Being 'faithful' to J.R.R. Tolkien's books is valued very highly by some Tolkien fans. They can be very protective of Tolkien's fiction. You mess with Tolkien at your peril. Most adaptions in film, TV and radio have taken that on board, and have tried, at least, to be 'faithful', even if they've often failed or veered away from that goal. Ralph Bakshi remarked that 'there isn't a page of *The Rings* that you wouldn't want to re-read a hundred times'. The reverence that Tolkien's stories generates has even increased since the professor's death. Everyone, it seems, has a view on what constitutes a decent, 'faithful' adaption of Tolkien.

It is possible to make a film with 22 principal characters, but it's very difficult. A film that shows how it could be done is the classy Country and Western backstage political comedy drama *Nashville* (1975), which follows 24 protagonists. To make a film with such a large cast work successfully begins and ends, really, not with the director, the producer, the crew or even the cast, but with the script and the writers.

Commercial filmmakers never have the luxury that Tolkien had when he was writing *The Lord of the Rings:* if he fancied it, Tolkien would start rewriting the book from the beginning. Hollywood calls that a 'page one' rewrite. That can be done if you're writing spec scripts, or don't have studios, executives and deadlines bearing down upon you. But with contracts agreed and signed and pre-production kicking in, you can't keep scrapping the script and rewriting it from the beginning. Director Peter Jackson said a totally faithful adaption of *Rings* 'just couldn't have been made and wouldn't have worked because it would have been slow and unstructured and very pedantic' (Sib, 411).

Tolkien's remarks in the essay "On Fairy-stories" about visual art and visual representations of fairy tales (including cinema) bears directly on the film adaptions of Tolkien's work:

> However good in themselves, illustrations do little good to fairy-stories. The radical distinction between all art (including drama) that offers a *visible* presentation and true literature is that it imposes one visible form. Literature works from mind to mind and is thus more progenitive. It is at once more universal and more poignantly particular. (MC, 159)

The reader, Tolkien suggested, offering a familiar argument of the differences between literature and visual art, imagines everything in literature subjectively as well as generally. When the text says 'bread', the reader imagines bread in general but also a 'peculiar personal embodiment in his imagination' (ibid.). But the film producer or visual artist has to show a particular piece of bread.

THE IDEAL TOLKIEN FILM

The ideal film of *The Lord of the Rings*, for me, would be made by a bunch of artists impossible to put together. The fights and battle scenes would be masterminded by Akira Kurosawa, whose *samurai* and historical films are truly, properly epic, as well as brilliantly conceived and executed (*The Seven Samurai, Kagemusha, Ran, Throne of Blood*). It would be tempting to opt for a great action director, like Paul Verhoeven, Anthony Mann, David Lean or Sam Peckinpah, but you might as well go for the best, and have Kurosawa.

For the big, visionary scenes in *The Lord of the Rings*, the recreation of a cinematic Middle-earth, I'd go for the New Zealand director Vincent Ward. As the extraordinary *The Navigator* showed, Ward can handle epic mediæval quests. And, in *What Dreams May Come*, a Dantean CG and vfx journey with extraordinary visuals.

To render a convincing archaic, pre-mediæval *mise-en-scène*, properly muddy, windy, shabby, rough and tough – as well as beautiful and sublime – it would be something out of the historical films of Pier Paolo Pasolini, Robert Bresson, Luis Buñuel or Ingmar Bergman (though none of these directors would be quite right for Tolkien's kind of story). Tolkien's grandson Adam (b. 1969) agrees with me here – in an interview he said something like the look of *The Seventh Seal* would be good for *The Lord of the Rings* (Adam Tolkien had found the Hollywood films too busy with CGI).

For the Shakespearean interchanges full of the clamour of war, in the later part of *The Lord of the Rings*, it would have to be Orson Welles (his Shakespeare films remain unsurpassed). For the elements of magic, myth and spirit, it would be obvious to try directors like John Boorman, or Terry Gilliam, but I don't think they'd quite carry it off (Gilliam's films, from 1997's *Fear and Loathing In Las Vegas* to the present, have been *very* disappointing, including his take on Tolkienesque territory in *The Brothers Grimm*).

CHAPTER 2

ADAPTING *THE LORD OF THE RINGS* FOR THE 2001-03 FILMS

'So much is lost', Galadriel says in the prologue of the 2001 movie *The Lord of the Rings: The Fellowship of the Ring*, 'so much is forgotten': these are the first words of Hollywood's live action version of *The Lord of the Rings*, almost as if they're reminding viewers of the costs of translating a book to the screen.

The 2001-2003 *Lord of the Rings* films didn't come out of nowhere, freshly minted. There's been a sizeable Tolkien franchise for decades, including action figures, posters, prints, illustrations, maps, jewellry, replica weaponry, costumes, toys, board games, wargaming, conferences, Ralph Bakshi's 1978 film, the 1980 TV *The Return of the King*, more TV adaptions (*The Hobbit* in 1977), various BBC radio adaptions of both *The Hobbit* and *The Lord of the Rings* (the first was in 1957, the second in 1981). There are probably more (other dramatizations, including plays, musicals). There have also been loads of references to *The Lord of the Rings* in popular culture: films (*Star Wars,*), heavy rock anthems (Led Zeppelin), hippydom, people dressing up, conferences, and some vicious parodies. And not forgetting the sword-and-sorcery fantasy flicks: *The Beastmaster* (1983), *Ladyhawke* (1985), *Willow* (1988), *Krull* (1983), *Conan the Barbarian* (1982), *Dragonslayer* (1981), *The Dark Crystal* (1983), *The Sword and the Sorcerer* (1982), and *Labyrinth* (1987).

Director Peter Jackson acknowledged that *The Lord of the Rings* was fabulous source material: 'we could never have come up with something as good as the raw material of those characters and this world'.[1] (There were times, though, when the filmmakers reckoned they'd improved on Tolk-ien's book).

The heart of the story of *The Lord of the Rings,* for Tolkien, was 'the journey of the Ringbearers' (L, 271), he wrote in a letter about the Morton Grady Zimmerman cartoon script of 1957. The 2001-03 films, for all their faults, do keep that part of the narrative in the foreground (although, in *The Return of the King*, there is a tendency to over-emphasize the Minas Tirith scenes – Faramir's force fighting at Osgiliath and his charge of the light brigade are expansions on the book, for example).

It's true that the problem of the ring does disappear from the story for long stretches, and Tolkien seems concerned with many other matters.

There's simply *so much* going on in *The Lord of the Rings,* that the ring sometimes gets lost in it. The writers of the 2001-03 adaption tried to find ways of reminding the audience about the ring – and about Sauron.

Because the 2001-03 films were remakes, they had previous adaptions of Tolkien's tome as guides on how *not* to adapt the book, on things to avoid, as well as which things worked. *The Hobbit* and *The Lord of the Rings* cartoons of 1977, 1978 and 1980 were very useful for the writers in reminding them of which aspects of the book work well on screen, and which aspects are harder to film. If someone's been there before it's handy to see how they coped with the adaption.

The adaptors of *The Lord of the Rings* could have consciously *avoided* seeing any previous attempts, but that's difficult, because not only are there film, TV, radio and theatrical versions of Tolkien's books, there are also forty-five years of illustrations and artwork. It would be impressive for a fan of fantasy art or movies not to have come across quite a few references to Tolkien's book or illustrations of characters from Middle-earth. (Besides, the writers knew the 1978 film version, the 1980 TV film and the 1981 radio adaption, and employed aspects of them in their take on Tolkien).

One wouldn't believe, without being told, that the *Lord of the Rings* films have been co-written by two women (Fran Walsh and Philippa Boyens). The attempts at 'feminizing' *The Lord of the Rings* for a contemporary audience have included: (1) Aragorn as a caring, sharing New Man hero (and casting an attractive actor for the romantic lead); (2) bringing Arwen from the appendix into the foreground (and Arwen taking over Glorfindel's role); (3) the Arwen-Aragorn romance plot; (4) Arwen's debate with her father about staying or going; (5) enlarging the role of Éowyn, and her love for Aragorn; (6) introducing mother figures (such as the mother Morwen in *The Two Towers* who sends her children to Edoras; mothers and wives saying goodbye to their loved ones before the battle of Helm's Deep); (7) the many cutie kid shots; (8) having Enya and other female singers on the soundtrack (including Elizabeth Fraser, Sheila Chandra, Isabel Bayraldarian and Emiliana Torrini).

FEAR OF COLONIZATION. Someone on the internet remarked that the 2001-03 *Lord of the Rings* films would get confused with the book in their head. That's a kind of fear of media colonization that David Cronenberg explores in his 'body horror' films.

For me, J.R.R. Tolkien's works and world are so deeply ingrained, it'll take more than the 2001-03 films to dislodge them. I have a very particular and very strong interpretation of a character like Frodo, for example, built over years of the reading the books, and an 18 year-old actor like Elijah Wood can't supplant it. It's odd that for some people their vision of Tolkien and Middle-earth, developed over 100s of hours of reading, will be supplanted by a few viewings of the films.

When the 2001-03 version of *The Lord of the Rings* is contemplated for any time, it's striking just how much the screenwriters invented. The novel is very long, dense, multi-layered, with plenty of characters and events, but the adaptors still introduced a huge number of elements and scenes. These included lengthy invented sections, such as:

   (1) the Arwen-Aragorn romance,
   (2) many Aragorn and Elrond scenes,
   (3) the ring going to Osgiliath,
   (4) Faramir's reversal,
   (5) the warg attack,
   (6) Aragorn's 'death' and return,
   (7) Saruman as chief villain (numerous extra scenes),
   (8) a wizard duel,
   (9) the collapsing stairs in Moria,
   (10) Aragorn and Frodo at Amon Hen with the ring,
   (11) Haldir and the elves at Helm's Deep,
   (12) much more for Éowyn (and for Éowyn and Aragorn),
   (13) Théodred's funeral,
   (14) the invasion of Rohan by Wild Men,
   (15) Gothmog and his troops,
   (16) attacks on Osgiliath much expanded,
   (17) telepathic communication between Galadriel and Elrond,
   (18) Boromir, Faramir and Denethor at Osgiliath,
   (19) Frodo and Sam under the elven cloak,
   (20) many additions to the Helm's Deep battle,
   (21) Arwen leaving for the Grey Havens,
   (22) Sam betrayed by Gollum at Shelob's lair, and so on.

Peter Jackson remarked that *The Two Towers* was the slightest of the books. Having cut out so much from an already 'slight 'book – Shelob, Cirith Ungol, the voice of Saruman, etc – the filmmakers proceeded to add more inventions to *The Two Towers* than to the other two films (the warg attack, Aragorn's 'death' and resurrection, Faramir taking Frodo and co. to Osgiliath, the face-off with the Witch-king, and so on).

As planned originally, the first film would have ended with Saruman's death, Pippin and the *palantír*, and the fellowship breaking up, with Legolas and Gimli going South. The second film would have begun with Frodo, Sam and Gollum at the Black Gate.

Peter Jackson said the filmmakers were conscious of trying not to make a bad film; if the films were good, the Tolkien fans might forgive them a little, but a bad movie would have been disastrous. 'We did obviously deviate from the books, but we knew there would be forgiveness if they [the Tolkien fans] drew some pride in what we had done'.[2] '*I want to make movies that I'd like to watch*', Jackson has remarked, a common view among filmmakers (Sib, 551).

Frances Walsh acknowledged that a film could only capture a small number of elements of a book, could only give a superficial indication of what a book was, and couldn't replace the pleasure a book offers. In adapting *The Lord of the Rings,* Walsh and Philippa Boyens hoped to honour some Tolkien's iconic moments and themes, and portray some of the memorable scenes, but couldn't hope to deliver a reader's enjoyment of the whole text.

Peter Jackson had admitted that the movie wouldn't be faithful to the book. Any book adaption is a thousand compromises: '*our adaption can't be faithful.* You can't just take the book and go and shoot it', Jackson said.[3] To film *The Lord of the Rings* in full would require probably 10, 20, 30 hours for each of the three books (and the text would still require a lot of work on it to appear 'faithful'). Christopher Lee reckoned that Tolkien 'would be very pleased. The spirit of Tolkien's work, the essence of the books, is still on screen'.

The job of the filmmakers was the difficult one of juggling a number of potentially conflicting requirements: (1) remaining true to Tolkien's beloved text (or the spirit of Tolkien); (2) not alienating the legions of fans (who had a lot of buying power); (3) producing a 'good night out' as Jackson called it, a fun and exciting two-three hours; (4) delivering a 'PG'-rated family adventure blockbuster to the studio, which it could market and sell (and on time, on schedule, on budget, with the agreed elements, and within agreed limits (the filmmakers clashed with the studio many times over these and other issues)); (5) to guarantee the financial investment, to deliver a profit on the investment, to shore up New Line Cinema for the future; and (6) to launch a franchise, licensing and merchandizing operation with a two-hour-45-minute advert.

The filmmakers were not duty bound or contractually obliged to please the Estate of J.R.R. Tolkien, however. Securing the film rights meant that they could (pretty much) do what they liked with the books, and the author's estate wouldn't be able to do anything – because Tolkien himself had signed away the film rights in 1967 (the estate would benefit financially from the films, though).

But it would have been foolish for the *Lord of the Rings* adaptors to deliberately irritate or put off the sizeable fan base for the books. The Hollywood studio would want that audience to come to the films, because a large percentage of that audience would see the films more than once in theatres, and would also buy the home entertainment editions of the films (as well as merchandizing). There was also a certain amount of goodwill built up towards Tolkien and the estate of the author (including Christopher Tolkien, who had administered so much of the Tolkien publishing empire after professor's death). It would've helped a little if Tolkien junior had blessed the films (he didn't, publicly, but he would have benefitted in secondary ways – not least in stimulating sales of the books of his father's he'd edited).

Some fans complained that the 2001-03 films of *The Lord of the Rings* would damage J.R.R. Tolkien's reputation. The point is, although there's lots wrong, mistaken, irritating or even depressing about the films, *in their arena* (the Hollywood blockbuster franchise), they have been regarded as very successful (economically and critically). Thus, the positive effects will overshadow the 'negative' ones, on the whole.

For me, far more 'damaging' to J.R.R. Tolkien's cultural status was the awful fantasy art that drew on Tolkien's works in the 1970s (and late 1960s, but mostly after his death in 1973). To me, that crappy fantasy art was far more offensive than anything in the 2001-2003 films (including all the changes and alterations). Heavy metal freaks, dungeons and dragons, muscular he-men slaughtering bug-eyed monsters while women with big boobs and bikinis cooed and waved from the battlements.

If you want to target the rise of fascistic fantasy art, a culture of pro-militaristic politics, men as Hitleran Supermen, backward-looking sexual politics (adolescent at best, misogynist at worst), women as virgins or whores (yes, true, there was the occasional warrior woman), and prowess measured in size of Schwarzeneggerian bicep and chest, to the sound of Richard Wagner or Carl bloody Orff, that's where it is.

1970s fantasy art in its macho, 'take no prisoners' mode was the visual equivalent of Led Zeppelin's 'Immigrant Song' ('wargasmic' music). But it could also be vomit-inducingly cute (*viz.* the hilarious footage of Mr Spock (Leonard Nimoy) singing about hobbits, aired again in the documentaries about the *Lord of the Rings* movies). Not all of 1970s fantasy art was bilge, but if any 'damage' was done to Tolkien's media image, it was there (and not forgetting the massive wave of merchandizing that followed the professor's death in 1973).

What's remarkable about the 2001-03 films of Tolkien's book, is that although there's more than enough dodgy hair, camp delivery, ponderous dialogue, leather, chains and improbable events to go around, the 1970s fantasy art look was, in general, avoided. The women in the Kiwi-Oz-US films, for example, have suitably demure costumes (no bare flesh here, no tits and ass), with flattened chests (like Princess Leia in the first *Star Wars* film). Of course, the male actors in the 2001-2003 films are prone to ridiculous flourishes with swords or bow and arrows, like macho Hollywood heroes (Viggo Mortensen and Orlando Bloom in particular), but some of excesses of fantasy art of the 1970s and 1980s or Hollywood action heroics are sidestepped. (Take the scene of Aragorn in the river in *The Two Towers*, for instance: Arny, Bruce, Jean-Claude, Kurt or Sly would certainly have used that opportunity halfway thro' *Lord of the Rings 2* to strip off or at least pose in a muscle-hugging vest). The only nudity on display in the 2001-03 films was, oddly enough, courtesy of Gollum – ironically, he's not only digital, he's the last person anyone would want to see naked (and there's the troll, and Lurtz, buried under two tons of prosthetic make-up).

Not only did the films bring new readers to the books, they brought old readers back too (and have done). Someone pointed out in a Tolkien newsgroup that new readers coming to Tolkien's work might be confused, might've had Tolkien misinterpreted or misrepresented for them.

That's a patronizing attitude, and a simplistic view of readers. If folk come to Tolkien's work via the 2001-03 films, the professor's prose and verse will soon work their enchantment on them. And if they love the fiction, great. And if they're jazzed enough to pick up a book and read it (as opposed to a billion other possible activities), they're probably also smart enough to realize there's loads they didn't put into the movies. No one *loses*. Having more readers is always a plus.

The two branches of the story, J.R.R. Tolkien asserted, were: '1. Prime Action, the Ringbearers. 2. Subsidiary Action, the rest of the Company leading to the 'heroic' matter. *It is essential that these two branches should each be treated in coherent sequence*' (L, 275). Pretty much any commercial filmmaking team wouldn't follow that structure, though. It's a daring element in the book, but would almost certainly alienate audiences.

It's absolutely necessary to have the whimsical, light-hearted scenes in the 2001-03 *Lord of the Rings* films, to balance the intensity and relentlessness of the dramatic, grim, gloomy, action-packed and death-filled scenes. The trouble is, the lighter, whimsical scenes come across as flimsy and uninvolving (partly because they're nearly always written and directed with far less passion and flair than the bigger, heavier scenes).

The staging of the scenes in the great halls of Rohan and Gondor was static and a little uninspired. These were the scenes that recalled Shakespeare's history plays in Tolkien's tome, but despite featuring actors who were known for playing Shakespeare (such as Ian McKellen), they were nowhere near even the standard of a rep or provincial theatre production of the history plays. With sets that impressive, the staging could have been much more dynamic. (When tiredness kicked in during the lengthy shoot, Peter Jackson said it 'was harder and harder to come up with inventive ideas', and scenes would be shot in the conventional manner [Sib, 490]).

And when it came to speechifying, some of the actors were not quite up to the job (principally Viggo Mortensen, who had to be Prince Harry rousing his troops at least twice, but couldn't really manage it). Mortensen was great as Strider the rough, gnarled, weary ranger and Aragorn the devoted, dreamy-eyed lover of Arwen, and the action and sword fights were fine, but the grandeur and dignity of Aragorn as King Elessar seemed to elude him somewhat (but that's the aspect of Aragorn from the books that's difficult to perform, as well as to take as a reader).

Weathertop is a less than satisfying sequence. But then, as a filmmaker, you're buggered with Tolkien's description in the book of the Weathertop attack: in other words, he doesn't describe it. He leaves it vague; it's lost in the gap between two chapters. Frodo swoons at the end of chapter 11: 'he caught a glimpse of Strider leaping out of the darkness with a flaming brand of wood in either hand'. Cut to the start of chapter 12, where Tolkien's narrator back-announces the attack, so to speak: Sam sees black shadows, not much else: 'they saw nothing more, until they stumbled over the body of Frodo, lying as if dead'.

The solution in the film showing how Aragorn defeats five nazgul isn't convincing. In a silly moment, Aragorn lobs a firebrand into the face of a nazgul, where it lodges. As camp and dumb as anything in Hammer or Roger Corman (actually, not as good as Hammer or Corman).

NOTES: ADAPTING *THE LORD OF THE RINGS* FOR THE 2001-03 FILMS

1. I. Nathan, 2004, 90.
2. I. Nathan, 2004, 90.
3. I. Nathan, 2002, 65; my italics.

THE SCRIPT

Director Peter Jackson said the most difficult part of making *The Lord of the Rings* was writing the script, cutting down the 1200 pages to a manageable three films of just over two hours each: 'the most difficult thing has been the script. Without any doubt, the scriptwriting has been a total nightmare', Jackson confessed [I. Nathan, 2002, 65]). Even a cursory look at *The Lord of the Rings* reveals how much detail and story is packed into it – names, places, genealogies, geography, histories, and tons of backstory. Making each of the three volumes as a two-hour/ two-and-a-half hour feature film inevitably means so much pruning that the films can't be much more than a 'greatest hits' of *The Lord of the Rings*. This's what the screenwriters, producers and studio went for: a series of the bits most people remember from the book, filmed with an international cast (not strictly 'international' – rather, an Anglo-America-Australian-Kiwi cast), and CGI special effects and old-style miniatures. Jackson said he intended to make something like the Ray Harryhausen fantasy films he'd enjoyed as a child, films like the *Sinbad* movies and *Jason and the Argonauts*. 'I wanted to make my 'Jason', or my 'Sinbad'', Jackson remarked (R. Harryhausen, ix).

Among the countless changes (discussed at length in this book) made in translating *The Lord of the Rings* to the screen were bringing a romance (between Arwen and Aragorn) from one of the many appendices to the main part of the narrative (to counter-act the masculinist slant of *The Lord of the Rings*). Tom Bombadil was dropped altogether, as was Old-Man Willow and many secondary characters (such as Prince Imrahhil, Elrond's sons, the Wild Men, etc).

To be fair to the adaptors of the 2001-03 films of *The Lord of the Rings* and the many alterations they made from J.R.R. Tolkien's novel, Tolkien himself had considered all sorts of variations, including having Sam wandering into Fangorn and being taken by Gandalf to Minas Tirith; having Frodo and Sam fighting nazgûl on the side of Mount Doom, having Frodo being taken to the Dark Tower; having Éowyn as well as Théoden dying at Pelennor; having Treebeard being an evil giant; having Aragorn casually chatting to a ringwraith over a hedge; and Lothlórien being razed by nazgûl, among many other alternatives.

In fact, the narrative variations that Tolkien contemplated as he was writing *The Lord of the Rings* between 1937 and its publication in 1954-55 were much more extreme than the ones that appeared in the two thousand one-three films, including the departures of Frodo as an 18 year-old kid, Aragorn's 'death' and return, Faramir taking Frodo and the ring to Osgiliath, and so on. (When the 2001-03 project was with Miramax, a script consultant made a number of suggestions for turning Tolkien's books into one film: drop Helm's Deep; combine Rohan and Gondor; combine Denethor and Théoden; cut Saruman, or use him better; combine Faramir and Éowyn; lose the attack at Bree; halve the Rivendell scenes; compress Moria scenes; delay Ganalf's return, and so on [Sib, 379-380).

For those who don't mind Tom Bombadil's omission from most

adaptions of *The Lord of the Rings* point out that not only does he not really add much to the quest to destroy the ring, he also doesn't appear again. He's mentioned at the Council of Elrond, and Gandalf visits him at the end of the novel, but he doesn't play a major role in the War of the Ring.

One of the most significant decisions in adapting *The Lord of the Rings* in 2001, as far as narrative was concerned, was to include scenes from the earlier life of the ring, of the Second Age and the Last Alliance, involving Isildur, Elrond, Sauron and, later, Gollum. Some of this material comes from Elrond's lengthy speeches at Rivendell. Some of it, such as the prologue to *The Return of the King,* about how Gollum acquired the ring, comes from Gandalf.

Making Galadriel the narrator of the film was perhaps another appeal to the female audience, because, really, in many ways the one character who should be narrating an adaption of the book was Gandalf. He was the one who had the most information (often in advance of the reader of the book or viewer of the film), who interacted with the most characters (from the lowliest to the noblest), who travelled around the most, and who told the most stories of the past. Also, as Elrond put it in the book, this adventure was primarily Gandalf's show. (Other characters would come before Galadriel as choices for narrators: Frodo obviously, and Bilbo, but also Sam, and maybe Aragorn). A narration by Frodo was written and recorded, as if he were looking back on events from the end of the story, but was dropped (Frodo does narrate parts of the films; the end section of *The Return of the King,* for instance, from the coronation of Aragorn to the journey to the Grey Havens). Bilbo narrating the prologue was also considered (in the extended DVD version of *Fellowship,* Bilbo does narrate quite a bit of the prologue, including the section 'concerning hobbits'). The 1981 BBC radio adaption was reworked in 2001, with Frodo as an older hobbit, looking back on the events of *Lord of the Rings.*

Bumping up Orlando Bloom's Legolas in *The Two Towers* and *The Return of the King* may have been inspired by wanting to attract the under 25 female audience; the studio and filmmakers knew that Bloom's elf was popular among young women, and that Bloom had star appeal in that sector of the audience.

ARAGORN. Curiously, Aragorn has little voiceover in the *Lord of the Rings* films. Most every other character narrates parts of the films – Gandalf, Bilbo, Frodo, Elrond, Galadriel, Saruman, Gollum. There seems to be more of an attempt to portray Aragorn in the films' present tense, not looking back from some point in the future, and not to explain events (i.e., 'Aragorn' meant action, not narration or explanation). The narration of the main characters noted above is largely for exposition, or to explain things which either were difficult to show, or would take too long to show.

With regard to Aragorn's story, screenwriters Frances Walsh and Philippa Boyens want to have it both ways: scriptwriters know from Vladimir Propp and the countless screenwriting bibles that quote Propp, Joseph Campbell, Mircea Eliade, Carl Jung *et al*, that the hero has to *refuse* the 'call to adventure' at first. But s/he has to accept it pretty soon, for the adventure to begin. But Walsh and Boyens stretched Aragorn's reluctance as long as possible, right into the third film: he really *doesn't* want to become king, to face up to his world-changing responsibilities. Poor dear. Yet, from the time he's introduced in Bree, Aragorn is right there, not only coming along for the ride, but taking charge of the travelling hobbits and guiding them to Rivendell. And at Weathertop, he's protecting them by fighting for his life. To make it more explicit, at the Council of Elrond he pledges his life to protect Frodo and help him carry out the task.

After that, Aragorn's fighting his way across all of Middle-earth, becoming Arda's greatest warrior. He doesn't seem very reluctant. Yet Boyens and Walsh introduced the notion of reluctance in Aragorn back in Rivendell, before the council, in that important duologue with Arwen in front of the shards of Narsil.

In short, the deep reluctance of Aragorn to accept his responsibility/ destiny as the king of Gondor and Arnor adds complications to his character that just aren't there in the novel, where Aragorn has accepted his royal, noble fate. The changes to Aragorn's characterization also helped to give the character a character development that would run over three films, not just the usual one film.

The Rivendell Arwen-Aragorn scene is utterly *vital*, for the *movies* – when Aragorn voices his doubts; it's an interiority scene, in which Aragorn reveals part of his emotional landscape. And the 'script Nazis', as director Jackson dubbed them – Walsh and Boyens – will milk that scene, and milk it, and MILK IT, to the point where the scene's a little shrivelled animal on the floor whimpering, 'no more, girls! I can't do this no more!' So the Script Nazis resurrect that weakness scene, using the Dark Magick all screenwriters learn in Hogwarts School of Moneycraft and Movie Wizardry. They re-animate the corpse, and continue to milk that sucker – right up to – where? – halfway through film three!

BODY COUNT. There are numerous deaths in the 2001-2003 *Lord of the Rings* films – but most of those deaths are also in the book. Some of the death scenes are spectacular – set-pieces in their own right: the troll, Lurtz, Boromir, Gandalf, the balrog, Haldir, the *mûmakil* rider, Gollum, the ringwraiths, the Witch-king, Saruman, Wormtongue, and most epic of all, Sauron. Other deaths include Háma, Gothmog, Faramir's lieutenant Madril, Shagrat, Grishnákh, Gorbag, the warg rider, and numerous orcs, Gondorians, Rohirrim, Haradrim, etc.

So many deaths!

Characters appear to die – Frodo, Sam, Gandalf, Aragorn – but somehow survive (Arwen wastes away, too, but revives, and Éowyn is near death). And there are death scenes where a character dies in another's arms: Aragorn and Boromir, Aragorn and Haldir, Théoden and Éowyn. But when you see them all strung together in the space of a few hours in a movie, the number of deaths does seem excessive. Really excessive. These are grotesquely violent movies.

Fans of the book pointed out that characters in the 2001-03 *Lord of the Rings* films always seem to fall into despair before rallying and deciding to fight: at Helm's Deep Legolas sinks into despair before rallying and apologizing to Aragorn; as soon as Théoden's revived, he decides to run away; the Entmoot decides to have peace instead of going to war; Aragorn breaking with Arwen, and so on.

Both *The Lord of the Rings* films and books are very clear-cut when it comes to how the audience is intended to identify with the groups of characters. It's simply good vs. evil forces. There isn't much ambiguity here. Tolkien's narrator is definitely on one side, the goodies. In some other forms of narrative, say a fugitive on the run from the police, an audience might identify with both pursuers and pursued. Stories about gangsters, for instance, encourage the audience to identify with criminals, as well as the people pursuing them (the cops, the FBI, etc). The *Godfather* films are a good example: Al Pacino, Marlon Brando, James Caan, Robert de Niro *et al* are nasty, vicious people, but the audience is encouraged to empathize with them. In classic literature, plays like *Macbeth* are good examples: the lead character Macbeth is a multiple murderer.

But there is no such ambiguity in *The Lord of the Rings*. Sauron and his forces are bad, bad, bad, and the audience is always encouraged to cheer for the goodies' side. Occasionally the narrator voices concern over the poor orcs, pushed around by the Dark Lord. And a character such as Gollum is an exception – he teeters between good and evil throughout the book (and Tolkien maintains the ambiguity around Gollum right to the end: Gollum takes the ring from Frodo by force, but he also destroys it, which Frodo couldn't do, apparently by accident when he slips and falls).

GANDALF. The 2001-03 Gandalf was a wizard who led armies into battle (as at Helm's Deep, where he's seen killing orcs with his staff, or on the battlements of Minas Tirith). This Gandalf tended not to use lots of magic or spells (the filmmakers were not fans of the common cinematic tropes of bolts of lighting or electricity). When the two wizards duel at Isengard, for instance, there is a strong physical component to the fight, although the staffs are employed magically too. When Gandalf fights orcs on the terraces of Minas Tirith, he uses his sword and staff, both as physical not magical weapons. Gandalf did use his magic throughout the films, though: to light the way in Moria, to battle Saruman, to exorcise Théoden, and to beat off the nazgûl in the retreat from Osgiliath.

Gandalf would also perform the role of the main vehicle for exposition, back-story, and the history of Middle-earth (along with Elrond and Galadriel). In contrast to the two figureheads of elven aristocracy, Gandalf could be in the thick of things, interacting with characters, and thus could be used by the screenwriters to carry a lot of explanations and history (Legolas and Aragorn occasionally provide exposition, as does Gollum on the journey to Mordor, though far less than the wizard).

The sections of the 2001-03 *The Lord of the Rings* films aimed at the global cinema audience and those aimed at Tolkien fans are easily discerned. It's almost as if the filmmakers had decided, as they went along with pre-production and shooting: this bit's for the multiplex audience (Treebeard squashing an orc), and this one's for the Tolkien fans (Legolas remarking that it was the elves who began to wake the trees).

Just as the potential for homoeroticism between Frodo and Sam was consciously avoided in the 2001-03 films (although the films weren't wholly successful in sidestepping it), the scenes between Frodo and Gollum were also kept asexual. But Gollum's subservient, pawing behaviour towards Frodo (and to Bilbo in *The Hobbit*), his touchy, feely gestures, have a sexual component which critics have drawn attention to (although Tolkien himself wasn't interested in that aspect of the characters; Frodo is ascetically non-sexual, while Sam has an earthy, more regular nature, and gets to marry his childhood sweetheart, Rosie Cotton).

The problems of the 2001-03 film adaptions of Ronald Tolkien's book is that the two forms are very different: one a novel written in the 1940s and 1950s in England and the other a big budget action-adventure blockbuster film made for a global market in the early 2000s. It's not just that cinema and literature are different forms, with different requirements, it's that the 2001-03 films were conceived as blockbuster action-adventure films, which are a very particular type of film. This kind of movie has a number of artistic, internal demands (among them, action, spectacle, romance, emotion, jeopardy, clarity, easily identified goals, motives, characters and settings), but also plenty of external, economic and social prerequisites: employment for a lot of people, a huge skills base (including money and time for training), tax incentives, a return on investment, profit potential, licensees and merchandizing, ancillary markets, and so on.

By contrast, Ronald Tolkien writing and publishing his book in the 1950s operated in a quite different socio-economic context. All that was required for the London publishers Allen & Unwin to make their investment back was to sell a few thousand copies (although shifting a few thousand units of a book can be difficult for even established publishers). Rayner Unwin remarked that he had been prepared to lose money on publishing *The Lord of the Rings* (he has quoted £1,000/ $1,600 as a figure). As a writer, Tolkien had only his publishers to please (but they were not 'hands on' editors of his work. As Rayner Unwin said, you did not dare to edit Tolkien's writing. They could – and did – turn Tolkien down, though; they rejected *The Silmarillion*, for instance). In other words, the manuscript that Tolkien delivered to his publishers was probably pretty much published in the form he desired (but they only agreed to publish *The Lord of the Rings* in three volumes, while Tolkien wanted a single book – it was never a 'trilogy' for Tolkien, but always a single piece).

A big Hollywood movie, by contrast, has all sorts of groups of people putting in their opinions and demands. All of those people – producers, writers, directors, lawyers, accountants, studio executives, marketers, advertizers, designers, illustrators, model makers, etc – putting their two cents' worth in would probably have driven Tolkien nuts. (The filmmakers of the *Lord of the Rings* films had some heated run-ins with New Line's executives, for instance. And there were plenty of arguments and disagreements behind the scenes – it would be impossible not to have tensions with so many artists working together).

RIVENDELL. The screenwriters confessed that the Rivendell chapters were the most difficult to adapt. There are many speeches, many new characters to introduce, and tons of back-story and exposition to dramatize. The elf, the man and the dwarf were introduced at Rivendell over Elrond's voiceover; the scriptwriters had toyed with different ways of introducing Legolas, Gimli and Boromir, including having a big feast. There wasn't time to include many sections of the Rivendell scenes in the book, such as the feast, Frodo speaking with Gimli's father, Glóin, Bilbo's song of Eärendil to the elves, or Elrond's lengthy history of Middle-earth, or Gandalf's accounts of his adventures, or new characters such as Glóin, Erestor and Galdor. (The addition of the Arwen-Aragorn scenes would have also pushed out the time available for other scenes). Some of the material in the Council of Elrond found its way into other parts of the films – in the prologue depicting the Last Alliance, for example.

THE RING. Another problem was to demonstrate the power of the ring. After all, the central conceit of *The Lord of the Rings* is that the whole fate of Middle Earth and all its people rests on a bit of metal, that so much power could reside in a ring. If only life were so simple! But this is the beauty of fantasy, its metaphorical or allegorical moves. In the 2001-03 films, the solution was to make the ring a 'character', to shoot it in close-up, use different-sized prop rings, and employ a variety of devices to express its magical powers (it was portrayed as having something like atomic energy), including Sauron talking through the ring, the ring whispering to characters, characters and fire reflected in the ring, and so on.

THE VILLAINS. The character of Lurtz, leader of the Uruk-hai orcs, was created partly because the filmmakers thought there was a lack among the villains: Sauron is merely a giant Eye, and doesn't move from Barad-dûr for the duration, and Saruman too stays put in his tower until the end of the story (the other old wizard, Gandalf, by contrast, is handily all over the place). Apart from the Nine Riders and the multitudes of orcs, the filmmakers decided some other villains were necessary. Thus Lurtz was invented, and the part he plays is that of muscle-man and chief bruiser sidekick for Saruman, a very familiar role in Hollywood blockbuster films (such as *James Bond, Die Hard, Lethal Weapon, Star Wars* and so on). But the addition of Lurtz to *The Fellowship of the Ring* isn't particularly problematic, even for the most ardent Tolkien fans, because Lurtz has a very familiar and useful cinematic role to play. More problematic for a Tolkien fan would be the elevation of Saruman as chief villain over Sauron.

In *The Return of the King*, the scriptwriters did the same thing with the Witch-king's lieutenant, Gothmog. In the book, he is referred to briefly, but in the film he's elevated to one of the chief villains (principally at the Battle of Pelennor, but also during the river crossing and battle of Osgiliath, and Faramir's horse charge). Like Lurtz, Gothmog is an under-written character in the film (no back-story for him!), whose primary function is to issue orders, look nasty, and lead the enemy forces to battle. Gothmog, the Witch-king's lieutenant, was a late addition to *The Lord of the Rings* as Tolkien was writing it.

Gothmog in the films is notable chiefly for the bizarre (and time-consuming) make-up job, all bulbous lumps, evoking the pitiful figure of the Elephant Man. And his voice is a silly, excessively gravelly bark.

(Unusually, the theatrical cut of *The Return of the King* didn't show Gothmog getting killed by one of the chief heroes, which is the typical Hollywood action film resolution: Éomer would an obvious choice, as he hadn't had the opportunity to demonstrate his military skill in that respect (well, yes, he did down a *mûmakil*). Gothmog's demise turned up in the *Extended Edition* of *The Return of the King* – polished off by Aragorn and Gimli before he can get to Éowyn).

The big baddie of J.R.R. Tolkien's book is Sauron, a Lucifer figure who's been around for millennia, and is so transformed by evil and magic he's become just a disembodied giant flaming Eye. In the book, much of Sauron's will is carried out by his minions, the Ring-wraiths or Nazgûl, and by the orcs and their leaders. Gollum also goes to Mordor and is subsumed into Sauron's master plan, as is Saruman. The problem for the filmmakers is to create a visible foe for the heroes to fight. The Ring-wraiths are obviously just messengers, not the top man. And with Sauron never moving throughout the book from his fortress of Barad-dûr, filmmakers have to look elsewhere for a good movie villain. The solution of the 2001-03 films was to make Saruman (Christopher Lee) much more prominent; he's the only wizard who can match Gandalf, the Jungian shadow of Gandalf's good wizard.

Sauron as the single giant eye was a concept that troubled the writers a good deal. I wonder if every viewer gets that the giant eye and the guy wielding the mace in the prologue of the 2001 film of *The Fellowship of the Ring* is the same, and what's his connection with Saruman? We see Sauron kill people in the first few minutes, but after that he's just an eye. I wonder if the film could've shown Sauron turning into that disembodied eye, to increase the sense of evil/ threat/ danger. It's not in the books, yeah, but neither is Faramir, Frodo and Sam at Osgiliath, Théoden's 'exorcism', Aragorn 'dying', Arwen at the ford, and many other things.

Seeing a little of Sauron's back-story (*showing* it, rather than having it narrated by Gandalf to Frodo) could be cool: hell, the producers included additions such as Aragorn and his wonder-horse, a silly wizard duel, Arwen appearing to Frodo as an angel or Jesus (cue the white light! cue the choir!), Gimli reduced to a humorous bumbling sidekick (so much for the grandeur of the dwarves), a skateboarding elf, farting hobbits, a stand-off between Frodo and a nazgul (eh?), Frodo thinking that Aragorn's going to take the ring, and dreadful movie-movie dialogue like 'nobody tosses a dwarf!' and 'let's hunt some orc!'.

It's a pity the filmmakers couldn't find a way to really get to grips with Sauron's character. He's the most interesting character in *The Lord of the Rings* in some ways. He's the Devil, he's all-powerful, all-pervasive evil. He's a shapeshifter, who turns into a werewolf and vampire in earlier legends, corrupts elves and men over thousands of years, has all manner of sieges, chases and battles, and brings about the downfall of Númenor and alters the shape of the world, no less. The problem is, he can't strut around a set, like a classic movie villain. He's only an eye! The upgrade in Sauron's look in *The Two Towers* film and again in *The Return of the King* is only cosmetic: and he hardly appears anyway. And nearly all of his (invented) dialogue was dropped (from the first film's depiction of Sauron).

How can the chief baddie be nothing but an eye? The solution in the 2001-2003 Tolkien films is to have someone in voiceover telling the viewer how bad he is, but cinema has to be 'show not tell'; it has to be visualization and dramatization. The other solution was to concentrate on Saruman, which unbalances Tolkien's book.

This is a major problem with *The Lord of the Rings* films, because the villain, in traditional narrative, drives the plot. Without him, everyone else would just get on their with their lives. The elves would be elves, the men men, the hobbits hobbits etc, and there wouldn't much of a story. Sauron is the evil step-mother of fairy tales, or Bluebeard, or the witch, the *James Bond* villain, or Darth Vader – except he can't be shown.

THE ENDING/S OF *THE RETURN OF THE KING.* For Peter Jackson, the ending of *The Return of the King* was always about the last 25 or 30 minutes, and the length of *The Return of the King* was edited in relation to that ending. So the longer *The Return of the King* became in editing, it lessened the impact of the ending.

Jackson's favourite of the three films was *The Return of the King*, because it was all pay-off, in terms of character and action, without needing more exposition or more new characters, and it was 'very emotional', with some high drama for the actors to embrace. *The Return of the King* also had all of the endings, too.

J.R.R. Tolkien was very careful to tie up all of the storylines at the end of *The Lord of the Rings*. So the reader finds out what happened to all the major characters, plus Saruman and Wormtongue, Treebeard, the ents, the huorns, the Wild Men, the Haradrim, the Southrons, Elrond, Galadriel, Celeborn, and also meets (or finds out about) many minor characters: Butterbur, Bombadil, Théoden, the Gaffer, Fatty Bolger, Rosie Cotton, and so on.

In the theatrical version of the 2003 *The Return of the King*, many of these characters are left out, as one would expect, but some of the ones who have played a prominent role in the previous two films – Saruman, Wormtongue, the ents – are dropped entirely. (The *Extended Edition* adds some more information, such as about the nascent romance of Faramir and Éowyn, the death of Wormtongue and Saruman, but from the Mount Doom scenes onwards there is nothing added to the theatrical cut).

The two *dénouement* scenes in *The Return of the King* (theatrical) do not seem to tie up enough of the storylines, or even fully explore the main storylines. The first *dénouement* has a joyful reunion of the fellowship at Frodo's bedside in (presumably) Minas Tirith (in the book it's the Field of Cormallen). The second *dénouement* takes place at Aragorn's coronation. In this big scene in the Citadel, all of the major players are present; Aragorn is crowned (by Gandalf); he sings (!); he walks past his subjects who bow (Legolas, Faramir, Éowyn, Éomer, etc); he is reunited with Arwen; and the four hobbits are applauded.

But in this scene, or any of the following ones up until the close, there is nothing about the healing of Merry and Éowyn; nothing abut the budding romance between Éowyn and Faramir; nothing about Théoden (or his funeral); nothing about Denethor; nothing about the Fourth Age, or the new political structure of Middle-earth.

The screenwriters were much concerned with the ending of *The Return of the King*. Frances Walsh was 'very worried' about the ending, more so perhaps than Boyens or Jackson. It had to end not one but three films. For Walsh, it was essential to pay off the Arwen and Aragorn romance, and also show Sam marrying Rosie Cotton. Walsh was acutely conscious of having the end drag on, of the multiple endings. Walsh found it 'very difficult', argued with the other writers about it, and admitted that it was unconventional.

CINEMATIC INFLUENCES

There are many movie allusions in *The Lord of the Rings* films, some conscious, some unconscious: the monsters recall Ray Harryhausen's movies. The CG wargs look back to the velociraptors in 1993's *Jurassic Park* (and the *mûmakil* recall the bigger dinosaurs in the Universal films). The fellowship running around staircases in Moria recall Irving Allen adventure films (such as *The Lost World*, 1960), while some of the stunts recall the *Indiana Jones* films. Aragorn and Gimli swinging on the rope at Helm's Deep is a Douglas Fairbanks or Errol Flynn moment. Saruman on the Orthanc balcony nods to *The Triumph of the Will* and Nuremburg. Saruman's crows appear in an aerial shot above the fellowship on a mountain which's a direct *hommage* to *The Birds* (1963). The wizard duel recalls martial arts movies (and *The Matrix*). The opening prologue consciously utilizes the action-led teaser in *James Bond* films (and Legolas snowboarding on a shield recalls the sillier stunts in *James Bond* films, and the *Bond* updates, like *XXX*, for the extreme sports generation). The big battles recall hundreds of mediæval and historical films (obvious references are *Zulu* and *The 300 Spartans* for Helm's Deep, and more recent epics, such as *Braveheart* and *Gladiator*). *Star Wars* occurs in the Frodo-Gandalf relationship (and Mr Lucas was in turn indebted to Ronald Tolkien – not only in his *Star Wars* saga, but also in *Willow*).

Westerns inspire scenes of the riders on horseback and the wide shots of people in a landscape (John Ford Westerns were conscious allusions by the filmmakers – such as the shots of Rohan being overrun by the Wildmen). And the orcs attacking the good guys from a distance with arrows in many scenes (often ambushing them) recall Westerns (cowboys and Native Americans). The battle scenes with thousands of orcs and elves recall countless Hollywood epics such as *El Cid*, *Spartacus* and *The Fall of the Roman Empire*. *The Lord of the Rings* nostalgically evoked the adventure films of the 1950s and 1960s: the monsters (such as the Watcher and the troll in *The Fellowship of the Ring*) recall Ray Harryhausen movies. The Argonath statues recall the giant bronze statue Talos in another Harryhausen classic, *Jason and the Argonauts* (1963). Peter

Jackson said his ideal movie version of *The Lord of the Rings* would have been 'a Ray Harryhausen version' (Sib, 48).

The filmmakers very likely looked at recent mediæval, historical and fantasy films prior to planning the *Lord of the Rings* films (the adaptors of *The Lord of the Rings* were clearly big film fans, and all of Peter Jackson's films are 'movie movies', films very much about – and *hommages* to – other films). In the 1990s, these inspirational movies would include *The Last of the Mohicans* (1992), *Braveheart* (1995), *Gladiator* (2000), *Messenger: Joan of Arc* (1999), *The 13th Warrior* (1995), *Rob Roy* (1995), *Star Wars: The Phantom Menace* (1999), two *Robin Hoods* (1991), *Dragonheart* (1996) and perhaps *The Matrix*. (During pre-production, Jackson called the look of the films a mix of *Braveheart* and 'the visual magic of *Legend*', but not with 'the meaningless fantasy mumbo-jumbo of *Willow*' [Sib, 410]).

The adaptors of *The Lord of the Rings* would also likely know (and love) pre-1990s films which share elements with *The Lord of the Rings*. To cite some famous examples from the 1970s and 1980s: *Willow, Highlander, Legend, Dark Crystal, Krull, Flesh + Blood, Ladyhawke, Dragonslayer, Labyrinth,* the *Sinbad* films, *Erik the Viking, Clash of the Titans, The Navigator, Return To Oz, Excalibur, Robin and Marian,* the *Conan* films, *Red Sonja,* and the *Star Wars* series. If the adaptors of the *Lord of the Rings* films were regular film fans, they would likely have seen most of those films, maybe a few times (Peter Jackson is a self-confessed Ray Harryhausen fan, for instance. And the influence of films like *Willow, Highlander, Excalibur* and *Star Wars* are easy to detect in the *Lord of the Rings* films).

THE ARAGORN AND ARWEN ROMANCE

The Aragorn-Arwen subplot in the 2001-03 *The Lord of the Rings* was not Boy Meets Girl, accompanied by the question: is the hero going to get the girl? In the *Lord of the Rings* films, the hero already has his lover. So the question is: is he going to lose her? Thus, the core of the Aragorn-Arwen romance was to explore the ways in which Aragorn would lose Arwen. The problem was, they were physically separated for most of the films (so he had already lost her, in some respects). All of the many options of Hollywood action-adventure movies could not be deployed: the heroine couldn't be captured by the villains (so the hero couldn't rescue her); she couldn't be menaced by the baddies; and the heroine couldn't have another lover (so that Aragorn would have to win her from his rival, perhaps fighting the cad in a duel).

So the screenwriters (principally Philippa Boyens and Fran Walsh) had to come up with obstacles and prohibitions, to create the conflict that a decent romantic subplot requires. In a typical romance, if the couple already love each other, and want to be together, what's the problem? Aragorn and Arwen were in love, and wanted to be together, so obstacles were thrown in their way. One was Aragorn's reluctance to embrace his responsibilities and destiny; another was Arwen prevaricating over leaving Middle-earth and choosing to be mortal (exacerbated by her dad); Elrond isn't just sad that Arwen has chosen Aragorn, he actively condemns her for doing so.

And in *The Two Towers*, the writers brought in another level of obstacle: Arwen was wasting away spiritually and now physically, because her fate was also tied to the ring. This latter obstacle sounded good on paper, gave Arwen more to do, and played nicely in the Arwen-Elrond scenes, but didn't bear up to examination. Why was Arwen wasting away now all of a sudden, and not in the past few thousand years, when the ring was still in existence (and affecting people like Gollum and Bilbo)? Why did the ring affect Arwen physically, but not affect the other elves in the same way (surely other High Elves, such as Elrond, Celeborn and Galadriel would have felt the effects of the ring)? And why was Arwen in particular suffering because of the ring, when she has had no previous connection with it at all? It's kind of emotionally true, but is full of holes, plot-wise.

Elrond doesn't want Arwen to die; it's that simple. He's already seen the effects of mortality on elves, when his brother Elros died, and doesn't want his daughter to suffer the same fate. For him, it's as if she's died. As Elrond puts it gloomily in *The Two Towers*, he can see only death in Arwen's future. What a nice, heartwarming, supportive dad he is.

Notice that Arwen, among all of the major characters, was significantly absent from the Council of Elrond. It was not explained or remarked upon at all (it's best not to draw attention to a major omission). The reason, narratively, is obvious: because if Arwen had been there, she would have been part of the fellowship (she would have volunteered – the viewer had already seen what a cool warrior-elf she was in the chase and Ford of Bruinen scenes; and she's not bad at bringing people back to life, too. A handy person to have around). Because up until that point, Arwen has been a significant presence in the film, from the meeting by the stone trolls onwards: she's been chased by nine Ringwraiths – the Enemy's chief henchmen, no less – and outfaced them *all* at the Ford. She's magically summoned up the river. She's the key person in Aragorn's life.

Then, when the Council of Elrond scene begins, she's suddenly absent. Yet there are some lesser elf characters present, who aren't introduced by name, and have virtually nothing to do, and no lines of dialogue. Perhaps the scriptwriters couldn't come up with a good explanation for Arwen's absence, so hoped the audience would ignore it. If the viewer knows their Tolkien, they could probably come up with many reasons for Arwen's absence, but in terms of the *film*, which has *already* elevated Arwen to a major female presence and heroic warrior role by this point, it's a gaping hole.

The screenwriters and editors of the *Lord of the Rings* films found various ways of bringing Arwen and Aragorn together. One was to have Aragorn thinking back to Rivendell (when prompted by Éowyn asking him about his necklace). Another was to have Aragorn dreaming at night of her. Yet another was to have Arwen appear to Aragorn as a kind of guardian angel, as he lies near death by the riverbank after the warg attack in *The Two Towers*. She kisses him and revives him, like an angel, then dissolves into the sunlight (she whispers something about grace of the Valar, too, as she did with Frodo at another river, the Bruinen. Maybe she's a kind of water sprite – after all, she lives in Rivendell, which's surrounded by rivers and waterfalls). In *The Return of the King* (extended version), Aragorn sees Arwen in the *palantír*. With Arwen staying in Imladris for the duration of the films until the ring is destroyed, the filmmakers finally came up with the solution of showing the love story in flashback.

One of the reasons that Arwen arrives at Helm's Deep with the elves (her presence being one of the main reasons for having the elves there at all) was because it was difficult for the screenwriters to find ways of conducting the romance between Aragorn and Arwen if they were hundreds of miles apart (a 'telepathic' love affair was considered but dropped). Thus, if Arwen were conceived as a warrior princess, she would be more mobile – able to leave Rivendell and go out to rescue Frodo, or help the Rohirrim at Helm's Deep (and she could believably arrive as one of the bunch of elven foot soldiers, rather than being separate as a princess, riding on a horse, say).

There were other alternatives considered but, in the end, the adaptors opted to have Arwen remain at Rivendell and to show the romance with Aragorn in flashbacks (sometimes couched also as dream sequences or memories for Aragorn). Thus, on the journey to Helm's Deep from Edoras, parts of the man-elf romance are played out in flashback, and also when Aragorn's recovering from his near-drowning, and later (in *The Return of the King*) when Aragorn's at Dunharrow and dreams of Arwen (there's also a trick played on the audience at Dunharrow, when the lone, hooded rider who could be Arwen is revealed as Elrond. What a nice surprise for troubled Aragorn if Arwen had appeared in his tent at night).

Parts of Arwen's older characterization as a warrior maiden survived in the films (the wild horse chase, for example, when she single-handedly outruns Sauron's nine most feared servants – whether Glorfindel or Arwen does it, it still stretches belief). The character of Arwen Undómiel was overhauled during shooting, though, in favour of Arwen as something of a distant muse or inspiration for Aragorn, with scenes between them relegated to flashback and dreams (in the appendices, Tolkien's narrator wrote that 'from afar she [Arwen] watched over him [Aragorn] in thought' [RK, 422]). The filmmakers admitted to being 'very uncertain' about what to do with Arwen's character (Sib, 431).

Scenes of Arwen fighting at Helm's Deep were shot (and Liv Tyler trained with sword fighting and stunts). Her characterization was the expected one: she would be a brilliant, fearless and ruthless fighter (when fans heard of this, they called Arwen a Xena character – *Xena the Warrior Princess* being an American fantasy TV show, shot in New Zealand in the Nineties. Quite a few of the *Rings* crew and cast worked on it and *Hercules: The Legendary Journeys*). Another idea was to have Arwen joining the Rohan army and dispatching the Witch-king at Pelennor, rather than Éowyn.

It took perhaps a year for that solution to the Arwen-Aragorn sub-plot to be discovered, the writers admitted, although it plays fairly logically in the films, as if it's an obvious answer to the problem. That was one of the pluses of a long shoot, a long lead-in (pre-production) schedule, and a lengthy post-production process. On most other films there wouldn't be an opportunity to go back and re-jig parts of the story like that; Arwen would thus have kept her warrior-princess status if the *Lord of the Rings* films had been made during a normal production cycle (and with union conditions).

As well as flashbacks to Rivendell, there was also a curious flash-forward, as Elrond outlined to Arwen what could happen to her and Aragorn. In this montage sequence (narrated by Elrond), Arwen was shown standing beside her dead husband, who lies on a tomb in full kingly garb. As the camera pulls back, Aragorn's corpse becomes a stone statue carved into the tomb, with Minas Tirith in the background, and Arwen now in widow's weeds. In the next shots, Arwen, black and hooded, is depicted wandering in sunlit, smoky woods (presumably it's Lórien after the departure of Galadriel). Classic tropes of decay and wistful melancholy are employed here – dead leaves blown by the wind, Autumnal greys, Arwen in black (J.R.R. Tolkien himself might've liked those images – an elf maid in the woods was a foundational image for him).

In terms of Tolkien's chronology, published as part of the appendices of *The Lord of the Rings* (like the Arwen-Aragorn romance itself), this scene is the furthest forward in time (King Elessar died in the year 1541 of the Third Age and the year 120 of the Fourth Age. So it's a flashforward of some 120 years).

One of the problems with the Arwen-Aragorn scenes was that they were relatively static, in terms of presentation (being largely dialogue scenes with characters standing or sitting around at Rivendell), and thematically and dramatically monotone. Once the romance between the mortal man and the immortal female elf had been established, and the oppositions outlined between elves and humans, immortals and mortals, Valinor and Middle-earth, the scenes did not really go anywhere. They did not develop much, but kept revolving the same issues: *should they, shouldn't they?* Should Arwen leave Middle-earth and go to Faërie? Should Aragorn persuade her to stay?

The repetition was enhanced in the extended versions of each film, which simply meant more of the same sort of scenes (or alternatives of the same sort of scenes). Complications were woven into the Aragorn-Arwen scenes, such as Elrond's relationship with his daughter and his desire for her to go with him, the addition of Éowyn longing for Aragorn with its love triangle complications, and Elrond reminding Aragorn to live up to his destiny.

CHAPTER 3

THE MOVIE STUDIO AND THE DEAL

THE QUEST OF THE RIGHTS AND THE JOURNEY TO THE SCREEN

And now, oh ye nobles, lords, ladies and great folk, gather round as we explore the weird and wonderful world of Hollywood, the studios, the deals, and that most magical and mysterious of things: money...

In this discussion of the Hollywood industry, in referring to New Line Cinema I'm really talking about all of the Hollywood studios (the big six – Disney, Sony/ Columbia, Universal, Paramount, 20th Century Fox, and Warners – and smaller studios, like DreamWorks and Miramax. Miramax played a big part in the story of the film from book to production).

According to observers, Ronald Tolkien sold the film rights of his book in order to provide money for his children and grandchildren. It wasn't that he particularly wanted to see a film made. Legend has it that Tolkien sold the rights for $10,000, in 1967. That figure has been disputed since: $250,000 was the real amount, according to some commentators (as well as a percentage of the royalties).[1] The lawyers for the estate of Ronald Tolkien acknowledged that it would receive royalties if the 2001-03 films of *The Lord of the Rings* took more than 2 1/2 times their costs. The Tolkien estate and family did not receive any money from the merchandizing (but still had 50% of the book sales profits).

The choice, Stanley Unwin told J.R.R. Tolkien in the mid-1950s, when *The Lord of the Rings* was gaining a name for itself, was that they would go for 'cash or kudos': either a great deal of money for the book rights, or a decent film treatment of the book (H. Carpenter, 1995). New Line Cinema and associated parties wanted both: they wanted a lot of money, and a lot of kudos.

John Boorman had spent a year preparing to film *The Lord of the Rings* in the late 1960s, before the project was abandoned. Boorman said that Tolkien had told him he didn't want to see a film version. After Boorman's film foundered, the rights were bought up by Saul Zaentz, who brought out half of *The Lord of the Rings* in 1978 with Ralph Bakshi, using animation and rotoscoped live action. Boorman said Bakshi's film was a travesty of the book, and luckily Tolkien didn't live to see it (he died in 1973). For more info on previous Tolkien adaptions, such as John Boorman's in 1967, the 1978 United Artists cartoon, the Rankin/ Bass TV shows (1977 and 1980), please see my book *J.R.R. Tolkien*.

It's conceivable that, had the 2001-03 Frodo films been made with Tolkien still alive, if they had been made, say, in the 1970s, like Ralph Bakshi's adaption, Tolkien might have been cut out of the loop. Saul Zaentz and his company might have gone ahead without Tolkien's blessing and made the films anyway (which happened after Tolkien's death, and against the wishes of the Tolkien estate). Had Tolkien been alive, he would very likely have kicked up a huge fuss about the films, which might have had a detrimental effect on the film's audience and Tolkien fans around the world.

As Peter Jackson related, he and Fran Walsh were casting around for their next project as *The Frighteners* was drawing to a close (and *Kong* was cancelled), and wanted to do something in the vein of *The Lord of the Rings*. It was Walsh who reckoned that if they couldn't do something as good or better than *The Lord of the Rings,* there was no point doing it. That led them to consider attempting *The Lord of the Rings* itself. At the time, 1995, no live action version of Tolkien's heroic romance had appeared. It was an 'impossible' project, though there had been attempts (the 1978 United Artists adaption did film *The Lord of the Rings* in live action, though, for its rotoscoping process. And plenty of live action remains barely disguised under the animation).

Doing *The Lord of the Rings* made sense in some respects: there were plenty of fantasy films in the Tolkien style around; they had been a staple of Hollywood throughout the Eighties, for instance, with *Krull, Legend, Labyrinth, The Dark Crystal* and *Willow*. And movies with a similar mediæval adventure flavour were doing good business in the first half of the Nineties: *Robin Hood* ($390 million global gross), *Braveheart* ($204m) and *First Knight* ($127m). But no one had done *The Lord* itself yet. Why? When Walsh and Jackson seriously began to consider doing it, they realized why: apart from the cost, and the rights issue, there was the structure, the large number of main characters, the settings, the Middle-earth histories, and the size of the story.

Everyone – John Boorman, Peter Jackson, Fran Walsh and others – who has had a go at it has spoken about the difficulties of turning Tolkien's book into a film, citing obstacles such as the lack of female characters, the dense layers of detail, the large cast, and the lack of a good movie-style villain.

NOTES: THE RIGHTS, THE JOURNEY TO THE SCREEN

1. F. Gibbons, *The Guardian*, Dec 11, 2001.

MIRAMAX, SAUL ZAENTZ AND PRE-PRODUCTION

Miramax were the initial developers of the *Lord of the Rings* films project, which was pitched to them in October, 1995 (with *The Hobbit* to be made first, to test the waters, But United Artists wouldn't let the rights of *The Hobbit* go to the Weinsteins). Miramax spent around $12 million (some say $15m) developing the film before getting cold feet (their $12 million was paid back by New Line Cinema). That money would count as a development fund, which covers everything a film requires before it officially begins pre-production.[1] In other words, to develop the project, budget it, research it, scout locations, shoot tests, and so on.

On the *Lord of the Rings* films, there wasn't just one producer and one writer, so that increases the budget quite a bit. Plus the *Lord of the Rings* films were a complex project, requiring model tests, make-up tests, tons of pre-visualization material, artwork, and so on, which would further bump up the development budget.

It does appear as if the *Lord of the Rings* films were one of those movie projects that grew and grew as the films were scripted, cast, designed, prepared, shot and edited. The filmmakers have acknowledged on many occasions that if they knew just how much work would be involved when they were starting out, they might have had second thoughts about undertaking the project at all. They have also admitted to being a bit naïve at the outset, not having produced films on this scale before.

The continual rethinks and reorganizations are plain to see – from obvious instances, such as recasting the third lead actor (Stuart Townsend) two weeks into shooting, to more behind-the-scenes battles between the studio (New Line) and the filmmakers, and the constant rewrites (and this despite the films being storyboarded entirely, as well as animatics produced of each film). The films were being reworked right up until the last possible moment. The slew of reshoots and pick-ups suggests that the films were being reconceived at every stage in the filmmaking process. Reshoots or pick-ups are not uncommon in Hollywood, but those for the *Lord of the Rings* films were far more extensive than most. The titles and logo – a critical element – were left until the final week of post-production on *The Fellowship of the Ring* (not uncommon).

Frances Walsh and Peter Jackson met Saul Zaentz, and he offered them an option for the rights. Saul Zaentz's Fantasy Film was based in the Bay Area. Zaentz had a reputation for critically acclaimed independent films, often based on novels, which were made with low budgets but high production values: *One Flew Over the Cuckoo's Nest, Amadeus, The Unbearable Lightness of Being,* and *The English Patient.*

Zaentz and Miramax had fallen out over *The English Patient* (which Miramax had picked up after Fox dropped it), with Zaentz claiming that he had not seen any money beyond the money that Miramax paid the crew and cast (but the cast and crew said they hadn't been paid what Miramax had promised). Harvey Weinstein takes a different view, of course: Zaentz did very well out of *The English Patient*, Weinstein said: it won the Best

Film Oscar, it made a lot of money worldwide, and he did very well out of *The Lord of the Rings,* which Miramax had been involved with: Zaentz 'will make $100 million personally on *Lord of the Rings.* Harvey made him a hundred fuckin' million bucks'.[2]

A 25 minute documentary on the pre-production that had been done so far was produced by the Kiwi team to take around the studios, including interviews with artists Alan Lee and John Howe, and photographs of the miniatures. As Jackson recalled 'we were desperate. The movie was collapsing around our ears – so we were all being interviewed for our documentary wearing happy, smiling faces whilst feeling utterly sick and appalled'.[3]

Miramax gave Jackson, Walsh and the *Lord of the Rings* team a very difficult turnaround time: just four weeks, plus the following terms: 2.5% of the gross for Miramax's Weinstein brothers (and 2.5% for Disney), and all of the $10.1 million back that Miramax had given Walsh, Jackson & co. (which had already been spent), immediately. In interviews for the *Lord of the Rings* films, Peter Jackson and the producers, discussing the studio set-up for the film, turned the story into a heroic last ditch attempt to save the project, when it was hiked around the studios, with everyone passing, until it got to New Line, their last hope, and Bob Shaye said yes – to three films. (Going from two to three films was great for the story – Lórien could be re-instated, scenes could be fleshed out, and there was simply more room all-round for characters and plot).

However, the reality was that Miramax's conditions for turnaround were very tough. As Jackson put it, the deal was 'beyond horrible'.[4] New Line's Mark Ordesky had been instrumental in brokering the deal, and setting up the meeting at New Line for Walsh and Jackson. New Line announced the project in August, 1998. Ordesky recalled that some of the Hollywood studios wouldn't even take the meeting with Walsh and Jackson. According to Jackson, only New Line Cinema and Polygram took a meeting with the *Lord of the Rings* team when they visited L.A.; everyone else was decidedly unimpressed – with Jackson's track record, and with the costly, complex project. 'You name any studio and they all turned *Lord of the Rings* down. I mean, that's an interesting little thing that not many people know about. But they, everybody said no, except for Polygram and New Line Cinema'. Among the studios who turned down *Rings* were DreamWorks, Sony, Universal, Fox, and companies like Centropolis and ImageMovers. Polygram wouldn't have been able to greenlight such an expensive project at that time.

Harvey Weinstein had a plan in case the deal with Peter Jackson and the New Zealand team didn't work out: he was going to hire John Madden to direct (Madden had helmed the Miramax hit *Shakespeare In Love*), with Hossein Amini to script alongside Walsh (he had adapted *The Wings of the Dove* and the dreadful *Jude*). And it would have been one film. The intervention of Jackson's and Walsh's agent (Ken Kamins at ICM) persuaded Harvey Weinstein to let the filmmakers take the project elsewhere (Miramax were very reluctant to put the project in turnaround). Jackson, meanwhile, was very concerned with the effect of walking away from *Rings* on the Weta company, especially after *Kong* had been cancelled too. So Kamins and his team sent the two scripts and animatics to the Hollywood studios, hoping one would bite (Sib, 392). (The relationship with Miramax was fraught at times: Jackson recalled that he was yelling at the producer Miramax sent to oversee pre-production on *LOTR* within days).

And when Bob Shaye first considered the project, he really didn't want to give a gross percentage to Miramax. Even without talking to Michael Lynne, Shaye knew that the Miramax percentage would be a stumbling block (Sib, 395). One of the attractions of the *Rings* films, though, was that the studio would get two sequels as well as the first film: at the time, New Line was having trouble continuing its franchises (such as *Dumb and Dumber, The Mask,* and *Nightmare On Elm Street*). The *Rings* films would mean two more big films that could be released down the line. It also meant three DVD and video releases, and three TV sales. 'I wanted to have three years of potential security and good business,' Shaye said (although it was a risk commissioning sequels when the first film wasn't released yet). Another attraction was the 'foundation interest: an incredible piece of material that had worldwide recognition and incredible marketing momentum', as Shaye put it (Sib, 402). And Shaye liked the designs, the ideas, the presentation that the filmmakers had put together, and he liked the idea that Weta could deliver vfx cheaper than ILM, who had been 'very expensive' on *The Mask* (although Shaye thought that Weta wouldn't be able to handle a completely digital figure like Gollum). Also New Line had recently cut their loses on developing Isaac Asimov's *Foundation* books for the screen (spending a rumoured $1.5 million), so that made *Rings* attractive too. (When the deal had been made, New Line immediately began negotiations the following morning with the lawyers of Miramax, Saul Zaentz, and Peter Jackson).

Harvey Weinstein had negotiated the rights to *The Lord of the Rings* from Saul Zaentz. Weinstein said that Zaentz didn't invest any of his own money, but as executive producer, he would be very well paid ($100 million was a figure bandied about for Zaentz's take).

Miramax put up $10.1 million for the development of the scripts and pre-production (producing models, designs, tests, location scouting). Miramax stipulated that the two-film deal would be $75 million for both films, a co-production between Miramax and Dimension. When the budget rose to $140 million during pre-production (the initial budget of $75m, Peter Jackson agreed later, was 'incredibly off the mark'), Miramax (and Disney) got cold feet. Harvey Weinstein blamed Miramax's parent company, Disney, for not getting behind the *Lord of the Rings* project. 'Disney didn't believe in it, wouldn't give me the money to make the film', recalled Weinstein.[5] Miramax hadn't tackled anything that expensive before. Bob Weinstein apparently didn't understand the project.

So Miramax asked Jackson and Walsh for a single film, 'One Great Movie', but the writers knew it would be impossible to put all of *The Lord of the Rings* into a single two-hour or three-hour movie without it departing too far from the book, and from their own conception (we would've had to 'get rid of a whole bunch of characters and a *lot* of the story', recalled Jackson). Miramax would not agree to a four-hour epic film; they wanted a two-hour movie. (Up until that point, around 1998-99, Miramax was not known as a producer of very high budget films, always preferring modest budgets. Jackson reckoned that the project finally died when Marty Katz showed the two hour thirty minute animatic to Miramax in New York: it had gone down 'incredibly badly' [Sib, 378]). Katz reckoned the one film version could have been made at Miramax, and it might have been a good movie. But it wasn't what the Walsh-Jackson-Weta team wanted to do. Miramax, though, ended up demanding one film; it could only be one film for them. Jackson suggested doing the first half, seeing how it went with audiences, then doing the second. Miramax declined.

The decision of all the major Hollywood studios not to get behind the *Lord of the Rings* films would of course be one of the worst in contemporary Hollywood, in view of how much revenue the films generated. And Bob Shaye and New Line's 'yes' was one of the best decisions they've ever made. Disney in the late Nineties didn't want to get in too many ultra-high budget features: they already had *Armageddon* in 1998 (costing $140m), *Tarzan* in 1999 (costing $145m), with *Dinosaur* (costing $200m), *Monsters, Inc* (costing $115m) and *Pearl Harbor* ($135m) coming up. Only years later would Disney have one of their own live action fantasy adventure franchises in the *Harry Potter* or *The Lord of the Rings* vein: *The Chronicles of Narnia*, debuting in 2005. Harvey Weinstein remarked that Disney's decision not to back them cost them in the region of $1 billion.

NOTES: MIRAMAX, SAUL ZAENTZ AND PRE-PRODUCTION

1. E. Grove, 2004, 346-7.
2. P. Biskind, 2004, 275.
3. J. Duncan, 2001, 67.
4. P. Biskind, 2004, 243.
5. P. Biskind, 2004, 243.

THE DEAL

Hollywood's finances (the financing and accounting of movies) is a vast and complex subject. There are only a few really good studies on the subject, and plenty of misunderstandings. Million dollar amounts are now employed in advertising (as in: '*Attack of the Hobbits* cost $145 million!'), and box office receipts are published in many places outside the trades ('*Killer Elves From Hell* grossed a healthy $52 mil on its opening weekend'). A box office gross of $100 million sounds great, for instance, but it's the *rentals* (about half that figure) that really count.

And one can also bet that if each Tolkien/ New Line film was grossing eight or nine hundred million bucks (or around the four hundred million dollar mark in rentals) then someone, somewhere, was making a lot of money out of them. Remember, too, that theatrical release represents only a *quarter* of the total revenue a movie generates (and the *Lord of the Rings* films weren't just movies, they were a vast licensing and merchandizing and computer game operation too).

Release dates were the Wednesday in the week before Christmas: Dec 19, 2001, Dec 18, 2002 and Dec 19, 2003. *Fellowship* opened in 3,703 theatres in the U.S.A. in total; *Towers* in 3,622, and *King* in 3,359 theatres.

New Line Cinema reckoned the films had generated $3 billion globally from their theatrical release. New Line haven't released figures for the DVD and home video sales (a figure of $6 billion has been suggested for the cinema, DVD and home entertainment revenue). Estimates for DVD and video sales of *Fellowship* are just less than 19 million; 17.3 million for *The Two Towers;* and 12m for *Return* (not including the extended cut).

How much money did the 2001-2003 *Lord of the Rings* films *really* make? It's difficult to get accurate figures: box office numbers are posted by the Hollywood studios, and sometimes they change their minds about how much a film has made. Distribution rentals are the key figure, but since the mid-1990s, *Variety* has taken to posting gross amounts. If we don't have the exact figures for the New Line Cinema *Lord of the Rings* films, we can work it out roughly:

The Fellowship of the Ring had a great opening weekend: $47.2 million over three days (from 3,703 theatres in the United States, making $14,055 per theatre). Those were record figures for a December opening, and the following two *Rings* outings beat that record (unadjusted for inflation). The second weekend is also vital, the drop between the first and second weekends helping to indicate how a film will perform in the long run: *The Fellowship of the Ring* fell by 18% (40% is typical). New Line, unusually, expanded the number of theatres to 3,381 for the 2nd weekend.

The Fellowship of the Ring was the top-grossing film for four weeks, until it was knocked off by *Black Hawk Down* (2002). But it only had *Orange County* (2002) and *A Beautiful Mind* (2001) to compete against in the U.S.A. It was in the top 10 for 7 weeks, was still playing in 1,000 theatres after 17 weeks, and stayed for 35 weeks in theatres.

The Return of the King was the top film of 2003 at the global box office, with $1,129 million gross. $377m was made in the U.S.A., and twice as much overseas: $752m. *The Return of the King* was followed in 2003 by *Finding Nemo* ($865m), *The Matrix 2* ($735m), *Pirates of the Caribbean* ($653m) and *Bruce Almighty* ($459m) in the top-grossing film charts.

In the lists of top 100 grossing films at the global box office, *adjusted for inflation* (the more accurate mode of comparison), *The Return of the King* was no. 48, *The Two Towers* was no. 57, and *The Fellowship of the Ring* was no. 72 (up to 2004). In the lists for US box office revenue, again adjusted for inflation, for films released since 1977, *The Return of the King* was no. 20, *The Two Towers* was no. 25, and *The Fellowship of the Ring* was no. 32.

The Fellowship of the Ring grossed $860.3m globally; *The Two Towers* took $848.7m; and *The Return of the King* made $1129m. So rentals for each film would be around the $425m mark. Say $1,225 million for all three films. To work out how much the *Lord of the Rings* films would have generated from other markets, such as satellite, pay-TV, cable, network and syndicated TV, home video and DVD sales, we can use *Batman* (1989) as a guide: theatrical release accounted for 34% of the franchise for Warners; 29% for home entertainment; 19% for merchandizing; 10% for US TV; and 8% for overseas TV. By 1994, only 16% of a studio film's revenue came from domestic (i.e., US) theatrical release. 16% was the international market; 45.9% was home video (26% from domestic sales, 19.9% from international sales); domestic TV accounted for 11%; with licensing and merchandizing at 11.1%.[2] (In the case of the *Lord of the Rings* films, international grosses were around 63% of total gross, so the films made two thirds of their revenue from overseas markets).

So if the *Lord of the Rings* films made $1,225 million in film rentals, and that was 34% of their total revenue, they might have generated $1,044m from home video and DVD; $684m from merchandizing; and $648m from TV sales, overseas and domestic. Or $3,600 million in total. Very happy figures for all involved (or least, for the key people near the top of each of the hundreds of companies involved; for everyone else, just the usual salary, as usual).

If *The Fellowship of the Ring* hadn't performed well at the box office, 'it would have been an absolute disaster', recalled director Peter Jackson, and 'New Line Cinema would have ceased to exist'. And maybe the 2nd and 3rd films wouldn't have been finished, 'because a lot of money gets spent on these movies in post-production'. Maybe New Line Cinema would've just shelved the films. Maybe. But probably not. Even if *The Fellowship of the Ring* had tanked, the other films could've been completed, at a lower budget. They'd make a great TV mini series, for example.

On a movie like *The Lord of the Rings,* the people with a profit participation deal would include the director, the main producers, and the main stars (Wood, McKellen, Tyler, Mortensen, and possibly also Astin, Blanchett, Rhys-Davies, Hill, Lee and others). Among the producers, the people with percentage deals would include: Barrie Osborne, Jackson, and writers Philippa Boyens and Frances Walsh, who also had producer credits. *The Lord of the Rings* had many producers, co-producers and executive producers, so it's more difficult to say exactly who would have received a percentage of the gross or net. Jackson was rumoured to have made $200 million from the films – but, folks, million-dollar figures are often thrown about like that – this is show business! *Show* + ***business***).

But the film crew on *The Lord of the Rings* would be paid a salary or fixed fee so that, no matter how well or badly the film fared, they would receive the same amount (the *Lord of the Rings* films were a non-union venture, too, and many people were working for less than their usual price). It's possible that a few of the crew also received points. Jamie Selkirk, for instance, has co-producer credit as well as editor. The Weinsteins brothers, who run Miramax, had compensation for initially developing the project (Jackson had a first-look deal with Miramax). In fact, the Weinsteins had 2.5% of the gross, which would have made them a lot of money (and 2.5% went to Disney).

Meanwhile Bob Shaye and Mike Lynne, New Line's co-CEOs, would have profited very substantially from the success of the *Lord of the Rings* films (probably more than any other individuals, including Jackson). As executive producers, Shaye and Lynne would likely have received gross percentages (one definition of an executive producer in the Hollywood system is someone who writes the cheques. The banks and backers of the *Lord of the Rings* films would certainly expect just a little profit on their investment too).

The Saul Zaentz Company was also a key player in the rights, merchandizing and licensing business created by the films. Zaentz's company, Tolkien Enterprises, controlled the licensing and merchandizing of Tolkienania. New Line had the license for the movie characters, but Zaentz had the wider merchandizing rights. A profit-sharing contract was in place between Zaentz and New Line, but Zaentz filed a suit against New Line, claiming he was owed $11 million from the profits of *The Fellowship of the Ring*.[4] And Wingnut and Jackson brought a law suit against New Line Cinema, about – what else? – money – $100 million they said was owed them ('I mean, I can't discuss the law suit, but it is just about rather dull audit issues, not people or projects', Jackson told an interviewer).[5] The Wingnut/ Jackson suit wasn't resolved until late 2007; Zaentz's case was resolved in 2005. But Zaentz sued New Line *again*, in 2007. (Zaentz and Jackson were given over $20 million each, when the case with New Line was settled).

Yet another case was brought against New Line Cinema, when the Tolkien Estate sued for £75 million ($120m) in February, 2008, claiming they hadn't seen a penny from the films, apart from receiving $62,500 for the 3 movies before production began. The estate wanted 7.5% of the gross receipts.

Zaentz, the Tolkien Estate and Wingnut/ Jackson claimed that New Line Cinema hadn't allowed them to audit their books (according to the *L.A. Times*, July 2, 2008). It's all very well for New Line and Time Warner to crow about how much money the *Rings* movies were making, but they should also have realized that other people would want a piece of the action. The Tolkien Estate gained a settlement of over $100 million in September, 2009.

The negative cost for the hobbit films was originally budgeted (in 1999) at around $270 million (i.e., about $90 million each film). Of course, that figure rose with each film (the figure of $109 million was published for *The Fellowship of the Ring*). The negative cost is the amount it takes to make the films. The average negative cost for a film rose from $9.4 million in 1980 to $26.8 million in 1990 ($39 million in 1995). The average cost for domestic p & a (prints and advertizing) rose from $4.3 million in 1980 to $11.6m in 1990 to $20 million in 1995. By 1998, the average cost of producing and marketing a movie was $75.6 million. The marketing budget for the three Tolkien films was reckoned to be $145 million; later estimates put it at $210m.

Accounts differ on the true cost of the *Lord of the Rings* films: tax breaks, investment from distributors, overseas investment, etc, all contributed towards paying for the films. The original budget was apparently $281 million (or $270m), and rose to $310m, or $330m according to some estimates. Peter Jackson thought the films cost around $130 million each. The final cost was probably more than that.

The tax break offered by the Labour government in New Zealand amounted to NZ$219 million. The Bank of New Zealand (Australian-owned) financed the films through a subsidiary company, who wrote off the expenditure as a tax loss. The subsidiary company was sold back to the producers. So, in effect, the New Zealand tax payers were financing the films to the tune of NZ$219 million

New Line's own investment was thought to be between $20 and 80 million. So New Line did not put up the whole $290m or $390 million or whatever the final negative cost was, nor all of the $210m spent on advertizing and PR. New Line, remember, were not a major Hollywood studio; they were one of the 'mini-majors'. The major Hollywood studios had in the region of $750 million for their production budget for a year of film production in the Nineties. So you can see how a big tentpole, event picture, costing say $140 million, takes out huge chunks of the annual budget. New Line's production budget was much smaller than that.

In terms of marketing and distribution, the *Lord of the Rings* films would have been among the most expensive movies of recent times, in the same price bracket as the *Star Wars* or *Harry Potter* films. The negative cost of a film is only the start of a long road of spending huge amounts of money for the studio, its banks and backers. Basically, you spend on advertizing what you think you'll get back from sales. So New Line and Time Warner knew the *Lord of the Rings* films could potentially rake in colossal sums, and knew they had to spend accordingly.

As a product, *The Lord of the Rings* had everything: it was a classic novel that had huge sales, it had a well-established audience (who had lots of spending power), it was a favourite book of millions, it had multiple points of entry for audiences, it could play to a broad spread in the audience (from the young to the old), and it had massive crossover potential into video games, toys, licensing, etc. And it had all of the crucial elements of a blockbuster film (action, spectacle, suspense, romance, etc). Plenty of punters already knew about the book: it didn't have to be sold from scratch, as a new subject in a film does. It was a 'pre-sold' product in many respects.

True, *The Lord of the Rings* was skewed too much towards fantasy and action for some of the older female segments of the audience, but for them the romance angle could be emphasized, as well as the old-fashioned adventure angle. (New Line's PR dept knew that the *Lord of the Rings* films had appeal across the board, but there was one age group that was difficult to reach: 50+ women (*Star Wars* also had trouble attracting older women to the theatre).)

Before New Line took on the *Lord of the Rings* films, they would have probably conducted market research. It's common for studios to preview films, of course (a nerve-wracking time for everyone linked to the film), but it's common practice to test titles, ideas, storylines, and so on. So a studio considering backing *The Lord* would go onto the street and ask questions like 'would you go and see a live-action version of *The Lord of the Rings?*' Pretty soon the market research would have revealed a high awareness of the book, and among many interviewees a 'must-see' response. That was why New Line asked for not just a 'rollercoaster' of a movie, they also commissioned documentary teams to record every last detail of the project for the home entertainment releases, every discussion, every prop, every set, every actor, every costume change, every moment, no matter how trivial or insignificant. Because they knew large segments of the audience would lap it up.

As before, the response from market research would have been favourable enough for New Line Productions to ask for (and pay for) the extended cuts for home DVD and video sales. After the theatrical grosses for *The Fellowship of the Ring* came in, after the weekend of December 21, 22 and 23, 2001, New Line would've been happy to authorize further shooting, editing, music, visual effects and sound dubbing necessary to produce the new extended versions of each film.

And yet another version: the 'Limited Edition' of 2006, which put the cinema cut and the extended cut of *The Lord of the Ring$* on one DVD disc, plus a new documentary by Costa Botes (Botes & co. had apparently shot 800 hours of footage for the five-hour documentary! God knows what those other 795 hours are like, because the documentary is excruciatingly boring. I am suing for $300 billion as compensation for those five hours).

Casting would likely have been an area New Line, like any Hollywood studio, would have definite ideas about. Stars sell movies above almost any other single element. No one goes to see a movie because so-and-so edited it, or a particular person was production designer, or because Joe Schmoo was third assistant sparks. Casting, as everyone in Hollywood agrees (except actors turned down for the *n*-th time), is vital. Producer Joel Silver (of the *Matrix* and *Lethal Weapon* films) puts casting at the top of the list for a film's success. Jim Carrey as the Grinch, Sean Connery as James Bond, the Rock as the Scorpion King, Arny as the Terminator, Mel as William Wallace – it's all-important.

New Line Cinema would've steered the producers of *The Lord of the Rings* towards names (although they had probably already agreed with the producers that *really* big names, like Toms Hanks and Cruise, would not need to be considered). However, New Line were probably completely happy with Elijah Wood as Frodo rather than some unknown British actor. Sure, Wood, Ian McKellen, Cate Blanchett and Liv Tyler may be a pricier than (virtual) unknowns, but the trade-off in terms of a little glamour, a little star quality, is immense, especially for the marketing of the film. New Line were certainly keen on Tyler, who would've helped to appeal to the overseas markets. According to Peter Jackson, there were certain actors, such as Richard Harris, which New Line told the filmmakers they could not have at all, and there were actors which New Line would not let the casting team even bring in for an audition (Sib, 430).

Miranda Otto might have been a little more troubling for the studio but, well, if she's good enough for a genius like Terry Malick (in *The Thin Red Line*), then perhaps she was enough for *Rings*. As it turns out, Otto was great as Éowyn, but it's likely that New Line would want a bigger name for only the third significant woman in a male-dominated series. Uma Thurman was considered, which would've enhanced the glamorous, star quality of the films. (New Line didn't like Stuart Townsend as Aragorn, and the filmmakers had to persuade them to accept him, and shot a test on film, standard practice, and not only when a studio's dragging its feet over a casting decision).

If you think about the casting of the *Lord of the Rings* films from the point-of-view of the *studio*, not the Tolkien fans, or other fascinated groups, a different picture emerges. New Line would be considering two primary markets: North America, and the international markets (with territories such as Japan, Germany, France, and the U.K., very important. I could provide tables and data of global markets for films here, but that's available in many other places). In short, the international markets often account for half a film's rentals. In the case of the *Lord of the Rings* films, *The Fellowship of the Ring* took $547 million overseas (gross sales), compared to $313m in the United States. *The Two Towers*, meanwhile, took $518m internationally, and $330m in North America.

In the *Lord of the Rings* films, New Line would happy with some of the casting choices, but not so much with others. Elijah Wood was an emerging lead following *The Faculty* and *Deep Impact*, Sean Astin was a Goonie, Liv Tyler was glam, and hot after *Armageddon*, Cate Blanchett was making a name as a 'serious' actor, Mortensen was moving into leading role territory. And, even better, Wood, Astin, Tyler and Mortensen were American. New Line would have no problem with Brits like Sean Bean, Christopher Lee, and Bernard Hill who were, respectively, the bad guy in *GoldenEye*, Dracula and the captain in *Titanic*. And Ian Holm had been in everything.

Ian McKellen was trickier. At the time of casting (mid-1999), he wasn't yet the bad guy in *X-Men* (in theatres, anyway). But Gandalf likely had to be an older character actor. Sean Connery probably wouldn't want to do it: too long a shooting schedule, and New Line might not have been able (i.e., willing) to afford to pay Connery a starring role fee (plus points) across three movies (it would've upped the budget by tens of millions). And Connery might not've agreed to the lower salaries which other actors accepted (Jackson, a huge *Bond* fan, would've loved to work with Connery). Connery was offered (via his agents CAA) in the region of 10-15 per cent of the movies, but he said no after reading the script. As Connery put it later, in 2005: 'I never understood it. I read the book. I read the script. I saw the movie. I still don't understand it' (in Sib, 429).

As far as casting goes, New Line wouldn't care a jot about hardcore Tolkien fans. The diehard fantasy fans might be sitting in tweeds in Senior Common Rooms in Yale and Cambridge, puffing on pipes and intoning 'James Bond as Gandalf?! The very idea!' The Hollywood studio would be thinking precisely the opposite: Connery (Peter O'Toole, Christopher Lee, etc) as Gandalf: perfect.

There was no time pressure to get *The Lord of the Rings* made: it wasn't a book that had to be released to coincide with audience interest. *The Lord of the Rings* had already been out in the public domain for forty some years by the time the Miramax and New Line deals were going through. The audience's interest in the book wasn't going to wane in a hurry. *The Lord of the Rings* wasn't a passing fad. (There were options, rights and contracts to consider, as always, of course).

Similarly, the fantasy adventure genre in Hollywood cinema wasn't going to go away, and had been a staple of the global film release schedules since the late 1970s, especially for Summer and Christmas family-oriented blockbusters. (The extraordinarily successful *Harry Potter* phenomenon might've helped to usher in another cycle of interest in fantasy and magic, too. So *Harry Potter* wasn't a rival to *The Lord of the Rings*, but an aid in revitalizing the fantasy genre).

Peter Jackson said that the production's relationship with New Line Cinema was not comfortable, and got 'pretty tense, and there has been some quite nasty sparring between lawyers'. A $15 million increase in the budget (due to the visual effects) occurred when the production was shooting Helm's Deep and New Line got tough, threatening legal action. 'Bob Shaye and Michael Lynne live under a whole different set of criteria to Peter Jackson,' noted Ken Kamins, Jackson's agent: New Line's a subsidiary of Time Warner, a Hollywood studio, very different from a group of filmmakers (Sib, 511). The filmmakers and New Line were very different companies, Jackson said, and they 'went through some pretty bad battles', and emerged with a 'grudging respect' for each other. In fact, they were getting so well that Wingnut was suing New Line over its accounting practices (the legal wrangle went on for years, and wasn't resolved until late 2007).

One of the key reasons for the wrangles between the filmmakers and New Line Cinema was that the script wasn't locked and the budget wasn't locked. The filmmakers were changing the script as they went along, adding more effects shots, and more complicated effects. Jackson acknowledged: *'we never had a locked script, and therefore never could arrive at a locked budget'* (Sib, 480; my italics).

As Peter Jackson related, as the films went along, the budget was increasing, the schedule for the visual effects was expanding, and the project was becoming much bigger than what New Line had intended. 'Which made them pretty angry, and threats would fly around'.[6] New Line would've realized, though, as every other Hollywood studio has when embarking upon a big and difficult project, that after a certain time it wouldn't have been economically sound to cancel the picture. They would just have to keep it going, to let the filmmakers carry on. Which meant throwing more money at it. Maybe New Line and Time-Warner considered abandoning the films from time to time, knowing that they would have to be very successful to return their investment (Shaye said he and Lynne 'always had the option of pulling the plug or cutting back', but after seeing the footage, they realized it was worth sticking with. But they would still not just throw money at the film: 'we argued long and hard about some things' [Sib, 484]).

Peter Jackson said that his job was 'to take responsibility for the investment New Line has put into the films and try to make them as good as possible'.[7] Jackson remarked that New Line's anxiety was understandable, because they hadn't seen any footage and the budget was going up. Jackson also said that filmmakers must drive studios mad with their ideas: 'I don't know how these studio executives do it! It would drive me nuts dealing with filmmakers like me!' (Sib, 479). Shaye later remarked that more experienced directors would probably have brought the films in costing much more.

NOTES: THE DEAL

1. S. Spielberg, 2000, 203.

2. L. Rice-Baker, 1996.

3. D. Biltereyst & P. Meers, in E. Mathijs, 2006, 73.

4. H. Davies. "*Lord of the Rings* Royalties Owner Issues £11m Writ", *Daily Telegraph*, Aug 20, 2004.

5. Zaentz held the film rights for the books for many years, and apparently thought that it was unlikely that a live action film would happen. Zaentz had also produced the 1978 cartoon, which was released through United Artists, so he would have seen revenue coming from the re-release of that film too.

6. In I. Nathan, 2004, 89.

7. I. Nathan, 2004, 89.

CHAPTER 4

CASTING AND PERSONNEL

THE CAST

Producer Barrie Osborne (b. 1944) made an important point on the extended cut DVD of *The Fellowship of the Ring*: that the *Lord of the Rings* films didn't need big stars to open the films (i.e., for the marketing, or to deliver an audience to the films), because the material had such a strong media profile already. These were much-loved books with over 100 million readers. In other words, the *Lord of the Rings* films didn't need Tom Hanks, Tom Cruise, Nicole Kidman or Julia Roberts to open them, because J.R.R. Tolkien's book was such a well-established property (and the movies' negative costs were already high, without bumping up the above-the-line costs with expensive talent). It also meant that the producers could look around for the best actors for the roles, rather than be tied to securing a big star. (At the time of casting, 1999, only Christopher Lee, Elijah Wood and Liv Tyler could be considered stars, but Wood and Tyler were only just then becoming stars. Maybe Cate Blanchett too. By the time of the first film's release, however, Ian McKellen, Viggo Mortensen and Orlando Bloom were stars. And Hugo Weaving, with his roles in *The Matrix* series and *The Lord of the Rings,* was, if not a star, then well-known for quirky roles).

The *Lord of the Rings* filmmakers stated that their intention had been to cast British actors where possible for the main parts. But it was clear from the beginning that a Hollywood blockbuster of this sort would include US actors as well as British, and also actors outside of the US-UK tradition (i.e., to become an 'international' cast – but 'international' this time meant white Australian and Kiwi actors as well as Anglo-Americans). In the end, three of the four main roles were filled by US actors.

Some parts were easier to cast than others: Gandalf and Saruman weren't too difficult: there were quite a few older male character actors who could have done either role (Peter O'Toole, Michael Gambon, Richard Harris, Sean Connery, Ron Moody, and my favourite choice, Paul Scofield, who was a brilliant Merlin in the BBC radio series *Arthur the King* [1990], and an extraordinary Sir Thomas More in *A Man For All Seasons* [1965]). (In a poll in April, 1999, fans voted for Sean Connery to play Gandalf). Gimli, turned into a comic foil for much of the action, wouldn't be too problematic (another older character actor). The elves were much trickier: they had to appear wise, ethereal, aquiline, sophisticated, tall, gentle and graceful without looking camp or hokey (in the end, they still looked camp). The two elves, Elrond and Galadriel, would be among the most challenging casting decisions, along with Legolas.

The villains in *The Lord of the Rings* were generally much easier to cast: the orcs were stunt folk or character actors, as were Gothmog, Lurtz, Sauron, the Witch-king *et al*. The baddies didn't have to look attractive, or speak much dialogue (many were looped by other actors), and they were often buried under prosthetics, make-up, helmets and costumes.

The orcs are among the least effective and convincing characters in the 2001-03 movies for me: they don't look right, they don't move right, they don't talk right, they tend to all look the same, they emit weird slowed-down grunts and snuffles, and they're suffocated under layers of special make-up. Tolkien's orcs are so much better.

The hobbits were probably the most difficult to cast, and Frodo and Sam in particular. Peter Jackson said the casting directors had looked everywhere for a British actor to play Frodo or Sam, but couldn't find one. So the parts went to two American actors. For me, both Sean Astin and Elijah Wood were too inexperienced or inadequate or just not charismatic enough to carry the three films. They both had a limited range (Astin in particular, though Wood soon ran out of anxious or painful facial expressions). Astin's limitations came to the fore in *The Return of the King*, when he had some big dramatic scenes to perform. It's hard to believe there wasn't a single actor in the U.K. that could have played Frodo better than Wood. The filmmakers had plumped for looks over ability (Wood, with his enormous eyes and pretty boy appearance, was attractive); and he also had a star caché (which most British actors of his age would not have had).

The producers tended to cast younger than the ages of the characters in the book: Frodo and Aragorn, for example, were cast younger than the book (the producers acknowledged their mistake in casting Stuart Townsend as too young for Aragorn, and recast with Mortensen). For critic Christopher Wrigley, Tolkien thought of his hobbit heroes as boys, and it was a 'great mistake' for film producers to cast adult actors as the hobbits (4). As a footnote, John Boorman had intended to cast ten year-old boys as the hobbits, to solve the scale issue, giving them facial hair, and dubbing them with adult voices (180). The idea, Boorman now concedes, having seen the 2001 *The Fellowship of the Ring*, would have been ridiculous.

Thinking more about it, many roles were cast younger than they are in the book: Denethor (I imagine him in his seventies; in the book he's in his late seventies); Arwen (Liv Tyler was 22 at the start of filming); Legolas (Orlando Bloom was also 22), and so on.

The *Lord of the Rings* films were tricky to cast in another respect: many of the characters were much-loved characters from fiction, which parts of the audience already knew very well (better than some of the actors eventually cast, who hadn't yet read the books). Gandalf, Bilbo, Frodo, Merry, Sam, Pippin, Gimli, Legolas, Aragorn – these were some of the most loved characters in 20th century fiction in a book which was often voted a favourite among readers. So the producers had to cast the film in that respect too (they didn't want to alienate potential movie-goers).

However, blockbuster action-adventure films such as *The Lord of the Rings* aren't really about 'acting' or 'performance'. The casting, while absolutely critical, was only one cog in the gigantic machinery of a Hollywood action-adventure blockbuster. It's the same with the *Star Wars, Jurassic Park, Die Hard, Lethal Weapon, Indiana Jones* and *James Bond* series. The actors become interchangeable. These colossal films are about spectacle, explosions, chases, monsters, special effects, costly production values, and the experience of going to the cinema. Oh, and merchandize, licensing and myriad tie-ins and spin-offs.

Casting and visual effects are two of the key factors in the action-adventure genre, according to Jon Lewis (2003). Star directors can help sell a movie – the Lucases, Spielbergs and Camerons (although many directors are far less well-known than their films: Roland Emmerich, Jan de Bont, Stephen Sommers and Wolfgang Petersen). Often they are marketed as 'from the director of…'

The casting process would have involved all of the usual questions: is the actor right for the part? Will they be able to play it? How do they look and sound? Can they do the accents? What's their fee? Are they prepared to work for less? What have they done before? Will audiences know them? Do they have star power? Are they easy to work with? Do we want to work with them? Can they commit to the project immediately? What do they have coming up that might clash? Will they agree to working in New Zealand for some time? Are they willing to help promote the film? Are they happy to be filmed many times for the 'making of' documentaries? And so on and on.

Because the *Lord of the Rings* schedule was an extended shoot for some of the roles, with some physical training required, additional questions might have included: are they willing to train (in sword fighting, canoeing, calligraphy, Elvish, etc)? Are there any additional costs – will they be bringing their family with them, for instance? Will they stay with the project for the entire schedule, including re-shoots and pick-ups? Will they agree to lower fees than they usually receive?

It's likely that the lengthy production schedule put off some actors, as well shooting in New Zealand (some actors aren't willing to move to another location for lengthy periods, leaving family and friends, etc). Some actors might've not liked the fantasy genre, or Tolkien, or the filmmakers' previous work.

ELIJAH WOOD. The star part (and top billing) in *The Lord of the Rings* went to Elijah Wood (b. 1981), 18 years old when shooting began in October, 1999. Wood's previous films had included big budget effects flicks such as the disaster movie *Deep Impact* (1998) and the teen horror flick *The Faculty* (1998, similar – though superior – to the horror genre stuff Peter Jackson made prior to *The Lord of the Rings*), as well as the *Flipper* remake (1996), Ang Lee's melancholy Seventies melodrama *The Ice Storm* (1997), *Forever Young* (1992), *The Adventures of Huckleberry Finn* (1993), and *Chain of Fools* (2000).

Elijah Wood had been found after a lengthy search to find hobbit actors in the U.K. and elsewhere. Wood had made a video audition tape of himself in a hobbit part, and sent it to the London casting office. Harry Knowles had encouraged the production to consider Wood. (Around 150 British actors were auditioned for the roles of the hobbits, which isn't that many, really. You can audition that many actors in a few days. On *The Shining*, for instance, Stanley Kubrick's assistant Leon Vitali personally video-taped *5,000* young actors for the part of Danny. That is an *extraordinary* amount of work to find one actor – but it paid off, 'cos Danny Lloyd was remarkable). The film production 'had been quite vocal and public in its reluctance to hire American actors' in order to stay close to Tolkien's vision, according to Sean Astin (2004, 191), but of course US actors prevailed in many of the lead roles.

The casting of Frodo was the most critical, perhaps, in the whole film project: Frodo was the chief hero, the audience had to spend a lot of time with him, had to identify with him and his situation. Crucially, Frodo would carry a good deal of the impact of the first film, and the first film had to do well at the box office and in home entertainment, to provide a solid base for the subsequent films. The hobbits were J.R.R. Tolkien's device of introducing the world of Middle-earth to the audience, and it would be the same in the film versions of *The Lord of the Rings;* so, as the chief of the hobbits, Frodo's role was vital. Before the audience got to meet Gandalf, Aragorn, Elrond, Galadriel, the elves, dwarves, orcs and monsters, they had to get to know Frodo and the hobbits. Note, for instance, how Frodo is introduced right after the prologue, over the title credit of the film (in the theatrical cut). Bilbo had been introduced in the prologue, of course (finding the ring, appropriately enough), but he's introduced as part of the history of the ring, not as a main character. It was Frodo who was established first, when the film comes out of the dense prologue (and in a cute reference to Tolkien, he's reading a book), and it's Frodo who meets Gandalf, and so on. According to Sean Astin, Elijah Wood never read the books in their entirety (2004, 149).

Among the cast marketed as eye candy were Wood, Mortensen, Bloom, and the three women, Tyler, Otto and Blanchett. Mortensen, as the romantic lead, was an obvious focus for attention in the publicity of *The Lord of the Rings* films, in particular *The Return of the King* (and whoever was cast as Aragorn would have to be handsome and believable as a romantic lead). Fans often drooled over Elijah Wood's angelic features and enormous eyes, but Orlando Bloom was the surprise hunk from *The Lord of the Rings* films, becoming a favourite with men and women, boys and girls (he was not only one of the most good-looking actors on the show, he was the coolest warrior, and the most athletic).

VIGGO MORTENSEN. Viggo Mortensen (b. 1958) had previously appeared in *G.I Jane* (1997), the *Dial M For Murder* remake, *A Perfect Murder* (1998), another Hitchcock remake, *Psycho* (1997), *Carlito's Way* (1993), *Witness* (1985) and *Boiling Point* (1993). Mortensen was known more as a character actor than a leading man (he was also regarded as somewhat eccentric, and was devoted to the project and the character). According to the publicity of the *Lord of the Rings* films, Mortensen was something of a 'Renaissance man', a published poet, and an accomplished painter. Mortensen, perhaps more than any of the other actors in *The Lord of the Rings*, took the role seriously (applying American Method principles): according to rumour, he wore his costume off-set, trained rigorously, and kept his sword close at hand (including driving round with it, and taking it into restaurants). He asked the people at Weta if he could keep the sword with him, and identified closely with it. Barrie Osborne often told the story of how Mortensen wanted to carry on shooting even after he'd knocked out a couple of teeth during a stunt. He also apparently slept in a stable with his horse, so it could get used to him. In playing Aragorn, Mortensen cited Toshiro Mifune in Akira Kurosawa's films, and Clint Eastwood and Gary Cooper: the silent, strong hero.

Because Viggo Mortensen arrived late to the production, when Aragorn was re-cast, he hadn't undergone the 6-8 weeks of training the other actors had, so took a while to get to grips with his role (one can see this in the first Aragorn scenes in *The Fellowship of the Ring* – the Weathertop attack and the *Prancing Pony* – compared with those in *The Two Towers* and *The Return of the King*). (Philippa Boyens knew they had made a good choice with Mortensen when the actor arrived carrying the *Volsunga Saga* that he'd brought from his own bookshelf).[2]

Viggo Mortensen used the media blitz surrounding the *Lord of the Rings* pictures to make political points (which few in the production did, and few in Hollywood ever do, and certainly not while publicizing a movie). Mortensen wore a 'no blood for oil' T-shirt on a PBS talk show, for instance. Mortensen wasn't the only one to make the links between Tolkien's tome and the West's attitude towards (and involvement in) the Middle East, Iraq, Afghanistan and North Korea.

STUART TOWNSEND. Irish actor Stuart Townsend (b. 1972) had originally been cast as Aragorn (Townsend had appeared in films such as *Shooting Fish* [1997], but certainly wasn't a 'star', or much known outside of British cinema. Perhaps the producers had been right to go for someone else. The *Lord of the Rings* films would have given Townsend's career a huge boost – as it did to, say, Karl Urban's and Orlando Bloom's film careers). Townsend went on to flicks such as *The League of Extraordinary Gentlemen* and *Queen of the Damned*.

One can see why Stuart Townsend had been cast as Aragorn: he had the right dark, handsome looks, and was moderately charismatic. He was, though, far too young for the Aragorn that's in the book (he was 27 at the time, being born in 1972). Townsend looked like someone in their late twenties (though he could have been aged up with myriad techniques – and not just the obvious ones of make-up). Townsend would've been a suitably good-looking foil for Liv Tyler's Arwen, and he would've been much cheaper than, say, Elijah Wood or Ian McKellen. It's impossible to say how Townsend might have fared in the later, more demanding aspects of the role, or how he might have handled the action. It would be fascinating to see the footage that was shot of Townsend (though it's highly unlikely that it will be officially released). To get an idea of what Townsend would've been like in *The Lord of the Rings,* have a look at the film he made instead – *Queen of the Damned,* where he played the vampire Lestat (not a great movie, but enjoyable. And Aaliyah made a superb villain). Peter Jackson said the team had cast Townsend because of 'his looks and his energy', and the 'gentle, slightly mystical side to him' (Sib, 432).

Having to fire Stuart Townsend very early in shooting, in late 1999, was probably the biggest obstacle the filmmakers faced in terms of actors and casting (the long shoot meant all sorts of other problems were possible: actors dropping out, illness, injury, other commitments, etc). But firing one of your lead actors when shooting is already under way is a nightmare. Delaying the film at that point would have cost 'a really frightening number of dollars a week' as producer Mark Ordesky put it.[3] There was no back-up plan: no Aragorn.

There were only five days to find someone who had to commit to a lengthy shoot. It was Ordesky who suggested Mortensen (New Line liked the idea of Mortensen). Phone calls went back and forth between the production office and Viggo Mortensen, between Jackson and Mortensen, between Walsh and Boyens with Mortensen, and as well as New Line's executives, as the actor decided whether to do the show (it took 48 hours to hammer out the deal, Ordsky recalled). If Mortensen had declined, Russell Crowe and Jason Patric were considered: but Crowe had just finished shooting *Gladiator,* and turned it down.

The exact reasons are difficult to ascertain, but some indication of the trouble surrounding Stuart Townsend can be gleaned from Sean Astin's book on the making of the *Lord of the Rings* films. Townsend was uncomfortable with the way his role was conceived by the writers and filmmakers, and wasn't happy with his costume. Sean Astin said Townsend was 'absolutely beside himself with discomfort – both mental and physical. He just didn't look right, didn't feel right, and he couldn't explain what needed to be done to correct the problem' (173). Other actors on the show had discomfort with their costumes and make-up (such as John Rhys-Davies with his prosthetic dwarf make-up), and getting Orlando Bloom's costume right had been agony. Costume problems could have been ironed out (they were a side issue) – but Townsend wasn't prepared to fuse his notions for the character of Aragorn with the filmmakers' vision. Ultimately, it was the filmmakers who would make the final decision about the characters, not the actors. So Townsend had to go.

Peter Jackson acknowledged that it had been partly his mistake in casting Townsend – 'I take full responsibility – I made a casting error' (Sib, 437). So on October 13, 1999, Jackson decided that Townsend would have to be replaced. Barrie Osborne agreed with him, and it was Osborne who told Townsend.

Ironically, both Peter Jackson and Fran Walsh had argued for using Stuart Townsend with the studio, because New Line didn't want him (the studio had ordered the producers to shoot a test on film, in costume, on sets, to see if Townsend could be Aragorn). That made the firing even more painful. Townsend felt bitter about it. As Sean Astin put it, it was 'cataclysmic' for an actor to be dropped like that. Some actors might've given up the business after an experience like that. Townsend told the *Los*

Angeles Times that *The Lord of the Rings* had been 'a nasty nightmare'. He also complained that he hadn't seen Jackson or the producers enough during pre-production,

As Sean Astin said, the film itself was the star, and 'rampant egoism would not be tolerated' by the production: 'you could and would be replaced' if you didn't want to fit in (2004, 172). So firing Stuart Townsend after a couple of weeks of shooting sent out a message to the performers: the film comes first, and if you don't subsume yourself to the show, you're out. Jackson said that all the actors had been stunned and upset, but Astin '*wasn't* devastated' (438).

One of my votes for Aragorn would be Liam Neeson. Even Bernard Hill might have been terrific as the rugged Strider and the lordly King Elessar (but perhaps not a good romantic lead for Tyler's Arwen – and he would have been a little old for Arwen, and not so good with the swordplay). Liam Neeson, of course, had already visited this territory with *Rob Roy* and *Star Wars: The Phantom Menace* (that 1999 film probably automatically excluded him from being considered as Aragorn: the *Lord of the Rings* films consciously distanced themselves from *Star Wars*, rather like Tim Burton asking for a design for Gotham in 1989's *Batman* film without neon and looking nothing like *Blade Runner*).

Neeson could easily have played the brooding, rough Celtic ranger, the Byronic ladies' man, the action hero (though he doesn't move brilliantly in *The Phantom Menace* – he's no Jet Li), and I reckon he could've have played King Elessar far more convincingly that Viggo Mortensen (that was the one aspect of the character of Aragorn I don't think Mortensen ever cracked). Neeson was sent the *Rings* script, for the part of Boromir, but declined. (On the basis of flicks like *Outlander* (2007), Jim Caviezel might have been an interesting Aragorn, though maybe not at the time of shooting, in 1999).

Liam Neeson did play two mentor warrior roles in subsequent films (in 2005): *Batman Begins* and *Kingdom of Heaven* (the latter Crusades film starred Orlando Bloom, but Bloom had the charisma of a cardboard box, as he had in *Troy*. He was truly dreadful. The Crusades film had been originally planned for Arnold Schwarzenegger with Paul Verhoeven directing). And Daniel Day-Lewis, one of the premier choices for casting, would likely have been a marvellous Aragorn.

IAN MCKELLEN. Ian McKellen (b. 1939) was known primarily as a stage actor, in the British theatrical tradition, rather than a TV or film actor (lots of Shakespeare, but also *Amadeus* and *Bent*). He had, like most British stage actors, many TV and film credits, though (but not nearly as many as other British veterans on the *Rings* films, such as Christopher Lee, John Rhys-Davies or Ian Holm). Most prominent of these, just prior to *The Lord of the Rings*, was the lead in *Richard III* (1995, which he also co-produced), *X-Men* (2000), and *Gods and Monsters* (1998), in which he had played the ageing British director James Whale (director of *Frankenstein*).

Ian McKellen's only role in blockbuster films like *The Lord of the Rings* was in *X-Men* (about a group of mutants with superhero powers, in which he played the chief villain, Magneto). The *X-Men* movies were fun action-adventure flicks, part of Hollywood's cycle of superhero movies (kick-started in the late 1970s by *Superman* and *Star Wars*, then in the late 1980s by *Batman*, and in the early 2000s by *Spider-man* – leading on to *The Hulk, Fantastic Four, Hell-Boy, Daredevil, Catwoman* and more *Batmans*). (Incidentally, McKellen's work on *X-Men* meant the *Rings* shoot had to re-jig their entire schedule, pushing Gandalf as far back as possible).

Ian McKellen was also known as an outspoken supporter of gay rights. He had come out of the closet in 1988, and was a high profile activist in the fight against the British Conservative government's Clause 28, which was seen by sections of the gay community as anti-homosexual. (This aspect of McKellen's media profile was played down (i.e., mostly ignored) by the New Line PR machine. Maybe they thought that an activist gay man playing a much-loved figure like Gandalf would have put off some of the target audience, who could be conservative. Instead, the *Rings* publicity dept concentrated on McKellen as Great British Shakespearean Actor, as well as his roles in *Richard III* and *X-Men*).

Discussing his characterization of Gandalf, Ian McKellen said he based some of it on Tolkien himself (such as the voice, low, precise, and rough from pipe smoking, and the stooping posture. McKellen had looked at video tapes of the professor in interview in preparing for the role. Actually, Tolkien was famous for speaking rapidly and indistinctly, making his lectures and interviews difficult to follow. But McKellen dropped that aspect of the voice). McKellen acknowledged that the characters in *The Lord of the Rings* were drawn in storytelling terms: 'I sometimes wish the relationships were more complicated, but they're not in the book', McKellen said.

McKellen underplayed Gandalf, holding back when many another actor would have grabbed a scene. Many of his lines were delivered in something close to a whisper. It wasn't wholly successful, and it meant that some important information and exposition wasn't wholly clear, but it did illustrate the screen acting tenet of doing everything by appearing to do nothing.

In *The Fellowship of the Ring*, the best scenes, acting-wise, were those between Gandalf and Frodo (partly because they are the heart of the book, where Tolkien outlines the key aspects of his life-philosophy). The scenes between Gandalf and Elrond (Hugo Weaving) were also solid (McKellen remarked that he and Weaving were same sorts of actors, with their background in classical theatre). Bernard Hill had been invited to play Gandalf but had declined (he later regretted his decision – though he did just fine as Théoden).

LIV TYLER. Liv Tyler (b. 1977), daughter of US rock band Aerosmith's lead singer Steve Tyler, had appeared in Bernardo Bertolucci's *Stealing Beauty* (1996), in which she played a precocious teenager at large in modern-day Bohemian Tuscany. Subsequent roles included Robert Altman's *Cookie's Fortune* (1999), *Plunkett & Macleane* (1999), *Onegin* (1999) and 1998's biggest grosser, *Armageddon*,.

Liv Tyler was known for dramatic roles, but was not considered a heavyweight actor like, say, Jodie Foster. Tyler had been eclipsed in the acting world by more accomplished contemporaries such as Bridget Fonda, Claire Danes and Winona Ryder (although her role in *Onegin* as the enigmatic, yearning woman Ralph Fiennes falls for was compelling). Tyler brought a movie star quality and youthful beauty to the role of Arwen, rather than character acting (she was 22 during filming, and played a character 2,777 years old). Reflecting her star status, Tyler was billed third, behind Wood and McKellen.

Liv Tyler did well with Arwen, though: Arwen was a tricky and underwritten role to play – she didn't have much to *do*, dramatically; she had to remain in Rivendell, talk with her father, and be an inspiration and spiritual guide for Aragorn via dreams and flashbacks.

JOHN RHYS-DAVIES. John Rhys-Davies (b. 1944) had lengthy credits, including (in movies) the *Indiana Jones* films (where he played Indy's Middle Eastern aide and fixer, Sallah), *The Living Daylights* (1987), *Victor/Victoria* (1982) and *King Solomon's Mines* (1985). Rhys-Davies, a loud, larger-than-life personality off-screen, was originally up for the part of Denethor. Acting in *The Lord of the Rings* for Rhys-Davies meant four and a half hours in make-up each morning; more than most of the cast, Rhys-Davies was buried under prosthetics, hair, make-up and a bulky costume (which he reacted to badly). Comedian Billy Connolly had been considered for Gimli.

CHRISTOPHER LEE. Christopher Lee's (b. 1922) credits are legendarily enormous – certainly more than any of the other actors in the *Lord of the Rings* films, and more than many of them put together, and more than almost any other actor then working in the film business. Lee's career had a resurgence in the years of *The Lord of the Rings:* he had appeared in Tim Burton's *Sleepy Hollow* (1999), and in George Lucas's *Star Wars: Attack of the Clones* (2002), where he played Count Dooku, a fierce Jedi master who overcomes Ben Kenobi and Annakin Skywalker in the climactic fight at the end of *Attack of the Clones* (he's killed at the beginning of 2005's *Star Wars: Revenge of the Sith*, and he's dispatched at the start of the extended edit of *The Return of the King*).

Among Christopher Lee's many film roles were the *James Bond* villain in *The Man With the Golden Gun* (1975) (Sean Bean had also been a *Bond* baddie), and of course, his most famous role was Count Dracula in the Hammer horror films (*Count Dracula, Dracula, Dracula A.D. 1972, Dracula, Prince of Darkness, Dracula Has Risen From the Dead, The Satanic Rites of Dracula, The Scars of Dracula*, and *Taste the Blood of Dracula*). (Peter Jackson was of course a big fan of the Hammer horror films, like thousands of other film buffs).

Christopher Lee also appeared in many other horror films (some of them from the Hammer studio): *The Curse of Frankenstein, The Devil Rides Out, Dr Terror's House of Horrors, The Curse of the Crimson Altar, The Hound of the Baskervilles, The House of the Long Shadows, The House That Dripped Blood, I, Monster, The Mummy, To the Devil a Daughter, The Two Faces of Dr Jekyll, Revenge of the Dead, She, Scream and Scream Again* and *The Skull*. He was also Fu Manchu in *The Brides of Fu Manchu*.

Chris Lee's favourite role, he claimed, was as Lord Summerisle in the 1973 cult horror film *The Wicker Man*, one of the great British horror films (for some critics, the best). Casting Lee as Saruman, then, was an easy choice: Lee had all the right credentials, and, importantly, a screen presence which could combine the strength, authority, pride, evil and intelligence that Saruman, now elevated to the main movie villain, required. Lee's Saruman also had to be a worthy adversary for Ian McKellen's Gandalf. Lee said he had wanted to play Gandalf for years (and even apparently had the blessing of Tolkien himself to do so), but when the time came he was thought to be too old.

SEAN BEAN. Dour Northern actor Sean Bean (b. 1959) was well-known to British TV audiences for his appearances in *Sharpe, Lady Chatterley, Clarissa* and *Lorna Doone*. In films, Bean's credits included *GoldenEye* (1995), *Ronin* (1998), *Black Beauty* (1994), *When Saturday Comes* (1996) and *Caravaggio* (1986). In big blockbuster Hollywood films comparable with the *Lord of the Rings* films, Bean only had *GoldenEye* and *Ronin* among his credits. (Sean Bean was also much in demand, like Ian Holm, as a voiceover artist in TV and radio advertizing). Bean often played villains, or the villain's henchmen, but in commercial TV's *Sharpe* he was the dashing action hero.

In *The Lord of the Rings*, Bean's was a supporting role, however: Boromir appears late in the first film, and dies by the end. It's something of a thankless role, too, because Boromir does more than most to break up the fellowship (he gets a heroic death, though, which lasts far longer on screen than Gandalf's). And Bean's Boromir did appear in the extended cuts of *The Two Towers* and *The Return of the King*.

IAN HOLM. Ian Holm (b. 1931) had appeared in many films before *The Lord of the Rings:* he was one of the British character actors most in demand by Hollywood, or 'British' films aimed at the international market (*Alien, Chariots of Fire, Time Bandits, Brazil, Greystoke, Frankenstein, The Madness of King George, Dance With a Stranger, The Fifth Element, The Sweet Hereafter* and *Night Falls On Manhattan*).

Ian Holm had played Frodo in the 1981 BBC radio version of *Rings* (which was a far superior interpretation of Frodo than Elijah Wood's). That gave Holm a welcome lingering association with Tolkien's fiction for many fans. Holm was apparently the first (and only) choice of actors to play Bilbo (there are other character actors who could have played Bilbo well, but Holm was terrific – he's one of those actors who's never bad). Like Lee and McKellen, Holm had become one of more respected 'knights' of British drama, turning in a memorable King Lear in the RSC's late 1990s production. With McKellen, Holm probably had the most experience in the theatre among the cast.

BERNARD HILL. Another British character actor, Bernard Hill (b. 1944), played the King of the Horse-lords. Hill had appeared in many TV and film productions (his big break was as jobless Yosser Hughes in TV's *Boys From the Black Stuff* in the early 1980s, which Peter Jackson had seen), but his highest profile role in terms of international cinema was the stolid, dependable but doomed captain in *Titanic* (1997). Hill had also appeared in Hollywood movies prior to *The Lord of the Rings*: *The Ghost and the Darkness* (1996), *A Midsummer Night's Dream*, *Wind In the Willows*, *The Mill On the Floss* and *Great Expectations*. Brit thesp Alan Howard, far less known to international audiences, was the voice of Sauron and the Witch-king (he had appeared in Peter Greenaway's *The Cook, The Thief, His Wife and Her Lover*). Of course, the voice of Sauron should be Bob Shaye of New Line – or perhaps the CEO of Time Warner.

CATE BLANCHETT. Australian Cate Blanchett's (b. 1969) credits prior to *The Lord of the Rings* included the lead in *Elizabeth* (1998), *Oscar and Lucinda* (1997), *An Ideal Husband* (1999), *The Talented Mr Ripley* (1999) and *Pushing Tin* (1999). Blanchett, on set for *The Lord of the Rings* for three weeks, was known as a 'serious' actress, who tended to pick 'interesting' roles, and actively shunned the media spotlight. After *The Lord of the Rings*, Blanchett continued to plump for prestige or unusual film projects (such as *The Aviator* [2004] and *The Life Aquatic* [2005]).

HUGO WEAVING. Hugo Weaving (b. 1960), another Australian (though born in South Africa), was probably best known for playing Agent Smith in another special effects blockbuster franchise, *The Matrix* (shot in Oz, like the *Star Wars* prequels, at 20th Century Fox's studios). *The Matrix* had been produced by Barrie Osborne, producer of *The Lord of the Rings*. The *Rings* producers had looked for a long while to find someone to play Elrond before Osborne suggested Weaving. One of Weaving's best film roles was as Mitzi, a drag queen in the gay comedy *The Adventures of Priscilla, Queen of the Desert* (1994). Like McKellen, Weaving was a veteran of stage productions.

MIRANDA OTTO. Another Australian, Miranda Otto (b. 1967), was the Rohirrim warrior Éowyn who falls for Aragorn. Otto's credits included the girl back home that Ben Chaplin dreams about in *The Thin Red Line* (1998), about the US assault in Guadalcanal. After *The Lord of the Rings* (and no doubt helped by the success of the Tolkien films), Otto appeared in The Hollywood action-adventure films such as *Flight of the Phoenix* (2005) and *The War of the Worlds* (2005).

One of the early choices to play Éowyn was Uma Thurman, with Ethan Hawke for Faramir. Ex-model Thurman, who made her name with *Pulp Fiction* (1994), has had an interesting Hollywood career (one of her first roles was as the Goddess Venus in Terry Gilliam's *The Adventures of Baron Munchausen* [1989]). Thurman moved into action-adventure leading roles in Quentin Tarantino's terminally dull martial arts *Kill Bill* movies (2003-04). Hawke, meanwhile, tended to pick 'serious' or 'worthy' roles, often in smaller or independent films, such as the lead in the contemporary version of *Hamlet*. (Thurman and Hawke had been a couple in the terrific sci-fi flick *Gattaca* [1997]). Hawke was keen, but passed. Stephen Dorff was another possibility.

SEAN ASTIN. Sean Astin (b. 1971) had visited Hollywood blockbuster territory previously – he was one of *The Goonies*, the Spielberg-produced children's adventure film of 1985 (directed by Richard Donner for Amblin). His other film credits before joining *The Lord of the Rings* included *Like Father, Like Son* (1987), *Memphis Belle* (1990), *Courage Under Fire* (1996) and *Bulworth* (1998). Astin was usually cast in supporting roles in dramas. His father, John Astin, had played a major role in the film Peter Jackson and Fran Walsh made prior to *The Lord of the Rings*, *The Frighteners,* and auditioned for the part of Gandalf (Astin senior had encouraged his son to consider travelling to New Zealand to take part in a Jackson-Walsh production). As Astin's account of making the *Lord of the Rings* films relates, Astin did have a tendency to harbour grudges and sulk, or shout his mouth off and say the wrong things, or want to get up there and direct the thing himself. At times Astin comes across as a frustrated film director who'd much rather be running the show, instead of being just a humble actor.

Astin said it was his work on *Rudy* and *Where the Day Takes You* that got him the part in *The Lord of the Rings* (2004, 47). Astin's audition for took place in L.A. and *The Lord of the Rings* involved the casting director, Victoria Burrows and an assistant. Astin reckoned he 'absolutely nailed the audition' (2004, 71). After that were further meetings with the filmmakers in New Zealand, before Astin was finally cast as Sam. Part of the casting process involved the filmmakers asking questions like, would we be able to work with this person for an extended period? The production meant that actors from the U.S.A. and U.K. would be working away from home and families for a long time. Being so far from home would have been a big sticking point for American and European actors, which's another reason why so many Australian thesps were cast (it's not so far to travel to Oz for weekends or breaks).

BRAD DOURIF. Character actor Brad Dourif (b. 1950), veteran of David Lynch's films and low budget horror films, was slimy royal aide and Saruman spy Wormtongue (Dourif's role was basically a replay of his part in 1984's *Dune*). Dourif's the kind of actor forever typed as strange and offbeat. One of the best things he's done recently was to appear as the narrator in Werner Herzog's brilliant documentary *Wild Blue Yonder,* and he turned up as an eccentric mountain climber in Herzog's stunning *Scream of Stone* (1994). Richard O'Brien, the total genius behind *The Rocky Horror Show*, was first choice for Wormtongue, but he declined. Pity.

Many of the other main roles were filled by relative newcomers (Billy Boyd, Orlando Bloom, Dominic Monaghan, and Lawrence Makoare). Orlando Bloom quickly became in demand following *The Fellowship of the Ring*, and entered the Hollywood mainstream with leads in *Pirates of the Caribbean* (2003, 2006 and 2007), *Troy* (2004) and *Ned Kelly* (2004).

ORLANDO BLOOM. Bloom was the star find among the cast; he was starring in big films long before the other newcomers in the *Rings* cast. Bloom had been a drama student in his 3rd year in the U.K. prior to being cast; he had played a minor role (as a rent boy) in the film *Wilde* (1998), based on the life of Oscar Wilde, as well as, like so many young actors in Britain, various walk-on parts in TV drama series. Bloom quickly became one of the more media-friendly of the *Rings* cast, enthusiastically talking up his extreme sports exploits, his accident-prone personality, and his willingness to try almost anything (these were the aspects of Bloom's profile the PR machine drew attention to, partly because extreme sports antics lend themselves so well to TV and magazine coverage. Also, when an actor hasn't done much else, career-wise, when they're young and just starting out, extreme sports are something neutral but exciting to talk about. And extreme sports, of course, link neatly to a key segment of the target audience – young males).

Notice how the *Lord of the Rings* films cast mainly from English-speaking actors, i.e., Oz, Kiwi, English and American actors. There are plenty of French, Spanish, German, Italian, Swedish, Russian, Chinese, Japanese and Indian actors (to name a few territories) they could have chosen. In fact, you could draw up a very tasty cast list from European actors (excluding Britain). The cinemas of France, Italy, Spain and Germany, for example, excel in mounting lavish historical dramas, and have actors comfortable with historical costumes, behaviour and dialogue (to name a few wonderful movies from recent years with affinities with the *Lord of the Rings* films: *La Reine Margot, Ridicule, Le Bossu, The Count of Monte Cristo, Germinal, Madame Bovary*, and *The Horseman On the Roof*). The leads in *The Lord of the Rings* could have been cast entirely from French actors. For instance, in the late 1990s, Isabella Adjani as Arwen, and Vincent Perez or Olivier Martinez as Aragorn, Faramir or Boromir.

How 'British' was the 2001-03 *The Lord of the Rings* film? Well, the source material was 'British', but the screen adaptors were Kiwi. Some of the actors and personnel were British (Ian McKellen, Sean Bean, Christopher Lee, Ian Holm, Bernard Hill, Andy Serkis, Orlando Bloom, John Rhys-Davies, hair and make-up artists Peter Owen and Peter King, sword master Bob Anderson, illustrator Alan Lee, and my friend from film school, location manager Nick Korda), but many of the actors and most of the crew were American, Kiwi or Australian: the production designer, DP, sound editor and costume designer were Australian, as were actors such as Cate Blanchett, Craig Parker, Miranda Otto, John Noble and Hugo Weaving. Karl Urban and Marton Csokas were Kiwi.

Among the many Americans were key personnel such as producers Osborne, Porras, Somers and Ordesky, visual effects supervisors Jim Rygiel, Joe Letteri and Brian Vant Hul, miniatures DP Alex Funke, sound designers and editors David Farmer, Michael Semanick and Ethan van der Ryn (a large proportion of the sound team was American), stunt co-ordinator George Marshall Ruge, and actors Elijah Wood, Sean Astin, Viggo Mortensen, Brad Dourif and Liv Tyler. Composer Howard Shore and illustrator John Howe were Canadian. The studio was of course American, the money was American (and, via tax loopholes, German), vfx came from the U.S.A. and New Zealand, the music was recorded in London and Watford, some of the film was edited in London (at Pinewood Studios), some looping took place in London and the U.S.A., foley work was by Redline Sound in Australia, digital grading was by the Posthouse in Australia, the wigs and hairpieces were manufactured in Bristol (UK), and principal photography took place in New Zealand.

Criticizing the acting in *Lord of the Rings* films is unfair for a number of reasons. Primarily, these sorts of high budget blockbuster Hollywood films are not about high quality acting, and it's not expected, or usually required (instead, actors are running away from explosions, wielding guns, driving cars, and so on). The large number of actors in the cast of *The Lord of the Rings* made it difficult to maintain a high standard of acting in every role. The films were shot over a lengthy schedule, which also made it tough to keep up standards for long periods of time. Also, some of the cast were young or relatively inexperienced. The films were also directed by a number of people (eight or so, including some uncredited directors). Finally, Peter Jackson is not known as an 'actor's director' (like, say, Ingmar Bergman or Robert Altman), and the acting in his films prior to the *Lord of the Rings* films was not particularly distinguished. (Jackson also has a weakness for over-the-top performances, especially in his villains).

NOTES: THE CAST

1. J. Hubbard, in E. Grove, 2004, 229.
2. In B. Sibley, 2002, 143.
3. In B. Sibley, 2002, 143.

BEHIND THE CAMERA

Some of the most important people working on *The Lord of the Rings* films in terms of production included producers Barrie Osborne, Rick Porras, Mark Ordesky and Ellen Somers; New Line execs Robert Shaye, Jon Davidson and Michael Lynne; Miramax execs the Weinstein brothers; director Peter Jackson; writers Fran Walsh, Jackson and Philippa Boyens (Stephen Sinclair had helped with early drafts, but wasn't one of the main writers); pre-viz supervisor Christian Rivers; illustrators Alan Lee and John Howe; the principal actors (noted above); composer Howard Shore; Richard Taylor, the eccentric head of Weta Workshop (which provided weaponry, props, miniatures and make-up); Ngila Dickson, costume designer; DP Andrew Lesnie (Alun Bollinger had been first choice); veteran sword master Bob Anderson; editors Jamie Selkirk, Michael Horton, Jabez Olssen, Heather Small, Annie Collins, Peter Skarratt and John Gilbert; Alex Funke, who lit and shot the miniatures; 2nd unit directors John Mahaffie, Geoff Murphy, Ian Mune and Guy Norris; Jim Rygiel, visual effects supervisor; make-up and hair artists Peter Owen and Peter King; production designer Grant Major; sound designers/ editors David Farmer and Ethan Van der Ryn; animator Randy Cook; and art director Dan Hennah. Each of these people had a huge impact on the final films of *The Lord of the Rings*.

On a film of this scale, the director does not direct everything. Apart from Peter Jackson, at least eight other people directed significant parts of the three films, including Barrie Osborne, Rick Porras, John Mahaffie, Geoff Murphy, Guy Norris, Ian Mune, Philippa Boyens and Fran Walsh, plus Alex Funke (miniature photography) and Jim Rygiel (visual fx).

At various times there were three or more film units, and sometimes five or more working at the same time. Some of the re-shoots of Merry and Pippin being carried by the orcs were shot by Geoff Murphy, who also shot most of the cave troll fight. Producer Barrie Osborne directed the fight between Aragorn and orc leader Lurtz, and other scenes, such as the orc chase across Rohan, the Three Hunters chasing the orcs, and the aerial images of the Misty Mountains at the beginning of *The Two Towers* (Osborne had experience shooting aerial footage, so was often drafted in to do that).

Scriptwriter Fran Walsh directed many scenes (including the pick-up scene of Arwen and Frodo at the ford, Gollum's schizophrenia scene (and many other Gollum scenes), the fellowship in the snow on Caradhras, the conversation between Éowyn and Aragorn in Meduseld, Gandalf and the Three Hunters in Fangorn, and others). Fellow writer Philippa Boyens also directed scenes. Co-producer Rick Porras directed the wizard duel and other scenes. John Mahaffie was the main director on the battle of Helm's Deep. Mahaffie also directed the warg fight (which was conjured up partly on the fly, on the day), and the Caradhras studio scenes (along with Fran Walsh). The miniatures, which contributed so much to the epic scale of *The Lord of the Rings* films, were shot by the unit headed up by Alex Funke (Funke's contribution to the *Lord of the Rings* films is huge).

Although the film director is regarded as an *auteur* in contemporary cinema, it doesn't work that way on big films like this. Of the people cited above, many can be properly regarded as co-authors of the three 2001-03 films: Fran Walsh, Philippa Boyens, Barrie Osborne, Richard Taylor, Mark Ordesky, Alan Lee, John Howe, Ngila Dickson, Grant Major, Dan Hennah, Andrew Lesnie, Rick Porras, Jim Rygiel, Jamie Selkirk, Michael Horton, Jabez Olssen, John Gilbert, Christian Rivers and Howard Shore. Certainly Walsh, Boyens, Lee, Howe, Taylor and Osborne can be classed as among the most important collaborators on the films, while Walsh and Boyens were co-creators (I'd cite Walsh and Boyens as significant as Jackson in the creation of the films, and helping to shepherd them from pre-production through shooting to release and marketing. And, as the writers, they were every bit as important as the director, if not more in some respects).

Not to mention the many other heads of department and key personnel, such as the casting directors (a much-underrated but absolutely crucial service), stunt co-ordinators and performers, matte painters, animatics designers, location managers, production managers, location managers, set builders, assistant directors, aerial photographers, camera teams, sound teams, editing teams, model makers, set dressers, sculptors, physical effects riggers, creature and prosthetic effects designers, make-up dept, hair dept, orchestras, choirs, sound editors, music editors, dialogue editors, foley artists, animal wranglers, catering and transportation, and so on.

Some of the key positions were taken by experienced filmmakers – such as Jim Rygiel, or US producer Barrie Osborne – but others were from Peter Jackson's team, much less experienced. Production designer Grant Major had few significant film credits, and nothing for this scale of movie, and it sometimes showed (he worked on Jackson's films, *Aberration, The Ugly, Angel At My Table* and the TV *Hercules* shows).

CHAPTER 5

PETER JACKSON

This book is not a study of Peter Jackson as a film director, or his other films, for a number of reasons. I don't reckon Jackson is a film director whose films stand up to an *auteur* analysis. True, there are some recurring themes and ideas in Jackson's films (a love of the horror genre, visceral gore and visual fx, for instance). Jackson seemed to be a filmmaker who clearly enjoys the whole process of making movies, and started out as a passionate amateur (making films with a Super-8 camera given to him by his parents, for instance, like so many filmmakers, or moving into low budget horror flicks, as so many others have done for their first films). There are some recurring modes of operation (staying within the New Zealand film industry, for example, or writing or adapting material with Fran Walsh). There are recurring members of the Jackson production team, many of whom worked on the *Lord of the Rings* films (such as vfx whizz Richard Taylor, or editor Jamie Selkirk). But I would not find it particularly productive to embark on an *auteur* analysis of Jackson as one might do with, say, Steven Spielberg or Paul Verhoeven or Ingmar Bergman. (It would be much easier to discuss Jackson's fellow New Zealand contemporaries in that respect, such as Jane Campion and Vincent Ward). The *Lord of the Rings* films were a team effort, of course. Jackson acknowledged that he didn't 'have all the great ideas, I don't have as much skill and expertise in certain areas'.[1] 'No one person can fully claim the authorship of the project', remarked Alan Lee.[2] Thankfully, the credit 'A Peter Jackson Film' was not attached to the *Lord of the Rings* films. That credit is rarely fully earned anyway – especially in contemporary Hollywood. But the *Lord of the Rings* films were truly a collaborative effort involving so many key creative personnel; films always are, of course, but in the *Lord of the Rings* movies you can see the imprint of many other personalities and talents.

Another reason for not discussing Peter Jackson's films at length here is that, prior to the *Lord of the Rings* films, I don't regard Jackson's films as that interesting. For many fans of the *Lord of the Rings* films, this is heresy: some regard Jackson as a genius above any other film director. I'd be much more interested in new movies from Fran Walsh than Peter Jackson.

No one's perfect, though. One of my favourite bits of hype surrounding the 2001-03 *Lord of the Rings* films comes from a 1999 interview that Jackson gave, in which he came out with the plainly ridiculous line: 'I don't think a classic fantasy film has ever been made'.

FRAN WALSH

Born January 10, 1959, Frances F. Walsh was raised in New Zealand. She studied at Wellington Girls' College and Victoria University (also in Wellington), taking English Literature. She began writing for television in New Zealand (*Worzel Gummidge Down Under* and *Shark in the Park*). Walsh later worked on films for Peter Jackson (whom she met in 1987), working on *Meet the Feebles* and *Braindead*. Walsh and Jackson collaborated again, on *Heavenly Creatures*; a film based on the true murder story from the 1950s had been Walsh's idea. After *The Frighteners,* their first Hollywood movie (made in New Zealand, but with US money and American actors), they began work on the abandoned *King Kong* and *The Lord of the Rings* (again, it was Walsh's idea to take on Tolkien's epic book). Walsh was in rock and punk bands in the Eighties (playing bass), and that interest in music was important for the *Lord of the Rings* films (Walsh contributed lyrics and helped to select Howard Shore as chief composer).

According to Jackson, he and Walsh were thinking of a fantasy adventure and thought, in considering an original idea, well, it should have battles like in *The Lord of the Rings,* and it should have creatures like in *The Lord of the Rings,* and after referring constantly to Tolkien's tome, they decided to enquire about the rights.

Walsh and Jackson must have been feeling very confident to be contemplating having a go at doing *The Lord of the Rings* in live action. But then, as they recalled after making the films, they might have thought differently had they known just how much work was involved.

CHAPTER 6

THE MAKING OF
THE *LORD OF THE RINGS* MOVIES

SHOOTING

Principal photography on *The Lord of the Rings* began on October 11, 1999. The first scene to be shot on the first shooting day was the four hobbits on the path in the Shire being menaced by the Black Riders (filmed in a park in the centre of Wellington; the master shot of the four hobbits hiding was the first to be shot). The first proper shot of a film is always an important moment, but the *Lord of the Rings* production had already shot tons of footage by then, such as make-up tests, models tests, creature tests, animatics, etc). Filming then moved on to the scenes in Bree, Frodo and Sam on their journey, and Weathertop.

The *Lord of the Rings* films began shooting in roughly chronological order, but that was soon abandoned due to the logistics of making three films simultaneously. Sometimes scenes would be shot from each of the three films in the same day.

Satellite link-ups were employed at times so that director Peter Jackson and his team of assistants could keep tabs on the various second units (such as the two models units, the fx unit, or the second unit doing stunts or background plates).

Producer Barrie Osborne was keen to promote feedback between the departments on the *Lord of the Rings* show, encouraging the exchange of information between the visual effects and sound departments, for instance. Osborne also established a 'think tank' for the production, comprising the heads of department (such as Richard Taylor, Alex Funke, Jim Rygiel, and Alan Lee), as well as the director and writers, who could brainstorm problems as they arose.

Sets were being demolished and constructed while others were being filmed, in the usual production manner on a film. During peak production, around 400 people were designing and constructing sets in the art department. It didn't help the art department that *The Lord of the Rings* was one of those movies where the script was being developed throughout production, with many rewrites and reshoots. The key to the production for designer Grant Major was 'all down to three things: budgeting, budgeting – and *budgeting!*'[1] It was nice to work on a big canvas, but it required collaborating with many people, Major said.

If there's a few people to single out amongst the 100s in *Rings'* production team, it would be Barrie Osborne for holding the whole thing together (he seemed to be making South Pacific fantasy blockbusters a speciality – overseeing both the *Lord of the Rings* series in NZ and *The Matrix,* shot in Oz. He liked to work outside the U.S.A., and loved New Zealand). Alan Lee and John Howe for their astonishing visualizations of Middle-earth. Visually, the most impressive stuff in *The Lord of the Rings* films comes from illustrators Lee and Howe – from the big views (Osgiliath, Helm's Deep, the Black Gate) down to the armour and props. The 2nd unit directors and assistant directors – the Helm's Deep battle in particular is a tribute to them. And the 2nd unit spectacle shots of horses and figures in wildernesses are wonderful. And Howard Shore. I wasn't that mad about the music for *The Fellowship of the Ring* (it didn't seem distinctive or clear enough for a fantasy blockbuster film, at first). But in the following two films he really went to town. Shore unleashing his augmented London Philharmonic on top of 2nd unit images of Gandalf or Aragorn on horseback were some of the highpoints of the films.

The *Lord of the Rings* films benefitted from the co-operation of the New Zealand military: the New Zealand Army provided extras – for the orc, Gondorian, Rohirrim and other armies. And the production was allowed to shoot in restricted areas (such as training areas and near firing ranges). The New Line films had their own Minister for the Rings in the Kiwi government, Peter Hodgson.

Maybe Sean Astin was right to say that the *Lord of the Rings* films wouldn't have happened the same way if they'd been made in Hollywood – from the point of view of economics, but also unions, and issues like health and safety. The *Lord of the Rings* project was a non-union undertaking. If it had been filmed in L.A., London, Toronto or Rome (other likely centres for this kind of big budget filmmaking), it would have been subject to stricter union regulations. (There was a death in the production – lighting gaffer Brian Bansgrove took his life in 2001. There were accidents: Mortsensen breaking his toe and a tooth; Astin cutting his foot; Hill cutting his ear; and Bloom cracking his ribs).

There was a movement amongst the crew to have the film shut down at one point. The producers responded by increasing their overtime payment a little, according to Sean Astin (2004, 190). Astin had been amazed at the difficult conditions of shooting the *Lord of the Rings* films, how people were pushed to the limit, and willingly went along with it. Astin later said it was amazing that nobody died making the film, because sometimes the safety measures were a little shaky.

Sean Astin's fee was $250,000, for three films. Astin reckoned that nearly everyone who worked on the *Lord of the Rings* films agreed to take less money than they would normally receive, or less than they would've got from other projects if they hadn't done Tolkien (2004, 84).

Training for the lead cast for the films included canoeing lessons, sword fencing (with Bob Anderson), weight training, and bonding sessions. All of that is fairly common on big films with a lot of physical action (they have to be *big films* to afford paying actors, trainers, accommodation and transport, etc, weeks before shooting).

The sword fights in *The Lord of the Rings* were choreographed by one of the legends of the movie business, Bob Anderson, then in his late seventies, who had worked on the *Star Wars* series, *James Bond* (*From Russia With Love*), *Highlander, Barry Lyndon, The Three Musketeers* and *The Mask of Zorro*. Anderson said he was after a 'brutal and heavy-handed' fighting style for the *Lord of the Rings* films.

The hobbits' accent was based, perhaps inevitably, on West Country accents (in this case, Gloucestershire). Dialogue coach Andrew Jack said that all of the material needed to render Tolkien's Elvish language could be found in the professor's appendices to *The Lord of the Rings* (B. Sibley, 100). (As well as dialogue coaches Andrew Jack and Roísín Carty, who were on set much of the time helping the actors with pronunciation, Tolkien linguistic expert David Salo also advised on pronunciation in the film. Fans of Tolkien's languages being legion, it would have been relatively easy to find someone to help with translation).

Quenyan and Sindarin Elvish were spoken, as well as Khuzdul (Dwarvish), and the Black Speech. Ian McKellen commented that he based the way Gandalf spoke partly on Tolkien's own speaking voice. Rolled 'r's were one of Tolkien's requirements for correct pronunciation (which McKellen, Weaving, Blanchett and others duly obeyed in the film: 'Morrrdorrr').

Not all of the actors quite had the accents down; Sean Astin's Sam and Bruce Hopkins' Gamling sometimes wavered (Astin recalled that doing a standard British RP wasn't too difficult, as American actors had to do occasionally, but West Country was much more challenging; 'I'm not sure that I did nail it, but I tried, and I think the results are good enough' [2004, 152]). For some reason, Billy Boyd was allowed to keep his native Scottish accent (an odd decision; maybe it sounded like it came from roughly the same part of the world as Britain's West Country, though many Scots might not agree). But as so much of the film was looped, accents could be allowed to waver on set. And the dialogue coaches were present during ADR sessions to advise performers, so accents could be polished through successive takes.

New Line wouldn't give the actors the scripts until they'd signed a confidentiality agreement, a not uncommon practice with big projects. Sean Astin commented that the agreement contained 'some of the most onerous language I had ever seen' (2004, 104). When the script arrived, it had watermarks on every page and was bound with circular binders, so the pages couldn't be ripped out easily. Each film was around 150 pages long (an average film script is 110 pages).

Shooting the council of Elrond scene was a nightmare, according to Sean Astin, because they were too many performers, too many monologues, too much to explain and show, and it was shot so many times. The scene was shot through once, concentrating on Gandalf, then again with shots taken from Gandalf's point-of-view. Shooting in the scaled-down Bag End set was difficult, Peter Jackson recalled, because it meant cramming thirty people into the small set with its low ceilings heated up by the lights for about a month.

One of the most disastrous days of filming on the *Lord of the Rings* films was the Grey Havens farewell scene. The actors playing the four hobbits (Elijah Wood, Sean Astin, Billy Boyd and Dominic Monaghan) had worked themselves into an intense emotional state. But when the rushes were screened, it was found that Sean Astin had forgotten to wear his vest after taking a break. The other actors were pretty mad. But when the scene was retaken, many of the shots were found to be out of focus. Needless to say, the actors were absolutely gutted when they found out the scene would have to be reshot entirely – again. (The chief focus puller on *The Lord of the Rings*, Colin Deane, had gone to Australia, and one of the assistant focus pullers had worked on the scene instead; the filmmakers said they begged Deane to come back).

Viggo Mortensen came up with ideas for his character all the time, according to some observers. Sometimes the filmmakers would take up his suggestions, and other times they wouldn't. He was involved in 'an on-going contentious creative discussion with Fran and Philippa and Peter', according to Sean Astin (2004, 203), and was 'absolutely relentless' with Walsh and Boyens about Aragorn. Astin reckoned that Mortensen maddened the screenwriters, and they hated and resented him for it, while also loving him and appreciating it (2004, 203-4).

In fleshing out the story of Aragorn and Arwen from the appendices, the scriptwriters had to add plenty, because the story is only ten and a half pages long. Boyens and Walsh said they only used the appendices and didn't anything, but of course, they had to add a ton of material to flesh out the scenes.

Ian McKellen, like Viggo Mortensen, had most definitely read Tolkien's books, and contributed much to the production in terms of offering views on the scenes and shooting. McKellen would approach writers Walsh and Boyens with ideas for his character or for the film, and contributed to the rewriting of Gandalf's character and scenes. The book of *The Lord of the Rings* was regarded as 'Bible' by the production (maybe so, but there were plenty of heretics, dissenters and outcasts from Tolkien's Biblical doctrine).

Jackson referred to Boyens and Walsh as the 'script Nazis', the 'script girls' who were, as Sean Astin put it, 'fiercely protective of their work' (2004, 200). *Lord of the Rings* was Philippa Boyens' first film script: as Jackson recalled, 'she's never written a script before in her life'. Boyens had provided scenes for actors previously, and had helped with plays, but she hadn't written a film script or worked in television. (It was 'a major turning point for the project… absolutely critical', when Boyens joined the show, Jackson said [Sib, 355]).

Elijah Wood's Frodo wasn't bulked up like Sean Astin's Sam (which Astin disliked intensely; Walsh and Jackson also disagreed about what size Sam should be). An odd choice, because Tolkien describes *all* hobbits as rotund. Keeping Wood slim made the transformation of Frodo by the ring more believable: he was already looking that way.

The *Lord of the Rings* production was dominated by guys, in front of the camera (though there were plenty of women in the crew), and the atmosphere was sometimes like a locker room, army barracks or prison, Sean Astin recalled (2004, 155). Lots of swearing and jokes and juvenile behaviour. That might have resulted in the *Lord of the Rings* films having more of a conscious gay male component. Sure, it's there in Tolkien's books, and in the films, but it was deliberately avoided, if possible. The scene where Sam cradles Frodo in his lap on the slopes of Mount Doom and talks about the Shire, Sean Astin thought was played more like a death scene on a battlefield than a love scene. But the scene where Frodo is reunited with the fellowship in Minas Tirith, that definitely had a gay element.

Gay or not, the *Lord of the Rings* movies are full of men weeping and weepy soldiers: Gandalf weeps, Aragorn weeps, Sam weeps, Frodo weeps, Boromir weeps, Denethor weeps, Faramir weeps, Pippin weeps, Merry weeps, etc.

During shooting, the cast wasn't often shown parts of the edited film, according to Sean Astin. Scenes would sometimes be screened after a break, and if the actors requested them (2004, 145).

Keeping track of continuity meant there were three sets of Polaroids and three sets of files (for the actors, the scale doubles, and the stunt doubles). Brett Beattie, John Rhys-Davies's scale double, did a lot of work with Gimli, to the point where some people in the cast thought he ought to receive co-credit with Rhys-Davies (but the older actor wasn't having any of that: 'I'm not in the habit of giving away the credit for my character', Rhys-Davies said).

The addition of Sam's speech at the close of *The Two Towers* was probably influenced by the events and aftermath of September 11, 2001. Andy Serkis remarked that 9/11 did affect the way he played Gollum.[3] Sam's speech, like Saruman's early in the film about the alliance between Isengard and Barad-dûr, were also responses to the pressure from some fans to have the title of *The Two Towers* changed because of the attacks on the Twin Towers.

REMAKING THE SAME FILM.

The *Lord of the Rings* films were made a number of times. The first time was when the scriptwriters read the book, wondering how to turn it into a script. The second time was the first draft of the script (this would have been rewritten too). The storyboarding process was the next time the films were made, when every frame of the three films was visualized, sometimes with only sketches, but other times with detailed drawings (again, there were a number of drafts of storyboards). The films were then turned into storyboard animatics, with local NZ actors voicing the parts (scriptwriting and storyboarding can be done on a very small scale, with one or two people – which's why it's used so often in film schools and on media courses. But as soon as the *Rings* films moved into full prep, then it got very expensive, and the production grew immensely). The script was overhauled after the animatic, because 'it was almost totally lacking in real heart and emotion', Jackson admitted [Sib, 371]).

There was a second level of animatics in 3-D using small models of sets and a lightweight video camera, and also involving more complex computer-generated visualizations. The films were made yet again during this stage, and the script was still being re-written. The film was then made during the lengthy pre-production period, in countless decisions about designs, costumes, sets, fx, props, etc, and of course the all-important casting sessions.

Note, then, how much of the films had been produced before actors were cast or sets built or cameras rolled. The screenwriters, director, storyboard artists and producers had already been through the films many, many times – they had already been living with it for a year or more. The really key period, when all the crucial decisions are made, is during pre-production – especially on a complex project like *The Lord of the Rings*. The Tolkien films benefitted from a long lead-in period (it was longer than usual partly because of the scope of the project, but also because of the lengthy negotiations between the filmmakers and Miramax, and then New Line). It really shows when big, complex films have been rushed into production.

During shooting, which's when many people think a film is created, the films were made for the n-th time. Editing is obviously a process where films are re-made time after time, and for many filmmakers (George Lucas, Orson Welles, Stanley Kubrick, Martin Scorsese, etc), editing is where a huge amount of a film's impact is created. Clearly, without editing, *The Lord of the Rings* would be hundreds of hours of rushes which would try the patience of the most ardent Tolkien film fan. Concurrent with the post-production stage were re-shoots and new ideas (chief among these was the late addition of the prologue, or the addition of the ents storming of Isengard in *The Two Towers*).

The films were made again when actors came in for ADR. At this stage, scenes could be completely rewritten, and lines could be inflected with different meanings (actors routinely loop the same scene a number of times before filmmakers are satisfied). And yet again when the sound effects team got to work (*The Lord of the Rings* without sound effects would consist of echoey dialogue, plane noise, cameras whirring, fans blowing, people yelling cues, and so on). And yet again when tons of visual effects work was added.

Finally, the music, which is one of the most important ingredients in any Hollywood action-adventure. The DVDs of the films don't allow for comparisons of the footage with and without music (as some DVDs do), but you can judge how they would play without music by turning the sound down (not fair, of course because that loses dialogue, atmos, and the crucial sound fx). And, ultimately, one could say that the films were made a zillion ways again when the audience watched them, in theatres, stores, jets, hotels, schools, clubs, inns and homes.

Little of the production sound (live, on-set sound) could be used for another reason: *The Lord of the Rings* were historical films. In a film with a contemporary setting, a stray police siren or distant jet doesn't necessarily ruin a take (well, not the visuals), but in a film set hundreds or thousands of years ago, it's no good (and the studios in Wellington were not proper sound stages). But even if the dialogue could be looped, and the actors know they can fix it later, it's still distracting for performers to work with loud noises.

The above budgets are not adjusted for inflation; adjusting costs for inflation (a much more meaningful comparison), the *Lord of the Rings* films would come out much less expensive than the epics of the Classical Hollywood era, such as *Ben-Hur, Cleopatra* or *The Ten Commandments*. There was another factor: the tax deal with shooting in New Zealand, which helped to bring costs down. (And the non-union nature of the production. Plus the German investment deals).

Filming in New Zealand, as Peter Jackson explained, meant the films could be made cheaper. Jackson estimated that the films were fifty or sixty million dollars cheaper than if they'd been made in Europe or the U.S.A. *The Return of the King*, for instance, would definitely have cost $200 million: 'if *Return of the King* wasn't a $200 million film, I don't know what is', as Jackson put it.

LOW BUDGET VS. HIGH BUDGET.

The *Lord of the Rings* films were through-and-through Hollywood productions, but that doesn't necessarily mean the day-to-day shooting was conducted in exactly the same way as a Hollywood film. Although viewers may get the impression that because the films cost hundreds of million of dollars, the studio facilities were plush and the techniques expensive. In fact, quite a bit of the films, as the filmmakers acknowledge, were created with some fairly crude methods. Most of the studios, for instance, were not the state-of-the-art sound stages of Culver City, Pinewood or Cinecittà. They were converted warehouses (and not sound proofed). Most of the pick-ups and re-shoots listed as exteriors in the script were shot in the car lot of the studios (i.e, not decent wet sets or tanks, or a proper back lot).

Clearly, the *Lord of the Rings* films were not low budget Roger Corman exploitation pictures, but they did use some of his techniques. The orcs pulling down a tree at Orthanc, for example, was shot, like many of the scenes in *The Lord of the Rings* films, with multiple cameras, and different angles were employed in the editing to suggest different trees. It's a technique that recurs throughout Hollywood cinema (especially on expensive or one-off stunts). When the Mustangs attack the Japanese prison camp outside Shanghai in *Empire of the Sun* (1987) for example, Spielberg and editor Michael Kahn unashamedly used two different angles of the same building blowing up.

There weren't enough stunt people in the core team on the *Lord of the Rings* films for each of the Middle-earth races (orcs, elves, men, etc), so they had to be different characters. Helm's Deep, for example, was shot with only 100 extras, whereas a Hollywood epic in the heyday of the epics (1950s-60s) might've had thousands of extras. Although the stunt people and extras on the *Lord of the Rings* films were augmented by thousands of digital characters, they still had to be blocked in front of the cameras so they looked like many more than there were.

Typically, there would be a core of ten or so performers in hero make-up and costumes (4-5 hours in make-up for the orcs), with pull-over foam masks for the 50 or so mid-ground characters, and pull-on masks for background characters.

NOTES: SHOOTING

1. In B. Sibley, 2002, 47.
2. In B. Sibley, 2002, 113.
3. In J. Smith, 2004, 10.

FILMING IN NEW ZEALAND

One aspect of *The Lord of the Rings* the films miss, and for me among the most memorable parts of the book, is the wistful nostalgia of the early chapters, the poetic evocation of a time that never existed. The atmosphere of melancholy, introspection and nostalgia J.R.R. Tolkien creates, embodied in the passages set in the Shire about the English Autumn, the season of bonfires, trees, mushrooms, streams, hills and leave-takings, a now-vanished Edwardian England, pre-First World War. This has a special resonance for me, as I first read *The Lord of the Rings* where Tolkien grew up and lived – in the English Midlands – the rolling English countryside which was his basis for the Shire. New Zealand can stand in for so much of the mythical pre-industrial Europe of the book, the epic vistas of mountains, lakes and rivers, but the flavour of the English Midlands, the streams, rivers, woods, trees, trackways, is harder to capture. There is little deep connection with the Earth in New Line's 2001-03 films, with particular places and, above all, Tolkien's beloved forests and trees.

Peter Jackson remarked that New Zealand provided a variety of scenery for the films – true, but the studio shooting could easily have been accomplished in Hollywood, Mexico, Rome, Sydney or London (and most of *The Lord of the Rings* was shot in the studio, including most of the exterior scenes: all of the Helm's Deep and Minas Tirith scenes, for instance, were exteriors shot in a local quarry, which could have been anywhere). And Peter Jackson and his film operation was of course based in New Zealand. (But in fact, many of the second unit shots of New Zealand were not straight images of the landscape: the plates were cleaned up and digitally graded, and traces of modernity, like roads, electricity poles, cars, cables, film equipment, crew and the like, were erased. Very often the footage of New Zealand was just the starting-point for a visual fx shot – using a sky from a shot, for instance, or just the foreground, with the rest of the image built up from mattes combined with models. So it was New Zealand, but it was New Zealand with millions of dollars of visual effects work done to it. In fact, New Zealand was just the starting-point, and was virtually unrecognizable beneath many shots).

It wasn't difficult for the *Lord of the Rings* production to make a big impact on New Zealand's cultural life: there are less than four million people in New Zealand, comparable with a medium-sized city. And Wellington has around 178,000.

Local businesses, airlines, the media and the government in New Zealand were involved with the *Lord of the Rings* production. Many locations can be visited, of course, but as fans and tourists have found, they don't often look like the locations in the films, which often use only a small section of a place. 'Hobbiton', the farmland in Matamata, is the only surviving setting. It became a tourist attraction in 2003, following 6 months of negotiations with New Line Cinema. It received 30,000 visitors in the 1st half of 2004. A guidebook, *The Lord of the Rings Location Guidebook*, became a bestseller. (Peter Jackson remarked that thinking about the real locations for *The Lord of the Rings* in New Zealand while watching the films 'defeats the purpose of a film like this').[2]

NOTES: FILMING IN NEW ZEALAND

1. Quoted in E. Mathijs, 2006, 113.
2. Quoted in I. Pryor, 2004, 263.
3. D. Cohen, "Lord of the Rings Brings Riches To City", *The Guardian*, Jan 20, 2001.
4. Quoted in L. Accinelli, "New Zealand Making a Pitch To Filmmakers", *Los Angeles Times*, Mch 15, 2000.
5. In D. Thornley, in E. Mathijs, 2006, 112.

LOCATIONS

The *Lord of the Rings* films were predominantly made in New Zealand. Farmland in Matamata in Waikato, was Hobbiton. Mount Ruapheu and the Whakapapa Ski Field in the Tangariro National Park were used for many scenes, including Mordor and Mount Doom (there are three volcanoes here; Ruapehu was the one used by the films). A park in the Town Belt area of Wellington was where the hobbits hide from the Black Rider, as well as part of Dunharrow. Harcourt Park in Upper Hutt, 20 miles North of Wellington, was Isengard. The Hutt River was the Anduin. Rivendell was constructed at Kaitoke Regional Park, 8 miles from Upper Hutt City (also used for Lothlórien and the Silverlode River. Other Lórien scenes were shot at Fernside Lodge, Featherton, Wairapa, 40 miles East of Wellington. It was appropriate, perhaps, that the garden at Fernside had been laid out in 1924 by the famous designer Gertrude Jekyll). Queen Elizabeth Park, MacKays Crossing, was part of Pelennor Fields (the scenes with the fallen *mûmakil*). The Brandywine ferry scene was shot at Manakou, North of Otaki (45 miles North of Wellington), as well as other Shire scenes. Waiterere Forest provided the woods near Osgiliath and the trollshaw forest. Bree was built on an old army camp at Fort Dorset, Seatoun, in Port Nicholson Harbour, Wellington.

Helm's Deep and Minas Tirith were constructed at a disused quarry, Dry Creek Quarry, Haywards Hill, Wellington, the largest builds on the show (there's nothing left of the sets, though), in Lower Hutt, outside Wellington. The Helm's Deep set was split into different parts of the Rohan stronghold, including the gatehouse and causeway and lower wall, the upper battlements, the lower area, the upper hall, and finally a quarter scale model. Each set was built into the cliff face of the quarry. The sets consisted largely of polystyrene blocks dressed to look like weathered stone. Barrie Osborne compared it to walking on to the large set to Kurtz's compound in *Apocalypse Now* or like something out of Cecil B. DeMille. Osborne wondered, at the time of *Apocalypse*, if sets that size and scope would be built anymore.

Many of the actors and crew found the quarry location inhospitable, cold, damp, and difficult. Shooting was complicated by the Helm's Deep battle itself taking place at night, in the rain. The battle shoot, largely overseen by 2nd unit director John Mahaffie, meant 9-10 weeks of night shoots, with up to 100 orc extras in prosthetic body suits, further groups of costumed extras for the Rohirrim and elves, plus principal players like Viggo Mortensen, Liv Tyler, Bernard Hill, Orlando Bloom, Craig Parker and John Rhys-Davies, big rain machines, many physical gags and effects, and plenty of stunts, co-ordinated by George Marshall Ruge, fight co-ordinator Tony Woolf, sword master Bob Anderson, and a core team of stunt people. (Mahaffie was responsible for Legolas's skateboarding gag at Helm's Deep; Mahaffie was a snowboarding fan).

Much was made in the marketing of *The Two Towers* of how gruelling the Helm's Deep shoot was, how Viggo Mortensen was a hero, giving a 120% effort every night, how brilliant the stunt people were, how the extras in full body make-up and costumes waited patiently every night to shoot, and so on. George Ruge described Helm's Deep as a nightmare: 'over fifty nights in the most arduous conditions: it was a brutal, surreal experience, exhausting to the point of hysteria'.[1]

There were only 20 people in the stunt team which was not really enough for George Ruge, especially when other units also needed stunt people. That number rose to 30, and at one point reached 65: 'that *really* was luxury!' recalled Ruge. But he really needed 300.

The extras on *The Lord of the Rings* wound up playing extras in many scenes, being used again and again. There was a core of 30 or 40 extras who stayed the course, and around 3-4,000 for the rest of the films.

All of those locations were on the North Island. On the South Island, locations included the Arrowtown Recreational Reserve outside Queenstown (used for the Misty Mountains, the West Road, Rohan, and Eregion, among others). Shotover River, Arrowtown, was the Ford of Bruinen. The Argonath were shot in Kawarau Gorge, Kawarau River. Closeburn, near Queenstown, was Amon Hen. Glenorchy, Paradise, beside Lake Wakatipu, was the location for the climactic woodland battle of *The Fellowship of the Ring*. The village ransacked by Saruman's minions was built at Poolburn Dam, Ida Valley. The Ben Ohau Sheep Station at Twizel was used extensively for the Battle of Pelennor, the charge on Osgiliath, the White Mountains and other scenes. Clutha River, Wanaka, was where the orcs attack the fellowship. Mavora Lakes Parks was also used, for the scenes by the River Anduin.

Takaka Hill, near Nelson, stood in for the hills near Bree. Mount Olympus, in Kahurangi National Park, was used for Eregion and more post-Rivendell trekking. Mount Owen was Dimrill Dale and outside Bree.

The Misty Mountains were the Southern Alps (which were also used for the beacons sequence). Weathertop was in Te Anau in Fjordland. The Kepler Mires in Fjordland were the Dead Marshes and Midgewater Marshes.

At Mount Sunday, Mount Potts Station, Canterbury, on the South Island, Edoras was constructed, another major build. Pretty much everyone who worked on the films remarked that the Edoras location was their favourite set: an outcrop of rock some 150 feet high that rose in the middle of a plain with two snow-capped mountain ranges on each side. It took the art department some 5-6 months to build the Edoras set, the pinnacle of which was the Golden Hall of Rohan.

For location managers Richard Sharkey and Matt Cooper, Edoras (Mount Potts) was easily the best location on the project; Cooper remarked that it was so impressive audiences would probably think it was another great effects shot.[2] Niagara waterfall was used in the Bruinen flood sequence. A Peruvian waterfall supplied the falls of Rauros (seen when Boromir's boat goes over it). Californian and Australian skies appeared in visual effects shots.

Many of these locations can be visited. There are tour companies who will take you round them (such as Rings Scenic Tours). Some were remote locations, accessible only via helicopter or 4 x 4. (It was typical for location shooting on *The Lord of the Rings* to involve a helicopter ride, a drive in a Jeep, then a walk. Sometimes drives of hours were required.)

Barrie Osborne described the location filming as a lot of travelling: 'we were here one day, and somewhere else the next: Wellington, Queenstown, Christchurch, Nelson... North Island, South Island, back up North again... Trucks, vans, ferries, aeroplanes and helicopters'.[3] Roads were constructed for the film (around 30 kilometres), and the crew reached 2,000.

STUDIO VS. LOCATION.

Although New Zealand's landscape was cited as one of the reasons by the producers and PR dept for shooting there, most of the 2001-03 films were made in the studio. Taking the extended cut of *The Fellowship of the Ring* as an example, which has 46 chapters on the DVD, one can see that between 70 and 80 per cent of the film was shot in the studio or on the backlot in Wellington (by far the greater part of the reshoots were filmed in the studio or backlot):

1. Prologue: mostly studio.
2. Concerning hobbits: location and studio.
3. The Shire: mostly location.
4. Very Old Friends: location.
5. A Long-expected Party: nearly all studio.

6. Farewell Dear Bilbo: mostly studio.
7. Keep It Secret, Keep It Safe: studio.
8. The Account of Isildur: studio.
9. At the *Green Dragon*: studio.
10. The Shadow of the Past: studio.
11. The Passing of the Elves: location and studio.
12. Saruman the White: studio.
13. A Short Cut to Mushrooms: location.
14. Buckleberry Ferry: location.
15. At the Sign of the Prancing Pony: backlot and studio.
16. The nazgul: backlot and studio.
17. The Midgewater Marshes: location and backlot.
18. The Spoiling of Isengard: studio.
19. A Knife in the Dark: studio.
20. The Caverns of Isengard: studio.
21. Flight to the Ford: studio and location.
22. Rivendell: mostly studio.
23. Many Meetings: studio.
24. The Fate of the Ring: studio.
25. The Sword That Was Broken: studio.
26. The Evenstar: studio.
27. The Council of Elrond: studio.
28. Gilraen's Memorial: studio.
29. Bilbo's Gifts: studio.
30. The Departure of the Fellowship: location.
31. The Ring Goes South: studio and location.
32. The Pass of Caradhras: studio and location.
33. Moria: studio.
34. A Journey in the Dark: studio.
35. Balin's Tomb: studio.
36. The Bridge of Khazad-dûm: studio.
37. Lothlórien: studio and location.
38. Caras Galadon: studio.
39. The Mirror of Galadriel: studio.
40. The Fighting Uruk-hai: mostly studio.
41. Farewell to Lórien: location.
42. The Great River: mostly location.
43. Parth Galen: location.
44. The Breaking of the Fellowship: location.
45. The Departure of Boromir: location.
46. The Road Goes Ever On...: location.

Some scenes were split between the studio or backlot and location work, and many scenes had miniatures or matte paintings or computer-generated imagery added to them, all of which count as studio-based work. The 2001-03 *The Lord of the Rings* films, then, were part of a long tradition of fantasy or big budget films which were mainly concocted in the studio or on the backlot – like *Sunrise* (1926) or *The Wizard of Oz* (1939) or *Mary Poppins* (1964) or *Batman* (1989).

NOTES: LOCATIONS

1. In B. Sibley, 2002, 149.
2. B. Sibley, 2002, 39.
3. In B. Sibley, 2002, 146.

RESHOOTS

The Lord of the Rings films of 2001-03 had the luxury of re-shoots and pick-ups, some of which took place two or more years after the initial, main production phase (October 1999 – December 2000). Scenes would be re-shot days or weeks or months or even years later, according to Sean Astin (183). As Astin put it, 'there was constant reworking, and thus a constant sense that it was never, ever going to be finished'. For the actors, that often meant learning new lines sometimes moments before a scene was filmed (which's another reason for the multiple takes, because the actors were still learning their lines in the early takes). Christopher Lee was from the old school, and liked to have his lines in advance, with plenty of warning for rewrites.

Scenes in *The Lord of the Rings* were rarely captured on the first take. Rather, multiple takes were the norm, to the consternation of actors like Lee, who complained 'I've never had a director ask me to do it this many times in my life!... This is ridiculous! I've done fewer takes in an entire movie!' (S. Astin, 2004, 197). Fairly soon, the cast realized they would be pushed to go for take after take, and to come back again to scenes they thought had already been adequately captured on celluloid. Sean Astin sometimes reacted badly: he recalled that he knew it was impossible that all of that material could wind up in the finished film. Even if each film were three hours long, there was no way it could all be part of the final cut:

> There were times when this presented a problem, when Peter [Jackson] asked for a tenth take, or a twelfth take, or a twentieth take, and I wanted to scream; I just started losing track of what I had done. (2004, 139)

Fran Walsh had a reputation for perfectionism, asking for numerous takes. Billy Boyd called her 'Franley Kubrick'.

Reshooting took place in July, 2002 and August, 2003. Some pick-ups and reshoots were for the theatrical cuts, and some were specifically for the extended edition home entertainment formats. Some of the pick-ups and re-shoots arose as the films were edited, and new shots were required, or new ways of playing particular scenes were discovered. Only as the films were edited would (some of the) gaps in the narrative appear. Often the pick-ups and re-shoots were employed to add dialogue or exposition to scenes, or to clarify story points, and often the pick-ups were for smaller or emotional scenes (such as, in *The Two Towers*, Merry and Pippin talking during the orc chase, or Gandalf and Aragorn discussing at night the political state of play in Middle-earth, or Gandalf and Pippin speaking about death in Minas Tirith, or Elrond conversing with Arwen, and so on).

Some of the re-shoots and pick-ups substantially altered the films: in *The Two Towers*, the most celebrated scene, Gollum's schizophrenia dialogue, was added late in post-production, and deepened Gollum's personality (they were late additions partly because the animation of Gollum was among the most complex visual fx for the film and took a long time to produce). Some of the pick-ups were entire re-shoots of scenes (such as the scenes between Elrond and Arwen).

Additional shooting included women and children and old folk sheltering in the caves behind Helm's Deep: these close-ups of scared people were inserted into the battle, intended to heighten the emotion, offering a more concrete and emotional reason for the battle (they weren't just defending an attack on a castle, said the filmmakers, but a way of life). Those extra cave shots, Peter Jackson reckoned, made it look as if Aragorn were leading a fight against an enemy that was threatening more than just some soldiers in a castle.

Some of the reshoots for *The Two Towers* had been undertaken partly because the film was deemed by the filmmakers to be a little too action-heavy, with not enough heart or emotion in it. That explains why additional scenes were shot – such as the mothers and children and old folk at Helm's Deep, or Sam's monologue over the closing scenes.

In *The Two Towers*, the scenes between Frodo, Sam and Gollum were considerably refined, so that the actors and crew revisited various versions of the Dead Marshes many times. Dan Hennah's art department became adept at reconstructing sets that had been packed away (or destroyed) sometimes two or three years earlier. Hennah said that Fangorn Forest was rebuilt eight times.

Generally, pick-ups and re-shoots are for smaller scenes: it wouldn't be so easy or cheap to re-build the whole of the Tower Hall of Minas Tirith on Stage A, for instance, so that another way of Gandalf conversing with Denethor could be shot. Once those big sets are down, that's it. Hence all that planning and discussion, to ensure everything has been covered. But it's common for filmmakers to realize days or weeks or months later (often during editing) that they didn't get *that one particular reaction shot* from so-and-so which would *really* have *made* the whole scene. (Even so, some of the rebuilds in the parking lot at the studios in Wellington were substantial – the stables at Edoras, and part of the Golden Hall, for instance, or the Dead Marshes, or Minas Tirith. And occasionally big sets, like the Golden Hall, were re-assembled).

The pick-ups and re-shoots came about partly because it's common for filmmakers (like any artists) to work up to the last possible minute, pushing as close to deadlines as the studio will allow. Many studios will not allow the budget or schedule or time for re-shoots or pick-ups. Often only prestigious directors, such as Woody Allen, have the option for substantial re-shoots built into their contracts (Allen's *September* [1987], for instance, was substantially re-shot).

But re-shoots and re-takes have been around for a long time. Alfred Hitchcock, for instance, would shoot re-takes of scenes (or parts of scenes) if he thought it would improve the picture. Despite Hitchcock having the reputation of planning every scene and every shot in pre-production, so that shooting was a chore, he often changed scripts and films during shooting, and allowed improvization. On *Notorious* (1946), for instance, Hitchcock re-shot many scenes (much to the consternation of mogul David O. Selznick, who wouldn't authorize them).

The *Lord of the Rings* films, however, were not a prestige project from Kubrick, Allen, Scorsese or Altman. They were blockbuster, tentpole pictures, which are far less often granted so many and so extensive re-shoots and pick-ups (partly because event movies are locked into an immovable release schedule). So the *Lord of the Rings* films were highly unusual in this respect. It's common practice in the Hollywood system to preview films, to measure audience response, and often for the studio to demand re-editing, and new endings. It depends on things like who has final cut, but a Hollywood studio has all sorts of ways of enforcing its decisions. Directors and filmmakers dislike previews and audience testing for many reasons. (The *Rings* films were not previewed; Jackson said test screenings would have been a 'disaster', because of the internet, and 'would probably have resulted in the movies being seriously dumbed down' [Sib, 533]).

When Bob Shaye and Michael Lynne flew to New Zealand to see the first footage assembled together, Jackson was surprised that they had been moved by the drama of the film. There was '*Hercules, Sinbad* and pure brainless sorcery' in the film, Jackson admitted, but there was also dramatic and emotional stuff too. Shaye was apparently moved to tears (Sib, 483).

Even when a film is meticulously storyboarded, with every shot carefully planned, all sort of things can suggest themselves once the actors are in make-up and costume and on set with the cameras are rolling. High budget blockbusters like the *Lord of the Rings* films – often likened during production to unstoppable trains – don't allow for lots of improvization among actors, but there was some. The way that John Rhys-Davies effortlessly upstages scenes, for instance, probably came from the way the actor played the scenes on the day they were shot.

One should also point out that some of the re-shoots and pick-ups in the *Lord of the Rings* films also came about because of a lack of confidence among the filmmakers and screenwriters – an uncertainty about how to stage scenes, what to include, whose point-of-view to cover. In short: what shots to get. A more seasoned, experienced filmmaker like, say, Michael Curtiz or John Ford in the days of the Hollywood studio system, might have churned through the script methodically and efficiently, knowing what they were after.

With the *Lord of the Rings* films, the filmmakers were discovering the film partly during shooting and editing. That often happens to some extent (filmmakers routinely rewrite constantly. And they often say a film is really made in the editing suite). On the *Lord of the Rings* films, though, this seemed to have occurred far more than with a usual feature film.

(Part of the reason could have been because some of the key personnel – the writers, the director, the heads of department – hadn't worked on a project this big. They also re-thought characters substantially: changing Arwen from warrior-elf to inspirational muse, for example, or shooting then dropping the idea of Aragorn sword fighting with Sauron. But it was also because *The Lord of the Rings* is such a complex, multi-layered narrative).

For the studio, New Line Cinema, the re-shoots and pick-ups on *The Lord of the Rings* films would not have incurred massive costs (partly because they were usually small scenes, involving only a few actors, and partly because the *Rings* films were actually cheaper to make than some other blockbuster films). Plus, New Line would have been encouraged by the massive interest in the films, prior to and during the release of *The Fellowship of the Ring* in December, 2001. When that film had been seen to do so well theatrically, and gain awards, Oscar nominations and favourable reviews, New Line would have been happy to authorize a few weeks of re-shoots and pick-ups. These took place, for *The Two Towers*, in the following Summer of 2002, ready for a release the next December (and ditto for *The Return of the King* in 2003).

There was another motive for the re-shoots and pick-ups, as far as New Line and its distributors were concerned, and that was the lucrative home entertainment market: the new scenes generated by the re-shoots and pick-ups could be used as come-ons in the marketing of the DVDs and home videos (especially to the legions of Tolkien fans). Indeed, some of the re-shoots and pick-ups were shot specifically for the extended DVD and video versions of the films (i.e., they were not shot for the theatrical versions). Part of the advertizing for the home entertainment extended cuts was the promise of new and extra scenes (around 30-40 minutes on each film), newly composed and recorded music, new visual effects, and so on.

The drive to re-shoot and re-edit and re-model the 2001-03 *Lord of the Rings* would not have come entirely from New Line Cinema: the filmmakers would also have to have been available to do the work, and also willing to do it. After some tough film shoots, some filmmakers would do *anything* but go back and revisit the material (and work with the production team again). There could be all sorts of personal or business reasons why a filmmaker might not want to go back to a film. There could be new projects to develop at the script stage, or new jobs looming, or new shoots, or personal stuff, like families and marriages and vacations and illness, or the filmmakers might be bored, or uninspired, or just too exhausted or ill to carry on.

One of the chief concerns of New Line Cinema, its lawyers, the banks and insurers, then, would have been about the ability of the filmmakers to keep going and complete the project – physically as well as psychologically. But, as Sean Astin put, 'New Line figured out how to make it beneficial to them all the way through, and thank God they did, because if they hadn't, we couldn't have got the movie made' (2004, 83-84).

EDITING AND POST-PRODUCTION

The large number of film units on *The Lord of the Rings* were churning out thousands of feet of film footage. One of the editors estimated *The Lord of the Rings* had used up to 4.5-5 million feet of film. Barrie Osborne reckoned that the most film that went through the cutting rooms in one day was 50,000 feet (the film laboratory processed 43,000 feet of film on one record day). That meant that viewing the rushes every evening could last three hours plus. The filmmakers tended to shoot many more takes than usual. About 70% of what was shot was printed (about 3.5 million feet of film). The shooting ratio was roughly 150 : 1. That meant for one of the films, at three hours long, 450 hours of film was shot. For all three films (each close to three hours long), something between 1,350 and 1,575 hours. New Line wanted *Fellowship* to be about three hours long (or less; it came in at 2h45m up to the end credits).

So much footage was shot for the *Lord of the Rings* films, it meant that there was always plenty of choice – but it also meant hours of whittling down footage for the editors and assistant editors. A scene of Théoden on a battlefield, for instance, had over 2 1/2 hours of film shot, but had to be cut down to 90 seconds.[1]

The sheer volume of footage drove some of the editors nuts. One of the assistant editors (Peter Skarratt), sick of seeing hours and hours of footage of the horse chase scene (enough for several feature films), said he had to escape back home to Australia for the weekend for the sake of his sanity. (Only a tiny fraction of the 2nd unit footage made it into the final cut).

The *Lord of the Rings* films were shot on conventional Kodak 35mm stock, in the conventional widescreen format. Some additional footage was shot on digital video cameras (such as the ones used in the *Star Wars* prequels). 21 cameras were used in all.

The schedule of the 2001-03 *Lord of the Rings* films was interesting. The main production period (of shooting) being Oct, 1999 to December, 2000 (274 days), that meant principal photography on film one was complete a year before it was due in cinemas (December, 2001). It meant that the bulk of *The Two Towers* and *The Return of the King* had been shot by December, 2000 (two years before it was due in theatres in December, 2002), with *The Return of the King* being released in December, 2003.

So why, for example, was the post-production on *The Two Towers* so difficult, and somewhat chaotic, if there were 2 years from the end of shooting to when the film was due out? There are many, many reasons. One is the pick-ups and re-shoots, which were taking place at various times from the end of principal photography (pick-ups and re-shoots meant many more rewrites, new conceptions of characters, new sets (or rehashed old sets), new schedules, and so on). Another is the changing shape of *The Two Towers* during editing. But the editing on movies typically starts as soon as rushes become available. Thus, *The Two Towers* was probably being edited from October, 1999 onwards. Visual effects (some 1,500 shots estimated after the release of film one) were being produced on all three films simultaneously,

Another, very major reason was that *The Lord of the Rings: The Fellowship of the Ring* had to be finished first, so from the end of principal photography in December, 2000, to the release in December, 2001, much of the resources had to be given over to completing *The Fellowship of the Ring*. Because if that film didn't do well, it could jeopardize the other two (even though the bulk of them was already in the can).

And don't forget the immense advertizing campaign for *Fellowship*, which required the cast to do the magazine, TV and radio and documentary interviews in mid-late 2001 (well in advance of the release date), and Cannes in May, 2001, and the further rounds of newspaper, radio and TV interviews as well as the personal appearances at premieres during December, 2001. And then, of course, the award ceremonies during early 2002.

Yet another reason is the *Special Extended Editions* of each film. In a way, it's better to think of the *Lord of the Rings* films as *six* films that had to be shot and edited and dubbed and scored and prepared for release, complete with enormous marketing campaigns, and all the rest of it. The extended editions were basically the same films, of course (and cynics could say they were released specifically for the legions of Tolkien fans. And they'd be right. You simply do not release further versions of a movie unless you're convinced it's got an audience.) So quite a bit of the schedule in early-mid 2002, which might have been for *The Two Towers*, was taken up with getting the extended version of *The Fellowship of the Ring* out on DVD, for an August, 2002 release date. Because the extended versions required new scenes to be shot (scenes which were filmed *specifically* for the DVD release), and editing, dubbing, music recording, visual fx and everything else. Plus the auxiliary material for the DVDs (commentaries, documentaries, etc – although those parts of the DVD were produced a different company – by Kurtti/ Pellerin, based in L.A., and produced by Michael Pellerin). The editing on the extended cut of *The Fellowship of the Ring* was completed in April, 2002. Later, in 2006, yet another version of the films were released: the 'limited edition' versions, which were the films plus a new documentary by Costa Botes.

Frances Walsh makes a waspish aside on one of the DVD commentaries: does New Line Cinema *really* need to make more money?

Well, no. But it loves to. And it can. So it does.

So those are some of the reasons why part of the post-production on *The Two Towers* had to be pushed back to mid-to-late 2002: once the extended edition of *The Fellowship of the Ring* had been delivered, the editing and visual fx for *The Two Towers* were ramped up further. The ents demolishing Isengard, for example, was a late addition to the film, even though, as Alex Funke remarked, everyone knew it had to be tackled, but somehow it kept getting pushed back. (One of the visual fx guys commented on the DVD that Barrie Osborne got tough when he called some of the vfx crew back and told them that if they wanted to stay on for the rest of the show, they had to do this last Isengard sequence, or they wouldn't be asked back at all). Other complications on *The Two Towers* included further demands for vfx shots late in the game (when Peter Jackson, the editors and filmmakers decided that a few more wide shots of Helm's Deep would be required, for instance).

The filmmakers acknowledged that everything on *The Two Towers* had been four or five weeks late, so the production was always battling against approaching deadlines. When the actors arrived for the reshoots, in August 2002, Fran Walsh said she hadn't finished the scripts for the new scenes.

The editing of *The Fellowship of the Ring* was taking place right up until the last minute – even during the recording sessions in England, and also during the sound mixing sessions. Peter Jackson and his team ended up staying in London for 12 weeks, much longer than intended. So electronic links (basically video conferencing with 5.1 surround sound) were set up between London and New Zealand, so that Jackson and the team in London could see the visual fx in Wellington, and also supervise the sound mixing.

The orchestra was recorded at Watford Town Hall, North of London, and Lyndhurst Hall in London. Music editing and recording was conducted at the famous Abbey Road Studios (as well as two other studios). The film editors were brought over from New Zealand and installed in a room at Abbey Road to complete the film. When Jackson and his team flew back to New Zealand, video conferencing was again utilized, this time so that the filmmakers could keep in touch with Howard Shore and the music editing team at London's Abbey Road. Because of the frantic post-production on *The Fellowship of the Ring*, electronic links were also set up for Howard Shore, so that he could supervise recording sessions taking place in other parts of Abbey Road, and other recording studios.

The final sound mix of *The Fellowship of the Ring* was completed on October 27, 2001. The film was delivered to the studio on Nov 1, 2001, which left a month and a half before the global release date (barely enough time for 10,000 prints to be struck).

An all-important point in the *Lord of the Rings* project, though, was the date of the weekend of December 21-23 in 2001, when the box office grosses came in. In amongst the champagne and the group hugs was the realization that *The Fellowship of the Ring* was a big hit, and that the other the *Lord of the Rings* films were very likely going to be hits too. That weekend was the single most important moment for *The Lord of the Rings* films as global market brands, as products which would move around the world, from territory to territory, making money, and films which would launch a franchise. It meant that work on *The Two Towers* could resume with the confidence that all three films would be massive on home DVD and video as well as in theatres, and thus, for the filmmakers, it meant operating from a very secure financial base. With *The Fellowship of the Ring* such a success, they could ask for money for re-shoots and pick-ups, for more visual fx, for more of everything. (Even if, for some unforeseen reason, New Line Cinema bailed out, any Hollywood studio would be more than happy to pick up the other two *The Lord of the Rings* films – even Miramax, which had passed on what would have been its biggest financial success. New Line later seemed reluctant to share out revenue from the films, however).

Editing on *The Return of the King* proved as problematic as on *The Two Towers*. There were five storylines to combine: Frodo and Sam; Aragorn, Legolas and Gimli and the Army of the Dead; Gandalf, Faramir, Denethor and Pippin in Minas Tirith; Théoden, Éowyn and the Rohirrim; and Arwen and Elrond in Rivendell. There were also scenes inherited from *The Two Towers* to include: the death of Saruman at Isengard; Arwen's vision of her son Eldarion; and the back-story of Sméagol and the finding of the ring.

In the end, Saruman at Orthanc didn't make it into the theatrical cut of *The Return of the King* – to Christopher Lee's great disappointment (but it was put into the *Extended Edition*). One of the reasons was that it was a scene dealing with the villain from film two, which didn't seem the best way to start film three. It was also a longish (seven minute) and talky scene (and not the best example of screenwriting or direction). It was one of the toughest decisions in the editing of *The Return of the King* to drop that scene (it's probably the single biggest omission from the theatrical cut of *The Return of the King*). (An early idea for the Isengard face-off had a flying nazgûl killing Saruman on top of Orthanc, then attacking Gandalf below; Frodo would have saved Gandalf by putting on the ring, sending the ringwraith back to Mordor. Saruman's death was going to end the first film, when the films were two movies).

With Saruman out of the picture, another way had to be found for introducing the *palantír*, which was one of the main reasons for going to Isengard after Helm's Deep in the first place (from the scriptwriters' point-of-view; in the book Gandalf guesses that Sauron will attack Gondor first). So it just happens to be lying under the water near our heroes, and Pippin spots it and picks it up. The other scenes inherited from *The Two Towers* were put in the only place they could go, really: early on in the film before the story had really started.

Another problem was how to begin *The Return of the King*. Then Peter Jackson had the idea of beginning it with Sméagol's back-story – partly because it introduced the ring again, and a major character, but also because it wasn't what the audience would be expecting (spectacular scenes had opened the previous two movies): so *The Return of the King* opened with a guy and a worm and a pastoral fishing scene.

The ending of *The Return of the King* was intensively worked on, because it was the most important part of the film, and the climax of the series (notice how the climax is unchanged in the *Extended Edition* from the theatrical cut, while there are plenty of other additions to scenes, as well as new scenes in the extended cut. Peter Jackson said he had halted the editing work in progress, and devoted some time to the final reel of *The Return of the King*, so it wouldn't be rushed at the end of the schedule).

One of the challenges of closing *The Return of the King* was the usual one of a Hollywood movie: how to combine the different storylines and actions into a coherent whole (and to top everything that had gone on before). Thus the crosscutting between the Black Gate battle and Frodo and Sam at Mount Doom. The classic device of delaying and stretching out the climax was employed here, with cuts back to the ring at it floats on the surface of the lava. Originally, the ring had simply disappeared with Gollum, but that was too fast, too anti-climactic. Having the ring sitting on the lava and cutting back to it three or four times stretched out the tension – but it also allowed the other action (such as Sam rescuing Frodo from the cliff) to unfold as well. It also carved out a little niche of time in which editors Jamie Selkirk and Anne Collins could cut to reaction shots of our heroes on the battlefield.

DIALOGUE AND ADR. There were a number of reasons why most of the dialogue in the *Lord of the Rings* films was produced in post-production. One was that many of the stages were converted warehouses, not sound stages, so there was plenty of outside noise (such as aircraft, the bane of filmmakers. It happens every time when you're filming: you set up the camera in a spot which seemed nice and quiet when you scouted it, but as soon as you're ready to starting shooting, World War Three breaks out. It was like that when we made *Ritual Magic*).

Another important reason was the accents: many of the actors were American, Kiwi or Australian, but the decision was made to have most of the characters speak in British accents: RP for the lords and kings, South Gloucestershire for the hobbits, bar Pippin, Mockney for the orcs, and so on). Dialogue coaches (Andrew Jack and Roisin Carty) were on set, but also on the ADR stages for all of the dubbing sessions. That meant that actors who weren't too sure about their accents and needed more time to rehearse their lines knew they could get it right months (or years) later, during post-syncing. ADR was also produced in London and Hollywood, among other places. For *The Return of the King*, for example, additional dialogue was recorded in London in September, 2003.

Leaving the dialogue to post-production also meant lots more control over it, of course. A filmmaker like Orson Welles could do extraordinary things with dubbed dialogue (have a look – and listen – at *Touch of Evil* for a terrific example). For the *Rings* films, it meant that all sorts of additions to dialogue or rewritten scenes could be included. There are many methods for slipping in new dialogue (over reaction shots, for instance, or cutaways to objects, or over long shots). One can see that occurring when the film cuts from close-ups of actors to a long shot and an actor is still heard speaking on the track. For instance, when Aragorn tells the hobbits they're going to Rivendell, when they're leaving Bree, Sam's heard saying 'did you hear that, Mr Frodo? We're going to see the elves', but he isn't shown saying it: instead, there are long shots of the characters walking.

While the lords and ladies of Middle-earth have British RP accents, and the hobbits have West Country accents, there were exceptions. For example, Frodo was given a Received Pronunciation accent, while Sam had a broad Gloucestershire accent. The difference in accent emphasized their class difference (as it still does in contemporary Britain). Billy Boyd's Pippin, meanwhile, seemed to stray into Scottish from time to time. Brad Dourif definitely had the oddest accent in the film (a strange fish, and Method actor, Dourif apparently kept up his accent on and off set, only giving it up when the gig was over).

One of the reasons so much of the films were shot in the studio was that it was decided early on not to use existing buildings (or props), but to build everything. Thus, much of what is up there on screen in the *Lord of the Rings* films was created specially for the films. That's not usual practice in the Hollywood film industry (though it does happen on some films, like *The Wizard of Oz* (1939) or *Bram Stoker's Dracula* (1992), for example, films which were largely put together in the studio). But the decision also meant that the production would not be employing existing buildings such as cathedrals, churches, castles and stately homes, the basic edifices in most costume or historical films. *Spartacus* (1960), for instance, used William Randolph Heart's Roman-style abode San Simeon, for Crassus's villa. That was constructed in the 20th century, and based on Roman originals, but it was accurate enough to be used without too much set dressing in the Kirk Douglas epic. Most fantasy and historical films whose production was contemporary with the *Lord of the Rings* films (*Harry Potter, Star Wars, Gladiator, Braveheart, Troy*, etc) used existing castles, or country houses, or banks, or public squares, or the foyers of big businesses, and so on.

SOUND DESIGN. Again and again the impact of much of the *Lord of the Rings* films derives from the sound recording, editing and mixing. So we ought to mention it yet again. Sound slips past unnoticed, perhaps, with so much eye candy and story to take in, but the sound is often 90% of the impact of the films. It's not just the replacement dialogue, the rewriting of scenes, it's also elements such as the balance of music, sound effects and dialogue: sometimes playing scenes with the music taking over, and everything else dipping away, or sometimes inserting a quiet moment without dialogue or music, or sometimes with sound effects doing the work of the music (in the 'ring moment' scenes, for instance, sound effects do the work of music).

The sound team on the *Lord of the Rings* films deserve as much as credit as any other department for the success of the films. Skywalker Sound and the Bay Area type of sound design is very much the influence here (some of the key personnel in the sound department had worked at Skywalker Sound). You can hear it in George Lucas's *Star Wars* films, or the films of Philip Kaufman, or Francis Coppola, or Walter Murch, or many other Hollywood pictures. It's a practice of sound design that prefers to record real sounds rather than create them in the computer or synthesizer.

BLUE SCREEN. Shooting against blue or green screens is not much different from the earlier techniques in Hollywood, such as back or front projection. To modern viewers, some of the back projections of the Classical Hollywood era may look creaky (two people talking in a car was one of the most common uses of it). But, in thirty or forty years, the combination of actors against models and matte paintings of the *Lord of the Rings* films will look clumsy (at the moment, the joins are simply more cleverly hidden than in 1940s or 1950s films. But they're all there if you look for them). However, it really doesn't matter a jot. Because in those films of the 1940s and 1950s, when Ingrid Bergman or Cary Grant was in shot, you certainly weren't looking at the rear projection, or even much aware of it. It's the story, the characters, the world of the film evoked that counts, and details of the production process soon fade away with good storytelling. As Dan Hennah, art director on the 2001-03 Tolkien films said, if you've done your job properly, no one notices it.

The blue/ green screen work on the *Lord of the Rings* films goes beyond back projections in the usual manner of Classic Hollywood cinema, however. It is more interactive, and closer to the way that Alfred Hitchcock used rear projection (the *Lord of the Rings* films were also using the methods developed by George Lucas on the *Young Indiana Jones Chronicles* and the *Star Wars* prequels). The *Lord of the Rings* films applied blue/ green screens to a wide variety of scenes, which many other filmmakers would automatically prefer to shoot outdoors.

NOTES: EDITING AND POST-PRODUCTION

1. In B. Sibley, 2002, 158.
2. Quoted in J. Boorman, 302.

CHAPTER 7

THE LOOK AND STYLE OF
THE *LORD OF THE RINGS* FILMS

THE LOOK

There appears to be more 'reality' in the *Lord of the Rings* films than, say, the *Star Wars* films or a Disney cartoon. In fact, the *Lord of the Rings* films are very much analogue-digital hybrids, films with tons of digital work, miniatures, sky replacements, motion capture, scale doubles and hundreds of other cinematic tricks. The *Lord of the Rings* films are every bit as 'fake', technological and fantastical as *Star Wars, The Matrix, Minority Report* or other hi-tech science fiction and futuristic movies. Take New Zealand, the much-hyped location for the Tolkien films: the spectacular setting for Edoras near Canterbury on the South Island was enhanced with digital buildings; and the impressive crumbly volcano locations of Ruapehu (for Mordor) had sky replacements in most of the shots.

That's why, if you visit New Zealand, it won't look quite like Middle-earth: Hobbiton, for instance, Matamata, won't be as green and golden as it is in the film, because the film was digitally altered to look like that. The Middle-earth you go in search of only exists on celluloid and in pixels: it was never 'real'. On film, Middle-earth is as much a place of the imagination as the books. The props may be 'real', the actors may appear 'real', but if you've only known the world of the films via a DVD player and a TV screen, or a laptop computer, or a cinema screen, it has no more 'reality' than a Pepsi commercial or a billboard for Nike sneakers.

One of the biggest decisions in adapting *The Lord of the Rings* was *when* to set the look of the films. Many readers consider *The Lord of the Rings* to be set in a mythical time, thousands of years before recorded history. But it's also a kind of Dark Age Northern Europe. And yet there's plenty of mediæval stuff in there too. Tolkien's book is full of anachronisms, when you look closer. The hobbits, for instance, draw on 16th, 17th and 18th century culture. Bilbo, for example, recalls landed gentry of the 18th century, in dress, language, customs, manners, and so on. It produces all sorts of clashes of historical periods: when Bilbo and Gandalf are in Bilbo's kitchen, they have a cup of tea out of a teapot like characters out of a Jane Austen novel. But when the hobbits are in Edoras, it's back a thousand years to iron pots on open fires and a fairly rough and ready existence. Edoras's Golden Hall drew on *Beowulf*, and Beorn's Hall in *The Hobbit*, as well as *Rings*.

Most of the elements in the films would be set in that Dark Age/ early mediæval period. That was what the audiences of the books expected, and that was what the films would deliver. The costumes presented numerous problems of period, as Ngila Dickson noted: the hobbits were dressed in clothes based on an English look of the 17th and 18th century, yet they had to interact with characters costumed in far earlier clothing.[1] When they meet the Gondorians or the Rohirrim, for instance, the hobbits are clad in clothes 600 or 1,000 years in the future, but no one must notice it.

What's so wonderful about John Ronald Reuel Tolkien's book is that few readers seem to notice how the story travels back in time from the 18th century a thousand or more years. The tobacco, the fish and chips, the cups of tea, it doesn't matter that the characters are using modern props in a Dark Age or Classical world.

The film adaptions had to tread a balance between all of the many historical periods, because they would be up on screen, not in a reader's imagination. The viewer of the films had to accept that Bree was designed as a 16th or 17th century English village (it could be a corner of modern-day Stratford-upon-Avon), but that Edoras had a Golden Hall out of *Beowulf*, and Minas Tirith was drew on the architecture of Istanbul, Venice and Rome.

The resulting look of the *Rings* films, in terms of production design, was a combination of South Pacific and European styles, a mixture of production designer Grant Major and costume designer Ngila Dickson (both Australian) and Tolkien illustrators Alan Lee and John Howe (British and Canadian). Plus the influence of a lot of Hollywood, including: Barrie Osborne (producer), Alex Funke (models), and Jim Rygiel (visual effects supervisor). The make-up and stylists were British (Peter Owen and Peter King, who'd worked on many historical pictures). Much of the rest of the key personnel were Aussie or Kiwi: Andrew Lesnie (DP), producers Tim Sanders and Jamie Selkirk, Dan Hennah, art direction, and Tania Rodgers and Richard Taylor, visual effects. And many of the actors were from Oz or NZ: Karl Urban, Cate Blanchett, Miranda Otto, Hugo Weaving, David Wenham, Marton Czokas, Craig Parker and Lawrence Makoare. Finally, a large proportion of the extras, stunt people, and production staff were from Oz or NZ.

John Howe provided the design of Sauron on the battlefield, much of the armour in the films, and many of the villains' environments, costumes and structures (such as the fell-beasts, Barad-dûr, Cirith Ungol, the Black Gate, and so on). Howe's designs were spikey, metallic, and darkly Gothic. Howe's illustration of the entrance hall of Bag End formed the basis for the set, and Howe helped design the rest of the Bag End set. Other Howe illustrations were employed closely: Gandalf fighting the balrog; the ringwraiths at the ford; Gandalf in Hobbiton; the Argonath; Cirith Ungol; Barad-dûr; Minas Morgul; and the Black Gate.

Alan Lee's illustration of Isengard was copied directly. Lee also designed Rivendell (as a kind of country retreat, in a forgotten valley, the kind of place, Lee remarked, that he'd like to retire to; DP Andrew Lesnie remarked of Hobbiton that it was meant to be a dream location, a paradise you'd like to visit for a vacation. Maxfield Parrish was cited in connection with Rivendell). Lee was very fond of the Rivendell set, and often visited it (in all of its forms, as a miniature, an outdoor set, and sound stage interiors). Rivendell has bowers and colonnades comprising *art nouveau* interlacings of wood. There were also raised walkways, bridges, bell towers; a stone bridge above a waterfall was a key feature.

Alan Lee provided the basis for the look of Bree, the Dwarrowdelf and tunnels in Moria, Fangorn, Treebeard, Helm's Deep, Edoras, the Grey Havens, Minas Tirith, Pelennor, and Lothlórien (including the design of the crucial Caras Galadon location). A Lee sketch for Helm's Deep was the basis for the models of the stronghold (which followed Lee's sketch very closely – it was another case of Peter Jackson wanting a 3-D version of a Lee drawing. Jackson said he had loved the painting Lee produced of Helm's Deep being besieged, and told his team he wanted something that came up to the same standard. Otherwise, why bother?). Lee also contributed immensely to *The Return of the King* – including the whole of the design of Minas Tirith, the Pelennor Fields, and the Grey Havens. The filmmakers had been much inspired by the anniversary edition of *The Lord of the Rings*, which Lee had beautifully illustrated. (The producers had been buying up Tolkien calendars, books and artwork all through pre-production).

One of the most significant contributions that Alan Lee made was to the whole look of the Moria sequence, the highpoint of *The Fellowship of the Ring* (and for some the best section of all three books, containing Tolkien's best writing). Lee produced an elaborate staircase drawing (for the part of the script which read 'the fellowship run down some stairs') which became the basis for much of the large miniature of Moria. Indeed, the giant stone staircases that Lee created became the setting for one of the key action sequences in *The Fellowship of the Ring*: the leaping across the gap in the stairs, the orcs shooting arrows, the approach of the balrog and the crumbling staircase. The Dwarrowdelf, though created as a wholly digital environment, was based on Lee's designs (with a few bases of columns being constructed full-scale).

One of the inspirations for the necropolis in the City of the Dead was Petra, a famous temple built into a cliff face (used in, amongst other films, *Lawrence of Arabia* and *Indiana Jones and the Last Crusade*). Moria was inspired partly by the angular, crystalline appearance of Tolkien's dwarvish runes. Moria was meant to look 'sophisticated and refined' commented Alan Lee, a place of civilization, though it was underground.

Lee cited the paintings of J.M.W. Turner as one of the influences on the look of the Grey Havens. It's easy to spot Turner and his wonderful Carthaginian paintings (and his hero, Claude Lorrain) in the image of the brilliant yellowy sun shining over the sea with Classical architecture ranged upon low hills on either side of the tranquil harbour. It's a landscape of coherence, peace and warmth.

For Minas Tirith, the designers looked to Mediterranean and European styles, in particular Italian and Middle Europe. Grant Taylor cited cities like Siena, Rome and Florence (although the filmmakers didn't use the warm Italian sunlight of those cities, or the distinctive reddish stone of Siena. Instead, they plumped for the cooler, white and black look of some Renaissance palaces, and the cathedrals in Firenze).

Alan Lee, who was primary among the designers of Minas Tirith, also referred to Mont St-Michel in France (the famous abbey and village on a granite island between Normandy and Brittany), and its counterpart in Cornwall, St Michael's Mount. Minas Tirith in the 2003 film was pretty much as Tolkien described it, with its seven levels, enormous prow, series of gates, citadel, great hall, houses of healing, courtyard and White Tree. Richard Taylor said that Weta's job in the miniatures department was 'quite simply, to facilitate Alan and John's combined vision, because we knew that it was going to be the *best* vision possible'.[2] For John Baster, one of the model builders, Howe and Lee had totally defined the look of *The Lord of the Rings:* 'these two incredible illustrators have given us the vision to create these extraordinary places in with such incredible richness and so much depth of design' (ib., 62). 'I've heard Peter [Jackson] talking repeatedly about using the art of Alan Lee and John Howe to gain inspiration', recalled Sean Astin (2004, 133).

The more I look at Alan Lee's Tolkien artwork, the more I think of the *Lord of the Rings* films as Alan Lee's *The Lord of the Rings,* not just Peter Jackson's *The Lord of the Rings* or Fran Walsh's *The Lord of the Rings* or Philippa Boyens' *The Lord of the Rings*. Richard Taylor was among many who enthused about Lee's contribution to the *Rings* films: commenting on the strength of Helm's Deep, Taylor said 'I sometimes think Alan should have been around nine hundred years ago and in charge of defending Britain!'[3]

So many Lee illustrations were copied directly: look at Gandalf and Pippin meeting Denethor, for instance: the throne's up some steps, Denethor sits below right, and holds Boromir's broken horn. There are black columns, and the wizard and hobbit stand before Denethor (without any others in attendance): it's all *exactly* like the movie.

An omission from the design of Helm's Deep was the great Dike, which plays an important role in the novel. The way Helm's Deep and the surrounding area was portrayed in the 2002 film, it seemed an empty river plain; in the book there are settlements, as well as the Dike. That also happened with Minas Tirith: below the city there are fields, buildings, and another wall. In the film, there's nothing but empty grasslands. Both Rohan and Gondor would have roads across them, and numerous marks of humanity, including walls, fields, houses, farms and livestock. The reason for making both Rohan and Gondor curiously empty of human traces in the 2001-03 movies is probably cost: villages, fields, houses, roads and the like could be evoked through models and matte paintings, but for the live action shoots full-size sets would be required.

Mordor had a distinctive look in the *Lord of the Rings* films: it's always overcast; the twin peaks of Mount Doom and Barad-dûr are usually visible; the plain isn't flat, but undulates with rocks and valleys (John Howe said he wanted Mordor to look as if an ocean had frozen and turned to stone). It's grey, plantless, and strewn with boulders. Smoke drifts; pockets of flames and steam rise. Colours are drained to near-monochrome. DP Andrew Lesnie said he wanted to keep shafts of sunlight cutting through in the Mordor scenes (although it's always cloudy. The harsh sunlight of New Zealand doesn't really match the gloomy skies. The Mordor I imagined was far grubbier, muddier, gloomier and more inhospitable).

The sky of the Black Land often has lightning flickering in it in the *Lord of the Rings* films, as well as orange glows reminiscent of the UFO lights in the clouds in *Close Encounters of the Third Kind*). Storms are often used in films because they look good, because they add a mood to a film (and they sound good too). In Mordor, the constant lightning activity suggests Sauron's uneasy psychological state, his nervy restlessness expressing itself in the fidgety animation of the Eye's spotlight beam in the third film. (Storyboard artist Christian Rivers remarked that the movement of the Eye was a tricky thing to bring off. The Eye needed to move, he said, for the purposes of storytelling, but exactly how was difficult to visualize. In the end, the filmmakers opted for a nervy, continuously restless motion which would express Sauron's doubt about the ring, as well as his anxious survey over his dominions and forces).

Both of Mordor's imposing peaks are topped with fiery lights: the Eye in its pointed crucible, sometimes with nazgûl flying around it – and, in *The Return of the King*, it has a spotlight capability. Mount Doom has a perpetually fuming summit, with black smoke boiling above it (and as the hobbits approach it, it's erupting, sending out showers of lava, and spewing out flaming boulders which crashland around the hobbits. The orange glow of Mount Doom – and the Eye – is used as a reminder of Mordor even when it's far away in the *Lord of the Rings* films.

NOTES: THE LOOK

1. In B. Sibley, 2002, 90.
2. In B. Sibley, 2002, 59.
3. In B. Sibley, 2002, 58.

COSTUMES

Though much of the film had already been designed by the time Ngila Dickson joined the production, the costume designer had plenty of work to do – including designing the hobbits' costumes. Ngila Dickson had previously worked on *Heavenly Creatures*, and the TV shows *Hercules: The Legendary Journeys* and *Xena, Warrior Princess* (many of the crew had worked on those shows, including Grant Major, Christian Rivers, and Philip Ivey). Although the costumes on the *Rings* show are superb, I wouldn't class Dickson among the star costume designers in the contemporary era

(Bob Ringwood, Jenny Beavan, Jeffrey Kurland, Colleen Atwood, Milena Canonero, etc).

The costumes in *The Lord of the Rings* are clearly part of the American TV fantasy drama tradition: some of the broad strokes look bold, chunky, hokey (other US TV series in this mediæval, mythological vein included *The Adventures of Sinbad* and *Robin Hood*). Peter Jackson said he wanted to avoid the 'cheesy fantasy we so often see in movies' (B. Sibley, 92), and in a July, 1999 interview with a New Zealand newspaper, Jackson said he was 'keen to avoid that American heavy metal look. It's a style that I don't think is appropriate but it's been used on a lot of Tolkien artwork and I think Tolkien would have been appalled'. And Richard Taylor remarked that they wanted to avoid the *Conan the Barbarian* look; unfortunately, Dickson's styling and costumes sometimes looked cheesy (or maybe it was the way they were filmed). Look at Gimli's make-up, or the orcs! Or the wizards! Or that endless sword fight at the end of *The Fellowship of the Ring*!

Many of the costumes for the orcs, the Haradrim, Easterlings and other villains were designed by the people at Weta Workshop. Some of Ngila Dickson's designs were beautiful – and not only the dresses for the three principal actresses (Liv Tyler, Miranda Otto and Cate Blanchett). However, Dickson's team clearly went to town on dressing the women, in such a boys' movie (though there wasn't any cleavage in this adaption of Tolkien's tome – no babes, then, although plenty of Hollywood mediæval movies – from the 1920s onwards – can't resist sexing up the costumes). As with most films, much of the detail, the embroidery, the undergarments, went virtually unnoticed by the camera. There were plenty of times when the filmmakers didn't shoot all of a costume (such as the eggshell blue dress ordered up to match with the scene of Éowyn sleeping in the blue cover. Despite Ngila Dickson designing an elaborate front to the dress, the filmmakers only shot Miranda Otto's head and shoulders).

Many of the costumes had fairly muted colours: the hobbits were in greys, browns and creams; the Gondorians were in black and silver; the high elves were in white, or dark cloaks. Among the more colourful costumes were those of Arwen and Éowyn, and the Haradrim. Dickson's designs concentrated as much on textures, weave and particular kinds of cloth, as on colour or cut (there was a good deal of embroidery in the *Lord of the Rings* wardrobe, which didn't always pop out of the screen in the midst of the rapid cutting and action).

Getting Legolas's costume right was difficult, and was being worked on right up to the last minute before shooting. As Ngila Dickson recalled, the wardrobe dept worked through a night and a day to nail it (because nobody could decide what it should be).

Clothing the elves was tricky, Ngila Dickson recalled, but it helped having the two actors, Cate Blanchett and Hugo Weaving, come in:

> suddenly, we knew that we had found a couple of the perfect Elves. Between the two of them, they defined "Elf" for us at last and we were able to create a design language that was rich and sumptuous and

which we knew would work.[1]

Aragorn's costume deliberately echoed the elves' costumes (as Aragorn had been raised among elves, in Rivendell). The shape of the Gondorian helmets recalls the war gear of the goodies (the Russians) in *Alexander Nevsky* (1938), a film regularly cited by filmmakers as a favourite historical epic.

Liv Tyler's costumes altered over the course of the films – from the warrior princess outfit of the beginning, through the floaty dresses of later scenes. Tyler's costumes developed from the same colour palette of the other elves to much richer hues – reds and blues, for instance, which suited Tyler's look. Arwen's make-up was revised: she had started out with dirt and blood on her face, but 'it didn't really work', commented make-up artist Peter King.

J.R.R. Tolkien's visual descriptions of his characters in *The Lord of the Rings* could be a little vague: he preferred to describe people as 'grim' or 'proud'. It was their mood, their attitude or their narrative function that interested him more (by contrast, his descriptions of landscapes could be detailed and vivid).

In the British *South Bank Show* documentary (broadcast December, 16, 2001), Peter Jackson spoke disparagingly of heavy rock and popular culture's appropriation of Tolkien in the 1970s, and the rise of the sword-and-sorcery genre. Bad move, inaccurate and ungenerous, because that's *precisely* what Jackson made with *The Lord of the Rings*.

WIGS. In the *Lord of the Rings* films pretty much everybody on screen wears a wig. The efforts of Peter Owen and Peter King should be acknowledged here; they did a terrific job in providing hair and make-up for so many characters (although some of their designs were a little silly, and often there was simply way too much hair on show – Gimli, for instance). The wigs were all made in Bristol, U.K., where Owen and King are based. Their previous films include *Dangerous Liaisons, The Draughtsman's Contract, Portrait of a Lady, Sleepy Hollow* and *Velvet Goldmine*.

In terms of make-up, the *Lord of the Rings* films contained plenty of transformations and transitions: Théoden and Gandalf came back renewed; Frodo went from youth through ageing; extras had to be turned into rosy-cheeked hobbits or ethereal, pale elves. Frodo's make-up was aged as the films progressed, with the make-up team deliberately pushing Frodo's youthfulness at the beginning, so the process of ageing would have farther to travel.

Caroline Turner spent hours creating the very long beard for Gandalf, but, after screen tests, it was abandoned. Peter Owen had told director Jackson that it wouldn't work, and he was right.

The look of Gandalf the White was different in terms of make-up from Gandalf the Grey: more colour was added to Ian McKellen's face, and his beard was fuller and closer trimmed. The idea was to create 'a feeling of rebirth', Peter Owen explained; 'he was the same character but renewed and ready to go on again'.[2] Ian McKellen described Gandalf the White as more driven, more grim, and with a better dress sense. But it was Gandalf the Grey that people thought of when they thought of Gandalf (even though Gandalf is the White longer than he is the Grey in the story). And McKellen, like Jackson – and me too – preferred the Grey wizard.

NOTES: COSTUMES

1. In B. Sibley, 2002, 92.
2. In B. Sibley, 2002, 118.

SHOOTING STYLE

Much of the time, the *Lord of the Rings* films were shot in a standard manner of traditional set-ups: wide shots followed by close-ups, observing the 180° rule, with one shot followed by a reverse angle. Some of the big set-pieces, which were storyboarded and animated before shooting, had a more stylized, elaborate shooting style. The scenes involving expensive elements – not only actors, but extras, miniatures, matte paintings, and digital characters and embellishments – were planned ahead. Sometimes, towards the end of the schedule, plans had to go out of the window, or if actors were only available for a day or so.

Peter Jackson's approach of pretending that *The Lord of the Rings* was a kind of history – that the events had really happened seven or eight thousand years and the actors were dressing up and visiting the places and recreating those events, has a similarity with docu-dramas, which were increasingly popular in the 1990s, and also reality TV, where participants would find out what it was like to, say, be in a trench in the First World War, or live as a mediæval peasant. And of course it was part of Tolkien's concept that Middle-earth had somehow existed 6 or 7 thousand years ago.

Shooting exteriors for *The Lord of the Rings* in New Zealand gave Middle-earth a spectacular look. Just as important, though, were the choices of *how* to shoot New Zealand (made by cinematographer Andrew Lesnie, designers Grant Major and Dan Hennah, director Peter Jackson, concept artists Alan Lee and John Howe, and other members of the production team). Lesnie opted for a glossy look to the cinematography, with lots of smoke and backlight (at times Lesnie admitted scenes looked like a pop music video). Nights, for instance, were rich with warm blues, rather than colourless blacks. The colouration of the films was enhanced by the use of digital grading throughout (achieved by the German company Posthouse, overseen by Peter Doyle. The digital grading, using Colourfront's Colossus, could scan a whole negative and select colours in any part of it. The system could alter highlights or shadows without affecting the rest of the frame; colour and grain and contrast could be altered anywhere. It was 'one of the greatest tools for a filmmaker that I've seen', enthused Peter Jackson).[2] (The films were shot in Super 35mm, on Kodak 500T/5279 film stock, with the film using digital intermediates. The scanned film was then printed onto EK 5242, with dupes being made on Eastman stock, and release prints (for theatres) on Fuji 3513D.)

The harsh light of the Southern hemisphere was diffused with filters, fog and smoke (to achieve the softer, storybook look of the artwork of Alan Lee and John Howe). In the Rohan scenes and in the 'world of men' in the second and third films, the colours and light are dirtier and more 'realistic' but, on the whole, the *Lord of the Rings* films tended towards a heightened, 'storybook' look. (The lighting and approach in the 2nd and 3rd films was more 'aggressive' and grainier when it came to lighting, Lesnie explained, while the first film was deliberately fantastical).

Although the visual approach suited J.R.R. Tolkien's fantastical world of elves, dwarves, hobbits and orcs, one wonders how different the films might have been if they had been shot in the Northern hemisphere. There's a particular quality to the light in Northern Europe, for example, in films shot in Germany, France, Britain, Norway, Sweden and so on. For instance, *Braveheart* (1995), shot mainly in Ireland (although set in Scotland), has the landscape of misty mountains, broad valleys and rocky streams that Tolkien described. There are exterior scenes in Roman Polanski's *Macbeth* (1971) which were shot in the mountains of North Wales which have a wonderful misty, rainy look, very much in tune with Tolkien's Middle-earth. And *Dragonslayer* (1982) is a beautiful film which used Scottish and Welsh locations. There are all sorts of little details in the landscapes of Northern Europe which differentiate them from New Zealand. They're not really important to Tolkien's story or the characters, and *The Lord of the Rings* could have been filmed in hundreds of locations around the world, but they subconsciously enhance the *mise-en-scène* of the film.

So many key scenes (as well as details and embellishments) were reshot, it's almost as if the *Lord of the Rings* films were two different films: the ones shot between October, 1999 and December, 2000, and the three films created during reshoots. And some scenes were shot more than twice. But it's a common practice nowadays with expensive blockbuster films to shoot them at least three times: first in rough video and computer animatics; secondly in principal photography; and a third time during post-production, when scenes are animated, reshot, and composited (combined with models, mattes, and tons of computer animation).

Another tribute to the filmmakers of the 2001-03 *The Lord of the Rings* films was to encourage audiences to take the whole thing seriously, the fantastical world of Middle-earth, the world of elves, dwarves, wizards, orcs and monsters. And also to take actors seriously who were in mediæval dress, swinging swords and spouting cod Shakespearean dialogue. This Middle Ages genre was already camp and self-conscious by the 1920s and 1930s, so to persuade viewers to take it straight sixty or seventy years later was tricky.

One of the solutions was to have the actors play their roles straight, with no winking at the camera or playing up to the gods. Acting styles were damped down somewhat, with much intense whispering taking the place of larger-than-life performances. Some of the performers hammed it up tremendously, though: Christopher Lee's Saruman, the orcs, Brad Dourif's

Wormtongue, John Rhys-Davies's Gimli, Andy Serkis's Gollum, and Dominic Monaghan's and Billy Boyd's hobbits. Let's face it, grown men riding on horses, brandishing swords, battling orcs and monsters, is difficult to pull off straight-faced in a movie, and especially to a movie audience which has already seen hundreds of similar films.

BLUE SCREENS AND SHOOTING STYLE. You'll notice that employing the blue screens in contemporary cinema tends to create a particular shooting style. The technology of filming actors against screens imposes certain kinds of styles (and where to put the camera). In the *Lord of the Rings* films, this tends to manifest itself in a kind of *tableau* style of shooting, which emphasizes frontality. That means for many scenes, there'll be a long sot, which might be a model with actors against blue screen superimposed on it, or digital characters. For the medium close-ups and close-ups, the actors are shot tight, against a partial set and a blue screen; for the reverse angles, it's the same set-up. And it means that angles from the side, or over-the-shoulder, or moving back and forth, are much rarer, because they are more difficult to achieve. Gandalf and co. emerging from Fangorn and encountering the hobbits on the wall at Isengard in *The Two Towers* is a good example: both sides of the scene are flattened, with the actors in a narrow space against screens which have matte paintings or models put in later.

NUDITY. It's striking how much nudity there is in the early 2000s *Lord of the Rings* movies. Only they're not the sort of naked bodies you probably want to see. Characters such as the cave troll are near-nude. A major character, Gollum, spends the entire movie in naught but a scraggy loincloth, like a squat, emaciated Tarzan or Mowgli. Thankfully, there's no Homer Simpson butt crack to Gollum. (Gollum's a supremely anti-erotic figure, of course, or erotic in an *uurrgghh* way, but the movie makes much, as the book does, of how creepily touchy-feely Gollum can be, especially when he's pawing at poor Frodo). At one point, Arwen and Aragorn were going to be depicted swimming naked in a rock pool at the Glittering Caves, with Legolas and Gimli discovering them (Sib, 368). Errr, right.

NOTES: SHOOTING STYLE

1. J. Howe, in D. Jude, 48.
2. In J. Duncan, 2001, 106.

VIOLENCE

The *Lord of the Rings* films are *extremely violent*, at least in terms of what they are trying to portray – a world war in Middle-earth. (The body counts of *The Return of the King* (836) and *The Two Towers* (468) far excel those in *Saving Private Ryan*, *Hard-Boiled*, *Braveheart* or *We Were Soldiers*, according to www.moviebodycounts.com). The movies are too violent, which unbalances Tolkien's book hugely (very close to an 'R' rated movie, as Peter Jackson confessed).

There isn't space in this book to explore the depiction of violence in cinema. Here are a few points about violence in movies, and the effects of watching movies and media consumption: it's worth remembering that movies are not 'real' in the usual sense of the word. They're a very particular form of cultural product (i.e., entirely cultural, ideological, political, æsthetic, social), which are subject to technological, industrial and economic pressures from many sources, and are consumed in very particular socio-economic contexts. They're not 'real': they use myriad devices to promote an illusion of what J.R.R. Tolkien called a 'secondary world': in other words, an abstraction on top of an abstraction on an abstraction. Very far removed from 'reality'.

CHAPTER 8

VISUAL EFFECTS

By the time *The Lord of the Rings* got to the screen in 2001, audiences had already seen plenty of computer-generated imagery and digital visual effects (at least eleven or so years of it, depending on how you define it). Viewers were very familiar with what CGI could do: giant bugs (in *Starship Troopers* and *Mimic*), huge reptiles in *Godzilla*, *Dragonheart* and *Anaconda*, dinosaurs in the *Jurassic Park* series, countless aliens in *Star Wars: The Phantom Menace*, mice in *Stuart Little* and *Mouse Hunt*, a pitch battle of apes in *Planet of the Apes*, robots in *The Terminator 2*, superheroes in *X-Men*, devilish tornadoes in *Twister* and killer storms in *The Perfect Storm*, talking animals in *Cats and Dogs*, the *Dr Doolittle* and *Babe* films, monsters in *Men in Black*, *The Odyssey*, *The Fifth Element*, *The Relic*, *Spy Kids*, *Lara Croft*, *Galaxy Quest*, *Evolution*, *Pitch Black*, the *Mummy* and *the Alien* series, amazing vistas in *Gladiator*, *Contact*, *Total Recall*, the *Batman* films, *The Grinch*, *A.I.*, and *What Dreams May Come*, World Wars in *Pearl Harbor*, *Enemy At the Gates*, and *Saving Private Ryan*, not to mention spectacular large-scale destructions in the cycle of mid-1990s disaster films *Independence Day*, *Armageddon*, *The Avengers*, *Mars Attacks!*, *Dante's Peak*, *Titanic*, *Volcano* and *Deep Impact*.

The visual effects in the *Lord of the Rings* films were by Weta Digital in New Zealand, GMD In Australia, and in the U.S.A.: Digital Domain, Sony Pictures ImageWorks, Animal Logic Film, Rhythm & Hues, and Oktobor Films, with matte paintings by Hatch FX and Michael Lloyd, and digital grading by The Posthouse, in Australia. Redline Studios in Australia provided the foley work; FX Rentals of London provided audio equipment.

The Lord of the Rings was typical among contemporary Hollywood blockbusters in farming out special effects work and taking bids from fx houses. Big movies like this are rarely produced totally in-house or by a single company – the way that the first *Star Wars* film used Industrial Light & Magic, for instance. There's simply too much work for one company to handle, especially as schedules decrease and workloads increase in the visual effects world and contemporary cinema. The number of fx shots on a show like *The Lord of the Rings* required the help of many other companies. (And New Line put added pressure on Weta, persuading them to fire some key personnel in the first months of production [Sib, 481]).

THE RING.
That friggin' ring! To convey the power of the ring, big close-ups of the ring, sound effects, music and rapid montages were deployed. The flaming Mordor script was added with CGI, while the lettering shining on Frodo's face was a practical lighting effect. Also, different sized ring props were used, as well as techniques such as a magnet on the Bag End floor set so it wouldn't bounce when Bilbo drops the ring (with an oversize sound effect). When Gandalf stoops to pick up the ring, a flash cut of Sauron's Eye startles him (accompanied by a burst of noise). It's the first time the device is employed in the films, and becomes, as a way of depicting Sauron's far-reaching power, a recurring motif.

During the Council of Elrond, a panorama of the gathering of free peoples arguing was reflected in a big close-up of the ring, with a wall of fire covering them. During the lengthy exposition scene between Gandalf and Frodo at the Bag End kitchen table (where some of the back-story in the prologue would have appeared if there hadn't been a prologue), the ring, lying beside them on the table, seems to whisper to them, and they both glance at it. It's a wonderful touch, the idea that Sauron's voice emanates from the ring (and can interrupt a conversation at a critical juncture, as if he's in the room with them).

Many of the ring shots ended up with a digital ring, after practical solutions had been tried. It was just easier to do things like change the ring's shape or have fiery letters appearing on it, in the digital realm (Wayne Stables had tried to matchmove 3D lettering to the practical ring, but it was very difficult – partly because the ring was shiny. So, in the prologue, the ring is mostly computer-generated).

SCALE.
The scale effects continually changed through the movie, as John Nugent explained, to deliberately shake up the audience, so they wouldn't have time to work out how the shots were done, and would focus on the story instead. Sometimes it was over-sized or under-sized sets, sometimes it was forced perspective, or scaled camera, or scaled composites, or scaled doubles.[1] The scale doubles and the like never convinced me, but it was certainly an improvement on John Boorman's idea for the hobbits of kids dubbed with adults' voices!

In pre-production, a tall actor and a short actor had been photographed from many angles, so the filmmakers could work out how to achieve the differences in scale for each scene. Tall Paul (Paul Randall) did many of the large scale double scenes, standing in for Gandalf and Aragorn, and practically every character in the films.

Some of the scale doubles had face masks, which were employed for longer shots. Some of the masks had basic facial movements, driven by a radio-controlled servor motor hidden under the wig. Dummies were also used, as well as 9-foot animatronic suits, with operators inside walking on stilts (you can see them in the Prancing Pony scene).

The moving forced perspective shot in Bag End was built by Brian Van't Hul and Harry Harrison; Illusion Arts' Bill Taylor had first proposed the idea, using a slaved motion control rig. Special tables, like the ones built to indicate the different scales of adults and hobbits in Bag End, were nothing new in movies: when Alfred Hitchcock wanted one of his unusual point-of-view shots in *Shadow of a Doubt*, an egg-shaped table was constructed, for one character's view of five other people at the table. *Under Capricorn* featured one of the more extravagant Hitchcock tables: it was built with 14 parts that could be pulled out of the way of the camera by the actors as it trucked along.

One of the key visual effects in the *Lord of the Rings* films, which many viewers might not notice, was sky replacement. New Zealand often has hard, blue skies, but *The Lord of the Rings* required cloudy, gloomy skies – especially as the story progressed towards Mordor. Sky replacement was a tricky (and thus also costly) process – pulling skies from around actors' heads and bodies, and putting a new sky in.

Set extensions also had to be added to the many studio-bound sets, or to scenes which were set outside. Bilbo's party at Hobbiton, for instance, was shot on in the studio, and needed a nighttime sky as well as other additions (such as the fireworks).

Alan Lee had designed Pelennor Fields, plotting the positions of the city, the mountains, the plain, Osgiliath, the mountains of Mordor, the river, and so on. Location photographs were tiled together in the computer to create a 3-D digital environment which would be used as the setting for the climactic battle. Pelennor Fields was constructed from New Zealand's mountains, rivers, grassland and skies (the skies above Wellington, for instance, were used for the cloudscapes, while Twizel, the location for the live action battle, was used to create the plain itself).

One of the reasons so many soldiers were used at Pelennor Fields – some 350,000 in Sauron's forces – was to fill out the vast arena designed by Alan Lee and the team. 50,000 soldiers wasn't enough to make the enormous area in front of Minas Tirith look full enough.

The underwater scenes in the *Lord of the Rings* films were shot 'dry for wet' (i.e., with cables and wind machines and other devices employed to suggest an actor being under water), partly because the New Zealand film industry doesn't (or didn't then) have a tank big enough. Wet sets were constructed for the *Lord of the Rings* project – for outside Moria, for instance, or for Osgiliath, or for the Dead Marshes – but those were shallow pools, not deep tanks. The producers could have gone to L.A. or London to use their tanks, but tried to keep much of the principal photography based in NZ. (Large tanks were constructed specially for films such as *Harry Potter 4* and *Alien 4*).

The Argonath sequence's hero shot lasts nearly a minute, and begins on the canoes and travels up to and past one of the statues of the kings of Gondor. It required digital boats, river, birds, scenic tiles, matte paintings, and a model.

The Eye of Sauron was a combination of practical elements such as flames, shot at high speed, coupled with digital fx driven by images of dry ice and underwater photography, fixed to the digital geometry of a taurus-shape like a cat's eye. In all, eight layers of particle systems and live-action layers made up the eye effect. As Jim Rygiel commented, the eye was a difficult concept to grasp: 'There were a lot of sketches done, but they were all different. What was the eye supposed to be? What it a menacing eye? Did it look like a real eyeball?'.[2]

The 'wraith world' effect took its lead from J.R.R. Tolkien's description, a world of shadows, with a tattered look around the edges, like heat distortion: it was a combination of 3D and 2D computer work, with 3D particle streams off a 2D plate. The particles would be streaked and tracked in 3D, so the image had depth, and shifted as the camera moved.

The matte paintings for the *Lord of the Rings* films were put together by art director Paul Lasaine, photographer Craig Potton, DP Alun Bollinger and Mark Stetson, vfx supervisor. Many of the scenic unit's work was put into a spherical digital environment, tiled together in 3D.

The Australian fx house GMD did the scary Galadriel visual effects, involving colour grading and 2D work. GMD split the live plates of Blanchet into 18 layers, applying Inferno and Flame software to them.

Animal Logic, based in Australia, provided the images of the Shire in turmoil, which included a miniature of the mill (designed by John Howe) and matte paintings. Images of Frodo were comped into the scene, as if they were a reflection in the water. They also did the scenes of Sam underwater and the *palantíri*. The scene of Sam underwater was achieved with fans blowing Astin's hair and clothes, and the camera running at 150 frames a second.

There was plenty of fire in the *Lord of the Rings* films – Moria, Mount Doom, Isengard – which, as Alex Funke pointed out, is one of the most difficult effects to pull off well.

Visiting Industrial Light and Magic and seeing their pre-viz pipeline had been an eye-opener for the *Lord of the Rings* team, largely because of the scale of the operation at ILM.

For example, in order to blend miniatures in the background with live action shot in the foreground, as in a scene set in a hallway in Rivendell, the camera department cleaned up the motion control file, supplied the technical breakdown, corrected the tracking mistakes that the motional control rig made, then scaled the information down to 1/24th, which was the scale of the miniature.

Animatics were created from the storyboards the team had designed when the film had been prepped for Miramax. Lipstick cameras were used on little cardboard sets. As shots were lined up with plastic figures on the mini sets, Christian Rivers would sketch them off a video monitor. The films were put together by Brian Van't Hul in 3D Studio Max, with temporary sound fx, dialogue and music. As shooting progressed, the live action could be cut into the pre-viz version of the films, so the filmmakers could look at the whole thing.

The Massive software incorporated motion captured live action, so, although it was a digital programme, it drew on real-life actions of running, falling, sword swinging, and so on (the vfx team used a physical fitness trainer as their basic NURBS model, scanned in L.A. with a Cyberware full-body scanner). The digital figures were used for the background of shots (usually), with live-action characters, in rows say four-deep, for the foreground, shot against a bluescreen. Passes were then added of atmospheric effects (such as smoke) and shadows. Films such as *The Phantom Menace* had already provided shots of thousands of digital extras with minds of their own (Massive software was developed in conjunction with ILM. Stephen Regelous supervised the Weta Digital side of Massive). As Fran Walsh pointed out, action could quickly become 'meaningless' if it didn't have an emotional point to it (Sib, 415), and big battle scenes could easily become just thousands of dots running around.

Information was shared between the units and departments to achieve the visual effects: camera information (like lenses, movement, etc), notes on set, motion control data, motion capture data, and so on.

MONSTERS.

The monsters in *The Lord of the Rings* were consciously designed to resemble Ray Harryhausen's animation. Animators Randy Cook and Adam Valdex were big Harryhausen fans (just like almost everybody in the visual effects industry), and the classic staging and theatricality of the creatures looked back to Harryhausen's peerless stopmotion. Cook, one of the chief orchestrators of the troll fight, said that it had been designed specifically like a Harryhausen scene:

> the monster shows up, fights with people, and is killed. But Harryhausen always tried to bring out the pathos of his creatures, and we did the same thing here.[4]

Peter Jackson said he wanted 'that monster fight to contain all the gags and moments I enjoyed seeing in Ray's [Harryhausen's] films' (R. Harryhausen, ix). Randy Cook and the pre-viz team came up with the complex action and gags for the Moria sequence, and Jackson came in and to pick the beats he liked, and maybe add some other gags.

MODELS.

Peter Jackson preferred models over matte paintings, particularly for buildings and cities, though came round to appreciating matte paintings, if they were based on photographic elements. The production built up a library of skies and scenes; if they saw a dramatic-looking sky as they were filming, they'd stop and film it.

As Alex Funke said, the emphasis on models in the *Lord of the Rings* films meant 'hundreds and hundreds of miniature shots for the three films; and that was a huge commitment of personnel, time, and equipment.'[5] 68 models were constructed for the three films. Shooting the miniatures began in October, 1999, and continued non-stop for all of principal photography, and right up to the release of each of the three pictures.

The filmmakers wanted to shoot miniatures in a sweeping, rapid camera style, when the scene needed it, though model photography has tended to be more conservative, often with the camera locked off. Although the camera moves might be 'impossible' – if the camera was meant to be move as if it were photographing a real object – Jackson thought they added to the drama, and made viewers forget they were looking at a model.

Rivendell comprised miniatures shot by Alex Funke's team (including DP Chuck Schuman), paintings by Paul Lasaine, photographs by Craig Potton, footage of waterfalls, and actors shot against blue screen. Lórien was built at 12th scale, but still took up a whole studio. Barad-dûr was one of the first models constructed for the show, back in early 1999, from a John Howe design.

Models were blended with 2D and 3D digital work, as well as matte paintings. Miniatures were shot in stacked layers, to maximize the sense of depth. For example, for the shots of Lórien, the model team (led by David Hardberger) shot their five or six hero trees for the foreground, then rearranged them for the middle distance, and shot them in a different grouping again for the background. Some shots were many layers deep. (Oktobor composited some of the Lórien and Rivendell scenes). The Lórien models were 60 by 80 feet, and filled the largest stage the production had (which was hired specially for the Lothlórien model shoot). Alan Lee led the design of Lórien, aided by art director Paul Lasaine, who devised the lighting (pinpoints of light in blue mist). As Lasaine explained, the Golden Wood was conceived as 'the Swiss Family Robinson treehouse, combined with a grove of sequoias, combined with the Ewok village'.[6]

Isengard was a combination of miniatures: one for the tower, one for the whole complex, and a variety of cave and mine models. Orthanc itself was shot with a bunch of photographs (taken at the Isengard park location) mounted on a physical cyclorama around the model, so that the colours would be reflected in the model, because Orthanc was meant to have a shiny, reflective surface. The circular fortress set was 60 feet wide, and in 35th scale; it was constructed out of concrete and urethane. In Los Angeles, Rhythm & Hues composited 9 shots of Isengard, and also enlarged the orcs' eyes in Moria.

The whole Moria sequence was largely a miniatures sequence. Nearly all of the environments of Moria were models. True, there were some CG sections (such as the Dwarrowdelf, or the bridge), and some digital additions to scenes (such as digital doubles for the fellowship, plus the balrog, and digital orcs), and digital extensions to some of the models. But the look and feel of the sequence was drive entirely by miniatures, combined with full-size sets. As Alex Funke proudly pointed out, from the time the balrog's approaching to the final scene when Aragorn's carrying Frodo, it's 'almost completely miniature sets. I believe it is the longest continuous all-miniature sequence ever done for a film'.

The stairs of Khazad-dûm was among the biggest models Weta built for the show, as well as one of the first built. It was 21 feet high and 66 feet long, constructed mainly from industrial tin foil and urethane rock castings. The miniature (at 14th scale, like most of the Moria models) included a set of doors, the stairs, the bridge to the great hall, the hall, the bridge of Khazad-dûm, and the stairs beyond.

GOLLUM.

Andy Serkis inevitably had to spend a lot of time on the postproduction of the *Lord of the Rings* films, when all the other actors had left

New Zealand. Originally, the filmmakers were going to animate Gollum digitally as a stand-alone character, but seeing Andy Serkis perform the character on set with the actors persuaded them to use Serkis's performance as the chief reference for Gollum.

Serkis's Gollum scenes were filmed three or four times: once with the actors, on set, once without other actors, and once again, on the motion capture stage. The other actors (often Elijah Wood and Sean Astin) also shot a pass miming reacting to Serkis's Gollum.

NOTES: VISUAL EFFECTS

1. J. Duncan, 2001, 93.
2. J. Duncan, 2001, 96.
3. J. Duncan, 2001, 130.
4. J. Duncan, 2001, 122.
5. A. Funke, in J. Duncan, 2001, 72.
6. J. Duncan, 2001, 127.

CHAPTER 9

MUSIC

Canadian Howard Shore (b. 1946) was best known for scoring most of David Cronenberg's films. But he also wrote scores for Martin Scorsese (*After Hours*); Jonathan Demme (*The Silence of the Lambs* and *Philadelphia*); David Fincher (*Seven* and *The Game*); and Penny Marshall (*Big*). The *Rings* score meant around three years of work, off and on, for Shore. He wasn't known so much for the big blockbuster franchises, like composers such as Danny Elfman, Alan Silvestri, Jerry Goldsmith, or John Williams.

In composing his music for the *Lord of the Rings* films of 2001-03, Shore said he had researched the chief sequences by going through the novel page by page, by examining the culture that had grown up around *The Lord of the Rings* since the 1950s, and by exploring the mythology that had influenced J.R.R. Tolkien's book.

The Moria sequence was the centrepiece of *The Fellowship of the Ring* for Shore, one that he had to get right. Shore explained the way he worked:

> *The Lord of the Rings* is the most complex fantasy world ever created, so I'm holding a mirror up to it, musically, and trying to create something that's the image of it. I had the idea of using the languages which, by putting them into the music, would express another layer of Tolkien's thinking, and put the mythology back into the film. Some of the texts came right from *The Lord of the Rings* book itself.

Howard Shore remarked that scoring *The Lord of the Rings* had 'gone *way* beyond cues! It's written in suites and, all told, we're talking about more than two-and-a-half hours of music!'[1]

Irish/ Celtic music was used for the hobbits' scenes, and for the scenes of the Rohirrims' exodus from Edoras to Helm's Deep (following a Hollywood convention of identifying the working class, the 'innocents', 'the people', with folk and traditional musical forms – *Braveheart* and *Titanic* were typical examples). For the theme for the Rohirrim in *The Two Towers*, Shore came up with a folky, vaguely Celtic melody (which was played on the Norwegian fiddle).

The title music for the *Lord of the Rings* films was what Shore called 'the history of the ring' music, and also Gollum's theme. A melancholy piece, when played at the head of the films, it introduced the pictures with a sombre, serious tone (very different from the military, martial themes of John Williams, say, or the percussive, playful vigour of Danny Elfman). My son Jake turned to me in the cinema at the start of each film and said the music was too sad – too sad for the opening of this kind of action-adventure movie.

For the scenes involving Gollum, Shore varied the theme for the 'Slinker' and 'Stinker' sides of Gollum's schizophrenic character. There was also a jokey version of the ring theme for the moment when the ring's discovered in the Sméagol prologue of *The Return of the King*.

There were ten soloists in the score of *The Fellowship of the Ring*: Miriam Stockley and Elizabeth Fraser sang in the Lothlórien scenes (for *Gandalf's Lament*); Edward Ross sang (in Elvish and English); Enya sang at Rivendell in Sindarin, and also later in English and in Quenyan.

Among the soloists in Shore's score for the three movies were Elizabeth Fraser, ethereal chanteuse with indie bands the Cocteau Twins and This Mortal Coil, Sheila Chandra, best known for Indian world music, and Irish/ Celtic rock-folk singer Enya (who provided a couple of songs). Enya is Ireland's bestselling solo artist, with 80 million album sales by 2009. 'Gollum's Song' in *The Two Towers* was sung by Emiliana Torrini (Shore said he wanted someone Northern European for this, and Torrini was a mix of Icelandic and Italian). *The Return of the King* was closed with 'Into the West' by Annie Lennox. Edward Ross, Mabel Faletolu, Ben Del Maestro and Isabel Bayrakdarian were the other soloists.

There were 200 musicians on the soundtrack, a 200-piece orchestra (it was a 100-piece symphony orchestra, a 60-voice mixed choir, a 30-piece all boys choir, and 10 vocal and instrumental soloists). The mixed choirs sang in the Quenyan, Sindarin, Black Speech, Adunaic, and Dwarvish, the languages of Middle-earth. And English.

It's interesting to note that many of the featured soloists and singers in the 2001-03 *The Lord of the Rings* films were female (Enya, Fraser, Torrini, Lennox, Chandra, Faletou, Bayrakdarian), and that many were associated with the Celtic fringe in British Isles: Ireland (Enya) and Scotland (Fraser and Lennox) (these singers were also linked to 1980s pop music, and gained their popularity in the 1980s). That the three pop acts chosen to sing over the end credits were female was significant (and two were from the British Celtic fringe, being Irish and Scottish). Also, many of the singers and soloists were either born in Britain (Fraser, Enya, Lennox) or worked in Britain (Chandra). Similarly, the orchestra was based in Britain (the London Philharmonic), and the music was recorded in Britain (at Abbey Road Studios, with the orchestra being taped in the unlikely setting of Watford Town Hall).

Enya was an obvious choice for *The Lord of the Rings* in other ways: she had an album with the very Tolkienesque title *The Memory of Trees*, and had written a song called 'Lothlórien' (found on her most well-known album, *Shepherd Moons*). And she had a deal with Warners (who released her album), the owners of New Line Cinema.

The soloists were often employed at key emotional moments: Aragorn near death on the riverbank (Sheila Chandra); Liz Fraser sang about

Gandalf in Lothlórien, and during Haldir's death on the battlements of Helm's Deep; boy soloists sang over the march of the ents, or Gandalf alone atop Orthanc.

Choral music was employed throughout the films – and not only at the climactic action moments. 'I thought of the choral music as another texture in the orchestra', Shore remarked.

The big choir sounds (by London Oratory and the London Voices) were often used in the big spectacle scenes: Treebeard leading the ents to war on Isengard; Gandalf fighting the balrog; Gandalf and Éomer and the Rohirrim storming down the mountain at Helm's Deep; the fellowship on the Moria staircase; the Black Riders leaving Minas Morgul; the horse chase to the Ford of Bruinen; and Frodo fighting Gollum at Orodruin.

Director Peter Jackson admitted he wasn't musical at all, and didn't know much about the technical side of music. He had ideas about the music for the films and oversaw the scoring sessions in England, but confessed he couldn't suggest much to Howard Shore beyond general remarks. Frances Walsh and Philippa Boyens seem to have had a big influence on the kind of music heard in *The Lord of the Rings* films, including the choice of Shore as composer (whom Walsh admired), and the selection of the many female soloists (in the commentaries on the extended versions of the films, Jackson rarely mentions the music, but Walsh and Boyens often do).

Both Fran Walsh and Philippa Boyens worked with composer Howard Shore on some of the songs for the *Rings* films, writing the lyrics (some of which were translated into Tolkien's languages, such as Elvish and Old English for the Rohirrim, by David Salo). It's curious that new songs had to be written for the films, when there are so many in the book. But the filmmakers wanted songs for specific dramatic moments (such as Théodred's funeral, for instance, sung by Éowyn, or the closing credits music).

Among the songs in the film of *The Fellowship of the Ring* are Gandalf and Bilbo singing 'The Road Goes Ever On and On', 'The Prophecy Song', 'Aniron' by Enya, a love theme for Arwen and Aragorn, 'Gandalf's Lament' by Liz Fraser and choir, the dwarvish chanting in 'Moria' (by the Samoan Choir), a *Green Dragon* song, etc. Further songs included four songs by the ents, Gollum's fish song, and Éowyn singing at the funeral. The attack of the ringwraiths on Minas Tirith had the choir singing in Adunaic. Pippin sings over the Osgiliath charge. Aragorn sings at his coronation.

Howard Shore said his music had to help with the constant shifts from one environment and mood to another. Shore often talked about his *Lord of the Rings* music in terms of opera. Rather than three separate films, Shore saw it all as one piece of music. It was the opposite of opera in terms of composition, because the visuals and staging had already been accomplished. 'What I'm trying to do is have the same feeling so that when you watch the film, it feels seamless, it's almost like the film was created to music'.[2]

Some of Shore's music was deceptively simple: the Mordor scene of Frodo crawling up Mount Doom, Shore employed a whistle very effectively, a welcome respite from the loud, big scenes of Pelennor and Minas Tirith. For the ents, Shore employed wooden instruments, and low, deep sounds on bassoons, double basses, log drums and bass marimbas.

Shore said he deployed wooden instruments for the Fangorn scenes, to offer an aural equivalent for scenes dominated by trees and a walking treeish giant.

Shore used leitmotifs or themes for each culture and group of characters: the heroic fellowship theme, the homely Shire and hobbit theme, the melancholy ring and Gollum theme, a bold Isengard march, dwarvish chanting, a heroic Rohirrim theme, and so on. Sometimes the themes were played on solo instruments (such as a fiddle or a flute or Norwegian Hardanger violin), and sometimes they were reprised as big choral cues.

There was a touch of ethnic stereotyping in Howard Shore's music for the villains: the music for Mordor and Isengard contained the Moroccan rhiata and Eastern or Arabic style music, aligning the forces of evil with North Africa. (Shore was among the few composers who've tackled Tolkien who purveyed the 'exotic' and negative aspects of the villains using Oriental styles.)

I guess some Tolkien purists might object to the music employed in the 2001-2003 *Lord of the Rings* films as anachronistic; maybe only 12th century courtly songs or minstrelsy from Dark Age Germany would do (if it were possible to reconstruct it). Or maybe no music at all, except for the songs Tolkien wrote in *The Lord of the Rings*. In fact, any kind of music from the 20th century or 21st century is anachronistic, in a purist sense. A film that was released the same year as *The Fellowship of the Ring*, Columbia's *A Knight's Tale* (2001) was a mediæval romp with a terrific rock and pop soundtrack (Thin Lizzy, Queen, War, etc) which fitted the Middle Ages setting and spirit of the film perfectly. One scene in *A Knight's Tale*, the mandatory dancing at the feast scene (which the *Lord of the Rings* films lacked), had a courtly dance cleverly segueing into David Bowie's 'Golden Years'. But using Bowie was no less silly than having Enya, Annie Lennox or Maori choirs warbling in the 2001-03 *Lord of the Rings* films.

NOTES: MUSIC

1. In B. Sibley, 2002, 179.
2. H. Shore, in R. Koppl: "Climbing Into Darkness: Scoring *The Two Towers*", *Soundtrack*, 21, 84, 2002.

CHAPTER 10

DIFFERENCES BETWEEN THE BOOK AND THE FILMS

DIFFERENCES BETWEEN THE BOOK AND THE 2001-03 FILMS

My discussions of the films will concentrate on the theatrical cut and the *Extra Special Limited Extended Platinum Edition* versions of the 2001-03 *Lord of the Rings* films, both available on domestic DVD and video.

In adapting *The Lord of the Rings*, there are a number of characters and incidents that would have to be in any adaption (the Fellowship, the Black Riders, Moria), but there are many less significant characters and sequences that many adaptors would probably drop (such as Bill Ferny at Bree, Gildor, Fatty Bolger and Crickhollow). Part of the disappointment with the 2001-03 adaption of *The Lord of the Rings* was that so many significant characters and scenes were dropped: Tom Bombadil, Goldberry, Glorfindel, Farmer Maggot, the Old Forest, Old Man Willow, the Barrow-wight, etc. (Some, like Maggot, Glorfindel and Elrond's sons, were in earlier scripts). Lórien was dropped in earlier drafts, with the Galadriel mirror scene shifting to Rivendell (and Bilbo as well Galadriel would have attended the council).

How would J.R.R. Tolkien himself have reacted to the Hollywood version of his epic book? With very mixed feelings, probably (look at the way he responded to the 1950s proposals for filming his book). No doubt the royalties streaming his way would have softened his response (from the book sales, not from the films), but, judging by the way he responded to book covers, illustrations, film scripts, and other interpretations of his works, he would have had a lot to say about the treatment by Hollywood. As he put it: 'I am a pedant devoted to accuracy' (Letters, 372).

If one looks at the *Letters*, one sees how very important many aspects of his works were to the author. He would have acknowledged that many omissions would be necessary to squeeze the books into manageable lengths. From *The Fellowship of the Ring*, the omissions in the film Tolkien would most have found unacceptable would be Tom Bombadil, Goldberry, and anything to do with the elves: Gildor and the elves in the Shire; Glorfindel and the feast at Rivendell. Tolkien would also have bemoaned the excisions of Old Man Willow, the Barrow-downs and the Barrow-wight.

Tolkien would probably have been pleased that parts of the accounts of Elrond, Glóin, Gandalf, Boromir, etc, at Rivendell were included in the prologue and flashbacks.

Incidents like the Bill Ferny and the Southerner at Bree, the dwarves at Bag End, Fatty Bolger and the Riders at Crickhollow, Gandalf's letter, the attack of the wolves/ wargs, Mirrormere, the night in the tree, and Gildor and the elves were lesser omissions.

Tolkien would probably have lamented the much shortened stay at Lothlórien, and Sam at Galadriel's mirror. Tolkien might not have minded the parting feast, but Galadriel's gifts were important.

But probably even more aggravating to the Oxford professor would have been the alterations and the additions. The idea that orcs can swarm down pillars would have likely appalled the professor, because it makes a mockery of his carefully planned world (and battles, such as Helm's Deep and Pelennor, would be drastically altered if the enemy can simply leap inside).

Tolkien would also have been saddened to find out nearly all of his songs, which he clearly laboured long and lovingly over, had been dropped. Nearly all of the songs were omitted from the film of *The Fellowship of the Ring*, and the other films (though aspects of the songs were included in Howard Shore's score, and some of the choral work).

As Tolkien's 8 page notes on Morton Zimmerman's 1958 script demonstrates, Tolkien might have objected to the early 2000s *The Lord of the Rings* films on many grounds. The following, using Tolkien's reaction to Zimmerman's script as a guide, are some of the alterations in the New Line films which Tolkien would very likely have disliked:

- The lack of a time scheme (one of his major criticisms of the Zimmerman script);
- Tolkien might have lamented Tom Bombadil being dropped but, as Zimmerman messed up Bombadil and Goldberry so much, 'I think she had far better disappear than make a meaningless appearance';
- As well as Bombadil and Goldberry, Tolkien would probably have missed:
  - Old Man Willow: dropped;
  - the Barrow-wight: dropped;
  - mushrooming and Farmer Maggot: dropped;
  - Glorfindel: dropped;
  - Galadriel's gifts: dropped;
  - Galadriel and Gimli: dropped;
  - Sam at Galadriel's mirror: dropped;
  - Merry and Pippin treated primarily as comic sidekicks;
- The too rapid introduction of Merry and Pippin;
- The crops the hobbits run through (Tolkien was meticulous about details like that);
- The Arwen-Aragorn romance (but Tolkien might have loved the allusion to the Beren-Lúthien romance, which's referred to on his tombstone);
- Arwen taking over Glorfindel's role;
- Arwen conjuring up the flood and Frodo being totally passive;
- The Weathertop confrontation between Aragorn, the hobbits and the Black Riders ('there is no fight', no screams or 'rather meaningless

slashings', Tolkien insisted);
- The depiction of the Black Riders: '[t]he Black Riders do not scream, but keep a more terrifying silence';
  - Ditto with the Balrog *'never speaks or makes any vocal sound at all'*;
  - Orcs climbing walls and pillars;
  - The emphasis on extended fights and violence;
  - Frodo, not Gandalf, deciding to go into Moria;
  - Frodo, not Gandalf, solving the riddle at the door;
  - Saruman conjuring up the storm over the mountain;
  - The Gandalf-Saruman *Matrix*-style wizard fight;
  - Strider being revealed as a king too soon;
- Aragorn meeting Frodo at the end of *The Fellowship of the Ring* and letting him go to Mordor alone.

The biggest omission in *The Fellowship of the Ring*, I reckon, is a clear hundred pages of the book, straight through, from halfway into chapter 3 ("A Short Cut to Mushrooms") to the end of chapter 8 ("Fog On the Barrow-downs").

Some of the omissions don't matter too much. Some do. A lot.

ROMANCE. The romance of Aragorn II and Arwen Undómiel is of course a curious one. When they met in Lórien, he was twenty and she was a sprightly 2,710 years old. And when he courted her in Cerin Amroth in Lothlórien (in TA 2980), he was 49; she was 2,739 years-old. The film (which had considered showing that early romance, but didn't in the end) played the ages of the lovers quite differently. Viggo Mortensen's Aragorn looked to be in his early forties, while Liv Tyler's Arwen appeared to be in her twenties (the differences between their ages in the book being 2,690 years). Thus, by the lights of his human life, Aragorn had had a lot of experience by the time of the War of the Ring, when he was 87, but Arwen was *2,777* (yes, I know age is different for humans and elves). Aragorn and Aragorn are also connected by blood ties, being second cousins far removed (and Elrond is Aragorn's distant great uncle).

So she had lived through the coming of the *Istari*, the invasions of the Easterlings, Sauron coming to Mirkwood, the height of Gondor's power, the emergence of the nazgûl, the Witch-king establishing a kingdom at Angmar, Angmar's invasion of Arnor, civil war in Gondor, the siege of Pelargir, Gondor's war with the Harad, the Wainriders and the Corsairs, the Great Plague in Gondor (which spreads to Eriador), the Witch-king over-running Fornost and Arthedain, the dwarves fleeing Moria, the nazgûl besieging Minas Ithil, the formation of the White Council, the ambush of Celebrían, orc invasions of Eriador and Rohan, and Gandalf going to Dol Guldur.

So Arwen's seen plenty before Aragorn's even born. Even if Arwen never left Imladris or Lórien for her entire life she would have heard about most of those events (the two elven realms being centres of news and communication). So, in a way, the configuration of the Aragorn-Arwen romance as older, experience-hardened tough guy and much younger woman should in fact be reversed. But that would never happen in the casting of the films, with Arwen being cast in her fifties, for instance

(Kathleen Turner or Meryl Streep, say). Arwen Evenstar's known as one of the great beauties among elves, so, by the rules of Hollywood's attitude to gender and age, she had to be an actress in her twenties or thirties (and the lower end of thirties): Uma Thurman, Sarah Michelle Gellar, J. Lo, Alicia Silverstone, Charlize Theron, Jennifer Love Hewitt, etc.

The screenwriters said they moved away from Professor Tolkien's tome in adapting it for cinema, but later found themselves moving back to it. Tolkien seemed to have the right solutions after all. One of the problems the screenwriters found was integrating their additions into Tolkien's narrative. Take two of the main female characters, Arwen and Éowyn. There were many additions to their characters in the films: the screenwriters thus had to come up with additional scenes for them, things for them to do and say. Sometimes they drew on the book – on the appendices for Arwen, and on the main text for Éowyn. But other times they wrote dialogue and actions which were based on their new conceptions of the characters. Arwen as spiritual inspirer to Aragorn as well as distant lover, and Éowyn as admirer of Aragorn and caged shield maiden.

However, once these new characterization had been decided upon, the screenwriters (in particular Boyens and Walsh, who took on the female characters) didn't seem to know what to do with them. The problem is that the role of spiritual inspiration for Aragorn doesn't translate into the right kind of drama for this kind of Hollywood action-adventure film. It's just the wrong genre, the wrong vehicle, for an exploration of spiritual issues.

While purists might complain that the Arwen-Aragorn romance doesn't appear in the main body of *The Lord of the Rings,* Arwen does appear in the foreground of the narrative (i.e, not in someone else's account, or in discussions about her). Indeed, it's Arwen who offers Frodo the chance to take her place on the ship that sails to Valinor: '"in my stead you shall go, Ring-bearer, when the time comes, and if you then desire it"' (RK, 306). Quite an important plot point but, oddly, the 2003 film of *The Return of the King* didn't use this bit that comes from the main text.

The new conception of Éowyn, meanwhile, is much easier to integrate into a Hollywood action-adventure blockbuster film, because she's right in there in the foreground action of the film (not stuck in Rivendell swooning on couches and gradually wasting away), interacting with characters directly (and in a position to fight too). So the screenwriters invented a number of scenes which would feature Éowyn: talking with Aragorn in the stable; meeting Aragorn in Meduseld; walking with Aragorn during the exodus to Helm's Deep; bringing Aragorn some stew; taking him a drink at the feast, and so on.

But each of these scenes simply repeats the same characterization, the same longing Éowyn has for Aragorn, the same conception of Éowyn as a caged bird. Éowyn loves Aragorn from afar all through the films, from the first scenes, where her fascination for him develops. But, once it's developed into love, it doesn't change at all, up until the moment he spurns her at Dunharrow. It's as if Walsh and Boyens, having created this new idea of Éowyn, didn't quite know where to take her.

Perhaps most damaging of all to her characterization in the films is that her story doesn't have a decent ending (in the theatrical cut of *The Return of the King*). After Dunharrow, she goes into battle and proves herself to be a formidable warrior, to the point of vanquishing Sauron's chief officer. And she gets to have a tender colloquy with her surrogate father before he passes away. But then she disappears from the film until she's seen smiling happily standing beside Faramir at Aragorn's coronation (with no suggestion of her passionate feelings for Aragorn, which have helped to keep her going all through the story. Indeed, she accompanied the Rohirrim troops to Dunharrow partly so she could be near Aragorn).

So, of the three aspects of Éowyn's character – her desire to fight and not be caged, her search for love, and her relationship with her surrogate father (Théoden) – only two are fully resolved in the *Return of the King* theatrical cut. She gets to show off her military prowess big time on the Pelennor Fields, and make a huge difference in the War of the Ring; and she has a fond farewell with Théoden. But the romantic angle is completely ignored. The single reaction shot of her standing next to Faramir (both of them miraculously brought back to ruddy-cheeked health) doesn't suggest if she's found (or is going to find) fulfilment in love. In fact, the romantic-erotic strand of her story was cut dead when Aragorn leaves her at Dunharrow, a cruel reward for the weeks of deep feelings she's had for Aragorn.

CHARACTER ARCS. Bemoaning the lack of character development among some of the characters (Legolas, Gimli, etc) in the 2001-03 *Rings* film is not due to the screenwriters. Or it may be, but it's also there (or *not* there) in Tolkien's novel. Turning Gimli into a comic sidekick is much more serious, I think, than the fact that he hardly changes through the course of three lengthy movies. It's true that the writers added aspects to the characterizations of Aragorn, Éowyn and Faramir, for instance, so they could have a more satisfying 'character arc'. Most of the principal cast does undergo some kind of transformation: Frodo, Sam, Merry, Pippin, Aragorn, Éowyn, Théoden, Gollum and Boromir.

Wormtongue, Éomer, Bilbo, Treebeard, Sauron, the Witch-king, Galadriel, Elrond, Arwen and others don't change much at all. Denethor just gets worse. Saruman and Gandalf hardly alter – they do remain pretty much how they start out: Gandalf's still the wise, compassionate leader of the free peoples, and Saruman's still a power-hungry son-of-a-bitch.

You can see, though, from the list of some of the key characters above, that it's not possible, really, to satisfyingly do justice to all of those characters and show how they've been changed. Or maybe it would be, but not in this particular conception of Tolkien's book as an ultra-high budget action-adventure movie.

Overall, the script of *The Fellowship of the Ring* was about right for a blockbuster franchise movie. Unfortunately, some of the additions, alterations and omissions were perplexing, and some were redundant. Some of the additions added zilch to the movie: Sam nearly drowning; Galadriel's monologue; and that pointless business with the crumbling staircase in Moria, which severely diminishes the subsequent bridge of Khazad-dûm scene.

TOM BOMBADIL. Some of the omissions are understandable in today's climate: for instance, it would be very difficult to make Tom Bombadil work, without falling into the silliness of Jar-Jar Binks, or some of Disney's characters. Who would you cast? Jim Carrey?! Danny De Vito?! Ben Stiller?! Bombadil's such a loud, larger-than-life character, he's almost impossible to play; plus, he's happy! Such a sunny character would look out of place in this version of *The Lord of the Rings*, which aims to be sombre and portentous.

Once the hobbits leave the Shire, the mood of the film darkens – Rivendell's an interlude, but there are few laughs there. You can see Old Man Willow and the Barrow-wight working, but Tom Bombadil? (On the other hand, you've already got crazy stuff such as Liv Tyler as an elf-babe, Cate Blanchett as a Disney Wicked Witch, tentacled monsters, balrogs, trolls, orcs, elves, dwarves, giant eagles, a giant eye, magical floods, invisibility, undead wraiths, and *Matrix*-style wizard fights, so why not Bombadil?!).

Another problem with Bombadil are his songs and his dialogue. He sings a lot. And he dances. On film, it'd be difficult not to have Bombadil come across as a Disney version of a Brothers Grimm woodsman, with his singing and dancing and bright blue jacket. He's also reminiscent of English Morris dancers, and folk singers (both folk music and 'hey nonny' Morris dancers are seen as very uncool and laughable in today's super-cynical culture, even if they are precisely part of the kind of 'authentic', historical English folklore Tolkien was trying to revive. And some of the members of various Tolkien societies around the globe look like folkies). With so many camp, over-the-top aspects to Bombadil's personality, it'd be tricky to stop audiences laughing at him, rather than with him.

But Tom Bombadil's very important in *The Lord of the Rings*. He rescues the hobbits not once but twice. He appears in three chapters of the book. And Tolkien gives him nothing less than a creation myth, as Bombadil sings about the creation and history of Middle-earth, about the natural world, about the elves, men, dwarves and other creatures. In chapter I.7 Bombadil is literally singing about existence, just as, in Tolkien's universe, the world is sung into existence by Ilúvatar.

GOLDBERRY. Goldberry, too, is important: she's the first major female character met in *The Lord of the Rings*. But her dialogue is also nearly impossible for an actor to deliver straight: 'Come dear folk! Laugh and be merry! I am Goldberry, daughter of the River', Goldberry tells the hobbits as they enter Bombadil's house. And Frodo responds by singing about her, standing in front of her. That, too, would be tricky to play straight.

Aspects of Tom Bombadil made it into the 2001-03 *The Lord of the Rings* films: some of Bombadil's dialogue was used (mainly spoken by Treebeard), and Treebeard rescued Merry and Pippin from being buried under the roots of a tree in Fangorn forest. This latter short scene (in the *Extended Edition* of *The Two Towers*) was a reworking of the scene with Old Man Willow in the book, though the scene had a different context and purpose (in the film, it's a relatively minor incident, and the halflings are rescued and carried off by Treebeard almost instantly; in the book, it's a severe set-back for the hobbits, which they are too inexperienced to deal with at that point, and have to be saved by Bombadil).

SONGS. Many, many songs were omitted from all of the films. Three songs were included in the first film (Bilbo's, Gandalf's, and the elves' lament for Gandalf; in the *Extended Edition*, Sam's sings a stanza for Gandalf, and the hobbits dance in the *Green Dragon*). But so many songs were dropped: from *The Fellowship of the Ring* alone, lost songs included: 'The Road goes ever on and on' (sung by Bilbo and Frodo), Pippin's bath song, Sam and Pippin's drinking song, the elves' song 'Snow-white', the hobbits' bed- and supper-song in I.3, Merry and Pippin's 'Farewell we call to hearth and hall!', Frodo singing in the Old Forest, Frodo's song at the *Prancing Pony*, Frodo summoning Bombadil, the Barrow-wight's song, Sam's troll song, Strider's songs about Gil-galad and Beren and Lúthien, the Rivendell elves singing about Eärendil, a song in Elvish ('A Elbereth Gilthoniel'), Bilbo's 'I sit by the fire and think', Gimli's song of the Elder Days, Legolas's song about Nimrodel, the elves' lament for Mithrandir, Frodo's lament for Gandalf, Galadriel's farewell song, Galadriel's 'I sang of leaves', another Elven-song (I.8), and of course Bombadil's many songs.

Indeed, so important are songs, poetry and music in *The Lord of the Rings* that just about every major character gets to sing or recite, and there are songs in most of the chapters in *The Fellowship of the Ring*.

LANGUAGE. Another aspect of J.R.R. Tolkien's work, difficult to render in cinema, is his continual stress of language, the notion of creating Middle-earth as an imaginative space in which he could introduce and explore his invented languages. *The Lord of the Rings* abounds in inscriptions, verses, chants, spells, songs, quotations, letters and proverbs. There is writing everywhere: on the door to Moria, Bilbo's book, the maps at Rivendell, Isildur's scroll, the Gondor records, the dwarves' book in the Chamber of Mazarbul, Balin's tomb, the many letters and of course on the ring itself.

GLORFINDEL. One reason that Glorfindel was dropped was because he would have been yet another character to introduce and explain. Fran Walsh remarked that the Rivendell scenes could have been one introduction of a new character after another, which would have been tiresome.

TREEBEARD. There was some doubt among *Rings* fans if Treebeard would make it into the film. He was another very difficult character to portray – a walking, talking tree (not strictly a tree; he's an ent). It would be all too easy for Treebeard to appear ludicrous (even though Tolkien provided him with humour, which was a way of persuading readers to accept the character). Treebeard could easily have become another silly fantasy movie character. The design team went through many variations, maquettes and tests before coming up with the final design for the old ent. The character was realized through a combination of a giant animatronic head, trunk and arms, a digitally created figure for the full body shots (with digital doubles for the hobbits), and the setting of model Fangorn forestscapes, the full-size Fangorn set, and matte paintings. John Rhys-Davies provided Treebeard's very deep voice.

In the end, the filmmakers pulled off a tricky challenge, saved by Tolkien's characterization, the humour, some interaction between the actors and the animatronic head, and the fact that (in the theatrical version at least) Treebeard was not on screen for too long. Treebeard was also a sympathetic character, which audiences could relate to: a peaceful creature whose life is disrupted when orcs come along and burn down his forest and his friends.

ARAGORN. In the book, Aragorn, at the Council of Elrond, gives an account of being a ranger, and how the efforts of the Rangers of the North have protected the Shire and Bree. He also states openly to Boromir that he is the heir of Isildur, that the Sword That Was Broken will be remade, and that he will come to Minas Tirith: 'A new hour comes. Isildur's Bane is found. Battle is at hand. The Sword shall be reforged. I will come to Minas Tirith' (FR, 325). In the film, it's Boromir who speaks about Gondor protecting the rest of Middle-earth from the threat of Mordor (only a reaction shot of Aragorn suggests that he doesn't agree with this, but he says nothing of the rangers' defensive work). Thus, the scriptwriters exaggerated Boromir's reluctance to accept Aragorn as Isildur's heir and heir to the throne of Gondor, and used Aragorn's reluctance to speak up about being the rightful heir of Gondor or come to terms about his destiny as dramatic tension between Boromir and Aragorn (and between himself and Elrond).

A recurring motif in *The Lord of the Rings* films was Aragorn's problematic attitude towards his responsibilities – chiefly his duty to come out of the wilderness and be a leader of people (this theme was even more prominent in the extended version of *The Fellowship of the Ring*). A number of characters remind Aragorn of his responsibilities: Elrond and Arwen at Rivendell, Gandalf, Galadriel during the farewell beside the Silverlode, and Boromir, and Éowyn too – she tells Aragorn that the Rohirrim have found their leader (and they continue their exhortations in the next two films. But Legolas and Gimli pointedly avoid even hints in that direction).

In a way, the biggest spiritual or emotional journey undertaken, at least in the film of *The Lord of the Rings*, is by Aragorn (from Ranger to king of Middle-earth). Indeed, with Gandalf's disappearance in *The Fellowship of the Ring,* Aragorn not only becomes the leader of the fellowship, he increasingly becomes the chief character of the films, at times over-shadowing Frodo. In *The Two Towers*, the narrative follows two main protagonists, Frodo and Aragorn. Even when Gandalf reappears, he seems to drive the plot forward less than Aragorn.

Aragorn's reluctance to embrace his fate in the film is far more exaggerated than in the book. Well, it isn't in the book. It becomes a key dramatic device not only in his relationship with the rest of the fellowship (and Boromir in particular, who wants the ring to go to Gondor), but also in his relations with Elrond and Arwen. Elrond wants Aragorn to accept his responsibilities and become a king, and Arwen persuades Aragorn not be be afraid of his destiny. In the appendices, there is another aspect to this dynamic between Aragorn, Arwen and Elrond that was omitted from the film: Elrond will only accept Aragorn as worthy of his daughter if he becomes king of Arnor and Gondor (along the Freudian, œdipal lines of 'only the best for his daughter will do for daddy'). Again, I reckon Tolkien would have objected strongly to the films altering Aragorn's character from the noble warrior-poet or soldier-scholar to an angst-ridden, continually-doubting modern Existential character).

The screenwriters wanted Aragorn to do something heroic towards the end of the film – not just to summon the Army of the Dead, defeat the Corsairs of Umbar, and fight at Pelennor Fields (as if that wasn't enough). They wanted some kind of heroic act, and came up with the idea of having Aragorn confront and fight Sauron. The concept was storyboarded, animatics were produced, and the fight was filmed over three days. Sauron was in his distinctive armour from the prologue of *The Fellowship of the Ring*, appearing on the battlefield in the midst of the conflict. Just before that, Sauron was going to appear in an angelic, Luciferan form, as he might have looked before he became evil (i.e., when he was still a Maia spirit). So plenty of footage was shot of our heroes staring at bright white light, reacting to a non-existent element that would be added later (a vestige of this idea is on the *Extended Edition* DVD of *The Return of the King*).

Why Sauron should suddenly appear like that, a form he hasn't taken for eons, and to Aragorn, is difficult to say. But the idea was dropped. Instead, a computer-generated troll substituted for Sauron, and Aragorn was nearly beaten by it (Legolas struggles to help him). A remnant of Aragorn interacting with Sauron was retained in the final cut of *The Return of the King*, when Sauron appears to address Aragorn from far off on the Dark Tower (which's visible through the Black Gates).

The emphasis on Aragorn and his story of struggling with becoming a king in 2001-03 films of *The Lord of the Rings* is understandable in another sense: Aragorn's character offers an action hero (and, just as importantly, a romantic lead), the kind of noble, heroic leader played in Hollywood movies by Mel Gibson (*Braveheart, The Patriot, When We Were Soldiers*), Kevin Costner (*Robin Hood, Dances With Wolves, Waterworld, The Postman*) and Daniel Day-Lewis (*The Last of the Mohicans*; Day-Lewis was one of the choices to play Aragorn).

Frodo, meanwhile, is a hobbit that trudges to Mordor with his faithful friend Sam. He has plenty of adventures, but Aragorn's story offers the bigger, action-filled spectacle that Hollywood entertainment cinema loves (and the romance it needs to appeal to a female and older general audience).

There're many sides to Aragorn's personality, too, or more aspects to him which lend themselves to the kind of spectacular, action-led blockbuster that the 2001-03 *Rings* films were. Frodo, meanwhile, has a much more internalized struggle, with his increasing addiction of the ring, and, although he's a heroic, noble, gentle hobbit, he can come across as a little dull. Aragorn, though, in the film, gets to kiss the elf babe Arwen, flirt with Éowyn, lead the fellowship, fight hundreds of orcs, lead the goodies into vast battles, journey through the underworld, get crowned king and have a royal wedding.

Aragorn's 'death' and 'resurrection' were added to *The Two Towers* film script to intensify Aragorn's character, to give him a more active role. Prior to the warg attack, Aragorn had been somewhat pulled along by events, rather than driving them, the screenwriters Philippa Boyens and Frances Walsh felt. Thus, Aragorn was separated from the others to give him, after his sight of the orc army, more of an incentive to protect the Rohirrim, and more ways of driving the narrative. The bits of business with the wonder horse Brego were also added to the story (although it's also a vision of Arwen which helps to revive Aragorn as he lies on the riverbank, as well as the horse).

Actor Viggo Mortensen was partly responsible for making the role of the horse Brego so prominent. Mortensen took to rehearsing the action with the horse and the horse trainer (even, apparently, going to the lengths of sleeping in the stable with the horse so the animal would get used to him, and so he could trust the animal wholly. *Sheesh*, those crazy American Method actors!). Producer Barrie Osborne, who worked a lot with Mortensen, was a little anxious that, during the revival scene, the horse might roll onto the actor.

Boyens and Walsh delved deeply into the backstory of Elrond, Arwen and Aragorn in expanding the love story of Aragorn and Arwen from *Rings'* appendices for the films, but there was one aspect of it they'd didn't use, curiously. That was Elrond's past: Elrond himself is the result of a marriage between an elf and a human, Elwing and Eärendil. And Elrond has seen his brother (Elros) and his parents die in the way of mortal humans. So having Elrond discuss his own background might've been another avenue the screenwriters could've taken.

SOME NIGGLES.

The multiple criticisms of the films of *The Lord of the Rings* might seem like niggling but, as J.R.R. Tolkien confessed, 'I am a natural niggler, alas!' (L, 313). So here are some more niggles:

There's no difference in the Frodo at the beginning of the film and Frodo seventeen years later, when the action hots up. The 2001 film of *Fellowship*, rather, played it as if a much shorter time had passed.

In the film, Frodo's surprised that Bilbo's at Rivendell, even though Gandalf's told him he's gone to stay with the elves. (In the book, Bilbo's gone on a holiday).

In the book, Saruman never intends to surrender to or go in league with Mordor, as he does in the film. He wants the ring for himself, to become a ruler in his own right. Even Saruman's efforts in the Shire show him attempting to create his own domain, where he is master.

In the films, Saruman is not only breeding Uruk-hai, which he definitely doesn't have the power to do in the book, he's also creating them from crossbreeding them with men.

For some fans, Aragorn's nobility's tarnished with selfishness when Elrond tells him that Arwen will waste away if the ring isn't destroyed.

In the film, Aragorn tells Arwen at Rivendell before leaving with the fellowship that they should part; 'it was only a dream', he tells her. It's played as if Aragorn is making a heroic sacrifice, giving her up so she won't be hurt further, so she can leave for the Blessed Realm. Arwen, meanwhile, is devastated, and rejects his suggestion.

Cynthia McNew complained that Frodo starts to deteriorate as soon as he's wounded by the knife at Weathertop, so he doesn't really get any chance to demonstrate his strength in resisting it.[1]

In the film, Gollum wants the ring at any cost, but there aren't any hints, as there are in the book, about what he's going to do with it once he obtains it. In the novel, he's planning revenge upon those who've hurt him.

In the 2003 *The Return of the King*, Éomer isn't named king of Rohan; rather, Aragorn is presented as king of all Middle-earth.

In the book, Treebeard isn't sure if the ents will decide to participate; in the film, he says they won't, and promptly takes the hobbits towards the edge of Fangorn.

For some fans, there was too little character development among the secondary characters. Legolas and Gimli don't develop much in *The Two Towers*, for instance, beyond their characters in *Fellowship*. Gimli, for example, retains his comic relief persona in *The Two Towers* (Peter Jackson admitted that, when in doubt, it was easiest to cut to an ad-lib from John Rhys-Davies).

There wasn't a follow-up to the scenes of the women and children in the Glittering Caves – no scenes showing them emerging into the light. Because they'd performed their dramatic function of punching up the tension before the battle.

The Eldar and Númenórean men were normally seven feet tall Tolkien stated in a late essay (HME, 12, 310). Well, that's not practical for a movie (only scale doubles, such as Tall Paul, were over seven feet).

Presumably, Éomer knows that Gimli will ride with Legolas when he gives them only two horses when he meets the three hunters on the plains of Rohan.

Many Tolkien fans bemoaned the rewriting of Tolkien's dialogue by Philippa Boyens and Frances Walsh, turning the speeches into banalities. Some Tolkien fans griped about this aspect of the 2001-03 films: the dialogue, for instance, with its 'trumped-up one-liners, twentieth-century jargon', reducing thunderous exchanges between Gandalf and Denethor to 'banal toss-off lines' so bad 'it almost makes me want to cry', complained Cynthia McNew.[2]

The Biblical coat of many colours for Saruman was dropped – he still wears white after his descent into evil (it would have been yet another plot point to explain).

There are no references to the nazgûl's Black Breath in the *Lord of the Rings* films – maybe that was deemed too tricky to visualize, or too silly to mention (villains with bad breath takes them into comedy, and the nazgûl must be kept scary). And the concept of the ringwraith's sniffing was only really used in the Shire path scene (the idea that the top villains were nearly blind and could only sniff our their targets wasn't the easiest of Tolkien's depictions to pull off).

Sam's Frodo's gardener in the book and film, but he doesn't share a drink with his master in the *Green Dragon* like an equal, as he does in the film. The filmmakers were always keen to play down the master-servant aspects of the relationship in the book, and make Sam much more like a loyal friend.

The whole journey of the Companions from Minas Tirith to Rivendell then the Shire is covered in *The Return of the King* with the classic film device of a map and the camera tracking over the familiar sites of Middle-earth until it reached the Shire (accompanied by Frodo's voiceover). As one can see from my list of omissions, that cuts out huge portions of the latter part of *The Return of the King*, the whole journey back and the many people met or left along the way.

Philippa Boyens gave a couple of reasons for the split between Frodo and Sam just before Shelob's lair in *The Return of the King*: one was to pay-off Gollum's character, because he's been struggling to scupper Frodo's plans and also have a chance at obtaining the ring for so long. The other was the increased suspense of having Frodo enter Shelob's lair alone.

The Return of the King doesn't satisfactorily conclude Faramir's (and Éowyn's) story, and makes Gandalf's rush to prevent Denethor killing Faramir in the midst of a battle seem a waste of effort for some viewers. The film doesn't show what happens with Faramir and Éowyn, apart from briefly hinting at their new attachment (in the extended version).[3]

NOTES: DIFFERENCES BETWEEN THE BOOK AND THE 2001-03 FILMS

1. In E. Challis, 307.
2. In E. Challis, 306-7.
3. As Jim Smith and J. Clive Matthews put it, 'it might also be considered odd that a film of this length (which contains many *longueurs* and frequent long-winded whimsical sequences) could not be edited in a way that would make it possible to include information about the eventual fates of all its leading characters' [194-5]).

OMISSIONS FROM *THE FELLOWSHIP OF THE RING* FILM

One of the reasons that the 2001 version of *The Fellowship of the Ring* could depict so many of the key moments from the book was that five whole chapters (out of 22) were dropped entirely (from chapter 4, "A Short Cut To Mushrooms" to chapter 8, "Fog On the Barrow-downs".) Or around 80 pages.

The Fellowship of the Ring film of course contains parts of the beginning of *The Two Towers* book. Omissions from *The Fellowship of the Ring* book in the *Fellowship of the Ring* film (theatrical and extended editions) included:

- Conversations with the Gaffer, Ted Sandyman and cronies in the *Green Dragon*;
- Most of Bilbo's speech (it's over two pages in the book);
- The dwarves with Bilbo at Bag End;

- Bilbo's gifts to friends and relatives at Bag End;
- The Sackville-Bagginses;
- Gandalf's second conversation with Frodo;
- Gandalf's further visits to Frodo in Hobbiton (up to TA 3008);
- Frodo's life at Bag End, up to his late forties;
- Sam, Ted and others discussing Frodo and elves in the inn;
- More of "The Shadow of the Past" chapter;
- Gandalf's story of Sméagol and Déagol (transferred to the opening of *The Return of the King*);
- Gandalf's account of hunting for Gollum with Aragorn;
- The interval between Frodo deciding to leave with the ring and his actual departure (between April and September TA 3018);
- Frodo selling Bag End;
- Gandalf staying at Bag End for over two months;
- Frodo waiting for Gandalf; the farewell party;
- Frodo overhearing a conversation between the Gaffer and a Black Rider;
- Frodo, Sam and Pippin leaving Bag End at night;
- Camping at night;
- Journeying towards Woody End;
- Hiding off the road from the Black Rider;
- Sam talking about the Black Rider visiting the Gaffer;
- Hiding in the hollow tree;
- The walking song;
- Hiding from another Black Rider, this time at night; it crawls towards Frodo but is scared off by Gildor and the elves;
- The elves' song;
- Meeting with the elves; food, drink, talk and rest;
- Frodo, Sam and Pippin talk before setting out again;
- The short cut;
- The hobbits sing, and hear a Black Rider wailing;
- In Farmer Maggot's fields;
- Meeting Farmer Maggot; talk about the Black Rider;
- Meal and conversation at Maggot's;
- Travelling by pony and cart with Farmer Maggot;
- Meeting Merry in the lane;
- Spotting a Black Rider on the far shore by the ferry;
- Journey from the Brandywine to Crickhollow;
- The house at Crickhollow; Fatty Bolger;
- Bathtime; more songs;
- Supper at Crickhollow;
- The 'conspiracy unmasked'; spies; the ring; Sam as chief spy;
- Merry and Pippin's song for Frodo;
- Plans for the next day;
- Frodo's dream of the white tower;
- Leaving Crickhollow at dawn;
- Farewell to Fatty Bolger;
- Through the Hedge;
- Talk about the Old Forest;
- The Old Forest;
- The forest closing in;
- Climbing out of the trees onto a hill;
- Descent to the River Withywindle;

- Merry goes ahead to explore;
- Drowsiness overcomes the hobbits;
- Frodo caught under a tree-root in the stream;
- Merry and Pippin trapped by Old-Man Willow;
- Frodo and Sam light a fire;
- Tom Bombadil rescues the hobbits;
- Bombadil's songs;
- The hobbits follow Bombadil to his home;
- At Tom Bombadil's house; more songs;
- Meeting Goldberry;
- Frodo's song for Goldberry;
- Bathing;
- Supper at Bombadil's; discussion;
- Another Bombadil song;
- Frodo's dream of Gandalf;
- The other hobbits' dreams;
- Breakfast at Bombadil's;
- Tom Bombadil's many stories (which practically constitute a complete history of Middle-Earth);
- Bombadil defines himself as Eldest;
- Another meal at Bombadil's;
- Goldberry's songs;
- Talk about the Shire;
- Frodo gives Bombadil the ring;
- Frodo puts on the ring;
- Frodo's dream which looks towards Valinor;
- The hobbits depart from Bombadil's house;
- The hobbits meet Goldberry on the hills;
- The hobbits approach the Barrow-downs;
- Fog descends on the Barrow-downs;
- The hobbits try to find their way across the downs;
- Frodo is separated from the others;
- The Barrow-wight captures Frodo on the hill-top;
- Frodo wakes up inside a barrow; Sam, Merry and Pippin lie cold beside him;
- The Barrow-wight's song;
- An arm gropes towards Sam; Frodo cuts off the hand;
- Frodo sings Bombadil's song;
- Bombadil appears and rescues the hobbits from the barrow;
- Bombadil vanquishes the Barrow-wight;
- The hobbits are revived;
- Bombadil finds the ponies; he brings his own pony;
- Bombadil finds swords for the hobbits;
- Bombadil rides with the hobbits to the road;
- Bombadil says farewell at the road;
- A description of Bree;
- Butterbur introduces the hobbits to the gathering in the common room, including hobbits and dwarves; minor characters Nob and Bob;
- Bill Ferny and the Southerner;
- Frodo meets Strider;
- Frodo sings *The Man in the Moon*;
- The second time, he falls off the table and vanishes; he crawls over to Strider;

- Butterbur tries to smooth things over;
- Strider introduces himself to the hobbits in their room;
- Butterbur talks with the hobbits in their room;
- Gandalf's letter and trusting Strider;
- Merry and the Black Rider;
- Fatty Bolger and the Black Riders at Crickhollow;
- Buying the pony from Bill Ferny;
- The crowds of Bree, Staddle, Combe and Archet watch the hobbits leave Bree with Strider;
- Bill Ferny;
- The hobbits see flashes in the night on Weathertop;
- Strider's song about Gil-galad;
- Finding the runes on Weathertop;
- Black Riders spotted on the road from Weathertop;
- Strider reads the tracks on Weathertop;
- Strider describes the Black Riders;
- Strider's story of Beren and Lúthien;
- They travel South and cross the road; they hear Black Riders;
- Twelve days of travel in the wilds before meeting Glorfindel;
- Strider finding an elf-stone on the Last Bridge;
- Finding a troll-hole;
- Sam's song about the trolls; talk about Bilbo's adventures in *The Hobbit*;
- Hiding off the road again and meeting Glorfindel;
- Glorfindel examines Frodo's wound;
- Glorfindel leads them towards Rivendell, with Frodo on Glorfindel's horse;
- The Black Riders approach; Frodo halts Asfaloth to look back; the Black Rides command him to wait;
- Frodo outpaces the Riders and faces them across the river;
- Frodo defies the nazgûl; he is stricken dumb by the Witch-king; his sword breaks;
- The river is raised by Elrond (not Arwen);
- Before he falls, Frodo glimpses Glorfindel as 'a shining figure of white light';
- A long discussion between Frodo and Gandalf at the bedside in Rivendell (including the ringwraiths, Bree, Butterbur, Strider, the wound, the wraith-world, the Eldar, Sauron, and what happened at the Ford);
- The feast at Rivendell;
- Frodo seeing Elrond, Glorfindel and Arwen at the feast;
- Frodo's long conversation with Glóin (the Dale, the dragon, Balin and Moria, and dwarf history);
- Bilbo's account of his life since leaving the Shire;
- Frodo dreaming in the Hall of Fire;
- Strider and Bilbo's song (3 pages long);
- The elves' (Lindir) reaction to the song;
- Frodo seeing Elrond, Aragorn and Arwen in the hall;
- Characters at the Council of Elrond: Glóin, Erestor, Galdor (and in the book, it takes place indoors);
- The accounts of Elrond;
- Glóin's account of the dwarves in Moria;
- The messenger from Sauron to the dwarves asking for friendship and the ring;

- Parts of Elrond's history of the ring were omitted from the film (about Númenor, Arnor and Gondor, the kingdoms by Lake Evendim, at Fornost, the waning of the Númenóreans, the siege of Minas Ithil, Osgiliath in ruins, for example);
- Parts of Boromir's speech were omitted (including Boromir's dream);
- Elrond's announcement that Strider was Aragorn son of Arathorn was given in the film to Legolas;
- Frodo says the ring should be Aragorn's, not his;
- Bilbo's song about Aragorn ('all that is gold does not glitter');
- Aragorn's account of himself and the Rangers;
- Aragorn's account of hunting Gollum;
- Bilbo's story of finding the ring;
- Frodo's account of the ring;
- Gandalf's account of the history of the ring, including Dol Guldur, Sauron's' move back to Mordor, the Wise, Saruman, spies around the Shire, tracking and finding Gollum, Denethor and Gondor, and so on;
- Legolas's confession that Gollum escaped from Mirkwood;
- Gandalf relating his encounter with Radagast;
- Gandalf's account of going to Rohan, and taming Shadowfax;
- Gandalf's tale of travelling North, visiting the Shire, meeting the Gaffer;
- Gandalf besieged on Weathertop;
- Tom Bombadil is discussed;
- Elrond talks about the three elven rings;
- Bilbo declaring he'll deal with the ring (there's no heated argument in the book at the end of the council);
- A discussion between Gandalf and the five hobbits; Gandalf says he might come on the journey;
- Nearly two months pass at Rivendell;
- Scouts return to Rivendell with news;
- Elrond selects the rest of the fellowship;
- Elrond and Gandalf consider adding Merry and Pippin to the group;
- The Sword That Was Broken is reforged in Rivendell;
- Aragorn and Gandalf prepare the journey;
- Bilbo's song, 'I sit beside the fire and think';
- Boromir sounding his horn at the farewell from the Last Homely House;
- Bilbo at the farewell;
- Sam checking through his pack;
- Days and weeks of travelling through the wilds;
- Aragorn remarking on the watchfulness of Hollin;
- A shadow passes over the Company (although at this point in the journey the nazgûl haven't crossed the river);
- Gandalf and Aragorn decide not to risk the Redhorn Gate, and aim for Caradhras;
- Gandalf handing out the cordial of Imladris;
- Gandalf uses magic to light a fire;
- Legolas searches around the mountain for a way forward;
- The Company navigates a snow drift and retreats; 'Caradhras had defeated them';
- The Company discusses what to do'; Gandalf chooses Moria;
- The attack of the wolves/ wargs on the fellowship defending a small hill; Gandalf uses a spell to create fire and light; Legolas kills a 'great wolf-

chieftain';
- Trudging over rocky terrain for many miles; the Sirannon; the Stair Falls;
- A meal in Moria;
- Leaping across a crack in the path;
- Frodo hearing Gollum's footsteps behind;
- Gandalf and Pippin on the night watch (there's no sense in the film that the company stops for meals or sleeps for two nights in Moria);
- Gimli's song of Moria;
- Frodo sees Gollum on the night watch in the great hall;
- An orc chieftain, rather than a troll, dodges Boromir and Aragorn to hurl a spear at Frodo (and he lunges forward to attack an orc);
- Gandalf seals the door behind them on the stairs, with the balrog on the other side ('"I have met my match, and have nearly been destroyed"'); he uses a 'word of Command', which smashes the door, the wall and the roof;
- A wall of fire separates the fellowship from the enemy; two trolls create gangways across the fire; Legolas spots the balrog;
- Aragorn and Boromir rush to Gandalf's aid on the bridge;
- Orcs guard the Eastern Gates; Aragorn kills their leader as the fellowship hurries out of Moria;
- The Mirrormere; Durin's Stone;
- The Silverlode;
- Aragorn tends the wounds of Sam and Frodo;
- Frodo hears Gollum again;
- The Company crosses the Nimrodel;
- Legolas sings of the maiden Nimrodel, and continues to tell the story;
- They meet Haldir and the elves who are up in the trees;
- The fellowship spend the night in the trees;
- Gollum climbing the trees;
- The fellowship cross the Celebrant on a rope bridge;
- The fellowship is blindfolded;
- The journey to Lothlórien;
- They spend a night, still blindfolded;
- They meet another group of elves, travelling North;
- The Lord and Lady of Lothlórien allow the fellowship to walk free;
- Cerin Amroth;
- Aragorn leads Frodo and Sam onto the hill of Cerin Amroth;
- A view of Dol Guldur;
- Frodo sees Aragorn transformed, now as a 'young lord tall and fair';
- The fellowship pass through the gates of Caras Galadon;
- Celeborn and Galadriel greet their guests one by one;
- Further discussions with Celeborn and Galadriel, such as about Moria and the balrog, the White Council, and Gandalf;
- The fellowship discusses the effect Galadriel had on them;
- Legolas shows Gimli around Lothlórien;
- More of Sam's song for Gandalf;
- Frodo and Sam discuss elvish 'magic';
- Sam at Galadriel's mirror; Sam's vision of the industrialized Shire; Sam wants to go home immediately;
- In the mirror Frodo sees Gandalf; Bilbo; ships; Minas Tirith (in the film Frodo sees the Shire rather than Sam);

- Galadriel shows Frodo the elven ring Nenya;
- Galadriel explains to Frodo about the relation of the power of the ring to its bearer;
- Celeborn, Galadriel and the fellowship discuss next move; Celeborn offers the boats;
- The fellowship debate amongst themselves the best course; Boromir speaks his mind about possibly wielding the ring;
- The elvish cloaks;
- Haldir leads the Company South through Lórien;
- The Company meet Galadriel and Celeborn on the Silverlode;
- Galadriel's song;
- The parting feast with Celeborn and Galadriel;
- They discuss Fangorn forest;
- Galadriel's gift of the Elfstone to Aragorn;
- Galadriel's gift of a box of earth for Sam;
- Galadriel unbraiding her hair and cutting off three golden hairs;
- Galadriel's parting song ("Ai! laurië lantar lassi súrinen");
- Sam's dream of a floating log with eyes – Gollum;
- Gollum approaches Frodo and the boats while Frodo's on the night watch;
- Travelling in the boats by night;
- The boats approach the rapids;
- The orc attack on the boats; the fellowship paddle to the other side of the river;
- A fell-beast flies over the fellowship; Legolas downs it with an arrow;
- The fellowship discuss how long they stayed in Lórien;
- The fellowship discuss again what to do;
- Aragorn and Legolas explore the path ahead, to miss out the rapids;
- The fellowship carry the boats and baggage along the path;
- The transformation of Aragorn into 'a king returning from exile to his own land' when he beholds the Argonath;
- Aragorn and Frodo on the night watch;
- Aragorn calls a meeting of the Company to decide their next course;
- Frodo is given some time to decide;
- Frodo seeing many parts of Middle-earth on Amon Hen (not only Barad-dûr and the Eye, as in the film), and 'everywhere he looked he saw the signs of war' (FR, 520);
- The others wonder what's happened to Frodo;
- Boromir returns; the Company runs off in different directions (Sam on his own, Merry and Pippin just after him, followed by Legolas and Gimli);
- Aragorn catches up with Sam, but Sam halts, thinks, and heads back for the boats.

ADDITIONS TO *THE FELLOWSHIP OF THE RING* FILM

The additions to *The Fellowship of the Ring* book in *The Fellowship of the Ring* theatrical film (2001) included:

- Gandalf visiting the archives at Minas Tirith;
- Gollum being tortured in Barad-dûr;
- Saruman speaking with Sauron via the *palantír*;
- Saruman hoping to join with Mordor rather than emulate it;
- Sauron commanding Saruman to 'make me an army worthy of Mordor';
- Saruman and his orcs;
- Orcs tearing down trees; orcs forging weapons;
- Saruman overseeing the birth of the Uruk-hai;
- Lurtz, Saruman's chief Uruk-hai;
- Saruman telling Lurtz how the orcs were formed;
- The introduction of Merry and Pippin in Farmer Maggot's field;
- The hobbits falling down a slope;
- The four hobbits hiding together from the Black Rider (in the book Frodo's on his own);
- The Black Riders chasing the hobbits to Bucklebury Ferry;
- Frodo's leap onto the ferry;
- Frodo seeing Sauron's Eye in the *Prancing Pony*;
- Strider giving the hobbits swords at Weathertop;
- Arwen appearing in the wilds;
- Arwen rescuing Frodo;
- Arwen conjuring the river to flood;
- Saruman conjuring the storm and avalanche;
- Gandalf visiting Saruman;
- Saruman, not Radagast, telling Gandalf about the Black Riders;
- Gandalf, Saruman and the *palantír*;
- The wizard duel;
- Saruman receiving news of the fellowship on the mountain from his spy birds;
- Saruman consulting a book which shows the door of Moria and the balrog;
- Boromir and the shards of Narsil;
- Arwen speaking with Aragorn beside the Narsil relic;
- Arwen and Aragorn romancing on the bridge at night; Arwen pledging to become mortal;
- Sam and Frodo talking about going home to the Shire;
- Gimli trying to destroy the ring;
- The quarrelling at the Council of Elrond;
- Merry and Pippin at the Council of Elrond;
- The fellowship being formed at the Council of Elrond;
- The fellowship being comprised of volunteers, rather than chosen by Elrond;
- Aragorn's reluctance to state openly that he is Isildur's heir and will come to Minas Tirith (thus creating the tension with Boromir that lasts for the rest of the film);
- Boromir handling the ring on the mountain;
- Frodo (not Gandalf) deciding whether to go through Moria;

- Frodo (not Gandalf) solving the riddle on the Moria door;
- The fellowship finding the corpses as soon as they enter the door of Moria;
- Lurtz, leader of the Uruk-hai;
- Much more screen time for Saruman;
- The troll fight in Moria (it's all orcs in the book);
- The collapsing stairs in Moria (and the dwarf-tossing joke);
- Orcs climbing pillars in Moria;
- The conversation of Boromir and Aragorn in Lothlórien;
- Aragorn's farewell with Frodo (with Frodo thinking Aragorn's going to take the ring);
- Sam drowning extended;
- Aragorn fighting Lurtz;
- And alterations between book and film included:
- The time between Bilbo's party and Frodo's departure compressed;
- Bilbo not present at the Council of Elrond;
- Bilbo not saying he'll take the ring;
- The break-up of the Fellowship.

ADDITIONS TO THE BOOK

Of the scenes added to the extended edition of *The Fellowship of the Ring*, the following were additions made by the Walsh, Boyens and Jackson to the book:

- Bilbo with his maps;
- A moment where Bilbo panics when he can't find the ring;
- Frodo, Merry, Pippin and Sam at the *Green Dragon* inn, dancing and singing;
- Frodo and Sam watching the procession of elves passing through the night;
- Aragorn at his mother's tomb;
- Arwen at the farewell at Rivendell;
- Gandalf warning Frodo that someone may try to take the ring;
- Haldir and the elves, preventing the fellowship from proceeding (also added: Haldir telling Frodo he brings great danger to Lothlórien);
- The conversation between Boromir and Aragorn.

ADDITIONS TO THE EXTENDED VERSION OF *THE FELLOWSHIP OF THE RING* FILM

There was extra footage included in the extended DVD and video of *The Fellowship of the Ring*.

- Additions to the prologue (such as Isildur putting on the ring and becoming invisible);
- A sequence following the prologue of Bilbo at his desk in his study

beginning his book, *There and Back Again*;
- Bilbo with his maps;
- A moment where Bilbo panics when he can't find the ring;
- Bilbo narrating an introduction to hobbits and the Shire (with Bilbo narrating over illustrative images: the film was originally going to start with the Bilbo bit 'concerning hobbits');
- Frodo, Merry, Pippin and Sam at the *Green Dragon* inn, dancing and singing;
- Sam, the Gaffer and Sandyman discussing the queer goings-on in the Shire;
- Frodo and Sam camping, with Sam unable to sleep;
- Frodo and Sam watching the procession of elves passing through the night to the Grey Havens (a severely abbreviated interpretation of Gildor and the elves in the book);
- Aragorn and the hobbits crossing the Midgewater marshes;
- Aragorn singing a little of Tolkien's beloved story told in the *Lay of Lúthien* and a few words with Frodo;
- A few more shots of the stone trolls (handheld shots, from Frodo's p.o.v., as Sam looms over him);
- The flight to the ford was enlarged;
- Gandalf reciting the Black Speech at the Council of Elrond (the scene darkens, there's the sound of thunder, though it's not certain whether Gandalf conjures the storm, or it's a reaction to the Black Speech being uttered. But Gandalf's aim it seems is to demonstrate how evil the ring is to Boromir);
- More dialogue at the council of Elrond (such as from Boromir);
- More of the exchange between Boromir and Aragorn before the shards of Isildur's sword;
- Another Rivendell scene, of Aragorn at his mother's tomb, conversing with Elrond about his responsibilities;
- The fellowship saying farewell at Rivendell, presided over again by Elrond, who mentions that none of the fellowship is bound to the task and can leave at any time. Arwen looks pale and washed-out, as if she's been crying all night. The reasons are explained in the extended edition of *The Two Towers*. (There's a nice joke where Frodo, faced with two paths, asks Gandalf which is the way to Mordor);
- A brief conversation between Gandalf and Frodo prior to Moria with the wizard alerting the hobbit that someone may try to take the ring, and that he (Gandalf) may be going to his doom in Moria (shot on Ian McKellen's last day in New Zealand, this wasn't one of the best scenes, and McKellen's make-up and hair looks a little slapdash);
- More shots of the fellowship traversing Caradhras;
- Additional footage of the fellowship in Moria (such as Gandalf explaining about the dwarves mining for *mithril*, with a big reveal of the dwarf mines, and Gimli remarking how precious Bilbo's *mithril* shirt was);
- The fight with the troll now seemed to drag on for even longer. All sorts of stunt work and bits of actorly business were added (more gore, more orcs being chopped up, Boromir thrown against a wall, etc);
- A little more of Haldir and the elves, including a conversation between Aragorn and Haldir on a flet, Haldir preventing the fellowship from proceeding, the fellowship looking at Frodo resentfully (these images had appeared in the theatrical version in the mirror of Galadriel), and some more images of Lothlórien (including a big reveal of Caras Galadon);

- Additions to the fellowship meeting Galadriel and Celeborn (principally dialogue);
- The gifts of Galadriel were back in the film (in the theatrical version only Frodo receives the gift of the phial). The gifts were intercut with images of the fellowship leaving Lórien in boats (thus being minor flashbacks). The farewell between Galadriel and Aragorn was moving – partly because it was the last time they would see each other, and partly because a couple of Tolkien's names were employed (Valinor, and Aragorn's elf name, Elessar). In the book, of course, Galadriel and Celeborn come to Minas Tirith, and say goodbye to Aragorn at Isengard;
- A short conversation on the riverside between Boromir and Aragorn was added (about Gollum tracking the fellowship on the river, and Boromir imploring Aragorn to come to Gondor, his usual refrain in the film);
- Additions to the lengthy fight scene with the Uruk-hai, and to Boromir's demise.
- But the extended *The Fellowship of the Ring* ended the same way the theatrical version did, with Frodo and Sam on hills overlooking Mordor.

OMISSIONS FROM *THE TWO TOWERS* FILM

Omissions to *The Two Towers* film (theatrical and extended versions) compared to Tolkien's book:

- Some of the dialogue between Aragorn, Legolas and Gimli;
- Aragorn searching the dead orcs for signs;
- Making a bier for Boromir;
- Preparing Boromir for the boat;
- Aragorn's song for Boromir at the riverbank;
- Legolas's song for Boromir;
- Aragorn searches for signs of Frodo and Sam;
- Aragorn loses the orc trail;
- They find orc corpses; Aragorn finds the trail in a stream;
- Aragorn's song for Gondor;
- Legolas sees an eagle;
- The hunters debate whether to continue the pursuit by night;
- Aragorn examines the orc tracks at dawn;
- They pass another night; Legolas dreams as he walks;
- The hunters spot the riders of Rohan;
- Aragorn explains about Rohan;
- Some of the dialogue between Éomer and the three hunters;
- Aragorn tells Éomer he knew his father, Éomund;
- Aragorn examines the orc tracks again;
- The hunters spend the night beside Fangorn forest;
- Aragorn tells them about Fangorn;
- Gimli sees an old man, perhaps Saruman, perhaps Gandalf;
- Pippin thinking to himself amongst the orcs;
- Pippin overhears the orcs discussing Sauron, Saruman and the halflings; more dialogue between the orcs;
- Pippin cuts his bonds;
- The orc scouts return;

- More of the orcs' arguments;
- Pippin sees the riders of Rohan pursuing the orcs;
- Merry and Pippin talk in the orc camp; the orcs wait for the attack;
- Merry and Pippin tease Grishnákh;
- Grishnákh is killed by a spear;
- Merry and Pippin walk beside the Entwash before entering Fangorn;
- The riders attack the orcs at dawn; Merry and Pippin hear the cries and watch the battle from afar;
- Merry and Pippin climb up a cliff in Fangorn;
- They meet Treebeard;
- Treebeard recites the 'lore of Living Creatures';
- More of the dialogue between Treebeard and the halflings;
- Treebeard mentioning Gandalf to the hobbits before he delivers them to the wizard;
- Treebeard discussing Lothlórien;
- Treebeard telling the hobbits about the history of the ents;
- Treebeard's song;
- Aspects of Treebeard's home (the rock wall, the glowing lamps, the ent draft);
- Treebeard lying on his stone bed;
- The hobbits telling Treebeard their adventures since leaving the Shire;
- Treebeard talking about Sauron and Saruman, and explaining at length about Saruman;
- Treebeard discussing his ent friends (Skinbark, Leaflock, Finglas, Fladrif, etc);
- Treebeard's story about the entwives; more of the entwife song;
- Merry and Pippin spend the night in Treebeard's house;
- Treebeard calls out to the other ents for the entmoot;
- Merry and Pippin discuss Isengard;
- Treebeard introduces Bregalad (Quickbeam) to the hobbits;
- Merry and Pippin explore Fangorn with Quickbeam;
- They spend the night at Quickbeam's house;
- Quickbeam's song;
- The entmoot continues; Merry and Pippin stay with Quickbeam;
- The ents storm out of Derndingle; Treebeard takes up the hobbits again;
- Treebeard's marching song;
- Aragorn, Gimli and Legolas discuss the old man they saw and the disappearance of their horses;
- They find the lembas and knife;
- They climb up the hill and find Treebeard's marks;
- The hunters see an old man in grey rags walking in the trees;
- They discuss the eagle, Frodo, Sam, Boromir, Saruman, Sauron, and the nazgûl;
- Gandalf explains about Treebeard;
- Much more of Gandalf explaining the current state of geopolitics in Middle-earth;
- Gandalf relates his time in Lothlórien, brings messages to Aragorn, Gimli and Legolas from Galadriel;
- Gandalf speaking about Edoras and the history of Rohan;
- Aragorn's song of the horse and the rider (given to Théoden in the film);

- The conversation at the gates of Edoras;
- More dialogue about the weapons left at the door of Meduseld;
- Théoden rising to speak with Gandalf in the Golden Hall (the equivalent of a page of dialogue; in the film he says barely a line);
- Much more of the interchange between Gandalf and Wormtongue;
- Gandalf's song to Théoden;
- Aragorn seeing Éowyn for the first time;
- More of the conversation between Théoden and Gandalf;
- Éomer comes forth to Théoden; they are reunited;
- Wormtongue tries to persuade the king a last time;
- Théoden offers Wormtongue the choice of going to battle or leaving;
- A meal in the Golden Hall;
- More dialogue between Gandalf and Théoden; Gandalf asks for Shadowfax as a gift;
- A conversation between Gimli and Éomer;
- The company see a gathering darkness (which may be Saruman's orc army, or the huorns);
- Ceorl, a messenger, reports to Théoden of the orc attacks;
- Gandalf dashes off on some errand;
- Another scout is met, near Helm's Deep; they meet roving bands of orcs;
- They see the orc host from Isengard in the valley;
- Gamling reports to Théoden that they have about 1,000 men; they discuss Erkenbrand;
- The orcs attack the Dike;
- The orc army fires many arrows over the battlements, but receive no answer for some time;
- Éomer is at Helm's Deep; he and Aragorn draw swords together; Aragorn uses Andúril;
- Éomer (not Gimli) accompanies Aragorn through the small postern-door;
- A group of orcs feign death then leap up and attack Éomer; Gimli comes to the rescue;
- Gimli aids Gamling in holing up the Deeping-stream with rocks;
- Gamling talking about the Dunlendings; the men of Dunland were not shown in the battle of Helm's Deep;
- Aragorn defending the stairway in the Deep with Andúril; he stumbles as he runs; Legolas kills an orc; the other orcs are dispatched by a great boulder;
- Aragorn is split up from Gimli, Éomer and Gamling, who did not make it up to the Rock;
- Aragorn reports to Théoden in a tower in the Hornburg;
- Aragorn talking with the orcs below the gate;
- Another gunpowder blast, which destroys the archway of the gate;
- Erkenbrand arrives at Helm's Deep with Gandalf (not Éomer);
- Éomer, Gimli and Gamling emerge from the caves;
- A discussion between the victors at Helm's Deep;
- Erkenbrand deals with the hillmen;
- The orc corpses are heaped up near the huorns;
- The next day the company passes through the forest of huorns;
- Gimli waxes lyrical about the caverns of Helm's Deep;
- Ents come forward to call other ents to the forest;
- The company passes a burial mound at the Fords;

- The company rides to Isengard;
- The forest of huorns passes by their camp at night;
- The Death Down is erected by the huorns overnight;
- The company reaches the great pillar of the Hand and the broken doors of Isengard;
- Théoden finds out about the hobbits, the holbytlan;
- More of the conversation between Aragorn, Legolas, Gimli and the hobbits;
- The hobbits tell of their adventures, including the attack on Isengard, watching the orc army leave, the huorns, etc;
- The ents attacked at night (by day in the film);
- Quickbeam spots Saruman near the gates and almost catches him as he hurries back to Orthanc;
- Merry and Pippin explore the circle of Isengard;
- Merry and Pippin meet Gandalf; Gandalf speaks with Treebeard;
- Merry and Pippin see more huorns travelling to battle at night;
- Wormtongue arrives at Isengard;
- The company meet Saruman;
- Saruman addresses Théoden, who finally resists;
- Gandalf offers Saruman the chance of a peaceful resolution;
- Gandalf casts Saruman out of the order and the Council;
- Wormtongue throws down the *palantír*;
- Treebeard meets the three hunters; Legolas asks Treebeard if he can bring Gimli to explore Fangorn;
- The company says farewell to Treebeard and the ents;
- More dialogue after Pippin looks in the *palantír*;
- A nazgûl flies overhead;
- Gandalf rides away with Pippin; they talk, about the *palantíri*, Saruman, Sauron and Middle-earth politics;
- More of Frodo and Sam discussing being followed by Gollum;
- More of Frodo and Sam talking about climbing down the cliff; Sam remembers his elven rope;
- a big storm;
- Frodo and Sam watch (and hear) Gollum from a distance crawling down the cliff;
- Frodo and Sam wait until Gollum reaches the bottom of the cliff, and pounce on him;
- Frodo and Sam pretend to rest, and capture Gollum when he springs away;
- Gollum's song;
- Frodo (and Gollum) sense the proximity of the power of Sauron;
- The 'gasping pits and poisonous mounds' near Mordor;
- Frodo dreaming of 'strange phantoms, dark riding shapes, and faces of the past' (TT, 297);
- The nazgûl fly over Frodo, Sam and Gollum a third time;
- Frodo threatening Gollum with the ring;
- More of Gollum's description of Minas Morgul, an account of his travels, conversations with orcs, and Gollum's view of how Sauron thinks about the defence of Mordor;
- Gollum talking about Aragorn;
- Gandalf in Isengard thinking of Frodo at the moment when Frodo debates whether to trust Gollum and the way past Minas Morgul;
- Sam spots the Black Riders in the sky;

- Sam's song about the oliphaunt;
- Gollum spying on the Southrons or Easterlings;
- A description of Ithilien in early Spring;
- Sam asking Gollum if he can find 'anything fit for a hungry hobbit' (TT, 323);
- Sam watching Frodo asleep;
- Frodo and Sam overhearing the Gonodrian men talk before they're captured;
- Frodo acknowledging Gollum to Faramir when they first meet (Frodo tells him that Gollum was someone they met on their travels);
- More of the conversation between Frodo and Faramir;
- Faramir leaving two guards (Mablung and Damrod) with Frodo and Sam;
- Frodo and Sam watching the battle between the Gondorians and the Southrons while two men guard them;
- Damrod and Mablung explaining about the Southrons and Sauron;
- Faramir interrogating Frodo surrounded by 200-300 of his men on a slope;
- Frodo tells Faramir about Aragorn, Isildur's heir (TT, 338);
- Sam squaring up to Faramir in front of his men;
- Faramir relating hearing Boromir's horn;
- Frodo and Faramir discuss Lothlórien;
- Faramir relating how the horn was washed up in the Anduin in pieces;
- Faramir talking in more detail about Isildur's Bane and the fellowship as they travel to Henneth Annûn;
- Faramir discussing the house of Denethor and the stewardship of Minas Tirith;
- Faramir talking about Gandalf, and how Gandalf questioned the Gondorians about the Great Battle of Dagorlad;
- Faramir states: '"I would not take this thing, if it lay by the highway. Not were Minas Tirith falling in ruin and I alone could save her, so, using the weapon of the Dark Lord for her good and my glory"' (TT, 348-9);
- Sam thinks he spots Gollum lurking behind them;
- Faramir consults with his scouts; they discuss Gollum;
- The meal with Faramir in Henneth Annûn;
- Frodo's tales of their adventures;
- Faramir discusses with Frodo and Sam the stewards of Gondor, the Rohirrim and the Númenóreans at greater length;
- They also talk about elves, Galadriel and Lórien;
- Sam talks about Boromir and mentions the ring by mistake;
- Sam follows Frodo and Faramir outside;
- Frodo tells Faramir that Gollum once bore the ring;
- One of Faramir's guards, Anborn, was left out;
- Gollum promises to Frodo on the ring;
- Faramir pronounces his doom upon Frodo;
- More of the dialogue between Faramir, Frodo and Gollum, including the discussion of the ways into Mordor;
- Faramir's gift of staves;
- Frodo, Sam and Gollum spend the night in a tree near the road;
- Gollum leads the hobbits to the Crossroads;
- The Witch-king on a horse leading his host;
- Sam talking about Beren and Lúthien and the *silmaril*;

- Gollum returning to find Frodo and Sam asleep;
- Frodo and Sam entering Shelob's lair (in the film, Frodo goes on alone);
- The hobbits seeing the 'two great clusters of many-windowed eyes' of Shelob (TT, 414); the hobbits approaching and the eyes receding;
- Aspects of the fight between Sam and Gollum;
- Sam's interior argument;
- Sam putting on the ring, and being aware of the Eye;
- More of the orcs' talk, about Sauron, the nazgûl and spies on the stairs.

ADDITIONS TO *THE TWO TOWERS* FILM

Among the scenes added to the film of *The Two Towers,* compared to the book, were:

- Grishnákh following the hobbits into Fangorn, pulling Merry down from Treebeard and being stamped on by Treebeard;
- The hobbits being trapped in a tree's roots and saved by Treebeard;
- Éomer being banished from Edoras by Wormtongue (in the book, the king's nephew remains loyal to the king);
- Wormtongue showing Éomer the order that Théoden has 'signed';
- Théoden's 'possession' and 'exorcism' (which's extreme, and isn't in the novel at all);
- Aragorn, Legolas and Gimli beating up the king's guards in the Golden Hall;
- Théoden threatening to kill Wormtongue (in the book it's Éomer);
- Théoden taking much longer to recover from his illness/ possession and decide to fight (in the book he is more assertive);
- Théoden in his chamber talking with Gamling (in the book Gamling is an old man who's used by Tolkien for exposition at Helm's Deep, about Helm's Deep, the Dunlendings, the Rohirrim, etc. In the film, he's made the king's aide, and younger too);
- A brief scene showing Éowyn overseeing the arrival at Helm's Deep;
- The banner that flies down from Meduseld and lands near Aragorn;
- A more subdued departure from Edoras (in the book the soldiers cry '"Our King and the White Rider!"' and "Forth Éorlingas!"', they clash spear on shield, horses neigh and rear, and 'with a rush like the sudden onset of a great wind the last host of Rohan rode thundering into the West' (TT, 159);
- Éowyn and Aragorn talking in the Golden Hall;
- Aragorn and Éowyn in the stables at Edoras;
- Aragorn and Gandalf talking in the stables; Gandalf telling Aragorn to watch out for him on the fifth day at dawn;
- Éowyn cooking an inedible stew for Aragorn and Aragorn telling her about being a Dunedain and 87 years-old, in the extended cut;
- Éowyn and Gimli talking about dwarf women;
- Théoden talking with Aragorn about Éowyn (how he should have been more of a father for her);
- A brief encounter between Aragorn and Háma's son Haleth (played by Philippa Boyens' 13 year-old son Callum Gittens, but voiced by an English

boy);
- The decimation of the villages of Rohan;
- Morwen putting her kids on a horse in the Rohan village;
- The warg attack;
- Háma killed by a warg;
- Aragorn falling off the cliff;
- Aragorn in the river;
- Arwen appearing to Aragorn like an angel and reviving him with – what else? – a kiss;
- Aragorn being rescued by his horse, Brego;
- Aragorn making his way alone to Helm's Deep;
- Aragorn seeing the Uruk-hai army marching;
- Aragorn arriving at Helm's Deep, meeting Legolas and Gimli, watched by Éowyn;
- The number able to defend Helm's Deep is 300 in the film, a thousand is mustered at Edoras in the book (TT, 166);
- A reunion between Morwen and her children at Helm's Deep (ah, bless!);
- Short scenes in the Glittering Caves of men and boys being led away from their womenfolk;
- A scene in the armoury, with boys and men being given weapons;
- An argument in the armoury, with Legolas doubting Aragorn (included to increase the pre-battle tension: Legolas also mentions the odds, of 300 against 10,000, where in the book there are some 1,000 men defending Helm's Deep);
- Aragorn, Legolas and Gimli putting on their military gear (a familiar moment in adventure and sci-fi movies);
- Haldir and the elves arriving at Helm's Deep in the nick of time (the unlooked-for arrival of the elves at Helm's Deep does have a precedent in the book: the band of Rangers from the North arrive, Aragorn's compan-ions, which cheers him up);
- A conversation between Haldir, Théoden and Aragorn by the entrance;
- Brief scenes of women and children in the Glittering Caves;
- The arrow loosed by an Rohan soldier on the battlements which starts the battle (this was going to be a young boy. In the book, the orcs begin the battle with hails of arrows);
- Legolas snowboarding down some steps;
- Théoden standing on the battlements of the Hornburg with Gamling and his captains (in the book, he's in a tower);
- The 'beserker' orc running with the torch to light the gunpowder while Aragorn and Legolas try to bring him down;
- Gimli leaping off a wall to help a beleaguered Aragorn (in the book he helps Éomer);
- Aragorn leading a charge of the elf warriors;
- Aragorn charging up stairs to save Haldir;
- Haldir's death;
- Aragorn leaping onto a ladder and falling down onto the orcs below, outside the wall;
- Gimli, not Éomer, sneaking out of the small postern-door;
- Gimli standing on top of the battlements, hewing down orcs as they climb the ladders;
- Théoden and others at the main gate, fighting orcs on the other side of the doors;

- Aragorn asking the king about ways for the women and children to escape;
- Aragorn remembering Gandalf's words (which are heard in voice-over) as he consults the next course of action;
- Aragorn suggesting they ride out to meet the enemy (in the book, it's Théoden who asks Aragorn if the ranger will accompany him. Reversing the roles makes Aragorn more pro-active, and Théoden more a reluctant ruler);
- Éomer arriving with Gandalf (in the novel, it's Erkenbrand);
- Éomer, not Erkenbrand, coming to the rescue at Helm's Deep;
- Conversations between Wormtongue and Saruman in Orthanc: about Aragorn and the ring of Barahir; about the Rohirrim travelling to Helm's Deep with women and children; about ways of attacking Helm's Deep; about an army to defeat Rohan, etc;
- Saruman addressing his orc army Nuremburg-style;
- Saruman commanding his warg riders on a mission;
- Saruman communicating with Sauron via the *palantír*;
- Merry and Pippin meeting Treebeard was combined with their escape from the orcs;
- Treebeard saving Merry by stepping on an orc;
- Merry badgering Treebeard into doing something about the war;
- Merry telling Pippin there won't be any Shire left;
- Pippin asking Treebeard to take the hobbits South;
- Treebeard's dialogue (some of it was taken from Tom Bombadil, some of it was ad-libs by John Rhys-Davies during looping);
- Aragorn dreaming of Arwen in Rivendell;
- A flashback to Arwen and Aragorn talking at Rivendell;
- Elrond telling Aragorn to let Arwen leave for the undying lands;
- A conversation between Arwen and her father at Rivendell;
- A flashforward or vision of the future painted by Elrond, depicting Aragorn dead in Minas Tirith, and Aragorn's tomb, and Arwen wandering alone;
- A scene of the elves leaving Rivendell at night;
- A flashback to the morning before Aragorn leaves with the Fellowship, and another conversation with Arwen;
- Elrond communicating with Galadriel by a kind of telepathy;
- Galadriel outlining to Elrond what'll happen in Middle-earth if Sauron succeeds in finding the ring;
- The ents attacking Isengard, killing orcs, destroying machinery;
- Ents flooding the site;
- Sam falling off a rock and down the slopes by the Black Gate;
- Sam buried in stones at the Black Gate;
- Frodo climbing down the hill to rescue Sam;
- Two Easterlings breaking off from the column of soldiers to investigate;
- Frodo and Sam hiding under the elven cloak;
- The Gondorians attack on the Southrons taking place before Frodo and Sam are captured by Faramir and his men;
- Faramir shooting a Southron who falls from the *mûmakil* and lands in front of Frodo and Sam;
- Gollum confessing to Faramir with his back to him, in a lengthy monologue (in the book the interrogation scene plays face to face, with more questions from Faramir);
- Faramir taking Frodo and Sam to Osgiliath;

- The Gondorians fighting the orcs at Osgiliath;
- The nazgûl attack at Osgiliath;
- Frodo encountering the Witch-king on the fell-beast and almost putting on the ring (a transposition and exaggeration of the scene at Minas Morgul);
- Frodo being saved by Sam;
- Sam's god-awful speech tying up the multiple storylines;
- Faramir leaving Frodo and Sam at the sewers in Osgiliath;
- Various 'jokes' in the dialogue (such as dwarf-tossing, or 'looks like meat's back on the menu, boys!').

ADDITIONS TO THE EXTENDED CUT OF *THE TWO TOWERS* FILM

Among the extra scenes or additional bits of business in the extended version (compared to the cinema release) of *The Two Towers* were:

- Merry and Pippin drinking the ent draft;
- The hobbits being trapped in a tree's roots and saved by Treebeard (a nod to the Old Forest scene with Old Man Willow);
- A couple of Treebeard's songs;
- A little more of the entmoot;
- The hobbits finding pipeweed in Isengard's ruins;
- Éomer finding Théodred at a riverbank massacre and taking him to Edoras;
- Additions to the scenes at Edoras;
- Wormtongue showing Éomer the order that Théoden has 'signed';
- A funeral scene for Théodred (quite a big scene, though its ends too abruptly);
- A 'stew scene', where Éowyn offers Aragorn some inedible stew (showing a 'lighter' side to Éowyn), and Aragorn talking about being 87 years-old and a Dúnedain (this wasn't one of Miranda Otto's favourite scenes);
- More action during the battle at Helm's Deep. Typically, the additions enhanced the violence and gore quotient: more heads and limbs being chopped off; a soldier skewered on the battering ram; another throttled;
- Aragorn running up the stairs;
- In the book, the orcs, fleeing from the king and his men riding out, meet the huorns first in the Deeping-comb; in the film, Gandalf and Éomer arrive and gallop down the slope, and the orcs flee into the huorns' forest (in the extended edition of *The Two Towers* only) after the battle has been won;
- Éowyn embracing Aragorn after the battle;
- Wormtongue and Saruman discussing Aragorn and the ring of Barahir (in the chronology in *The Return of the King* this ring was actually given to Arwen by Aragorn in TA 2980);
- Frodo and Sam and the elven rope;
- More of Gollum leading Frodo and Sam through Emyn Muil;
- Brief debates between 'Gollum' and 'Sméagol';
- A Dead Marshes conversation developing the three characters further;
- A longer introduction of Faramir (where he compassionately dis-

cusses a dead warrior);
- Faramir's men beating up Gollum;
- Faramir meeting his brother and father at Osgiliath;
- Boromir addressing the troops at Osgiliath;
- Denethor comanding Boromir to bring the ring to Gondor;
- Frodo, Sam and Gollum leaving Faramir in the city's sewers, with Faramir brutally questioning Gollum about the route they were to take;
- A nighttime scene of Gandalf outlining the current state of political affairs in Middle-earth to Aragorn;
- Gimli and Legolas reckoning up their body count after Helm's Deep;
- A flashback to Osgiliath, an important scene showing Faramir, Boromir and their father Denethor. Apart from showing how Denethor prefers Boromir over Faramir, and Boromir giving a speech to the soldiers who've recaptured Osgiliath, this scene had Denethor commanding Boromir to travel to Rivendell to secure the ring for Gondor.

Some of the scenes cut out from the theatrical version of *The Two Towers* were expansions of character scenes, such as: Gollum debating with Sméagol, Aragorn talking about being 87 years-old, and Faramir portrayed as more compassionate.

Some scenes had a few extra shots added to them which didn't alter the narrative at all. Some scenes were ones many fans of the book remember but which didn't change the narrative in any way: the elven rope, the ent draft, Treebeard's song.

A couple of the deleted scenes were big scenes: Théodred's funeral, and Boromir, Faramir and Denethor at Osgiliath. The funeral scene, on the slopes below Edoras, was a pleasant interlude in the helter-skelter pace of the film (it was very much an Alan Lee-designed scene, a Nordic or Viking or Anglo-Saxon kind of burial). Best of all in the funeral scene was Éowyn singing (to words which had been translated into Old English). Unfortunately, the scene ended all too suddenly, cutting to Théoden speaking about simbelmynë.

The Boromir-Faramir-Denethor scenes were probably the most significant deletion from the theatrical cut, in terms of the narrative (producers Barrie Osborne and Mark Ordesky wanted them in; maybe in retrospect, they ought to have been included). These scenes, which were not in the book, were flashbacks to the time before Boromir had departed for Rivendell. Apart from showing Boromir and Faramir together, and Boromir giving a heroic victory speech to the troops from a battlement, the scenes introduced Denethor, depicted as a stern, intense patriarch. Denethor's commands to Boromir explained very clearly for the audience what he was after: the ring. Elves, dwarves and wizards will try to claim it, Denethor tells Boromir, but it must come to Gondor. The scene also explained how Faramir knew about the ring (in the theatrical version he guesses all too easily that Frodo has the ring), and also foreshadows some of the dialogue (about a 'mighty gift', and 'the chance for Faramir, captain of Gondor, to show his quality').

Another scene that was shot for *The Two Towers* but didn't make it into either the theatrical or extended versions had Éowyn presiding over

Morwen giving birth in the caves (Morwen's the mother of the two children, Éothain and Freda, sent away when the Wild Men attack Rohan). When some orcs burst in to the caves Éowyn finally gets to draw her sword and defend women and children. Another scene that was shot but not used had Éowyn rescuing Morwen's children from an attack by some wargs (Sib, 502).

The earlier scene of Morwen putting her two cute moppets on a horse was an addition to Tolkien's book, of course, added probably to humanize and individualize the sack of Rohan (and to offer a link between Rohan and Edoras, because the kids turn up there and tell Théoden, Gandalf and the others about the attack on their village). Introducing a birth scene (entirely led by women) would have been a big departure from Tolkien's kind of manly, heroic fiction. (Jackson acknowledged that such additions were 'cheap and cheesy: Hollywood spewing itself over Tolkien's book, via us!' [Sib, 502]).

OMISSIONS FROM *THE RETURN OF THE KING* FILM

Omissions from *The Return of the King* (the theatrical version) compared to the book included:

- Halbarad, the rangers and Dûnedain;
- Aragorn looking into the *palantír*;
- Denethor and the *palantír*;
- The Dûnedain accompanying Aragorn on the Paths of the Dead;
- The journey to the Stone of Erech;
- Conversations between Théoden, Éomer, Éowyn and Merry; at Dunharrow;
- Denethor sending the Red Arrow to Théoden;
- The Rohirrim encountering the Wild Men and Ghân-buri-Ghân;
- Prince Imrahil rescuing Faramir and taking him to Denethor;
- Beregond;
- Beregond and Pippin exploring Minas Tirith (and lots of back-story about the city);
- Pippin talking to Denethor for an hour;
- Gandalf encountering the Witch-king at the gate;
- The Dûnedain and Elrond's sons at Pelennor;
- Aragorn camping outside Minas Tirith;
- Aragorn entering the city;
- The houses of healing (many conversations, and accounts of the battle);
- Éomer at Théoden's death, and fury at finding Éowyn on the battlefield;
- Ioreth;
- Aragorn healing Merry, Faramir and Éowyn;
- Pippin with Merry in the houses of healing;
- Legolas and Gimli in Minas Tirith; meeting Merry and Pippin;
- Accounts of the Umbar fleet, Pelargir, the dead attacking the ships;

prisoners and slaves set free;
- The voyage up the River Anduin;
- Elrond's sons, Elladan and Elrohir (they had been in earlier drafts);
- Prince Imrahil (Michael Stanton pointed out that Imrahil, a Gondorian Dúnadan of Dol Amroth, was a major figure among *Rings*' secondary characters: he ruled Minas Tirith for a while; fights at Pelennor and the Morannon; found Éowyn at Pelennor; enters the white city with Aragorn; is Faramir's cousin and Denethor's nephew (via Denethor's wife); he's in the Last Debate; and he's the equal of Éomer and Aragorn [RK, 167]); and Imrahil does much more than, say, Legolas or Gimli, in the later parts of *The Lord of the Rings* (at the Morannon, for instance). The writers recalled that Imrahil had been in earlier drafts of *The Lord of the Rings*, but he was another character too many;
- Imrahil governing Minas Tirith in Denethor's absence;
- The battles around Lothlrien and Mirkwood;
- Much more of the last debate;
- In the book it's Gandalf, not Aragorn, who suggests an attack on Mordor to draw out Sauron. In the film, Aragorn suggests it as if he's just thought of it; but in the book, Gandalf has clearly considered at length their next move (RK, 186-7);
- Prince Imrahil saying that assaulting Mordor with only 7,000 soldiers was '"the greatest jest in all the history of Gondor"' (RK, 189); Gimli's comic line, though, links with that idea;
- The journey of the Host of the West to the Morannon (including the crossroads, an ambush, heralds, scouts and deserters);
- The Mouth of Sauron;
- Pippin being attacked by a troll (in the film this was transferred to Aragorn);
- Prince Imrahil, the knights of Dol Amroth, the Dúnedain and the sons of Elrond at the battle of the Morannon;
- The Captains fighting on separate hills;
- Frodo, Sam and Gollum at the crossroads;
- The Morgul-king sensing Frodo and the ring (this was transferred (and expanded) to the climax of *The Two Towers*);
- Gollum attacking Sam in Shelob's lair;
- Sam using the phial to enter Cirith Ungol;
- Sam taking the ring from Frodo;
- Sam wearing the ring;
- Sam using the ring to enter Cirith Ungol;
- Further conversations between the orcs in Cirith Ungol;
- Sam singing in order to find Frodo in the tower;
- Sam and Frodo escaping from Cirith Ungol;
- Sam and Frodo using Elvish cries and Galadriel's phial to get past the Watchers;
- Further meals, conversations and events as Frodo and Sam cross Mordor;
- The hobbits overhearing a conversation between an orc soldier and a tracker;
- The tracker killing the orc;
- Sam spotting Gollum tracking them in Mordor;
- Frodo and Sam being overtaken by an orc band and falling in with them;
- The Field of Cormallen; a song celebrating the halflings; many re-

unitings;
- The feast at Cormallen;
- The journey down the Anduin to Osgiliath and Minas Tirith;
- Éowyn and the Warden at Minas Tirith;
- Éowyn and Faramir;
- An eagle singing over Minas Tirith ('sing and rejoice, ye people of the Tower of Anor');
- The Captains of the West entering Minas Tirith (again partly narrated from Ioreth's viewpoint);
- King Elessar and Beregond;
- King Elessar and Éomer;
- The Companions in Minas Tirith;
- Gandalf showing Aragorn the 'scion of the Eldest of Trees';
- The arrival of Glorfindel, Erestor, Elrohir, Elladan, Elrond, Galadriel and Celeborn in Minas Tirith;
- The Companions leaving Minas Tirith for the North;
- The Companions in Edoras; Théoden's burial; the minstrel's song; the funeral feast;
- More farewells;
- The king's heralds giving the Wild Wood to the Wild Men;
- Helm's Deep; the elf and the dwarf in the Glittering Caves;
- Isengard; Treebeard;
- More farewells (including to Aragorn);
- The Companions meet Saruman and Wormtongue on the way North (Saruman heads for the Shire);
- Elrond, Celeborn, Galadriel and Gandalf communicating 'from mind to mind';
- Celeborn and Galadriel depart to Lórien via the Redhorn Gate and Dimrill Stair;
- Rivendell; reunion with Bilbo;
- Bilbo's birthday;
- The four hobbits and Gandalf leave Rivendell; Bilbo's gifts;
- The journey to Bree;
- Meeting with Butterbur at the *Prancing Pony*;
- Things going ill in Bree; Bill the pony;
- Gandalf turning aside to visit Tom Bombadil;
- The hobbits return to the Shire, talk of Bill Ferny, ruffians, Shirriffs and the 'Chief';
- The hobbits 'arrested' by the Shirriffs;
- The industrialization of the Shire at Bywater;
- Confrontation with ruffians;
- Raising the Shire;
- At Farmer Cotton's; planning to fight back;
- Another face-off with the ruffians; one dies;
- Farmer Cotton telling the hobbits about events in the Shire while they've been away;
- The Gaffer visits Farmer Cotton;
- Pippin and the Tooks arrive from Tuckborough;
- The Battle of Bywater between the hobbits and the ruffians;
- The hobbits reach Hobbiton; Ted Sandyman;
- Meeting Saruman at Bag End;
- Saruman tries to kill Frodo;
- Wormtongue cuts Saruman's throat, and is then shot dead;

- Meeting Fredegar Bolger;
- Repairing the Shire;
- Frodo as deputy mayor;
- Sam planting trees all over the Shire;
- 1420: the bounteous year in the Shire;
- Sam's children;
- Frodo and Sam meeting Gildor, Elrond, Galadriel and Bilbo; the elven rings;
- Meeting Círdan at the Grey Havens;
- Gandalf arriving with Merry and Pippin at the Grey Havens.

Some of these omissions were restored in the *Extended Edition* film of *The Return of the King*. Among the more significant were Aragorn and the *palantír*; Gandalf encountering the Witch-king; the houses of healing (Aragorn healing Éowyn, Éowyn and Faramir); Éomer finding Éowyn on the battlefield; and the Mouth of Sauron.

The theatrical cut of *The Return of the King*, incredibly, leaves out the fates of Saruman, Éowyn, Éomer, Faramir, Legolas and Gimli; the *Extended Edition* includes the fate of Saruman (and Wormtongue), but still not the others. The 'voice of Saruman' scene was shifted three times: it was going to be in *The Two Towers* theatrical, then *Towers* extended, then *The Return of the King* theatrical, and finally made it into the extended version of *Return*.

ADDITIONS TO *THE RETURN OF THE KING* FILM

Additions to *The Return of the King* book in the 2003 theatrical version of the film included:

- Gandalf sending Pippin to light the beacon;
- The Witch-king suiting up (presumably in Minas Morgul), while Gandalf explains that the Enemy has yet to unveil one of its weapons;
- Orcs attacking Osgiliath by night and Faramir and his men defending it;
- Faramir and his cavalry attacking the orcs at Osgiliath (in the book the battle and the retreat are described from the viewpoint of someone looking out from Minas Tirith across the plain; in the film it's a more detailed action sequence, and covered in a curious montage between Pippin and Denethor in the great hall, Faramir and his men, and the orcs);
- Sauron's eye as a searchlight;
- Arwen and the elves riding and walking through the woods;
- Arwen turning back for Rivendell;
- Elrond and Arwen talking in Rivendell;
- Arwen's vision of the future of her child with Aragorn in what appears to be Minas Tirith (with Aragorn appearing older and greyer);
- Arwen urging Elrond to reforge the sword Narsil;
- Elrond holding Arwen's hands and realizing that she is dying;
- Elrond linking Arwen's fate to the ring;
- Elrond bringing the restored sword Narsil to the muster of Rohan

(introduced as another tease for the audience);
- The Witch-king riding a fell-beast instead of a horse at Minas Morgul;
- Gandalf and Pippin (and some Gondorians) seeing the light streaming upwards from Minas Morgul;
- Sauron addressing Aragorn at the Black Gate;
- Aragorn leading the charge (yelling 'for Frodo!');
- Another conversation between Gollum and Sméagol;
- Gollum saying he'll kill the hobbits in the conversation with himself that Sam overhears;
- Gollum framing Sam with the lembas bread;
- Frodo going into the tunnels alone;
- Sam going back down the stairs, finding the lembas bread and returning;
- Gollum watching as Frodo is trapped in Shelob's lair;
- A conversation between Frodo and Gollum in Shelob's lair;
- Frodo being helped up by Galadriel (as if he were back in the Shire).

CHAPTER 11

SELLING THE 2001-2003 *LORD OF THE RINGS* MOVIES

MARKETING AND PUBLICITY

Boy oh boy was the marketing and PR great for the *Lord of the Rings* films! It had a lot of people fooled with its aggressive spin. There was a lot of information flying around which had even diehard cynics like me believing some of it for a nano-second. For instance:

• The 2001-03 films were the biggest movie project ever undertaken. No they weren't.

• The *Lord of the Rings* movies were the most expensive films ever made. No they weren't (estimates hover around $130 million per film).

• The *Lord of the Rings* films had the longest schedule ever for a movie. Noooo! (I've cited a few films elsewhere for endless schedules).

• The *Lord of the Rings* films could only have been made in New Zealand. Rubbish. (They could've been shot in many, many places).

• More people worked on the *Lord of the Rings* films than any other motion picture project. Utter garbage.

• Only Peter Jackson could have made the films of *The Lord of the Rings*. Junk. What? Like there's no filmmaker as good, as talented, as hard-working as Peter Jackson around?

• Gollum was the first fully-formed CGI character. Nope. (There were many predecessors).

• The PR machine claimed that director Peter Jackson and the film-makers read Tolkien's book on set before every shot (utterly unbelievable, as anyone who's been on a film set would know).

And on and on it went, and the PR was so good, so slick, so all-consuming, so in-your-face, it convinced quite a few people. It's true that all of those points were not made by the filmmakers themselves, but by the studio, New Line Cinema, by Time Warner, and by the publicists – and the media, the magazines, the radio stations, the newspapers and the internet lapped it all up. Even now, years after the films have done the rounds of the global media outlets, they are still written about as the 'biggest' this or 'most expensive' that.

You have to remember: **THIS IS HOLLYWOOD**. And marketing and PR have one overriding aim: to sell, to raise awareness, to do the whole aggressive consumer capitalist thing. Expansion. Sales. Accumulation.

Colonization. Sales. Invasion. Production. Sales. Consumption. Sales.

This is Hollywood. THIS IS HOLLYWOOD. Or 'Wellywood'. Same thing.

Marketing. It's odd (well, not really) what a short memory the PR depts at New Line and Warners have, citing *The Lord of the Rings* as the biggest undertaking of its kind. Eh? Say the Tolkien saga cost, finally, $300-400 million for 9 hours, or around $100-130m per film. Well, *Titanic* supposedly cost $200m. And *Cleopatra* cost $40 million plus, and that was in 1963, at 1963 prices (i.e., some 15 times the average cost of a feature). If you do the math, adjust for inflation, $300-400m is a lot, but it's by no means the most shelled out to make a movie (each *Lord of the Rings* film cost about three times the average for a feature). Ambitious, then, but not the biggest film ever made, nor the most expensive, nor using the most people.

The marketing strategy for the *Lord of the Rings* films would include: teaser posters in July; trailers in theatres in October; releasing the extended DVD and video in September; putting out the computer games, competitions and tie-in promotions in November; launching the TV, radio and web publicity campaign in mid-November; installing final posters, banners, postcards, lobby displays, etc, in theatres in early December; retail store campaigns and tie-ins in December; world premieres in December; special and marathon screenings in December; promotions such as holidays, competitions, etc, in December; various parties in December; press junkets in December; TV commercials, newspaper ads and billboards in mid-December; and merchandizing such as music, toys, action figures, etc, throughout this period. The marketing campaign was timed to peak around the week of the film's release, like similar campaigns, with media interest at its height between the 12th and 19th December.

The award season would see a fresh spate of marketing and PR, for the Golden Globes, Academy Awards, BAFTAs, etc. (*Return* gained 161 nominations for awards, and won 11 Oscars).

Marketing to schools, the Ministries of Education and educational establishments was another tack that New Line Cinema took with the *Lord of the Rings* films: this occurs only with a few films. But the *Lord of the Rings* project had the aura of a literary prestige project, with its storytelling, its fairy tale and fantasy elements, and its 'classic novel' status. The *Lord of the Rings* films were put into an educational context, with the pedagogical aspects emphasized. For instance, in Belgium distributor Cinéart organized a 'Fantasy and Film' day for teachers in three cities.

A vital part of the *Lord of the Rings* films' marketing and distribution was that international distribution was not handled by the major distributors, not by Warners. Rather, New Line brokered many individual deals with distributors in overseas territories on a company-by-company basis ('a handcrafted approach to marketing that would be impossible for a studio to achieve', as *Variety* put it).[2] Sometimes they wouldn't choose the biggest fish in the pond in each territory. In Belgium, for instance, instead of releasing through a major distributor like UIP, New Line chose Cinéart, known for distributing arthouse films, like those by Theo Angelopoulos or

Pedro Almodóvar. But Cinéart had done well releasing New Line's *Magnolia* (1999).

New Line, though, kept a close eye on their independent distributors in each territory: they laid down strict guidelines and deadlines, controlling when and where to market the films, and had the distributors reporting back to California regularly. (Cinéart's marketing *nous* enabled them to be successful in certain areas of the media: 220 articles in *Der Standard* newspaper, for instance, mentioned the *Lord of the Rings* films from Dec, 2003 to Jan, 2004).

A key component in New Line's marketing strategy for the *Lord of the Rings* films was to target upscale and highbrow newspapers, magazines and media outlets. *The Lord of the Rings* was thus positioned as a quality, prestige, serious film, not simply a big, dumb, hyped populist movie.

There were various groups of people to please with the *Lord of the Rings* films – the legion of fans of the book and fantasy film fans, the sticklers who wanted the films to be accurate and faithful; the studio and its backers (and accountants, lawyers, etc); and the general audience. The general movie-going audience was addressed on a number of levels. One of the obvious come-ons was targeted at the older female audience: the inclusion of two romantic plots: Aragorn and Arwen, and the triangle of Aragorn, Arwen and Éowyn. (The emphasis on scenes between Elrond and Arwen in the 2001-03 pictures also alters the masculinist slant of Tolkien's tome, which is chiefly concerned with fathers and sons (such as Denethor and his offspring).) An older audience was tackled by emphasizing the films as old-fashioned epics. The younger audience was addressed in multiple ways: the inclusion of childish humour, the action-adventure aspects, the gore and violence, and the myriad tie-ins and licences.

The 2001-03 *The Lord of the Rings* films were a site of a struggle between different social groups. Director Peter Jackson wanted a monster movie and fantasy adventure movie, in the Ray Harryhausen tradition; scriptwriters Fran Walsh and Philippa Boyens wanted a romantic historical saga (a kind of *Braveheart* with magic); New Line Cinema demanded (and got) a 'rollercoaster' of a movie, a big event, tentpole movie; licensees, manufacturers and merchandizers wanted a powerful advert for their wares; the record company wanted to sell CDs; publishers wanted to shift books, audio books and tie-ins; Tolkien fans wanted a decent interpretation of the book; the Tolkien estate didn't want a film at all; and movie audiences weren't that bothered, as long as it was a cool movie they might go see at the local multiplex – or they might see another movie instead, or go to a nightclub, or a bar, or rent a DVD or video, or watch TV, or go bowling, or play the lottery, or surf the net, or play a computer game, or a million other leisure activities.

Early on New Line clearly decided that the *Lord of the Rings* films were going to be their big tentpole movies for 2001, 2002 and 2003, and would represent their biggest advertizing spend. The *marketing*, not the films themselves, would put them in the same company as the series of *Star Wars, James Bond, The Matrix* and *Harry Potter* films. By sheer force of money and a massive PR campaign, the *Lord of the Rings* films would be made into New Line's event pictures. As producer Jerry Bruckheimer remarked, you have to make films seem something special, to build into them reasons for the audience to want to leave their homes and visit a cinema. Stars, action, spectacle, visual fx, are some of the tools or come-ons employed, but only if carefully orchestrated by a brilliant PR campaign. For that reason, the people who designed the *Lord of the Rings* PR campaign and the companies who produced them, can be regarded as very significant elements in the success of the films (or even as co-authors of the films).

The marketing of the early 2000s Tolkien films emphasized a number of aspects, all of them tried and tested in the advertizing and publicity of big motion pictures. The artwork for *The Fellowship of the Ring,* which graced the posters, billboards, print ads, video and DVD box covers, and 100s of items of merchandizing, emphasized first of all the stars: the three top-billed stars were grouped in the centre of the artwork (Elijah Wood, Ian McKellen and Viggo Mortensen). Liv Tyler and Cate Blanchett were positioned to either side of this group. Supporting actors, such as Orlando Bloom, Sean Bean, John Rhys-Davies, Sean Astin, Dominic Monaghan and Billy Boyd, were dotted around the central group of stars, and much smaller in the composition. At the bottom of the picture, the Black Riders were shown, crossing the Ford of Bruinen.

The palette of *The Lord of the Rings*' advertizing was predominantly browns, greens, blacks and whites. The colour of the title (in gold) blended with the palette. The use of the colours, the typeface, the costumes, the lighting, all suggested a storybook or olde worlde quality. The look of the *Fellowship of the Ring* artwork also drew attention to action: Legolas, Aragorn and Gimli were all brandishing their weapons, as were the ringwraiths (and Boromir was blowing his horn, and Arwen was clad in her warrior princess garb, rather than the more 'feminine' dresses she sported in other parts of the film, and later on in the other films). The expressions of each of the stars was dour, grim, and very serious (only Blanchett's Galadriel had anything approaching a smile, and that was more of an enigmatic smile, as befitting her character). Aragorn was wearing chain mail, not his ranger outfit. The central character, Frodo, and top-billed star, Elijah Wood, stared out at the viewer, the blue of his eyes exaggerated, the lighting from above creating deep shadows around his eyes. Frodo wore the elven cloak of the journey, not his Hobbiton costume. Superimposed over Frodo was the inscription on the ring. (Many eyes and eye-lights were exaggerated in the *LOTR* movies, as with so many contemporary movies – using contact lenses, or using digital grading, which makes them look weird).

Combined with the colours, the brooding facial expressions, the brandishing of weaponry, the impression was that this was definitely not a fluffy romantic comedy, or a lightweight melodrama. This impact was: this is a serious movie, with lots of action, some fantasy elements, but more of a war movie perhaps than a fantasy movie. Pull quotes were used (from, on the DVD box cover of *The Fellowship of the Ring* in the U.K., *Empire* magazine, as well as the BAFTAs and Oscars the film had received).

The advertizing artwork for *The Two Towers* followed a similar pattern to that of *The Fellowship of the Ring:* browns, greys, whites, blacks and dark greens, a smoky, misty background, and the four stars at the centre (although there was a slightly different emphasis now: McKellen and Mortensen were slightly larger in the composition than Wood, although Wood was slightly higher up). Gandalf was clad in his Gandalf the White costume, and was no longer holding a sword.

As if to literalize the title, two towers were depicted in either edge of the picture (Barad-dûr and Orthanc). Curiously, Sauron's eye was missing from the top of the Dark Tower (maybe he had a NO PUBLICITY clause in his contract?).

The supporting characters were grouped below the four stars (Legolas this time brandishing a sword, Gimli with his axe again, and Saruman holding his staff. Even Éowyn, in a brown tunic and white dress, has a sword, although she only uses it once in either version of *The Two Towers*, and that's to practise with it in Meduseld as she converses with Aragorn). Curiously, no sign of Merry and Pippin, though Sam was more prominent. The image of Gollum was the one taken from *The Fellowship of the Ring,* when he's in Moria, crouched on a rock, seen in silhouette (as if prolonging the secrecy surrounding how Gollum would finally look).

The artwork for *The Return of the King* focussed on Viggo Mortensen, who was one of the chief leads chosen to market *The Return of the King*, appearing prominently in advertizing, and in the trailer (delivering the 'we few, we happy few' speech at the Gates of Mordor).

The *Lord of the Rings* logo was created to look like beaten, embossed gold. The words 'The Lord of the Rings' were much larger, with the title of each film in a smaller font below the main title. Rather a long title, the words in *The Lord of the Rings* emphasized were 'lord' and 'rings', with 'the', 'of' and 'the' printed much smaller (and the 'l' and 's' bookmarked the title as drop capitals).

The following copyright notice was pasted on everything to do with the *Lord of the Rings* films:

> © New Line Productions, Inc. The Lord of the Rings, and the names of the characters, events, items and places therein, are trademarks of The Saul Zaentz Company d/b/a Tolkien Enterprises under license to New Line Productions, Inc. All Rights Reserved.

And every time *The Lord of the Rings* appeared in writing, it was always accompanied by the trademark sign: *The Lord of the Rings*™. Tolkien was now a copyrighted, trademarked brand, like Coca-Cola, Disney or McDonald's. The same symbols – ™, ©, R – appear with franchises such as *James Bond* ('© 1962-2004 Danjaq, LLC and United Artists Corporation'), or *Spider-man* ('TM & © Marvel Characters, Inc and Columbia Pictures, Inc'). HarperCollins held the rights to some of the artwork and images that weren't linked to the New Line Cinema films.

There were at least three versions of each film on DVD: the two disc set of theatrical cut of the film (retailing in the U.K. at £14.99/ $24.00; also a single-disc edition); the four disc box set of the extended version (£27.99/ $45.00); and the four disc 'special pack' which had the extended cut plus 'a collectible Gollum statue' (£39.99/ $65.00). This latter was sold in a cardboard box package. (And the later 2006 *Limited Editions*).

It's interesting to see how the making of the films was described in the many commentaries on the DVD releases, and the many interviews made during the production and release of the films, theatrically and for home entertainment. The same stories are replayed endlessly: how Viggo Mortensen cracked his front tooth and asked for superglue to stick it back on; how Sean Astin cut his foot in the Amon Hen boat scene and had to be helicoptered to hospital; how Sean Bean preferred to walk up a mountain to a location rather than take a helicopter; how Mortensen suggested camping out to catch a sunrise for the orc chase scene in *The Two Towers*, resulting in a bunch of actors and crew in the great outdoors; how Mortensen was totally dedicated to the film, kept his sword with him at all times, trained hard with horses and sword fighting; how the four hobbit actors bonded; how Orlando Bloom and some of the younger actors pursued extreme sports; the boot camp regime for canoeing, sword fighting and training; and how arduous the Helm's Deep shoot was (with T-shirts commemorating the event: 'I survived Hel(m)'s Deep').

The melding of on-screen and off-screen personalities was encouraged by New Line in the marketing of the films. Ian McKellen was thus the wise old wizard of the production, offering pearls of wisdom on adapting Tolkien from the book, or on acting, and the hobbit actors were portrayed as a group of adventurous young men like their on-screen counterparts.

Had J.R.R. Tolkien been alive when the 2001-03 *The Lord of the Rings* films were being planned, prepared, shot and released, he would very likely have been a nightmare to work with, if he had chosen to be deeply involved in the adaptions of his books. Because Tolkien was absolutely tireless in his pursuit of total exactitude in all matters to do with his beloved Middle-earth. It's likely he would have driven the films' producers mad with countless suggestions, demands, provisos and questions about the films (not to mention the merchandizing and tie-in games). There are so many aspects of the 2001-03 *Lord of the Rings* films that Tolkien might object to, it would be impossible to begin listing them. One has some idea of the scale of Tolkien's objections to screen adaptions of his work from the lengthy letter he sent to the first group of filmmakers to approach him about filming *The Lord* in the 1950s. Taking liberties with Tolkien's sacred text – like having Aragorn appear to die, or having the ring go to Osgiliath, or Arwen becoming a warrior princess and saving Frodo, or changing Faramir's character – would simply not have got past the professor.

In the lead-up to the release of *Fellowship*, sales of Tolkien's books increased (including the audio version on 10 CDs, which was $70.00). Ballantine reported that 'sales are going through the roof'.[4] Sales of *The Fellowship of the Ring* increased to 1.8 million in 2001 (compared to 600,000 in 2000).

Christopher Lee was a big fan of the film. Only John Rhys-Davies, among the actors, talked it up more enthusiastically. There were things in the film that weren't in the book, Lee acknowledged, but for him they were improvements (a statement tantamount to blasphemy for diehard Tolkien fans). Lee claimed to read *The Lord of the Rings* every year. Both Lee and Rhys-Davies reckoned the three *The Lord of the Rings* films would be regarded as ground-breaking.

A big problem in selling *The Lord of the Rings* in the global marketplace is the thoroughly masculinist tone of the book and films. *Star Wars* had (and has) the same problem, with the adult female audience resistant to the war-mongering, violence, techno-fetishism, dumb heroism, and boys being boys. *The Lord of the Rings* is such a masculinist tome, indeed, one of the most masculinist of all modern fantasies (*viz.* the films' strategies to counteract this sexism: dredging up a romance from the appendices, casting two high profile female stars, playing up the love triangle, using Enya on the soundtrack, etc).

There are only three significant female characters in the book. Where are all the female friends, girlfriends, partners, wives, daughters, mothers and grandmothers of those bloody hobbits in Tolkien's book? Nowhere. And the Aragorn-Arwen romance in the book is about the most antiseptic, cold and unsexy love affair you could imagine. Instead, you get lots of men being tough men together, and homosocial bonding between Frodo and Sam, etc. The suspicion, fear and dislike of women in *The Lord of the Rings* is sometimes scary: for example, the giant spider Shelob, loathsome in her fecundity (women as begetting children, or as a deadly preying mantis, the castrating mother), who's dispatched with Sam's trusty phallic sword. Then there's Gollum, thoroughly (and negatively) feminized. Called a 'Ring junkie' by some of the filmmakers, it's odd that one of the chief villains in this version of *The Lord of the Rings* is a gay Welsh drug addict.

Sean Astin remarked that the *Lord of the Rings* films generated such a huge amount of interest, months before they were released, that New Line's senior vice-president of marketing, Gordon Paddison, 'felt like he had the best job in the world' (2004, 288). The trailer for *The Fellowship of the Ring*, released on the internet, received 1.7 million downloads from New Line and Time Warner sites (it was shown in cinemas in January, 2001, with fans. The movie's official website had 62 million hits in its first week online. Having Ian McKellen narrate the trailers for *The Lord of the Rings* emphasized the distinguished, 'Shakespearean' aspect of the production.

The *Lord of the Rings* films had a massive audience in the U.K.: cinema admissions for *The Fellowship of the Ring* were 16 million; 14.4 million for *The Two Towers;* and 15.2 million for *The Return of the King*. (As a guide, cinema admissions in the U.K. were 12-19 million per month in 2002 and 9-18 million per month in 2003, and 160-175m per year. So the *LOTR* movies had a sizable proportion of the British cinema audience).

New Line co-opted Tolkien fans by including them in the filmmaking process via a number of officially sanctioned websites and information points. Rather than working against the fans, New Line actively encouraged a sense of inclusion in the production. The official *The Lord of* the *Rings* website was overseen by Gordon Paddison, marketing VP at New Line, which expanded beyond short news items about the film to online shopping, interviews, production videos, trailers, screensavers to download, photo galleries, etc. Movie websites such as Harry Knowles' *Ain't-It-Cool-News* were also included in the marketing of the film on the internet. About ten Tolkien websites were given insider information, with about 40 other websites receiving information about the films from New Line. TheOneRing.Net, WETA, aint-it-cool-news.com and ringbearer.com were among the websites New Line encouraged. Some of the actors, such as Ian McKellen, had their own websites which discussed the *Rings* films (such as McKellen's 'The White Book'). New Line monitored chatrooms, message boards and websites, and kept in personal touch with selected webmasters, so that views of the films could be controlled, with negative spin being headed off early.

The secrecy and security surrounding the *Rings* films wasn't about the story – everyone knew the story. It was to do with how the story had been achieved. In particular, what the characters would look like.

The One Ring was founded by Erica Challis, Christopher Pirotta and William Thomas to spread information about the films (Challis had been thrown off the film set in New Zealand and given a court order not to appear there again. Later, the production decided to allow access).

Tolkien fan websites included information on fan conventions, actors appearances in the media, FAQs, character backgrounds, archives, fan clubs, games, spy reports, interviews, DVD releases, collectibles, downloadable photos and graphics, and fan polls (even years after the films' releases). New Line offered Tolkien fans the chance of appearing in the credits of the DVD versions of the films when they joined the official *Rings* fan club.

There was some talk during 2001-02 that the title of the second film, *The Two Towers*, might be changed in the wake of the terrorist attacks on New York and Washington on September 11, 2001 (Manhattan's Twin Towers having been destroyed and thousands of lives lost). The title wasn't changed, but the filmmakers were sensitive to the impact of 9/11 (the fall of the Dark Tower, for instance, was conceived to consciously avoid the harrowing images of the collapse of the World Trade Center).

The filmmakers might've had more marketing problems if Tolkien had chosen one of his other possible titles for the three books: *The Ring Sets Out*, *The Ring Goes South*, *The First Journey* and *The Journey of the Nine Companions*, *The Journey of the Ringbearers*, *The Treason of Isengard*, *The Ring Goes East*, *The Shadow Grows*, *The Ring in the Shadows*, *The War of the Ring* and *The End of the Third Age*.

The War of the Ring(s) is probably the best alternative to *The Lord of the Rings* (and is more accurate and descriptive title than *The Lord of the Rings*), but titles such as *The Treason of Isengard* or *The Ring Goes East* would have been unwieldy for a postmodern blockbuster film. And *The War of the Ring* would have had 'war' in the title, which puts off some audiences, and can also prove problematic (as George Lucas found with the title *Star Wars*, which put some people off seeing the film, emphasized certain aspects of the film over others, and was also appropriated by the Republican Reagan administration, and used as a name for its S.D.I. military defence system).

Headlines in newspaper and magazines about the *Lord of the Rings* films give some of the flavour of the media's response: "Lad of the Rings Advert", "One Film To Rule Them All", "Why Tolkien Lords Over It All", "The Bore of the Rings", "The Epic To End All Epics", "Hobbit Forming", "Ears To You Orlando", "The Orlando Bloom Effect, Or How Sisters Are Doing It For Their Elves", and "I Was Stroked Into Submission, Then Soppy Farewells Put Me On the Orcs' Side".

By the time of the release of *The Return of the King*, Orlando Bloom had become one of the *Rings*' films biggest assets, in terms of celebrity and publicity. If there was a crowd to see the cast of the films, 80% of them would be to see Bloom, according to Sean Astin (2004, 295).

Curiously, Frances Walsh opted to stay out of the publicity for the *Lord of the Rings* films: she's not in the 'making of' documentaries, the puff pieces, the celebrity chat shows, or the Tolkien biographies. Odd, because, as co-writer, co-producer and co-director, Walsh's one of the most important members of the production (she did appear on the commentaries on the DVDs, however, and provided some of the best insights into the show. And, if shy, she also made speeches at the Oscars).

2001's *Fellowship* was nominated for 13 Oscars (including best film, director and screenplay), and won 4 (the expected technical categories, though Howard Shore was awarded for his score). *The Two Towers* was nominated for 5 Academy Awards and won two (visual fx and sound editing). But *The Return of the King* won 11 Oscars from 11 nominations, a 'clean sweep' as Steven Spielberg put it.

Andy Serkis was promoted by New Line Cinema as a possible Oscar contender, despite being a mainly digital character, at the time of *The Two Towers*. With the release of *The Return of the King*, Sean Astin was 'Oscar Boy for New Line' for a while (2004, 302).

The Lord of the Rings had its world premiere in London; the studio's spin on that was it was fitting to show *Rings* first in Britain, because that's where it was written. The premiere party had food comprising 'Barliman Butterbur's Famous Sausage and Mash' and 'Gandalf's Secret Recipe of Pan-fried Guinea Fowl'. The rooms were decorated as Rivendell and Lórien.

26 minutes of *The Fellowship of the Ring* was screened at Cannes on May 13, 2001, with 14 minutes of the mines of Moria sequence as the centrepiece. It was the first time that many of the production saw the film with visual effects and sound effects and music added. Again, the art department and marketing people put on a big display for the film and media crowd at Cannes, with Tolkien-themed areas, food, and PR material. (The 2003 party at Cannes cost $2.5 million).

New Line's Shaye, Lynne and Mittweg helped to chose the material for the Cannes showreel: Jackson and his editors had focussed on Moria, but Shaye wanted to reflect more of the rest of the first film and to give a taste of the following two films. The Cannes gig was vital for New Line: it was the first public showing of the film. As Shaye put it, he and Lynne were anxious and 'felt responsibile, not only to our own company but to the twenty different companies [investors and distributors] throughout the world that had risked more than they had ever risked for a motion picture' (Sib, 496). Rolf Mittweg, marketing head, said he probably wouldn't have shown the film at Cannes: it was a big gamble, but when it paid off, it did mean the end of the press muttering about 'New Line's Folly' (Sib, 497).[5]

Actor Viggo Mortensen made an interesting comment in one of the documentaries on the extended DVD of *The Fellowship of the Ring* (2002): that the heat being generated by the film (the amount of money the film was grossing in theatres, the awards and attention the film was receiving) was something like the ring, something seductive but evil. And all that buzz detracted from the creative work of the film itself.

NOTES: MARKETING AND PUBLICITY

1. C. Sylvester, ed. *The Penguin Book of Hollywood*, Penguin, London, 1999, 356.
2. D. Harris & A. Dawtrey, "Can B.O. Postman Ring Twice?", *Variety*, Nov 27, 2001.
3. In B. Hayward, *Haywire*, ICM, 1977.
4. "Hobbits Take Revenge On America", *Sunday Times*, July 1, 2001.
5. The International Lord of the Rings Research Project, based at University of Wales (at Aberystwyth), did a survey of the release and reception of *The Return of the King* in 20 countries. Many of the results were published in the book of essays edited by Ernest Mathijs (2006).

TOLKIEN MERCHANDIZING

Ronald Tolkien said that when *The Lord of the Rings* became successful, in the 1960s, he received all sorts of commercial offers – for *Lord of the Rings*™ puzzles, sculpted soap, puppetry rights, TV and film rights, and musical comedy rights (C. Plimmer, 1968). By the time of the release of the Hollyweird *Lord of the Rings*™ films, there had already been 35 or more years of Tolkien merchandizing.

New Line said in 2000 that they were releasing the merchandizing slowly, 'to build on the property slowly', as David Imhoff, New Line VP said.[1] No doubt New Line were acutely conscious of the costly over-hyping of *Star Wars: The Phantom Menace* and the over-production of merchandizing in the previous year.

Estimates have put the global merchandizing sales of the *Lord of the Rings©* films at $1-1.2 billion. New Line claimed that $2.5 billion had been generated by home entertainment releases and merchandizing.

Marvel's Toy Biz owned the 'master licence', producing up to 500 toys. Marvel's action figures were particularly popular. Up to 300 licensees were operating for the *Lord of the Rings*™ films, though the real number may have been lower than that.

Licensees included Burger King, JVC Electronics, Barnes & Noble, phone company Verizon, A & W, Cadbury, Bassett's Candy, National Geographic, France Telecom, Cheerios, Pringles, HP Baked Beans, and Air New Zealand. Telecom in New Zealand provided data, voice and video links for the production (enabling them to advertize their help with the show).

The internet was used to sell thousands of *Lord of the Rings*© items, at websites such as the Tolkien Enterprises™ website (tolkien-ent.com) and the Lord of the Rings Fanatics Shop (lotrfanshop.com). New Line sold its own line of merchandizing, at the New Line Cinema Store (newline.com and newlineshop.com).

Among the merchandizing produced for the *Lord of the Rings*™ 2001-03 films were posters. Not just one poster, but many, many *Lord of the Rings*™ posters (posters of individual characters – Frodo, Aragorn, Legolas – and a 'heroes door poster', Middle-earth maps, and one-sheet posters). Postcards of each character, reproductions of the map of Middle-earth in different colours on postcards. Planet Report and New Line sent out millions of *Lord of the Rings*™ bookmarks and posters to school children (26 million for *The Return of the King*™, distributed in the two weeks before release).

NOTES: TOLKIEN MERCHANDIZING

1. In T. Howard, "Now Playing At a Toy Store Near You", *USA Today*, Dec 8, 2003.

THE EXTENDED VERSIONS OF *THE LORD OF THE RINGS* FILMS

It's typical for Hollywood movies to exist in a number of versions. The theatrical cut, for instance, is not always the only version of the film released in cinemas. Sometimes changes are made for different territories. Even prior to the theatrical cut, there are versions previewed to test audiences, or studio heads, which can be different. Or special premieres, with different sound mixes. Then there are IMAX versions. On DVD and video and laser disc, films often differ again. Consumers know about theatrical studio cuts and 'director's cuts' ('director's cuts' are not always sanctioned by the director, or made by the director), but there can be further versions again. Foreign language and dubbed versions add to the confusion. Versions of the film shown on cable, pay-TV and satellite channels can differ too (often for censorship issues). For television, new versions are sometimes prepared (panned and scanned, for example, or with different soundtracks). Sometimes versions of the films have toned-down violence, sex or sensitive material (with different dialogue, say, for censorship reasons). Often versions of 'R' rated movies are re-cut for a 'PG' rating (*Saturday Night Fever* is a good example), with violence, sex and 'bad' language being excised. Finally, when TV stations broadcast films, they sometimes chose to edit films themselves, and cut out whole scenes or sections (sometimes to make them fit into time slots and advertizing schemes, sometimes to take out offending bits. *The Lost World* (*Jurassic Park 2*) has been broadcast in Britain at least twice with the waterfall scene missing, where a guy gets chomped by the T-rex). Many of these things will have occurred with the *Lord of the Rings* films.

When the Hollywood film of *The Fellowship of the Ring* was released in 2001, in amongst the slew of documentaries and puff pieces on *The Lord of the Rings* were extracts from the 1968 BBC documentary *Tolkien in Oxford*, which the old writer had not liked making at all. The BBC programme was bogus, 'gimmicky and nonsense', Tolkien complained, and tricked him into being portrayed as a 'fuddy not to say duddy old fireside hobbitlike boozer' (L, 389-390).

After its run in theatres, *The Lord of the Rings* was released in a number of formats. There was a home video and DVD of the film, and an 'extended version' of the film, released on DVD and video. The extended edition of *The Fellowship of the Ring* was packaged in a box that looked like a bookcase (it also came with book-ends), as if appropriating some of the olde worlde feel of dusty books and literature (even though the DVD format, like the digital technology used to make the film, was cutting edge, state of the art and very modern).

The *Special Extended DVD Edition* of *The Fellowship of the Ring* was issued in a box set of no less than 4 DVDs, two for the extended cut of the film itself, and two for all sorts of additional material: storyboards, pre-visualization animatics, costumes, production design, set tests, photo galleries of costumes and designs, a discussion of the adaption and screenplay, a biography of Tolkien, Weta Workshop, Weta Digital, shooting the miniatures, interviews with the cast and filmmakers, the digital grading process, post-production, sound design, the music, New Zealand as a location for Middle-earth, and an atlas of Middle-earth.

Like many DVDs of the time, some of these were conventional documentaries, some were more like short 'infotainment' pieces, some were lightweight celebrity clips, some were photo galleries, and the film itself had commentaries from the writers, producers, directors, actors and crew (the *Lord of the Rings* DVD documentaries were directed by Michael Pellerin, and by Costa Botes in the *Limited Edition* release). 113 of the 163 cast and crew who worked on *The Two Towers* were interviewed for the DVD version of the film.

The audio commentaries were easily the most interesting element in the DVD packages: Peter Jackson, Fran Walsh and Philippa Boyens provided the director's and writers' commentary; among production personnel, the art department and designers had their own commentary (including Grant Major, Dan Hennah, Alan Lee and John Howe); as did the visual effects, producers, DP and sound designers (including Barrie Osborne, Mark Ordesky, Howard Shore, Ethan van der Ryn, David Farmer, Jim Rygiel, and Rick Porras).

Some scenes in the extended DVD and video tape of *The Fellowship of the Ring* were enlarged, and some were new scenes (about six). Most of the additions did not add anything significant to the narrative, or introduce new characters, or plotlines, or themes. Most of the additions were expansions of existing scenes. As with most deletions which reappeared on video or DVD or in other formats of films in the global entertainment industry, it was easy to see why the scenes or additions had been cut out in the first place.

There were one or two new characters, however: the Gaffer in the *Green Dragon*, for instance. The Sam-Rosie romance was given a little more screen time (though hardly developed beyond a few looks and a little teasing dialogue between Frodo and Sam). There was more background information about hobbits and their society (in Bilbo's part of the prologue, "Concerning Hobbits"). There was a little more of Isildur, Gollum on the river, Elrond saying farewell, new scenes of the elves in Lórien (including Haldir), and more of Galadriel. Aragorn was seen singing (as were the hobbits in the *Green Dragon*).

Perhaps the biggest enlargements to characterizations were Bilbo and Aragorn: Bilbo played a bigger part in the extended cut. Many of the additions to the extended version of *The Fellowship of the Ring* concerned Aragorn, his back-story, his responsibilities, and his destiny. Aragorn's character now included more pining for Arwen, some singing, tending his mother's grave, and more people holding him to his responsibilities. Plotwise, Galadriel's gifts was a substantial addition, a scene which should have been in the theatrical release (partly because the gifts turn up later in the story).

The extended DVD version of *The Fellowship of the Ring* (released in 2002) was three hours and 13 minutes long (not including the credits, which wend on for a further 26 minutes! The theatrical cut was 2h45m to the end credits). So the *Special Extended Edition* is not a three and a half hour film, but three hours 13 minutes. The end credits on the extended cut of *The Two Towers* included hundreds of members of the Official *Lord of the Rings* Fan Club. They were listed in the credits to acknowledge their help in preparing the film (or perhaps to ensure further sales of the DVD and video: if those 100s of members got free copies of the film, there was always their friends and relatives). It was a bit like casting a theatre show with all your friends, to ensure you get an audience comprised of friends and relatives.

The extended versions of the *Lord of the Rings* films add much to the characters and situations of Éowyn, Faramir and Denethor, among others, and help to explain them. Without those extra scenes, the motivations and complexities in the theatrical versions seem vaguer and more confused.

The *Special Extended DVD Editions* of the *Lord of the Rings* films were shameless attempts to exploit two fanbases hungry for more: the Tolkien fans, and the fantasy and action-adventure film fans. The main selling point for the *Special Extended DVD Editions* was the extra footage that had been integrated into the film. The distributors – Entertainment in Video who released the DVDs in the U.K. and New Line Home Video – were keen to emphasize that each film had been 'reimagined' for the extended version DVD releases (i.e., that they weren't the usual DVD practice of releasing the film itself, plus some deleted scenes, plus interviews with cast and crew). *The Fellowship of the Ring*, for example, was substantially re-edited for the extended cut, rather than new scenes simply being inserted. This demanded new visual effects sequences, and all the rest of the post-production process, including music (Howard Shore wrote new music).

There is also an *Extra Special Extended Platinum Diamond Collector's Edition* of the movies, which runs to 450 hours. It's all of the rushes printed end-to-end, and is only available directly from www.satan.com. You have to give up your soul to buy it. Only the most diehard Tolkien fans have taken up the offer so far (but sales have run to 33,905 souls).

To counter charges of exploiting fans not once (the theatrical release) or twice (the home video and DVD of the theatrical version) but *thrice* (the DVD *Special Extended DVD Edition*), two discs of supplementary material were included. A lot of this stuff, though, was pretty bland and uninspired, and tended towards 'infotainment' television (and wasn't much different from the studio's publicity materials).

For Peter Jackson, the extended version on the DVD was an 'alternative' version of the film, but not necessarily the main version (Jackson said he disliked the idea of a 'director's cut' coming out after a film's theatrical release, because that would imply that the theatrical version wasn't the film the director and producers wanted in theatres; it debased the theatrical cut. In the case of the *Rings* films, the producers and studio were very happy with the cuts that were released theatrically). Jackson regarded the theatrical versions as 'the definitive versions. I regard the extended cuts as being a novelty for the fans that really want to see the extra material'.

For *Fellowship* editor John Gilbert, the extended edition was a chance to go back and tweak some scenes in the theatrical version, to add some of the scenes that had been cut for reasons of pacing, or narrative, or duplication of information. As Gilbert explained, the extended cut wasn't simply a matter of inserting deleted material in its already existing form. Howard Shore had to compose new cues and new music; actors had to add more dialogue; a few pick-up shots were filmed; and new visual effects shots had to be produced. Visual effects shots in the *Rings* movies amounted to 500 shots in *Fellowship*, 800 in *Towers* and 1,300 in *Return*.

The usual practice with deleted or additional scenes released for home entertainment was to put them after the main film, in a sequence (or on an additional DVD disc). Sometimes the deleted scenes would have a commentary or introduction from the writer, director or producers. Most often deleted scenes were short, small-scale and less costly than other, bigger scenes. Deleted scenes were seldom really big or expensive scenes (if they had been, it would suggest the filmmakers were pretty hopeless at planning the shoot). Occasionally, a big scene would be relegated to an additional or deleted scene status on a DVD or video. Deleted scenes tended to be about character, or details, or exposition, or bits of back-story. In short, information which had either been covered elsewhere in the picture, or was deemed unnecessary, or could confuse, or slowed up the pace.

The *Lord of the Rings* films were unusual because some of the deleted scenes were not part of the principal photography shoot, or part of pick-ups for the theatrical release, but were specially shot for the extended versions of the films (in between the theatrical release dates and the home entertainment release dates).

The DVD documentaries and commentaries went on and on about how wonderful the *Lord of the Rings* films were to make, how great everybody was to work with, how friendly they all were, how they all stayed friends afterwards, how brilliant Peter Jackson was, how true to the spirit of Tolkien the production tried to be, how everyone gave their best, how everybody worked beyond what was expected of them, etc.

What all this blather did was to try to create an aura of friendship, creativity and authenticity around the film production, which would reflect on the films themselves, so that the movies would be quests in themselves – the quests of the actors and the crew to make the films, even the quest of New Zealand itself to star in and help promote the pictures.

The DVDs were one of the more prominent elements in a brilliantly executed marketing campaign which wrapped up the *Lord of the Rings* films as this wonderful creative enterprise which took in the whole of New Zealand and everyone who lived there. The impression given was that the whole population was celebrating the fact that *The Lord of the Rings* was being produced in New Zealand (while forgetting that the money was coming from the U.S.A. and elsewhere, and that the production contained a large proportion of European and American talent).

Hardly anyone talked about money on the DVD commentaries, or whinges about the shooting conditions, or gripes about their agents, or about travelling, or about being separated from their families and friends. Hardly anybody talks about arguments (of which there are many on even the smallest films), or the crew threatening to walk out. No one mentions the hotels, the affairs, or the gossiping and bitching about other people. Listening to the commentaries and watching the documentaries of *The Lord of the Rings*, you'd think that professional filmmaking was a riot of jolly japes and childlike camaraderie. (Costa Botes said that New Line had edited his documentary, including cutting scenes where the cast/ crew swear. There's an argument between my friend Nick Korda (production manager) and Carolynne Cunningham (first A.D.), but the camera stays meekly around the corner, out of sight).

CHAPTER 12

RECIPE FOR A SWORD AND SORCERY MOVIE

In the last few days before *The Lord of the Rings: The Fellowship of the Ring* hit 10,000 screens worldwide on December 19, 2001, I made a list of some suggestions for the basic requirements of a fantasy/ sword-and-sorcery blockbuster movie (and most these duly turned up in *The Fellowship of the Ring*):

• Silly and unpronounceable names for people, creatures and places.
• Wacky costumes (fur, leather, chains). High fashion meets S/M by way of pantomime and Hallowe'en (and some of the *Lord of the Rings* costumes duly wound up as Hallowe'en and party costumes – with Legolas's wardrobe coming out the most popular). Designer Richard Taylor was adamant about *LOTR*: 'this was never going to be a *Conan the Barbarian*-style film', meaning the phony fantasy look (actually, the 1982 film of *Conan* has a great look, designed by Ron Cobb, including the $350,000 Thulsa Doom 'Temple of Set' set constructed on a mountain).
• Fairy tale wizards, princes, warriors, princesses.
• Cute animals.
• Cute li'l creatures (E.T.s, Ewoks, hobbits, Nelwyns, munchkins, dwarves).
• A range (and hierarchy) of creatures and beings (including the cute furry ones).
• Humorous sidekicks (the fat, lazy slob; the fussy, camp neurotic; the clumsy clown; the laconic beefcake).
• The useless wimp who accidentally discovers some wonderful talent (and helps to save the day).
• Fathers and sons (wise men and acolytes, martial arts teachers and novices, ageing kings and young, would-be warriors).
• Male-male bonding, the buddy formula, patriarchy in action (Frodo and Sam, Qui-Gon Jinn/ Anakin Skywalker and Obi-wan Kenobi, the white cop and the black cop, etc).
• Dumb dialogue (awkward, convoluted, obvious).
• Minimal (under-written) characterization.
• Men in fright wigs.
• Women with Pre-Raphaelite locks and long dresses (women as wise crones, or mothers, or helpers, or 'love interest' only). If they're lucky,

an actress may get to don the low-rent-Goth-meets-Jean-Paul-Gaultier costume to play a witch or sorceress.

- Actors practising their scowls, grimaces and – crucially – looks of awe and amazement to blue screens (film director yelling: 'now you see a really scary monster, Chuck, and it turns into a semi-naked vixen!').
- British/ European actors playing the villains.
- Hunky, macho warrior types (bare torsos; hours in the gym to get – and maintain – those abs).
- 'Magic' visualized with bluish streaks (*de rigeur* from *Star Wars* and *Raiders of the Lost Ark* onwards).
- A 'magical' transformation of a person or creature (usually live and on-screen).
- Sword fights (preferably with lots of jumping, swinging and stunts, *à la* Errol Flynn, ending with the hero nearly getting stabbed, until the villain trips and falls over the battlements).
- A magical sword (Excalibur, Narsil, Green Destiny, dad's lightsabre).
- Emphasis on weaponry (every hit and thud mixed very loud on the Dolby digital super surround sound soundtrack).
- A silly gadget or weapon or trick.
- Heroic acts (with maybe the worthy sacrifice of a sidekick or helper).
- The hero ought to have some amazing athletic skill: swooping martial arts (Jet Li, Jackie Chan, Stephen Chow), or a circus trapeze act (Burt Lancaster), or swordplay (Errol Flynn), or brute strength (Arnold Schwarzenegger and Vin Diesel).
- A big battle or three (one of them must show a small band of brothers winning against overwhelming odds).
- The hordes of baddies have to be both fearsome *and* hopelessly useless at fighting (orcs, stormtroopers, vampires, bugs). The goodies (even the tiny or weedy ones) must be able to dispatch them with a single sword or axe stroke.
- Someone has to swing on a rope, or a chandelier, or some rigging on a ship.
- A stuntman or woman has to fall into some water (a pool, a river, a moat or the sea). Some high falls are mandatory too (usually when shot with arrows or spears).
- Stunt people have to fall off horses, chariots or carriages when shot.
- A raid on a village, which's burnt (*Conan, The Vikings, Pathfinder, The Masque of the Red Death* – those shots of burning buildings in *Red Death* crop up in every Roger Corman film).
- Bustling towns, villages and markets (it's impossible to make a fantasy or mediæval or sword 'n' sorcery flick without at least one bustling village scene, usually in the first act).
- Thousands of extras (if you can't afford that many, use computer-generated people, which can turn out to be nearly as expensive – except they do act how you want them to, and you don't have to feed 'em, transport or house 'em, or clothe 'em).
- Secondary characters who wouldn't look out of place at Glastonbury

Festival, a Marilyn Manson concert, or a tattoo parlour.
- Horse rides in spectacular scenery (mountains, lakes, rivers, forests – cue the music!).
- Drinks round the camp fire (or a mead hall, or a tribal gathering).
- A camp of tents in a forest scene, or a caravaneserai in the desert among palm trees.
- Amazing sets (one of these *must* be a royal hall where the king/ queen/ emperor/ chief/ villain dwells).
- The climax of the film must take place on the biggest, most expensive set, which is then destroyed (there was always a lot more gunpowder, dynamite, gas jets and petrol than you realized in ancient castles, as well as wind machines, dry ice machines and smoke machines, and sometimes lasers and spotlights).
- Castles and towns are seen in the distance (models, mattes, CGI, or the real thing, if you can afford to go to Spain, Hungary, Wales, etc).
- There must a king, or queen, prince, or emperor, and a throne, and someone nasty plotting its overthrow.
- A banquet, dance or a tavern (a feast around a big table is essential – preferably with someone unexpected turning up, like Robin Hood).
- A joust (the hero's always in disguise, and wins, like in *Ivanhoe* or *A Knight's Tale*).
- There's always a scene in the lady's chamber, when she's alone in the evening, and the hero scales the walls. (The room always looks very comfy, well-lit, and vast, and not like a cold, drafty, dark castle. It recalls a mediæval-style bridal suite at a Las Vegas hotel).
- Long dark tunnels lit by perpetual torches (torches, always with the torches).
- Candles must be *everywhere*, on every surface (always with the candles).
- Caves, dungeons, arenas of death (there *must* be prop skeletons and skulls, rubbery cobwebs, dripping water, and some rats).
- A torture scene, and a weirdo met in the dungeons.
- A chasm or cliff (and someone has to jump or fall off it, as in *Jason and the Argonauts* and every fantasy film ever made).
- Gratuitous gore and blood.
- Storms, thunder and lightning.
- A snow, fire or rain scene (preferably all three).
- A few great monsters (if you can't get Ray Harryhausen, you make do with any of hundreds of visual fx wizards who can turn in *hommages* to the great man).
- Moments of gut-wrenching sentimentality and bathos.
- Unintentionally funny bits (you don't need to plan for these – they will occur spontaneously).
- Camp humour (ditto).
- A bourgeois, heterosexual romance (always adolescent, not mature, no matter what the age of the lovers).
- The villains meeting a juicy, inventive death.
- Big 19th century orchestral music with Wagnerian overtones (when

in doubt, raid Carl Orff's *Carmina Burana* for the *n*-th time, just like everyone else does).
- Maybe some New Age/ Celtic AOR warbly music (as in *Braveheart* or *Gladiator*).
- Quotes and references to other movies.
- Conservative, right-wing WASP, First World ideology (pro-war, pro-family, pro-establishment, pro-class, pro-élite, pro-Christian, etc).
- America vs. the rest of the world, followed by an affirmation of US new world order.
- Celtic, Dark Age, Western European culture and history.
- Raiding Western mythology (Homer, Norse saga, Arthurian legend, ancient Greece, Egypt, Rome, etc) via Joseph Campbell.
- Simplistic, Manichean morality – good vs. evil.
- Spiritual mumbo-jumbo (including a curse, prophecy or magical formula).
- An enchanted crystal or key or sword or spell or statue that'll impossibly save the world (well, I suppose a ring'll do).
- Total closure (of plot strands) at the end.
- Absolutely no ambiguity whatsoever.
- Happy ending (utterly essential – and it's built into the form from the beginning, as J.R.R. Tolkien recognized).

The Lord of the Rings films did of course contain nearly all of those ingredients (and went to town on some of them: the fright wigs, the Ray Harryhausen monsters, the CGI extras, the magical weapons, and the gore, for instance).

CHAPTER 13

THE FELLOWSHIP OF THE RING FILM (2001)

The Road goes ever on and on
    Down from the door where it began.
Now far ahead the Road has gone,
    And I must follow, if I can.
Pursuing it with weary feet,
    Until it joins some larger way,
Where many paths and errands meet,
    And whither then? I cannot say.

J.R.R. Tolkien, *The Fellowship of the Ring* (107)

When I first watched *The Lord of the Rings* part of me loved it, while the literary/ critical part (and Tolkien fan) was thinking, at various times: 'What?!... Eh?... But... No!.... You're kidding!... Come on!' I've since revised my view of New Line's movies, but it's still love/ hate (love/ dislike). Basically, the films could have been a lot worse, were a lot better than expected, and if they weren't so good they wouldn't be generating so much debate (or making so much money). Just think what could have happened: *Dune*... or *Excalibur*!... or – by Ilúvatar's halo! – *Battlefield Earth* (actually, each of those movies have their fans, and *Battlefield Earth* has some *astounding* visual effects, superior in many respects to the *Lord of the Rings* films. Unfortunately, there was so much wrong with the Ron Hubbard adaption).

The studio and the filmmakers clearly knew they couldn't win against the Tolkienites and hardcore fantasy fans, in terms of being 'faithful' to the 1954 book. It's impossible to second guess audiences, to know how they're going to react (and even delivering a film tailor-made to a specific segment of an audience is very tricky).

Whatever they were going to do, the filmmakers on *The Lord of the Rings* films would make certain they were going to produce entertaining movies that'd work on their own (i.e., that wouldn't require the audience to know the book), and launch a franchise. So they did – as an action-adventure flick, the *Lord of the Rings* films are terrific. I don't know if they're 'great' movies, like the films of Ingmar Bergman or Akira Kurosawa (but they're not meant to be that kind of great art), but they are certainly superb and very entertaining blockbuster movies.

POOR SCREENWRITER! The filmmakers of *The Lord of the Rings* rightly opted for a 'greatest hits' movie – they had to get the basics, the set-pieces, the action beats, in there at the very least (what Stanley Kubrick called 'unsubmersible units'). Incredibly daunting for a scriptwriter, though, is all the other stuff, the layers of *The Lord* which have been analyzed in terms of politics, religion, spirituality, ethnicity, industrialization, Christianity, 20th century ideology, war, the First World War, the Second World War, the Norman Conquest, mediæval history *et cetera*. Then there's all those layers of linguistics: the Germanic, Finnish, Icelandic, Anglo-Saxon and other Northern European texts and traditions, not to mention the influence of mediæval romances, British and European fantasy fiction, etc. Then there's the intricate geography of Middle-earth. The rhymes with the Christian calendar that Tolkien built into the book were another layer that the films did not take up. A host of places with tricky names. And the two most difficult elements: tons of story, and the huge number of characters (a massive problem in a 2-3 hour movie).

And there are further imposing elements to incorporate in the script: the vast histories and back-stories of characters, races, places (150 pages at the back of *The Lord of the Rings*, plus all the stuff in 'The Silmarillion' and various tales.) And those genealogies and family trees. Some of these histories have direct bearing on the plot and characters of *The Lord of the Rings*, but weaving them into the narrative of a movie which is supposed to zip along and not bore millions of viewers is very tricky (limiting them to brief flashbacks, or narrated resumés from characters – principally Gandalf – is about the most you can expect from a Hollywood blockbuster).

If the screenwriter isn't exhausted to the point of copious amounts of drugs, drinks, rehab or madness by squeezing in significant chunks of all of the above into the screenplay, not forgetting keeping up with all the usual stuff like characters, events, settings and plot, then what about the most difficult of all aspects of adapting *The Lord of the Rings*: what the hell is it about? Is it a parable of life? A *Bildungsroman*? An allegory of 20th century history? A linguist's reworking of pre-Norman European literature? A Christian (Catholic) epic? An anti-industrial treatise? The creation of a national 'British' myth or cycle?

DEATH AND IMMORTALITY. J.R.R. Tolkien said the real theme of *The Lord of the Rings* was *death* and *immortality* (not power and domination). War, power, dominion, Tolkien said, were the *settings*, the narrative drives to reveal the characters. The power and dominion plot 'only sets the wheels going', so that the real theme, of 'Death and the desire for deathlessness', can be explored (262). Tolkien wrote:

> The real theme for me is about something much more permanent and difficult: Death and Immortality: the mystery of the love of the world in the hearts of a race 'doomed' to leave and seemingly lose it: the anguish in the hearts of a race 'doomed' not to leave it until its whole evil-aroused story is complete. (*Letters*, 246)

The inevitability of death, the longing for immortality, runs deep in *The Lord of the Rings* (the lure of Valinor/ Paradise, the farewells and departures, the many deaths and mournings, the restless travelling, the immortal elves, and the movement from the age of the elves to that of man). Everyone seems to be about to lose something (the ring, power over others, their homeland, their friends, their sovereignty, their time, their epoch). But how to capture the abstractions of the theme of death and the desire for deathlessness in a 2-3 hour Hollywood blockbuster, to the extent, detail and seriousness that J.R.R. Tolkien demands?

ROUGH CUT. The first rough cut of *The Fellowship of the Ring* had come in at four and a half hours. That contained all of the material that the filmmakers wanted in the film. Everyone agreed that the film had to be cut down. Scenes were subsequently shortened, and others were dropped in the usual manner of editing but, as New Line Cinema's Mark Ordesky remarked, the trimming process wasn't entirely successful until an 'epiphanic' moment occurred, and the filmmakers realized that *The Fellowship of the Ring* was Frodo's movie: it was about Frodo carrying the ring to Mordor. Any scene that wasn't directly to do with Frodo and the ring was taken out (the film was meant to be 'Frodocentric'). Some scenes in which neither Frodo nor the ring appeared (such as Saruman and Gandalf) were retained, because they were crucial to the story. But others, such as Aragorn at his mother's memorial or Aragorn and Boromir discussing Gollum, were excised (the non-Frodo scenes appeared in the extended cut). Among the most significant casualties was Galadriel's gifts; and when the extended version of *The Fellowship of the Ring* was released, this was probably the most important re-instatement.

OMISSIONS. There are so many omissions it's impossible to list them all (I've had a go). As long as it's a good movie, though, it doesn't matter. A film isn't a book, as Orson Welles said. It's completely different. Trouble is, if you're not going to stick to the book, why bother? Why not write your own sword-and-sorcery epic?

Curiously, Bilbo is absent from the Council of Elrond scene – perhaps so that Frodo can stand up and declare he'll take the ring to Mordor. It's an omission you might not notice for a while, because there are so many characters in that scene. And Arwen has by then been established as a powerful elf who can take on all nine nazgûl, but she's also absent from the council.

In the film, Sam calls Frodo 'Mr Frodo', rather than 'Master'. Sam calling Frodo 'Master' would perhaps have dubious, ethnic connotations.[2] It would send the wrong messages about subservience: Sam isn't portrayed as a servant in the film, but Frodo is still his superior socially (the film implies that in many ways, including the difference in the hobbits' RP and regional English accents).

The Gaffer, one of the chief older hobbits, only makes an impression in the *Extended Editions* of the 2001-03 Tolkien films. Indeed, aside from the five hobbits – Bilbo Frodo, Sam, Merry and Pippin – very few hobbits have any significance in the films. Rosie Cotton, of course, but few others.

In the theatrical version, Proudfoot (Noel Appleby) is more prominent than the Gaffer or his cronies.

It's Alan Howard who is the 'voice' of the ring, whispering to characters; it's the same as the voice of Sauron. It does also suggest, though, that the ring has a life of its own, separate from its master. Ultimately, it's Sauron speaking through the ring. As Gandalf states, Sauron and the ring are one. Jim Smith and J. Clive Matthews suggest that the ring may even be more powerful than Sauron himself, that Sauron has become a slave to it, or that he has created something he can't control, and that the ring is ultimately the Lord of the Rings. No. That's not right – not in the 1950s books, nor in the 2001-03 films.

It's Gandalf who gets to say the title of the film (in the Isengard scene, where he escapes from Saruman), and he states, correctly, that there is only one lord of the ring/s, and he doesn't share power. The ring embodies Tolkien's concept of the 'Morgoth-ingredient', i.e., evil at work in the world. Remember that Tolkien called all of Middle-earth 'Morgoth's Ring'.

Peter Jackson later justified the decision to not even shoot the Tom Bombadil and Old Man Willow scenes in the same terms as were used to make the final edit on *The Fellowship of the Ring*: that the movie had to be about Frodo and the ring, and anything that wasn't tied in to that overriding narrative line was dropped. For Jackson, the Bombadil and Old Man Willow scenes didn't add much about Frodo and the ring (even though there was ring material in those chapters); plus they slowed the movie up too much. New Line's proviso to editor John Gilbert was to edit *The Fellowship of the Ring* as a rollercoaster of a movie. Hence, the *Lord of the Rings* films were never going to contain many layers of Tolkien's masterpiece, such as the nature mysticism, or the delight in invented languages, or the songs, or the detailed accounts of the different cultures of Middle-earth, or the metaphysical exploration of the theme of death, or the theological and philosophical comparisons between the two related 'dooms' of death and immortality. Fran Walsh acknowledged that the films could never replace the book, or offer the same experience as reading the book.

ARAGORN. The Aragorn in the films is *much* more troubled, reluctant, doubtful, less obviously 'noble' and less prone to speak in a high and mighty tone (and thus also less patronizing). In the 1954 book, Aragorn is proud to be the heir of Gondor; in the film, he's very ambiguous about his inheritance, sometimes treating it as Frodo does the ring, and wishing it had never befallen him. When Legolas tells Boromir that Aragorn is Isildur's heir, Aragorn seems almost embarrassed.

In the films, it's suggested that the line of kings was broken when Isildur died, and his death was of course partly engineered by the ring. So that's another link between Aragorn and the ring. A few characters refer to Aragorn as 'Isildur's heir' (Elrond, Arwen, Boromir), hinting that he may have the same weakness that defeated Isildur. Part of Aragorn's reluctance to embrace his destiny as the king of Gondor is thus aligned with the ring: he thinks he might have inherited the same weakness. That's a negative way of justifying his own reluctance to act, but the reluctant hero is a staple of Hollywood movies. Philippa Boyens and Fran Walsh have simply pushed it much further than usual (in your standard Hollywood flick, the hero isn't still reluctant halfway through – he's accepted his journey by then. Otherwise a film becomes a series of nagging scenes).

The films suggest that both Théoden and Aragorn have longer journeys to endure before they become true kings, and are recognized as such by their people. They have to earn and be worthy of their leadership and royalty; it isn't a given, a product of heredity. In the film, Théoden is king, and his people kneel before him after his rebirth, but he's not the fearless leader needed in the War of the Ring; he has to grow into that role. Similarly, Aragorn doesn't come out all guns blazing as a noble, heroic, strong, confident leader. He takes over the leadership of the hobbits' fellowship swiftly, protecting them from the Black Riders at Bree and later at Weathertop. But when they reach Rivendell, Aragorn is riven by doubts again (expressed in his conversation with Arwen in front of the shards of Narsil). The notion of the 'weakness' of Númenor flowing in Aragorn's blood is *completely foreign* to Tolkien's conception of Aragorn, who's always proud of his lineage in the book.

ROMANCES. There are only three romances of any significance in *The Lord of the Rings*, the novel: Sam-Rosie, Aragorn-Arwen (which takes place in the appendices) and Éowyn-Faramir (with Arwen-Aragorn-Éowyn as a potential love triangle that comes to nothing). Those romances tend to occur in the background, or are summarized by Tolkien's narrator. The only romances that occur in the foreground in the book are the unrequited desire of Éowyn for Aragorn, and Éowyn and Faramir.

The movies concentrate on Aragorn as a romantic hero, turning his romance with Arwen into a minor sub-plot. In the extended version of *The Fellowship of the Ring*, Aragorn is the only character who gets involved with women: he has two farewells with two elven women as he leaves their elven kingdoms: Arwen at Rivendell and Galadriel at Lórien.

Liv Tyler and Viggo Mortensen asked for more lines in Elvish, and conducted some of their love scenes in Elvish, with subtitles. Tyler dropped her voice as low as possible, and spoke softly. (Lines were translated into the various forms of Elvish by David Salo).

LEGOLAS. The elf with much the most screen time was Legolas, played by an actor, Orlando Bloom, with (at the time) far less acting experience than the other elves (Blanchett, Weaving, Tyler, etc), and in his films since then, Bloom still for me has poor acting skills and the charisma of a cardboard box.

Legolas's costume and hair and make-up went through many iterations before it was finalized (and was being refined throughout shooting). As Legolas was a woodland elf, browns and green were obvious choices for his costume. Legolas's look also included a very long blond hair-piece, with other hair attachments. Legolas's signature prop was his bow, arrow and quiver (he also carried a pair of knives and a sword). He was shown as a deadly shot with his arrows (he never seemed to miss), and could also fire faster than anyone else (best displayed at Parth Galen). (Legolas's arrows were digital because the filmmakers wanted the elf to fire off arrows very rapidly.) He was basically Robin Hood with supernatural senses. Legolas was portrayed as warrior elf, always ready for battle, always the first to draw his bow, always at the front of a group, looking for the enemy with his far-seeing eyes (he also seemed to be able to sense the enemy before seeing them).

Legolas was also the most acrobatic character in the films: snowboarding down stairs while firing his bow at Helm's Deep, leaping onto a horse, walking across snow without sinking, and his set-piece at Pelennor Fields: the single-handed attack on a *mûmakil* and all its occupants. (This had been added by the filmmakers partly because the audience's reaction to Legolas leaping onto a horse during the warg attack had been so positive. The horse jump was what Bloom called 'a Leggy moment'. Ironically, that had come about because Bloom had broken one of his ribs early in the shooting of the warg sequence and was unable to complete the scene. As animator Randy Cook put it, halfway through a shot, Legolas turns into a bunch of pixels, in daylight, in a full body shot. It's a shot that occurs in loads of Hong Kong martial arts movies, though achieved practically not digitally).

GALADRIEL. Galadriel's costume consisted of white, diaphanous beaded dresses in mediæval cuts, and long curly blonde tresses. Like all the elves, she wore pointy ears (made from gelatin). She was shot with haze filters and *tons* of backlighting. (DP Andrew Lesnie created a special 'Galadriel light' rig with his gaffer, Brian Bansgrove – a cluster of lights that would reflect in Cate Blanchett's eyes, to recreate Tolkien's description of Galadriel's eyes having stars in them: Galadriel and Celeborn are described as having eyes 'keen as lances in the starlight, and yet profound, the wells of deep memory').

All of the elves were cast tall, over 6ft if possible, and Blanchett said she wore glam rock platform boots to make her taller. The movements of the elves were graceful and balletic, and Blanchett's Galadriel glided rather than walked. Make-up on Galadriel was kept very pale, with almost no colour in the lips and cheeks (and with those sharp cheekbones, she could've taken someone's eye out).

In the film the elves are played by tall, white androgynous looking actors in long blonde wigs. They resemble white, Nordic, Northern Europeans (and for Tolkien's detractors, they have Aryan, racist overtones).

The voices of the elves were modelled in a slow version of English received pronunciation (with Blanchett slowing her delivery down to a portentous pace, as well as lowering her voice a few tones). Another technique with dialogue was having Galadriel communicate with Frodo telepathically, in voiceover, so that in the mirror of Galadriel scene they look at each other, mouths not moving, but speaking in narration. (The spiritual link between Frodo and Galadriel was established as soon as the fellowship entered Lothlórien, with Frodo appearing to hear Galadriel in his head, and being startled by a big close-up of Galadriel's eyes, as if she's entering his consciousness as abruptly and unexpectedly as Sauron's Eye). Galadriel had been seen briefly in the prologue, holding up one of the three elven rings; she had also narrated the prologue. Only when she's met at Caras Galadon does the viewer link her voice with her face. Later, in

Shelob's lair, Galadriel will perform her role as intercessor in the Virgin Mary mode when she helps Frodo up when he falls to the ground, and provides the star glass which helps Sam defeat the monster.

Galadriel's big scene in the *Lord of the Rings* pictures was the mirror of Galadriel (played with Frodo alone, without Sam). A nighttime scene, the palette limited to blue, silver, green and white, with plenty of glowing lighting around the elf-queen. Blanchett played the other-worldly, solemn character of Galadriel to the hilt.

ARWEN. Arwen's able to stand up against nine Black Riders on her own, out-run them in a lengthy chase, heal Frodo, and summon up a magical flood. Messianic overtones colour the scenes where Arwen tends Frodo: she appears like an angel, in over-the-top white light, accompanied by a choir (there was a good technical reason for this addition of white light, because the stunt woman, Jane Abbott, standing in for Liv Tyler, was wearing the wrong costume, so the effects team loaded the shot with radiance to distract from the mistake. Tyler was nervous of horses, particularly riding a horse into a crowded studio, so the stunt rider took over).

Arwen appears to Frodo first in a white dress, like an angel. When the viewpoint shifts to Aragorn and the hobbits looking at her, she's clad in her green and brown elf huntress garb. At the ford, Arwen performs Christ-like healing, clutching the ailing Frodo to her breast and hoping that some of her 'grace' will heal him. (The films depict the elves as ethereal, rarefied figures, and also saintly, drawing on the tropes of religious movies).

It turned out that the actress cast as Arwen, Liv Tyler, wasn't comfortable with the physical aspects of the new conception of Arwen's character as warrior princess. That only came out during production. Arwen's character might've played out differently in the final cuts of the *Rings* films had the actor playing Arwen been an accomplished sword fighter and action heroine (like, say, the wonderful Michelle Yeoh).

Arwen could've been made to look like an all-around action expert, of course, with stunt doubles and careful editing: a film like *Hero* (2002) turned Maggie Cheung, no martial arts star, into a tornado of quickfire moves. Similarly, the fabulous Brigitte Lin in the marvellous *Bride With the White Hair* and *Swordsman*, two Hong Kong action movies, isn't an action heroine, but she became one.

Tolkien himself said the Arwen-Aragorn romance was the most important of the appendices, and it would have been a part of the main text of *The Lord of the Rings*, but

> it could not be worked into the main narrative without destroying its structure: which is planned to be 'hobbito-centric', that is, primarily a study of the ennoblement (or sanctification) of the humble. (L, 237)

THE PROLOGUE. The prologue to 2001's *The Fellowship of the Ring* was added very late in the production schedule (both the 1978 UA film and the 1981 BBC radio series had included a prologue). For the writers, it had been very difficult to convey a lot of information in a short time, so it was in and out of the screenplay at various times. It had been shot, but was left out of the final cut. New Line, however, wanted a prologue to set the story up, and the filmmakers struggled with the studio over the prologue. It was edited in London, where the scoring sessions were held at Abbey Road, on an Avid machine set up in a side room.

Originally, the film was going to open with Bilbo in his study at Bag End, narrating an introduction to hobbits and the Shire, just before his birthday party. As it turned out, the prologue was one of the masterstrokes of *The Fellowship of the Ring*, an exhilarating introduction to the scale of the War of the Ring. For director Peter Jackson, the prologue to *The Lord of the Rings* functioned like the teaser in a *James Bond* movie, which was always a big budget action sequence. It introduced the audience to the fantasy world of the film, and pulled viewers away from their everyday world; it also offered an idea of the scale of the show, and what was at stake.

Thus, although one of the goals of the prologue was to show the smaller scale story of how the ring passed from Isildur to Sméagol to Bilbo, the key element was the Last Alliance battle on the slopes of Mount Doom, with thousands of elves and men pitted against thousands of orcs. The other important story point was to introduce Sauron early on, to show how powerful he was, and how he was diminished when the ring was cut from his finger. (Further story points included the sword Narsil, how the ring betrayed Isildur, by slipping off his finger. The film states clearly that the ring 'betrayed' Isildur, and sort of knew what it was doing when it slipped from his finger, so the orcs could see the man and kill him with arrows. If the ring's that clever, it might've slipped off Isildur's finger earlier, dropping onto the ground, and allowing the orcs to find it, so it would've got back to Sauron).

In the film's prologue, it's suggested that Sauron made all of the rings of power, and gave them out to elves, dwarves and men in order to corrupt them; in the book, Sauron makes only the one, ruling ring. That's always been a little confused in Tolkien's writing. (The writers were worried about confusing people with a barrage of strange names in the prologue, and that they might alienate viewers for the rest of the film [Sib, 344]).

The scene where Elrond and Isildur are at the Crack of Doom isn't in the book; the reader knows that Isildur was advised to destroy the ring, and that only a few of the nobles were present to see him to take it and keep it. The book's a little more ambiguous about Isildur and the ring, but Elrond says it led him to his death. In the film, this's illustrated by Isildur being attacked by orcs and escaping to the river, where's he's shot and loses the ring.

When Sauron appeared in warrior form in the prologue, some Tolkien fans were worried that he might return in that form later on in the following two films. It might have been tempting to have Sauron appear in the flesh at the Battle of Pelennor – the audience had already seen Sauron in military mode in *Fellowship*'s prologue. But the filmmakers resisted it (instead, Sauron appearing at the Morannon was filmed, but not included).

Without the prologue, *The Lord* would have cut to the 'story' quicker, introducing three key characters in rapid succession: Bilbo, a brief section 'concerning hobbits', then Frodo and Gandalf. The exposition of the prologue, about the history of the ring, would have been included (pretty much as it is anyway) in the scenes of Frodo and Gandalf in Bag End. The scale of the film would thus have been built up gradually, but with the prologue, the film achieves an 'epic' scale very early, with the battle scenes.

New Line Cinema wanted a prologue at the front of *The Two Towers*, as a recap for the theatrical audiences who would have seen the first film a year ago. The filmmakers resisted, preferring to cut straight to the stand-off between Gandalf and the balrog. They felt that would be sufficient to remind viewers of what happened in *The Fellowship of the Ring,* to re-introduce viewers to the world of Middle-earth.

The balrog fight was also, of course, a large-scale action sequence, giving the film a suitably high voltage opening. Although New Line insisted on a prologue, this was inserted instead into the middle of the film, following another of the scenes between Arwen and Aragorn. This bit of exposition occurred between Elrond and Galadriel, who seemed to be having some kind of telepathic conversation (scenes with Elrond visiting Lothlórien had been shot but discarded). Instead, Galadriel is seen talking to the camera in mid-shot (as if from Elrond's p.o.v.), while Elrond gazes anxiously out of a window at Rivendell.

The prologue/ exposition continues with Galadriel speaking in voice-over over images of the key locations and characters of Middle-earth (Barad-dûr, Isengard, Saruman, the Uruk-hai army, etc). Galadriel is on screen for brief moments (some four or so shots), but she reprises her role as one of the God-like narrators of the events in the films. It was a scene that came together in the editing of the film, being largely a series of images, scenes and characters linked by Galadriel's voiceover.

The same thing happened late in the editing with Sam's narration of the climaxes of *The Two Towers*. In this case, the ending of *The Two Towers* was arrived at very close to the deadline (endings are often a problem for any film, but especially one in the middle of a three film set). In the script, *The Two Towers* was going to close with a lengthy dialogue scene as Gandalf, Théoden, Éomer and others ride to Isengard and meet Merry, Pippin, Treebeard and Saruman. The filmmakers found that the scene was too long or too slow or too talky after the excitement and spectacle of the intercut battles at Helm's Deep and Isengard, and the nazgûl attack at Osgiliath. In one of the first cuts of *The Two Towers*, Sam standing at the window watching the fell-beast depart had been a short scene, without voiceover. Philippa Boyens related how she and Walsh had written themselves into a corner, reaching a dead-end with Sam talking about the people struggling on in stories and Frodo's retort 'what are we fighting for?' Boyens suggested that Sam say something along the lines of 'that there is some good in the world worth fighting for'. Thus was inaugurated Sam's narration of the final scenes of *The Two Towers*, over images of Gandalf, Théoden and Aragorn fighting at Helm's Deep, and the ents flooding Isengard.

Unfortunately, it didn't work, partly because the writing was execrable, partly because Sean Astin's performance was cheesy and unconvincing, and partly because the sentiments were so bathetic and awkwardly expressed ('that there's some good in the world, and it's worth fighting for'). Nothing wrong with deep emotion, with searing drama, with great speeches of hopes and dreams, with uplifting outbursts of idealism, but the filmmakers, the scriptwriters and the actors were not up to this big moment. This was where one really does need a writer of the calibre of William Shakespeare, and an actor as good as, say, Paul Scofield to bring if off.

THE VILLAINS. I always imagined the Eye of Sauron as some brooding, fiery presence *inside* a vast black hall at the top of Barad-dûr, staring out of a huge slit in a stone wall (rather than *on* the tower). The force of its deadly stare would be derived partly because it was glimpsed through a slit, not seen whole and naked. In the 2000s films, the Eye had to work quickly and memorably as a visual device, so placing it atop the Dark Tower, between two horns, makes it an easily recognizable image, which would work well in big long shots as well as close-up (and the Eye supported by two horns suggested some kind of electrical field, some kind of electromagnetic support for Sauron's spirit, which's a familiar movie conception. And twin horns suggest the Satan, too). (I'm not sure if the Lidless Eye being so exposed on top of Barad-dûr fits in exactly with Tolkien's conception of Sauron and Mordor: presumably the Eye would see everything going on in the Black Land, but also every orc and troll and minion could see it too. Sauron at Lugbúrz would be a gigantic Camera, a Voyeur, the ultimate surveillance and control system where everyone would feel 'naked in the dark' as Frodo described it).

It's curious how Tolkien and the films talk about the nazgûl being 'disguised' as Black Riders. Yep, that 'disguise' of scary dudes in black really makes 'em fade into the background of Middle-earth! Wouldn't it be better to do a Ulysses, when he returns home and comes in as a weedy old man no one would glance at twice? What was Sauron thinking when he bought his boys those heavy black robes, spiky gauntlets, and Hallowe'en costume hoods?

NOTES: *THE FELLOWSHIP OF THE RING* FILM

1. R. Wood, 174.
2. J. Smith, 2004, 165.

CHAPTER 14

THE FELLOWSHIP OF THE RING, SCENE BY SCENE

PROLOGUE AND ACT ONE

In these scene-by-scene explorations of the 2001-03 *Lord of the Rings* films, I'll be using the theatrical term 'acts', as it's a convention. Really, as many commentators have argued, cinema isn't the same as theatre and doesn't have 'acts' (or even scenes) quite the same as theatre. Also, instead of the more usual 30-40 minutes 'acts' of film criticism, I am employing the approach of Kristin Thompson, developed in her excellent book *Storytelling In the New Hollywood* (1999), which uses 25-30 minute acts or sections in movies.

    The prologue of *The Lord of the Rings: The Fellowship of the Ring: The Motion Picture* is narrated by Galadriel: she is not properly introduced on screen until Lothlórien, and appears only very briefly in the rest of the films (Cate Blanchett was on the *Lord of the Rings* films for three weeks). The choice of Galadriel as narrator is curious: Gandalf would be the obvious one, and Frodo next (both had been scripted as the narrators, and some recording had been done). Elrond or Bilbo or even Sam or Aragorn might be next in line, before you reach Galadriel (both Bilbo and Sam are, like Frodo, chroniclers and narrators of the War of the Ring). Choosing Galadriel might be partly to do with bumping up the female input in a heavily masculine movie, or wanting to use Cate Blanchett's voice (a reason scriptwriter Philippa Boyens referred to). So Blanchett performs the function here rather like, say, Orson Welles or Charlton Heston in historical epics of the 1950s and 1960s: a grave, authoritative voice to introduce the world of the films and provide some back-story.

    The narration employs bits of Tolkien's dialogue and prose from different characters, which's rewritten. The opening phrases, for instance, come from Treebeard at the end of the book, when he parts from Galadriel and Celeborn: '"the world is changing. I feel it in the water, I feel it in the earth, and I smell it in the air"' (RK, 314-5).

    Note that the voiceover also features Cate Blanchett's voice speaking in Elvish, quieter in the mix; it's a curious effect, as if Galadriel is really addressing the viewer in Elvish, but is being translated into English, rather like those documentaries and news bulletins which employ voiceover artists instead of subtitles for interviewees. There might have been a decision to have Galadriel speak in Elvish here, with English in some subtitles, as in some parts of the rest of the films. Either way, there's Elvish and English. And there's a soft but atmospheric choral cue from Howard Shore: in this film, Galadriel will ever be accompanied by singing choirs, as if she's the Virgin Mary. Indeed, the film employs all of the cinematic language used for saints, gods and messiahs for Galadriel (and for the resurrected Gandalf): white costumes, bright light, backlighting, choirs, slow motion, awed reaction shots, etc.

The prologue concentrates mainly on the history of the ring, and depicts, in a rapid montage (with much sombre fading in and out of black), Sauron at the Crack of Doom wielding the ring, the ringbearers of the lesser rings (men, dwarves, elves), and culminates in the big CG images of the Last Alliance below Mount Doom, introducing characters such as Elrond (Hugo Weaving), Isildur (Harry Sinclair), Elendil (Peter McKenzie) and Gil-galad (Mark Ferguson) (Elrond, fittingly, is the first person to speak in the film, issuing commands in Elvish). In his 1954 book, Tolkien wrote:

> Thereupon Elrond paused a while and sighed. "I remember well the splendour of their banners," he said. "It recalled to me the glory of the Elder Days and the hosts of Beleriand, so many great princes and captains were assembled." (FR, 318)

The battle itself, while impressive (it's the first glimpse of the Massive computer technology, which I still think makes the tiny figures look like the creatures in a computer game), isn't as important as the plot point that the ring is very powerful, that Sauron appears to be destroyed when it's cut from his hand, and that Isildur picks it up (there are little details, too, like the black powdery ash of Sauron's finger which Isildur crushes, or the way the ring shrinks in the second flashback, when Gandalf's at Minas Tirith, and the fiery writing fades).

The prologue could continue with Elrond encouraging Isildur to destroy the ring inside Mount Doom, but that scene was inserted as a flashback in the Rivendell scenes, or more of how Gollum found the ring (that became the prologue of *The Return of the King*). (The battle had been included late in production, blocked out on a clay model with a lipstick camera, and shot from that and storyboards).

The prologue also allows the filmmakers to depict Sauron as something like a real person. His face isn't shown (but that's a classic movie villain device, and anyway, what would Sauron look like? Tolkien is vague on that point), but it does offer a chance to show the Dark Lord in full effect, as a superhuman warrior (pure comicbook, superhero imagery, with Sauron wielding the mace like a video game weapon – *'PRESS <A> FOR EXTRA MACE POWER'*). (There's no satisfying account in Tolkien's tome or the films of how Sauron went from being a man to a giant eye. Gandalf mentions it, but I bet a few movie-goers seeing *The Fellowship of the Ring* without knowing the book were a little confused about who the true villain of the films was. Somehow, a giant eye just doesn't seem as fearsome as a ten foot soldier in cool armour with a mace. What's a giant eye going to do

– stare you to death?).

Continuing in the fragmentary fashion of this very satisfying montage, which is dense with visual and verbal information, the viewer learns that the ring was lost in a river when Isildur was ambushed (the extended cut adds a few more shots here), and was later found by someone very unexpected. Gollum's introduced very briefly, holding the ring (in a real hand) and murmuring 'my precious' over it, on his rock.

The prologue continues with a very brief description of Bilbo finding the ring (with Ian Holm made over to look a little younger – thirty years for Holm, sixty years for Bilbo). Along the way are glimpses of Middle-earth – the rivers and mountains (the helicopter shots of mountains will be revisited numerous times in the three films). By the time the prologue reaches Bilbo, it has come close to the time frame of the rest of the film (this last part of the prologue takes its cue from the prologue published in the book, the pages entitled "Of the Finding of the Ring").

At this point, on the basis of the prologue montage, *The Lord of the Rings* looks to be a classy movie: confident, slick, with lovely visuals and an antique look, and fairly true to Tolkien's treasured book. It's all classic stuff from the sacred texts, *The Hobbit* and *The Lord of the Rings*: the elves, dwarves and men with their rings, the Last Alliance battle, Elrond and Isildur, Sauron and the ring, Gollum on his rock by the underground lake, and Bilbo finding the ring.

I say it's 'true' to the book, but it isn't, of course. *The Lord of the Rings* does open with a prologue (which follows the short, somewhat spiky foreword, with its famous assertion that *The Lord of the Rings* is *not* an allegory, thank you very much), but it concerns the events surrounding the ring from *The Hobbit* onwards (TA 2941), not the grander events going back to the Last Alliance at the end of the Second Age, or the forging of the ring (the opening shots of the whole film trilogy), in c. SA 1600 (this is as far back as the films go, in terms of memories, dreams, flashbacks and the like, and it's absolutely apt that the birth of the ring should be the oldest moment depicted in the films, chronologically, and the first couple of shots. To be *really* picky, there are (verbal) references to older events, like Beren and Lúthien, for instance, and of course Treebeard is one of the oldest living things).

The extended cut of *The Fellowship of the Ring* moves into Bag End from the end of the prologue (using the lead-in of tilting up from a map of Middle-earth), and introduces Bilbo fully: it's a very Tolkienesque moment: Bilbo is in his study, writing, surrounded by piles of books and papers, with an open fire blazing (in keeping with the rest of the Hobbiton scenes, it's a peaceful, sunny day. It doesn't rain in the Shire – that starts at Bree). It could be an idealized view of a cosy Oxford study, or a room prepared for a meeting of the Inklings.

The film mines J.R.R. Tolkien's prologue to *The Lord of the Rings*, with a sequence loosely based on the "Concerning Hobbits" section of the prologue: it's still in a montage style, with Bilbo narrating over *tableaux* of hobbits in the Hobbiton (basically sunny, pastoral images of hobbits at work and play). According to Barrie Osborne, the film was going to open at one time with Bilbo's own form of a prologue, before moving on to the arrival of Gandalf. The scenes with Bilbo were shot later, with Ian Holm being brought back to New Zealand. Producer Mark Ordesky said that New Line Cinema preferred to have just one prologue, and felt that Bilbo's narrated prologue following the other prologue was too much (for audiences), and it was better to get into the story. So that was one reason why the "Concerning Hobbits" section was dropped (and not inserted elsewhere: it's tricky going into a narrated montage then back out to regular continuity editing. Filmmakers like Orson Welles or Martin Scorsese are geniuses at it).

The extended cut of *Fellowship* has Gandalf coming to Bag End to see Bilbo, as in the book, but the theatrical version segues from the prologue to Frodo in the woods (a scene added later). In the cinema version of *The Fellowship of the Ring*, Frodo is introduced reading a book, propped up against a tree, when he hears Gandalf singing in the distance. Here's where the film departs dramatically from the book: the hero has been cast as way too young; he's portrayed practically a child, a teenager who must be protected by the rest of the fellowship on their journey (the film feminizes Frodo as well as makes him much younger, and the fellowship treat him at times like a young woman). Elijah Wood, who could've been aged up a decade or so with make-up and other devices, plays Frodo as very young (in fact, Wood plays Frodo pretty much as the age he was at the time of the first weeks of shooting in October, 1999 – 18).

But this is nothing to do with Elijah Wood – it's the decision made by the producers (and the studio and others) to cast their hero many years younger than the book (they wanted a star: they got one). In the book, Frodo's 50 when Gandalf visits Hobbiton in TA 3018 (actually, Gandalf first visits the hobbits in TA 3001, for Bilbo's farewell party, but because the film effectively elides those years, the film really starts in TA 3018).

Don't forget, too, that Frodo has the ring:

> As time went on, people began to notice that Frodo also showed signs of good 'preservation': outwardly he retained the appearance of a robust and energetic hobbit just out of his tweens. 'Some folk have all the luck,' they said; but it was not until Frodo approached the usually more sober age of fifty that they began to think it queer. (FR, 67)

In the book, Frodo has already been using the ring from time to time (he puts it on at Tom Bombadil's, for instance). He's not yet feeling 'stretched' or 'thin' like Bilbo, but he is heading that way. In the film, there's no suggestion that Frodo ever put on the ring until Bree, which makes that moment so much more dramatic. So dramatic, in fact, that Sauron himself appears to Frodo in the *Prancing Pony* (the first time the viewer sees that the guy in the cool armour in the prologue has become a thirty foot-wide eye).

The opening Hobbiton scenes of *The Fellowship of the Ring* show Gandalf arriving by horse and cart and Frodo encountering him in a country lane somewhere near Hobbiton (Frodo is introduced the same way in both cuts of *The Fellowship of the Ring*). The first couple of shots portray Gandalf on a cart in a lane, sunlight shining through the trees, and heard humming 'the road goes ever on'.

It's a critical scene: it introduces two of the four most important characters, and the chief hero of the films. Not only that, it introduces the two top-billed stars of the three films. Among the rules of Hollywood scriptwriting are: introduce your money (your stars) early on, give them a good entrance, and make sure the introductions say a lot about their personality (are they are happy, sad, angry, bored, on their own or with people, what are they doing, what are their goals?, and so on). In a way, it's one of the scenes (like the following party scene) which will always be nostalgically evoked by the hobbits during the rest of the films (and it shows that Frodo has known and been friendly with the wizard for some time). It's a scene before the story has really started, before the characters are changed by all those amazing events. The scene is played out in a relaxed, friendly manner (Frodo even leaps at Gandalf for a big hug, like a child rather than a 33 or 50 year-old) in a pastoral, sunlit setting (only the sound of birds, the creaking of the cart wheels, the jangle of the bridle, Gandalf's mumbled song – no wind, or rain, or ominous sounds which dominate the rest of the films). And Frodo is in causal (though smart) clothes, a mid-green shirt and dark green pants. The scene could easily be out of a fairy tale:

Once upon a time there was a hobbit. One sunny day he met a wizard in the woods.

It was decided by the filmmakers that *The Fellowship of the Ring* would be 'Frodo's story', so he had to be established very early on. In the book, Gandalf is visiting Bilbo; the film does the same thing: Gandalf is on his way to Bag End. But he meets Frodo along the way. It sounds simple and obvious, how Gandalf just happens to encounter Frodo, but it's vital. Without that scene, Frodo might have been introduced later, during the party scene, say, where he would have been one amongst hundreds of hobbits. Having Frodo and Gandalf meet alone neatly separates them from the rest of the hobbits, gives their meeting more impact (no other actors or characters to contend with), and identifies Frodo as the premier hobbit in the three films. Frodo should be the first hobbit encountered after the prologue, and in the theatrical version of *The Fellowship of the Ring* he is (very Tolkienesque imagery: the book, the tree, the forest).

When Frodo's first seen, he's reading a book: he's the aristocratic man of leisure (characters such as Gandalf will be shown with books, as well as Aragorn at Rivendell, and Bilbo). The book emphasizes Frodo's intellectual, upper-class origins and lifestyle far more than the film does. The screenwriters said they didn't want to make Frodo appear too much of a higher class character – especially in relation to Sam. They dropped Sam using the term 'Master' for instance, and downplayed the master-servant relation. Sometimes Sam's relationship to Frodo, especially in the later part of the films, resembles a parental one – making sure his friend has been eating, and sleeping, and resting, and so on. The more humorous elements of Sam's character were toned down for the films. (In the extended cut,

Sam is first seen tending a plant: he's a worker, a gardener, though Sean Astin's wide-eyed gawp makes Sam look as if he's never seen a plant before).

Notice that Frodo is introduced alone, not with Sam, not with Merry or Pippin, not in the inn, drinking and, God forbid!, not with a female hobbit (if this was a Michael Bay or Jerry Bruckheimer movie, Frodo might be smooching a cute hobbit babe). Frodo's solitariness in the woods fits in with Tolkien's characterization of Frodo as something of a social outsider, someone, like Bilbo, who doesn't quite fit in (at first, Frodo is basically a younger Bilbo for Tolkien).

Frodo and Gandalf are soon laughing – staring at each other (when Frodo reproaches Gandalf for being late) and laughing (the moment will be echoed when Frodo comes round in Rivendell, and again, joyously, in Minas Tirith when Frodo's rid of the ring, and Gandalf says nothing but laughs). The scenes between Ian McKellen and Elijah Wood are some of the best in the films, far more satisfying than most of those between Wood and Astin, for instance.

The cart scene is essentially a two-hander dialogue scene that needs to establish both main characters, and the relationship between them. The *relationship* is vital: how Gandalf regards Frodo (indulgent, tender, thoughtful), and how Frodo regards Gandalf (warmly, and respectful when reproached). It needs to signal upcoming events (the party), and so on. But it also adds a little note about the ring, the primary plot, when Frodo mentions that Bilbo has been acting strangely (after all, the film's called *The Fellowship of the Ring*, and the book is *The Lord of the Rings*. Notice how often the filmmakers remind the audience about the ring: it's even placed on the kitchen table when Gandalf and Frodo talk).

Continuity is up the spout in the *Extended Edition* version of *Fellowship*, though, with the cart conversation cut into scenes of Bilbo and scenes of the hobbits in the village, so now the cart seems to go through Hobbiton at least twice, and cuts back to the same road, before the wizard reaches Bag End. (Among the hobbits portrayed at Hobbiton are Mr and Mrs Proudfoot – Noel Appleby and Megan Edwards, who also appear the party and in the closing scenes of *Return*).

When Frodo meets Gandalf in the country lane in the film, there are other things at work. Crucial among these is the scale issue, which much concerned the filmmakers: Frodo in C.U. is Elijah Wood, but in long shot, he's Wood's hobbit stand-in, Kiran Shah (and, just by chance, he happens to be standing on an embankment, which handily puts him close to the same head height at Gandalf). That introduces the first of many visual tricks (some simple and in-camera, some in-camera and tricky, others very complex and digital) to portray different sized people and creatures. When the stand-in jumps onto Gandalf's cart, for instance, there's a complex face replacement visual effects shot (when Elijah Wood's face is re-sized and fitted over the face of Shah). A forced perspective shot occurs next, between Frodo and Gandalf on the cart (with Frodo sitting further back in the cart). Two different-sized horses pulled the cart (a Welsh mountain pony, and a thoroughbred hack). When Gandalf reaches Bag

End, further cinematic trickery is employed to sell the scale issue: different-sized doubles, blue screen work, and shots designed to foreground the scale issue (the hand-over of the hat in the hall, for instance, which took all day to shoot, or the shot where Bilbo walks all the way around Gandalf next to the fireplace, or when Gandalf lifts the teapot lid on the split forced perspective table). The scale doubles did a lot of acting in the *Lord of the Rings* films – Kiran Shah, Tall Paul, 'Phon' Chansantor, Paul Randall, Jeff Barber, David Muzzerall, Steve Reinsfield, Tim Wong and Brett Beattie, among others. (Some of the scale doubles were young, but some, like Shah, were veterans of films like *Return of the Jedi*).

Another element in the first present-tense scene of the film of *The Fellowship of the Ring* is Howard Shore's music, the jaunty Hobbiton theme (with light flutes and strings) which will recur at key moments throughout the films (with most poignancy at Sam and Frodo's darkest hours in Mordor).

The Hobbiton scenes telescope lengthy sections of *The Lord of the Rings*: to depict the whole area (and to show off the expensive outdoor set), Gandalf on his cart is used as a device to link together images of Hobbiton (it's a visual tour of Hobbiton, in other words). The cart trundles over the bridge, past the mill, and eventually up to Bag End. The same narrative device is used to introduce Minas Tirith and its levels in *The Return of the King*, when Gandalf gallops up the streets to the citadel. (There's a brief scene of hobbit kids clamouring for fireworks, and being rewarded with a minor display around the back of the cart. Note how Frodo climbs down from the cart – for no particular reason – leaving Gandalf to visit Bilbo alone).

Hobbiton is depicted as an idealized rural village, impossibly sunny and painless. A pleasant retirement spot, as DP Andrew Lesnie put it (he said the same of Rivendell). Plenty of cinematic sleight-of-hand is employed to give Hobbiton the look and feel of a comfy, safe enclave: digital grading to heighten greens and golds, backlighting, gentle, expansive crane shots, shooting in full sunlight, and extras told to smile, smile, smile. (Hobbiton looked like the rustic, pantomime village out of *Babe*. Or Disneyland *circa* 1957. Not a speck of mud or dirt anywhere. An 18th century movie version of Disney's Celebration town in Florida.)

For Peter Jackson, Hobbiton (and the Shire) had to be represent what Frodo and Sam were fighting for, what was at stake in their quest to destroy the ring. Neither Frodo nor Sam had a family to fight for, or wives or lovers, or children (Sam's future family and marriage to Rosie Cotton is waiting in the wings, in the future, so to speak). Frodo didn't have parents either (and Sam's parents weren't established really – the Gaffer's more prominent in the book). So, to personalize their struggle (remember, Hollywood films always have to dramatize feelings or tensions in terms of individuals), Hobbiton was used as a point of reference.

But though Hobbiton was intended to represent what was at stake in the *Lord of the Rings* films (losing the Shire, losing freedom, etc), I don't think it really worked. Although Hobbiton, Bilbo, the Gaffer and Rosie

Cotton were evoked by Frodo and Sam at times in the films, as they wandered through Ithilien or Mordor, it didn't really resonate as it should have done. (Rosie's glimpsed in the *Green Dragon* scene, for instance, and at the party, but the Gaffer, in both cuts, is a vague presence (the relation between the terms 'gaffer' and 'father' isn't clarified). So when Sam, facing the Black Gate of Mordor, mutters 'my gaffer would have a thing or two to say if he could see me now', it remains abstract).

But that lack of individualization of what's at stake is also a part of J.R.R. Tolkien's novel. Tolkien, as commentators such as Tom Shippey have noted rightly, does things a professional writer just wouldn't do. If you were rewriting *The Lord of the Rings* as a film script and didn't care too much about being 'faithful' to the book, you'd probably have the Black Riders or orcs invading Hobbiton during the party (after carefully establishing the main characters and the rural idyll of the place), and capturing or killing Bilbo, just as he's giving his speech. Somehow, Bilbo would manage to get the ring to Frodo before he's carried off or killed. Gandalf, detained by Merry and Pippin, or on some other errand, returns to drive off the villains (but not before they've butchered plenty of hobbit extras). Frodo would see Bilbo die right before him, and thus his quest is fairly clear: to avenge Bilbo as well as to destroy the ring (or, if Bilbo isn't dead but captured, to rescue him from the Dark Tower). All sorts of other clichés of Hollywood action-adventure films could be introduced as well here.

What *The Lord of the Rings* (the book) doesn't have is a big dramatic event to *motivate* Frodo taking up the ring and leaving the Shire. In both book and film, it takes *a lot* of talk from Gandalf to put the case to Frodo that the ring should be destroyed (rather like an endless pitch from a filmmaker to a studio to persuade them to make a film. And then they say no).

In the book, Frodo doesn't hear from Gandalf for a long time, and eventually decides to leave on his birthday, in September, without waiting for the wizard. Months drift by, in other words. A Hollywood screenwriter, urged by film producers, distributors and the studio, wouldn't let it play like that at all. Frodo's village would be burnt down, his child would be kidnapped, his best friend might be slaughtered, something of that magnitude would be required to motivate someone to leave their idyllic life and embark on an immense journey towards the nastiest place in Middle-earth. In *Thelma & Louise* (1991) one of the women kills a guy; in *Star Wars* (1977), Luke's surrogate parents are killed; in the man on the run movie (*Minority Report*, say, or *North By Northwest*), the hero's framed for a murder he didn't commit (or did he?).

Take one of the models for the *Lord of the Rings* films, *Braveheart* (1995). (*Braveheart* is consciously evoked in the *Lord of the Rings* films a number of times, and the music was used as temp music in the animatics, and in the trailers) In that 20th Century Fox movie (written by Randall Wallace, it was a star vehicle for Mel Gibson), those nasty English soldiers encamped in Scotland slaughter Mel's girl, Murron. Her death, on top of everything the snooty British invading imperialists have done, encourages William Wallace (Gibson) to take up the Scottish cause big time (note that, in the classic conception of the Hollywood hero, Wallace initially declines to be involved in the politics of the time, preferring a nice family life with his woman. The hero being reluctant at first is straight out of the screenwriter's handbook. Boyens, Jackson and Walsh used it too – not so much for Frodo, but very much for Aragorn and, to a lesser extent, Théoden. Indeed, the scriptwriters stretched out Aragorn's reluctance to accept the hero's role across three long films).

Bilbo Baggins' party scene is a classic movie device for introducing more characters. It depicts the hobbits in their natural habitat, not bothered by the calamitous events in the rest of Middle-earth. It was a big scene (lots of extras, costumes, make-up, sets and props, plenty of minor incidents), but it wasn't about the ring, or Frodo and ring, which was the main plot in *The Fellowship of the Ring* (the party occurred before Frodo is given the ring). The ring did feature, of course, when Bilbo uses it to disappear once and for all from his fellow hobbits. (A curious departure from the book has Gandalf looking surprised when Bilbo disappears, whereas in the book he's knows what's coming, and adds a little smoke and mirrors of his own: 'a blinding flash of light' [FR, 52]).

Note that Frodo is introduced at the party dancing with (or next to) a young female hobbit, smiling at her. When he comes over to Sam, he encourages his gardener to dance with Rosie Cotton, pushing him clumsily towards her. So, these two guys, who spend the rest of the films together (sometimes very closely together), ain't gay. No sir! At the party they're doing young guy stuff, like drinking and flirting with women. (Hell, even Gandalf gets down and boogies, after a fashion.) But these heterosexual moments are few and far between (it's the only time Frodo's seen side by side with a female hobbit), in what some commentators have called the gayest movie to come out of Hollywood for years.

Merry and Pippin are introduced here, in a comic, mischievous mode (which's not in the book – they come in much later), where they steal and light Gandalf's fireworks (the dragon firework is a nod back to *The Hobbit*). Gandalf catches them and punishes them with some washing up. J.R.R. Tolkien complained that some readers made too much of Gandalf and fireworks. He grumbled about being taken to a bonfire party by a BBC documentary film crew in 1968, when they wanted to film the professor and fireworks. 'Gimmicky and nonsense' Tolkien called the documentary *Tolkien In Oxford*. Fireworks are in the book, though, and the passage where Gandalf's display is described must make a deep impression on some readers. As far as hobbits are concerned, Gandalf to them is just one of the 'attractions' of the party, just an old guy who's great with pyrotechnics (in a way, it is a foreshadowing of Gandalf's magic, which's often linked with fire and light – either battling the Balrog, or driving off the nazgûl. Which's fitting, as he holds the ring of fire, Narya, and if a wizard's going to do any magic, in literature or film, it usually has to be bolts of lightning, flashes of light, fire, and the like).

So linking Merry and Pippin with fireworks was a cinematic shorthand which had to more to do with the common view associating

Gandalf and fireworks, rather than Tolkien's intention. At the party (and the build-up to it), Tolkien's narrator in *The Lord of the Rings* is much more concerned with the many gifts Bilbo gives (and their individual notes), or with the food and drink at the party, or with the gossip among the hobbits about the party, than with the fireworks. Introducing Merry and Pippin chatting or dancing with female hobbits or carousing loudly with their chums might've been closer to Tolkien's book.

The next time Merry and Pippin are met in the film is a much further departure from the book. The road movie has already begun, and Sam and Frodo are well on their way. They bump into Merry and Pippin (literally) at Farmer Maggot's fields, filching vegetables (in the book, Merry and Pippin know Maggot well, and Maggot is very helpful). Merry and Pippin are still introduced and depicted as basically comic relief; they're fundamentally helpers, sidekicks, and don't make any serious decisions.

One of the most glaring omissions from the 2001 film of *The Fellowship of the Ring* is any discussion of why Merry and Pippin opt to come along with Frodo and Sam. There's no suggestion of the conspiracy, or that the other hobbits all knew about the ring, or that Sam was their chief spy, or about what was going on, and, crucially, that they intend to accompany Frodo. It's wonderful (and very silly) that in contemporary Hollywood cinema characters can simply join up with a team or embark on a perilous journey without any time for planning, discussions, or even packing a few clothes. They just *go*. (It reminds me of a moment in *Indiana Jones and the Last Crusade* (1989) when Indy visits a library in Venice and needs to get into the crypt. A pedantic, timid writer would have had a cautious, stealthy Jones come back at nighttime, when nobody's about. But no: Indy just smashes away at the floor in daylight, when the library's still open. And he times the hits with a librarian stamping books).

The insertion of a simple piece of discussion might have clarified this plot point. Let's say that Merry and Pippin have helped Frodo and Sam reach Bree.

EXT. NIGHT. BREE
The HOBBITS stand in the road outside Bree at sunset. FRODO turns to face MERRY and PIPPIN.

FRODO
You must go back. You don't know what lies ahead.

SAM
Neither do I... Or you, Mr Frodo.

MERRY
(Decisively)
We're coming with you.

FRODO
(Reluctantly)
Very well. *(Pause)* I'm glad.

MERRY grins at PIPPIN.

But there's no discussion at all, although it would've made sense to clarify the point – certainly by the time of the attacks at Bree and Weathertop.

After Bilbo's party come the most important scenes in *The Fellowship of the Ring* – indeed in the whole three films: the conversations between Bilbo and Gandalf, and between Frodo and Gandalf, which set out the goals, the motivations, what Frodo must do, and develops the backstory of the prologue. (Note that there's no wraithworld scene for Bilbo: he pops the ring on and off and simply disappears: the wraithworld is saved for later, for Frodo).

The Gandalf-Bilbo scenes are some of the best in the films (as one would expect from the two knighted actors). Hollywood has been casting British knights like this, for these sorts of roles, for decades (Laurence Olivier, Alec Guinness, Ralph Richardson, Freddie Jones or Michael Hordern might have played Gandalf or Bilbo – indeed, Guinness was the Gandalfesque Obi-wan Kenobi in *Star Wars,* and Hordern played Gandalf in the BBC radio 1981 *Rings* – when Ian Holm had been Frodo).

The most important narrative outcome of the Bilbo-Gandalf scenes is very simple: Bilbo must give up the ring and leave it for Frodo. Along the way, all sorts of bits of exposition are being slid under the audience's nose while the two Ians play out a terrific scene: the effect of the ring on Bilbo (which viewers'll see in detail later, with Gollum and Frodo, and Bilbo uses the same phrases, such as 'my precious'), and Bilbo's deep reluctance to give up the ring (and Frodo's, throughout the films, but most importantly at the Crack of Doom).

The Bilbo-Gandalf scene starts off in a friendly fashion, intensifies to the point where Gandalf reveals some of his wizardly power, and culminates with Bilbo finally giving up the ring. Visual effects are in abundance in these scenes, which seem to be very domestic and modest – indeed, this's the most fundamental scene in all drama: *two people talking in a room* (but there are different size sets, blue screen work, stand-ins, different-sized props, forced perspective shots and the like).

Acting-wise, both Ians let go a little (Holm especially), producing what McKellen called some 'big acting'. But what Holm expertly conveys is the effect the ring's had on him: there's the critical moment when he drops the ring on the floor by the front door of Bag End, but just as vital is the moment right afterwards, the deep sigh of relief, the way he can finally walk away from it (reprised after Frodo displays the ring at the Council of Elrond and sits down with a sigh. And, more poignantly, at the Crack of Doom). Dropping the dwarves from the book at this point makes Bilbo seem an even more forlorn figure as he walks away from Bag End (humming, of course, 'the road goes ever on and on').

There's an interesting scene that follows: it's the only scene in the films with Gandalf and the ring (i.e., Gandalf and Sauron) alone together, the two chief rivals in the War of the Ring. A nice moment has Gandalf reach down to pick up the ring and receive a sudden flash image of Sauron as a giant fiery eye. The scene shows that even Gandalf is afraid of touching the ring (the audience finds out why when Gandalf explains its all-pervading corruption in the following scenes), and it also introduces the audience to the visual concept of the Dark Lord as a giant flaming cat's eye. That's a little taster of what the ring can do when you are near it or put it on, and what Frodo will experience with the ring. (Note that, in Hollywood movie logic, Gandalf's sudden vision of Sauron, which doesn't occur in the book, doesn't occur at other times (when he puts the ring in an envelope, for example). Instead, Gandalf's vision takes place in a horror genre setting: the quiet, dark house, and Gandalf on his own. The sound is faded down just beforehand, so that when the flash cut of Sauron appears it is accompanied by a loud cracking sound, just like the moment in a horror film when the monster suddenly appears, or the murderer grabs someone from the shadows. Gandalf could be reaching down to a serial killer's sacrificial knife, or a suicide note with spots of blood on it.)

At this point, Gandalf doesn't know this is the one ruling ring. But the image of Sauron's eye must trouble him. He'd know that you wouldn't see that vision from just any old ring. Clearly Gandalf suspects something, because he's quick to have the ring put into an envelope and hidden away when Frodo arrives.

The following scene, where Frodo comes back to find Bilbo gone and Gandalf at Bag End, is pretty much from the book in essence (it includes the scene of the following day in the book too). Note how, in the background of a depth of focus two shot, Frodo bends down and picks up the ring. The sudden flash cut to Sauron is withheld (having just been set up when Gandalf nearly picks up the ring): this is not the right time in the narrative (i.e., in Frodo's psychological journey) for that particular dramatic moment. In other words, the filmmakers, having set it up, will be saving it for later.

> Frodo came in soon afterwards, and found him sitting in the dark, deep in thought. "Has he gone?" he asked.
> "Yes," said Gandalf, "he has gone at last." (FR, 59)

In the film, Frodo doesn't know that Bilbo's planning to leave. (Jim Smith and J. Clive Matthews suggest that the ring is already exerting an effect on Gandalf, who sits by the fire muttering 'my precious'. Maybe. I don't think so: Gandalf seems to be musing on the ring, certainly, but using the phrase 'my precious' appears more like a reference to Gollum). (Visually, it's another Alan Lee painting).

The key line in this part of the film, when the ring is still 'Bilbo's ring' (i.e., it hasn't really passed to Frodo yet, or started to have an effect on him), is Gandalf's command to Frodo: 'keep it secret, keep it safe' (the 1981 radio version also emphasized and repeated that line). As in the book, Gandalf disappears suddenly, taking off for foreign climes.

The film then cuts to Barad-dûr, Minas Morgul, and images of

Gandalf horseriding to Minas Tirith (for some Tolkien fans, this 'gave away' the city before it should've been seen); the scene opens out the film considerably, foreshadowing the big landscapes and cities that will be encountered later (but it's not a full reveal of the Minas Tirith model, but a side view).

The scene in the library of Gondor (no meeting with Denethor or his sons) now has Gandalf narrating the film over flashbacks of Sauron and Isildur at the Last Alliance, which reprises images from the prologue. These are visual reminders of Sauron, Isildur and the ring. Even Tolkien himself would've applauded the library scene, and Gandalf as Middle-earth's private detective, being so close to his own experience in the dusty old libraries of Oxford, and years of historical research, and to his conception of Gandalf as a wise old man who works his way through the material to confirm his suspicions (some critics have seen it as a Middle-earth version of Tolkien himself).[1] The scene is an addition to the novel (it is more implied than described by Tolkien's narrator), but a very welcome one (in complete contrast to, say, the warg attack, or Frodo at Osgiliath).

(The film alters the chronology of events considerably around this point. There are more comings and goings of Gandalf in the book, but the film suggests that Gandalf's in Minas Tirith when the nazgûl are leaving Minas Morgul, and that they soon reach the Shire. In the novel, Gandalf visits the white city in TA 3017, and the Black Riders cross the Isen in September 3018.)

Just prior to the library scene comes one of the best shots in the whole show, the lengthy aerial shot of Barad-dûr. Wonderful design by John Howe, great model-building by Weta Workshop, and superb cinematography by Alex Funke's miniatures team – and, not least, one of Howard Shore's big villain themes. It's night (of course) when the Dark Tower's first glimpsed: rivers of lava below, a vast bridge teeming with activity, orcs manning the irregularly-shaped tower, torches flickering all over the building, and the angry volcano of Mount Doom in the distance. As if this is not enough, there's more narrative information piled into the shot – Gollum's shrieks of 'Baggins... Shire'. At this point, it's not exactly clear what this voiceover refers to (or whose voice it is), but it's gotta be bad, because right after the shot is a cut to a low wide angle of the entrance of Minas Morgul and the Black Riders galloping out. OK, the film departs from the book at this point (Gandalf visits Minas Tirith in TA 3017, 16 years after Bilbo's party and a year before he's in Hobbiton with Frodo), but when the 2001-03 Hollywood adaption of Tolkien is this good, it doesn't matter. (And no matter how good the visual imagery, models and matte paintings of tons of people might be, it's Howard Shore's music, in a grand choral tradition, which *really* rounds off the scenes of Barad-dûr and Minas Morgul.)

The narrative pattern of the film is now established: the backbone will be scenes of Frodo and his journey (gathering companions along the way), occasionally intercut with scenes of the wider geo-political developments in Middle-earth: Saruman in Orthanc, Gandalf riding to Minas Tirith or Isengard, or Barad-dûr, or the nazgûl leaving Minas Morgul and getting closer, and so on. By the time the film has launched Frodo on his way, the film has introduced the primary villains, their dwellings, and their chief henchmen. That's crucial in Hollywood movies: Saruman, for instance, doesn't appear in the flesh of the book, in the foreground of the narrative of *The Lord of the Rings*, until the scenes at Isengard, halfway through. He is, of course, discussed by Gandalf at Rivendell, but that's within Gandalf's dialogue (Gandalf also mentions him during "The Shadow of the Past" chapter). If the screenwriters had followed the book, Saruman (and Sauron) would've been introduced too late for this kind of action-adventure movie.

When Frodo next meets Gandalf for the pivotal "Shadow of the Past" discussion, it's over nine years since he last saw him in the book (FR, 71), but a few months perhaps in the film. Again, the movie doesn't suggest for a moment that Frodo has ever used the ring (in the film he digs it out of a chest where's it buried under papers and stuff, and still in its wax-sealed envelope. It's great how Frodo can find it within seconds – hunting down a small envelope after nine years could be a lot more difficult, especially in my house). In the book, he's been using it from time to time, so that he appears well-preserved by the age of 50. (The ring itself was made by the Dutchman Jens Hansen; Hansen made 15 rings before the final one was chosen.)

"The Shadow of the Past" section of *The Fellowship of the Ring* is again introduced with a creepy horror film moment (presumably to keep up the tension, though it's only actually old Gandalf visiting Frodo). Frodo returns from another night's carousing at the *Green Dragon* to find the windows open, papers blowing about, Bag End all shadowy, low cello stabs on the soundtrack, and the camera covering the action with deliberately loose handheld shots. Again, it's a scenario familiar from the hundred-plus year history of cinema: a person on their own at night in a dark house.

This opening of the Gandalf-Frodo scene is partly a trick played on the audience: they've just seen the Riders galloping like bats out of hell out of Minas Morgul (and we can guess where they're headed), so maybe they've already reached the Shire? Look at the framing and staging of the moment when Gandalf meets Frodo. No nice 'hello', no friendly smile, no pot of tea waiting beside the fire from Gandalf, but a hand looming out of the shadows which grabs Frodo's shoulder, from behind.

The trick on the audience is that, for a brief moment, it's been fooled into wondering if Frodo's been caught by the baddies. But no, it's Gandalf (and a very haggard, anxious Gandalf, looking as if he's just ridden from Minas Tirith without stopping.) He immediately asks 'is it secret? Is it safe?' (The repetition of 'is it safe?' from the earlier scene brings back memories of *Marathon Man* [1976], when a young American actor [Dustin Hoffman] was menaced by an older British actor [Laurence Olivier]). Ian McKellen's performance is a little over-cooked here, the way he swivels to the noise from the window as if the Gestapo are going to come crashing through it at any moment, brandishing revolvers and orders to take the halfling and the ring to the Führer.

It's a terrible lapse from the book, really, because Gandalf would *never* frighten the bejesus out of Frodo like that, jumping on him out the shadows. What kind of friend is that? It's amazing that Frodo doesn't yelp and yell 'what the fuck are you doing? You almost gave me a heart attack!' Is Gandalf suddenly turned into a practical joker, perhaps? No. If there's one thing Gandalf never jokes about, it's the ring. After all, Sauron and the ring are the reason he's been sent by the Valar to Middle-earth, his whole *raison d'être*.

The overriding narrative function of the "Shadow of the Past" scene is to tell the audience a number of vital plot points:

(1) that Sauron is back in business,
(2) that his power is increasing,
(3) that Bilbo's ring is indeed the One Ring and
(4) that it's very dangerous,
(5) that Gandalf won't accept the ring when it's offered to him,
(6) that the enemy is searching for it,
(7) that he knows it's in the Shire, held by a Baggins (there's a brief but vivid flashback to Gollum being tortured in Barad-dûr),
(8) that it must be removed from the Shire,
(9) that Frodo must volunteer to take it, and finally
(10) that Sam is to be Frodo's companion on the journey.

All of that information is quite a bit for the audience to handle, so it's parcelled out in segments, and in a particular order, so that the climax of the whole sequence is Frodo volunteering to take the ring. (That Frodo *volunteers* is absolutely vital, as Gandalf and Elrond recognize. In the book, Bilbo volunteers to do it, and Gandalf and Elrond tell him that the ring has passed on others).

(Going East might seem to be the wrong direction, in the book at least, East being towards Mordor. But Gandalf is clearly thinking that the ring should go to Rivendell first, before deciding what to do. Of course, Gandalf has now realized there's only one solution, really: that's revealed to him when it's conclusively shown that Bilbo's ring is the One Ring).

Co-writer Philippa Boyens acknowledged that the back-story

> was very difficult to do. It's finding the places where it isn't just exposition, it should never be just exposition. It should be character driven, it should be as much as possible character driven, it should be action driven. It should, again, feel real.

Weaving it into the piece without boring the audience was tricky – to know just how much back-story to give the audience, and how it related to the primary narrative.

As in the book, "The Shadow of the Past" is the *all-important* scene in *The Fellowship of the Ring:* if the audience doesn't get all of the information here, large parts of the film won't make much sense. The *Lord of the Rings* hasn't got Frodo's village being burnt, or his wife/ lover/ son/ father/ friend being killed or captured, but it does have the cool narrative hook of the baddies hurtling on horseback towards the Shire to get back the ring for their master. Once it gets going, the narrative in *The Fellowship of the Ring* is gripping stuff in the classic adventure mode: Frodo's got to destroy the ring before the villains get it, and if he doesn't, it's the end of the world. It's basically a dual chase, in Alfred Hitchcock's definition (with the ring as ultimate MacGuffin).

This is called the 'set-up' in Hollywood screenwriting, when everything the audience needs to know is laid out for them: the main characters, the relationships, the goals, the obstacles, what's at stake, and the motivations (sometimes the motivations are included later, or they alter as the narrative progresses).

The set-up usually occurs, as Kristin Thompson (among many others) has shown, 25-30 minutes into a film, at the end of act one. The traditional way of looking at the form of a film narrative is three acts: introduction (situation), development (complication), and conclusion (happy ending). Thompson has suggested that four or five or more sections is more accurate (each one being in the 25-30 minute range).

With *The Fellowship of the Ring* (theatrical version) coming in at around two hours and forty-five minutes (up to the end credits on the DVD), imposing a three-act structure on it isn't very helpful. Instead, *The Fellowship of the Ring* contains six or seven acts. Act one would be the events up to Frodo agreeing to leave the Shire with the ring; act two follows the travellers to Rivendell; act three comprises the many scenes at Rivendell; act four runs up to Khazad-dûm and Gandalf's demise; act five takes the film to Lórien, until the fellowship leaves; act six is the Great River to the end of the film. (Peter Jackson said that the films had been written and edited using Robert McKee's well-known rules for screenwriting. When Frodo takes up the ring, that where the story starts: it's about Frodo and ring).

The book of *The Lord of the Rings* is not a 'classic' movie narrative (to the frustration of all those who have attempted to adapt it, from the 1950s to the late 1990s), but it had to be turned into one, for some important reasons: every blockbuster film of this type has to be a 'high concept' narrative, narratively clear, easy to sell to audiences, simple enough to be turned into merchandizing and licensing, and so on. What *The Fellowship of the Ring* turns out to be is a road movie or chase movie (in fact, the three films are road movies, as well as war movies. The road or chase movie is the driving narrative form, done in an action-adventure style, but overall the *Lord of the Rings* films are essentially war movies).

W.H. Auden estimated that Frodo spent 80 days on the road (excluding rests) and traversed 1,800 miles, mostly on foot.[2] In a way, as commentators have noted, all of contemporary Hollywood's action-adventure films boil down to chase narratives (Alfred Hitchcock called the chase fundamental to cinema; it was cinema in its purest form). The *Lord of the Rings* films are no different. For all of *The Fellowship of the Ring*, Frodo is on the move, with only two stop-overs, in elven kingdoms (and that fundamental road movie narrative structure continues all the way to Mount Doom). Throughout, he's pursued by ringwraiths, orcs, trolls, crows, men (Boromir), and monsters. (It's a pretty eventful time for Frodo:

he's attacked by nazgûl (saved by a man, and later an elf), grabbed by the lake monster, speared by a troll, falls into the Dead Marshes, is captured by a giant spider, and captured by orcs, then rescued, tormented by the ring and Sauron, and so on.)

Jean Lowerison in the *Reel Story* wrote of the 2001 picture: 'to reduce Tolkien's odyssey story to a series of physical battles with phony-looking monsters is to miss his point, which is that the real struggle is the internal one between good and bad instincts, heroism and cowardice'. For Lowerison, the monsters and characters had been borrowed from *Star Wars, Planet of the Apes, Princess Mononoke* and other fantasy and sci-fi films.

Structurally, *The Fellowship of the Ring* is a road movie filled with narrow escapes and dramatic incidents (not all are nasty or action-based: some are breathtaking and inspiring – Moria, Lothlórien, Rivendell). But if the viewer doesn't identify with Frodo, or with his quest, everything that the filmmakers conjure up is just more show, more extras, more sets, more stunts, more noise, more sounds, more visual effects, but without emotional impact. If Frodo's character and his quest to destroy the ring isn't compelling, then the audience is watching one nice second unit shot of mountains or rocks followed by another, one group of actors with oversize hair extensions and unpronounceable names following another across windswept hilltops, and one fight with orcs, trolls, nazgoolies or monsters following another.

The viewer *has to* identify wholly with Frodo and go along with him, just like the viewer has to identify with Dorothy and her journey through Oz to find the wizard in *The Wizard of Oz* (1939), or with Phillip Marlowe solving a sleazy murder case in *The Big Sleep* (1946), or with the alien trying to reach home in *E.T.* (1982) and the boy trying to save him from the scientists. The film, Peter Jackson explained (Sib, 342), is 'a story about a hobbit with a ring and the need to destroy it'.

For my money, the 2001-03 adaption of *The Lord of the Rings* isn't wholly convincing in this respect (which seriously damages the three films), partly due to the casting of Elijah Wood, partly due to the way he played the part and was directed, and partly due to the script (somehow, the film just doesn't do the dramatic work of persuading the viewer to identify with Frodo, even though the viewer desperately wants to, and knows it has to). But it's also due to the faults in Tolkien's book, in which Frodo never really seems to be in jeopardy (or is it rather that the reader knows Frodo's going to be OK in the end?). So much happens to him, but he's always miraculously rescued. It's worth recalling, when considering the *Lord of the Rings* films, that some of the faults with the films are actually already there in Tolkien's novel.

As the film's narrative rushes headlong from one action beat to the next, there are little snippets from the book, like concessions to the book (and to Tolkien fans), as if the filmmakers are saying 'we haven't forgotten you fans, dears'. For instance, when Frodo and Sam meet Merry and Pippin there's a very brief appearance by Farmer Maggot (well, his scythe, anyway, glimpsed through giant crops, and sound designer Mike Hopkins' voice yelling), and a reference (in the dialogue) to the chapter title "A Short Cut To Mushrooms". In the book, of course, the hobbits spend some time with the wily Maggot, and he's another unexpected aide on their journey (earlier scripts had included more of Maggot).

Other touches include the stone trolls from *The Hobbit*, which are glimpsed behind Sam when Frodo comes round after Weathertop. There's a nice touch in the first scene in Bag End when Gandalf moves over to a table in the living room and picks up a map of the events in *The Hobbit* (while the music moves into a quietly mysterious mode). It's 'Thror's Map', creased and tatty, with the Lonely Mountain and the dragon in it, and it's (based on) the map which Ronald Tolkien drew himself for *The Hobbit*. It may be one of the only instances in the films of something the professor drew himself appearing on screen, and it's the perfect fan moment.

There are quite a few references to the events depicted in *The Hobbit* in the early scenes of *The Fellowship of the Ring*: Thror's map, the dragon firework, Gandalf talking to Frodo on the cart, Bilbo with Gandalf in Bag End, and so on. The references to *The Hobbit* serve a dual purpose: they are back-story, suggesting, in movie terms, that Gandalf has known Bilbo and Frodo (and the Shire) before, that he and Bilbo have been on adventures before. And for people who know Tolkien's books, they are allusions to an earlier book and adventure.

The *Special Extended Edition* added some material to the hobbit scenes, such as Bilbo hiding from the Sackville-Bagginses at the party (his ear twitches as he hears them from afar), and talking alone briefly to Frodo (a scene which seems to be going somewhere, but doesn't), and the hobbits dancing and singing at the *Green Dragon* inn (that was a nice scene which showed the hobbits doing innocent hobbit stuff, and tied in with the *Green Dragon* scene at the end of *The Return of the King*). And there were additions to the early part of the journey in the *Extended Edition*: the Midgewater Marshes, for instance (with the hobbits struggling through pools), or Sam and Frodo seeing some of the elves leaving for the West (the hobbits hear them in their camp and watch the elves, lit glowingly, walking through the trees in the distance, accompanied by ethereal music – another scene which looked forward to the close of *The Return of the King*), or some more of Sam and Frodo camping (Sam unable to sleep on a tree root, for instance, and Frodo sitting in a tree smoking a pipe).

NOTES: PROLOGUE AND ACT ONE

1. G. Fuller, 2001.
2. W.H. Auden, The Quest Hero", in N. Isaacs, 1968, 53.

ACT TWO

Saruman the White was introduced at the time the hobbits leave the Shire. A big departure from the book, he was basically a scheming movie villain (how could he be otherwise? When you cast Christopher Lee, you're deliberately drawing on the audience being familiar with the dastardly parts Lee's played over the decades). No surprise, then, that Lee's Saruman is imposing, dignified, intelligent, confident, and increasingly nasty (though he never gets his hands dirty himself, preferring lackeys for that, except when he fights Gandalf – a contender for the silliest scene in the films).

When the first Black Rider appears (in the Shire), the first indication of Frodo's heightened awareness is introduced (although he isn't wearing the ring). A track-zoom shot (out of *Vertigo* [1957], by way of *Jaws* [1975] and countless Hitchcock imitators) of the empty path (with leaves blowing along it, as in *The Conformist* [1970]) sets up the idea of Frodo having some kind of special consciousness of danger (unfortunately, it seems to desert him later – at Weathertop, for instance, or when he enters Shelob's lair, knowing the tunnel stinks and looks pretty bad).

The Black Rider scene has some great touches: apart from the wide crane shot, it's mainly covered with very big close-ups: of the horse, its hooves, the gauntlet, the bugs crawling (this may be a nod to a wonderful scene in *Excalibur* [1981], where insects, snakes, owls and creatures appear as the 'dragon' surrounds Merlin and Arthur, or it may be to *Dracula*), and the sound paring down to echoey, distant noises (the flapping of a bird's wings), the clink of a bridle, footsteps, and the Rider snuffling.

But the key sound in this sequence is the low pulse which accompanies Frodo trying to put on the ring (dubbed the 'ring's heartbeat' by the film's sound designers). This is a subjective sound effect, not heard by anyone in the film; it's the embodiment of the lure of the ring, of evil, of Sauron. Later, some high-pitched wordless singing will accompany the ring's spell over people, which has the same spooky, warbling function as the theramin from 1950s sci-fi and horror movies. (Incidentally, the BBC radio adaption of 1981 had a similar high-pitched ringing to suggest the lure of the One Ring). At key points, the ring's 'heartbeat' also changes: it becomes smoother and sweeter as the ring gets closer to Mordor, to home, as sound designer Mike Hopkins explained.[1] And at the climax of *The Two Towers,* in the face-off with the nazgûl at Osgiliath, the pulsing sound of the ring is combined with the throb of the fell-beast's wings, so they seem to be part of the same thing (as Gandalf tells Frodo at Bag End, the Dark Lord and the ring are one).

> A sudden unreasoning fear of discovery laid hold of Frodo, and he thought of his Ring. He hardly dared to breathe, and yet the desire to get it out of his pocket became so strong that he began slowly to move his hand. He felt that he had only to slip it on, and then he would be safe. (FR, 109)

So this scene is vital in many respects, not least because it's the first time in the film the ring is seen being used, though not quite put on (apart from by Sauron in the prologue, and by Isildur). It shows the power of the ring over Frodo, and Frodo's struggle to resist it, and how important Sam is (because he prevents Frodo from putting it on). It also establishes the hair-breadth escapes Frodo manages, time after time.

This Black Rider scene is also replayed a number of times in the films, and it's always Sam who saves poor Mr Frodo from succumbing to the dark side of the force (the most spectacular replay of this scene is employed as the climax of *The Two Towers*, when Frodo faces the flying nazgûl at Osgiliath, but it's exactly the same scene, narratively and dramatically). Unfortunately, the outcome of that scene is the god-awful speech Sean Astin's teary-eyed Sam delivers.

After the Black Rider on the path scene, there are some brief walking and hiding scenes (expanded a little in the extended cut), all smoke and backlighting in the trees, and parallel action cuts to the Riders in various parts of the countryside. A vestige of Merry's decisiveness and confidence from the book is played out in the film – it's Merry, for instance, who throws something to draw off the Black Rider in the previous scene. And it's Merry who suggests aiming for Bucklebury ferry (and he also suspects that the riders are looking for something, or someone). That's the only vestige, too, of the 'conspiracy' surrounding Frodo.

But there's still not a word in the film about how and why Merry and Pippin tag along with Frodo and Sam, nor anything about their background or lives. There's not even a question from Merry or Pippin about where Frodo and Sam are going, or why. The viewer understands that these guys know each other (Merry and Pippin were at Bilbo's party, for instance), but there's no concessions to believability in terms of motivations or reasons.

The 2001 film of *The Fellowship of the Ring* pumps up the action enormously at this point. In the book, one of the Black Riders is glimpsed on the other side of Brandywine River in another of Tolkien's understated, eerie moments: 'it looked like a dark black bundle left behind. But as they looked it seemed to move and sway this way and that, as if searching the ground' (FR, 140). Well, *forget that for the film!*, you can hear the producers saying; *we've already had snuffling nazghoul, once was enough: and they look ridiculous! No, what we need here is a full-on horse chase!*

So, as the hobbits discuss what to do next, the Black Riders come of nowhere and pursue them. Naturally, it's Frodo who gets cut off from the other hobbits, and just makes it to the ferry with a leap over the water. Also introduced around this time are the high-pitched screams of the riders (voiced, apparently, by Frances Walsh, one of the writers), as if the riders're communicating to each other like birds or animals. And the wraiths' steeds bay like hounds rather than horses. (The fell-beast, later on, had the howl of a donkey). The sounds of the nazgûl were a late alteration by the sound designers in post-production on *The Fellowship of the Ring*. (The wraiths' voices included lions, camels, possums, owls, all speeded-up. And 'the sound of a plastic cup being scraped over concrete!' as sound designer Ethan Van der Ryn explained.[2]).

It's at Bree, in the next scene, that the scale issue in the films really comes into its own. In Bree, the hobbits really are out of their depth (literally), as everything is too big and unfriendly: the buildings loom over them (with angles deliberately built off square by the art department); there are huge men everywhere; it's dark, cold and raining; and the *Prancing Pony* is a shadowy, unknown realm (lit, according to DP Andrew Lesnie, with a 'piss yellow' hue, accomplished partly by digital grading).

The inn extras were hired from Weird Looking Guys, Inc. The men (there are no women, or female hookers here – well, maybe a couple of old crones) are covered with wide angle, tilted (unflattering) close-ups, dribbling drink, cuddling sharp-toothed critters, and generally looking dishevelled and scary (it's basically a child's view of a bar or public house, and also the very familiar saloon scene in a Western movie when innocents come to the Big Bad Town for the first time). It's much more oppressive than the *Prancing Pony* in the book. And, just when the hobbits are settling down to a nice mug of ale after a damp, long hike, who should show up to disturb their drink, but the bloody Dark Lord himself!

Compare the Bree scene with the book here: Frodo, a little drunk, and encouraged by the crowd, sings a drinking song about the Man in the Moon, slips and puts on the ring (or the ring slips on his finger on purpose, to reveal itself). He crawls into a dark corner, near Strider:

> Frodo felt a fool. Not knowing what else to do, he crawled away under the tables to the dark corner by Strider, who sat unmoved, giving no sign of his thoughts. Frodo leaned back against the wall and took off the Ring. (FR, 217)

That's nowhere near dramatic enough for the filmmakers. They want a full-blown 'ring moment' here. After all, it's the first time Frodo's put on the ring, and the first time the viewer will see what it feels like to put on the ring. Tolkien describes some of the 'wraithworld' later, on Weathertop, but the filmmakers decided to put it here, at Bree. So this 'ring moment' will foreshadow Weathertop, but also the other times Frodo puts on the ring. So it's got to be good.

Before Frodo puts on the ring (or the ring slides onto his finger) he moves into that odd, dreamy, druggy state which he slid into when the Black Rider spooked the hobbits earlier. As he fingers the ring, Elijah Wood's rolling eyes and lolling mouth are presumably meant to suggest the pull of the ring, like a nasty desire that should be repressed. As this goes on, Sauron's voice speaking through the ring is heard again, whispering 'Baggins', until, as Frodo comes back to awareness in the inn, Pippin's voice is heard saying 'Baggins', and the sound returns to normal. The writers explained that having Frodo sing made the hobbit look a little silly; they wanted to show that it was partly Pippin's fault, by giving away Frodo's identity, but it was also the ring that decided to make itself known at that moment. The blame was taken away from Frodo, then, and put onto Pippin and the ring.

One of the iconic moments from the film, employed in the advertising, had Frodo on the floor of the *Prancing Pony*, looking up at the ring, with the ring spinning above his outstretched hand and finger (later spoofed in *Shrek 2*). The shot, a bird's-eye-view of Frodo (really a 'ring's-eye-view') was much reproduced in the marketing (and was rhymed visually when Gollum's at the Crack of Doom). Just as Frodo puts on the ring (in the film), there are cuts to Strider's reaction and, significantly, to the Black Riders in the woods, who appear to have instantly sensed its presence (although they seem to be miles away).

What happens is the viewer is put into the subjective experience of Frodo at this moment, and enters the 'wraithworld', with its wind tunnel sound effects (rushing wind and flapping), its snarls, its shimmering visuals, and the appearance of Sauron right there in the *Prancing Pony* inn. The Dark Lord as a giant eye was established earlier, when Gandalf nearly touched the ring at Bag End, but at Bree he's on screen for much longer, swamping the frame (a wall of fire, with the figures of the men drinkers visible on each side as quivering silhouettes). There are also snippets of Sauron speaking: 'I see you'... 'you cannot hide' (Alan Howard's voice, as expected, is treated with electronic effects, which draws out the words, roughens them up with wind sounds, and mixes them underneath the roaring, flapping sounds of the wind tunnel 'wraithworld').

The result is an important departure from the book. It's at Amon Hen that Frodo sees the Dark Tower, and Sauron nearly finds Frodo (with that vivid image of the giant groping finger or arm), before he takes off the ring (aided by the voice of his conscience that is of course Gandalf). By the time Frodo reaches Mordor, he feels 'naked in the dark', with Sauron searching for him. But Sauron *does not see him*, just as he *didn't* see Frodo at Amon Hen. Because if Sauron *did* see someone putting on the ring, and see Frodo with the ring, it would change things considerably. The filmmakers altered all that, though, and had Sauron spot Frodo as soon as he puts the ring on for the first time. Sauron says: 'I see you'. Maybe it's in Frodo's mind-screen, his experience when he puts on the ring. (In the book, Sauron sees Aragorn and Peregrin in the *palantír*, but not Frodo putting on the ring, until it was too late, at Sammath Naur).

Incidentally, there are plenty of ambiguities about the business of putting on the ring in the book, which J.R.R. Tolkien doesn't satisfactorily resolve. For instance, Bilbo has been putting on the ring intermittently for years, so how is it Sauron didn't see or sense him? Same with Gollum, who may have worn the ring for hours at a time or longer in Moria (and Moria's a den of plenty of the servants of the enemy, including a balrog). And Isildur, too, may have worn the ring (and he was closer to Mordor).

In a way, the solution of the screenwriters makes more sense than Tolkien's book: *when you put on the ring, the big bad guy can see (or sense) you*. It's adds more jeopardy, and clarifies the effects of the ring. So that, every time Frodo seems about to put on the ring (in the Dead Marshes for instance), the audience will be yelling 'don't do it, Frodo! He'll see you!' Like playing hide-and-seek, and putting on the ring reveals your hiding place.

The introduction of Strider at Bree is handled in an economic fashion at first, with Frodo glancing at the ranger lurking in the shadows. In the time-honoured style of Hollywood movies, one character tells another character (but really the audience) who a third character is (David Weatherley plays Butterbur). But Strider's a much rougher characterization than the book in some respects at this point, because he grabs Frodo harshly and man-handles him (or hobbit-handles him) upstairs and gives him a good talking to, like an irate teacher. Aragorn may be 87 years old, but that's no way to treat a 50 year-old hobbit! (87 and 50 are the ages of Aragorn and Frodo in the book).

Strider berates Frodo for acting as he did in the inn downstairs. The hobbits' doubts about accepting Strider as their guide, and the business with Butterbur and Gandalf's letter, are dropped, and the film moves swiftly on from the scene where Sam and his chums burst into the room to defend Frodo to later on that night. Building up to the nazgûl attack at Bree are some striking images of the riders battering down the Bree gate (and flattening the poor watchman), riding up the street of Bree, and entering the *Prancing Pony* (accompanied by a Wagnerian choral cue – *Carmina Burana* in all but name – an expansion of the one heard over the images of the nazgûl leaving Minas Morgul). (The ringwraiths had power powder dusted over their robes, so their movements showed up nicely in back-lighting, a favourite technique with martial arts performers to give their moves a cool look).

The Narsil sword narrative was altered in the film; in the book, Strider shows the broken sword to the hobbits at Bree, but Peter Jackson thought that moment would risk getting a laugh from the audience. So the sword was introduced at Rivendell, in the scene between Boromir and Aragorn. To make sure the audience gets the connection, the sword is placed opposite a painting (by Alan Lee) of Sauron and Isildur (who's wielding the sword). There are also cuts back to the moment the ring's chopped off the Dark Lord's finger.

In the movie, the sword's delivered to Aragorn (in *The Return of the King*) by Elrond himself, at Dunharrow. This comes in the middle of scenes of Aragorn being troubled by the sight of the narrow way between the mountains at Dunharrow, and having dreams of Arwen and Elrond at Rivendell, with the central tensions between father and daughter being aired yet again (about Arwen pining for Aragorn and Elrond maintaining that she should sail for the West). There's no explanation, though, why Elrond doesn't accompany the Rohirrim to Gondor – after all, the audience had seen Elrond in military mode, leading the elves into battle in the prologue, so why he suddenly vanishes from *The Return of the King*, only to appear at the end, beside Arwen, is a mystery.

One of the biggest teases played on the audience occurs in the dead of night scenes in Bree (the *Lord of the Rings* films are very fond of teasing the viewer, down to appearing to kill Aragorn). The editing pattern and framing suggests that the hobbits are sleeping in the room the ringwraiths enter. The trick is stretched to the limit when Sam is shown waking up suddenly right after a ringwraith's stabbed one of the beds. Only after the beds are shown to be stuffed with pillows and the wraiths scream in frustration are the hobbits, safe and sound, depicted in a nearby room. The point-of-view in the narrative, unusually, is with the nazgûl for a brief time. At most other times – all through Weathertop for example – it is with the good guys. (It's incredible that Aragorn and the hobbits use an old boarding school gag of dummies in their beds, and even more incredible that the nazgûl fall for it. These ringwraiths are hopeless villains).

Strider provides the exposition about the Black Riders, which's heard over cuts to the horsemen in the Bree street, and in the woods, at dusk (the film moves out from the present tense of Bree with these cuts).

I miss, in the 2001 film version of Bree, the bustling, non-stop talk of Butterbur (in the movie he's a very different, soberer characterization), the encounters with Butterbur's assistants (Nob and Bob), the Bree hobbits, Frodo singing, Merry wandering outside (and receiving 'the Black Breath'), Gandalf's letter, and the company leaving Bree by daylight with the pony (with Sam hitting Bill Ferny with an apple; Aragorn does throw one at Pippin, though). One can understand some of the omissions. Presumably the Bree hobbits in the *Prancing Pony* were dropped to make Frodo and his pals seem more like fish out of water in an unfriendly zone ('the Bree hobbits were, in fact, friendly and inquisitive', comments Tolkien's narrator [FR, 211]).

Another omission, Merry wandering outside and encountering a Black Rider, would've meant a whole new sequence (building up tension, having Merry creep along the road, overhear the Black Rider and Bill Ferny (or the 'squint-eyed southerner') talking, and be assailed by the Black Breath). It would've taken up too much time, perhaps (though it was depicted in a short scene in the 1978 *The Lord of the Rings*), but the scene would also have shown, again, that the Black Riders aren't great villains when it comes to capturing their prey and making off with it. You don't want to show how ineffective your villains are too often, because they lose their impact. (The whole Bree sequence in the 1981 BBC radio version of the book is much superior to the 2001 film).

There were numerous changes from the book in the Saruman and Isengard scenes at this point (no many-coloured robes for Saruman, but he does have a *palantír*). And of course the wizard duel. The Orthanc interior scenes were covered with Dutch tilts all over the place, and rapid Steadicam work (in one memorable shot, the Steadicam operator runs down a corridor up to Saruman, as if he's chasing Danny riding his kart around the Overlook Hotel in the Stanley Kubrick film *The Shining* [1980]). These are the techniques deployed to spice up that most common scene of drama, two people talking in a room. (But what a room! The Orthanc interior chamber set is a masterpiece of hard, brittle, shiny, irregular vertical forms, like a flow of lava that's frozen, been chiselled into blades, painted black and polished daily by Saruman's grotesque orcs. Orthanc really does look as if it's been carved by magic from a single piece of rock).

Saruman delivers the exposition about the movies' chief villain: Sauron, and how he is now a lidless, fiery Eye that sees all. There's been a flashcut of the Eye in Bag End (and one a moment after the Saruman-

Gandalf scene, when Gandalf touches the seeing stone). But Saruman's exposition about the Eye of Sauron explains what happened to Frodo in Bree, and puts the flaming Eye together with Sauron for the movie audience. Giving the Sauron exposition to Christopher Lee (and Saruman) helps to sell the idea of the main baddie being a giant Eye, because Lee has that great voice, and authority. You know Lee's not kidding when he talks about Sauron being reduced to a giant Eye. Coming from, say, Pippin (the Pippin in the film), the Sauron exposition wouldn't be nearly so effective.

Less said about the wizard duel in Orthanc the better. But the filmmakers almost make up for it by turning in a marvellous setting for the roof of Saruman's obsidian skyscraper, the stunning vistas of Isengard below, and the enormous pull-back on Gandalf huddled in his robes against the rain. Not to mention the marvellous visuals of Gwaihir flying behind the gloating Saruman as if right out of the moon. (Although Orthanc was built by Gondorian Dúndedain, it looks in the film as if Saruman has always lived there. He's actually been there about 64 years – not long in Middle-earth terms). (The wizard duel was created largely by the stunt team, who made it up as they went along: it wasn't storyboarded years before shooting. It was Bob Shaye who told the filmmakers that he hoped the duel would be as inventive, dynamic and original as the fights in *The Matrix*. It, err, wasn't [Sib, 473]. I've mentioned *The Matrix* in connection with the wizard duel a couple of times, but that's quite fair, really, because the action in *The Matrix* was choreographed by Yuen Woo-Ping, one of the absolute legends of Hong Kong martial arts cinema. His action scenes are truly astonishing).

One wonders if the screenwriters Walsh, Boyens and Jackson pondered for a while whether to include Gwaihir. After all, it's a scene where the good wizard escapes the bad wizard by jumping onto the back of a giant flying bird. It could easily have got some laughs (probably did in some theatres). But the filmmakers got away with it with some tasty visuals, and sweeping music, and keeping it short). Hell, Gwaihir's nearly as good as Pegasus in *Clash of the Titans* (1981), the Ray Harryhausen extravaganza. Nearly. (And notice that the eagles are never shown in close or medium shot, but always in long shot, and always making slow, graceful movements in the sky. And accompanied by big orchestral cues. And, as in Tolkien's fiction, they are only used sparingly. And, perhaps most crucially, Gwaihir doesn't talk in the film, as he does in Tolkien's tome. One thing the eagles *won't* be doing in the *Lord of the Rings* films is flying over Minas Tirith crying: 'sing and rejoice, ye people of the Tower of Guard', as they do when the ring's destroyed).

With the big crane up over the Isengard model set and the flight over the newly-built mines, teeming with digital orcs, Howard Shore's masterful Saruman theme is heard: big percussive cues, low brass, with thumping drums. (It's as if Shore thought a bit of John Williams would do nicely here – Williams being well-known for his brassy, military themes. In a way, the Saruman theme is Shore's version of the Darth Vader march in *Star Wars*, a cue with a very similar cinematic function).

Note, too, how the entry into the Isengard fly-by is linked by Frodo's cry of 'Gandalf!' when he's wounded by the nazgûl. A nice touch, suggesting that in moments of agony and desperation, Frodo calls out to the father figure wizard. (The shot up to the tower was achieved by moving the camera over the 35th scale Isengard, then handing over to a digital Orthanc tower, and finally up to Ian McKellen on a partial full-size set, raised off a blue-screen floor. CG orcs, atmospheric elements, interactive lighting in the caverns, smoke plumes, and a flying moth were comped into the shot (the moth has Gandalf talking to the animals like Dr Doolittle or Tarzan, and hints at Radagast the Brown, who in the book sends Gwaihir to Isengard). As fx designer Adam Valdez pointed out, the moth was really a supermoth: he had to fly at 1,000 mph to reach the top of the tower. 'The most fun part of the shot was trying to create the feeling that this little moth was answering a call... he was there to have a chat with Gandalf and see what was going on').[3] The production team would argue with the studio, New Line, over particular shots, such as the moth shot, because they were costly. Jackson wanted the whole thing, of course, but New Line reckoned it would be too complicated (i.e., too expensive).

The cross-fade to the choral cue which follows the magical moth that flies up the tower of Orthanc to Gandalf is a little awkward (it's a rough fade-out). The solo English choirboy music is heard briefly, before the camera topples over the roof and flies down into the mines again, ending up on weapons being bashed into shape. (The subsequent montage of orcs hard at work creating weaponry is a kind of tribute to the team at Weta Workshop, the art department, the armourers, the designers, the metal workers, and many others).

The next scene, where Saruman visits the mines to oversee the 'birth' of his new half-men half-orcs is simply another of countless transplants the screenwriters conducted in adapting the book from Sauron to Saruman. In Tolkien's Middle-earth books, the Uruk-hai were bred by Sauron and appeared some 550 years before the events of the War of the Ring (in TA 2475). Only Sauron, and his master Morgoth before him, would have been capable of breeding orcs. It's an unintentionally funny scene, memorable as much for the look of perverted appreciation on Christopher Lee's face as for the orc Lurtz (played by Lawrence Makoare). (Lurtz is a time-consuming full body make-up and prosthetics job. This scene shows off Weta Workshop's efforts).

The film of *The Fellowship of the Ring* elides the hobbits leaving Bree and puts them on their way again, with some second unit long shots of figures in the landscape, and a bit of dialogue explaining that Strider is taking them to Rivendell, to see the elves. A brief comic scene has Merry and Pippin asking about food (second breakfast), and there's a remnant of the hobbits expressing doubts about trusting Strider. The hobbits acquiring weaponry is explained by the ranger handing out swords. Soon, while Strider goes to scout around, the hobbits are cooking some food over a fire in a dell at the side of the hill. The viewpoint alters from the hobbits to the ringwraiths – a long shot of Weathertop at night shows the fire clearly.

Strider has been taken away specifically so he can leap in to rescue the hobbits (in the book, he's with the hobbits when the nazgûl attack). His heroic act at this point will largely define his character as the primary action hero of the films, who single-handedly takes on five bad guys in order to save the cute, friendly hobbits. There will be no doubting his character or dramatic function in the films after this point – though Strider's self-doubt concerning his kingly – and romantic – responsibilities will be milked by the screenwriters to breaking point and beyond.

The Weathertop attack acts as that very familiar scene in action-adventure movies when the villains get close to capturing or killing the heroes, but the goodies manage to escape. Usually, this occurs in the middle section of a movie (often it's a chase, or a duel, or the villains invading the heroes' dwelling). It's there: (1) to provide some action and thrills (and bump up act two, which can often sag), (2) to show off the heroes' ingenuity and teamwork in escaping, (3) to remind the audience of the villains and their pursuit, and (4) to remind viewers of the goals of both heroes and villains. *The Lord of the Rings* is unusual among movies to have the hero severely wounded (rather than a sidekick or secondary figure). And notice that none of henchmen die (there's usually a few deaths of faceless henchmen in action-adventure movies at this point). But there are full body burns for the stunt team.

None of the business with Gandalf being at Weathertop earlier is covered in the film (such as Strider finding the stone with Gandalf's message). A high-pitched scream announces that the nazgûl have discovered their prey; they advance on the hill in a God's-eye-view shot straight out of Hammer horror films: converging on the hill as black, cloaked shapes looming through dry ice. Frodo leads the halflings up to the ruined fortress on the crown of the Weathertop. The hobbits gather in a huddle in the middle of the ring of ruins, statues and pillars. The wraiths rise ominously from beyond the walls, and advance on the hobbits, with Angmar in front, drawing his sword (big close-ups take in the nazgûl's feet, hands, and weapons).

A significant departure from the book occurs here: in the film's Bible (i.e., Tolkien's novel), Frodo *doesn't* instantly fall to the ground and crawl away in panic and fear, then put on the ring. He draws his sword, leaps at the Witch-king, and wounds him in the foot, while crying *'O Elbereth! Gilthoniel!'* (FR, 262) In the film, Sam attempts to stand between the villains and his master, but is thrown to the side, against a wall. Merry and Pippin are cast aside. Frodo falls to the ground, crawls backwards, and puts on the ring. In the white, ghostly wraithworld, the nazgûl are revealed with complex facial make-up (the Witch-king looks like all the blood and muscle's been sucked out of his skull).

When Strider arrives to save the day, Frodo sees him from inside the wraithworld. Frodo's wounded pretty much as in the book, and soon after takes off the ring. The sword fight between Strider and the five ringwraiths certainly wouldn't rank as one of the great action scenes in cinema history. It's not just because it was Viggo Mortensen's first days on the show, nor that it was an early scene to be shot, and the filmmakers hadn't got up to speed with staging fights and action, it's also because of the nature of these mid-film chases or fights: the heroes have to be good enough to escape the villains, and the villains have to be good, but not *too good*. They can't slaughter all of the heroes at this point. So the success of such scenes is to show both heroes and villains as trying their best, but the heroes must always escape. (But the fight is still badly staged).

After the Weathertop scene, the group are holed up underneath the trolls from *The Hobbit*, with Sam pleading that they need help for Frodo. The film elides twelve days and many miles of travelling in the book.

Arwen has one of the best introductions in the films. It's unashamedly over-the-top: slight slow motion, ringing choirs, and bright white light shines behind her and around her. Indeed, this particular saint of Middle-earth is so full of light she even illuminates Frodo, as he lies on the ground, and turns to look at the source of the brilliance. Has the *Close Encounters of the Third Kind* mothership just landed and are aliens streaming out down a mirrored ramp flooded with light? Is Jesus performing miracles on the nearby desert set of a Biblical epic? Is the ring really a portable nuclear device and has Pippin just triggered it by accident? No. Arwen's light is in Frodo's mindscreen. It's how she *ought* appear to him in his stricken state, except that he's fading, sinking into the darkness. The notion comes from the book, where Glorfindel first appears to Frodo:

> The rider's cloak streamed behind him, and his hood was thrown back; his golden hair flowed shimmering in the wind of his speed. To Frodo it appeared that a white light was shining through the form and raiment of the rider, as if through a thin veil. (FR, 279)

It's a view of an elf on the other side, as Gandalf explains.

(Actually, the excessive light came about partly due to a mistake: the stunt rider, Jane Abbott, was wearing the wrong costume and had the wrong hair style. So Chris Godfrey and others had to place a heavy glow around her, achieved with Softimage and Mental Ray software, to hide the error. Bushes and trees were also built digitally, and the light rays made to look as if they came from behind her). (Liv Tyler didn't get on well with riding horses).

When Arwen clutches Frodo to her breast it's not only a mother and child image (because he's small enough to appear as a child), it's a clear *Pietà* image – the Virgin Mary holding the dead Christ. And Arwen murmurs 'come back to the light', as if she's Orpheus calling to Eurydice, imploring his beloved not to step into Hades. (Erica Challis wondered if Arwen were 'trading her immortality right there', by giving up her life for Frodo.)[4]

In its way Arwen holding Frodo is one of the tenderest moments in the films (part of the scene was re-shot by Frances Walsh). Arwen speaks in voiceover of allowing her 'grace' (whatever that is) to pass to Frodo. (We know Frodo's in a bad way, apart from the wound, because he's wearing those weird bluish-white contact lenses and each breath is a gasp).

The scene with Arwen, Aragorn and the hobbits has to do one

important thing: to show Aragorn and Arwen together, and introduce the romance theme: Arwen's the first major female character to show up in the films. A nice touch here has the lovers shifting into speaking in Elvish, like two parents who don't want their kids (the hobbits) to know what they're talking about. (Galadriel speaks the first Elvish in the films, but it's Arwen who does it up close and personal, announcing to camera (to Frodo), 'I'm Arwen' in Elvish, with English in the subtitle. It works, and the filmmakers deftly avoid another potentially embarrassing or silly moment, because although having a character walk up to the camera and intone 'I'm Arwen' in that solemn, low voice could be laughable, in Elvish it sounds great. And particularly when a radiant Liv Tyler is whispering it: when Tyler's got those enormous eyes fixed on the viewer in giant close-up, they can't possibly giggle. Tyler dares the viewer to giggle. But they might mumble something inane before helplessly swooning).

The horse chase has some spectacular second unit photography, but there's nothing remarkable about it (that hasn't been seen in countless Westerns, for instance. But it does provide some good footage for the trailer). At the end of it, Arwen's got one slender scratch on her cheek. But otherwise she still looks luscious.

As Arwen's is the first female costume that's seen up close, it's worth commenting upon it. Her costume is a close-fitting dark green and brown huntress outfit. (Not Xena the Warrior, but not far off it either. It's kinda like what Robin Hood would wear to meet his bank manager: serious and sober. This costume means business!). If that costume was sold in an off-the-peg version in high street stores, it'd do well (like many of the other costumes in the *Lord of the Rings* films). It's just the thing for the young woman who likes to get out and about, a spot of power jogging perhaps, or kickboxing at the local gym, or maybe being chased on horseback by nine ringwraiths with the fate of Middle-earth resting upon her.

Arwen has her hair pulled back in unusual plaits. And, yes, Arwen's sporting pants this Paris fashion season (did women wear pants in mediæval/ DarkAge times? They do here). No impractical pencil skirts for Arwen! This girl's not gonna trip in high heels like a typical movie heroine, or snag her ankle when she's hanging on to the hero's wrist and escaping the mafia hoods! (In the event, it was Orlando Bloom's elf costume that became the most popular among fans – ironically, because the costume department sweated tears over it right up to the last minute).

At the close of the chase Arwen confronts the ringwraiths from the other side of the river (the ringwraiths being reluctant to enter the river was difficult to sell. It's there, but only briefly). Again, the film departs from the book – it doesn't just switch Glorfindel for Arwen, it has Frodo too far gone to offer any resistance to the nazgûl (in the book, Frodo yells at them to go back to the land of Mordor, but gradually falters).

In the film, he can barely keep on Arwen's horse. So it's the elf princess who does the brandishing of swords and defiant cries. And it's Arwen, not Elrond, who summons the flood. The following scene, where Arwen tries to keep Frodo from fading away, is an addition to the book. The brief scene (inevitably another reshoot) has Arwen keeping Frodo alive by the sheer force of her spirituality – her 'grace' as Philippa Boyens and Fran Walsh insist on calling it. (Digital Domain in America took 11 weeks to produce the vfx for the flood sequence, using photographic elements shot at Niagara Falls, as well as slo mo footage shot at 72 and 96 f.p.s. in the studio in L.A. from dump tanks situated 40 feet above the floor. Arwen and Frodo were rotoscoped into the foreground).

NOTES: ACT TWO

1. M. Hopkins, *The Two Towers* DVD documentary.
2. In B. Sibley, 2002, 159
3. In J. Duncan, 2001, 98.
4. In E. Challis, 141. Certainly she's sacrificing much of her strength for Frodo.

ACT THREE

And so to Rivendell.

No one could argue with the quality of the visualization of Rivendell: it's Alan Lee at his best (and most obsessive too: the Rivendell model set goes back and back, and back and back, with more and more buildings being added, creating the illusion of so many layers by Alex Funke and his miniatures team (Chuck Schulman shot the models that made up Rivendell, which were mounted on islands on casters, so they could be shifted around easily. The model background had to line up with the live action footage. Because the Rivendell miniatures were shot in layers, backgrounds could be constructed months later, built from separate layers.) Lee admitted he loved the Rivendell sets – in miniature or full-scale, and hung around them a lot.)

Rivendell was shot at Kaitoke Regional Park, and in the studio, and also comprised models, paintings and CG elements. The CG cyclorama that wrapped around the Rivendell miniatures was created from photographs taken in Fox River Valley on the South Island of New Zealand. The weather was misty during the shoot, although Paul Lasaine had wanted a Mediterranean blue look for Rivendell. But the misty, hazy look suited Rivendell. Waterfalls were filmed in New Zealand and placed into the images.

But before the eye candy of Rivendell's model and matte paintings and animated waterfalls are revealed, the outcome of what happened to our hero at the ford needs to be resolved. (And so it is, straight away).

The Rivendell scenes are introduced with a simple but very effective device: a s-l-o-w, carefully controlled fade out of white on a close-up of Frodo in bed (just prior to that, one should note a brief Hollywood montage (i.e., a series of superimpositions), including Elrond in C.U. looking down into the camera and speaking in Elvish, and pans of the room, a familiar method of suggesting that Frodo's been slipping in and out of consciousness for some time): 'Frodo woke and found himself lying in bed.

At first he thought that he had slept late, after a long pleasant dream that still hovered on the edge of memory' (FR, 287).

The scene, which follows the book fairly closely (and will be repeated in Minas Tirith in *The Return of the King*), has Frodo waking after an ordeal to find Gandalf at his bedside. The screenwriters altered Gandalf's dialogue considerably here. The revelation that Strider is really 'Aragorn son of Arathorn' (FR, 289) was given to Legolas at the council. The account of Gandalf at Isengard was inserted here, moved from the council scene (in the novel).

The bedside scene closes with Elrond (introduced by Gandalf as 'Lord Elrond') welcoming Frodo to Rivendell. Then follows two of the best visual fx images in the *Rings* films, and one of Howard Shore's loveliest cues, as Frodo walks out onto the balcony to take the air. The long shot reveals Rivendell nestling in a steep gorge, with waterfalls and rivers, and paths winding around rocky hillsides (the images closely resemble the painting Alan Lee made of Imladris for the 1992 *The Lord of the Rings* edition, down to many details but also Tolkien's description).

The happy reunion with Merry and Pippin plays in slight slow motion, with muted local sound. The subsequent scene between Frodo and Bilbo (now considerably aged, and looking 128 years-old) is a distinctly Tolkienesque moment, as Frodo examines the book Bilbo has been writing (the book seen in the opening Bag End study scene. Why Bilbo should have aged so swiftly, though, is odd – because in the film the gap between Bilbo leaving and the hobbits arriving at Imladris is, say, a few months. Maybe that's what being without that darned ring does to ya). Flooding these scenes, and the subsequent ones at Rivendell, is a warm, comforting Autumnal light: it is perpetually a sunny mid-afternoon in late September in Rivendell.

The council of Elrond material at the beginning of *Book Two* (included in the chapters "Many Meetings", "The Council of Elrond" and "The Ring Goes South") was the most difficult sequence to adapt in *The Fellowship of the Ring*, and in all three films. The screenwriters didn't transmute "The Council of Elrond" chapter straight, or even a compressed version of it (and the chapters on each side). Instead, they concentrated on the most important plot points, and then took other parts of it and used them elsewhere in the film.

For instance, Gandalf visiting Minas Tirith and discovering the account of Isildur and the ring was described by Gandalf to the council (i.e., a second-hand depiction, not in the foreground of the narrative). The screenwriters took that small scene out and inserted it much earlier in the film, when Gandalf leaves the Shire for the first time.

Another Gandalf-related scene, Gandalf with Saruman at Isengard, was placed right after Frodo wakes up at Rivendell. That gave the scene of Gandalf's battle with Saruman and being imprisoned a different emotional slant: now it wasn't part of the lengthy tales Gandalf told to the council, but a more personal account of what happened, told to one person.

A key scene was to how to introduce the elf, the dwarf and the man: it was done in a rapid montage narrated by Elrond (the film could've spent ages here introducing Legolas, Gimli and Boromir, with all sorts of scenes of interactions and fleshing out characters). Just prior to that was a flashback recounted by Elrond of the fatal moment at Orodruin when Isildur claimed the One Ring for his own. It's brief but vital, foreshadowing the end of the film trilogy.

What's missing from the Rivendell scenes is plenty of the book. Clearly, everything in the Rivendell chapters couldn't be included in the films, because those chapters could take up a whole film in themselves. It would've been nice to see the feast, to see Arwen and Aragorn and Elrond presiding over a little merriment, and maybe even squeeze in a half a stanza of Bilbo's song ("Eärendil was a mariner"). Everyone knew that the history of the dwarves from Gloín, or accounts of Gondor (from Boromir), or the wood elves (from Legolas), or the rangers (from Aragorn), or every detail of the lengthy tales of Elrond and Gandalf, and so on, would never have made it into the picture, or would have to be severely compressed. (There is an elderly dwarf, glimpsed behind Gimli during the arrival montage, that might be Gloín; in the book, Gloín is much more prominent). But a bit of a celebration at this point would have enhanced the film greatly (and the elves could be seen letting their (considerable lengths of) hair down). In the 2001 film of Tolkien's tome they are always so solemn and restrained – more reticent than in the book).

One of the chief reasons for so much going out of the window at Rivendell, of course, was the romance of Arwen and Aragorn. The women working on the script, Philippa Boyens and Fran Walsh (and the producers, too, mindful of their target audience), seemed determined to get at least one decent romantic story into the film. So Aragorn is elevated from rough and ready ranger, action hero and king in exile to romantic lead. While audiences might swoon over the good looks of Elijah Wood or Orlando Bloom, it was Aragorn who gets the girl, who has the romance.

(There are numerous other narrative solutions. The romance of Éowyn and Faramir could be bumped up to grand passion; Aragorn could have an affair with Éowyn; Sam could get it on with Rosie before leaving. Even Frodo, who's more like a prim maiden aunt than a healthy middle-aged hobbit at times, could have a fling with a hairy hobbit babe. But perhaps that aspect of *The Lord of the Rings* is best left to fan fiction, or the secret 'R' rated version of the films which the filmmakers prepared without New Line's knowledge. No, I made that last bit up. But there is fan fiction that eroticizes *The Lord of the Rings* in abundance. My favourite is the cocaine orgy at Rivendell involving Arwen, two orcs, a nazgûl and the shards of Narsil. As for the ring...).

Three scenes were added to the 2001 adaption of *The Fellowship of the Ring* in the centre of the Rivendell sequence: one between Boromir and Aragorn, chiefly to establish Boromir's character (proud, noble, but a little shifty, and too easy to dismiss history, and Isildur and the sword). The Boromir-Aragorn scene includes Isildur and Sauron yet again, in the Alan Lee painting (a further reminder of the prologue), and also when Boromir turns to the shards of Narsil. The moment when Boromir cuts his finger and bleeds is straight out of fairy tales (Sleeping Beauty cutting herself on a spindle), and marks him out (perhaps as a future victim). Aragorn replacing the sword and bowing tells the viewer enough about his respectful attitude to history, to his forefathers, and to his future destiny.

It was a subtle touch having Aragorn reading a book at Rivendell (it's *Tolkien For Dummies*). A book! Not many macho heroes do that in blockbuster films. Not often you see Bruce Willis or Arny popping into the library to pick up *The History of the Second Peloponnesian War* on their way to the LAPD HQ, or the UFO crash site in an Iowa field, or the rendezvous with Don Sorrenzo and his boys on the Strip in Vegas.

The next scene is a continuation of the previous one, with Arwen appearing (now in a shimmering white number, as if Ingrid Bergman had come to find Cary Grant to take him back to the party for a cocktail). Inevitably, Arwen and Aragorn start ruminating on the weight of history and fate on Aragorn's shoulders, his doubts about taking up his responsibilities, about being the person everyone (except Boromir and Denethor) seems to want him to be. It will be the main topic of conversation between them for the rest of the films. They will tackle it from every direction the screenwriters can come up with (rather like a soap opera worrying away at a plot strand involving, say, terminal illness or sexual betrayal, like a dog with a bone).

For her part, Arwen's all loyalty, devotion, love (she's basically the dutiful, stay-at-home wife). *She's* already made her sacrifice, offering to become mortal and stay with him (what a woman!). Aragorn's reluctance to bind his lover to a mortal fate is all very noble and compassionate, but it's a little hard to believe as well, when he's got Liv Tyler in his arms offering herself to him. Is he nuts? (You know Aragorn must have *serious* problems when he's turning down a beautiful, loving woman like that).

The interior library scene between Aragorn and Arwen segues into a classic love scene (cue Enya on the soundtrack, and birds chirping, tons of smoke and backlight, and water ripples reflected on a small bridge. We wouldn't be surprised if a couple of cute li'l Disney creatures hop onto the bridge, smiling, while twittering bluebirds fly around the lovers' heads).

It's a love tryst to make the Goth girls and neo-romantics in the audience go goo-goo. Kissing and whispering and love pledges. Here the prop of the evenstar is introduced (a perfect piece of merchandizing for the female audience). Boy, will that jewel do a lot of narrative work! (Éowyn draws attention to it, it's pried out of an orc's mitt, Legolas returns it to Aragorn at Helm's Deep, it smashes in Aragorn's dreams, and so on.)

After that poignant, gooey interlude, the films returns to the primary narrative strand – Frodo and the ring – with the Council of Elrond – the committee meeting from hell, the watering-hole scene to end all watering-hole scenes. (Philippa Boyens recalled that writing the Rivendell sequence 'nearly killed me. Nearly killed Fran. We were like, 'Don't make us go back there''. I can believe that: if you think this script was easy, try this test: condense the Council of Elrond chapters in the book into ten minutes of screen time, with a satisfying dramatic shape and every important ingredient, plot point, incident and character included. Whew! Can we have another coffee break first?! Where's the cocaine?).

The council scene has a number of subsidiary functions (such as elaborating the enmity between elves and dwarves, fleshing out the characters of Gimli, Legolas and Boromir a little more, and so on). Two important sub-plots are foreshadowed: that Strider is actually Aragorn, heir of Gondor (revealed, oddly, by Legolas, not, as in the book, by Gandalf to Frodo), and that Boromir wants to use the ring or take it to Gondor. Both these plot strands pay off big time later.

(All sorts of subtle aspects of the relationships between the characters are revealed too: the cut to Aragorn, for example, when Boromir expounds how it's Gondor who keeps Middle-earth safe. If you know the book, that huffy reaction shot of Aragorn refers to the effort over hundreds of years of the rangers to protect places like the Shire; if you don't, it under-scores the tension between Boromir and Aragorn, with Boromir as a rival for leadership of the fellowship – especially after the demise of Gandalf).

But the council scene has three overriding dramatic functions: Frodo has to volunteer to the ring, its fate has to be decided upon, and the fellowship has to be formed. Along the way there are some interesting touches, as the scriptwriters struggle to invent new ways of making a scene comprising people sitting around talking into good cinema (that's why it's really the Committee Meeting From Hell: if you've been to that kind of meeting, you'll know what I mean. Good examples occur in *A Man For All Seasons* (1965). And in *Jesus of Nazareth* (1977) there's a long council scene of religious elders which involves some big names: Laurence Olivier, Anthony Quinn, Ian Holm, James Mason, etc).

One of these added flourishes has Gandalf reciting the Black Speech (in the *Special Extended Edition*): there's thunder, and darkness (it's basically a bigger version of the scene in Bag End, when Gandalf scared Bilbo). Note the cuts to Elrond and Legolas, who seem most disturbed by hearing the Black Speech.

When Frodo brings forth the ring, he sits down with a sigh of relief (like Bilbo did when he finally let go of it). He seems to smile a little, as if he imagines, at that point, that he's rid of the ring altogether. There's no stone pedestal in the book (Frodo just holds up the ring), but it adds to the dramatic tension to have the ring on permanent display throughout the council (a precious object that only the foolhardy dare to touch), and allowing it to work its magic.

When Gimli leaps up with his axe to smash the ring, it tells the viewer plenty about his character (it's the first decisive action Gimli's taken so far). That action is there for the disbelieving dudes in the audience who're going, 'hey, just smash the thing!' The ring (i.e., Sauron) talks at this moment, when the axe shatters and the ring's unaffected. A reaction shot of Frodo suggests that the hobbit has a twinge of pain, which Gandalf notices, as if he's already linked to the ring and wouldn't want any harm to come to it (the moment will pay off, of course, at the Crack of Doom, when he claims the ring for himself).

The ring murmurs again when Boromir approaches it (in the

extended cut) and Gandalf responds with the warning of the Black Speech (the ring 'speaks' to Frodo, Gandalf, Gimli and Boromir, among others). But the stand-out moment in the Council of Elrond scene comes when the giant close-up of the ring reveals the reflections of the council members arguing in it (people arguing is OK as drama, but turning them back onto the ring is heightened drama).

The wall of flames that wraps around the ring is a masterful touch, because the first time Sauron is introduced, at the Sammath Naur, flames were superimposed over his figure. Fire is always a Sauronic device; whether it's the fire that created the ring in Orodruin, the burning village in the Westfold, the lanes of lava at Barad-dûr, or even the fires Saruman creates at Isengard. (As DP Alex Funke remarked, fire is everywhere in the *Lord of the Rings* films. Funke was referring to the difficulty of reproducing fire in visual effects, but he's right: there's fire in the prologue, the lava streams surrounding Barad-dûr, Mount Doom, the Sammath Naur, the Rohirrim village, the balrog, the wall of flame in Moria, Isengard, the attack on Minas Tirith, and of course Sauron himself.)

This is great cinema, a superb solution to the problem of showing how evil the ring is, how Sauron can manipulate people, via the ring, over huge distances. And over the sound of people yelling, the flames roaring, is Sauron's voice. It's as if Sauron himself is orchestrating this descent into dissent in the council, through the ring. The reaction shots of Frodo (still seated, like Elrond) emphasize that idea (as do the alterations of sound from a third person to a first person soundscape). For Frodo, more connected to the ring now than anyone else there, it rightly appears that it's Sauron's evil that's inciting the conflict. As of course it is. But, just in case some parts of the audience haven't got that idea (which Gandalf and Elrond have explained at length), the use of the sound mix, the addition of Sauron's voice, the visual fx of reflections and fire, the cutting pattern, all ram it home. (Diehard Tolkien fans might retort that no way could Sauron have that kind of influence in Rivendell, which's protected by Elrond's ring Vilya from Sauron's influence).

As drama, *this* is the right moment for Frodo to stand up and declare he will take the ring (it's the moment when Frodo becomes a true hero, an even more dramatic extension of his decision to carry the ring at Bag End, although Frodo was already a true hero when he agrees to take the ring in Hobbiton, which Gandalf rightly recognizes). In the book, it occurs right at the end of "The Council of Elrond" chapter, when Bilbo has stood up and been placated by Gandalf, and everyone is downcast and deep in thought. So Frodo's 'small voice' comes out of a quiet, uncomfortable moment, very different from the film.

> An overwhelming longing to rest and remain at peace by Bilbo's side in Rivendell filled all his heart. At last with an effort he spoke, and wondered to hear his own words, as if some other will was using his small voice.
> "I will take the Ring," he said, "though I do not know the way."
> (FR, 354)

But the film, rather, has been building up the suspense precisely so that Frodo can announce he'll take the ring. Like so much in the film, it's kinda what happens in the novel, but amped up ten notches dramatically.

Swiftly after that, the fellowship is formed. In the book, Tolkien delays the formation a few pages, and it occurs in another debate between Elrond, Gandalf, Aragorn and the hobbits (yes, another debate. And it's *Elrond* who picks out the members of the fellowship, rather than having them offer their services heroically here, at the council).

Any film adaption would want to get the members of the company together much quicker than that (and particularly after a long talky scene without any monsters or action). When the formation occurs, each of the members of the fellowship pledge their allegiance in a manner rather like knights with kings (when Aragorn kneels before Frodo and offers his sword, you're not supposed to snigger). The order of members (Gandalf first, then Aragorn, Legolas, Gimli, Boromir and the hobbits) is in keeping with their character, and function in the films. Boromir's somewhat cautious, reluctant acceptance ('if this is indeed the will of the council') is closed with an ominous rejoinder: 'you carry the fate of us all, little one'. The message to the movie audience is clear: watch out for this guy.

In the book, Elrond is reluctant to allow the other two hobbits to join the fellowship, and wants to send them back to the Shire, aware that things may be happening there. Gandalf responds by saying that hobbits might do just as well as anyone else in this quest: '"it would be well to trust rather to Friendship than to great wisdom"', Gandalf tells Elrond (FR, 360). And not even an elf-lord like Glorfindel could storm the Dark Tower, Gandalf adds.

The Council of Elrond sequence closes (finally!) with one of the iconic moments in the three films: the nine companions standing side by side in two rows (short guys at the front, natch), as if posing for a school or wedding photograph (indeed, the cast – and crew – will pose like this many, many times during the marketing of the movies). The bit of humour arising from the hobbits scurrying in functions to lighten the mood after the long talks and serious council scene.

So the ring goes South. (One of the best jokes in the film, on the extended cut, has Frodo asking Gandalf which turning is the way to Mordor as they leave Rivendell's gates). The *Special Extended Edition* of *The Fellowship of the Ring* also added a couple of brief scenes before the boys are on their way.

In the theatrical cut, there's a touching scene between Bilbo and Frodo (with a jump moment when Bilbo becomes 'a little wrinkled creature with a hungry face and bony groping hands' [FR, 304], achieved by substituting a devilish Bilbo puppet for a few frames). After Bilbo's given Frodo Sting and the mithril shirt, he won't be seen until the final reel of the three films. Bilbo, the only person in the history of the One Ring to give up the ring willingly, wisely decides to sit this one out.

After the Bilbo gift-giving scene, the film cracks on with the road movie format. The extended cut, though, has time to dwell a little longer at

Rivendell. There's an opportunity for Aragorn to visit his mother's grave (which embellishes his character a little further). A sidenote: both Elrond and Aragorn have lost the women in their lives to orcs: Celebrían, daughter of Galadriel and Celeborn, was ambushed by orcs in TA 2509 (509 years before the events in *The Lord of the Rings*). The poisoned wound she received was one of the reasons she left for Valinor in TA 2510. (Elrond and Celebrían were married for 2409 years before she left for the West; so she's been a widow for hundreds of years). Aragorn's mother Gilraen, meanwhile, was killed by orcs in TA 3007 (that is, eleven years before the events of *The Lord of the Rings*. The screenwriters may have been tempted to portray that scene, to give added impetus to Aragorn's need or desire to avenge her death. But that would have meant delving into Aragorn's backstory further, which would've held up the film again.)

There's a short departure scene at the gates of Rivendell overseen by Elrond in the extended edit. In this last scene, Liv Tyler's Arwen looks at her worst (and closest to 'realism' – whatever that is), as if she's been up weeping all night (a 'no make-up' look, as if she's too distraught by Aragorn leaving to bother with making up her face).

Although Aragorn II and Gandalf are often compared to King Arthur and Merlin the magician, it's Elrond (aided by his daughter) who takes up a good deal of the role of adviser to Aragorn, not Gandalf, encouraging him to 'become who he was born to do be' as the old elf puts it at Gilraen's memorial. Gandalf, meanwhile, acts as Merlin did with the young Arthur with Frodo, guiding him, advising him and supporting him. The bond between Aragorn and Gandalf is much stronger, more satisfying and more poignant in the novel. The idea that Aragorn was (and still is) a pupil of Gandalf's is transferred in the film to Elrond (and Faramir, similarly, is something of a pupil of Gandalf's but that's not in the picture either).

Following the departure from Rivendell there are short sequences of the fellowship amid epic scenery intercut with short scenes which explore a teensie bit more of the characters, but chiefly Gandalf's wavering about the decisions for the route. There's also a 'hero fellowship shot', as the filmmakers called it, of the company walking past the camera against a mountainscape (but shot in the studio, not on a distant Kiwi summit). This was devised partly for the trailers and marketing – a shot which would feature all of the fellowship together. Peter Jackson shot the beginning of it, but Barrie Osborne completed shooting it (at different slow motion speeds, such as 36 and 48 f.p.s.).

On the lower hills of the Misty Mountains the Company halt for a little food (a Samwise Gamgee fry-up again), sword practice (fun and games as Merry and Pippin learn from Boromir how to be warriors), and discussions about where to go next (with Gimli, with a little bit of a Welsh accent, suggesting to the wizard that they head for Moria where his cousin Balin will give them a royal welcome. Gimli's response to going to Moria is different in the book – eager, but also cautious). In the book, it's Aragorn who's afraid of going into Moria, not Gandalf. Shifting the fear to Gandalf makes sense in terms of prefiguring Gandalf's demise.[1] In the film, this section is built up as a battle of wills between the two wizards, which isn't in the book.

What was a rest on the journey turns into a minor action beat for the movie audience, as the crows fly overhead (with a nod to 1963's *The Birds*, a direct recreation of the famous God's-eye-view shot of the birds flying over Bodega Bay. A shot, incidentally, that took two women three months to complete, by rotoscoping seagulls shot from a 90 foot cliff in California. It lasted ten seconds on screen in Alfred Hitchcock's film).

What's so striking in the scenes prior to the Nine Walkers reaching the West gate of Moria is just how prominent Saruman is in the narrative. In the book around this point, yes, there are references to his spies, and to Saruman's presence at the Gap of Rohan, but he is certainly far in the distance behind the looming, brooding form of the Lord of the Rings (and his henchmen, the nazgûl). In the book it's *ALWAYS SAURON* whose long arm can be felt stretching far over Middle-earth, *NOT* Saruman. The orcs were put in Moria by Sauron; the wargs, if they're in league with anybody, it's with Sauron; and the spies (including the birds) are Sauron's too. The film reverts all of that influence in Eregion to Saruman.

But the film does much more than that. It doesn't just suggest that Saruman, back in Isengard, is sending out spies, it suggests that Saruman is following the progression of the fellowship through Eregion closely (even though he doesn't know anything about it in the book). It does this by cutting back and forth between Gandalf leading the Company of the Ring across hills and wildernesses and Saruman in Orthanc. Thus, when Gandalf's worrying about entering Moria (over big close-ups of Gandalf in the snow on the mountain), the film cuts to Saruman leafing through a book and talking about the nameless fear the dwarves woke when they dug too deep (though how Saruman knows there's a balrog in Moria is not explained. The film doesn't quite have Saruman peering into a magic pool or crystal ball that shows him the fellowship, as in *The Wizard of Oz* or *The Clash of the Titans*). The book that Saruman consults functions in the film to foreshadow the balrog, with an illustration by Alan Lee in the style of William Blake (and also, incidentally, a version of the elegant design of the West gate which Pauline Baynes drew for early editions of *The Fellowship of the Ring*. It's nice to see Baynes' art in a Hollywood flick).

And when Gandalf turns to contemplate Caradhras, after the Dunland crows have spooked the fellowship, Saruman's on hand again to tell the viewer about the dangers of that particular road (the arrival of the crows back in Isengard is accomplished with one of the wilder model shots in the *Rings* films, as the camera flies behind the birds in crazy swoops. The boldness of this apparently continuous aerial shot helps to hide the fact that this mine is – like the mine in *Total Recall* (1990) or *Indiana Jones and the Temple of Doom* (1984) – a model. In fact, it's three 1/14th scale models, with matted hook-ups between each miniature. The crows were digital, and the orc workers were digital figures).

The batting of wizardly strategy back and forth between Gandalf and Saruman (all suggested through editing and scriptwriting) culminates with the avalanche Saruman calls up on the Redhorn. Legolas's line that there are 'fell voices on the air' is snipped from the warg attack scene earlier (in the book). But the voices are not wargs, or orcs, or other creatures, or Caradhras the Cruel itself (in the book the strange noises the Company hear may or may not be in league with Sauron), but Saruman on top of Orthanc. *Everything* is telescoped down to *Saruman*: the movie personalizes all possible obstacles for the fellowship as stemming from Saruman (which severely limits the scope of J.R.R. Tolkien's book).

The swooping helicopter shot of Saruman with his arms outstretched incanting is one of the best in the films (it begins in long shot, careens past the imposing form of Christopher Lee and pulls back to reveal an angry, cloudy sky, handing over and back from miniatures and matte paintings and CG elements to live action). It's such a truly great movie moment, the viewer can forget for a moment that the scene bestows on Saruman powers of a godly nature (equal to Sauron's). Now the white wizard can command the natural elements hundreds of miles away, causing a lightning strike to dislodge tons of snow and rocks onto the fellowship (it's cool, too, that Gandalf attempts a counter-spell, which doesn't seem to do the trick. The avalanche was achieved on the miniature of the mountain-side with table salt and bicarbonate of soda, falling from dump tanks set up above the model, pushed by hydraulic rams).

Now comes the moment when Gandalf – bizarrely, unfairly and cruelly – asks Frodo (poor Frodo) to make the decision about going through Moria. (And Saruman's had time to run down hundreds of flights of stairs at Orthanc, smoothing his long windswept hair on the way, ready for his next telepathic *tête-à-tête* with Gandalf). When I look at these snow scenes, however, I think of the cast's stories of the uncomfortable conditions of filming them, when cast and crew, directors Fran Walsh, John Mahaffie and Rick Porras, all complained about the fake snow in the studio which got everywhere. And the snow in the film does look very fake.

Let's face it, despite a scene set on a real mountainside, the *Lord of the Rings* films are not great snow movies like, say, *Pathfinder* (1987) or *Andrei Rublyev* (1966) or even *Fargo* (1996). Those movies were shot in real snow. (Why is it that Hollywood films use such bad artificial snow, even in an age of incredibly sophisticated visual and digital effects? The only really exceptional fake snow scene is in *The Magnificent Ambersons* (1942), with its famous sleigh ride scene shot by Orson Welles over 12 days in an ice factory in L.A. It helps, of course, that this matchless scene was part of one the greatest films ever made.)

Talking about mountain scenes, let's have a look at the one where Boromir takes up the ring (one of the very few, incidentally, shot on a location with real snow). It's not in the book; in essence, it foreshadows what'll happen later between Frodo and Boromir at Amon Hen (and also the way that Aragorn will be nearby, trying to protect Frodo – note that in the mountain scene Gandalf is way off, up the slope). But when Boromir encounters Frodo at Parth Galen, Aragorn isn't there. The scene is also a call back to the scene in the prologue where Isildur keeps the ring for himself, and the continuation of that in the Council of Elrond three thousand year flashback to the Orodruin, where Isildur refuses to destroy the ring.

Some of the images of the Caradhras scene were used so often in the marketing of *The Fellowship of the Ring* (the helicopter shot of the fellowship, the close-up of the ring in the snow using an oversize prop ring), it seemed as if the cast were helicoptered up there to do the scene specifically for a little production value and material for trailers and promos. Nothing wrong with that of course. It's what Hollywood does so well. As written, the scene, where Boromir's tempted by the ring yet again, could've been set anywhere. But the real mountain, the light, the snow, all enhanced the film a little at that point (and also, from that point onwards, the film was going to dive into the studio for next half-an-hour, with the Moria scenes. So the actors in the snow in daylight was a little bit of fresh air before oppressive, gloomy Khazad-dûm). (For marketing purposes, though, it would've been the other way around: the PR dept would trawl through the film and extract the images and short sequences they thought best sold the film.)

MORIA.

What a gift for a filmmaker. It's got everything: relentless build-up of tension, suspense, monsters, orcs, fights, tunnels and caves, abysses, skeletons, narrow escapes, the death of a major character, the works. It would be good even in a low budget film, even in a pantomime on stage in a small, provincial theatre. With so much to play around with, you'd have to be a terrible filmmaker to mess it up. Moria's the set-piece action sequence of *The Fellowship of the Ring,* as Helm's Deep is in *The Two Towers* and the Battle of Pelennor Fields is in *The Return of the King.* Peter Travers in *Rolling Stone* quipped of the Moria scenes in *Fellowship*: 'these action sequences play like gangbusters. And when Gandalf faces the winged demon Balrog on a bridge and thunders, 'You shall not pass!' well, even the Taliban would quake'.

Before Gandalf's remembers how to get inside Moria (aided by Frodo), there are a couple of brief scenes. One scene, included in the *Special Extended Edition* of *The Fellowship of the Ring* (and probably a pick-up scene), has Gandalf warning Frodo about the possibility of danger inside as well as outside the fellowship (referring to Boromir, who walks past them at that moment). Gandalf also hints that he might not always be around for Frodo, that there are some foes against whom he has not yet been tested. It's such a clumsy scene – badly written and badly acted. Bad writing, because it foreshadows too much. Yes, in the book, Gandalf has a growing unease about Khazad-dûm, but he never tells Frodo he might not always been around like that. Yet, when the film stays a little closer to the book, as in the scene where Gandalf talks about mithril a few minutes later, it's much more satisfying. The end of the scene has Gimli gasp 'the walls of Moria!', Gandalf looking up and a cut to an impressive and ominous matte painting of the rock walls.

If one wanted to offer an example of Ronald Tolkien's talent for writing to those detractors who emphasize what a bad writer he was (adolescent, immature, simplistic, repetitive, they call him), Moria would be a good choice. It's good writing because it's simply good storytelling. It engages the reader completely and immerses them in a vividly evoked environment. The reader's with the characters every step of the way. There's a sense of Tolkien following his nose, of his narrator making it up as he went along, and discovering the horrors in Moria along with the reader. He uses a classic device to get the Company into the mines swiftly – the Watcher in the lake (there's no going back). There are days of walking in darkness, the feeling of cold, claustrophobia, oppression, a tomb-like deadness. A sense of huge areas of the dwarf kingdoms stretching on for miles, of tunnels no one wants to enter, of endless stone stairs, of decay and dust, and of being followed by the pad-pad of Gollum. It's marvellous stuff, and anybody adapting it, whether for radio, TV, theatre, film or whatever, couldn't help but have a great time, feeding off so many tremendously vivid images and sequences that Tolkien provides.

For all those reasons, I don't reckon Moria would have disappointed if it had been shot by Irving Allen, king of disaster and adventure movies, in, say, 1961. Or if Ray Harryhausen had got hold of it in, say, the mid-1960s or mid-1970s. Or George Lucas or Ridley Scott in the mid-1980s. The acting doesn't really matter in the Moria chapters, nor the sets, the costumes, the lighting, the editing or the visual effects, or whatever. (It doesn't *need* CGI and digital jiggery-pokery either – a huge part of Moria is miniatures anyway in the 2001 *Fellowship of the Ring*). It's the *storytelling* that counts, the scope of it, the chilling, oppressive atmospheres Tolkien generates:

> *Doom, doom* it rolled again, as if huge hands were turning the very caverns of Moria into a vast drum. Then there came an echoing blast: a great horn was blown in the hall, and answering horns and harsh cries were heard further off. There was a hurrying sound of many feet.
> "They are coming!" cried Legolas.
> "We cannot get out," said Gimli.
> "Trapped!" cried Gandalf. "Why did I delay. Here we are, caught, just as they were before. But I was not here then. We will see what –"
> *Doom, doom* came the drum-beats, and the walls shook.
> "Slam the doors and wedge them!" shouted Aragorn. "And keep your packs on as long as you can: we may get a chance to cut our way out yet."
> "No!" said Gandalf. "We must not get shut in. Keep the east door ajar! We will go that way, if we get a chance."
> Another harsh call and shrll cries rang out. Feet were coming down the corridor. There was a ring and clatter as the Company drew their swords. Glamdring shone with a pale light, and Sting glinted at the edges. (FR, 420)

It's sequences like Moria that have helped to make *The Lord of the Rings* one of the most popular books in the modern era. It may not be 'great literature' like *Ulysses, The Magic Mountain, Gravity's Rainbow* or *The Tin Drum*, but it is a *cracking good read*, a book that sucks the reader in and carries them along on a compelling and exciting journey. It's the same with authors such as Michael Crichton, Joanne Rowling, Jackie Collins, John Grisham, Tom Clancy and Stephen King, writers that literary critics regularly denigrate, but that readers love to read. Not to judge, to analyze, to compose essays about, but simply to read for the sheer joy of reading. Wanting to know what happened next.

This talent for storytelling shouldn't be under-estimated. It's not that easy to create books that people buy and read in tens of millions (or films that viewers consume in their millions). No one *forces* consumers to buy books. So if they do, there must be something about the book and the story that they enjoy. But because it's couched in a fantasy genre, or an action-adventure genre, this kind of fiction is persistently undervalued by the literary establishment. For many literary critics, Tolkien will never live alongside Thomas Mann, James Joyce, Günter Grass or Thomas Pynchon, but also, to their continuing bafflement and resentment, Tolkien will outstrip the sales and reader figures for any of those modernist novelists.

The scene in the 2001 film of *The Lord of the Rings* outside the West gate of Moria follows Tolkien's tome closely. (A little of the journey was cut, as was the animosity between Legolas and Gimli, and the warg attack was wholly omitted). Classic horror film devices were employed to suggest the approach of the Watcher in the Water (a cut to a handheld point-of-view shot of the fellowship below the wall, for instance, which is presumably meant to suggest the monster's viewpoint). When the Watcher appears, there are nods to Ray Harryhausen movies, as well as Disney's *20,000 Leagues Under the Sea* (1954), which has a classic (and very expensive) fight with a giant squid.

In J.R.R. Tolkien's book, Frodo's dragged along the ground by a tentacle and Sam hacks at it with a knife, until it lets go and the hobbits manage to reach the doors (FR, 401). It's a nice heroic moment for Sam, too, because everyone else is rooted to the spot – usually it's Aragorn or Legolas who're the first to react (FR, 402). As expected, the film ramps up the action, and has cable work, practical effects, model work, computer generated tentacles, and all sorts of additions to sell the action: Frodo's lifted into the air, and Aragorn and Boromir chop at the tentacles. (The scene was shot by Guy Norris and stunt co-ordinator George Ruge, with the crew holding sticks to help the actors with eyelines. It was one of the tricker scenes to accomplish because of the water element, which used a mixture of real water and CG water. The scene was going to be dropped, due to budgetary and schedule reasons, but using 2nd unit directors to shoot it enabled it to stay in the film [Sib, 476]).

The film also shifts the timing and suspense of the scene from the book (as well as making Aragorn the hero, not Sam – the screenwriters never lost an opportunity for building up Aragorn's character ever higher). For instance, in the book Gandalf has just stepped into the tunnel when 'several things happened' (FR, 401). In the film, the Company all move through the doorway, and have time to discuss Moria for a moment (Gimli promises a roaring fire and good food), and find out that there are skeletons everywhere, a classic haunted house movie moment ('it's a tomb', says Boromir), before the monster attacks. The film, then, offers a common device: to extend the suspense: the audience knows, from the stones thrown in the water, the close-ups on ripples, and the cutting pattern, that something's in the lake. They also guess that the ripples and handheld p.o.v. shots will pay off in a short time (the audience are ahead of the characters here: it's a 'it's behind you!' pantomime moment). The filmmakers then tease the audience by delaying that pay-off.

Once inside Moria, the film sticks to the overall narrative structure that Tolkien had devised: long journeys through dark tunnels, Gandalf's indecision about the route, Pippin throwing something in a hole which alerts the enemy, Gollum pursuing the Company, Balin's tomb, the Book of Mazarbul, the orc fight, and the whole sequence culminating in the bridge and the balrog and Gandalf's death.

The extended cut on DVD and video added some minor embellishments. One of them refers to the history of the mines, and what the dwarves were really there for: mithril. This scene allows for some further impressive images of the mines, including a floating bird's-eye-view way above the Company walking along a ledge, an Irving Allen kind of shot (cue choral music from Howard Shore for this 'wow' shot), and also foreshadows Frodo's mithril coat. (Digital grading took down the colour in the Moria scenes, particularly on the actors' faces).

An important segment of chapter two of *The Lord of the Rings* ("The Shadow of the Past") was inserted here, when the Company halt beside the three doorways with dwarvish-looking decorations (in the book it's Pippin who sits up with Gandalf during a nightwatch). The scene, a quiet two-hander between Gandalf and Frodo, sitting slightly apart from the others (and covered in tight close-ups), puts forward some of the moral philosophy of the films and the book: about Bilbo (and Frodo) being 'meant' to find the ring, '"that may be an encouraging thought"', remarks Gandalf (FR, 84), about using one's own time wisely, and the dialogue about pity or mercy:

> "What a pity that Bilbo not stab that vile creature, when he had a chance!"
> "Pity? It was Pity that stayed his hand, and Mercy: not to strike without need... Many that live deserve death. And some that die deserve life. Can you give it to them? Then do not be too eager to deal out death in judgement. For even the very wise cannot see all ends"'
> (FR, 89)

The conversation between Gandalf and Frodo contains some of J.R.R. Tolkien's humanist, pragmatic life-philosophy. Not Christian or pagan, not pessimistic or optimistic, but practical. If critics wanted to link Tolkien's philosophy of life to his experience in the First World War, and losing all of his friends bar a few, or to losing both parents by the age of twelve, it's easy (and has already been done). As Tolkien scholars have noted, this conversation is pivotal, because it looks forward to the climax of the book, when Frodo and Gollum fight for the ring at the Crack of Doom, or the moment when Frodo has an opportunity for killing Gollum and declines (when he could give a signal to Faramir), or when Gollum's part in the fate of the ring is unseen by even the wise.

The dialogue in the film has also been inspired by the sight of Gollum. Much of the "The Shadow of the Past" chapter concerned the ring and Gollum (and Bilbo), so it's apposite that Gollum should appear now in Moria. (Two shots introduce Gollum: a very long shot, with his scrawny figure leaping from rock to tock, and a big, shadowy, creepy close-up. The story of Gollum which Gandalf relates at Bag End will be transposed to the opening of *The Return of the King*).

Note that Frodo doesn't kill anyone in either book or film, and that he rarely uses his sword. In this incredibly violent set of films, the hero is no action hero, no Arny or Sean or Keanu. Unusually, the film went even further than the book on this point, turning Frodo into even more a pacificist or non-participant in terms of violence and death. In the book, for example, Frodo leaps forward and stabs the troll's foot in Balin's tomb (while Boromir's sword glances off): '"One for the Shire!" cried Aragorn. "The hobbit's bite is deep! You have a good blade, Frodo son of Drogo!" (FR, 422). The film excised that moment, and Frodo was simply hunted down by the troll. Frodo also leapt at the Witch-king and stabbed his foot in the book, but the film lost that too.

Note that the music cue in the troll fight action scene starts when Frodo draws his sword and it's glowing blue; but though Frodo appears to move forward with the other hobbits towards the danger, he's not depicted in any encounter with an orc in this scene, or any subsequent scene. (In the book of *The Lord of the Rings* for example, Frodo hacks off the barrow-wight's hand. About the only time the viewer associates Frodo and his sword and conflict in the 2001-2003 films are the two times he draws it on a character lying on the ground: when Gollum first appears to the two hobbits in the Emyn Muil, and Frodo tames him by brandishing Sting, and the mirror of that scene, at Osgiliath, with Sam). The film, then, 'feminizes' Frodo beyond the book (although in the book Frodo is a 'feminized' hero, lacking the macho heroics of Aragorn or Éomer). The fellowship don't take a woman along with them (Arwen), as some Tolkien fans feared when the film was being made, but they do take Frodo (and Frodo's treated a little like young women are in action-adventure movies).

Some of the members of the fellowship in the 2001 film pile up bodies by the tens, with Leggy, Gimli and Aragorn having the highest body count (and the elf and the dwarf have a running gag about their death tolls), followed by Boromir, Faramir, Éomer, Gandalf, Éowyn, Théoden, Haldir, Háma and others, who all kill people in hand-to-hand combat (the *Lord of the Rings* films are decidedly un-PC when it comes to multiple on-screen deaths). Even Merry and Pippin have their moments of heroic slaying (and Sam gets grisly at Cirith Ungol). But not Frodo.

The troll fight in the Chamber of Mazarbul was designed as one of the key action scenes in *The Fellowship of the Ring*, and became instrumental, for instance, in the film being shown at Cannes, as well as the marketing during release. It's a very over-the-top slice of Hollywood action: Aragorn and Boromir are thrown against the wall by the troll with a force that would kill anyone else (in the extended cut). Merry and Pippin become impossibly heroic, and leap onto the troll's shoulders (as does Legolas).

The fight with the troll in Moria was ridiculous if you thought about it for even a moment. While exciting, it was unbelievable that the hobbits would be in any serious danger from a cave troll and a few orcs with Gandalf around. Only Sauron himself in all Middle-earth, as Tolkien says, could be a fearsome adversary for Gandalf (and the Witch-king and the balrog, of course). But not a troll and some orcs. After all, in *The Return of the King,* Gandalf vanquishes the flying nazgûl single-handed (when he rescues the retreat from Osgiliath, in both book and film). And Gandalf's not alone to protect the hobbits: there's Aragorn (according to the films and book, the greatest warrior in Middle-earth at that time), Gimli, Legolas and Boromir, and every one of those four guys is depicted by the films as a skilful and very successful fighter who happily and effortlessly pile up corpses ('19... 20... 21!' Gimli cries as he hews orcs down at Helm's Deep in the film of *The Two Towers*). So with five extraordinary combatants, Frodo wouldn't really be in jeopardy, and there's no sense of danger for the Company.

But the biggest gripe about the troll fight is it goes on for absolutely ages, longer than the Third Age of Middle-earth (and that's only in the theatrical version). Narratively, it has only one purpose: Frodo is menaced by the troll and then speared by it. And he survives. And for some supernatural reason, the troll (portrayed by the filmmakers as very stupid, but kinda lovable too, though he's not quite Shrek yet), somehow knows who Frodo is, and can distinguish him in amongst the other hobbits and the chaos of the fight.

Another thing: while Aragorn is busy rushing to Frodo's aid a number of times (and even more times in the extended edition than the theatrical cut), *what the hell* is Gandalf doing? Is he painting his fingernails in a corner? Or perhaps most of the orcs have orders to keep the wizard busy? Note how, unable to really explain the long delay before Gandalf goes to Frodo's aid, he is largely cut out of the fight by the editors, who concentrate far more on the elf, the dwarf, the hobbits, and the two men. All of the other characters have little bits of business particular to them: Legolas leaps onto the upper level, dodges the troll's chain, leaps onto his back, fires arrows into the troll, and later waits patiently for the troll's throat to be exposed to he can finally kill it with an arrow. Boromir has some stunt action with orcs, as well as being thrown by the troll, coming round, and being saved at the last moment by Aragorn throwing a sword into an orc's neck (in the extended cut). Meriadoc and Peregrin, meanwhile, throw stones at the troll, leap onto the troll's back when they see Frodo wounded, and get whirled around, upside-down, in the troll's fist. Gimli has some slashes at the troll, throws an axe at it, and leaps off Balin's tomb just before the troll demolishes it with his club. Sam uses his frying pan to bash orcs on the head ('I'm getting the hang of this', he quips). Aragorn struggles to Frodo's side, is swiped against a wall by the troll, uses a spear to try to pierce the troll's hide on its chest, and is eventually knocked unconscious (Frodo calls to him but he can't answer). There are plenty more stunts and gags in this troll fight.

While Frodo is being hunted by the troll, Gandalf is glaringly absent: yet he has dominated all of the Moria scenes up his point, and dominates all of them after it. One can see, from the descriptions of just a few of the many incidents in the troll fight, that the filmmakers cheat considerably by erasing Gandalf (not entirely: Gandalf is shown fighting briefly, and he does hurl away his hat – the last time it's used in the *Lord of the Rings* movies). Frodo is not shown having any kind of encounter with an orc, however, and isn't a great fighter. He spends most of his time in the troll fight running away from the troll, hiding behind a pillar, thinking he's free, then being spooked by the troll, and so on.

Gandalf's absence may have stemmed from the filmmakers being unsure about what to do with Gandalf in this kind of *melée*. What *does* an elderly wizard do? A wizard would probably use magic, but, maybe, having decided to save Gandalf's big moment for the balrog fight, the filmmakers opted to take him out of this one (including saving the magic for the later scene).

In the book, of course, Gandalf does have an encounter with a powerful presence on the other side of a door (which's the balrog: '"I have never felt such a challenge"'), and eventually seals up the door, and the passage, when it all crumbles behind him when he comes flying down some steps (FR, 425). Another reason may have been more practical: that a fighting style (plus rehearsal) hadn't been decided upon for Gandalf. At the end of *The Return of the King* a way of having Gandalf use both staff and sword was devised (a kind of swirling, clubbing style). Some of the Gandalf fighting scenes in *The Two Towers* and *The Return of the King* may have been re-shoots (when there had been time to develop a satisfying way for the grey and white wizard to fight).

Next up is Dwarrowdelf. The film rightly keeps Gimli and Gandalf prominent throughout the Moria scenes (as well as Frodo, as always) – Gandalf and the dwarf are the two characters who comment most often on the different environments the Company of the Ring passes through in the dwarf realm. Dwarrowdelf offers a moment of respite from the action (and time for a little awe and wonder). In a successful and satisfying action film, the breathers and pauses (and the contrasts) are just as important as the action itself.

Dwarrowdelf is a depiction of the dwarf kingdom which's pure Alan Lee in every detail. The film at moments like this is like looking at an illustrated book with moving pictures (a moving version of the anniversary illustrated edition of *The Lord of the Rings* which Lee produced in the early Nineties, and which was often used by the writers). And the film's not superior to an illustrated book either, it's just a different medium (in a book, for instance, the eye can wander at leisure over the amount of detail that an illustrator loads into their images; in a film like *The Fellowship of the Ring,* it's a five second shot before the next action beat is being set up).

The next scene is a classic snake-pit or cliffhanger situation, which films have been employing since the birth of cinema. Every action-adventure film has to have one (or two hundred, more like). Here, the Nine Walkers are surrounded by hundreds of goblins and orcs who crawl down pillars and rush out of holes (the bug-eyes were added digitally, by Rhythm & Hues in L.A.). The audience has been here ten zillion times, and they know too that there's no real danger. Maybe a character will stumble and receive a scratch, but not much more. (And, if they know their Tolkien, they'll know that Tolkien only extremely reluctantly sacrifices a character, and never a hobbit).

The pleasure of such snake-pit scenarios for the audience is: how will they get out of this one? (And the pleasure for the scriptwriter, if you can call it that, is devising ways for the heroes to escape. Of course, the heroes have only seconds to come up with something, but screenwriters have days or months or years). This time, it's not the heroes' ingenuity that helps then, but the introduction of the balrog.

The orcs don't surround our heroes in the book as they do in the film. In fact, the picture departs from the book in many details at this point in Moria: in the book, the heroes make it to the First Deep. Trolls employ slabs of stone to form bridges over the walls of fire across the Second Hall, and there are hundreds of orcs behind them (FR, 426f). And when the balrog appears, the trolls and orcs have long fled.

The build-up to the balrog employs well-known cinematic techniques. Firstly, to show that something is very scary in a story, have someone react in fear to it. In this case, hundreds of orcs are suddenly terrified, and soon clamber back up the columns, disappear down holes, or run away. That's the primary method the film employs to suggest that Something Bad Approaches. Next, to hint at the scale of the monster, and its power, light shining at the end of the hall, accompanied by a low roar. Finally, have your heroes quake in fright, with even your top hero (Gandalf) looking scared.

The film employs those techniques, and reprises them two or three times, to show the balrog is getting nearer. Gandalf's advice is sound as always: 'RUN!' (maybe that's a nod to *Monty Python and the Holy Grail* and the exhortation: 'run away!'). The film could cut straight to the bridge and abyss now and the balrog fight, which would be plenty for many filmmakers and audiences. Instead, yet another action sequence is inserted, a literal cliffhanger: the crumbling stone steps (in the book, the characters have to leap a gap). The logic employed in the 2001 flick is the familiar one of the whole action-adventure genre: obstacles piled on top of obstacles. Or as producer Joel Silver said, one 'whammo' followed by another 'whammo'. Or as scriptwriting manuals put it: your characters must always be facing 'difficulty, difficulty, difficulty!' It's no use having your hero/es escape easily; they must suffer, they must be pushed to the limit, they must go down to the depths, so that when they rise back up, their ascent is all the more glorious (and rapid). When the ring's been destroyed, for instance, at the Crack of Doom in *The Return of the King*, and everything seems OK, the filmmakers add another literal cliffhanger, with Frodo hanging from the rock, and Sam saving him for the last time. Notice how the editors have worked in that scene to cheat time, and delay the eruption of the volcano for a minute or so).

A good example is the famous opening of *Raiders of the Lost Ark* (1981), a film which revived many of these cliffhangers and heroic escapes, as well as being a film which was probably more instrumental in revitalizing the action-adventure genre in contemporary Hollywood cinema than almost any other single film: its influence was being felt twenty years later, with the *Lara Croft, XXX, Spy Kids, The Mask of Zorro, Blade, Shanghai Noon* and *The Mummy* films, for instance (and *The Lord of the Rings* films owe a big debt to the *Indiana Jones* films, of course, and very obviously in the Moria sequence).

Two 'countdowns' or 'clocks' (as they're termed in scriptwriting handbooks) control the staircase scene: the balrog getting closer, and the stairs collapsing (the two are linked – it's the balrog that's causing the stairs to crumble; but the stairs don't crumple all at once, but in stages). A tried and tested example of adding another obstacle for the heroes here are the orcs on a distant ledge firing arrows (i.e., just when it seemed as if leaping across the gulf was enough, there are orcs attacking the fellowship. Luckily, Thranduil's son happens to be a praeternaturally brilliant shot – that skill, established here for the first time with an impossible shot flying behind an arrow (out of Warners' 1991 *Robin Hood*) and hitting an orc in the head, will be part of action scenes in the rest of the movies). It's all standard, hokey movie stuff, a very movie-movie moment (down to the mini-beats within the action beat, such as Gimli nearly falling, and Legolas grabbing his beard, and Aragorn and Frodo scrambling up the stairs as they disintegrate beneath them). Its very familiarity is what's great about the sequence, but also what's naff about it.

Again, the *order* in which the characters leap over the chasm, and the characters who are left behind (Frodo and Aragorn) is all in keeping with the rest of the films. For instance, Gandalf jumps second, because he's an old man (and can't jump so far), and because his big moment is just coming up. Legolas effortlessly leaps the gap, and it's Leggy, naturally, who hangs on to Gimli's beard to pull him back (developing the love/ hate relationship between elf and dwarf further). Boromir makes it over clutching Merry and Pippin under each arm, while Sam, poor thing, is unceremoniously thrown over. And that leaves the two main heroes of the films, after Gandalf and Sam: Frodo and Aragorn. The final shot of the sequence, a wide shot of the staircase miniature, the structure crumbling, and the digital doubles running down, was reproduced in the marketing many times.

The balrog finally appears, and doesn't disappoint. Of course, he's enormous (a ten or twenty foot balrog just wouldn't cut it after that big build-up). Thus, the balrog's a giant demon, 50-60 feet tall, recalling the one at the end of *The Night of the Demon* (a.k.a. *Curse of the Demon* [1957]), one of the great British horror films (*The Return of the King* references this film again – as well invisible man films – when Frodo puts on the ring in the Sammath Naur, and his footprints are visible). The balrog's whip is handily very, very long – so that it can grab Gandalf up on the bridge even when the balrog's already fallen. And it's also glowing with fire, so the viewer can see it.

One of the big, complex visual effects shots (lasting 516 frames) introduces the bridge, the abyss, and the characters (some bluescreen, some CGI) running over it one by one. It's one of the signature shots of the Moria sequence, and involved a combination of live action, digital characters, bluescreen shooting, miniature sets, and digital extensions to models.

The fight between Gandalf and the balrog is one of the iconic moments from the book, and thus has to deliver. Everything the film adaptor requires is already there in the book, except for small details such as: what the dilly-oh does the balrog look like? How big is the bridge? How do the wizard and the demon fight? Because Tolkien's narrator offers glimpses or vague impressions (however striking) of the balrog and the fight, the filmmakers followed suit, and evoked a balrog swathed in fire and smoke, darkness and rapid editing. In other words, they partly adhere to the movie precept concerning monsters that: the less you show the better. The balrog was a combination of a dog and a bull, with bat wings and a lizard's tail. The skin was congealed, cold lava. The fire and smoke was added much later, to the animation, and ended up hiding much of the creature in the 25 shots of it.

The blocking and staging of the action favours either Gandalf's viewpoint or the fellowship looking on in horror from a distance (with Frodo's p.o.v. predominating). Note how high up the fellowship already are, on a level with the balrog, so that Gandalf looks small in the distance, and it gets them out of the way (the scene could've been viewed much closer, with the fellowship waiting at the end of the bridge, for instance.)

Big wide shots capture the tiny figure of the wizard on the bridge with the fiery, shadowy, smoky balrog towering above him, 'grey and bent, like a wizened tree before the onset of a storm'. (Models, live action and many digital additions comprise this very complex scene, which represents months of work in post-production). The film includes some of the iconic images and dialogue from the book, and follows the book in its key beats. Ian McKellen's Gandalf, sweaty and intense, defiantly yelling 'you shall not pass!' is one of the most memorable images in all three films (it's 'you cannot pass' in the book).

Although the filmmakers disliked the blue lightning bolts of traditional screen magic, this is the scene for some magic, if ever there was one. Although it's a spectacular scene, the magic is still kept restrained. When Gandalf unleashes the 'Secret Fire', the 'flame of Anor', it's envisioned as spherical glow of white light which envelops the wizard. There's also a big clashing of swords.

The fall of the balrog is particularly effective, his form now a boiling mass of flames and smoke, and a tumultuous roar on the soundtrack (a bit like the roar the demon truck makes when it goes over the cliff in *Duel* [1971], which in turn was taken from either *Godzilla* or *The Creature From the Black Lagoon*). Howard Shore's score pounds with drums and dies away, leaving a big empty space on the track for Gandalf's whispered cry of 'fly, you fools!' (The scene involved bluescreen footage of the actors, digital doubles, matte paintings, miniatures, a CG balrog and highspeed photography of the break-away bridge).

Immediately after Gandalf's fall, the film rightly cuts to reaction shots of Frodo and Aragorn, the two characters that Gandalf's death most affects, and the two main heroes along with the wizard. This kind of action beat is what you pay your eight bucks for. (Yet another omission is Aragorn rushing to Gandalf's aid, crying '*Elendil!* I am with you, Gandalf!', closely followed by Boromir [FR, 430]. Instead, Aragorn and Boromir hold back the hobbits).

Jean-Luc Godard summed up cinema in one word: *emotion*. In the Hollywood system, people go to the cinema for emotion, for an experience, above all (or emotion and experience before anything else). The audience *wants* to be moved, they *expect* to be moved, and very often it's the people who can move them the most (Steven Spielberg, Walt Disney, Cecil B. DeMille, Charlie Chaplin) who are treasured the most (by the studios as well as the audience). It's the same with Ronald Tolkien: there may be a thousand things 'wrong' with *The Lord of the Rings* as literature or 'high art', but there's no doubting the emotion that the book generates.

Absolutely incredible, the mourning for Gandalf scene, the move to slo-mo, no local sound, and the elegiac music after Gandalf's death outside Moria. That scene stuns because there's hardly another like it in contemporary blockbusters – *Godzilla, Star Wars, Star Trek, Spider-man, James Bond, The Mummy,* etc. To move into that kind of emotional territory with such passion is unexpected and very welcome. But it is in the book, of course:

> *Doom.* Grief at last wholly over came them, and they wept long: some standing and silent, some cast upon the ground. *Doom, doom.* The drum-beats faded. (FR, 431).

There are differentiations according to character as to how the Company's weeps, too (i.e., they're still in character when they mourn): Legolas looks puzzled and downcast, as if he's never seen death up close before (death and the elves, one of the great mysteries in Tolkien's *legendarium*, is later explored with Haldir at Helm's Deep), while Frodo is turned away from the camera, a little way from the others. (The scene was shot on Mount Nelson, and was a good shoot, according to Sean Astin, with the actors working easily in a perfect setting [2004, 225]).

Isn't it cool that the audience probably thinks it's looking at really complex computer-generated visual effects in many parts of the *Lord of the Rings* films, including much of Moria, when it's actually looking at models built out of foam, paper, metal, resin and polystyrene and painted, with matte paintings as backgrounds? True, digital additions are made to many miniatures to sweeten them and help sell them, but the fundamental work is done by the models. In Moria, CGI was employed for the hordes of orcs, for Dwarrowdelf, for the troll, for the arrows, for some of the fire, for the fellowship running over the bridge, and for the balrog. But linking everything together are miniatures and partial full-scale sets. (Dwarrowdelf was digital partly because the big camera moves couldn't be achieved on a set; similarly the actors couldn't be filmed moving across that space, because it wasn't possible to have the camera shoot them from far enough away and show them in scale with Dwarrowdelf. There were cheats, too: when Gandalf says he'll risk a little light, the light seems to come from his staff, but rim light was added, to show up the columns, which were altered slightly, so they wouldn't look as if they'd been duplicated in the computer).

Talking about the filmmakers playing tricks on the audience (as at Bree, when the ringwraiths seem to stab the hobbits), so does Tolkien. One of his biggest cheats in *The Lord of the Rings,* as he acknowledged, was killing Gandalf only to bring him back.

Frodo is always the keystone of the film of *The Fellowship of the Ring.* Every time the travellers enter a new environment (Bree, Rivendell, Weathertop, Lórien, or wherever), there is always a cut to a close-up of Frodo. When the fellowship are introduced to Lothlórien, for instance, and walk through the woods accompanied by Haldir and the elves, Frodo's is the only close-up. When the company climb the stairs around the mallorn trees, there's a cut to Frodo. Rivendell isn't fully revealed until Frodo's well enough to walk out onto the balcony and the camera follows him. And so on. *The Fellowship of the Ring* is always a movie seen through a hobbit's eyes, and the hobbit is nearly always Frodo.

That isn't the only way *The Fellowship of the Ring* could have been adapted. If the point-of-view had been wholly with Gandalf, for instance, a completely different film could have been shot and edited: it might begin with a prologue outlining Gandalf's earlier life as a Maia spirit called Olórin, for instance, in Valinor. It might include the Valar giving the quest of defeating Sauron (a fellow Maia) to Olórin. Flashbacks to Gandalf's arrival in Middle-earth might be sprinkled throughout the film, and to some of his more notable achievements: his first visits to the Shire, for example, or entering the dungeons of Dol Guldur, or the White Council meetings. And on and on. An adaption of *The Lord of the Rings* doesn't have to be just like the 2001-03 films. There are many approaches and, hopefully, some other adaptions will be undertaken (after all, the New Line films are themselves remakes of United Artists and Rankin/ Bass Productions films of the late 1970s).

NOTES: ACT THREE

1. J. Smith, 2004, 125.
2. J. Duncan, 2001, 116f.
3. A. Hitchcock, 1995, 117.

ACT FOUR

The speech about distrusting the Golden Wood, as the fellowship enters Lórien, was given to Gimli (in the book it's Boromir who expresses it). Lothlórien could've been set up by Aragorn or Legolas, but the filmmakers plumped for Gimli, i.e., a character suspicious of the elves, which gives the Golden Wood a particular slant, a place possibly scary or dangerous. The introduction of Lórien would be different if Aragorn or Legolas had had the exposition dialogue (the long shot of Lórien, though – the first view of it – was cut with a reaction shot of Aragorn smiling, as he runs ahead of the Company and looks down on Lórien from the lower slopes of the Misty Mountains. Readers of the book know that Lórien was where Aragorn first encountered the elf Arwen).

Frodo has another of his telepathic moments here (not in the book), with a flash cut of Galadriel's eyes in E.C.U., and her voiceover telling Frodo he is bringing great evil to the Golden Wood. What that does is yet again to set up *obstacles* for Frodo and his quest (just as Lórien is set up initially as a mysterious, threatening place). In the book, only Gimli and Boromir are really wary of Lórien and Galadriel (while Aragorn goes off into dreamy recollections of meeting the love of his life, Arwen Undómiel, and Legolas speaks of the mysterious, powerful reputation of the elves of Lothlórien.)

For J.R.R. Tolkien himself, Lórien is a magical kingdom, a haven of peace and elvish lore – along with Imladris (Rivendell), it's one of the professor's favourite places in Middle-earth (Tolkien limited himself to two main elven realms in the Middle-earth of the Third Age and the time of the action in *The Lord of the Rings*, Thranduil's realm being off-stage – in his stories of earlier ages in Arda, there were many elvish kingdoms: Gondolin, Doriath, Nargothrond, Maedhros, and Menegroth, among others).

The flash cut of Galadriel transposes the link between minds that Frodo experiences in the mirror of Galadriel scene to the introduction of Lórien in the film of *The Fellowship of the Ring*. The empathy with Galadriel is only experienced by Frodo in the book when he's face to face with the Lady of the Wood. The film, though, establishes that spiritual link earlier. (And Galadriel summons Frodo from the depths of sleep, too, to come to the mirror dell. In the book, she comes upon Frodo and Sam in person and leads them to the mirror). Galadriel's telepathic powers will also be employed later on – in the 'Galadriel montage' in *The Two Towers*, for example, the elf queen seems to communicate with Elrond in Rivendell.

But the cut to Galadriel at the front of the Lothlórien scenes also serves to remind viewers of the whole quest in the film: the ring. So Galadriel says that Frodo brings great evil to Lórien (i.e., the ring). In the extended cut, Haldir also mentions that, so that the impression is that the fellowship is being held up by Haldir and his company of elves because of the ring, rather than any other reason (such as dwarves). That changes the book in small details, so it appears that even elves such as Haldir know about the fellowship and the quest. In the book, Haldir receives a message from Galadriel and Celeborn, but only after blindfolding the fellowship (including Legolas) and leading them to Caras Galadon.

The build-up to the introduction of Celeborn and Galadriel features some lovely model photography as the fellowship climb the mallorn tree, with Lórien shown as a mass of elegant trees, flets in the trees dotted about, and lights disappearing into the distance, with a warm blue of the night behind it all (quite a Disneyesque scene, really). Howard Shore provides a strident choral cue, and extended string drones (which also use dissonance. Indian bowed lutes and North African flutes were employed). The music is mixed loud, and there is no local sound or sound effects (no sound of the wind, for instance, or birds, or elves talking or singing on the other flets). The fellowship appear on the flet which acts as an elven court and line up in a row, silently.

With the music still dominating, Celeborn and Galadriel approach, hand in hand, down some steps (in slight slow motion). They are pretty much how a viewer might expect them to be portrayed in a movie: tall, clad in white, with very long hair pieces, pale white skin, smooth make-up, no blemishes, no facial hair. Haughty looks, and s-l-o-w English accents. And they're bathed in light, with auras produced by back-lighting. The fellowship actors are encouraged to do their best awed expressions as the film cuts from the high elves to the group of hobbits, dwarves, elves and men, now moving into close-ups. The filmmakers trying their hardest to suggest awe and wonder.

All of the techniques employed here are the same ones used in Biblical and ancient world epic films depicting Christ, or saints, or deities. And walking down the steps to meet the fellowship is a classic device, familiar from Middle Ages dramas depicting kings and queens. (In the book, the flet is much bigger, and there are many elves seated on either side; Celeborn and Galadriel, meanwhile, sit motionless and silent on thrones before rising to greet their visitors).

> The chamber was filled with a soft light [writes Tolkien in *The Lord of the Rings*]; its walls were green and silver and its roof of gold. Many Elves were seated there. On two chairs beneath the bole of the tree and canopied by a living bough there sat, side by side, Celeborn and Galadriel. They stood up to greet their guests, after the manner of Elves, even those who were accounted mighty kings. Very tall they were, and the Lady no less tall than the Lord; and they were grave and beautiful. They were clad wholly in white; and the hair of the Lady was of deep gold, and the hair of Lord Celeborn was of silver long and bright; but no sign of age was upon them, unless it were in the depths of their eyes; for these were keen as lances in the starlight, and yet profound, the wall of deep memory. (FR, 460)

The *strangeness* of the encounter between the fellowship and the lord and lady of Lórien derives mainly from invisible devices: editing, voiceover and music. The scene is one of the more complex, from an *editing* point-of-view, despite the *staging* of the scene being fairly straightforward – it's two people talking with a group of eight people. But the dialogue from one shot is laid over other shots, and a lot of the impact of the scene comes from following big close-ups of eyes with reaction shots (such as when

Galadriel turns her Medusa glare on Boromir).

Finally, at the close of the scene, the filmmakers overlap regular dialogue with voiceover (one of the few times in the film they opt for that kind of disorienting device), when Galadriel tells the Company to rest up but addresses Frodo telepathically (with a cut to another E.C.U. of Galadriel). This may be a nod to *The Shining* (1980), when Halloran (the wonderful Scatman Crothers) communicates with Danny (Danny Lloyd) telepathically while he's speaking to Danny's parents (the staging of the Lórien scene is very similar, too, in terms of space, sightlines, and so on).

So the encounter with Celeborn and Galadriel is not really a dialogue or dramatic scene where information is exchanged or action explored, but more a visual and musical experience in which the overall mood is more important than details of dialogue. It's a scene about the spiritual enlightenment, power, and sophistication of the elves. A glimpse, if you like, of how things might be in Valinor, the elven paradise.

There *are* plot details, though: the viewer does see (1) that Boromir crumples a little under Galadriel's gaze, while Gimli looks uncomfortable; (2) that most everyone else is lost in awe; and (3) that the first matter to be addressed (brought up by Celeborn) is the absence of Gandalf, who has fallen into shadow.

Following one of the most high-flown moments in all three films, the fellowship are back on the ground again, settling in to their quarters (no rooms, no gyms, no jacuzzis and no bars for them, but kind of open-plan hollows built into the mallorn tree roots). Distant singing is heard (led by Liz Fraser). If you ordered up 'ethereal', 'other-worldly' and 'melancholy' from a composer, it might sound like this. Legolas explains that the elves are singing a lament for Gandalf, but he hasn't got the heart to translate the Elvish for them, because his grief is still too deep. The *Extended Edition* of *The Fellowship of the Ring* added a brief scene, taken from the book, where Sam makes up a song of his own for Gandalf (inevitably, the writers have chosen the stanza from Sam's song about Gandalf's fireworks, but Sam also sings of other things in the novel). There's a bit of comic business between Strider and Gimli (Gimli seems to be asleep and snoring disrespectfully).

One of the more interesting visuals during the Lothlórien sequence occurred during the mirror of Galadriel scene. No, not Cate Blanchett's Disney evil queen moment, but the scenes when Frodo looks into the mirror. The shots of the rest of the fellowship looking at him darkly and accusingly were taken from the earlier scene, on the borders of the Lothlórien, when the fellowship's prevented from carrying on by Haldir. The images of the hobbits being enslaved (with Sam prominent among them, being whipped) was the only significant nod to the Scouring of the Shire chapter in *The Return of the King*. Last of all came Sauron (he has to be last – nothing can follow the giant Eye, really).

But note the point-of-view shot which portrayed the ring on its chain hanging over flaming Eye of Sauron. That may be the only time in the films when Sauron and the ring are shown within the same frame (apart from the prologue, where Sauron's wearing the ring). It's interesting because it's a superimposition shot (i.e, *not* one that's conjured up by the editors in the occasional montages in the *Lord of the Rings* films), and a view of what Frodo might actually be seeing as he leans over the water which shows him the Eye of Sauron.

Galadriel's gifts in the book include the magic cloaks, rope, seeds of elanor, golden hair, and the phial of light. Galadriel gives Sam a box of earth from her orchard.

The gifts of Galadriel in the extended cut (in the book it's actually Galadriel *and* Celeborn who offer gifts) are one of the more complex montages in the films (often it's easier to cut an action scene like a fight than something like Galadriel's gifts, which moves back and forth in time, and weaves in dialogue and voiceovers. For instance, the editors set up Gimli's gift scene, then go to something else, then come back to it. But even then, they don't show the actual moment when the elf queen plucks out her hair and hands it to Gimli; that, too, is handled in Gimli's dialogue).

Curiously missing is a gift to Boromir; he must've really made a bad impression on the lords and ladies of the Galadhrim (in the book, he gets a belt from the Lady of the Wood). Aragorn didn't get the sword sheath as he does in the book, because the films altered the story of the Sword That Was Broken (Aragorn wasn't carrying his broken sword). And he didn't get the silver brooch either, because the scriptwriters had created the Evenstar at Rivendell as a token of Arwen's love (so when the film cut to a close-up of the brooch, it was a visual reminder of Arwen, so the filmgoers in Melbourne, Seoul, Copenhagen or wherever could say: 'oh yeah, he's got that elf girl waiting for him in that other elf place').

Samwise Gamgee, meanwhile, didn't get the box of magic soil because the Scouring of the Shire had been dropped, and there wasn't time at the end of *The Return of the King* for some gardening, planting, and waiting for plants to grow (a gift is often a foreshadowing of its use later on, but there's no point foreshadowing something that doesn't crop up later. And Galadriel and Celeborn were cast in the role of magical helpers at this point in the films, as they are in the novel). So, instead, Sam had some rope (in the book, the elves give him that anyway), because the rope would be employed in a later scene in the Emyn Muil (a little wooden box, which Sam carries and drops at Emyn Muil in the *Extended Edition* cut of *The Two Towers*, was a nod to Galadriel's gift).

Curiously, the gifts from Galadriel to Meriadoc Brandybuck and Peregrin Took were switched from belts to knives (presumably knives are cooler than belts – maybe belts would've got a laugh from sections of the audience, particularly adolescent males, a crucial segment of the global audience ('what? they get a *belt*?'). Hence also Sam's awkward complaint when he's lumbered with the runner-up prize of rope and fancies 'one of those nice elf knives'. Like a nurse handing out sour medicine to a five year-old child, Galadriel merely smiles at him patronizingly).

The film entered a new phase of narration when the Company left Lórien. By that time, the film had already cut from the tranquillity and stasis of the Lothlórien scenes to the scenes of Saruman presiding over sending off the Uruk-hai in Isengard (waking the audience with a jolt from the languors of Lórien). The intercutting of the two scenes cast this part of the film as that all-purpose climax of so many (of all) action-adventure movies: the chase. Now the fellowship are to be hunted down and killed. A couple of brief scenes between the white wizard and his chief Uruk, Lurtz (an invention of the film: if Saruman's going to be elevated to major villain but isn't going to leave Nan Curunír, he needs a chief bruiser), spelt out to audiences that Saruman was going after the ring, that all he really cared about was the ring. An intriguing snippet of Tolkien's *legendarium* was included at this point in both film versions of *The Fellowship of the Ring*: that the orcs were originally corrupted from elves by the 'dark powers'.

Now the 2001 movie cuts back and forth between the fellowship on the river in the boats and Saruman's orcs closing in on them from Isengard (accompanied by the martial version of the Saruman theme music). The insert shots of Legolas and Aragorn in the boats looking at the riverbanks helped to evoke the approaching villains. This part of the film signals to the audience that a confrontation is on its way, that the fellowship face further obstacles. (There are hints, too, that Boromir is getting restless).

This is always one of the less engaging passages of the book of *The Lord of the Rings* for me. It almost seems as if J.R.R. Tolkien is doing what Aragorn is also doing: allowing the fellowship to drift along with the current of the River Anduin, because the characters are moving in roughly the right direction (for the time being at least). It's as if Tolkien's narrator is also putting off the decision that has to be made: what to do next? Strike out towards the Emyn Muil and Mordor? Or continue down the river to Gondor? Have the fellowship split up voluntarily? Have Gollum make a move for the ring? And so on. (The 2001 film didn't find an equivalent for the barren, unwelcoming lands the river winds through, either; in the picture they look heavily wooded).

A recurring quip in Hollywood action movies is: 'I'm just making this up as I go along'. (It's a phrase Indy uses in *Raiders of the Lost Ark*). But it does describe the spontaneous, improvized aspect of writing and storytelling, and the idea that characters have some kind of spontaneous independency, and are not the puppets of writers. It's one of the strengths of *The Lord of the Rings* that it does appear as if Tolkien were making it up as he went along, as if he too doesn't know what's coming next. It's a cool trick to maintain, because it keeps a freshness to the narrative.

It's like that bit in *E.T.: The Extraterrestrial* (1982) when one of Elliott's brother's friends complains about the alien: 'why can't he just beam up?', and Elliott retorts: '*this is reality, Greg*'. Similarly, Tolkien's book is fantasy and fantastical, but it is also, for his narrator, *reality*. The characters can't 'beam up' *à la Star Trek*. They can't fly with the eagles the 250 or so miles direct to Mount Doom (that's *too* easy. The story would be over in a few hours). And they can't just call down a chopper to airlift them out of trouble (though the actors and crew can, and did at the Parth Galen location (Mavora Lakes Park on the South Island), when Sean Astin had an accident in the water, cutting his foot on some glass, while shooting the scene where Sam wades into the water after Frodo).

A sequence which was scripted, planned and scouted would have occurred around here: the river rapids scene, with the fellowship carrying their boats and being set upon by orcs. Sets were built but the floods at Queenstown destroyed them. Frodo was to be dragged into the river by an Uruk, fighting over the ring, with Frodo struggling free (Sib, 503). These were ways in which the river journey would've been livened up with action; an early idea had Gollum trying to take the ring on the river, and Frodo being saved by Legolas and Aragorn.

The extended cut of *The Fellowship of the Ring* added one or two brief scenes around this point in the river journey. One shows Gollum riding a log in the river; this image leads to Boromir trying to persuade Aragorn to take the road to Gondor (with the ring, of course). This is Boromir's overriding narrative goal, and has been part of most of his scenes since his introduction in the film at Rivendell. This's also the fiercest argument in the film between the two men, when Boromir accuses Aragorn of ignoring his responsibilities, and grabs him (Frodo overhears Boromir). Sure as eggs is eggs, that set-to is definitely *not* in the book.

It is followed by a brief two-hander between the lead hobbits, the essence of which is to remind the audience of Sam's loyalty, his willingness to help, but also the Loneliness of the Long Distance Ringbearer. Frodo tells Sam that he can't help him this time. It's a hint of the way the ring will take hold of Frodo big time in the second and third films. It was cut from the theatrical version probably because it wasn't necessary, and is explained in more detail in the second film anyway.

Time enough on this road movie (or river movie, as it is now) to pause for some spectacle and awe, and the six foot high polystyrene models of the Argonath certainly provide it, with some memorable eye candy of the canoes riding past the stone feet of the Pillars of the Kings (which originally marked the Northern borders of Gondor), and the camera swooping upwards in the next shot, across the grim visage of one of the kings, to reveal Tol Brandir and Nen Hithoel beyond.

ACT FIVE

Ah, if only Aragorn listened to Thranduil's son and kept to the other bank of the river... So, at Parth Galen, Nen Hithoel and Amon Hen, the film's narrative reaches its climax (in both versions): with a big fight and an even bigger 'TO BE CONTINUED' ending. Someone has to disrupt things from inside, and if it's going to be anyone, it's got to be Boromir (Gimli and Aragorn may be next in line).

Despite warnings from wizards, and elf lords, and elf queens, and future kings, and even hobbits, Boromir still goes ahead to try to persuade Frodo to head for Gondor with the One Ring. Boromir's is the all too human course of action, familiar, like Sauron's, from thousands of years of human history. Boromir's act is in fact the most obvious one in many respects. So many leaders, regimes and nations throughout history would have taken that course of action: if persuasion doesn't do it, force will (behind Boromir lurks Stalin's Russia, say, or Mao's China, or Britain under Queen Victoria, or modern America). In a way, it's surprising that Boromir hadn't made a move for the ring earlier (kidnapping Frodo in the night, say, and wresting the ring from him). In fact, it's a tribute to Boromir and his sense of honour or loyalty that he tries the more diplomatic methods of verbal persuasion first. (Note how Tolkien places Aragorn with Frodo and Sam in one boat, and Boromir with Merry and Pippin in another).

First, Amon Hen. Here's an opportunity for a filmmaker to really go to town with the visuals. It's the first truly awesome vision of the whole of Middle-earth in the novel: Frodo sees a huge chunk of Middle-earth spread before him: the Great River, Mirkwood, the Misty Mountains, Lórien, Isengard, Rohan, Minas Tirith, Osgiliath, Minas Morgul, the Harad ships, the Easterlings, Mordor, Mount Doom and finally Barad-dûr. And everywhere is teeming with war:

> But everywhere he looked he saw the signs of war. The Misty Mountains were crawling like anthills; orcs were issuing out of a thousand holes. Under the boughs of Mirkwood there was deadly strife of Elves and Men and fell beasts. The land of the Beornings was aflame; a cloud was over Moria; smoke rose on the borders of Lórien.
>
> Horsemen were galloping on the grass of Rohan; wolves poured from Isengard. From the havens of Harad ships of war put out to sea; and out of the East Men were moving endlessly: swordsmen, spearmen, bowmen upon horses, chariots of chieftains and laden wains. All of the Power of the Dark Lord was in motion. (FR, 520)

Some critics have likened that image of Frodo's of war everywhere to Tolkien's experience in the First World War, the endless devastation, the pits, corpses, barbed wire, and ant-like activity. Curiously, despite all of those gifts to the illustrator and adaptor of *The Lord of the Rings*, the filmmakers avoided them, perhaps because those images were being saved for the second and third films, and would have given away too much, or perhaps a satisfying way of introducing the idea of the Seat of Seeing was too difficult, or perhaps the visions would have been too complex or confusing for the viewer (certainly it would have been a very costly sequence to put together, with live action, matte paintings, models, and lashings of digital hocus-pocus).

Instead, the filmmakers of the 2001-03 version of *The Lord of the Rings* opted to concentrate mainly on Frodo's first sight of Barad-dûr and the Eye of Sauron (although they did follow Tolkien in his description of the Dark Tower of moving from the base to the tip, the camera rushing up the model: 'wall upon wall, battlement upon battlement, black, immeasurably strong' and so on upwards: '[t]here was an eye in the Dark Tower that did not sleep' [FR, 521]).

A rapid track-and-zoom effect is intended to slam Frodo up against Barad-dûr. It's an intense moment, with Frodo wrapped up in the torment of the wraithworld. The voice in Frodo's head ('*Take it off! Take it off!*') was dropped (maybe it was tried but didn't work, or wasn't needed). In any case, Gandalf's voice comes up later, in voiceover, as Frodo stands by the river deciding what to do.

The final reel of *The Fellowship of the Ring* altered the events in Tolkien's book considerably. While Frodo's encounter with Boromir followed the general drift of the book, as did the subsequent scene of Frodo on the Seat of Amon Hen, the rest departed from the book. For instance, there is an important conversation between Aragorn and Sam (principally) in the novel which the early 2000s film of *The Fellowship of the Ring* dropped (it occurs just before Boromir returns, and Aragorn acknowledges that Sam speaks wiser than the rest [FR, 524]. Boromir's return was also cut, where Aragorn talks to Boromir.) Also, in the picture, it appears as if Frodo has already decided to go on to Mordor alone, but in the book he's still undecided.

Part of the chaotic events were also depicted in the book from Sam's point-of-view, when Tolkien's narrator unusually steps away from Frodo for a moment (unusual because Tolkien's narration has kept Frodo in the foreground throughout the novel, up until this point). In the Parth Galen sequence, it's Sam who's now portrayed up front, with the narration switching from Frodo's to Sam's interior monologue: '"Whoa, Sam Gamgee!" he said aloud. "Your legs are too short, so use your head!"' (FR, 526).

So Sam heads back for the boats, in time to catch Frodo. And that's where the book of *The Fellowship of the Ring* ends, with the hobbits reaching the other side of the river. That wouldn't be right for any movie, because it leaves the fates of the other key characters in limbo. Thus, the 2001-02 film carries on into *The Two Towers,* and includes the first chapter, "The Departure of Boromir". The motion picture, in short, wasn't very satisfactory in depicting what happened to Sam: there's no clarification where he is in the chaos of Nen Hithoel, or if he ran into (or hid from) orcs. The extended cut of *Fellowship* includes two shots of Sam rushing through the trees, but that's not enough, really. Sam couldn't really have accompanied Aragorn to Amon Hen, because Aragorn has to have his ring moment with Frodo alone (having Sam there would alter things considerably. And what would happen to Sam when Aragorn takes on 2,500 orcs single-handed?). So much of the final reel of *The Fellowship of the Ring* is narrated from Frodo's, not Sam's, point-of-view.

One of the chief alterations from the book at this point is what happens to Aragorn. First of all, he gets a farewell scene with Frodo in the film. That would be all fine and dandy (although the book makes Aragorn's ill-fated day, when everything he tries goes wrong, even more frustrating for him, because he *doesn't* meet Frodo or Sam again until at the end of the book), but the scriptwriters make an unforgivable error here and turn it into another ring moment. For a moment, Aragorn wavers in front of Frodo, and it looks as if he is tempted by taking the ring (it calls out to him in Sauron's voice: 'Aragorn').

The scene was included presumably to have Aragorn also 'pass the test', like Galadriel and Gandalf, and also to emphasize Aragorn's potential for weakness (which the screenwriters made much stronger in the films than it is in the book. Well, it *isn't* in the book). The adaptors wanted a more 'realistic' or believable Aragorn, not the unconquerable Aragorn of the book, who feels doubt and uncertainty far less than in the films. The screenwriters were right in thinking that audiences would find it harder to accept an Aragorn who was so noble, so intelligent, so morally right, as he is in the book. And, partly because they included the Arwen romance, but mostly because they wanted to bring Aragorn down to a more everyday or less rarefied level, they opted to emphasize his self-doubt and crises of indecision (to make his 'journey' or 'character arc' more intense).

The films suggested that maybe Aragorn had been in exile for too long, that he was seriously considering not facing up to his responsibilities. Elrond, Gandalf and Arwen (and Boromir and Éowyn, in their way) are on hand to remind Aragorn of his true path. Boromir, for instance, berates Aragorn in the riverbank scene in the DVD extended cut that he is afraid of his responsibilities, that he has been too long in the wilderness, that he is too frightened to go to Gondor (some fans might find that scene a sorry addition to the novel: no one should be allowed to talk to Aragorn like that!). The tension between the men is kinda resolved in Boromir's death scene, when Aragorn promises he will not let the white city fall, nor 'our people' fail (in the 1954 book, Boromir implores Aragorn to do that: '"Go to Minas Tirith and save my people! I have failed"' (TT, 12). Boromir dies reconciled a little to Aragorn (and Aragorn forgiving him a little): the Dúnedan mentioned 'our people' for the first time, and Boromir seems to see, for the first time, that Aragorn may possibly be the king some folk in Gondor have been searching for.)

In short, what the screenwriters did was to take the common element in adventure and hero stories of the *reluctant hero*, and apply it to Aragorn. It's the part in hundreds of Hollywood movies where representatives from a community go to a one-time leader or hero and ask him (beg him) to help them, and he denies them. Turns out that *only* Joe Schmoo (Bruce Willis, Arny, Owen Wilson, whoever) can pilot that space shuttle and save the planet from a meteor. *Only* FBI agent Clint Eastwood (decorated in Vietnam and the Gulf) knows the security system of the prison camp in Afghanistan where Osama bin Laden's being held captive by the Chinese. And though there're sometimes two or three attempts before the hero say yes, the viewer knows they will for two obvious reasons: they're the star (so they'll be in every important scene), and if they decline the hero's task, there's no movie.

The screenwriters (Philippa Boyens, Peter Jackson and Frances Walsh) altered the 1954 book in another important respect at this point in the final reel of *The Fellowship of the Ring, Aragorn doesn't fight*. At all. Not a single stroke. He dashes up to Amon Hen on the hill, doesn't see much, hears Boromir's horn, and rushes to the rescue, arriving just as Boromir expires. Well, *forget that* for the movie!

One can imagine the response of Hollywood MBA studio execs reading a faithful adaption of the scene:

What? Our main action hero $tar doesn't even get to fight *one* filthy orc? You're $$$$ing kidding! Give us action! Blood! Gore! More action! More blood!

So the film orders up an extended fight scene from Big Sword Fights, Inc., for Aragorn: first off, he's up against around fifty orcs beside the Seat of Seeing after he's sent Frodo away safely. Even the filmmakers realized that Aragorn couldn't take on *that* many orcs (he's not Jet Li or Jackie Chan), and so Gimli and Legolas hurry into the *melée* to help him (some odd continuity blips in this sequence: at one point, Aragorn seems to be dashing away from the area, then he's back again a shot or two later).

And yet another departure from the book: all of the fighting between good guys and the orcs is related in dialogue in the book by Legolas and Gimli to Aragorn when they meet him. In other words, it doesn't occur in the foreground action of the book. This would be another of those instances where professional writers look at what Ronald Tolkien did and sigh wearily. *Tut, tut, Herr Professor.* A big fight to the death of a major character (Boromir) and the capture of two more major characters (the hobbits) cannot be back-announced by a character. It has to be shown in the foreground: it's something audiences would want to see.

So all sorts of mini action beats were added to the book: the orcs bearing down on Merry and Pippin, Boromir rushing up help them (in slow motion), Boromir dispatching orcs, Lurtz approaching in the distance and preparing his bow, Boromir being hit with arrows in slow motion (conscious nods to Akira Kurosawa and Sam Peckinpah), and finally crumpling, the agonized reactions of Pippin and Merry, the orcs carrying them off, and the orcs walking past the kneeling Boromir, leaving him to die. (The extended cut added more gags in the fights with the orcs, including footage of Merry and Pippin stabbing some orcs: the extended edits of the films made these two hobbits much more aggressive and warlike, while the theatrical versions focussed on their comedy. Editor John Gilbert didn't think the hobbits throwing rocks was very convincing, especially when the stones bring down the hulking orcs, so the shots were cut from the theatrical version. But they're back in the *Extended Edition*).

Another scene invented for the film had Frodo running into Merry and Pippin on his way to the boats. As with the Aragorn-Frodo scene, it allowed a farewell between the hero and two sidekicks (and was an addition to the original script). Merry, usually quicker on the uptake than the hapless Took, realizes that Frodo means to leave on his own (note that Frodo doesn't speak in this scene, not even a murmured 'goodbye'), and so creates a diversion by jumping up and hollering to the orcs. It succeeds in drawing off the orcs, but also means that Merry and Pippin are captured. (The scene also turns Merry into something of a hero, sacrificing himself– and Pippin – for the sake of Frodo and the quest).

Lurtz was an orc character invented for the films, and that was in the time-honoured Hollywood movie tradition of giving a face and an individuality to the villains, so they're not just a mass of faceless baddies who're dispatched in the end by the heroes. If Saruman ain't gonna come down out of Orthanc, someone's got to: so Lurtz is there to be, first of all, the chief henchman (and also the primary Uruk-hai that Saruman's been breeding). Lurtz doesn't have a personality as such: all the viewer needs to know is that he's a mean motherfucker. Lurtz's in there so that he can lead the orc band heading for the fellowship (personalizing Saruman's orcs), so that he can kill Boromir, and so that the hero can go head to head with him and avenge Boromir's death.

(There is a brief scene, however, between Saruman and Lurtz, back at Isengard, where the white wizard gives Lurtz his motivation, so to speak, like a director with an actor (Saruman shares some attributes with film directors, and even more with old-time movie moguls). Saruman explains that the orcs were originally corrupted by the dark powers. In that case, then, Lurtz should be mad at Morgoth, not men or elves or hobbits, none of whom have the ability to create orcs. In the book, only Morgoth and Sauron have the power to breed orcs. It doesn't make sense, though, 'cos Saruman has just created the Uruk-hai! Saruman is that 'dark power'. It's Frankenstein and his monster – and of course Chris Lee has played those characters).

Lurtz, like all henchmen and henchwomen, is just a function of the plot, just a narrative device. And when he's fulfilled his function, he's dispensed with, just like all henchmen are when those uncaring, morally corrupt dudes – no, not movie villains – *Hollywood writers* get hold of them. It's Hollywood producers and writers who happily discard characters when they've done what they were created to do. (In this case, Lurtz's ultimate function *is* to be dispensed with, like Oddjob in *Goldfinger*, or Darth Maul in *Star Wars: The Phantom Menace*.)

A couple more notes about the climactic fight in the 2001-02 adaption of *The Fellowship of the Ring:* Lurtz has to be dealt with by Aragorn. As Boromir's brother in many respects, but also as the main action hero in the *Lord of the Rings* films, it's fitting that Aragorn should kill Lurtz. To do so, he first has to be split off from Legolas and Gimli (most action-adventure films do this in the final minutes: only James Bond, for example, can dispatch the chief villain in a *James Bond* movie. Absolutely no one else can.) It's the same here: Aragorn is separated from the others precisely so that he can fight Lurtz alone (it's odd that Legolas, usually so swift, takes so long to reach Aragorn, although he hears Boromir's horn at the same time as the ranger. It's one of those things you're asked to quietly ignore by the storytellers).

The filmmakers (in this case, producer Barrie Osborne, who directed the Aragorn-Lurtz fight with schoolboy glee) also opted to push obstacles in front of Aragorn. So the future king of Gondor doesn't simply waltz in and nonchalantly lob a sword into Lurtz's heart, striking him instantly dead. No, he has a tough duel with the seven foot Uruk-hai, and the orc gets the better of him a few times. The fight involves all sorts of gags and stunts: Lurtz throwing Aragorn against a tree truck, then hurling a shield at him, which pins the guy to the tree (Aragorn escapes just as Lurtz whacks a sword into the bark where his head was). Punches and headbutts follow:

it's an ugly, messy fight.

In another gag, after licking the blood off the knife Aragorn's stuck in his leg, Lurtz hurls it at Aragorn who just about deflects it (the filmmakers liked to point out that it was a real metal knife that Viggo Mortensen batted away. Actually, an orc does lick a blooded knife in Tolkien's novel, in a different place). In another gag, at the end of the fight, the two are now face to face: Aragorn chops off Lurtz's arm. The Uruk seems unphased, and yanks on Aragorn's sword when it's pierced him in the gut, grinning in the man's face as he pulls the sword through his body. The final gag is a swift decapitation (decapitations are always swift in Hollywood movies – not only because of censorship and gore, but because holding a shot longer than a flash image on a dummy makes it look like a dummy).

The best moment in this lengthy fight sequence in the final reel of *The Fellowship of the Ring* is undoubtedly the bird's-eye-view cable camera master shot, with the brassy, percussive cue from Howard Shore. The fights also include some cool images of Legolas in full attack mode, wielding the bow and arrows with amazing speed on the left of the frame, bringing down five or six orcs one by one. The orcs die easily and quickly in the *Lord of the Rings* films, just like the henchmen and women in any action film, for the simple reason that if every man or woman out of two hundred baddies requires even thirty seconds of a fight to die, action films would be ten hours long. (The filmmakers dropped the fact that the orcs were a mixture of Misty Mountains orcs, orcs from Sauron, and Saruman's white hand orcs, because they had chosen Saruman as the chief villain for much of the films).

But one thing the battle at the end of *The Fellowship of the Ring* doesn't do much of, and that's storytelling. It's fun, it's spectacle, it's visceral and loud, but it doesn't advance the story much. For that, there is Frodo and the ring. A scene invented for the film (it was also re-shot) had Frodo standing at the water's edge having a crisis of conscience. What should he do next? Luckily, his spiritual guide (Gandalf) is there (in spirit, at least) to tell him. Frodo is heard in voiceover, speaking the lines from Bag End (transplanted to Moria in the film) about wishing the ring had never come to him. When Gandalf's voice appears on the soundtrack, it's played over the puzzled expression on Elijah Wood's face as if he's hearing Gandalf at the same time as the audience. There's a brief visual flashback of Gandalf at Moria, reminding Frodo of the ethical aspect of his quest. And *that* is the impetus Frodo requires, because the next shot after Frodo's close-up is a M.S. of Frodo walking towards the boats.

The next scene is the famous Hip-Hop Orc Dance Number, secretly shot and withheld from the trailers and subsequent versions. It's the one the fans have been talking about, because underneath the orc make-up is every principal player in the three films. It's a cross between Michael Jackson's *Thriller*, something out of *Annie* or *The Wiz*, and a P. Diddy video. No, no, wrong film again. I'm thinking of *Troy*...

The riverbank Frodo scene clarifies what all that fighting was all about, and what the central quest of the films is all about. Although it could be played quite calmly and matter-of-factly, Frodo's inner conflict scene is played *emotionally* because the film requires an emotional climax, as well as the emotional one provided by Boromir's death and the kidnapping of Pippin and Merry. And it's depicted in a heightened manner because this kind of film needs that kind of ending. That's why Frodo is weeping. That's also why Sam's drowning seems to go on forever: to amp up the emotion. Because *The Fellowship of the Ring* isn't the end of the line, and it isn't a proper climax to a film, or to a book.

Boromir's death scene was close to the book, except that the dialogue was of course rewritten. The main alteration was having Boromir provide the plot point that Merry and Pippin had been taken by the orcs; in the book, he dies before he can tell Aragorn. That meant that the scene where Aragorn does his Sherlock Holmes tracker bit and decodes the signs left behind could be dropped from the movie. The film followed the book in its depiction of Boromir being redeemed in part by dying while defending the hobbits. (It's a scene involving some forgiveness, some expiation of sins, some atonement). An early idea had Saruman also redeeming himself as he dies, with Gandalf forgiving him, and Saruman telling Gandalf that Sauron means to attack Minas Tirith.

Unusually, Aragorn kisses Boromir – I bet that idea came from the actor. Actor: 'what if I kiss Boromir?' Director: 'err, not on the mouth!' Actor: 'no'. Director: 'show me'. (In Tolkien's story, Gondorians do greet each other like that sometimes).

The extended cut allowed for a brief funeral scene, with Boromir in the boat floating on the river lying on his back, with his weapons, and falling over Rauros (no ten lines of song from Aragorn for Boromir from the book, though, followed by ten lines from Legolas and another ten lines from Aragorn). (Boromir's Viking death was the last piece filmed for *The Fellowship of the Ring,* shot by Barrie Osborne on the sea at Wellington, when Peter Jackson was away in London overseeing the scoring of the film).

As they leave, Aragorn's parting shot in the film is 'let's hunt some orc!' That's far too short for Tolkien, who has Aragorn say:

> "But come! With hope or without hope we will follow the trail of our enemies. And woe to them, if we prove the swifter! We will make such a chase as shall be accounted a marvel among the Three Kindreds: Elves, Dwarves and Men. Forth the Three Hunters!" (TT, 20).

And on and on he goes. Maybe 'let's hunt some orc' (though more casual and vaguely American) is better. It's certainly shorter. But it is a dumb-ass line.

The film closes with the establishment of the characters and goals of the three splinter groups of the fellowship: Merry and Pippin as victims to be saved by Aragorn, Legolas and Gimli; Gandalf and Boromir dead; and Frodo and Sam taking the ring to Mordor on their own.

It's a downbeat and moody final moment: a brief snatch of dialogue is inserted to remind viewers of the goals, and also the relationship between the characters: how Sam, for instance, remains optimistic that they might find a way to achieve their quest. Frodo and Sam are now in the hills, approaching the Emyn Muil (the Mount Doom scenes at the end of *The Return of the King* look very similar, because they shared the same location).

The last image of *The Lord of the Rings: The Fellowship of the Ring* is a wide shot of Frodo and Sam walking down a slope, with distant mountains and an overcast sky, and slow strings and choir on the track, and a sombre, respectful fade to black...

Certainly *The Fellowship of the Ring* doesn't have the upbeat happy ending of total closure and smiles all round that the Hollywood film industry prefers. The ending of *The Fellowship of the Ring* was always going to be a problem, but not, in a way, as much of a problem as the ending of *The Two Towers*. *The Fellowship of the Ring*, after all, did have the death of a major character to give the film an emotional close of heroic sacrifice (and a few Hollywood movies go that way from time to time, having the hero die: *Saving Private Ryan* (1998), *The Perfect Storm* (2000), *Gladiator* (2000), *Titanic* (1997), *The Matrix 3* (2003) and *Braveheart* (1995) for instance). And viewers were primed by the marketing and the book that this was part one of a three film set.

New Line Cinema, though, wanted a different ending for Frodo. They asked for more of an action ending, and one was duly written and shot. It involved orcs attacking Frodo and Sam in the boat: one of those endings where you think the heroes have escaped the villains, but the baddies turn up one last time. In the sequence, Frodo loses the ring, but an orc goes after it, to the point where he drowns in order to obtain it. The scene ended with Sam recovering Frodo – and the ring – and continuing on their journey.

The filmmakers weren't happy with that ending. Philippa Boyens said the end should be about Frodo and the ring, not an action scene with orcs. So it was re-shot, with Frodo now alone, having a crisis of decision, with Gandalf speaking to him from beyond the abyss. The climax for Frodo was thus him deciding to carry on with the quest to take the ring to Mordor. The emotional climax continued into the scene where Sam rejoins Frodo, and Frodo saves him from drowning (so it's Sam who nearly drowns, not an orc). It was directed by Fran Walsh.

Notice how *The Fellowship of the Ring* closes with sombre, 'serious' cinematic devices: the image of Frodo and Sam in the hills against a moody landscape, and the slow, elegiac music, and the fade to black. It could be the ending of an intense Chekovian family melodrama where the mother dies of terminal cancer after being briefly reunited at the end with her estranged daughter.

I think one of the functions of the ending of each *Lord of the Rings* film was to bring the films back to a 'serious' dramatic mode, to remind viewers that the films were an honest approach to J.R.R. Tolkien's book, rather than action-adventure fantasy movies with lots of battles and fights and monsters and orcs and weird hairy creatures and magic. In other words, to bring them closer to Oscar-worthy, prestige cinema mode rather than the popcorn entertainment genre (which's what they are, really).

Notice, also, how the film continues with its solemn tone *after* the fade to black and the credits (which're in white over black, inevitably). The music segues into an Enya song, which's slow and brooding. (I can't think of an Enya song which *is* fast, even her work with Gaelic folk-pop faves Clannad was s-l-o-w). There is no sudden blast into upbeat, triumphal music, as at the end of so many contemporary Hollywood movies. Enya's theme song is not the cheerful piece of pop fluff employed by many Hollywood movies (the nu metal reworking of heavy rock favourite 'Kashmir' at the end of *Godzilla* (1998) for instance). Later on in the credits, Howard Shore runs through the film's theme tunes. He has to: the credits are hours long (and there's no incentive to create a wholly new piece of music for way down the credits, because nobody watches them).

Some global movie franchises in the same market as the Lord of the Rings films: clockwise from top left: Spider-man, James Bond, Harry Potter, Star Wars, Studio Ghibli, Jurassic Park, and Indiana Jones.

(© Warners. Lucasfilm/ Fox. Eon Productions/ MGM/ Columbia. Sony/ Columbia/ Marvel. Studio Ghibli/ Tokuma. Lucasfilm/ Paramount. Universal).

A tiny fraction of the merchandize and toys generated by J.R.R. Tolkien's books.

CHAPTER 15

THE FILM OF *THE TWO TOWERS* (2002)

*The days have gone down in the West behind the hills into shadow.
Who shall gather the smoke of the dead wood burning,
Or behold the flowing years from the Sea returning?*

J.R.R. Tolkien, *The Two Towers* (137)

In 2002, when *The Lord of the Rings: The Two Towers* was released in cinemas, other blockbuster fare of a similar kind that year, and aimed at a similar global audience, included *Spider-man, XXX, Scooby-Doo, Minority Report*, and the usual rash of sequels: *Star Wars: Attack of the Clones, Spy Kids, Stuart Little, Die Another Day, Harry Potter* and *Men In Black*. (2002 was a year of five other big franchises bringing out sequels: *Harry Potter, James Bond, Men In Black, Austin Powers* and *Star Wars*. So *The Two Towers* was in good company, as another big franchise movie.) And the release window of *The Two Towers* coincided with two other American movies based on British writers, *James Bond* (*Die Another Day*) and *Harry Potter* (*Harry Potter and the Chamber of Secrets*), which were both released in the run-up to Yuletide, 2002.

The Two Towers is the least satisfying of the movies: too many additions, too many omissions, too much silliness and violence, etc. It can come across as multi-million dollar fan fiction, as the filmmakers riff on Tolkienesque scenarios.

I wonder if the *Lord of the Rings* films are so popular among John Ronald Reuel Tolkien fans (though not *all* fans) because the fans know all of the background from the books. I wonder how well the *Lord of the Rings* pictures resonate with people who don't know anything about Middle-earth and have never read a word of J.R.R. Tolkien. When I watch the films, I can fill in what's happening with hundreds of pages of information and backstory. As Tolkien used to say, one of the intentions with *Lord of the Rings* was to have all of the vast historical background of Middle-earth glimpsed through characters, or dialogue, or narration. But in a movie, even one touching two-and-a-half-to-three hours (or eight-nine hours total theatrical and say eleven hours on the extended DVDs for the three flicks), only a fraction of that Middle-earth history can reach the viewer. So the

Lord of the Rings films, though they're far from perfect (having many faults), at least have enough energy and Tolkienania in them to persuade some people to go back to the books, or take up the books for the first time. And there's enough in them to remind Tolkien fans of all the stuff they couldn't include (i.e., the bulk of Tolkien's vast Middle-earth writings).

No one who knows anything about the economic and industrial structure of the global entertainment industry could have expected a Hollywood studio and the films' producers to make something other than an action-adventure blockbuster version of J.R.R. Tolkien's beloved fairy tale. Everyone knew that the people who were spending $300-400 million (negative cost) and, say, $100-200 million (on marketing) would want a sexy, action-packed high concept product that would do everything it could to guarantee a return (and profit) on their investment, take a substantial market share, increase the profile and clout of the studio (New Line Cinema), enhance the standing of the studio's executives (Shaye, Lynne, Mittweg, Emmerich, Einhorn, Ordesky, Tuckerman, Schwartz – and the lawyers, accountants, agents, etc), bolster the share price of the studio and its parent company (AOL Time Warner), stimulate sales of affiliated companies' products, and inaugurate 100s of licensees and a huge range of merchandize.

If you put yourself in the shoes of the people stumping up the $400-600 million, their primary considerations would *not* be: how can we satisfy Tolkien obsessives with the films? Sure, they want Tolkien fans to come along (the various DVD and video editions of the films have shamelessly targetted that market), but the investment of 100s of millions of dollars could not be recouped with a profit from literary and fantasy fans alone. Rather, the audience has to be as wide as possible, with maximum cross-over potential. If you keep in mind the intended audience of the 2001-2003 Tolkien flicks, everything about them falls into place:

-> every casting choice,
-> the emphasis on action,
-> the breathless pace,
-> the exaggerations,
-> the additions (the romance plot, for example, the action set-pieces),
-> the clarification, compression (simplification) of the plot,
-> the pop culture references, many aimed at male teens (skate-boarding, farting, jokes),
-> the vast licensing and merchandizing operation,
-> every aspect of graphic and visual design,
-> the marketing, etc etc etc

Ultimately, the *Lord of the Rings* films were (1) better than expected, (2) contained a surprising amount of Tolkien's Middle-earth, (3) had moments of visionary splendour, and (4) were way above the average Hollywood blockbuster.

But the *best* fantasy films made since 1895? No. I'd put the mooovies up alongside *Jason and the Argonauts*, as wonderful mythic fantasy, but for many viewers they wouldn't be in the same class of fantasy as Jean Cocteau's *La Belle et la Bête* or Todd Browning's *Dracula* or as *The Seven Samurai* as action-adventure.

One of the many reasons that for me the *Lord of the Rings* films aren't wholly successful is that I don't feel any sense of jeopardy for the characters (Elijah Wood and Sean Astin, and other casting decisions, are part of the problem for me). When the giant eye appears in the inn at Bree, or the black riders on the hills, it's all very nice cinematography, vfx, editing, sound and music, but if you don't really care for the characters in the first place, if you don't ever feel they're in real danger, the whole thing crumbles. Hence that decision to have Aragorn appear to die in *The Two Towers* was a cretinous, hokey, utterly unconvincing attempt to increase the level of drama and suspense. That's not how to play drama or build tension. Ditto with Frodo seeming to expire in *The Fellowship of the Ring*. It's not a question of already knowing the story 'cos we've read the 1954 book, so we don't really care for the characters. It's about the skill in storytelling that persuades the audience to pretend for a moment, to suspend their disbelief. Even a puppet show in a back street, or a shadowplay with paper figures, or a comedian on stage, or someone reading a book aloud, can produce that all-important suspension of disbelief – and without the aid 100 million dollars of visual effects and the most up-to-date technology. It's about the *performance*, the conviction, the flair, the storytelling skill – and having great material.

The sense of doom and menace which J.R.R. Tolkien so brilliantly evoked in the books is distinctly lacking in the films at times. It's acutely palpable in the books, but it's only there in dribs and drabs in the films. But compare to the sense of dread in films like the 1931 *Dracula*, or *Night of the Demon* (1957), or *Nosferatu* (1922), or *Vampyr* (1932). There's a creeping claustrophobia, a graceful and assured evocation of truly dark atmospheres in those films which the New Line *Lord of the Rings* films only possess in fits and starts.

The Two Towers opted not to provide a short summary of the plot of the first film, perhaps due to time restrictions. New Line wanted a prologue, but the filmmakers preferred to use that time for other scenes. A prologue for *The Two Towers* was scripted, storyboarded and an animatic (video and computer storyboard) made of it, but it was ultimately shelved.

However there are plenty of other ways for a good screenwriter to bring an audience up to date. In *The Two Towers* there were reminders of the some of the key events in the *Fellowship of the Ring* film, in the dialogue, and in some flashbacks. *The Two Towers* opened, for instance, with a short retread of one of the highlights of *The Fellowship of the Ring*: Gandalf and the Balrog on the bridge of Khazad-dûm (this duel offered an action-based opening for the film, *à la* James Bond, as with the first film, and was/ is common practice in contemporary Hollywood cinema. It also, importantly, revives the character of *Gandalf*, as he disappears from *The Two Towers* for ages).

Frodo and Sam were introduced next, clambering around mountains, with Gollum met soon after. The orcs carrying Merry and Pippin, and their three pursuers (Aragorn, Gimli and Legolas), were also introduced very early on in *The Two Towers*. Saruman reprised his role in *The Fellowship of the Ring* as the voice of the villains, and acted as a narrator, providing exposition (such as over the scenes of the invasion of Rohan). (Saruman's role is again bumped in *The Two Towers*, especially during the second half of the film, as all roads lead to Helm's Deep and Isengard.)

After Frodo, Sam and Gollum have been introduced, *The Two Towers* then sets about bringing on the other main players: Aragorn, Legolas and Gimli, now tracking the two hobbits and the Uruk-hai West, towards Rohan. Saruman was once again seen at Isengard, plotting villainously. New characters and a new location were also part of the first act: Edoras, Éowyn, Théoden, Éomer and Wormtongue.

Thus, by the twenty minute mark, *The Two Towers* had (re)acquainted the audience with the chief characters of the film. A couple of major roles were brought on later (when they were encountered for the first time as they were in the book, by the characters as they meet them): Treebeard and Faramir.

There was hardly time in *The Two Towers*, with so much narrative to get through, for exploring characters. Thus, the political and social situation at Edoras, between Théoden, Éowyn, Wormtongue and Éomer, and the kingdom of Rohan, was described at a lightning pace, depicted with broad strokes.

Having Éomer arrive to save the day with Gandalf at the end instead of Erkenbrand makes sense in one way, because it makes good the subplot, invented for the movie, of the feud between Théoden and his sister-son, which has been encouraged by Wormtongue.

In the 1954 book, it's Treebeard who makes all the major decisions concerning attacking Isengard and dealing with Saruman. The writers have taken Gandalf's suggestion that the arrival of the hobbits have been the pebbles that start an avalanche and expanded upon it: now the hobbits seem to be orchestrating the rising up of Treebeard and the ents. It kind of works, except in scenes like Merry yelling at Treebeard to do something because his friends are suffering. No, no, *no!*

The beginning and ending of *The Two Towers* film presented a big challenge to the scriptwriters. Somewhere George Lucas has remarked that the first 5 minutes and the final 20 minutes are the most important in a film. As it was in the middle of a three film set, *The Two Towers* film could not offer any major resolutions of the story at the end, and had to begin with a story in the midst of its telling. As a film being released a year from the first film (in December, 2002), *The Two Towers* also had to remind viewers of the first film (although a year wasn't the usual gap between sequels in contemporary Hollywood, which was typically two to three years, but was also often four or five or more years). *The Two Towers* also had to work for people who hadn't seen the first film, who didn't have the backstory and background information on the characters: it had to work (like any sequel) as a film on its own.

There were many pluses of being a sequel, however: the key characters had already been established, and screen time did not have to be expended on introducing most of the key protagonists (so more screen time could be given over to the new characters in *The Two Towers*, such as Faramir, Treebeard, Wormtongue, Éowyn, Éomer and Théoden).

One of the biggest script decisions was not to follow Tolkien's structure of one book following another (an easy decision: even the most 'faithful' of literary adaptors would find that format very difficult to adhere to – and impossible in a big budget Hollywood movie). And to lose the climactic scene in Shelob's lair. Thus, the terrific cliffhanger at the end of *The Two Towers* was not available to the scriptwriters: '[h]e was out in the darkness. Frodo was alive but taken by the Enemy' runs the last line of *The Two Towers* (TT, 442).

So scriptwriters Frances Walsh, Philippa Boyens, Peter Jackson (and Stephen Sinclair in early drafts) struggled to concoct a different climax to the Frodo-Sam storyline, taking them to Osgiliath and having Faramir now act as an obstacle not a helper as he is in the book. As Philippa Boyens explained, Faramir didn't change enough in the book, he didn't have a satisfying story or character arc, which was one reason why he became an obstacle for the hobbits. Boyens said, as written in the novel, Faramir would not pick up the ring if it lay by the roadside, and that would undo all of the dramatic work that been expended in the films on making the ring such an evil force. Also, Frodo and Sam, by the end of *The Two Towers*, would still be walking, but 'to where, to what?' So Faramir and the Osgiliath episode was a suitable obstacle in their path. Hence also the nazgûl appearing, and Frodo's encounter with the Witch-king: further evidence (the clincher, in fact), for Faramir, of the evil of the ring and why it should be destroyed. (The Osgiliath sequence also functions crucially as a climactic sequence for the Frodo and Sam story, now that the Shelob sequence was shifted to film three; otherwise, their story wouldn't have a satisfying or exciting conclusion in the picture, they would simply fade from view as they struggle towards Mordor.)

The addition, during editing, of Sam's voiceover, which draws together the plot strands in a montage, offers what the filmmakers hoped would be an emotional climax to the film (Helm's Deep being a big action climax). (Having Sam turn narrator here isn't so far-fetched: Sam often wonders, in the course of the book, how their experiences will be written up later by chroniclers, and he becomes a writer himself when he completes the *Red Book* which Bilbo and Frodo have been writing. It's just that Sam's narration is badly handled, and the dialogue is bathetic).

Sam's speech was designed to add some heart to the movie; one wonders also, because the speech defines what the whole quest of the ring is about, if the filmmakers were thinking in terms of a response to the events of September 11, 2001. Films such as *Spider-man* had been rewritten in order to incorporate the bullish liberal reaction of Hollywood to what were interpreted as attacks on the American way of life. (Théoden's line, 'what can we do against such reckless hate?' also had links with 9/11, and suicide bombers in the Middle East, political factions who were willing to kill themselves for the cause. An orc does just that in *The Two Towers* –

the 'beserker' orc carrying the torch kills himself (and plenty of his comrades) in order to breach Helm's Deep).

The Two Towers also did not have any big emotional climaxes: apart from Helm's Deep, everyone else and everything else just continues, only being resolved in the final film. And even at Helm's Deep there is a victory with no real losses. In *The Fellowship of the Ring*, the deaths of Gandalf and Boromir provided some deep emotional resonances, and the ending of the film with the fellowship broken apart and in disarray, while not wholly satisfying as a narrative conclusion, at least provided some exciting moments, with audiences conscious of the story continuing in film two. *The Two Towers* didn't have any significant deaths, so it invented some (Haldir and Aragorn), and invented an action and thematic climax for Frodo and the ring by taking Frodo and Sam to Osgiliath and encountering the nazgûl.

The other problem, of how to open *The Two Towers*, was solved by retreading one of the key moments in *The Fellowship of the Ring*, the balrog-Gandalf fight (which, in terms of the chronology of the 1954 book, took place some weeks before the ending of the first film, with the break-up of the fellowship. The chronology of the whole of the 2002 movie of *The Two Towers* is vague; the events seem to take place in a few days). The balrog battle was a suitably spectacular opening for the film, a kind of thrill ride or theme park ride, as Gandalf and the Maia spirit roar down to the foundations of the Misty Mountains (and it was cheaper, by re-using existing footage). If the scriptwriters had followed the book, the much smaller scale scenes of Frodo and Sam would have opened the film, cross-cut with the orcs carrying the hobbits and the elf, dwarf and ranger pursuing them.

In some respects, the adaptors altered *The Two Towers* more than the other two books: adding the ring going to Osgiliath, the encounter with the Witch-king, dropping Shelob, adding Haldir and the elves at Helm's Deep, changing Faramir's character, as well as Théoden's, adding the warg attack, and 'killing' Aragorn. Certainly it looked as if the scriptwriters had made the greatest changes with *The Two Towers* in adapting *The Lord of the Rings*. In fact, among the most severe departures from the novel occurred in *The Fellowship of the Ring*: casting Frodo as an 18 year-old (and turning him into a young hobbit); losing the lengthy chronology; losing Tom Bombadil, Goldberry, Old Man Willow, and many secondary characters; leaving out the Old Forest, the conspiracy and the Barrow-downs; bumping up Saruman to chief villain; Arwen taking over Glorfindel's role (and moving her from the appendices); turning Merry and Pippin into comic sidekicks, and so on.

The Two Towers is not like the usual sequel or follow-up in the Hollywood film industry. Most sequels rerun the same material (same plots, characters, situations, etc) as the first film, becoming a series of films which are all essentially remakes of the original: *Jaws, Jurassic Park, Indiana Jones, Hallowe'en, Scream, Scary Movie, Austin Powers, Pirates of the Carribean, Die Hard, Rocky,* and so on.

The Two Towers was part of a continuous story, which had been split into three parts by the publishers in the 1950s (for economic, not artistic or æsthetic, reasons), and into two by United Artists and Rankin/ Bass in the 1970s, and two again by Miramax in 1997-98, and then three by New Line Cinema in 1998-99. Also, because the *Lord of the Rings* films were adapted from an existing property, they were not, like the *Star Wars, Alien, Scream, Lethal Weapon, Indiana Jones, Austin Powers* or *Die Hard* franchises, written solely *as* movies (i.e., they were not books before they were movie scripts). Finally, there was only ever going to be three films (or six, if you count the *Extended Editions*). They were not a franchise would be extended and reinvented many times, over and over, with the stories running on almost indefinitely, as in the *Batman, James Bond* or *Star Trek* franchises.

Among the multitudinous problems for the filmmakers in making *The Two Towers* were: how to keep audiences abreast of the multiple storylines; how to portray the ents (how do walking trees go into battle?, how do they talk?, what do they look like); whether to have one book follow another (the way Tolkien intended it to be read – although this was never seriously considered an option by the filmmakers); the banter of the orcs (go for Tolkien's not entirely satisfactory (or funny) Cockney speech?); and, most interesting of all, how to deal with the story collapsing down to three characters, Frodo, Sam and Gollum, struggling across marshes and mountains, one of them a computer-generated ring junkie with a curious Welsh accent.

In *The Two Towers* as scripted at one time, Elrond visited Galadriel in Lothlórien to discuss the weighty matters of the elves and the War of the Ring. These scenes were also shot, but discarded when it was decided that Arwen (and thus Elrond) should remain in Rivendell for the duration of the films. (This was altered a little, when Elrond delivers the reforged sword to Aragorn at Dunharrow in person. But an echo of the Arwen plot persists, when at first it appears as if Arwen is visiting Aragorn; and Arwen may be in the band of elves that turn up just before the battle of Helm's Deep).

Instead of the prologue going at the front of *The Two Towers*, it was inserted into the middle – the Galadriel-Elrond montage (although it wasn't really a prologue anymore, but a summing up of the state of affairs in Middle-earth seen from the elves' perspective). Here, Elrond doesn't visit Galadriel bodily, but in spirit, and they have a kind of telepathic exchange. This was entirely constructed in the editing, by combining scenes of the actors shot at different times and linking them narratively with voiceover. Now Elrond and Galadriel were communicating on the long distance Elf Line. (It was handy having the idea of Galadriel speaking in *voiceover* while a C.U. or medium shot of her *not speaking* was introduced in film one (the way she communicates telepathically with Frodo, a fellow ring-bearer), because it meant that any voiceover could be deployed over the same sort of shots (instead of, as is usual practice, adding new dialogue to establishing or long shots, or reaction shots). Thus, Cate Blanchett is shown in *The Two Towers* in medium shot or a big close-up of her eyes, while she's talking to Elrond. The extreme close-ups were also useful, because different dialogue could be inserted over them).

Actually, the idea of the elves communicating without speaking was introduced by Tolkien himself, in a short but vivid scene right at the end of *The Lord of the Rings*, when the elf leaders (and Gandalf) commune with each other. It's one of my favourite scenes in *The Lord of the Rings*:

> They [Celeborn and Galadriel] had journeyed thus far by the westways, for they had much to speak of with Elrond and with Gandalf, and here they lingered still in converse with their friends. Often long after the hobbits were wrapped in sleep they would sit together under the stars, recalling the ages that were gone and all their joys and labours in the world, or holding council, concerning the days to come. If any wanderer had chanced to pass, little would he have seen or heard, and it would have seemed to him only that he saw grey figures, carved in stone, memorials of forgotten things now lost in unpeopled lands. For they did not move or speak with mouth, looking from mind to mind; and only their shining eyes stirred and kindled as their thoughts went to and fro. (RK, 319-320)

SOME FIRST THOUGHTS ON *THE TWO TOWERS*.

The Two Towers, like *The Fellowship of the Ring*, doesn't need to rush from one digital matte of a landscape to the next castle set to the next CGI-enhanced miniature to the next battle scene at 1,000 mph. *The Two Towers* film can work – and does work very well – when it slows down. I mean, it was very important in *The Fellowship of the Ring* film that Gandalf stopped for a moment in Moria to talk to Frodo about Gollum and pity, which becomes hugely significant later.

The Fellowship of the Ring showed that millions of viewers were willing to come along for the ride, so *The Two Towers* had earned a certain latitude amongst its audience (the packed venues of the opening few days proved that audiences will follow the Tolkien films anywhere). It could have included lots more non-action scenes and spent much more time with, say, the hobbits and Treebeard (mercilessly rushed), or found time for some songs (OK, perhaps not), or, best of all, had a scene or three of Elrond or Gandalf delving into the history of Middle-earth (that stunning opening montage in *The Fellowship of the Ring* about the Last Alliance and the ring was crying out for a re-cap or development in *The Two Towers*).

The visual effects team came up with some superior moments to *The Fellowship of the Ring*: Merry and Pippin running under a horse – wonderful; the trolls opening the Black Gate; Gollum; the warg attack; a tremendously effective cut to an extreme long shot of Gandalf and the Balrog; and, best of all, the most daunting fx task in *The Two Towers* – the ents. It was nice to see a map unfurled in the Faramir scenes – that was one of the apposite touches in *The Fellowship of the Ring*.

Gollum was surprisingly good – from the integration of live action and CGI animation point-of-view. The part's a gift to any actor to steal the show, and Andy Serkis certainly threw himself into it.

Bernard Hill was great as Théoden (and might've made a good Aragorn). But *The Two Towers* was Aragorn's film, with Viggo Mortensen dominating the action (when Gollum wasn't on screen). Apart from Serkis, watching Mortensen launching himself wholesale into the role was a delight. Gimli, now charged with carrying most the humour, had some cool moments – the biggest laugh in the theatre at one screening I saw was Gimli below the parapet.

Advance rumours that the Helm's Deep battle would last for 45 minutes 'boded ill' for me (as Gimli might put it). It showed how the filmmakers unbalanced their adaption of Tolkien's tome in favour of endless battles. In my copy of *The Two Towers*, the "Helm's Deep" chapter was 21 pages long – out of 432 pages in the 1954 book. In other words, 5 per cent; in the film, at 45 mins, it's so expanded that it unbalances Tolkien's fiction way too much.

Yes, *Lord of the Rings* is about a war (*War of the Ring*, one of Tolkien's alternative titles, is a more accurate title for the whole book). But Tolkien's depiction of war at the end of the Third Age of Middle-earth doesn't mean one CG action sequence after another.

Some Tolkien gripes. The biggest gripes with the 2001-2003 adaptions of *The Lord of the Rings* are to do with the script and the casting. It seems a pity that so much time and effort was spent on getting details right (Aragorn's sword flaming when Gandalf reappears, for example, or the piney woods of Ithilien), but huge chunks of the book were dropped, and some of the changes were far-reaching. There's clearly so much enthusiasm for Tolkien's material on screen – rendered by the film departments in art direction, armoury, costume, leather, make-up, miniatures, and practicals – but so much buggering about with the story.

FURTHER THOUGHTS ON *THE TWO TOWERS* FILM.
I reckon some two-thirds of the main action of *The Two Towers* book was shown. The last 4 chapters of *Book Three* were left out, as were the last 4 chapters of *Book Four*. Plus chapter 1 of *Book Three* had been covered in the first film. So only 12 out of 21 chapters were in the film. That makes *The Two Towers* more like 'One and a Half Towers' (and the second tower, Barad-dûr, hardly featured – if one thinks of the Dark Tower as the second tower). About 60-70 pages were cut from each book, or 120-140 pages from *The Two Towers* book as a whole. Roughly, *The Two Towers* flick covered 280 pages of the 430 pages in *The Two Towers* book.

This means that each film is pushing deeper into the next, so that *The Return of the King* will have to cover masses of material – i.e., not only the 370 pages of *The Return of the King* book, but also the other 120 pages of *The Two Towers* book. Tom Shippey noted that when he was watching the first and second movies, realizing how much story the filmmakers still had to cover.

So much was left out of *The Two Towers*. Some major cuts, some minor. I missed: Aragorn's parley with the orcs at Helm's Deep ('we are the fighting Uruk-hai!'); the sighting of Saruman in Fangorn; the lengthy arguments the orcs have about the hobbits (Grishnákh and Uglúk); and the great *Macbeth* moment, when the forest comes to Helm's Deep and devours the orcs (included in the extended cut).

Gandalf was such a big presence in *The Fellowship of the Ring*, it's a shame he takes a backseat in *The Two Towers* (even though that's how the book plays him, shifting attention to the rest of the Company). Apart from relating his experience with the Balrog, healing Théoden and providing the *deus ex machina* rescue at Helm's Deep, he's not on screen much (but that should be enough!).

There were many additions, too. When the additions to Tolkien's book are done with such style and vigour, no one could argue with them. But when the additions don't add anything to the narrative or substance of the films, it's a waste of time. For instance, Aragorn in the river, pretty pointless. And much of the Osgiliath sequence. (It would have been nice to indicate that Galadriel was Arwen's grandmother; instead, the filmmakers emphasized Elrond as the stern daddy who presides over his daughter Arwen's fate, and cautions her against staying in Middle-earth with Aragorn.)

The warg attack was originally planned to take place at Edoras at night, and would have been a major reason for the exodus of the Rohirrim to Helm's Deep. In the end, the scene proved too costly to shoot (due to problems such as paying for night shoots in a remote location, and rigging the Edoras location at Canterbury with lots of lights), and was transferred to the journey to Helm's Deep. (Some of the filmmakers felt that the warg attack wasn't wholly satisfying; the planning of it was left until close to shooting).

The elves arriving at Helm's Deep had another narrative function: they brought Arwen with them (which's why they say they've come from Rivendell). But the idea of Arwen as a warrior princess elf was later dropped (although Liv Tyler did shoot scenes at the Lower Hutt quarry set. The scene where Haldir dies and Aragorn runs up the stairs to rescue her was originally going to be Aragorn rushing to save Arwen from orcs). In some respects, then, Haldir is a direct replacement for Arwen. Another alteration was the return of Aragorn: in the released versions of *The Two Towers*, Éowyn sees Aragorn return and meet Legolas, who gives him the evenstar; an earlier version had Éowyn watching Arwen being reunited with Aragorn (which would've ended the Éowyn-Aragorn plot right there).

One of the problems the scriptwriters said they felt they had with *The Two Towers* was that none of the major characters die. In other words, an event which would have intensified the drama. In *The Fellowship of the Ring*, Boromir dying heroically at the end of the film gave the film a big climax (a dramatic scene, which was heightened with overblown action sequences). And of course, Gandalf falling to his doom also racheted up the sense of jeopardy and suspense. Thus, in *The Two Towers*, the screenwriters resorted to bringing the elves to Helm's Deep: it wasn't just an addition to the novel which even Tolkien might have liked a little, it was also a way of introducing the character of Haldir, the only significant character who dies during the battle (oddly, although Haldir says he has come from Rivendell, he's seen in *The Fellowship of the Ring* at Lothlórien). Thus, as Aragorn, Legolas, Gimli, Éowyn, Éomer, Gandalf or

Théoden don't die at Helm's Deep, a minor character like Haldir could be introduced and killed off. It gave the battle some kind of weight – otherwise, the good guys are victorious yet again, without seeming to suffer much.

Another script problem with *The Two Towers* was the ring: it fades into the distance, and is rarely glimpsed. Frodo doesn't put it on at all in the film (or in the 1954 book). So the adaptors had to find a way of keeping the ring in the foreground, and of reminding viewers that the whole of *The Lord* was about the War of the Ring.

This was done in various ways: Frodo was seen stroking the ring obsessively at night (which led to a discussion with Gollum about his past); Frodo brings it out and nearly puts it on twice (when the ringwraith hovers nearby), and is saved both times by Sam; Gollum tries to take the ring when he first encounters Frodo and Sam; Faramir lifts the ring with his sword as he contemplates what he'll do with it; and Sam and Frodo discuss the influence the ring is having on Frodo. One of the ideas of showing the effect of the ring on Frodo was tried out – Elijah Wood was dressed in grotesque make-up to show him turning into something like Gollum, to illustrate to Faramir what was happening to him, but didn't make it into the final cut of either version of *The Two Towers*.

One could hear the narrative creaking louder than Howard Shore's pounding score in the final 30 minutes or so of *The Two Towers* film, as scriptwriters Frances Walsh and Philippa Boyens struggled to come up with a decent ending. Hence the Osgiliath sequence. Narratively, it didn't add much: the Frodo-Faramir confrontation over the ring could have happened anywhere (in the book it takes place at Hennen Annûn). The visualization of Osgiliath as a bombed-out Hiroshima or Dresden or Bosnia or Beirut was interesting (the filmmakers took London during the Blitz as an obvious comparison).

The most significant addition, aside from the alteration of Faramir's characterization, was the stand-off between Frodo and the flying nazgûl, with Sam saving the day. But this was already a re-run of a previous scene in the same film. Didn't the scriptwriters ask the basic questions about film narrative when they were concocting the Osgiliath confrontation (i.e., what is the point of the scene?). The scene with the nazgûl dramatized the relationships already existing between the characters: Frodo being seduced by the power of the ring and nearly putting it on; Sam looking after his master and saving him; and Faramir finally understanding the influence of the ring.

It's also amazing just how quickly Faramir realized that Frodo and Sam were carrying the One Ring. In the 1954 book, it takes Gandalf, probably the best mind in Middle-earth, years and years to discover if Bilbo had found the ruling ring, including trips to Minas Tirith and to see Saruman. And it's only when Sam blurts out about the ring, after a very lengthy scene of dialogue between Faramir, Frodo and Sam about big chunks of the history of Middle-earth, in the novel, that Faramir realizes the whole story. In the film of *The Two Towers*, Faramir grasps the truth in a minute or two.

The Osgiliath sequence was there to provide a suitably action-filled ending to Frodo and Sam's story in *The Two Towers*. This was partly due to the decision not to shoot all of *The Two Towers*, but to stop short of the Shelob and Cirith Ungol sequence. Thus, the Frodo and Sam storyline would not have had a big finish. It would've petered out. Another reason to leave Shelob until the next film was due to the problem of intercutting the Frodo and Sam story with the Helm's Deep battle and ent attack on Isengard. One of the reasons offered by the scriptwriters was because it would have been too much, too much to fit in, and too tricky to intercut with the Helm's Deep battle. Actually, the movie goes to the action climaxes of the Treebeard-hobbit story and the Frodo-Sam story *after* Helm's Deep, so there are other ways of intercutting the narratives. (The Frodo-ringwraith scene was a remnant from the Miramax script, when the film was going to be split into two parts; at that time, it would have provided the climax to the first film, where Frodo would have encountered the nazgûl at Amon Hen. It was economic, too: going to Osgiliath meant using the same set).

Frances Walsh and Philippa Boyens acknowledged that *The Two Towers* gave them the most trouble in terms of adapting it for the screen. It didn't have the simple form of *The Fellowship of the Ring,* which was basically a journey narrative. In *The Two Towers*, the story fragments into three groups of people (centring around Frodo, Sam and Gollum; Aragorn, Legolas and Gimli; and Merry, Pippin and Treebeard). Tolkien, of course, risked much on having the narrative split into two books and two distinct parts. The busy scenes involving Treebeard, the ents, Rohan, Merry, Pippin, Gimli, Legolas, Gandalf, Aragorn, Éowyn, Saruman, Wormtongue, Théoden, Helm's Deep and so on come first, in *Book Three*, then the narrative shrinks dramatically, down to three little figures, Frodo, Sam and Gollum. The film of *The Two Towers*, of course, was never going to have *Book Three* followed by *Book Four*; it was always going to intercut the stories throughout.

But it seemed as if the filmmakers had forgotten or not realized that the real point of Tolkien's narrative structure was the *difference* between the clamour of war and two little hobbits – that no matter how loud, chaotic, exciting, violent and catastrophic the war scenes were, they were not the really important events: what *really* counted was whether Frodo and Sam would reach the Crack of Doom. By taking Frodo and Sam to war-torn Osgiliath, the scriptwriters gave Frodo and Sam suitably big scenes to close the picture, but that severely detracted from the narrative scheme that Tolkien had created (what C.S. Lewis called 'structural invention of the highest order'). And anyway, Frodo and Sam had plenty of action in the final chapters of *The Two Towers*, including an encounter with a giant spider, chases in dark tunnels, and the wonderful cliffhanger of Frodo being captured in Cirith Ungol:

> Sam yelled and brandished Sting, but his little voice was drowned in the tumult. No one heeded him.

> The great doors slammed to. Boom. The bars of iron fell into place inside. Clang. The gate was shut. Sam hurled himself against the bolted brazen plates and fell senseless to the ground. He was out in the darkness. Frodo was alive but taken by the Enemy. (LR, 770)

It would have been a cinematic cliffhanger in the old style, the sort of cliffhanger that George Lucas had revived to close the second *Star Wars* film. At the time, in 1980, cinema audiences had to wait three years before they found out what the enemy had done with Han Solo in *Return of the Jedi*.

Tolkien fans objected to the change in Faramir's character in the 2002 movie of *The Two Towers*, having him much tougher, less sympathetic, and having the ring taken to Gondor. One of the points of the Faramir episode in the 1954 book was to demonstrate that not all people, and not all men, are tempted to take the ring. One of the functions of Faramir's character was to show that he was different from his brother Boromir, and that his response to having the ring right in front of him with a band of loyal men at his call was a noble refusal to do what Boromir did.

> "And here in the wild I have you: two halflings, and a host of men at my call, and the Ring of Rings. A pretty stroke of fortune! A chance for Faramir, Captain of Gondor, to show his quality!" (LR, 707).

In the 2002 film of *The Two Towers*, the critical confrontation between the halflings and the captain of Gondor is placed right after the nazgûl has buzzed Frodo and Sam's saved him. The scene is played quite differently, with Sam now standing in between Frodo and Faramir, bullishly defending his master, and standing up to Faramir with a bilious remonstration (there is a scene like this in the novel, but it's not played like this). In the 1954 book, Faramir considers how to respond for a moment, and gravely reassures the hobbits that he won't take the ring. In the film, Faramir is berated by Sam, in front of Faramir's men, and told how Boromir tried to take the ring. This sure ain't right!

Scriptwriter Philippa Boyens remarked that the decision to take the narrative to Osgiliath and change the character of Faramir and the nature of his confrontation with the hobbits was to give Faramir more of a 'character arc' or journey (a screenwriting term which Tolkien would have detested – but then, he wouldn't haven't liked any part of contemporary screenwriting, theory or practice!).

It's typical of the 2001-03 films of *The Lord of the Rings* (and contemporary Hollywood movies in general) that what happens in the book is exaggerated, emphasized, hyped up, sometimes to point of laughable pomposity (Galadriel's speeches), or gory battles (the ending of *The Fellowship of the Ring*), or horror film clichés (Théoden's 'exorcism').

Philippa Boyens and Frances Walsh also remarked that Faramir was changed to give Frodo and Sam an obstacle on their journey. Without the cliffhanger ending of Frodo being captured by orcs and Sam on the outside of Cirith Ungol, the filmmakers were faced with the prospect of Frodo, Sam and Gollum toiling onward to nowhere in particular. For Boyens and Walsh, the Faramir scenes lacked drama, and a dramatic resolution.

Yet another reason, Boyens explained on the DVD commentary, was that having Faramir simply resist taking the ring detracted too drastically from the rest of the films: it took away the setting up of the power of the ring, how it had affected Galadriel and Gandalf and sent Boromir mad. If Faramir had calmly turned away from the ring, and set Frodo free, as he does in the 1954 book, it would have lessened the impact of the ring in the film, and perhaps been confusing to viewers who didn't know Tolkien's tome. The scriptwriters always kept in mind spectators who hadn't read *The Lord of the Rings,* and having a man refuse the ring when others had been sorely tempted by it, could have been confusing. I disagree with the solution that Walsh and Boyens came to in regard to Faramir and the Frodo and Sam story in the last quarter of *The Two Towers.* The Faramir and Hennen Annûn scenes had always been problematic, the scriptwriters acknowledged, so they decided to amp up the drama and suspense.

With the visuals still coming thick and fast, the final reel of *The Two Towers* film was entrancing, but clunkily strung together. The pacing was off, with myriad groups of people and locations tied together with all sorts of voiceovers (from Gandalf, Frodo and Gollum). Even Sam got to do some narration: his execrable liberal, would-be Martin Luther King speech, an appalling piece of screenwriting. It didn't help having Astin delivering it in teary-eyed, po-faced fashion. At this point, writers Frances Walsh and Philippa Boyens, director Peter Jackson and editors Michael Horton and Jabez Olssen seemed to be suffering from George Lucas syndrome – when in doubt, cut cut cut, chopping up myriad plot strands into unsatisfactory bites (*viz.,* the ending of *Star Wars: The Phantom Menace*).

The self-consciousness of the nods to different segments of the global audience in *The Two Towers* was acute: Legolas skateboarding down some stone steps at Helm's Deep for the *XXX/ Blade/ Matrix* action crowd, and the Elrond-Aragorn-Arwen 'should-she-shouldn't she?' soap opera for (older) women, one of the unashamed attempts at reaching a *Titanic* demographic (also aimed at this female audience were the woefully underwritten Aragorn-Éowyn scenes, and the constant cross-cuts to the women and children in the caves during Helm's Deep. The filmmakers milked the build-up to the battle with a gut-wrenching sentimentality that Walt Disney or pre-*Schindler's List* Steven Spielberg would be proud of (all those endless slo-mo shots in the caves of women saying teary farewells to their men-folk. Actually, *Spartacus* had employed montages of peasants in exactly the same way).

The best action-adventure film ever? The outrageous stunts and moves in countless Hong Kong action movies easily trounce *The Two Towers* for imagination, power, speed, agility, humour and skill (and they're on the whole practical or physical gags, done on set, without expensive post-production).

What about the battles in *The Two Towers*? Well, Helm's Deep can't be the best battle ever, even for complete fans of *Lord of the Rings* movies, because by rights the biggest and best confrontation has to be in the last film.

In a comparable recent Hollywood blockbuster, the battles with the giant bugs in *Starship Troopers* outdo those in *The Two Towers* for scale, imagination and visceral excitement (*The Two Towers* consciously refers to *Starship Troopers*). The attack on the abandoned Whiskey Outpost towards the end of *Starship Troopers* takes some beating (and it occurs in full daylight, too, without the aid of added atmospherics used in Helm's Deep – rain, backlighting, storms, lightning and night. Paul Verhoeven also gleefully kills off most of his leading players). (The thousands of orcs are impressive in *The Two Towers*, but *Starship Troopers* got there first with the enemy swarming in countless numbers, using Dynamation and particle software).

Reviewers have forgotten their movie history, too, in calling Helm's Deep *à la* New Line Cinema the best ever battle in a film. What about *Alexander Nevsky*, or *El Cid*, or *Napoleon*, or *Waterloo*, or *Spartacus*, or *Andrei Roublyov*, or *Intolerance*, or *Lawrence of Arabia*?

Or Akira Kurosawa's *Ran* and *Kagemusha* and *The Hidden Fortress* and *Yojimbo* and and *Throne of Blood* and *The Seven Samurai*? Have a look at the end of *The Seven Samurai* to see how a beleaguered few beat a host of baddies becomes one of the best battle scenes ever shot (and inspired *many* imitators).

Or *Chimes At Midnight* (done with a couple of horses, one or two soldiers, and lots of smoke). I urge you to track down *Chimes At Midnight* (a.k.a. *Falstaff*). More recently, *Platoon, Full Metal Jacket,* and *Apocalypse Now*. All incredible. The battles in all of the above films are serious competition for Helm's Deep, and for many films fans out-do the 2002 film.

My own pick among recent battle scenes is *Alexander* (2004): incredible staging, extraordinary visuals, brilliant stunts, outstanding sound effects and technical aspects, and some truly amazing music by Vangelis.

Reviewers have also been calling *Lord of the Rings* films the best-looking movies for years. Yeah, right. To name but three recent examples in a comparable Hollywood blockbuster fantasy category which can match and outclass the *Lord of the Rings* films: *Sleepy Hollow* ('Chivo' Lunezki, DP, Rick Heinrichs, production designer), *Bram Stoker's Dracula* (Michael Balhaus, DP, Thomas Sanders, production designer) and *The Adventures of Baron Munchausen* (Giuseppe Rotunno, DP, the great Dante Ferretti, production designer).

This is a reminder of cinema's history (one of the overriding themes of Tolkien's fiction is never forget the past). *The Two Towers* is a superb blockbuster from the Hollywood system, yes, but it's not the greatest film ever made (that's *Showgirls*, as everyone knows…)

CHAPTER 16

THE TWO TOWERS, SCENE BY SCENE

ACT ONE

The Lord of the Rings: The Two Towers: The Motion Picture (2002) opens, after the titles over black, with helicopter shots of the Misty Mountains, backtracking hundreds of miles and about six weeks of story time (from the beginning of the 1954 book) to the balrog fight (why go back to Gandalf and the balrog, backs weeks of time and 100s of miles?: to remind audience that Gandalf is back in business). Voiceover is again employed to set up the scene, though this time it is not Galadriel or Elrond or someone else, but excerpts from the dialogue of that particular moment from film one. But there's enough information in Gandalf's cries to the balrog (and Frodo's shouts to Gandalf) for viewers to gain some idea of what's happening. Even if the words aren't clear, it's the *tone* of the dialogue that's important. The camera rushes towards the mountainside as if gaining the momentum it requires to crash through the rock. It's an impossible move for the camera, of course (unless it's one of those billion-dollar cameras fitted with tunnelling machinery, like in *The Core* (2004) or *Thunderbirds*).

The camera's headlong flight into the hill self-consciously draws attention to itself, rather like those camera moves between two rooms in a studio past a wall (most filmmakers keep those transitions 'invisible', but sometimes, like Francis Coppola in *One From the Heart* (1982) or David Lean in *Hobson's Choice* (1954), they deliberately draw attention to them). That camera crash through the mountainside, then, reminds viewers they're watching a movie, but it also acts as a storytelling device. It's not quite a time-honoured device like 'once upon a time', but it has a similar effect. Movies have always enjoyed those sorts of devices. In fact, the *Lord of the Rings* films use quite a few of them, including a variation on a C.U. of hands turning the pages of a book which open Disney animated fairy tales (in this case, it's the book that Bilbo writes, the *Red Book,* which Frodo browses in Rivendell, and later adds to himself, before finally passing it on to Sam). Remember that Ronald Tolkien always thought of *The Lord of the Rings* as a fairy tale. And note how the animated menus in the DVD editions of the *Lord of the Rings* films include images of books and pages turning. In another place, the films cut from images of Gandalf reading written parchment in Minas Tirith to events thousands of years earlier.

The Khazad-dûm bridge scene uses the same footage as in *The Fellowship of the Ring,* with some minor variants (and it still focusses primarily on Gandalf's point-of-view, and Frodo's view of Gandalf). However, when Gandalf falls this time: instead, the camera swoops in from the side, over and down, to follow the falling wizard. (For those boys in the audience worried about Gandalf losing his tasty sword, there's a shot of Gandalf zooming down to grab it. Actually, he needs it, as he rides on the balrog's chest and shoulders and repeatedly stabs him (how do you kill a balrog? Tolkien's description emphasizes Gandalf battling the balrog, but how do you show that?). And while towards the end of *The Fellowship of the Ring* Gandalf fell helplessly backwards into shadow, at the beginning of *The Two Towers* he soon turns about, and zooms purposely towards the camera head first).

Within this action beat are some smaller dramatic units: the gag of the balrog batting Gandalf away, for instance, or the monster smashing into the sides of the chasm, and the balrog rolling over and over. Gandalf seems to think his only hope is to stay close to the balrog, and he hangs onto the demon's horns towards the end of the descent (the filmmakers have clearly thought a little about how Gandalf could stay with the balrog when they're both travelling at high speeds).

Throughout this sequence, the sound designers and editors provide whooshes of air, balrog roars, sword zings, and fiery crackles (of course, swords make that sound when they fall, don't they? When was the last time you heard a sword falling in a chasm?), and Howard Shore offers a grand choral cue. The abrupt cutaway to an extreme long shot of Gandalf and the balrog is definitely one for the theatre screen, not television (it's a piece of Gustave Doré or John Martin). The camera then flies behind the wizard and the monster as they fall towards the water. Cutting to Frodo waking at this point suggests that the hobbit was haunted by the wizard, that the wizard's death had been a great loss for the hobbit. (Incidentally, a lengthy sequence was planned – written, sketched and storyboarded – to show the rest of the Gandalf-balrog fight, with a skeletal 'slime balrog', fighting on the lakeside, then up the stairs, and so on. It was cut mainly for budgetary reasons).

The two versions of *The Two Towers* differ considerably. The scenes involving Rohan and Edoras were shifted around and enlarged for the *Extended Edition*. Much of what was written by me here was after seeing the film in theatres, and then again after viewing the longer version on DVD. Consequently, some sections repeat the same information. Instead of re-editing this chapter, I have left the repetitions in. Apologies!

The second scene in *The Two Towers,* with Frodo and Sam, establishes their characters again for the audience, and quite a bit of exposition: their quest, their relationship, some of the obstacles they face, where they are, how far they've got to go, and so on. The film has also departed from *The Lord of the Rings* in combining books three and four, of course, and also going to Frodo and Sam first, not, as the 1954 book of *The Two Towers* does, to Aragorn. Putting Frodo and Sam here reinforces the major quest of the story: that it's about Frodo and Sam taking the ring to

Mordor.

Tolkien didn't want the two books of *The Two Towers* to be intertwined, advising Morton Zimmerman and his team adapting in 1957 that they were 'totally different in tone and scenery'. Maybe so, but no film adaption in the commercial marketplace would adhere to such a structure.

The film has pushed the hobbits along a bit, to the Emyn Muil hills (between the end of *The Fellowship of the Ring* and *The Two Towers*), but with the Dead Marshes, the Black Gate and the rest still to come. The introduction of Gollum is of course a pivotal moment in the quest of the ring, and in the lives of Frodo and Sam. Before Gollum is brought onto the stage, however, the movie is careful to make sure the viewer is familiar first with Frodo and Sam. Hence the scenes of the hobbits getting lost and going round in the circles in the Emyn Muil, sitting under a cliff in the rain, climbing down a cliff with a rope, and so on (some of these scenes, shot in Tongariro National Park and the studio, were added in the extended cut). The rope scene plays differently from the book but some of the alterations aren't particularly significant (Sam mentions that the rope was a gift from Galadriel, a way of getting in a pay-off reference to Galadriel's gifts), though the big storm sequence on the cliff was lost. The scene in the fog was grabbed on the hoof when mist descended over the Mount Ruapehu location; digital fog had to be added though, when the filmmakers waited for more fog which, of course, never came.

There was one crucial difference with the book, however: a 'ring moment', when Frodo, gazing at Mordor in the distance, has another vision of Sauron's Eye (now Frodo can see Sauron from 200 miles away without the aid of seeing seats or elf queen's mirrors. In which case Frodo would see the Eye any time he's up on a hill, but we'll quietly ignore that). It gives him a nasty turn, as your Aunt Frieda might put it, and Frodo clutches the ring in his pocket. Yep, and just to make sure the audience knows what's going on, dear old Sam says 'it's the ring, isn't it?' Well, yeah, *duh,* it is.

This 'ring moment' serves to remind viewers of the ring, of its effect on Frodo, of why the hobbits are clambering around rocks at all. A minute earlier, too, Sam had re-stated the quest: to get to Mordor. So the shots of Mount Doom's glare beyond the mountains, and the characters staring in that direction, are spatial clarifying shots. (Even though the fires of Mount Doom don't loom so large for observers far away from Mordor in the novel, the filmmakers chose to have a glow visible (plus smoke, and thunder and lightning), to show that the object of the quest was beyond the mountains. It lent a visual, geographical reference, without having to resort to the map).

The vision of Sauron also introduced the Eye early on in the film, to remind viewers of another major character. (Apart from this moment, Sauron is glimpsed during Saruman's montage, but isn't seen again for most of the film of *The Two Towers*). The shots of the Eye serve to remind audiences around the world that this is that movie where the baddie is a giant Eye. A giant Eye? Are you kidding? You mean, not a dragon, an evil emperor, a bastard Nazi, a shark, or a monster? *An Eye...* uhh, are you sure about this?

Every time you see Sauron atop the Dark Tower, he's thinking to himself, 'why oh why am I a Giant Eye? And the filmmakers are thinking that too.

Another hobbity reminder was the prop of the wooden box of salt and seasoning that Sam brings along with him in the hope of cooking some chicken (Sam is often linked with food in the films, his highpoint being the rabbit he stews in Ithilien, and his low point the lembas that Gollum steals and uses to frame him). It's an intentionally lighter moment, too, for Frodo, before things get darker and grimmer.

The box is there in the 2002 film (it's not in the 1954 book) as a visual reminder of the Shire, it's literally what the hobbits have left behind (Frodo also says as much, just to make sure the audience gets it. This's *Scriptwriting Basics: How To Adapt the Classics: Book One*, page one). It's a reminder, too, of how far away from the world of the Shire the hobbits are now (there's not much chance of chicken or any decent grub in the misty Emyn Muil. You'd be lucky for a couple of bugs). And it's a visual stand-in for what Frodo is fighting for: not his wife, or child, or father, or mother, nor even his friends, but the Shire and his way of life. There's classism and deference even in the film, which has softened the ideology of the book somewhat: Frodo is fighting for the Shire, but his own way of life within that community is of a relatively wealthy citizen, who doesn't have to work (he's shown reading a book under a tree in his very first scene of the films, and is never depicted at manual labour). And he has a servant (although the film soft-pedalled on the master-servant relationship in the book as well as the classism. Philippa Boyens or Fran Walsh mentions in one of the DVD documentaries that they wanted to have Frodo and Sam more as equals or friends).

Actor Sean Astin recalled in his autobiography that the relationship between Sam and Frodo had been regarded by Peter Jackson and the filmmakers as central to the books, a specifically *English* relationship, that was based for them on Tolkien's experiences in the First World War (2004, 74).

The 2002 Hollywood adaption of *The Two Towers* played the entrance and taming of Sméagol quite differently from J.R.R. Tolkien's 1950s heroic romance. In the film, the hobbits are asleep, with no indication that they are being followed by Gollum (apart from a brief hint from Frodo): it's night, and the wretched creature crawls head down a rock face above the sleeping hobbits. The only part of that which comes from the 1954 book in the film is Gollum making his way down the cliff head first (animator Randy Cook likened it to Dracula crawling down the walls of his castle – beautifully done in the 1979 Universal *Dracula* movie, and reprised in the 1992 Columbia film. This first full look at Gollum certainly distinguishes him from the other characters in the film – although the Moria goblins were able to climb down pillars).

What Tolkien created in the text was a scene at the cliff which Frodo and Sam have just climbed down (aided by the elven rope). They look back and spy Gollum. They decide to ambush him, and wait for him in the shadow of a boulder at the base of the cliff. It's an important point, that the hobbits have a head start on Gollum, and decide to waylay him.

> "It doesn't sound as if he knew we were here, does it?" whispered Sam. "And what's his Precious? Does he mean the —"
> "Hsh!" breathed Frodo. "He's getting near now, near enough to hear a whisper."
> Indeed Gollum had suddenly paused again, and his large head on its scrawny neck was lolling fom side to side as if he were listening. His pale eyes were half unlidded. Sam restrained himself, though his fingers were twitching. (TT, 273)

The film plays the encounter more for suspense, with the creature approaching the unaware hobbits full of menace, muttering to himself that he *wantsss it*, his *preciousss*. For viewers who don't know the story, anything could happen here. Gollum may have superhuman powers, or a bite like a vampire. He might be able to attack both hobbits at the same time, and take the ring from Frodo. At this point, he's still an unknown quantity. (The hobbits are ready for him, though, as they are in the book, but the build-up to the encounter puts the audience with Gollum, not the hobbits: the camera is behind and above Gollum, looking down past him at the hobbits, i.e., from his point-of-view. So it appears as if the hobbits are going to be surprised by Gollum. The very first shot of Gollum on the rockface, though, with the moon large behind him, seems to be from the hobbits' filmic space).

The introduction of Gollum is important also from the point-of-view of selling the character as a computer-generated element in the film, though, as is obvious from the first shots of Gollum, he is based very closely on human models, just like Snow White and the Prince in Disney's 1937 film (who were partly rotoscoped from live action footage). And the audience had already seen plenty of CG characters within live action films before Gollum (to pick a few immediately prior to *The Two Towers:* Spider-man in *Spider-man*; the wonderful mouse in *Stuart Little*; the visceral invisible man in *Hollow Man*; the vicious dinosaurs in the *Jurassic Park* films; Dobby, the centaur, Voldemort, Fluffy and the troll in the *Harry Potter* films; and Jar-Jar Binks, Watto, Sebulba and many others in the *Star Wars* prequels. And then there were the gorgeous CG characters in *Toy Story, A Bug's Life, Monsters, Inc* and *Shrek,* genius examples of animation). So Gollum as a wholly digital character was not as big a deal as the marketing department would have punters believe (though the serious lobbying for a supporting actor Oscar for Andy Serkis was new).

The subsequent violent confrontation between the hobbits and Gollum follows Tolkien's description quite closely, as far as Gollum grabbing Sam, who can't escape, until Frodo forces Gollum to him to let go at sword-point. Another slice of Alan Lee was ordered from director Peter Jackson for this moment, and the Lee illustration of Gollum pinning Sam from behind (from Lee's illustrated *The Lord*) was used on set for the actors to recreate it precisely. In the film, Gollum attacks Frodo first, going for the ring immediately. Sam pulls him off Frodo twice, and Gollum attacks Frodo twice (Frodo just about manages to stop Gollum's hands taking hold of the ring). Both hobbits are thrown around by Gollum, and he bites Sam's neck at one point.

Tolkien had Frodo thinking back to Gandalf's words in Bag End about Gollum in this first scene with Gollum, Frodo and Sam in the Emyn Muil, in particular Gandalf talking about pity (TT, 275). The filmmakers had already employed Gandalf speaking in a flashback voiceover at the end of *The Fellowship of the Ring,* which may be one reason why they opted not to use it here. But they did repeat the moral teaching of Gandalf in the key scene in Moria – about pity. Very early on in the encounter with Gollum (in the second or third line), Frodo says that now he sees him he does feel pity for him.

Other changes from the 1954 book in the 'taming' of Sméagol sequence were the alterations in the emphasis in Gollum's mutterings and whingeings. Gollum mentions Sauron far more in the book: telling Frodo that he won't let *him* have it. He talks about Sauron being 'over there', in Mordor, and 'he's lost his Precious' (TT, 277). Maybe the adaptors thought it would be too confusing having Gollum refer to Sauron too often, so made the scene more about Gollum wanting the ring for himself. But in the book, Gollum has already guessed that the hobbits are taking the ring to Mordor.

Also in this scene in the 1954 book, Gollum seems to re-live – or remember all too vividly – his encounter with Sauron for a moment: '"Leave me alone, *gollum*! You hurt me. O my poor hands, *gollum*! I, we, I don't want to come back. I can't find it"' (TT, 276). This too was dropped. (Gollum is, intriguingly, one of the few people in the foreground action of *The Lord of the Rings* who has met Sauron in person, or at least been to Barad-dûr).

The struggle between Gollum, Sam and Frodo includes some wonderfully fierce faces from Gollum, and low angle close-ups of Frodo (equally fierce). The scene'll be echoed at Osgliath at the end of the film. It shows not only how desperately Gollum wants to the ring, but also how ferociously Frodo defends himself and won't let Gollum have it. The scene has to be intense, and acted a little over-the-top, because it plays out and pays off in the Crack of Doom scene at the end of *The Return of the King.*

The scene closes with Gollum's wail and a cut to (a painting of) the hills (a pause and breather shot), then the three folk travelling the next day, Gollum now with the elven rope around his neck (and his hands tied behind his back. Presumably the hobbits didn't get much sleep with Gollum complaining loudly about being tied up).

Gollum writhes like a mad thing among the stones (including employing the hysteric's arching of the back). At this point, the elven rope is taken off and Gollum swears on the precious (repeating the phrase 'on the precious' a number of times as he cowers before Frodo). (Sensibly, in both book and film, Frodo doesn't show Gollum the ring: '"you know it would drive you mad"' [TT, 278]). The book also featured an earlier scene which the screenwriters thought was perhaps redundant (or they didn't have time in the film for it): the scene where Sam and Frodo sit each side of

Gollum and pretend to be asleep, and Gollum leaps away. That's when they catch him and put on the rope (TT, 277-8).

The film of *The Two Towers* kept to the general tone and drift of "The Taming of Sméagol" chapter in the book. Fundamentally, what needed to happen was Gollum encountering the hobbits, being 'tamed' (after a fashion), swearing on the ring, and agreeing to lead them to Mordor (and also pointing up Sam's distrust of Gollum, and Frodo's pity for him: both attitudes towards Gollum would play out again and again in the rest of the movies).

It was important to get the relationships, the attitudes, the goals and the structures right for the introduction of Gollum scenes, because Frodo and Sam, the movie's heroes, are going to be stuck with him (along with the audience) until the Crack of Doom. So the filmmakers don't play Gollum too obnoxious, too crude, too nasty or too evil, because it wouldn't convince audiences that the hobbits would take him with them. If Gollum hadn't also been depicted as a sympathetic wretch, the kind of hapless but ultimately likeable or pitiable (if not lovable) kind of character that, say, Peter Lorre played in the 1930s and 1940s, it would not convince viewers. Play Gollum too vicious, and audiences would cheer if Sam stuck him with a sword. Play him too humorously, and he wouldn't be any threat to Frodo or Sam, he'd be just another sidekick, like Merry and Pippin were in film one.

But any adaptor of *The Lord of the Rings* would be pretty dim if they didn't recognize that the introduction of Gollum into the story of Frodo and Sam going to Mordor is a masterstroke of the book (and it had to be done exactly right). It's one of Tolkien's best creations in *The Lord of the Rings,* and turns the quest of the ring into an undertaking much more *morally* and *psychologically* complex, as well as more exciting as an adventure (on the physical, action level, because you never quite know what Gollum's going to do). Without Gollum, Frodo and Sam's journey would still be incredibly hazardous, full of suspense and suffering. But with Gollum, it intensifies the jeopardy, the suspense, the suffering, but also adds layers of moral and ethical complexity and ambiguity. It's when Gandalf's remark to Frodo hundreds of pages earlier, about pity, Bilbo and the effect of the ring on its bearer, really pays off. With the addition of Gollum in the mix, *The Lord of the Rings* cannot be dismissed as simply a tale of good vs. evil, of obvious and clear moral choices. The whole matter of the ring is more multi-layered than that, and what Gollum does is bring all of that moral, philosophical ambiguity right into the foreground action. Thus, it's not just about Gandalf battling Sauron with vast armies on the plains of Middle-earth, all those big, 'epic' elements in the book: the conflict is brought right into the daily lives of the hobbits struggling to reach Mordor.

Once the trio of hobbits and Gollum has been established and they are on their way, the film of *The Two Towers* cuts away to other groups of characters: there's still Saruman to be introduced, and the Three Hunters, and the orcs carrying Meriadoc and Peregrin, and also the leaders of the Rohirrim. The film doesn't return to Frodo, Sam and Gollum for quite some time – not until after Merry and Pippin have encountered Treebeard and

Gandalf. (The extended cut of *The Two Towers* adds a short scene of the schizophrenic Gollum as he begins to lead them to Mordor – presumably the filmmakers thought that the audience will already have seen the theatrical cut, so it wouldn't spoil it by seeing the Jekyll and Hyde Gollum much earlier. In the extra scene, Gollum is muttering to himself about Mordor, orcs, Sauron, and his precious).

Frances Walsh enjoyed writing for the schizophrenic Gollum. Walsh admitted that Gollum was written partly from an autobiographical area – she said that Gollum was 'my family dynamic', that she had 'a dysfunctional family background', and that Gollum was 'my father'. As Walsh put it, 'I understand the persecutor-parent and I understand the child who wants to please their parent but who also wants to be free of that conflict'.

One of Saruman's chief functions in the first reel of *The Two Towers* is to proffer quite a bit of exposition to the audience. He does this mainly in voiceover (Christopher Lee definitely has the best voice in the *Lord of the Rings* films, so he's always a good choice for narrator. Note, though, that Saruman's narration never mentions the elves – that side of things is given to Galadriel, Elrond and Gandalf).

At this point, the editors, Michael Horton and Jabez Olssen, went back to many images from the first film, creating an explanatory montage: images of Isengard; Saruman consulting the *palantír*; Barad-dûr, seen via the *palantír* (this's one of Alex Funke's team's best model shots, spiralling around the tower model until it reaches the Eye at the summit); the orcs ripping down trees; orcs stoking fires; orcs hammering out weaponry; trees falling into the mines; the birth of the Uruk-hai, and so on. Most all of these shots were from the first film (with some variations or alternate takes): the montage actually represents weeks of time in the story, of Saruman building up his army.

And throughout it all, Saruman is narrating, telling the audience about the alliance between Isengard and Barad-dûr, about invading Rohan, about destroying opponents, and so on. Quite a bit of time is spent with Saruman, the Wild Men, the orcs and the enemy at this point in the film, for all the usual reasons (summarizing the first film, providing antagonists, getting a good look at the baddies, and so on). Saruman narrates this section of the film because this's precisely why his role was greatly expanded from the book: to put a face to the enemy, to say and show what the Eye could not (having Sauron narrate events wouldn't work at all: it would demystify his character. Instead, other characters – Gandalf, Elrond, Galadriel, even Merry – tell the viewer what they reckon Sauron may be thinking).

A scene where one of the Wild Men swears allegiance to Saruman in his throne room was added to the extended cut (it's pretty much redundant, the only glimmer of interest being Christopher Lee's nasty grin when the Wild Man cuts his hand. And the Wild Man has a bizarrely slightly slowed-down voice). So Saruman sends off the Wild Men to Rohan (further additions to the 1954 book), a mass of hairy, wide-eyed guys (like the mosh pit at a Deep Purple reunion concert).

As Saruman personifies the enemy in the film, so the family of mother

Morwen (Robyn Malcolm) and two children, Éothain (Sam Gomery) and Freda (Olivia Tennet) humanizes the plight of the good guys (the Rohirrim in the Westfold. The name Morwen is Welsh for *maid*; in Tolkien's *legendarium*, Morwen's a key elf, married to Húrin and mother of Túrin. A different Morwen was mother of Théoden. The name Éothain comes from a member of Éomer's éored, a Rohan cavalry unit).

These characters are not given much characterization beyond being tearful, desperate mother, weeping daughter, and elder son trying to be brave. It's a scene (directed by Geoff Murphy) familiar from plenty of Westerns. The characters are functions of the plot, really, ciphers to stand in for the homely, well-meaning side of the Rohirrim (as opposed to their war-like aspect, which's depicted in abundance by Éomer and his buddies). There's also one of the first mentions of Edoras (Morwen tells her son to raise the alarm at Edoras, though the audience is asked to forget for a minute why a ten-year old boy would be sent as a messenger with such an important message, or why Morwen doesn't ride off herself with the kids, or run along beside them).

And so to Merry and Pippin, introduced on the backs of the orcs running through a gully, where they halt (there are some impressive helicopter shots of the band of running orcs too). The extended cut of *The Two Towers* added a little more business here – for instance, the other group of orcs (led by Grishnákh), and the arguments over who's in charge of the halflings. And a brief scene of Merry being force-fed orc-licquor. The orc scenes also introduce two of the orc leaders of the different groups: Uglúk and Grishnákh (Nathaniel Lees and Stephen Ureboth in gruesome prosthetics). They don't hang around very long on screen before they're slain by men and ents, but they do have a couple of fun moments (Uglúk beheading an orc and yelling 'looks like meat's back on the menu, boys!', and Grishnákh chasing the hobbits. Curious that the filmmakers left out the scene where Éomer fights Uglúk 'sword to sword' and dispatches him [TT, 73]; even a brief shot would've enhanced Éomer's character, as well as showing the hobbits' oppressor biting the dust. Chief bad guys must always be dealt with in movies).

Needless to say, huge chunks of orc dialogue in the book couldn't make it into the film: the rivalry between the orc bands, for instance, or where the orcs come from, or about Saruman and Sauron, or the nazgûl. One of the most significant omissions was the teasing conversation between the hobbits and Grishnákh about the ring. A remnant of this found its way into Merry's lines: 'they think we've got the ring'.

When the orcs move off, after an orc (Sala Baker) catches the scent of 'man flesh', the film cuts to the last group of our heroes to be introduced: Aragorn, Legolas and Gimli. Aragorn is now back in his tracker mode, his ear to a rock, listening to the orcs far away. The Three Hunters are introduced in the order in which they are seen throughout this sequence of running shots followed by more running: man, elf and dwarf (Legolas's just behind Aragorn, but Gimli's way behind). The scenes of the pursuit are depicted in a return to the heroic mode of the fellowship journey scenes:

helicopter shots of tiny figures in wilderness landscapes accompanied by a grand cue from Howard Shore. (Gimli also introduces a little humour).

It's Merry who handles the exposition about Fangorn and the ents, during the scene where the orcs chop up the trees at the edge of the forest, and the low groans of the trees are heard (though why the orcs don't pick up dead wood from the forest floor, which's easier, quicker, and better for burning than cutting up living trees, is a mystery, especially as Fangorn's an ancient forest – i.e., it has tons of dead wood – and the orcs are exhausted by their long run – it takes much more effort to hack down living trees to picking up dead wood).

Shots taken from the depths of the forest and looking to the edge and zooming out, as if receding into the trees, suggest the forest's own point-of-view, or perhaps the p.o.v of ents (or huorns). Thus, the idea that the trees are alive in a new way is introduced to the audience before they meet Treebeard (with Faramir, he's the last of the major new characters to be introduced in the 2002 film of *The Two Towers*).

Gandalf's first appearance as the white wizard is handled in a similar teasing fashion as it is in the 1954 book: J.R.R. Tolkien withholds the true identity of the mysterious wizard figure seen around the forest for a while as the picture does (right up until he's standing in front of the hobbits). The percussive music cue here is used again, when the Three Hunters face the wizard.

It also means that the audience is still uncertain about Treebeard, and which side he's on. He crushes the hobbits in his fists (a nod to *King Kong* perhaps), and seems to be taking them to Saruman. (However, if the audience is attentive, it's fairly clear: Treebeard's first acts are to kill an orc and save Pippin from falling. And when Merry asks him which side he's on, he replies no one's side, because no one's on *my* side).

Closing the scene of the hobbits meeting the wizard on an over-the-shoulder shot of Gandalf offers a neat link with Frodo: the film cuts at this point to Frodo, Sam and Gollum. Throughout the films a psychic or symbolic connection is made between Gandalf and Frodo, and the films often cut from one of them to the other, especially at crisis points: when Gandalf faces the balrog, Frodo is most prominent in the reaction shots, or when Frodo seems to be dreaming of Gandalf on top of Isengard, or when Frodo agrees to take the ring at the Council of Elrond, and the first reaction shot is Gandalf's (followed by Aragorn, Gimli & co.).

It's one of the great strengths of the Hollywood films that the editing puts Frodo and Gandalf together so often, making their relationship the strongest in the films, along with Frodo and Sam (and this's also why the troll fight in Moria is so bad, because it's such a lapse and error by the filmmakers, separating Gandalf and Frodo for far too long. But it's a tricky dramatic problem, because for Frodo to be in jeopardy, he must be separated from Gandalf, yet they're in the same room. But the solution in the troll fight – simply not cutting to Gandalf – is not satisfactory).

Pippin is a kind of stand-in for Frodo, in both book and film, because Frodo and Gandalf are physically apart for the whole of *The Two Towers* and *The Return of the King*. When Gandalf takes Pippin under his wing, and tutors him (an unofficial pupilage, but Gandalf, like Tolkien himself, can't help acting like a teacher, and both are always partly a professor), the reader can assume that Gandalf educated Frodo in a similar fashion.

The Three Hunters section was edited like a chase, but without the frenetic editing of, say, a car chase, horse chase or spaceship chase: because the orcs were a day or so ahead, the film broke up the chase into full scenes played out in each group (rather than the rapid crosscutting of a typical movie chase). This part of the film was low on plot but big on spectacle, as second unit footage (much of it shot by Barrie Osborne around Poolburn) depicted elf, dwarf and man running over hills and rocks (Gimli's double, Brett Beattie, did a lot of the running). A brief scene (expanded a little in the extended cut) revealed that Merry and Pippin, while alive, were not doing too well either (Merry is forced to drink some nasty orc stuff). Pippin has the foresight to drop one of the elven brooches (which hints at Pippin beginning to mature a little, and to use his head).

The encounter of the Three Hunters with the riders of Rohan was fairly faithful to the novel, and only differs in relatively minor details (such as the fact that Éomer has been banished from Edoras by Wormtongue. Oh, and there's *lots* more talk in the novel).

The scenes at Edoras introduce each of the major characters early on in *The Two Towers:* Éomer, Éowyn, Wormtongue and Théoden (all recognizable types: a brother and sister in the aristocracy of Rohan, both warriors and leaders, an ageing, decrepit and wifeless king, and his sly, conniving adviser). I'm jumping between the theatrical release and the home entertainment release here, so it gets a little confusing.

An added scene in the extended cut has Éomer in heroic mode, a man of action and chief among soldiers, arriving at a riverbank (the Fords of Isen) in the rain after a battle between orcs and Rohirrim, finding Théodred (the king's son) barely alive among the corpses (the colour palette here is limited to sombre greys and cold blues) and taking him back to Edoras. This offers the visual lead-in to Edoras, as Éomer carries Théodred there on horseback. (The actor playing Théodred (Paris Howe Strewe) has the thankless task of being near-dead, then a corpse). Notice, however, that the big reveals of Edoras on its rock in the valley are saved for later, for the time when our heroes (Gandalf, Aragorn, Legolas and Gimli) arrive there. So the film cuts from second unit shots of Éomer and his soldiers into the studio sets of Edoras.

Éowyn is introduced as the caring cousin of Théodred, rushing to Théodred's side in the bedroom. Brother and sister exchange a dark look after seeing Théodred's wound, as if they're thinking that with the king's son nearly dead, they don't know what's going to happen at Edoras now. The banishment of Éomer swiftly follows. This scene introduces Théoden and Wormtongue. Éomer and Éowyn are first depicted standing before Théoden, informing him that his son is gravely wounded (Meduseld looks dark and lifeless, just a pool of light around the throne). Five banners hang behind the king, each containing horse emblems and sun patterns. A close-up of Théoden reveals Bernard Hill in full old age make-up, a cliché of a doddery, senile king (it's basically the fisher king or wounded king of Arthurian legend, with Rohan dwindling into a rulerless waste land).

Wormtongue's entrance is as a pantomime villain from the start – the audience is encouraged to yell 'boo! hiss!': he slinks around a door behind the throne with a sinister music cue and a sly question about troubling an old man. Wormtongue's look is pale, veiny, bad skin, no eyebrows, contact lenses, and long, lank, greasy black hair, with dandruff (but he does have a tasty black robe). The look is Richard III designed by a Milan fashion guru (though the filmmakers stopped short of giving him a hunchback or limp).

Wormtongue holding up the warrant for Éomer's arrest is a wonderful idea (though it's probably a little anachronistic by a few hundred years to have that kind of bureaucracy for this *Beowulf*-era society). The films have beautiful calligraphy (handled by Daniel Reeve), and Tolkien was a passionate devotee of the written word with few equals in modern times, so seeing Théoden's feeble scrawl is a terrific (and piteous) embodiment of his mental decline.

Wormtongue's first act in the film is to banish Éomer: as well as the act itself (accompanied by Éomer being thumped in the stomach a couple of times by Wormtongue's guards), the blocking of the scene also suggests how Wormtongue stands next to the king, and operates in the political as well as physical space in between the king and everyone else. The face-off between Éomer and Wormtongue is handled with big close-ups on the American and the Kiwi (with Éomer grasping Wormtongue's jaw tightly, a favourite gesture in the *Lord of the Rings* films – the Witch-king does the same with Éowyn at Pelennor, and Aragorn grabs the Dead King, and Faramir with Gollum, and Sam with Gollum, and Frodo with Gollum, while Gollum opts straight for strangulation, strangling Frodo, Déagol and Sam. Maybe these are strangulation fantasies on the part of the director, in the manner of Alfred Hitchcock. It wouldn't be the first time a film director's wanted to strangle their cast – and vice versa).

Brad Dourif is always watchable (if often over-the-top), but relative newcomer Karl Urban is terrific in these scenes. Some of Éomer's dialogue comes from Gandalf, when he confronts Gríma after Théoden's recovery:

> "Down, snake!" he said suddenly in a terrible voice. "Down on your belly! How long is it since Saruman bought you? What was the promised price? When all the men were dead, you were to pick your share of the treasure, and take the woman you desire? Too long have you watched her under your eyelids and haunted her steps." (T, 153)

Note how Éowyn slips away, as if she doesn't want to be involved in another confrontation between her brother and the king's aide, as if there have been a few of these arguments already (it's a little cowardly of her, isn't it? Wouldn't she stand up to Wormtongue – she'd have some leverage with him, too, as he fancies her. Oh well, let's just quietly ignore that). But one reason is perhaps so that Éowyn can be glimpsed from afar by Wormtongue in a point-of-view shot (Éomer follows his gaze and tells Wormtongue that his steps have for too long haunted his sister's. The lines are spoken by Gandalf in the book, and are transposed from after Théoden's revitalization). And the main reason is to have Éowyn step off-stage so that Wormtongue can banish Éomer.

When *The Two Towers* returns to Frodo, Sam and Gollum, they are now at the marshes. A scene was added in the *Extended Edition* containing two dramatic elements: hunger and the ring: first, Gollum complains about being unable to find anything tasty to eat in the marshlands; Frodo and Sam are sitting nearby, munching on *lembas* (there being a distinctive lack of good restaurants, diners, stores and fast food outlets in the Dead Marshes). Gollum eats a worm, sucking it up like spaghetti. Sam scowls. Frodo throws some *lembas* to Gollum, but of course the creature chokes on it. The move to snatch up the *lembas* gives Gollum a chance to edge closer to Frodo.

The scene then turns from something slightly light-hearted into another ring moment (i.e., back to the main plot of *The Lord of the Rings* again), with Gollum muttering about the *preciousss*, and Frodo warning Gollum not to touch him when he does that subservient pawing thing. Even ardent Tolkienites and anti-film Tolkien fans couldn't find too much to complain about in such modest scenes, which stick closely to the spirit of the book (and many of the details of the scene).

A very long, long shot, a helicopter shot flying slowly over the marshlands, clarifies the geography of the area: it shows the tiny dots of the hobbits and Gollum, the vast expanse of the Dead Marshes and, when it tilts up slightly, the outer line of Mordor's mountains, with the sullen red of Mount Doom beyond. While this shot's on screen, though, the voices of Gollum and the hobbits are heard as if up close (i.e., continuing from the previous shot). Gollum provides the exposition of the history of the Dead Marshes. A low angle tracking shot covers the introduction of the hobbits walking past the marsh fires (most of the marsh scenes were shot on the studio lot, a car park, with gas jets for the flames). A montage of C.U.s of the faces just under the surface of the pools comes next (practical dummies, not actors). Faint cries are heard on the track (as well gloopy sounds): the dead haunt the place.

The Dead Marshes' first action sequence occurs when Frodo topples face first into the water (lured by an elf corpse, which opens its eyes). Sam yells and rushes towards him. Naturalism is jettisoned now in favour of storybook fantasy, as spectres zoom up at Frodo from below in a series of point-of-view shots lit by lurid green and white. Ghostly faces grimace and bony hands grasp towards the camera, very familiar stuff from films like *Raiders of the Lost Ark* (1981) or *Casper* (1995). Gollum pulls Frodo out of the water. A nice touch has Frodo saying 'Gollum' deadpan on the bank, as if he's either astonished at having been rescued, or that he was saved by Gollum, not the ever-reliable Sam, or is still in shock after his vision.

Much of the time Frodo, Sam and Gollum travel by night, in the novel; but in the film it's usually daytime, or sometimes a kind of dusk. When the ringwraith flies overhead, for instance, it's a moonlit night in the book.

A short night scene, a two-hander between Gollum and Frodo,

humanizes Gollum somewhat, with Frodo questioning the one-time Stoor hobbit about his origins. The camera begins with over-the-shoulder shots on Gollum, winding up with big close-ups of that strange CGI face. The scriptwriters use the idea of Frodo speaking Gollum's real name, Sméagol, as a way of enabling Frodo to appeal to the softer sides of Gollum underneath his neurotic, defensive, ugly exterior (in the book, the name Sméagol occurs in the taming of Sméagol scene). Perhaps more could have been made of these scenes, between the ringbearer who's feeling the effects of the ring increasing every day, and the twisted creature whose life's been extended hundreds of years by the power of the ring. But the scriptwriters also needed to pace themselves, to allow the discussions and confrontations between Frodo and Gollum over the ring to be doled out gradually, over the course of this film and the next one.

One of the masterstrokes in J.R.R. Tolkien's book, of course, is the kernel of pity (and fear of the ring) inside Gollum that prevents him from simply wringing the necks of both hobbits in their sleep and taking the ring for himself. After all, Gollum has both hobbits miles away from anywhere and has killed before (and not just his brother Déagol). It adds to the complexity of the book that although Gollum desperately wants it, he's almost reluctant to take it. He embodies the love and hate – and fear – of the ring (early in the Dead Marshes scenes in the movie, too, there's a brief shot of Frodo caressing the ring in his palm. And Gollum, without looking, his back to Frodo, knows what's going on – another nice touch of the psychic link between the two. Frodo caressing the ring turns it into a fetish object – you don't need your eighth grade Sigmund Freud to know what's going on here – fetishism and masturbation).

The second action sequence in the Dead Marshes section is much more significant than Frodo's plunge into the pool of the dead, because it foreshadows the climax of the *Two Towers* film: the flying nazgûl scene. As in the book, it's the cry of the fell-beast that alerts the hobbits and Gollum to the ringwraith: 'a long wailing cry, high and thin and cruel' as Ronald Tolkien wrote in the 1954 book (TT, 293). The pace of the film alters abruptly, with flash cuts back to Weathertop, and Frodo's point-of-view shots of the Witch-king when he was in the wraithworld (partly there to remind viewers that the flying nazgûl are the same bad guys as the ones on horses in *The Fellowship of the Ring*). Frodo clutches his shoulder and staggers. Gollum wails. More flashes of the ringwraiths at Weathertop occur, intercut with close-ups of Frodo in the marshes, followed by a cut to a very different point-of-view: a close-up on the ringwraith's gauntlets holding the reins of the fell-beast (the camera pulls back, flying beside the wraith, to tease the audience momentarily: the nazgûl's not riding a horse, as in *The Fellowship of the Ring*, but a fell-beast, a creature that will feature prominently in *The Return of the King*).

It appears to be the Witch-king himself riding the winged beast (not stated in the book), swooping over the characters below, who hide under a bush. The beat of the creature's wings is mixed loud on the track, as well as its roar (the Witch-king himself makes no sound). The beating of the wings here functions as the ring's 'heartbeat'. The Witch-king and the fell-beast will appear at Osgiliath at the climax of *The Two Towers,* and also in *The Return of the King,* leading his army into battle out of Minas Morgul, and at Pelennor Fields.

Gollum tells the hobbits that they – the 'Wraiths on wings!' – are searching for it – a redundant line, but it leads to the struggle Frodo's having, lying on his back, reaching for the ring, with Sam beside him. Sam saves him, and this scene will be replayed in very much the same dramatic form at Osgiliath, with Frodo left alone for a moment about to put on the ring, Sam rescuing him, and Gollum watching nearby.

A cut to a big C.U. of Gimli's fingers picking up some dark orc blood on some leaves (a close-up shot of this kind is a time-honoured way for editors to begin a scene). Gimli tastes it (urrrgh!) and announces that it's orc blood (best not to ask how Gimli knows what orc blood tastes like). Wider shots reveal the Three Hunters now in the depths of Fangorn Forest, still on the quest to find Merry and Pippin. There are brief beats with Gimli voicing doubts about the forest, and lowering his axe at Aragorn's bidding, Aragorn searching the ground and finding unusual tracks, and Legolas explaining about the ents, how the elves woke up the trees long ago. Gimli's reaction about 'walking trees' stands in for the audience's response to such far-fetched ideas (the filmmakers had to sell the idea of walking, talking trees to the jaded, seen-it-all-before audience – not only because of Treebeard, but because the ents play a big part towards the end of *The Two Towers.* The 1954 book, of course, had already introduced the idea of sentient trees with Old Man Willow and the Old Forest in *The Fellowship of the Ring*).

When the orcs halt beside Fangorn, the movie indulges in some camp orc humour: an argument breaks out, and an orc is slain. The big Isengard Uruk-hai, Uglúk, wants to protect the halflings from being eaten by the others (as instructed personally by Saruman). Uglúk is basically Lurtz reincarnated, and is virtually indistinguishable from him. One of the orcs wonders if the halflings 'give good sport' (TT, 54). When an orc makes a grab for Merry and Pippin, he's swiftly killed (the film, which delights in orcish violence, is unusually more restrained than the book here: three orcs are slain in Tolkien's text). As the orcs tuck in (with bits of the orc's body flying in the air), Uglúk yells 'looks like meat's back on the menu, boys!' A good line, guaranteed to raise a laugh in the audience, and one which incited some debate in Tolkien fan circles about whether an orc would know about sophisticated things like menus and restaurants.

In order to follow Uglúk's orders to 'get a fire going', the orcs start chopping down branches from the edge of Fangorn: it's the first glimpse of yet another magical forest in Middle-earth. However, it's not the combination of model trees, matte paintings and live-action orcs that's memorable about this part of the film, but the *sound* of Fangorn, the slowed-down cries of cows, whales, donkeys (or whatever animal was employed) to create the impression that the trees themselves are groaning in pain, or alerting ents or huorns or trees deeper in the forest. It's a moment that Tolkien, arch tree-hugger among writers, might applaud.

In the book a whole section of argument between the orcs was dropped from "The Uruk-hai" chapter. It was partly about the different groups of orcs in the band (some are from Isengard, some from Sauron and Barad-dûr, and some are from the Misty Mountains), as well as some orcs disliking sunlight, and many orcs being afraid of the 'whiteskins' (the orcs' term for the Rohirrim. In the politically correct environment of Hollywood in the 2000s, that kind of racial term wouldn't be welcome in *The Lord of the Rings*, even if it was a fantasy film. Because if the orcs think of the Rohirrim as 'whiteskins', it brands the orcs as possibly black or Native American or another non-white ethnicity. And such racial stereotyping wouldn't do, because the orcs are slaughtered in their thousands in the films, and portrayed in a wholly negative light.)

The orc Grishnákh is depicted as a suitably grotesque creature (there's always one dumb orc and one that's a bit cannier in Tolkien's orc scenes). Another minor point was dropped in the film: Grishnákh is an orc from the Dark Tower, and seems to know about the ring. So when Grishnákh picks up the hobbits (who've managed to crawl away while the orcs fight over the orc corpse), he wants the ring for himself. The picture cut out the idea of the three orc bands dividing up and travelling in separate groups; it also left out the scene the orcs are pursued by the 'filthy horse-boys', as they call them (TT, 66).

Both the 2002 film of *The Two Towers* and the 1954 book were dramatic in their depictions of the escape of Merry and Pippin. In the book, Grishnákh is enticed by the hobbits about possibly obtaining the ring, as they stall him and try to find a way of escaping ('"Do you want it, or not?"' Merry asks Grishnákh [TT, 67]). In the confusion of the Rohirrim's attack on the orc camp, the hobbits are saved by one of Tolkien's many miraculous incidents: Grishnákh is hit with an arrow 'aimed with skill, or guided by fate' (i.e., guided the Valar perhaps), and then run through with a spear' (TT, 69). In the film of *The Two Towers,* much of the nervous interchange between Grishnákh and the hobbits was dropped: instead, the orc carried the hobbits away from the camp, but is hit by the Rohirrim. The hobbits run into the forest, but Grishnákh is one of those movie villains that just won't die when you want him to, and he lopes after them.

Like children, the hobbits' method of dealing with the situation is to climb a tree. The death of Grishnákh was then combined with the encounter with Treebeard. The final action beat of this sequence had Pippin climbing the tree, Merry being grabbed by Grishnákh before he can get high enough and pulled to the ground, Pippin doing a double take on Treebeard's face, and just before Grishnákh can open up a 'maggot hole' in Merry's belly, Treebeard lifts a leg and squashes him.

In this way, when Treebeard scoops up Merry, the hobbits have been introduced to Treebeard, and are already riding along in his fists. It's a much shorter way of getting the hobbits to this point in the story, rather than having them wander into Fangorn, climb up the rock, talk, and so on. Tolkien's encounter between the hobbits and the ent in the book *The Two Towers* is much more static, much calmer, but the biggest difference is the element of fear and suspense. In the film, Treebeard's just stamped on an orc, and he appears just a little imposing, so the hobbits could be, as

Bilbo might put it, 'out of the frying pan and into the fire' (the first thing a character *does* in a film is always important – it defines their character somewhat – and here the hobbits see that Treebeard can kill big orcs by squashing them. That gives Treebeard's character a quite different slant, delaying his true nature until a while later). Eventually, of course, the hobbits manage to persuade Treebeard that they aren't orcs, *hrum, burrarum.*

The *Lord of the Rings* films seem to portray every new character encountered as potentially a threat, whereas the book is clear that Treebeard is friendly towards the hobbits from the get-go, and certainly doesn't squeeze them warningly (plus he's already been primed with information about them by Gandalf). The Treebeard scenes involve plenty of movie chicanery, from an animatronic ent, a CG head, model forests, to full-size forests, matte paintings and photographic backgrounds. Treebeard's designed as very treeish, with leaves, twigs and branches all over him (although he tells the hobbits very early in their encounter that he isn't a tree). With his eyes closed he might be a tree, though with its upper branches lopped off. In the novel, the ents are less obviously tree-like.

The meeting with Treebeard closes on yet another cliffhanger: the ent tells the hobbits that the white wizard will know what to do with them. As he places them on the ground before Gandalf, the film teases the audience (as Tolkien does in the Fangorn scenes), by having the hobbits look up at the wizard who's clad in bright white light, who might be Saruman. (An over-the-shoulder shot looking down the hobbits withholds the identity of the wizard by not granting a reverse angle). (A sidenote: if Gandalf had been so close to the orcs, why didn't he help them himself?).

And so to the meeting with Gandalf. The Three Hunters ready themselves (cue close-ups on their weapons) and turn to face a figure in white standing above them on a rise lit from behind by brilliant light. The figure bats away their weapons and fries Aragorn's sword (a subtle detail that's in the book). When the film cuts to close-ups of Gandalf, the shots are bleached out so intensely, his face can't really be made out (the selective over-exposure resulted from altering the plates in post-production, as well as practical lighting on set). The voices of Gandalf and Saruman are blended together, speaking the same lines (apparently, Ian McKellen was asked to do a Christopher Lee voice, and vice versa).

It's an intriguing (and economical) way of prolonging the confusion between the two white wizards (other solutions used by filmmakers for this kind of scene include the superimposition of one piece of film onto another, or cutting rapidly between two different actors, or using make-up, to show Ian McKellen looking like Christopher Lee, and so on). Éomer suggested earlier that Saruman's been spotted wandering around. As in the book, it's the elf who recognizes Gandalf first (in the film, he kneels humbly and says 'forgive me'; in the book, he gives 'a great shout' of 'Mithrandir!' and fires an arrow into the air which vanishes 'in a flash of flame' [TT, 119]). Aragorn stares at Gandalf disbelieving.

Gandalf steps forward, the white-out effect fades away, and Ian McKellen appears as Gandalf the White, in white robes, long, straight, white hair, and a white beard (and he looks younger, if anything – literally reborn. Although Gimli complains that the new Gandalf is grumpier than the old one, and Aragorn remarks that he still talks in riddles, the reborn wizard is still played much the same way. The new Gandalf is a little more focussed, less humorous, and becomes a military leader).

The music cue is a choral song, and the three characters stare in awe at the figure (in the book Tolkien writes: '[b]etween wonder, joy, and fear they stood and found no words to say' [TT, 119]). In fact, the cinematic techniques employed at this point – the white light, the ringing choirs, the low angles looking upwards, the awed reaction shots – are all those of the religious film genre. Aragorn, Gimli and Legolas could be looking up at Jesus or a god in a Biblical epic (Gandalf of course has many affinities with saints and deities). But the whole staging of the meeting with Gandalf in the film is very different from the book. The film plays it much more for exaggerated drama, with bright light, choirs, sound effects and visual effects, whereas the book is more suspenseful, more subtle, and more drawn-out.

Fairly soon after the meeting and the recognition, Gandalf is giving an account of his fate, as he did when Frodo woke up in Rivendell. Before the rest of the talk, the planning, and so on, then, the writers presume that the burning question the audience wanted answered first is: what happened to Gandalf after he fell with the balrog? (which was the scene which opened the film of *The Two Towers*, of course). Gandalf narrates his story in voiceover. Three or so tremendous fx shots (combining models, CGI and live action) depict the final blow of the fight at Zirak-zigil (a stab to the balrog's heart in a shot over Gandalf's shoulder, not with zapping spells or magic, but lightning zigzags from the sword to the creature – how *do* you kill a balrog?), and Gandalf lying on his back on Durin's Tower (the shots are long shots, keeping balrog and wizard small in the frame, a Wagnerian battle of titans on the snowy peaks, accompanied by stabs of lightning).

A series of visual effects (rotating camera, fades out of white, and the Stargate effect from *2001: A Space Odyssey,* but with clouds and stars rather than Pop Art neon) serve to illustrate in shorthand Gandalf's experience of being sent back to Middle-earth, closing with a shot of what is presumably a naked Gandalf (though only head and shoulders are shown – we're not about to see full body nudes of old Gandalf just yet). (One wonders if the filmmakers were tempted to show where Gandalf went – some Tolkien commentators assume that Gandalf was 'sent back' by the Valar. It might've been nice to see Gandalf's spirit winging back to Valinor for rest and relaxation, followed by recuperation and refitting in Lórien in white wizard's garb). If the audience's confused about Gandalf's return from death, the film keeps it mysterious: it shows that Gandalf struggled with the balrog and eventually dispatched him; maybe the old Gandalf 'died' at that point, collapsed on his back in the snow of Zirak-zigil. The fades to white, the Stargate effect, and McKellen's narration suggest a death and rebirth, but it's not made definite.

And then we're back with Gandalf in Fangorn in the film's present tense. (Plenty of the material from the book was elided of Gandalf's story, including more of the fight with the balrog, Gwaihir the eagle saving Gandalf and carrying him to Lothlórien, Gandalf's restoration in Lórien, and messages from Galadriel for Legolas and Aragorn. The eagle, meanwhile, didn't really need to be shown, as the audience had already seen Gandalf being rescued by Gwaihir from Orthanc. It could've been intriguing to see Gandalf in Lórien, but there isn't time for everything in a 2 hour 45 minute-plus movie.

An exposition scene follows, in Fangorn, with Gandalf explaining a little about the state of things, as the figures moved towards the edge of the forest. The extended cut adds some more information from Gandalf about the rising up of the ents (with a hint of the ent music cue on the track, which reaches its fullest expression when the ents march on Isengard). Legolas is prominent in the reaction shots to Gandalf's dialogue about the ents (nods to the book, in a way, because Legolas falls in love with Fangorn, and persuades Gimli to revisit it after the War of the Ring is over).

The wizard explains (to a concerned Gimli, who's often used as the audience's stand-in) that Merry and Pippin are in safe hands (Gimli remarks – to no one in particular – that the new Gandalf is grumpier than the old one, but in fact it's Gimli who complains most). In the book there's hours more talk, of course: the four characters sit down in Fangorn Forest and Aragorn tells Gandalf everything that's happened since they parted in Moria (this might have been a place for a prologue or summary of the first film. It's curious, isn't it, that Gandalf doesn't ask the Three Hunters much at all about what *they've* been doing. It's just assumed that he knows everything already). Then Gandalf launches into a lengthy monologue about the state of affairs in Middle-earth, the betrayal of Saruman, the ents, and finally his story of fighting the balrog (quite a bit of this was featured in the next but one scene).

The 2002 interpretation of *The Two Towers* doesn't pause long, though, after the meeting with Gandalf: fairly soon the travellers are at the treeline, with Gandalf summoning Shadowfax with a whistle. The slo-mo images of the white horse running towards the camera (plus a choir singing) could come from a TV advert for washing powder or health insurance. The music segues into one of Howard Shore's heroic themes, over second unit shots of the riders in wilderness landscapes (one of many John Ford Western moments in the films, but too brief, I think).

Treebeard's song of the ent-wives was inserted here in the *Extended Edition* of *The Two Towers*, one of the nicer additions, because it includes a song (there are four songs in the "Treebeard" chapter), and there are too few in the films (it has the refrain: 'Come back to me! Come back to me, and say my land is fair!' [TT, 95]). The form it takes is of Treebeard singing (well, John Rhys-Davies speaks it rather than sings it) and the film cutting away to a montage of helicopter shots of trees and hills (most of them featuring dawn mist), then cutting back to the hobbits, now asleep (the scene began with C.U.s of Merry and Pippin, with Merry yawning, as they listened to Treebeard's song). Treebeard places them on the forest floor like children (Dominic Monaghan said he included a gesture of the hand raised because he'd seen babies sleep like that).

The extended cut added a scene with Gandalf and Aragorn talking at night as they look towards Mordor (presumably as they halt on their trip to Edoras), covered in standard close-up shots. Actually, Aragorn has little to do but listen to Gandalf and nod, because the wizard churns rapidly through a couple of pages of dialogue. Gandalf's monologue brings the audience up to date on Sauron and his plans, on Saruman and his army, on Rohan, on the decrepitude of Théoden, and what needs to happen next. It won't have entered Sauron's and Saruman's darkest dreams, says Gandalf, that we should hope to destroy the ring (in the book, Gandalf only talks about Sauron's darkest dream, not Saruman's:

> "That we should wish to cast him down and have *no* one in his place is not a thought that occurs to his mind. That we should try to destroy the Ring itself has not yet entered into his darkest dream." (TT, 122)

It's quite a dull scene, really. Actually, it's as dull as could be imagined: two people talking quietly, without moving, without any change in the staging from start to finish. Which's one reason why the theatrical cut dropped it. But it does contain a lot of information. (In a way, the buyers of the extended cut DVD and video don't need this scene, because presumably many of them've already seen the theatrical cut in theatres or at home, and they know the score. So, in a way, it was a scene that would have been better to include in the theatrical cut for non-Tolkienites. It was also a reshoot: small-scale, two actors, lots of dialogue). The two-hander with Gandalf and Aragorn discussing Frodo was reprised in the Edoras feast scene towards the beginning of *The Return of the King*.

The close of Gandalf's monologue mentions Frodo, and Aragorn tells Gandalf that Sam went with him, which pleases the wizard (his dialogue here follows the book closely). That serves as a link to the next scene, which's back with the hobbits and Gollum, opening with a C.U. on Sam climbing a rock. A crane up follows the travellers to reveal the Black Gate, accompanied by a loud, ominous orchestral cue – classic Hollywood epic filmmaking, and a standard 'reveal' (the scale of the miniature is enormous). Some lines are directly from the book (such as Sam saying if the Gaffer could see him now). Gollum cowers at the sight of the Morannon, covering his face with his hands like a child (a nice touch). Gollum and the hobbits are situated on a rocky outcrop on the other side of the valley from the Gate, with a few hundred yards of level ground in between. (The topography is very close to Alan Lee's illustration in the 1992 edition of *Rings*).

The 2002 *The Two Towers* follows the book with a scene of soldiers marching towards the Black Gate. The soundtrack mixes the sound of marching feet and cries of orders very loud. The costumes of what are presumably a legion of Easterlings mix Arabic and Pacific cultures, with elaborate helmets, and black kohl around the eyes of the actors like Bedouin or desert people in the Middle East or Magreb.

The opening of the Black Gate itself becomes a major visual effects sequence in itself, with trolls on top of the gates hauling them open, orcs blowing horns, and soldiers pacing around on the battlements. (The idea for the shot of the trolls opening the gate came from animator Randy Cook: Cook said that Alex Funke invited him to suggest some other coverage when he was visiting the miniature stage. Cook suggested having a shot showing how the gates worked. Hence the image of the trolls being woken up and pulling and pushing the gate mechanism. Suffice to say that Tolkien didn't go into how the Black Gate worked).

At this point, an action beat is inserted, drawn from a scene where Frodo and Sam are inside Mordor and are nearly discovered by orcs. In the film, Sam crawls onto a rock at the edge of the outcrop, which tips over, he falls, and Frodo hurries after him down the slopes. The idea of the elven cloaks hiding the hobbits from unfriendly eyes is used twice here: two soldiers break off from the phalanx of marching soldiers to investigate: first, a point-of-view shot of a soldier looking up at the slope and seeing dust kicked up Frodo, but no Frodo. Secondly, in the second half of the scene, where Frodo, thinking quickly, covers himself and Sam (who's landed up to his waist in stones) with his elven cloak, but the soldiers see only a rock. It's kids' stuff, with the two hobbits hiding from the soldiers right in front of them, the camera offering point-of-view shots from underneath the cloak, like children who put their hands over their eyes and say: 'you can't see me!'. And it's the stuff of fairy tales, that a cloak can hide good guys from baddies (this was vaguely set up during the Galadriel's gifts scene, but only in the extended cut).

At the base of the hill, the scene where Gollum persuades Frodo to take the road South to Cirith Ungol while Sam disagrees, is a heavily condensed version of the book, but it follows the general drift of the novel closely. The hobbits discuss whether to go ahead: Frodo plunges forward three times, but Gollum pulls him back, and yanks on Sam too (the actors said that this was a particularly bad day of filming, on a cover set; Randy Cook commented that the animators had to work hard to give Gollum all of the right facial expressions and moves: in this scene, Gollum is acting up as much as he can, to persuade Frodo to try the other route into the Black Land). The third time Gollum hauls Frodo back, he tells him that there is another way into Mordor.

NOTES: ACT ONE

1. R. Foster, 1978, 269.

ACT TWO

Once the three diminutive travellers are set up on their way again, the film is able to cut to one of the other stories. This time it's back to Merry and Pippin in Fangorn, with a scene cut from the theatrically released version of *The Lord of the Rings: The Two Towers*: the ent draft scene (shot as a pick-up, it's one of the least engaging sequences in the three films). The whole scene is depicted from Merry's point-of-view, beginning when he wakes up to find himself in one of Treebeard's houses, hears the sounds of ents in the distance, and starts to sense something different about Pippin. It's a lighthearted scene, played for comedy, with jokes about hobbit height (Pippin claims he's pushing three foot seven). Eventually, Merry realizes it's the ent draft that Pippin's guzzling that's the cause, and grabs the bowl from him. As the hobbits playfully chase each other, the film moves into an action beat (the hobbits' movement helpfully puts them in the right place, clambering over thick roots), culled from the Old Forest scenes in *The Fellowship of the Ring*, where Old Man Willow trapped the hobbits under its roots. And when Treebeard rescues the hobbits from under the roots and piles of dead oak leaves, he employs some of Tom Bombadil's dialogue in the book when he saved the hobbits from Old Man Willow. By the end of the sequence, as Treebeard explains about some of the trees going bad, the characters are in motion again (Treebeard walking through the forest, carrying the hobbits), on their way to the ent moot.

Fangorn Forest, in the matte paintings and digital additions to live action plates, seems to climb far up the slopes of the surrounding mountains, much higher than the treeline in the real world in similar mountain ranges. That helps to give Fangorn Forest its other-worldly look, as if it's spreading each year further up the mountains. Fangorn is also depicted as a solid mass of trees stretching as far as the eye can see, without any breaks.

The scenes in Edoras go back over weeks and months, which's already a little confusing, because they are intercut with the continuous present of the film. So they appear as if in the present, but they're not. There are further confusions, because the Edoras scenes are split up, some appearing earlier, and some as the Three Hunters and Gandalf approach Edoras. (And even more confusing when you add the *Extra Special Must-Have Gotta-Get-It Extended Edition*).

The group of short scenes at Edoras served to introduce the culture of the Rohirrim, the wizened old king, the scheming counsellor, the lonely shield-maiden and the balance of power in the ailing kingdom. Without the time to dig deep into the back-stories of the characters or the wealth of detail that Tolkien provided about the Rohirrim, the film stuck to the most salient points about the characters and the society. Thus, Théoden was introduced on his throne, but in a virtually catatonic state (sporting make-up impossibly wrinkled and aged). Like Bilbo in *The Return of the King*, Théoden is extremely old, senile, virtually on death's doorstep. He speaks in a barely audible croaky whisper. The filmmakers have up taken the notion of the fisher king, the ailing, wounded king of mediæval Holy Grail legends whose kingdom has become a waste land (typically, an Arthurian knight comes along and helps to bring life back to the nation). Éomer underlines that portrait of Rohan as a mediæval waste land by telling the king that orcs roam the country unchecked.

Wormtongue, meanwhile, was portrayed as a larger-than-life movie villain:. And Wormtongue sported a peculiar English accent, as befitting an outsize vaudeville or pantomime villain in an American film (although, this time the villain wasn't played by a British character actor, but a US character actor).

Both Théoden and Wormtongue were grotesques, close to caricature, exaggerated presumably so that no one in the audience could mistake their roles. Early in the Edoras sequence is the depiction of the return of Théoden's son, Théodred, fatally wounded at the Fords of Isen. Also, his death cannot have much impact on a movie audience (and it doesn't in the books, either), because he wasn't established in any substantial form (including in the extended cut).

Cut to a close-up of Théodred, dead, in the same room of the earlier scene with Éowyn and Éomer. This time, Éowyn is grieving for Théodred, her cousin. In a C.U., Éowyn is weeping. The scene is a very brief prelude to the scene where Gríma Wormtongue enters the chamber and speaks with her (he slinks into the scene in *boo! hiss!* pantomime style). When Wormtongue slides around the door, as he did before, it gives the impression not only that he's a creepy guy, always hanging around, but that he stalks Éowyn. Éowyn rises and a two-hander scene ensues, with Gríma doing most of the talking. She calls him a snake, and says his words are poison, but for a moment she listens to him. The camera circles with Wormtongue as he moves around Éowyn, using the words of Gandalf's about Éowyn, taken from much later in the book, which he says to Éomer:

> "But who knows what she spoke to the darkness, alone, in the bitter watches of the night, when all her life seemed shrinking, and the walls of her bower closing in about her, a hutch to trammel some wild thing?" (RK, 170)

Some of Wormtongue's dialogue, taken from Gandalf in the much later Minas Tirith chapters, Philippa Boyens thought Tolkien would dislike.

In this scene at Edoras, the words serve a dual function – as Wormtongue's seduction of Éowyn (that he's quite perceptive about her psychological state), and also to inform the audience a little about her character (because Éowyn hasn't been given actions yet which can really illuminate her character for the audience. So far, she's been seen mainly as someone who cares for the king and his son). Interestingly, the words of Gandalf's in the Houses of Healing in Gondor are spoken to Éomer while Éowyn lies asleep beside them, and in the film Éowyn and Gríma stand beside another recumbent Rohirrim. Another connection is that just before Gandalf's lines about Éowyn he's talking about Saruman and Wormtongue.

At the end of the Edoras scene, Wormtongue puts his hand to Éowyn's cheek; she's still crying; the camera edges in slightly and the actors stare at each other in the preamble to a love scene. But Éowyn shakes her from the spell and storms out (just before a cut from the two-shot, Wormtongue looks at his left hand, as if thinking that it was the closest he ever came to his beloved).

The blocking of the scene has Éowyn standing still listening to Wormtongue as he circles her, covered with tight close-ups. The audience is teased for a moment when it appears as if Éowyn will respond to Wormtongue's advances (ugh!), as he leans in close (the staging and framing hints at a kiss). But she rightly rejects him with a put-down that would have the fan-girls in the audience cheering: 'your words are poison'. (Well, as a mate for Éowyn, Wormtongue is ugly and creepy, but he does have a great Gothic costume (a high velvet collar to create the illusion of a humpback, an over-robe in black, with a fish-tail extension that dragged on the floor, and sleeves that end up at the hands in points).[1] And he's available – Aragorn's swooning over Arwen, although she's hundreds of miles away). Boyens recalled that the scene was intended to show something of Éowyn's lonely lifestyle in bleak Edoras, and her craving for human contact.

Éowyn's abrupt movement offers a visual link to the travellers on horseback below, when Éowyn rushes through the main doors of Meduseld to get some fresh air. A close-up of Éowyn (perhaps contemplating the accuracy of Wormtongue's words about her being cooped up in a hutch) is followed by the image of the flag flying loose and floating out over the main gate below. It lands near Aragorn (shown riding in slight slow motion). This offers a visual link between Aragorn and Éowyn before they've met (one wonders if that idea came about because the Mount Potts Station location was so windy. Maybe it's symbolic of Rohan's decline, the banner with its horse motif falling to the ground).

Much more significant than Théodred's death is the scene of Théoden mourning him, and (in the *Special Extended Edition*, his funeral). This latter scene is notable for Éowyn's song for Théodred in Old English (translated by David Salo from Philippa Boyens' lyrics) and a scene that looks as if it were shot in a force nine gale (wind blowing hair and clothing is a nightmare for wardrobe, hair and make-up, and one thing digital technology can't clean up easily or cheaply). The funeral also has an awkward and most abrupt ending (chopping Éowyn's song like that just doesn't work). (Miranda Otto loved the dress: it 'was *fabulous*. It carried its own personality – dark and heavy, beautiful but stifling').[2]

Wormtongue holding court from beside Théoden on his throne is of course a scene familiar to movie viewers, as well as being a staple of historical and fantasy fiction (or contemporary thrillers based in the White House, with Vice Presidents or aides who actually run the country). Pretty soon an example of Wormtongue exercising his power is depicted, when Éomer is banished from Edoras (and the filmmakers have established that Éomer seems to be the one person noble and active enough to reverse Rohan's decline).

Many of the scenes at Edoras were not related in *The Lord of the Rings* in the foreground; the content of them was inferred from the book, and also invented for the film. Éowyn mourning Théodred, her encounter in the chamber with Wormtongue, Wormtongue banishing Éomer, and so on, all of these were constructed for the film, to flesh out the characters *before* Gandalf and the Three Hunters turn up.

The timeline of the book was also altered, bringing the Edoras scenes forward: in the book, Edoras is only reached *after* Aragorn, Legolas and Gimli meet Éomer and the riders of Rohan, *after* Treebeard, and *after* they meet Gandalf. The scriptwriters likely decided that it would be too late in the film to introduce Théoden, Éowyn, Éomer and Wormtongue and that it would have more impact if the audience knew about them before Gandalf and the others arrive at the Golden Hall (otherwise, it would have meant more delay and more talk to establish their characters). The scene where Gandalf and cohorts sweep into Meduseld and storm up to Théoden's throne makes for impressive (if rather silly) drama. Thus, in a way, placing all of the character-based scenes earlier allows for this climactic moment when Gandalf releases the king from Saruman's spell.

To Edoras now, as the four travellers approach it on horseback: a sweeping crane shot reveals the Edoras location as the horsemen halt and contemplate it. For many in the cast and crew (such as Barrie Osborne, Miranda Otto, Bernard Hill and Brad Dourif), the Edoras location, at Mount Sunday, near Canterbury on the South Island of New Zealand, was the most impressive set in the three films. Access was difficult (roads had to be built), and it took the construction team 5 or 6 months to complete the build, sometimes in high wind or very cold conditions and, as usual in a big movie, it would only be used for 8 or so days. Apart from the centrepiece, the Golden Hall (which has elaborate carvings picked out in gold, and horses above the doors), out-buildings and stables were constructed, with an access road and space for parking vehicles hidden behind structures. There were digital additions around the hill, too, to make Edoras look like the capital city of Rohan. It was a world of timber and stone, rounded Romanesque windows, interweaving Celtic patterns, and plenty of horse emblems and statuary. Rough and windswept, a place for the 'Vikings on horses' concept of the Rohirrim.

In the theatrical version, Gandalf handles the exposition about Edoras (if Gandalf's in a scene, it's commonsense to have him handle the exposition), and his dialogue continues as a voiceover on top of a cut to a high, wide shot of the dimly-lit interior of the Golden Hall. At this point, the film moves backwards in time, as a reminder to the days after the death of Théodred (it continues from the earlier Edoras scenes). Éowyn is kneeling before the king, holding his hands, and telling him softly that his son Théodred is dead (Wormtongue is absent). Then a cut back to Gandalf and the others approaching Edoras. Gandalf tells them to mind what they say, and 'do not look for welcome here' (the film omitted that Gandalf had already been there after escaping from the balrog).

As the four travellers ride up the road to the Golden Hall, there are mobile point-of-view shots of the inhabitants staring at them on each side.

Gimli mutters something about finding more cheer in a graveyard. A couple of shots are taken from Aragorn's point-of-view, looking up towards Éowyn standing outside the Golden Hall. These are presumably meant to express the sentiments of Aragorn in the Houses of Healing in *The Return of the King,* when he says in the book:

> When I first looked on her and perceived her unhappiness, it seemed to me that I saw a white flower standing straight and proud, shapely as a lily, and yet knew that it was hard, as if wrought by elf-wrights out of steel. Or was it, maybe, a frost that had turned its sap to ice, and so it stood, bitter-sweet, still fair to see, but stricken, soon to fall and die? (RK, 169)

The screenwriters have dug around in *The Lord of the Rings* text to find material to shape into a filmic portrait of Éowyn, teasing out every possibility of approaches to Éowyn's character, and occasionally adding new scenes (such as the one between Éowyn and Aragorn in the stable, or the one with them in the Hall). With Galadriel stuck in Lórien for the duration of the film, and Arwen in Rivendell, Éowyn was the only major female character to be out and about, interacting with the other characters, and travelling with them. And those two elf women were ethereal, distant, spiritual inspirers of people, *elves,* very different from regular women, and not like flesh-and-blood women who live amongst ordinary people. Éowyn, though royalty (privileged, well-off), is also much closer to everyday folk than Galadriel or Arwen. Thus, Éowyn has to carry much of what the scriptwriters want to put in the film about women and women's issues.

It might have been tempting for the filmmakers to give Éowyn superhuman or extraordinary fighting powers, because many action films or superhero films contemporary with the *Lord of the Rings* films did that, turning women into kickboxing, karate experts: *Charlie's Angels, X-Men, Spy Kids, Lara Croft, Catwoman, James Bond, The Incredibles, The Matrix* and the best of the bunch, the wonderful *Crouching Tiger, Hidden Dragon* and *Hero.* (Éowyn did turn out to be a fearsome fighter – though not until Pelennor Fields).

In the film, Éowyn's role is bumped up from loving Aragorn from afar to a soap opera-style romantic involvement with Aragorn. It may all be one-sided, but she's still mad about him. In one of the flashbacks to Rivendell, Aragorn appears to break off his relationship with Arwen, telling her it was just a dream that couldn't last. When the film cuts back to the present, Aragorn is with Éowyn on the way to Helm's Deep, hinting that Aragorn is now free to romance Éowyn.

Arwen is an inspirational figure in the films: when Aragorn's in doubt, he thinks back to Arwen and she reminds him what he has to do. Both Elrond and Arwen in the flashbacks are continually encouraging Aragorn to live up to his responsibilities. They act as the fates or the gods in Greek mythology movies, or as angels in Christian movies, appearing to advise Aragorn.

The scene with the travellers' weapons being given up at the doors of

Edoras follows. All fairly routine. Gandalf's clad in a grey robe, so that his unveiling a moment later will have a greater impact (he also takes Legolas's arm when he walks, like an old man). As the travellers approach the king, across the length of the hall, for the key Edoras scene, there's time for a little more dialogue and information. Wormtongue is now in his usual spot, sitting beside the king, and whispering in his ear about Gandalf not being welcome. The camera tracks with the travellers as they approach, and cuts to their point-of-view of Wormtongue's guards following them at the side of the Hall, glancing darkly in their direction. Only Gandalf talks at first, the other three acting mainly as his bodyguards. Either Gandalf has primed them about what he's going to attempt, or they have the *nous* to keep the area clear for him.

After Théoden's feeble address to Gandalf Stormcrow, Wormtongue approaches the wizard. Gandalf's words to Wormtongue about keeping his forked tongue behind his teeth and not 'bandying crooked words with a serving-man' hop out of the book into the film. Wormtongue's cry that the guards didn't take the wizard's staff is the signal for the Rohirrim heavies to pounce on our heroes. One of the silliest moments in the films occurs here, as Aragorn, Legolas and Gimli beat up the guards (with completely unconvincing staging and combat. Where were the stunt co-ordinators?).

With all of the guards defeated (and Gimli watching over Wormtongue), Gandalf approaches Théoden and begins his spell. The unveiling of the white wizard is accompanied by the now familiar religious film devices of a choral music cue, whooshing sound fx, white light, and awed reaction shots.

The struggle between Saruman and Gandalf for control of Théoden (and Rohan) ensues. The voice of Saruman is mixed with Théoden's voice, in the same way as it was earlier between Saruman and Gandalf. There are no lightning flashes or electrical rays in Gandalf's spell, but plenty of sound effects. The film only cuts to Saruman in his throne room right at the end of the exorcism, when Théoden is hurled backwards, and visual fx morph Théoden's face with Saruman's. The wizard is thrown onto the hard, shiny floor as in the wizard duel earlier (the film depicts Saruman as actively controlling Théoden from afar – a huge departure from the book, where no character is controlled puppet-like from a great distance).

Éowyn rushes in during the exorcism, and is held back by Aragorn (it has to be Aragorn to hang onto her – the filmmakers never waste an opportunity to put Aragorn and Éowyn together). When Théoden is finally transformed, Éowyn runs to his side (in the book, this is the moment when Éowyn recognizes Aragorn as a 'tall heir of kings, wise with many winters, hiding a power that she yet felt', and he sees her as

> strong... and stern as steel, a daughter of kings. Thus Aragorn, for the first time in the full light of day beheld Éowyn, Lady of Rohan, and thought her fair, fair and cold, like a morning of pale spring that is not yet come to womanhood. (TT, 146)

Instead, the filmmakers keep the momentum of this scene with

Théoden and Gandalf. In the next couple of scenes, Théoden is now a character driving the action, with Aragorn, Gandalf and the others secondary, rather than a passive character, manipulated by Wormtongue. Théoden pursues Wormtongue outside to the steps of the Hall, and threatens to kill him; Aragorn restrains him (in the book, it's Théoden who's merciful to Gríma). The action is covered with loose handheld shots. A beat where Wormtongue spits on Aragorn's hand (it's Théoden's hand in the book) was added to the extended cut (it's when Wormtongue glimpses Aragorn's ring of Barahir). The people kneel before the king, as does Aragorn, but it's not the heroic affirmation of leadership of the book. Théoden musing on his son Théodred is a lead-in to the subsequent scene, of Théodred's funeral. Again, very different from the king in the novel, which has him restored to vigour rapidly, and crying out *'Arise now, Riders of Théoden!'* In the film, Théoden's first thought after taking up his sword is to deal with Wormtongue.

The style of the film changes here, with slow, stately tracking shots appropriate for a sombre scene, most everyone clad in black, with soldiers in full armour. Éowyn in a black dress, hair tied up, stands to one side, in front of weeping women. (Gandalf, though, retains his white robes: from now on, this will be his chief costume for the rest of the films). Éowyn's song, in Anglo-Saxon (with a bit of *Beowulf* in there for good measure), is tricky to pull off, but the filmmakers get away with it (the song, like the funeral scene itself, is an addition to the book. However, the funerary rites have little *emotional* impact, and no dramatic value, partly because they concern a character who was nearly dead in the first place, hasn't played a significant role in the story, hasn't been given any characterization whatsoever, and has no dialogue or interaction with anyone. The viewer knows they're burying the king's son, but it could be anybody).

The following scene presumably takes place later that day, with evening light on the distant mountains, and the burial mounds in shadow. A curious scene, it has Gandalf standing some way off from Théoden, who stands before his son's tomb (no aides or companions for the king – no one else's about at all). A big close-up shot of a *simbelmynë* flower falling to the ground in slight slow motion introduces the scene (it took 98 takes to get that shot, according to DP Andrew Lesnie. You could have shot a whole low budget movie with the film stock). Théoden weeps; Gandalf comforts him with some well-chosen words about reaching the halls of his fathers (a bit of Viking mythology). At the close of the scene, Gandalf spots the horse carrying Morwen's children who escaped from the Westfold in the distance. The exhausted Éothain falls off the horse, paying off the scene in the Saruman invasion montage.

NOTES: ACT TWO

1. In B. Sibley, 2002, 93.
2. In B. Sibley, 2002, 97.

ACT THREE

The next scene, half-an-hour later in the Golden Hall, is decision time for Théoden. Éowyn stands next to the children (she's typed here as a mother figure, as she was in her first scene, when she tended the ailing Théodred). It's a night scene in the Hall, with fires, people eating (Gimli and the children), and others smoking (Aragorn). (In fact, it's one of Ronald Tolkien's favourite moments from mediæval mythologies: evening in the Northern European mead hall, which was evoked by the various literary clubs Tolkien founded or joined. Tolkien would be quite at home here).

A subtle touch has Gandalf now replacing Wormtongue as the adviser at Théoden's right side, encouraging him to particular courses of action (the king glances down as Gandalf places his hand on the arm of the throne). Having just been a puppet for so long, Théoden isn't in a hurry to become another one. Maybe Saruman's spell, and the whisperings of Gríma, have had some lasting effect. And when Aragorn takes up Gandalf's cause ('open war is upon you'), Théoden reminds him who's king around here. Finally, Théoden announces that he will lead his people to safety at Helm's Deep.

It's quite different the book, where Théoden isn't suspicious and reluctant, but decides (on his own) to lead his people to Helm's Deep (Gandalf doesn't expect this). Indeed, when the king grasps his sword he chants 'in the tongue of Rohan a call to arms. *Arise now, arise, Riders of Théoden! ... Forth Eorlingas!'* (TT, 149). The filmmakers saved Théoden's battle cries for later. Théoden's played much more anxious, reluctant, and unsure, a weaker personality, so that his rise to heroic status will seem more impressive in *The Return of the King*. But it's *not* the king of the horse lords of Tolkien's tome, who is keen to go out to hunt down enemies straight away. In the book, Théoden is in a fey, dark mood sometimes, in his bid to go out and fight, and not stay cooped up in Edoras or Helm's Deep, but he's also pro-active and brave. He's not the doubting, worried man of the 2002 film; the traits added to Théoden's character make him more amenable to a contemporary movie audience, because out-and-out nobility and heroics are more difficult to accept and believe in, perhaps. The adaptors did the same thing with Aragorn's character. Certainly it adds more shadings to Théoden's personality, and Bernard Hill is terrific at bringing them out.

Cut to Háma (John Leigh), the captain of the king's guard, telling the people of Edoras that the city must empty and make for Edoras (the scene is presumably the following day). Two scenes now follow which are set, appropriately enough for this kingdom founded on horses, in the stables at Edoras (the designers and art department had situated the stables near the Golden Hall, figuring that the Rohirrim worshipped horses, valuing them highly. That's the æsthetic reasoning: the practical reason for it is that the Golden Hall and the stables are in the same dramatic space).

First, Gandalf leaves to find help (from Éomer), and then a scene between Aragorn, Éowyn and... a horse. Yes, a horse (but it's not *that* kind of scene). A nice touch in the two-hander between Gandalf and Aragorn has the wizard mentioning his age, saying that he's walked the earth for 300 lives of men and now hasn't got any time. He tells Aragorn that Helm's Deep must not fall, and reminds the Dúnadan of his responsibilities (again). He also foreshadows his miraculous arrival in the nick of time at Helm's Deep. So there's no suspense: the viewer knows that all will be well, 'cos Gandie will return.

The film stays in the same time and space for a scene which begins with a wild horse that's rearing up in the middle of the stables, which no one can seem to tame. But our hero can, whispering to it in Elvish. As he's stroking the horse (it's Brego, Théodred's horse, according to Éowyn, which emphasizes the personal connection), the shield maiden of Rohan slips into the scene. The subtext of the scene appears to be Éowyn's becoming more enamoured with Aragorn; for Aragorn, though, it seems to be about the horse. (According to producer Barrie Osborne, Viggo Mortensen disagreed with writers Walsh and Boyens about the real content or subtext of the scene. Mortensen often brought ideas to the screenwriters about his character, which might have been great many times, but sometimes it must've been a pain).

Essentially, the scene brings Éowyn and Aragorn together under the pretext of the taming of the horse. Thus, it's another opportunity for Éowyn to get to know Aragorn (but not vice versa, it seems). Unfortunately, for some reason or other, the scene doesn't appear to be about anything: it's kind of pointless (and wasn't in the theatrical cut of *The Two Towers*). There's some talk about elves being known to tame wild animals, and Aragorn growing up in Rivendell, but it's muddled. As directed by, say, Michael Curtiz or William Wyler in the Classical Hollywood era, the point of the scene might've been clearer. In short, the actors and writers aren't playing the same subtext.

Back to Saruman now, after a long gap (since the first reel, in fact). He's still in Orthanc, scheming wickedly (but now joined by Wormtongue whom he derides as 'smelling of horse'). Saruman, pacing around the throne room (lit in blue), gripes about Gandalf's new guise as the white wizard. It's an addition to the book, but does come out of Sarumam's character as competitive and mean-spirited (revealed in the confrontation between Gandalf and Saruman at the door of Orthanc in the book, for instance.). And the way Christopher Lee plays it, it comes across as the petulance of the movie villain who's been bested by his rival. (If Saruman's many-coloured guise had been used, maybe Saruman wouldn't mind Gandalf being white so much. Everyone hates it when someone else turns up wearing exactly the same outfit).

When Gríma mentions the man with Gandalf, Saruman's interested. Wormtongue describes the ring. Cut to a dramatic continuation of the previous scene, but Saruman's now seated in his library, contemplating a big black-and-white drawing of the ring of Barahir (the shot of the large sketch of the ring helps to inform the audience that this new ring ain't the One Ring).

In fact, Barahir's ring (a.k.a. Felagund's ring) was an elven ring, made by the Noldor, given to him by Finrod during Dagor Bragollach, the fourth great war of the First Age of Middle-earth. Barahir's hand (and ring) was cut off after his death in Dorthonion, but Beren got hold of it and brought it to Nargothrond. The ring later passed on to the Númenóreans in the Second Age, and then to the Northern kingdoms in the Third Age. It eventually found its way to Rivendell, and the scriptwriters had Aragorn wear it. Barahir's ring thus has plenty of back-story attached to it (there's more, too) – chiefly, as far as Aragorn's concerned, its direct link to Beren, because Aragorn plays Beren to Arwen's Lúthien. None of that back-story could possibly make it into a Hollywood movie or even a multi-part TV series of *The Lord of the Rings*. But Elrond does give Aragorn Barahir's ring, along with the shards of Narsil, in the appendix of *The Lord of the Rings*, so maybe Walsh and Boyens thought'd be nice if Aragorn also had a ring (Tolkien had toyed with the idea of Galadriel giving Aragorn her ring).

The 2002 *The Two Towers* film alters the chronology as well as the manœuvres of Gandalf and the Rohirrim at this point (there's no Second Battle of the Isen, for instance). In the movie, Théoden mentions that Éomer is three hundred leagues away: that means Gandalf has to ride 900 miles there and 900 miles back – with an army, so he can save the day at Helm's Deep. Just a *little* unlikely. Effectively for the film, Gandalf now disappears from the story until his miraculous reappearance at Helm's Deep. So it's all up to Aragorn and his chums, bumping up Aragorn's role considerably. (Notice how, though the book explains Gandalf's reappearance, in the film it's timed to coincide with Aragorn urging Théoden to ride out with him. In the book, Gandalf's away for one night only: Gandalf heals Théoden on March 2, 3019, and the Rohirrim ride against Saruman that very day; Théoden is at Helm's Deep on March 3; and on March 4, 3019, Théoden and Gandalf ride for Isengard (RK, 470). In the film, the journey to Helm's Deep takes some time, maybe a few days. Gandalf tells Aragorn in the stables to watch out for him at sunrise on the fifth day.)

The writers extended the trek to Helm's Deep for a number of reasons: (1) one was because Helm's Deep would be the climax to *The Two Towers*, so they didn't want to get there too quickly; (2) they had other stories to develop, such as Merry and Pippin and the ents, and Frodo, Sam and Gollum; (3) they wanted to insert scenes concerning Aragorn's anxieties about assuming his responsibilities of being a leader, and also leave time for (4) the subplot of the romance between Aragorn and his elf lover (those romantic interludes could not occur *after* Helm's Deep, or in the run-up to the battle. In other words, quite a bit of the book has to be dealt with before the beginning of the build-up to the siege).

The 2002 film of *The Two Towers* handled the exodus from Edoras and the subsequent journey to Helm's Deep very differently from the book. For a start, the Rohirrim leave Edoras with an army a thousand strong ('their spears were like a springing wood'); Éomer's there (but Éowyn's left behind, in full armour, outside the Golden Hall); and Gandalf and Théoden lead the army, with Gandalf revealing himself in white and Aragorn crying '"Behold the White Rider!"' (TT, 159). Trumpets sound, spear clashes on shield, and 'with a rush like the sudden onset of a great wind the last host of Rohan rode thundering into the West' (ibid.). Wow. Rousing, heroic stuff:

> Then suddenly he threw back his grey cloak, and cast aside his hat, and leaped to horseback. He wore no helm nor mail. His snowy hair flew free in the wind, his white robe shone dazzling in the sun.
> "Behold the White Rider!" cried Aragorn, and all took up the words. "Our King and the White Rider!" they shouted. "Forth Eorlingas!"
> The trumpets sounded. The horses reared and neighed. Spear clashed on shield. Then the king raised his hand, and with a rush like the sudden onset of a great wind the last host of Rohan rode thundering into the West. (TT, 159)

Well, the 2002 film plays it completely turned about. Now it's a downbeat, straggling procession of horses and figures leading out from Edoras, a lot of them women, children and old men (including a brief shot of the Westfold kids of Morwen's on a horse), with Théoden looking back longingly on his capital. Prominent in the scene is Howard Shore's folky, Celtic Rohirrim theme, played on the Norwegian Hardanger violin. Clearly the bold, proud, brassy Rohirrim spirit will be saved for later, for Helm's Deep, and for the ride of the Rohirrim in *The Return of the King*. It's sometimes surprising in this film adaption of Tolkien's book that so many opportunities for a bit of exuberance, laughter or rejoicing are damped down. So many songs were cut, for instance. Although cinema is commonly regarded as more 'dramatic' or 'exaggerated' than literature, it ain't necessarily so here.

The film of *The Two Towers* thus contrasts strongly with Tolkien's book at this point. Instead of Théoden and Gandalf leading an army of more than a thousand spears (with more collected along the way) to Helm's Deep, there's a ragtag caravan of women, children and old men, some on carts and horses. It's as if the filmmakers decided to play Edoras and Rohan while Théoden was under Saruman's spell like the fisher king myth in Arthurian legend, where the kingdom becomes a wasteland (with Gandalf as Lancelot, Galahad or Perceval or some knight who revitalizes the land – there is some of that in Tolkien's book). Or as if a plague had ravaged the land, or wars lasting years, killing all of the able-bodied men.

In actuality, what the screenwriters opted to do was to exaggerate the suspense and tension of the book by increasing the odds stacked against the heroes. So, at Helm's Deep, the free peoples have far less soldiers than in the book (300 vs. 10,000). And Théoden presides over a kingdom close to the end of a long decline. Tolkien might have objected to that, because it severely altered the fundamental conception of one of his favourite cultures in Middle-earth.

Just prior to the exodus are a couple of interior scenes. A brief one, between Théoden and Gamling (Bruce Hopkins; Gamling in the book is an old man, probably Erkenbrand's lieutenant), in Théodred's chamber re-dressed as the king's chamber, has Théoden's telling Gamling that they are not retreating (but they are, really, of course: it's another departure from the book).

The second Edoras scene is more interesting: set in the Golden Hall, with background action consisting of people preparing tables or generally readying for the exodus, it features a little moment with Éowyn alone, trying out a sword, before Aragorn turns up. The scene was directed by Fran Walsh (according to the 'making of' documentaries, no one in the crew knew how to handle a sword, so a member of the visual fx team was brought on set to work out some moves with Miranda Otto). It's the first appearance of Éowyn as a shield maiden of Rohan. It's a more satisfying scene than the muddled stables scene. The subtext is undoubtedly erotic: one doesn't need to know about William Shakespeare's bawdy language and the symbolism of swords and clashing blades to see what's going on here. The best moment is Éowyn's startled look when Aragorn stops her mid-flow with his dagger, as if no one's ever dared do that to her before. The heart of the dialogue here is taken almost word-for-word from another scene between Aragorn and Éowyn, just before Aragorn leaves for the Paths of the Dead:

> "What do you fear, lady?" he asked.
> "A cage," she said. "To stay behind bars, until use and old age accept them, and all chance of doing great deeds is gone beyond recall or desire."
> "And yet you counselled me not to adventure on the road that I had chosen, because it is perilous?"
> "So one may counsel another," she said. "Yet I not bid you flee from peril, but to ride to battle where your sword may win renown and victory. I would not see a thing that is high and excellent cast away needlessly." (TT, 63)

From the Edoras exodus, *The Two Towers* cuts back to Saruman in Orthanc, with Wormtongue telling his boss what he thinks Théoden will do (i.e., head for Helm's Deep, along with women and children). Saruman gives a Dracula smile. Wormtongue's speech is placed over a couple of shots of the Rohirrim caravan walking beside a lake in daylight. Cut to Saruman now in his caves below Isengard, paying a visit to his warg riders, and ordering them out. A shot of the shadows of the wargs on the walls of a pit lit by flame is a classic action-adventure device of foreshadowing (literally shadowing) the ferocity of the wargs without yet revealing them in full. (It's cheaper than digital critters).

The middle of *The Two Towers* breaks up each narrative strand of the book into smaller, shorter sections, and the viewer spends less time with each group of characters. The editors of *The Two Towers* (Michael Horton and Jabez Olssen) commented that they explored many variations on putting the jigsaw puzzle together, because there were many narrative strands to intertwine: Saruman in Orthanc; Arwen and Aragorn in Rivendell (a flashback); Arwen and Elrond in Rivendell; Aragorn alone; the Edoras exodus; the warg attack; Merry, Pippin and Treebeard in Fangorn; Frodo, Sam and Gollum in Ithilien, and so on.

The solution, of cutting around to each narrative plot more and more rapidly, wasn't entirely satisfactory. One can see why *The Two Towers* had such a protracted and difficult editing period, and why it was still being edited during sound dubbing and music recording sessions, as close to the deadline as possible (or with each deadline being pushed back again and again).

After Saruman in Isengard, the film shifts to Ithilien, opening on the shots of Gollum in the river hunting fish. Gollum is shown crawling through the river, over rocks, trying to catch a wriggling fish. The PR dept made much of Andy Serkis's bravery in performing this scene in icy conditions (the location was snow-covered and the practical effects department used heaters, fans, hoses and anything else they could find to melt the snow and ice. Brave of the actor, maybe, but he certainly didn't have to do it – stand-ins can be obtained for difficult scenes or scenes that an actor can't or won't perform). For the animators, this Gollum scene was a big challenge, mainly because it used water (always difficult in vfx). And it was Gollum in full body shots in daylight.

But Gollum chasing a CG fish was only the prelude to the meat of the scene, which was an argument between Frodo and Sam, with Frodo much more abrupt than before. The scene, blocked in a very routine fashion (with the two actors standing near some ruined masonry), illustrated the shifting allegiance and sympathy of Frodo towards Gollum, and his impatience with Sam for not understanding what possessing the ring means. Set in Ithilien, which was meant to be early March (i.e., equivalent to early Spring in Europe), it looked very sunny and Summery.

The following night scene, written and directed by Fran Walsh, was the most famous in the *Two Towers* film: the Gollum-Sméagol schizophrenia scene. It was a moment, as animator Randy Cook noted, when direction, writing, performance and visual fx came together really well to tell the story and reveal character. It was a triumph for Andy Serkis, his stand-out performance in the films, but it also meant months of work for the digital animators and compositors. It wasn't just a case of copying (or rotoscoping) each of Serkis's movements and expressions from a video monitor into a computer, and letting motion control data drive a bunch of pixels. As Jim Rygiel and Cook explained, the portrayal of Gollum went through many iterations before everyone was happy (the green light in Gollum's eyes when Stinker has the upper hand was dropped, but the facial expressions were altered from the Slinker side of Gollum).

As far as staging went, the schizophrenia scene was deceptively simple: Gollum is crouched on a fallen block of stone and talking to himself. But the camerawork and the editing, as well as the animation, is more subtle and complex. To introduce the idea of one side of Gollum's personality arguing with the other, the camera dollies rapidly a couple of times, back and forth. Then the film cuts from one shot to the other, but carefully controls the size of Gollum's head in the frame. Gollum also stares into the camera, or just past it. To remind viewers of the subject of the whole argument, the scene opens with a very big close-up of Frodo's hand clutching the ring as he sleeps nearby. And it closes with an elated Sméagol, who seems to have vanquished his nasty side, crying 'Sméagol's free!' and leaping on the ground. This mobile, 'happy' Sméagol will segue into the following scene, where Sméagol dashes into frame carrying rabbits.

The schizophrenia scene was a big success and was revived for the beginning of *The Return of the King* (but this time with Gollum staring into a pool while the hobbits slept nearby), and also the extra scene added in the extended cut of *The Two Towers* (and one or two other places, with Gollum arguing with himself in the midst of scenes). And it provided the basis for the final scene in *The Two Towers*. (The schizophrenia scene in *The Two Towers* was added later, however: the one in *The Return of the King* was scripted before shooting).

It's in the book (and reprised at the start of *The Return of the King*):

> "But the Precious holds the promise," the voice of Sméagol objected.
> "Then take it,": said the other, "and let's hold it ourselfs! Then we shall be master, *gollum*! Make the other hobbit, the nasty suspicious hobbit, make him crawl, yes, *gollum*!"
> "But not the nice hobbit?"
> "Oh no, not if it doesn't please us. Still he's a Baggins, my precious, yes, a Baggins. A Baggins stole it. He found it and he said nothing, nothing. We hates Baginnses."
> "Not, not this Baggins."
> "Yes, every Baggins. All peoples that keep the Preious. We must have it!"
> "But He'll see, He'll know. He'll take it from us!"
> "He sees. He knows. He heard us make silly promises – against His orders, yes. Must take it. The Wraiths are searching. Must take it." (TT, 298-9)

The chapter "Of Herbs and Stewed Rabbit" is next, a favourite with Tolkien fans, dominated by the bickering of Sam and Gollum over food (Frodo doesn't say anything throughout). It opens with Gollum springing into the scene and dropping two rabbits into a dozing Frodo's lap (Gollum's depicted as the dog or servant eager to serve its master). A C.U. of Gollum biting the rabbit and pulling out rubberized guts puts Frodo off his lunch a little bit. Sam takes over.

A cut to a C.U. of the stewed rabbit smooths over an hour or so of real time. Sam and Gollum chirp back and forth with chides and put-downs about food. Frodo is now up and about, in the background of the scene. The comic repartee between Sean Astin's Sam and Andy Serkis's digital character of Gollum dominates the scene. For the animators, this was one of the most difficult scenes to achieve, because it was a lengthy scene, because Gollum was seen in daylight and in full body, and because he had to interact closely with another actor, and really had to act.

In the midst of the banter, Frodo hears a bird call which sounds unnatural. Frodo moves off on his own, ending up lying on a rise above a valley. One of the armies travelling to Mordor lies below, shown in a big reveal. Sam and Gollum join Frodo on the rise. Gollum fills the audience in about the army over a brief montage of medium shots of the extras in costumes that fuse Arabic and Pacific cultures (these are probably Haradrim, as they have *mûmakil*, though are not named as such in the film. The troops seen at the Black Gate are presumably Easterlings. It gets confusing, as producer Mark Ordesky noted, which of the groups of men are allies and which are enemy. At the battles at the end of *The Return of the King*, including the Battle of Pelennor Fields, you've got Haradrim (Southrons), Easterlings, Corsairs, Wainriders, Wild Men and Variags as well as orcs). Cuts from the three characters watching on the rise to a wide shot of the valley now reveals two enormous *mûmakil*: basically they're elephants with towers and soldiers on top, though much larger, and fierce (they have gigantic tusks). Again, Alan Lee had drawn the oliphaunts like this, in battle, though these were bigger.

The next scene continues from the previous one, as Faramir (David Wenham) and his men attack, hidden in bushes and trees. The whole battle is depicted mainly from the point-of-view of Frodo and Sam up on the ridge (Gollum slinks away). The battle is basically an ambush, with the hooded Rangers firing arrows from a distance and the Haradrim running for their lives, covered with long lens shots to evoke the p.o.v. of the hobbits. This kind of ambush with hooded forest men and arrows flying everywhere is very familiar from Robin Hood movies (though the filmmakers stop short of having Faramir and his buddies swinging on vines or ropes, jumping on horses from branches, leaping down from trees or using nets to string up the enemy). Faramir's costume (with the white tree of Gondor prominent on his chest) could easily be Robin Hood's.

Frodo and Sam are transfixed, although they know they have to leave (Frodo says they have to get out of there, but Sam wants to stay and watch the oliphaunts). The *Extended Edition* of *The Two Towers* adds a little more of Faramir: now he seems to know that the hobbits are on the rise, and aims to protect them, by shooting down one of the Haradrim on the *mûmakil* that's careening towards them. The beast runs wildly to one side of the ridge, but close enough to the hobbits so that the Southron killed by Faramir falls out of the *mûmakil's* tower right in front of them. That act dubs Faramir as an ally, but when the hobbits meet him face to face, his allegiance is left uncertain (yet again in the movies – how many times did the adaptors milk that particular dramatic device?).

Another act separates Faramir from the enemy (and from most soldiers), because he immediately launches into a short soliloquy about death and war, using the victim from Haradwaith lying face-up on the ground before him as a pretext (in the extended version). Who was this man? Faramir muses, and wouldn't he have preferred to stay at home rather than go to war? That kind of speech, which not even Aragorn has offered, marks Faramir out as a different kind of hero: the philosophical soldier or warrior-poet. War will make corpses of us all is Faramir's parting-shot.

Establishing Faramir initially as a mediæval Wilfred Owen or Rupert Brooke renders his decision to take the ring to Osgiliath and Minas Tirith even more unconvincing; if he's such a sensitive guy, he probably wouldn't do that (the *Extended Edition* adds further œdipal tensions between Faramir and his father, which might explain how he wants to do his duty now, and do what Boromir could not: bring the ring to Gondor).

Frodo and Sam are captured (Sam manages to draw his sword to aid Frodo, but he's thrown to the ground). Faramir orders their hands bound. A spiky line from Frodo – about enemies of the Enemy not hindering them – was dropped from the theatrical cut.

The intense family relationships between the steward and his sons is partly explained in the book by Gandalf, who remarks that both Denethor and Faramir have the blood of Númenor in them, but not Boromir (HME, 8, 281).

Back to the Rohirrim by the lake. A light-hearted bit of banter first, from Gimli, on horseback, to Éowyn, talking about differentiating dwarf men and dwarf women, taken, according to Boyens and Walsh, from the appendices (a different gender politics is at work in this mediæval cosmos: Lady Éowyn is walking beside Gimli on the horse). Gimli's horse suddenly speeds up and Gimli takes a tumble. Aragorn laughs. Éowyn rushes to help him (falling from a horse can be extremely dangerous, of course, but here it's played for laffs).

The point-of-view shifts, in the second half of the scene, which has Théoden telling Aragorn about Éowyn and her back-story (how he should have been a father to her after the death of her father at the hands of orcs. That would chime with Aragorn, because his own mother was killed by orcs). Éowyn is now depicted from Aragorn's point-of-view, in a fitted brown dress (more practical – the Rohan court's equivalent of jeans, sneakers and a T-shirt), with Miranda Otto looking her best in warm, sidelit close-ups.

These images, and the cuts back to Aragorn looking at her, are presumably meant to indicate the first time that Aragorn really sees her for what she is:

> Grave and thoughtful was her glance, as she looked on the king with cool pity in her eyes. Very fair was her face, and her long hair was like a river of gold. Slender and tall she was in her white robe with silver; but strong she seemed and stern as steel, a daughter of kings. Thus Aragorn, for the first time in the full light of day beheld Éowyn, Lady of Rohan, and thought her fair, fair and cold, like a morning of pale spring that is not yet come to womanhood. (TT, 146)

A halt in the mountains on the way to Helm's Deep next. Rohirrim sit about eating and resting on a grassy hillside, against an impressive backdrop of snowy peaks. Éowyn brings some stew to Aragorn (offering it to Gimli first, who declines). The scene, a two-hander between Éowyn and the Dúnadan, has its light-hearted components (i.e., Éowyn handing around food, using the food as a pretext to get near Aragorn, and her stew being inedible, with Aragorn humouring her and accepting some and tasting it. It doesn't look as good as the stew Sam made in the earlier scene).

As producer Barrie Osborne noted, there was some concern that Éowyn would appear too coquettish, that her behaviour in the scene might detract from her otherwise stern and serious personality. Like the stable scene, the stew scene is not entirely satisfactory as a marker in the developing relationship (not yet a romance) between the shield maiden and the future king of Gondor (it's the kind of scene that Leigh Brackett could write so well – in, say, one of her many movies for Howard Hawks about tough men and strong women). It does, however, proffer some interesting information – about Aragorn's age (87), and that he's one of the fabled Dúnedain of the North. Éowyn mentions that she's heard that Aragorn fought with Thengel, her grandfather (Thengel was Théoden's father, and Éomer and Éowyn are Théoden's nephew and niece).

It's tricky finding the *right* context, reason and situation to put Aragorn and Éowyn together. The screenwriters opted to do that many more times than Tolkien does and, generally, they had Éowyn coming to Aragorn, rather than Aragorn approaching Éowyn (he's already pledged his love to Arwen, remember, even though, confusingly, he's also rejected her in a Rivendell flashback). So Éowyn comes him with a drink (in the Golden Hall), walks beside him in the caravan, brings food to him, and so on. And Aragorn has to respond politely, sensitively, but never giving a hint of a suggestion of the thought of seriously considering her romantically or erotically. The writers kept the erotic desire strictly one-way in the films. There were numerous opportunities for a love scene, of course, and many another Hollywood adaption of *The Lord of the Rings* might demand one. When Aragorn ventures into Meduseld at night, for example, and finds Éowyn sleeping on a couch (doesn't she have a room of her own?), it's an ideal opportunity for the discussion about Tolkien's childhood nightmare to slip into caresses and then sex.

A cut to Aragorn at night in a similar grassy landscape to the previous scene (but on his own), smoking his thin-stemmed pipe, lost in thought. Arwen's voice (speaking about the Evenstar) announces her first appearance in *The Two Towers* (quite a late introduction, really – indicative of her sub-plot and back-story status). The film moves into a flashback mode, linked by the idea of Aragorn sitting and musing, because he's in the same position in the flashback to Rivendell (lying on an elaborate wooden couch). When Aragorn says he must be dreaming, Arwen replies that it is a good dream (adding to the ambiguity about the scene – it's both memory and dream). She kisses him. All dreams have an erotic component, and Aragorn's are erotic too in this film.

A wide shot reveals the couple in yet another part of Rivendell, a bower open to the elements with a view of the valley beyond (Alex Funke, model DP, said that the idea in *The Two Towers* was to extend the Rivendell sets even further, to reveal other parts of the realm, that hadn't been seen in film one. In Tolkien's tome, Rivendell is the Last Homely House, big but not enormous, but in the 2001-2003 films it's more of a small village or town).

The lovers converse in Elvish, with English subtitles. Arwen wears a floaty pale mauve number. Aragorn stands; they kiss, embracing closely, and talk about Aragorn's destiny and responsibilities (what else do they talk about? – food, gossip, shopping, clothes, pop music, make-up... do you think this dress suits me? How about the Knicks last night, eh? Oh Aragorn, did you take the trash out? Oh, honey, when are you going to *shave* already?). The camera tilts down slowly to reveal... that flipping Evenstar brooch again. A choral cue on the track, with a solo English choir boy warbling.

Cut to: the Rohirrim column in daylight and a big close-up of the Evenstar around Aragorn's neck and a tilt up to Aragorn lost in thought. Éowyn, walking beside Aragorn, asks a question she wishes she hadn't asked (but can't help asking), about the woman who gave Aragorn the brooch. When Aragorn tells her about Arwen (this's the first time he's mentioned Arwen to Éowyn), she walks off ahead of him.

Poor Éowyn. The idea of a love triangle at the heart of the *Lord of the Rings* films was always a non-runner (producer Mark Ordesky admitted that a love triangle was suggested by the marketing, but it didn't really exist in the films themselves). The *Lord of the Rings* films, which added plenty of gore, blood and fight scenes to Tolkien's beloved tome, were surprisingly chaste when it came to presenting the aspects of love and romance (surprising, because so many liberties were taken with Tolkien's text, and the climate of Hollywood cinema favoured expressions of sexuality. There's certainly no suggestion of sexual relations between Aragorn and Arwen. Arwen may be the only two thousand seven hundred and seventy-seven year old virgin in the history of movies. (I haven't checked, but I bet there are 1,000s of examples of fan fiction and images around depicting Arwen and Aragorn getting freaky, or Aragorn tupping Éowyn, etc).

Aragorn never makes a move towards Éowyn in the films. He's so bloody perfect. He remains the faithful lover to Arwen at all times. He never even encourages Éowyn verbally. They barely touch at all, except when handing over a cup (she hugs him in joy after Helm's Deep). They could be the chaste lovers in a Japanese melodrama by Yasujiro Ozu, always standing apart. It might have been tempting to allow one lapse into erotic contact, to have Aragorn clasp Éowyn to him just once. But no, the screenwriters resisted all temptation. How noble of them! (In an early draft, Aragorn and Éowyn were shown in bed together with, improbably, Arwen arriving at their chamber and embracing Aragorn while Éowyn watched).

Yes, Aragorn says nothing to suggest to Éowyn that he's interested in her romantically. On the other hand, he doesn't actively *discourage* her. One word to Éowyn could explain that he's utterly devoted to Arwen. But the screenwriters Philippa Boyens and Fran Walsh (who handled the romantic storylines, as well as everything else) probably reckoned that if Aragorn had spurned Éowyn too early in the films, it would have wrecked the romantic tension between them (they wanted to keep it fizzling along with the will-they?-won't-they? tension beloved of TV soap opera and sit-com writers, and romance novelists). The sub-plot would've folded too soon.

So Aragorn also acts like an egotistical male who quite likes the fact that Éowyn fancies him, and delays putting her right on that score. Or maybe he's keeping his options open, if it doesn't work out with Arwen, and the elf maid heads for the West. Some might say that Aragorn's behaving a little selfishly and immaturely, wrongly giving Éowyn hope that one day they might...

Back in Rivendell again, this time at night (it's always late afternoon, evening or night at Rivendell, never full-blown noon), and this time Elrond is talking with Aragorn (presumably it's the night of the previous flashback scene). Elrond takes a more stern, paternalistic line with Aragorn, but they're still talking about Aragorn fulfilling his destiny (ever get the feeling this storyline has been stretched very thin, like butter over too much toast, like Bilbo says of the ring?). Screenwriting manuals suggest 'difficulty, difficulty, difficulty' for your characters, and Fran Walsh and Philippa Boyens rack their brains to come up with obstacles.

The third Rivendell flashback depicts Aragorn kitted up and ready to go (with the fellowship), walking along a corridor in another part of the elven kingdom. Arwen waylays him, saying he can't leave like that, without saying goodbye (so presumably they didn't sleep together last night, then – perhaps their last night ever together. How honourable of them!). Moving in and out of Elvish and English, the lovers are again discussing their relationship. Aragorn wants to return the Evenstar to her, but she won't have it (it was a gift, she tells him). Aragorn tells Arwen that it was a dream they had (he's effectively ending their relationship). This's why Arwen looks pretty washed out at the parting of the fellowship at Rivendell's gates in the *Extended Edition* of *The Fellowship of the Ring,* because she's just heard that lover boy has jilted her.

Aragorn sells Éowyn the same line when he scuppers her hopes of romance just before he leaves for the Paths of the Dead in *The Return of the King*. Note how the screenwriters stretched the potential for romance between Aragorn and Éowyn right up until the last possible moment, when Aragorn splits off from the Rohirrim and heads for the Battle of Pelennor Fields by his own route. There wouldn't be another decent moment for that encounter between Aragorn and Éowyn, not just because Aragorn is going to be in a different place geographically, but also because it's a point in the film when the narrative has to begin intensifying and building up to the climax.

Other screenwriters might've played the Aragorn-Éowyn (non) romance differently, building in twists and turns. It would've been very cool if Éowyn had turned about 180 degrees in that final encounter at Dunharrow: Aragorn might've approached Éowyn and said there was something he had to tell her.

EXT. NIGHT. DUNHARROW.

ARAGORN
It was a dream.

Thus ARAGORN hands her his favourite line. ÉOWYN, taken by surprise for a beat, is swift to respond.

> ÉOWYN
> What?

> ARAGORN
> It was dream, Éowyn, you and me. But it can't be.

ÉOWYN can't believe what she's hearing.

> ÉOWYN
> What are you talking about? You thought I *liked* you? You are very wrong, my lord!

ÉOWYN laughs. ARAGORN steps closer to her. She swiftly draws her sword. At that moment, THÉODEN happens by. He glances quickly from ÉOWYN to ARAGORN.

> THÉODEN
> What's going on here?

And so on and on.

Let's face it, the romantic aspects of the *Lord of the Rings* films were fairly unengaging. The glossy photography, choral music and pretty gowns couldn't hide the fact that there wasn't a lot of chemistry there. A filmmaker from the golden age of Hollywood – Howard Hawks, Max Ophüls or George Cukor, say – might've made the romance wittier, pithier, sexier, faster and cooler.

Up next in the 2002 *The Two Towers* mooovie is the warg attack on the Rohirrim caravan. The warg skirmish acts in the same fashion as a chase or confrontation between the heroes and the villains in the middle of a film. It's an act two chase or battle, in which the heroes have to meet the villains (or the villains' henchmen), suffer some losses, but get away, able to continue their quest. In a typical Hollywood movie, there's a car chase in act two (a subway chase, a plane chase), or a bar brawl, or a fencing duel, or a raid on the villains' stronghold, but the heroes slip away at the end of it intact.

The warg attack is the kind of scene that Hollywood producers demand of filmmakers to spice up the sagging centre of a film, when all of the components of plot, desires and character have been laid out and the heroes are working towards their goal. (And the film adaption of *The Two Towers* does need spicing up here, from the typical Hollywood producers' point-of-view, because a lot of the preceding scenes have been talky, dealing with Edoras, the funeral of Théodred, the exodus, Aragorn dreaming about Arwen and Rivendell, and so on.)

The warg-Rohirrim skirmish, like a mid-film fight or chase, doesn't really move along the plot at all. The only significant story point to come out of it (Háma's death doesn't really count) is Aragorn's disappearance, which's also played, *very falsely*, as a death, with Legolas, Théoden and Gimli, and later Éowyn, grieving for him. That fake death is silliest aspect to come out of the warg attack, and one of the biggest mistakes in the *Lord of the Rings* films. The filmmakers tease the audience with the apparent death of a major character when the punters know full well that Aragorn can't have disappeared halfway through the second film of a three film set (especially when he has been signposted in forty-foot high neon throughout as the future king, and the last film's called *The Return of the King*).

As originally scripted, the warg attack on the Rohirrim would've taken place at night at Edoras. Presumably, Aragorn would have been separated from the others in the *melée*, and found his way to Helm's Deep in a similar manner as in the final film. The warg battle might have been a better scene at Edoras at night. As filmed, the warg episode was a haphazard piece of filmmaking, put together on the fly by the second unit, directed by John Mahaffie (there's a nice shot in one of the documentaries of storyboard artist Christian Rivers working away in an anorak sitting on a rock at the location, rapidly putting together shots that would be filmed that day. Many films wind up being made this way, with last minute alterations and additions. Even a filmmaker like Alfred Hitchcock, who liked everything to be planned in advance, would alter scenes on the spur of the moment).

Before the wargs and orcs attack, there is a prelude: Háma and Gamling ride ahead; Legolas stands on the brow of a hill, looking into the distance; a warg leaps down from some rocks and kills Háma; there's a skirmish; Gamling's fighting the orc rider with swords; Legolas downs the warg, and swiftly dispatches the out-rider. A cut back to the column: Aragorn is now alert to the danger; Gimli climbs onto a horse, which doesn't quite obey him to charge forward; Théoden commands Éowyn to lead the women and children to Helm's Deep, but she wants to stay and fight; as the men ride on horseback to head off the wargs, there's yet another Aragorn-Éowyn moment, as she watches Aragorn turning his horse (in slow motion).

A wide shot, from Legolas's point-of-view, reveals the wargs streaming over a hill like a pack of dogs or wolves. Orlando Bloom broke his rib during shooting of the warg scene, so the shot where he climbs onto the horse couldn't be completed. Instead, Bloom acted the beginning of the slow motion shot, then, as Randy Cook explained, he turned into a bunch of pixels in broad daylight, in a full body shot, in the middle of the frame, and leapt onto the horse (i.e., it was a hand-over from live action to digital effects. But it wasn't the first example in a movie by any means). It became a favourite Leggy moment with fans.

These shots, of the Rohirrim riding into battle, are heroic images, in slight slow motion, with a big drumbeat cue from Howard Shore. A whip pan between the two sides (wargs and horses) shows them rushing headlong towards each other (and when they clash, the music stops abruptly. Exactly the same device was used for the charge of the Rohirrim at Pelennor Fields).

The gags and beats during the skirmish include Théoden stabbing a warg in the jaw; Gimli falling off Legolas's horse; Gimli facing off against a warg and being saved by Legolas's arrow ('that one counts as mine', Gimli tells Legolas); Gimli gets trapped under a warg carcass, lying on his back; an orc climbs on the beast but Gimli kills it by twisting its neck; when Gimli thinks he's safe at last, yet another warg menaces him, appearing over the top of the warg crushing him; Gimli is rescued this time by Aragorn, who grabs a spear out of the ground while galloping his horse towards Gimli and hurls it at the warg.

Finally, Aragorn is unhorsed by a diving warg. He runs alongside a warg rider, climbs up to fight with the orc rider (Sharku, leader of the wargs), knocking him out with a head butt; Sharku falls off the warg, but Aragorn is dragged along by the animal, unable to get his hand loose from a leather strap (like the famous car race in *Rebel Without a Cause*). Aragorn goes over the cliff with the warg. That is the signal for the end of the fight. Subsequent shots show the survivors surveying the field and calling for Aragorn.

The orc rider, Sharku (Jed Brophy's buried under inches of prosthetics and make-up) is still alive. Legolas pries the Evenstar out of his clutches, and Sharku tells them, before he dies, that Aragorn fell (it's appropriate that Legolas takes up the Evenstar, not Gimli or Théoden, because Legolas is an elf, a link to Arwen, Rivendell and Aragorn's elvish associations. The notion of using the Evenstar yet again was added later).

Théoden joins Legolas and Gimli staring down at the river way below. The sequence closes with Théoden acting ruthlessly: leave the dead he commands (would the Théoden of the book order that? The filmmakers have *completely misunderstood* or *misrepresented* the heroic, noble Anglo-Saxon or Viking king and Rohirrim that Tolkien envisaged). Legolas and Gimli aren't happy about that. They remain at the rock's edge, staring down, unwilling to abandon their friend. That they don't head off down the cliff instantly, to look for their friend, or at least to recover his body from the river, is *completely ridiculous* (the viewer's already seen them give Boromir a proper send-off, so it's the least they'd do for a noble lord and loyal friend like Aragorn). Aragorn's 'death' and return makes everyone who cares about him – Legolas, Gimli, Éowyn, Théoden – look like *dicks*. The more you think about this sequence, the more dork-like it becomes. It's *ABYSMAL. IT STINKS*.

ACT FOUR

The warg-Rohirrim battle is an event dramatic and violent enough to separate Aragorn from his companions (nothing less would make him leave them, but they just wander off when Théoden tells them to), and puts him at his lowest point – near death and all alone (there were a couple of dicey moments in the shooting of this sequence, when actor Viggo Mortensen disappeared under the river, and when Mortensen trained his horse to nuzzle him and bend down to let him climb on. As Barrie Osborne remarked, it was a nerve-wracking time watching one of his lead actors lying next to the horse, when a slip-up could have put Mortensen out of the schedule for some time).

Separating Aragorn allows him to commune psychically, as it were, with Arwen. She even appears to him, as in the earlier dream, to kiss him back to life on the riverbank. Then, her duty done of reviving him, she fades away. Instead of the warg attack, a solution more in keeping with Tolkien of linking with Arwen might've had Aragorn thinking about her in the halls of Helm's Deep at night, with maybe Legolas asking him about Arwen. There are numerous ways of having your hero dream about his lover faraway without appearing to kill him.

Yes, Aragorn does also get to see the orc army marching on Helm's Deep, which gives the vision more power than if an anonymous Rohirrim out-rider had seen it, and when the information's related to the king, it has more impact than coming from a messenger.

A brief scene has Éowyn and the women, old folk and children walking to Helm's Deep and seeing it from a distance. It nestles below mountains, with a very wide plain in front of it. The following images offer descriptive shots of Helm's Deep, introducing the last major location of *The Two Towers* (and a sizable portion of the budget). A powerful orchestral cue accompanies a Steadicam shot tracking behind Éowyn as she enters the main gate of the fortress. Extras are dotted around performing the 'general background action' that extras typically perform. Éowyn appears to act as an overseer of preparations. A huge crane shot is the hero Helm's Deep shot at this point, moving up very high over the whole complex (with plentiful digital extensions to the set built in the quarry, including the whole lower level, with its people walking about, and walking up the causeway to the main gate). This kind of major visual effects shot demands a big piece of music, and gets it, with the Rohirrim theme now played by the orchestra. (These first glimpses of Helm's Deep also introduce the different miniatures which depict the fortress at different scales, built for different shots. But the full-scale set construction was also substantial, so these shots also show off the money).

A very minor subplot is resolved here, with a brief scene of the mother (Morwen), seen earlier during the sack of the Westfold sending her kids Freda and Éothain to Edoras, being reunited with her offspring. A big hug. Ahh, bless...

The king enters Helm's Deep next, returning from the warg attack (the first day of shooting for Bernard Hill and Miranda Otto). The viewpoint is again with Éowyn: she runs to the greet them. The bad news of Aragorn's death is not delivered to Éowyn by Théoden (another alteration of his character from the book, as Tolkien's Théoden wouldn't shirk from that duty, even though it was invented for the film); instead, Théoden seems keen to avoid her anxious gaze. It's up to Gimli to tell her 'he fell' (the clue to his imminent resurrection is in the dialogue: the same was said in the films of Gandalf: 'he fell'). The film shifts into slightly slow motion and a solo choral cue over a close-up of Éowyn's face in grief, for another of those emotional movie surges we all know and love.

Helm's Deep in the film consists of the main keep or fortress, the Hornburg; the Deeping Wall which stretches across the valley and protects Helm's Deep behind; and the caves behind the stronghold. There was also a long, curving causeway up to the main gate. The filmmakers followed Tolkien's descriptions of Helm's Deep closely (with Alan Lee leading the design of the miniatures and matte paintings). But the great Dike, the settlements, and the other elements, such as roads, were left out. Once again, the area in front of a stronghold, as with Minas Tirith, is oddly empty, which it so wouldn't be.

The next scene is up on the battlements (the Deeping Wall), with Théoden issuing orders to his soldiers. A slow track past Théoden and his guards moves into a M.S. of the Deeping-stream. Wormtongue is now heard in voiceover explaining that Helm's Deep has one weak point – right after Théoden has just said that the defences are impregnable. The shot offers moment of suspense, with the filmmakers placing the audience ahead of the heroes. The culvert is foreshadowing which will pay off later, and will be pivotal in the battle.

Wormtongue's voice continues with a cut to the interior of Orthanc. A C.U. and pull back reveals Saruman pouring gunpowder into a large egg-shaped metal container that resembles a mine. To underscore the danger this device possesses, Saruman grips Wormtongue's arm when he brings a candle a little too close. Wormtongue's question about an assault on Helm's Deep requiring a huge force is answered by a visual device: Saruman leads Wormtongue out onto the balcony above Isengard, and the camera follows. (DP Andrew Lesnie said the filmmakers were after a casual kind of movement with the camera, as if a character were simply moving from one room to another, so that the reveal of Saruman's orc army would be casual).

Dubbed the 'Nuremberg scene', for obvious reasons, Saruman addresses his army while Wormtongue looks on in awe. Saruman encourages his army: 'to war!' The orcs are chanting in Black Speech (this was recorded at a cricket match in New Zealand by the crowds in the stands; the sound team of *Spartacus* had recorded a cricket match forty years earlier, for the 'I'm Spartacus!' scene).

The quotation from Leni Riefenstahl's famous 1935 film *Triumph of the Will* is a shorthand way of defining Saruman's character and intentions (the scene had also appeared in the 1978 *The Lord of the Rings*. Here, as in 1977's *Star Wars*, it's used without irony. It's not as controversial as it is in *Star Wars*, because Saruman and the orcs are the baddies, and equating them with Nazis is OK in Hollywood movies).

Although Tolkien's book may be set in some mythical pre-mediæval period (i.e., the land of Faërie), the narrative devices employed by the filmmakers (and Tolkien too) were very modern. Possibly only a relative few among the global cinema audience of the *Lord of the Rings* films will have seen *Triumph des Willens*, but many of them will have seen allusions to it. (Let's face it, *Triumph of the Will* isn't shown regularly – or at all – on TV; you won't see it after a re-run of *Friends* or *Family Guy*).

At the end of the brief Nuremberg scene, when Saruman-Hitler cries 'to war!' there's a rapid track backwards from Orthanc, past a forest of spears (another quote from *Triumph of the Will*, and also used by Terry Gilliam in *The Adventures of Baron Munchausen* [1989]). The mood (and music) continues into the following scene, which comprises impressive shots of the orcs of the White Hand marching to war (they carry long pikes which form clusters as they march past the camera).

For some critics, the quotation from *Triumph of the Will*, and the conscious equation of Saruman with Hitler, was problematic. One critic remarked that Hitler would have loved the *Lord of the Rings* films (and so would Leni Riefenstahl).

Treebeard and the hobbits are next up, after quite a gap. The filmmakers slam Merry, Pippin and the ent into the same frame as the previous scene: a L.S. has Treebeard carrying the hobbits in the lower half of the screen and Isengard in the upper section. Cut to a C.U. of Pippin first (because it's Pippin who comes up with the idea of telling Treebeard to go South) and then Merry. The hobbits climb up onto the upper branches of Treebeard: they can see over the tops of the trees (that's handy, because, at 14 feet tall, Treebeard wouldn't be the tallest thing in the forest at all). An extreme long shot, tracking with the hobbits' movement on top of the ent, shows the orc army in the far distance, spreading out across the plain. Merry states the obvious: 'it's Saruman'. *Duh*.

A cut to Aragorn, unconscious, floating in the river (you might say, 'why doesn't he drown?' And the film answers: 'don't ask such stupid questions!'). A montage of images, many in dissolves and superimpositions, comprises this scene (images of water, Aragorn, Arwen lying on her back in Rivendell). The solo female vocalist on the track emphasizes that Aragorn is travelling in different realms (psychological or spiritual), not simply a river somewhere between Edoras and Helm's Deep.

Aragorn winds up lying on the riverbank, with sparkling water behind him. A low angle profile close-up offers an unusual view of the unconscious Aragorn when Arwen appears above him, leaning down to kiss him. In voiceover, she says 'may the grace of the Valar protect you', then she fades away, and his eyes open.

One of the funnier moments in the *Lord of the Rings* films occurs next, featuring Brego the Wonder Horse. Big, low angle C.U.s portray the horse nuzzling Aragorn awake, kneeling, and Aragorn hitching a ride. Images of an exhausted Aragorn riding through Rohan follow. According to the writers, actor Viggo Mortensen wanted to show how Aragorn gets back to life and back to Helm's Deep. Why the filmmakers bothered to show this, when they didn't bother to explain hundreds of other narrative points, is a mystery (maybe they wanted to indulge one of their main stars. Mortensen offered up numerous suggestions about the narrative during production). In terms of the grand scale of the film, seeing how Brego kneels and allows Aragorn to climb aboard is fairly minor, compared to the outrageous scene earlier, where Legolas and Gimli accept Aragorn's death and abandon him to the river.

Back to Arwen, now revealed as still in Rivendell. The cut to the same shot of Arwen lying down as in the Aragorn riverbank montage hints that Arwen somehow visited Aragorn in spirit, helping to revive him (the audience had already seen Arwen perform a little of that elvish magic in *The Fellowship of the Ring*, when she brought Frodo back to consciousness at the Ford of Bruinen, using the same phrase of 'the grace of the Valar'). These Rivendell scenes are set in the present of the film; they are not flashbacks to the time of the earlier scenes between Aragorn and Arwen, when Aragorn left with the Fellowship.

Daddy shows up to interrupt Arwen's astral travelling. He begins with an ominous parental injunction: 'it is time' he tells her in Elvish. The ships are leaving for Valinor. The *mise-en-scène* is white curtains blowing in the wind, subdued colours (all in the blue, black and grey end of the spectrum: it's blue and muted because life is draining out of Rivendell, out of the elves, and out of Arwen, as later developments of this scene reveal). Elrond moves around the room slowly, while Arwen remains sitting on another of those elegant elvish couches. He introduces the most painful subject for humans: mortality. As he does, there's a cut to a big close-up of Arwen, looking into camera, a wide-eyed, melancholy look, wind suddenly blowing her hair (Liv Tyler at her best in a Goth but also glossy manner). Fade out to white after an even bigger C.U. of Elrond's face. (The looks into camera here in the Galadriel montage are effective).

Then comes a favourite shot for Alex Funke and Randy Cook, heads of the models and animation teams on the films. For Funke, it's a spiritual image that contains a lot of narrative information. The picture Elrond paints for Arwen is one of her future life if she chose to remain in Middle-earth with Aragorn. And it's one particular moment from the life she might have with Aragorn: his death (as if Elrond wants to frighten as well as warn his daughter of what's to come).

The movement of the shot is a slow track out from Aragorn lying on a tomb, in Minas Tirith, with the White Tower visible in the centre of the frame, and many domes and buildings (so presumably this is Aragorn lying in state in the House of the Stewards, in the year 120 of the Fourth Age). The shot combines live action, practical effects, miniatures for the city beyond, and matte paintings. Aragorn dead has grey hair, a crown, a red robe, his sword on his chest, while Arwen is in an elegant black widow costume (there are other mourners nearby). There's a dissolve in the middle of the shot, from Aragorn dead to a stone statue of the king, in exactly the same pose.

In the second half of the shot, Arwen is now alone, standing beside her husband's tomb, with dead leaves blowing. Elrond is speaking in voiceover throughout this scene, so it is very much his view of his daughter's future that he lays out for her. And he continues to narrate the scene when it moves from Minas Tirith to a shot of Arwen in black walking in a wood (presumably to suggest the time after Aragorn's death when Arwen returned to Lórien, where they had first courted, to die at Cerin Amroth, in Fourth Age 121).

So there is plenty of narrative detail packed into the shot, although it unfolds on screen in a deceptively simple manner. If the audience doesn't know all of the back-story behind that shot, it still has the impact of showing that Arwen will be alone after Aragorn's death: the film has often reminded viewers that Arwen is an immortal elf and Aragorn's a mortal human. But Elrond's vision stops short in one important respect: that Arwen died not long after Aragorn, in 121 of the Fourth Age, and that she *chose* to die rather than live without Aragorn. There is also a child, which Elrond may have foreseen but omitted from his vision (as Arwen suggests to Elrond in *The Return of the King*, after she's had a vision of the future himself and sees her child).

The idea for the flashforward to Aragorn's death was Frances Walsh's; she recalled that a Tolkien fan had written to her, drawing her attention to the passage in the appendices evoking the scene. Walsh wanted to honour that scene, and directed the sequence. (So although Peter Jackson usually receives all the credit for everything in the *Lord of the Rings* films, this scene, a favourite for some viewers, was conceived, written and directed by Fran Walsh).

> But Arwen went forth from the House [narrated Tolkien in *The Return of the King*], and the light of her eyes was quenched, and it seemed to her people that she had become cold and grey as nightfall in winter that comes without a star. Then she said farewell to Eldarion, and to her daughters and to all whom she had loved; and she went out from the city of Minas Tirith and passed away to the land of Lórien, and dwelt there alone under the fading trees until winter came. (RK, 425)

As far as Elrond is concerned, Arwen agreeing to be mortal means agreeing to die in what to an elf seems like a very short time (she has 120 years with Aragorn, which's a blink of an eye by elven standards). There are, of course, many moments from Arwen's future that Elrond could chose to illuminate for her, but he has a point to make, so he shows her just one aspect of it. In a way, this 120-year vision, though an addition, is in the spirit of Tolkien's book. Remember that Tolkien remarked that the big theme of *The Lord of the Rings* was death and immortality. The scenes between Arwen and Elrond in part explore those two choices (or 'dooms' as Tolkien called them), the choices of elves and humans. 'For Elrond... all chances of the War of the Ring were fraught with sorrow', as Tolkien put it (HME, 12, 257).

A white-out fade brings the scene back to the Rivendell, and to that luscious close-up of Arwen, now weeping. A female voice sings on the soundtrack, the aural embodiment, perhaps, of Arwen's quivering, melancholy soul. Daddy now approaches Arwen on the couch, sitting beside her and saying (in Elvish), 'do I also not have your love?' (So that's it! Elrond's getting a little jealous and possessive, envious of the intense, world-shattering love Arwen has for Aragorn. It's almost as if Elrond is suggesting, as so many fathers have done, that no man's good enough for his daughter. Not even the most eligible bachelor in Middle-earth – who's also the greatest warrior, and the future king). Remember, though, that in the story related in the appendix of *The Lord of the Rings*, one of the reasons that Aragorn wanders in the wilds, and aids the 'free peoples', is to prove himself worthy of Arwen in her dad's eyes. He has to become king of the world to be good enough for Elrond.

Father and daughter hug. Ahh, how sweet... The mood of the scene continues into the next scene, of the elves leaving Rivendell (at night, presumably that same night, or one soon after). They are hooded, sombre, carrying white lamps, and drifting along in slight slow motion. Elrond is watching from somewhere above. Arwen glances up at him. He frowns. Howard Shore's loveliest elf music wafts over the scene (the music cue for the reveal of Rivendell in *The Fellowship of the Ring*).

Next up is the 'Galadriel montage', where the elf queen and the lord of Imladris appear to commune with each other psychically. The montage sequence is a summing up of the state of affairs in Middle-earth from the *elves'* point-of-view (Saruman performed a summary from the villains' p.o.v. earlier, and Gandalf laid out his view of things to Aragorn in the halt on the way to Edoras). The ring theme music, which opened the whole three films, reminds viewers that the ring is foremost in Galadriel's communication with Elrond. (The sequence is narrated (and thus controlled) by Galadriel in voiceover; Elrond doesn't say anything, but is shown standing at a window, and in his library).

Galadriel is introduced in a giant close-up, speaking to camera in Elvish. Cut to Elrond at a window in Rivendell, doing his best mean or worried stare. Galadriel now continues, but in English, in voiceover: a cut to Saruman in Orthanc, consulting the *palantír* (suggesting that Galadriel knows that Saruman has been communicating with Enemy, in which case Gandalf would also have known). Shots of the orc army. The Eye. An extreme long shot of the Osgiliath miniature, a big, vaguely circular city surrounded by endless plains. A cloud shadow creeps over it. A cut to Frodo and Sam being blindfolded and led by Faramir's men (the blindfolds handily cover the faces of the body doubles, as Philippa Boyens pointed out). Back to Galadriel, speaking slightly off-camera, in English. Then one of the iconic images in the three films: the spinning One Ring shot, taken from the prologue (odd, in a way, that this shot wasn't employed more often – there is a fade to black before the spinning ring image, to give it more impact). More talk from the elf queen of the One Ring, and its affects on the elves. A cut back to Frodo. A long shot of Ithilien. A medium shot of Frodo and Sam being handed from one ranger to another, now in Henneth Annûn. A cut to Sauron's Eye and Barad-dûr, with nazgûl flying nearby. A shot of Elrond shows him now in his library (still alone) and contemplating the Alan Lee painting of Isildur and the Dark Lord. Galadriel wonders whether they should leave men to their fate.

In the midst of the Galadriel montage there are images describing what is happening to Frodo and Sam in the present: being taken captive by Faramir and his boys and led to the Window on the West. Galadriel says that the Captain of Gondor will try to take the ring. The montage could continue indefinitely, to show Gandalf riding to find Éomer, or Aragorn lost in the wilderness, or the preparations for war at Helm's Deep, and so on.

But the overarching purpose of the 'Galadriel montage' is to remind viewers of the ring, the ring, the ring.

Another map scene follows, between Faramir and his lieutenant, Madril (John Bach). This scene was added very late in post-production (it was put together by Peter Jackson at short notice in London on a domestic video camera to illustrate what was required, with the production team back in New Zealand drawing the map and shooting it). It was thought that the audience would benefit from another clarifying scene of the forces, politics and geography at this point in the story. So Faramir explains that Sauron will attack from this direction, and Saruman from that (all done with voiceovers and inserts of the map). Once again, the 1980 Rankin/Bass cartoon got there first, with a hand and a map explaining things.

A rapid pull-back from Frodo and Sam having their blindfolds taken off is next; they're standing in the middle of the cave, revealing the Henneth Annûn set, with the rangers busying themselves in the background, and the waterfall beyond. Frodo and Sam are comped into the scene (rather than doubles being used). Faramir begins questioning the hobbits. There are numerous departures from the book at this point: no mention to Faramir of Aragorn as Isildur's heir and the Sword of Elendil, no Sam standing up to Faramir, no Faramir tricking Frodo with words, no Faramir mentioning Gandalf, or Lórien, no lengthy disquisitions on Isildur's Bane, and so on. (Note that Frodo doesn't mention that their mission was overseen by Elrond and Gandalf – Faramir's the 'wizard's pupil', and telling Faramir that it was Gandalf's and Elrond's idea to destroy the ring would be enough).

The *Special Extended Edition* of *The Two Towers* adds a fascinating series of scenes here, which would have enhanced the theatrical cut greatly. At the end of Faramir's initial conversation with Frodo and Sam, he is alerted by Frodo mentioning Boromir. That offers a link to the next scene: Faramir's vision of Boromir, dead, in the boat on the Anduin. First, Faramir is shown alone, holding Boromir's cloven horn. Cut to a shot of Faramir wading in a wide river with mist in the distance. The eerie high-pitched singing and low rumble help to announce this new narrative segment (part-dream, part-memory), as do the dissolves and fades to white. The boat floats past Faramir and he stares at it but doesn't approach it. Inside, Boromir is in exactly the same pose as he was when set afloat at Rauros by Aragorn, Gimli and Legolas.

Cut to Faramir, back in the cave, alone, holding the broken horn. Sounds of the crowd cheering at Osgiliath are heard for a few moments before the scene cuts to Boromir at Osgiliath. He's holding a standard in his left hand, with the White Tree of Gondor on a flag. He's standing on a building above a square, with hundreds of soldiers listening to him below. A big vista of the city of Osgiliath is shown. Boromir is addressing the troops. He draws his sword and gives a short speech about Osgiliath being taken from the enemy, 'For Gondor!'

A brief reunion between the brothers occurs next, down on the ground, with the characters surrounded by soldiers in armour. Boromir sports elaborate armour, with the White Tree engraved on it. This's the first time the viewer's seen the brothers together; Boromir calls Faramir 'little brother' and jokes with him. They share a drink, but are soon interrupted by the approach of Denethor (John Noble; there are extras in armour all around them). An aside to Faramir, about Denethor not giving them a moment's peace, illustrates the resentful attitude Boromir has towards his father (Faramir never goes that far). Denethor makes his way through his soldiers, congratulating them on their victory (he's clad in a dark grey robe, shoulder length grey hair, but no beard, like Faramir and Boromir. It's quite a Nordic look, with the fur collar, not really an equivalent for Minas Tirith as Rome or the Holy Roman Empire, which's how Tolkien described Gondor at one time. Denethor's intense, forbidding, patriarchal – but aren't all of Tolkien's older male characters like that? Few ever laugh, or even smile).

As soon as daddy reaches his sons, and has given his elder son a hug, and praised him on his success, he's already handing them the line of preferring one son over the other. Poor old Faramir, he can't do nuttin' right for big daddy. Whatever he tries, whatever he says, daddy don't like it. Denethor castigates Faramir with not being able to protect Osgiliath (in the films, Osgiliath will be Faramir's bane: he fails to protect it this time, he has to retreat from it again in *The Return of the King*, and makes a suicidal attempt at taking it, winding up nearly dead).

The model for the scenes in the picture between Faramir, Denethor and Boromir, which seem intense and grown-up, are still fairy tales, with the favourite son and the outcast son, and also Biblical and Shakespearean sources. Boromir pipes up with some positive words for Faramir, but Denethor will hear none of it.

The sequence shifts when Denethor leads Boromir around a corner, turning it into a two-hander scene. Denethor launches into a long speech about Elrond calling a meeting at Rivendell and Denethor's guess that it's about Isildur's Bane, a great prize which he wants Boromir to go and get for him (Noble's Denethor becomes quieter and more intense as the speech progresses, leaning closer to Boromir).

Just as significant as the father bestowing a mission upon his son is Boromir's reaction to it. Sean Bean's Boromir moves into that doubtful, anxious mode which the audience has already seen from the Council of Elrond sequence onwards. 'Isildur's Bane', Boromir mutters darkly (no, don't laugh), quaking at the very thought of it. Bean's performance here, and the script, emphasizes in green neon that our Boromir is not scared by the journey to Imladris, but by the fact that he's got to obtain the One Ring. (It's rather silly that Denethor, one of the wisest minds in Gondor, and who's clever enough to guess that Elrond's called the meeting because of the ring, should imagine that Boromir will be able to obtain it single-handed).

The actors move apart when Boromir attempts to decline his father's task, bringing Faramir into the loop. Faramir offers to go to Rivendell. But, oh no, the stern patriarch won't give the mission to Faramir; he will entrust it only to Boromir.

The next scene is a different time, and a slightly different place (i.e., another section of the Osgiliath outdoor set). It could be the next day, or a week later, or a month later, whatever. Boromir is on horseback, kitted-up and leaving for Rivendell (he's wearing the same costume as his first scene in the films, the entry at Rivendell). It's a short parting scene. Boromir tells Faramir: 'remember today, little brother'. And, hey, what is Faramir doing in the very next shot: remembering. (The relationship, right down to the phrase 'little brother', recalls the central buddy relation in *The 13th Warrior*).

An officer enters and whispers in Faramir's ear, presumably about the discovery of Gollum. The next scene has Faramir waking Frodo (by just standing there, it seems, or maybe Frodo's a very light sleeper) and telling him to come with him (it's a reprise of the scene where Galadriel woke Frodo in the night; and in the book, Sam went along with Frodo both times). A pretty matte painting wide shot reveals Ithilien by moonlight – like looking at an illustration of *The Lord of the Rings* on a poster or in a calendar. Faramir waxes lyrical for a moment on this vista:

> '"Moonset over Gondor. Fair Ithil, as he goes from Middle-earth, glances upon the white locks of old Mindolluin. It is worth a few shivers."' (TT, 365)

The camera takes Frodo's point-of-view above the Forbidden Pool, with the waterfall beside it, and Gollum a tiny figure on the rocks below.

Cut to Gollum with a fish, sitting on a rock in the pool. He bashes it on a rock to kill it and sings a brief, humorous ditty about juicy sweet fish (ad-libbed by Andy Serkis on the motion capture stage, but the words are in the novel, Book 4, Chapter 2, "The Passage of the Marshes"). Serkis's Gollum is more playful than the Gollum in the 1978 film (or the BBC 1981 radio series). Portraying Gollum in a light-hearted mood is a dramatist's preparation for the violence of the next scene: his capture and punishment. The scene is intended to elicit the audience's sympathy with Gollum, but also to illustrate some of Frodo's own growing empathy with the 'wretched and hungry' former ringbearer (TT, 368).

The next scene has Frodo approaching Gollum alone. Gollum eventually comes along, with a fish in his mouth. Frodo repeatedly asks him to trust him, to trust master. When Gollum is captured by men on either side of some rocks, and covered with a hood, Frodo tells Gollum not to struggle. Frodo's pangs of pity are palpable.

Cleverly, the filmmakers aim to have it both ways: to have the audience partly behind Faramir and his rangers who capture Gollum (this's also Sam's view in the scene in the book), but also partly behind Gollum (and Frodo). But in the next scene the sympathy for Faramir and his soldiers evaporates under the cruel, over-the-top treatment they deal out, punching and kicking the creature, and throwing him about. That turns them not into noble men of Gondor, but brutes. Notice that Frodo is absent from these harsh scenes (even Sam might wince and feel sorry for Gollum). And Faramir himself doesn't hit Gollum, but he's still very much involved, being the leader of his men. Even more violent torture scenes were shot, apparently, with the Gondorians stamping on Gollum's fingers. Ridiculously over-the-top and wholly unnecessary, and the violence was trimmed back (but it's still way too much in the *Extended Edition*).

Finally, Gollum is hurled against a wall, where he remains, with his face to the wall. The subsequent scene where Faramir interrogates Gollum is quite a departure from the book. In the Henneth Annûn scenes in the book, it is often Faramir who speaks at length, and some of his speeches are fairly long. In the film, it's Gollum who has a monologue at this point. A curious scene it is too: it is played for the most part with the camera looking at the back of Gollum, trucking in slowly, while the audience hears Gollum's voice. (Concentrating on Gollum's back view does have a positive effect on the film's budget: it means that the face doesn't have to be animated – it's often the face in animation that consumes weeks of labour). The scene sees the return of the Gollum-Sméagol schizophrenia, with the Gollum side of the character gaining supremacy.

Faramir prompts Gollum a couple of times with questions: 'where are you taking them?' and 'what did they steal?' It's not really enough for Faramir to guess that it's the One Ring that Gollum's talking about (which he announces to Frodo and Samwise in the next but one scene. The extended cut, though, added the scene of Denethor handing Boromir the mission to go to Rivendell). Gollum also has a couple of schizophrenia moments, and so let's Faramir in on the psychological struggle in the creature between the slinker and stinker sides.

A brief two-hander scene is next, between the hobbits, in the corner of the cave where they sleep (presumably this scene is occurring while Faramir questions Gollum). Sam urges Mr Frodo to use the ring and escape. Frodo declines, and uses the reason that if he puts on the ring 'He'll see' (i.e., Sauron). It's a precursor of Frodo's experiences later in the book (in Tolkien's tome there is more the sense that the Dark Lord will be able to 'see' Frodo if he puts the ring on *inside* Mordor. After all, Frodo's put on the ring a few times outside Mordor, including once – at Parth Galen and the Seeing Stone – which was dangerously close).

In the next scene Faramir approaches the hobbits sitting on the cave floor. Faramir drives this scene, bearing down on Frodo and drawing his sword. The hobbits stand up; it looks as if Faramir means business, and might even attack them. It's time for another 'ring moment', and it's definitely *not* in Tolkien's novel. Frodo backs up again the cave wall. The sound editors fade up the ring sound effects; the ring's 'heartbeat', the high-pitched voice, and the theramin-like warbling. Sam stands to one side. Faramir lifts up the ring on a chain with the point of his sword (now the ring is handily around Frodo's neck, making it a more dramatic moment than Faramir's sword pulling it out of Frodo's pocket or hand). Handheld wide angle shots lurch the ringbearer into close-up. Frodo enters the 'ring trance', and the captain of Gondor looks mighty fascinated by the One Ring. At the end of this ring moment, Sauron's voice is heard, and the sound fx go zoooooop up to a climax. The spell is broken, and Frodo hurries into a huddle in a corner (Frodo in wraith-like make-up was tried out for this portion of the scene, which would have been Faramir's view of what Frodo would become, and what the ring was doing to Frodo. It was a visual translation of Sam's dialogue).

Sam now faces up to the man, and tells Faramir that Frodo is going to Mordor to destroy the ring. To intensify the drama of this moment, the screenwriters add an artificial, rather hokey device: an officer coming in to tell Faramir that Osgiliath is under attack and what are his orders. Faramir is still digesting the information that his prisoners intend to destroy the ring in Mount Doom (and in the *Extended Edition*, viewers will remember the scene of Faramir's father commanding his brother to travel to Rivendell to bring back the ring). The officer asks Faramir again about his orders (very silly, but it does encourage Faramir to hurry up with his momentous decision. And, in a three-hour movie, you've got to move things along at a lick). So Faramir decides. Badly. 'The ring will go to Gondor', he announces. And it sucks.

Next: Aragorn on his horse, alone, by day, seeing the army of marching orcs from a hill. Long shots of man and horse riding. A big aerial shot circles around Aragorn to reveal a wide river plain with Helm's Deep nestled below the mountains in the distance (shot near Canterbury). Cut to Aragorn riding into the lower level of the fortress. He is greeted by Gimli, while extras mutter in the background (presumably about this new arrival). Aragorn is straight down to business: 'Gimli, where is the king?'

The next scene picks up the Aragorn-Éowyn-Arwen romantic subplot when Aragorn encounters Legolas in the colonnade outside the hall. Legolas returns the Evenstar to the Dúnadan, saying (in Elvish), 'you're late'. (If viewers and fangirls wanted to emphasize the homoerotic undertones in the relationship between Aragorn and Leggy, it's in scenes like this, where they stand very close, facing each other and whispering in Elvish). The viewpoint then cuts to Éowyn, with p.o.v. shots of the man and the elf. Her disappointment when she sees the Evenstar being returned to the object of her affection is clear.

With the romantic and elvish subplot out of the way, the film resumes with the primary narrative, which will dominate the final stretch of the film: the battle for Helm's Deep. Aragorn enters the main hall of the stronghold in a signature shot that was subsequently employed in all of the marketing for the film (he pushes open the heavy doors of the hall with intense backlight behind him. The backlighting will become even more substantial in Théoden's 'where is the rider?' scene. The lighting serves a practical purpose, of course: to hide the fact that this is another studio set, and neatly does away with using another diorama or matte painting. Extras stride to and fro in front of the lights).

The king is on his throne (as kings should be in mediæval movies). Apart from one or two wide shots of the hall, the scene is played mainly in close-ups between Théoden and Aragorn, with no cutaways to other characters. Aragorn delivers his news about the approaching Uruk-hai army.

Next, Théoden is issuing orders in the Hornburg in the following scene, in the lower level. Théoden tours the fortress, accompanied by Aragorn, Legolas and Gimli. This scene, and the subsequent ones, are classic devices to explore the spaces of the stronghold which will feature in the battle. They introduce the audience to the various areas – the gateway, the causeway, the battlements and so on – in daylight, so they can see everything (the actual battle takes place at night), and with Théoden talking about the areas in voiceover, or standing in front of them.

Throughout the early Helm's Deep scenes, the film script keeps two people centre stage in almost every scene: Aragorn and Théoden. Aragorn, for instance, seems to be everywhere: touring the fortress with the king, chatting with nervous boy soldiers in the inner court, arguing with Legolas in the armoury, talking with Éowyn about going to the caves, and so on. If you didn't think of *The Lord of the Rings* as a war story, this segment of the film of *The Two Towers* makes it very clear: the primary narrative is the build-up to a giant battle (and, as Gandalf intones at the end of the film, the battle of Helm's Deep is but one part in the battle for Middle-earth). Tolkien often subtitled *The Lord of the Rings* 'the War of the Ring', and the 2001-03 films go along with that to the hilt.

Really, from halfway through the film of *The Two Towers* to the close of the film of *The Return of the King*, it's all a war story. Just look how often weaponry and armour is fetishized in the second half of *The Two Towers*: Aragorn extolling the virtues of a sword to Háma's son; Éowyn swinging a sword in the Golden Hall; Théoden gripping his sword at his resurrection; spears and swords being handed out in Helm's Deep; armourers sharpening swords; the close-ups of the main characters donning armour, and so on. And Aragorn and Andúril in *Return*. The films are a virtual commercial for a 'Swords R Us' store (and of course, weaponry from the *Lord of the Rings* films did appear in many stores, including weaopns made and sold by Weta Workshop).

The 2002 film of *The Two Towers* continues the tour of the castle with an impressive, very complex visual fx shot of the battlements and the lower levels. It's a big crane shot which combines the full-scale top level battlements with digital extensions for the lower areas, digital extras, model work and matte paintings. It's one of the dozen or so really big Helm's Deep shots that clarify the different areas. The shot's endpoint is Théoden, in medium shot; Théoden is telling the others about the upcoming battle. An argument ensues between the king and the future king about the defences, about potential allies, and Théoden's insistence that Rohan fights alone. Théoden's gripe about where was Gondor when the Westfold fell is a silly line – they are separate countries.

A link scene has Théoden outside the Burg, with crows gathering above the Deeping Coomb (a nice touch of the gathering of the storm, and a visual reference to Saruman and his spy birds). Théoden seems confident, but Gimli reminds him that these are fierce Uruk-hai they're dealing with.

Cut to Fangorn, with Treebeard carrying the hobbits and entering the Derndingle (true to its name, the set is a sunlit, grassy glade, surrounded by trees and very dingly. There's even a prehistoric megalith in the centre, a pointed stone). The setting, though, is not particularly important: what counts is the introduction of the walking trees. They are wonderful digital creations, gnarly, twisted, decidedly asymmetrical and 'organic'-looking.

Even in a short and apparently unimportant scene like the arrival at Derndingle, the viewpoint of the film subtly shifts. For instance, it is Treebeard who is driving the action at this point – he is carrying the hobbits (they just ride along); he does all the talking, and so on. But the introduction of the ents is viewed from the hobbits' point-of-view, not Treebeard's: there's a cut from a C.U. of Merry to the ents, first, followed by a pan right from Pippin to more ents. The hobbits are again the viewers' way into the world of Middle-earth.

Back to Helm's Deep again: crowds of extras shuffling through the gateway and around the lower levels of the stronghold. Notice in this section of *The Two Towers* that the narrative stays for the most part with Helm's Deep (with Aragorn the most prominent character), and cuts away only to Fangorn (and once or twice to the approaching orc army), but not to Frodo, Gollum and Sam, or to Arwen and Elrond in Rivendell, or – the most notable absence – Gandalf. Many of those plot strands were dealt with in the preceding part of the film: Arwen and Elrond in Rivendell, Frodo and his companions, Faramir, and the Boromir/ Denethor flashback in Osgiliath.

Legolas and Aragorn discuss battle plans, to keep the upcoming battle foremost in the minds of the audience. As the filmmakers put it in interviews, the build-up to a battle is as important, and perhaps more exciting, than the conflict itself (rather like making a film, where all the really good stuff – and important decisions – occur in pre-production). So when the film cuts to Aragorn or Théoden or subsidiary characters at Helm's Deep, it's always to emphasize the approach of the battle.

There is time, occasionally, for the film to step aside from this overriding narrative, as in the next scene, involving Aragorn and Éowyn. This brief scene develops their one-sided romance a little further: the shield maiden tells Aragorn that the soldiers would follow their leader anywhere, because they love him. The subtext is writ in neon (Éowyn loving Aragorn and Aragorn keeping his distance). The scene also tells the audience what's going to happen to Éowyn during the battle (and how she would rather fight). And it leads into the caves scenes, which are next up.

Extras (mainly women and older folk) crowd the Glittering Caves sets (these are small sets with rocks and stalactites in the foreground and matte paintings and digital extras beyond). A wide shot establishes the scale of the setting, with people and torches stretching below into the distance. A brief shot of Éowyn in the extended cut of *The Two Towers* suggests that she is about to do something, pulling back her hair, but it's not followed up (it's a remnant of the subplot involving Éowyn fighting orcs that break into the caves, and helping a woman – Morwen – give birth. You can see Mirando Otto rehearsing the scene where she takes on a bunch of orcs in one of the 'making of' documentaries).

Notice that when *The Two Towers* cuts from Helm's Deep to the women and children and old folk in the Glittering Caves, Éowyn is absent, even though she is by far the major character in that situation (there is

Morwen too, a minor character, but everyone else is an extra not to be seen again after Helm's Deep). As the viewers've already seen Éowyn in warrior mode (at Edoras) and seen her willing to help fight on at least two occasions (with Théoden when the wargs attack, with Aragorn in Helm's Deep), it is curious that Éowyn doesn't figure at all in many of the caves scenes. She is shown comforting a woman when the orcs have broken through to the inner court (but wouldn't she also be drawing her sword and preparing to defend the others in the caves?). Maybe the filmmakers thought it would detract from Éowyn's character to have her standing around not doing much. If you haven't got anything for your characters to do, it's best not to draw attention to that fact by cutting to them.

The Glittering Caves scene segues into a slow motion montage, accompanied by an elegiac cue from Howard Shore, depicting the menfolk leaving their wives and families to fight. Tearful farewells play silently, closing with two women comforting each other. These scenes are about the costs of war, and remind the audience what is at stake, and what the men are fighting for. (They are additions to the book, needles to say: women hardly feature in Tolkien's description of the run-up to the battle: instead, it's all men talking grimly about how to defend the castle).

Into the armoury next: swords are being handed out. The room is thick with extras in beards and straggly hair (and further crew cameos). Aragorn, Legolas and the dwarf discuss the soldiers around them – they are too old or too young (the dialogue comes from Gamling speaking to Théoden and Éomer in the book). Legolas states that they are 300 against 10,000. This conflicts dramatically with the novel: Gamling says they have a thousand on foot at Helm's Deep – and the arrival of the king's army (including cavalry) bumps up those numbers further. I wonder if the number 300 was chosen in the film of *The Two Towers* because of the famous story of the Spartans fighting the Greeks at Thermopylæ (subject of a good 1962 movie, *The 300 Spartans*, and a 2007 movie). It's 300 versus 10,000 not just to make the conflict all the more exciting, but also because Erkenbrand and his army have been removed from the film (in the book, Erkenbrand leaves reinforcements at Helm's Deep, and he fights orcs at the Fords of Isen, and also returns to Helm's Deep to help defeat Saruman's army).

Now the film moves to Théoden and Gamling in the main hall of the Hornburg. Excessive backlighting pouring through the open doors dominates the scene. After Théoden having doubts about the battle and his leadership, the film moves into montage mode again (in slight slow motion, with Théoden having his armour put on by Gamling). This time, Théoden delivers the 'where is the rider?' speech (in the book it's chanted by Aragorn as the travellers pass the burial mounds of the Rohirrim). In the film, the horse-lord's poem becomes an elegy of a leader for his troops, with obvious links with the two World Wars.

Intercut with Théoden's speech (which continues in voiceover) are close-ups of Gamling putting on Théoden's armour (with the clinks and creaks enhanced by reverb), shots of marching orcs, a swordsmith sharpening a blade on a wheel (a cameo from editor Mike Horton), a slow motion shot of spears being handed out in the armoury and, best of all, images of children being given weapons and fitted with armour. Talk about milking a moment for maximum sentiment and emotion. It's all build-up, of course, a way of making the battle seem even more perilous. But the images of young boys receiving weapons and equipment are there unashamedly to provoke sympathy (notice that the boys are younger than sixteen or seventeen, which's the more usual age for the youngest soldiers in war movies).

Back to Fangorn again (introduced with an aerial model shot, flying over the trees) at night. The ents sway back and forth (how *do* you show a group of ents talking?), accompanied by the low rumbles of their voices. Merry begins to display his pro-activity again when he informs æons-olds Treebeard that they're running out of time.

Helm's Deep again, introduced via another big crane shot. Extras are busying about (extras in movies never seem to do anything specific or useful – they're just responding to the assistant director yelling for 'background action!' – and 'background action' is usually interpreted as skittering to and fro). A brief respite from busy-ness is inserted here, with the conversation between Aragorn and Haleth about fighting. (If everyone is so busy, why is Aragorn, one of the two leaders, sitting down doing absolutely nothing?). A tiny detail, that the audience might not pick up on, is that the boy (played by Philippa Boyens' son Callum Gittins, but voiced by an English actor) is the son of Háma, doorwarden at Edoras (and first victim of the wargs, so poor little Haleth now has no daddy).

A sword is yet again the pretext for the dialogue between Aragorn and Háma's son: *The Lord of the Rings* is a film where quite a few characters talk about swords: Bilbo and Frodo with Sting at Rivendell; Aragorn handing out swords at Weathertop; Boromir and Narsil; Aragorn and Narsil; Aragorn and Elrond and the reforged Narsil; Théoden after his exorcism; Éowyn in Meduseld, and so on.

The cuts between the preparations at Helm's Deep and the Entmoot suggest not only that these events are taking place simultaneously (in the book, the chronology is different – it takes the ents much longer to decide to act, for instance), but also that the ents are important for the outcome at Helm's Deep. The film suggests that, if anyone's going to come to the rescue, it will be the ents (although the film did also add a band of elves from Lórien). The *deus ex machina* rescue in the film comes from Gandalf and Éomer and their army (which's foreshadowed by Gandalf telling Aragorn to watch for him at a particular time). The book offers more detail about the various forces away from Helm's Deep (including Erkenbrand and his infantry), while the film withholds information from the audience to create a bigger surprise (and a greater sense of relief) when the rescue finally comes (but not really, 'cos Gandalf tells us when to expect him). Having Éomer arrive with Gandalf to save the day at Helm's Deep was used in the 1978 United Artists film. It makes sense dramatically, now that Éomer's character had been changed to a still-loyal but banished soldier.

Long, general high angle shots of Helm's Deep reveal the good guys lined on the battlements, waiting for the enemy to march up the Deeping

Coomb. By now, the filmmakers have laid all of the groundwork for the battle: they've shown our heroes organizing the defences, they've shown what the guys are fighting for (the families in the Glittering Caves), they've cut away to Treebeard and the hobbits, they've given the audience a bit of hope with the arrival or the elves, they've given viewers a whole tour of the fortress, and they've foreshadowed the one weak spot (the culvert).

The audience knows full well that the heroes will prevail, of course, but it also pretends that they might not survive. To ensure the audience can suspend its disbelief to the utmost, the filmmakers have piled on the sentiment, by depicting the teary farewells of combatants with their families, and cutting back to the women and children quaking in the caves. They have also greatly exaggerated the odds (300 against 10,000) from the book (as well as throwing in a slither of hope with the elf army).

But the filmmakers were right in considering the *build-up* to the battle as more interesting and exciting than the battle itself. True, Helm's Deep is a great movie conflict – while the hand-to-hand combat is fairly routine, those enormous aerial images give it a terrific sense of scale and breadth. But it's the individual stories and characters that audiences are often really interested in and rooting for. In that respect, the battle itself is viscerally thrilling, but emotionally flat. None of the heroes, bar Haldir, even seems to get seriously hurt (they're all beaten about, of course, and Théoden is speared, but the damage is never lasting). Part of the fault is not the adaptors', but Tolkien's: the professor tended to have miraculous rescues, last minute escapes, and was very reluctant to kill off his characters. (For Burton Raffel, the miraculous rescues and *deus ex machina* events weakened *The Lord of the Rings,* though Tolkien clearly enjoyed putting them into the story, showing how good will prevail.)

ACT FIVE

The preamble to the battle itself moves in a series of steps, regimented like a marching army (it's filmmaking by storyboard):

(1) wide general shots of the stronghold (plenty of smoke, flaming torches, and wind blowing);

(2) the sound of the orcs' marching feet, heard offscreen first (kind of impossible, as they are still over a mile away; off-screen sound was used so effectively in *Zulu*);

(3) a push over the heads of the soldiers on the battlements reveals the orc horde, a long lines of flames;

(4) Aragorn joining Legolas and Gimli on the battlements (Gimli lightens the mood a tad – he's too small to see over the battlements);

(5) Théoden flanked by Gamling and others;

(6) thunder rolls and lighting flashes;

(7) the rain begins;

(8) cuts to the orcs;

(9) brief images of the women and children in the caves (accompanied by a plangent version of the main Rohan theme);

(10) the orcs coming to halt before the walls;
(11) the orcs banging their spears on the ground (which apparently emerged from the stunt people passing the time between set-ups, but it's a classic part of any battle preamble);
(12) the Rohirrim and elves drawing their bows;
(13) the old timer who looses an arrow and fells an orc;
(14) the orcs baying, maddened, then rushing forward on the signal of their commander, who stands on a rock.

The battle proper then begins, with a powerful cue from Howard Shore.

> It was now past midnight [wrote Tolkien in *The Two Towers*]. The sky was utterly dark and the stillness of the heavy air foreboded storm. Suddenly the clouds were seared by a blinding flash. Branched lightning smote down upon the eastward hills. For a starting moment the watchers on the walls saw all the space between them and the dike lit with white light: it was boiling and crawling with black shapes, some squat and broad, some tall and grim, with high helms and sable shields. Hundreds and hundreds more were pouring over the Dike and through the breach. The dark tide flowed up to the walls from cliff to cliff. (TT, 168-9)

The sound designers use classic techniques in the battle of alternating quiet with loud passages: just before the mines explode, for instance, the sound drops away, to make the detonation more impressive. And just before the battle, quiet, mundane sounds, like rain drops, wind noises and the creak of wood, prepare the audience for the aural assault to come.

Musically, the Helm's Deep battle revives many of the key themes of the *Lord of the Rings* films up until this point. It's two-thirds into the three film set, and by this time Howard Shore has developed a range of cues which can be applied to each sequence with different instrumentation or emphasis. For instance, when Haldir's elves appear, the elf theme is given a military turn. The heroic fellowship theme – heard over the 'hero fellowship shot' when the Company leave Imladris – is deployed for the 'Leggy moment', when the elf skateboards down the staircase. When the orcs attack with ladders, Shore revives the bombastic Isengard theme. The orcs' Black Speech chant is revisited when the bomber runs towards the wall, and so on.

The action, stunts and gags in the battle of Helm's Deep are all standard Hollywood fare: high falls, tumbles, a few leaps, slashing and swinging in the swordplay. As orchestrated by swordmaster Bob Anderson, stunt co-ordinators George Ruge and Casey O'Neill, and second unit director John Mahaffie, Helm's Deep is unashamedly old-fashioned in its fighting styles, stunts and action. Some new techniques are deployed (such as wire work for the leaps, with the rigs and cables hidden in post-production), but most of the stunts rely on tried and tested techniques going back to the early days of Hollywood movies. Compared with even a run-of-the-mill Hong Kong action film, Helm's Deep is fairly routine.

Unquestionably the star of the battle of Helm's Deep – onscreen – is Viggo Mortensen's Aragorn. He's depicted everywhere: commanding the elves, fighting on the battlements, trying to bring down the bomber, leading a charge of elves, rescuing Gimli, struggling to save Haldir, leaping off the battlements on a ladder, running up the stairs, fighting at the gatehouse, leaping onto the causeway, holding back the orcs, pulling Gimli up on a rope, and finally urging King Théoden to ride out to meet the orcs head-on.

By comparison, Théoden does little in the battle. Legolas and Gimli have their moments: Gimli with his two leaps, and Legolas's skateboarding shield. But it's Aragorn who dominates the whole battle. It's as if the filmmakers had decided they were going to put all of their favourite moments from mediæval war films into Helm's Deep: lengthy build-up, siege towers and ladders, fighting on the battlements, daring leaps, last minute rescues, whistling arrows, chopping axes and swinging swords, and various snakepit or cliffhanger scenarios. And Aragorn is at the forefront of most of those situations.

Aragorn offers a resumé of former action stars: Errol Flynn and Douglas Fairbanks as Robin Hood and pirates, Charlton Heston and Kirk Douglas as heroic leaders, and crazy stunts and brutal combat of later stars like Mel Gibson and Bruce Willis (there's also Monty Python hacking of limbs in there).

And there's a feeling that the Helm's Deep has been plotted in the computer as well as on paper, that it looks like a video game, tailor-made for gaming with a range of battle scenarios and regions of the castle (and different characters to be – Aragorn, Legolas, Gimli, Théoden, Haldir or an orc chieftain). And it *was* a computer game. Of course, with only a hundred extras or stunt people on set, a large part of the armies are digital. And the sets, though some were full-scale (the gatehouse and lower levels, the battlements), were mostly models, paintings and digital extensions.

Another problem with spending so much time with the battle of Helm's Deep is that it is not the primary ring story of *The Lord of the Rings*, and doesn't concern Frodo's quest to destroy the ring. So in the film of *The Two Towers* there is a long stretch where the ring and the quest is not mentioned at all. Again, that's not the fault of the adaptors, but Tolkien's tome (for some critics and fans it isn't really a fault, it's just that the Rohirrim are so busy preparing to repel Saruman's forces, they haven't got any time to think about the ring). In the film, there are a number of ways that viewers could have been reminded of Frodo and the ring (from obvious ones, such as having Aragorn and the others talk about it, to more complex ones, such as flashbacks, or intercutting with Frodo and Sam). But the filmmakers clearly decided to deal with Helm's Deep in long chunks, and to cut away only to Merry, Pippin and Fangorn. Only when most of the battle for Helm's Deep has been fought does the film cut back to Frodo and the ring.

Before the battle, Aragorn suits up, in the armoury (now empty of extras). Cue more fetishized close-ups of weaponry. Legolas makes it up with the Ranger. Gimli's also there, to offer a bit of light relief (about the chain mail) before the battle (he does so again, on the battlements, with a running joke about his size and not being able to see over the battlements). A loud horn blowing off-screen calls Aragorn and Legolas away, and they scurry up some stairs.

Accompanied by a martial version of Howard Shore's elvish cue, three columns of elves arrive in the lower levels of the stronghold, clad in dark grey cloaks and hoods, with metal helmets underneath, clutching long bows. They are led by Haldir, who greets Théoden. The stairs and walls are lined with extras playing Rohirrim in full armour. Théoden looks simply baffled (offering no words of welcome, none of the formal greetings that Tolkien loved); when Aragorn and Legolas turn up, there's a happy reunion between Haldir and the Dúnedan. It's Haldir's line, about elves fighting alongside men, that inaugurates the real start of the battle.

The elven army fire arrows under Aragorn's command, still maintaining that military precision for a while. Plenty of orcs fall in the hail of arrows. The first casualties among the heroes occur when the orcs get closer and employ crossbows – cue the first of the high falls from the battlements (the orcs, throughout the battle, are seen with more technologically advanced weaponry: the crossbows, the ladders, the siege towers, the catapults, and their *pièce de résistance*, the bombs). The rows of archers – one row firing while the other row reloads – is a standard manœuvre in Hollywood action-adventure films (and it's used in *Zulu*). Great as the mass of arrows and archers is in the *Lord of the Rings* films, a film like the martial arts epic *Hero* (2002) easily trumps it.

'Ladders!' yells Aragorn, and the elves draw dutifully their swords. Howard Shore revives the tub-thumping Isengard/Saruman theme at this point, and the action is caught with a marvellous wide shot from above the orcs of the ladders going up. It's one of the signature shots of *The Two Towers* (the scene closes with another L.S. travelling alongside the wall – apparently one of the first model shots of Helm's Deep, used as a test, which the filmmakers then decided they wanted to use in the final film, so a lot of work had to done by the vfx team to clean it up. The inspiration for this part of the film is Alan Lee's great illustration in the 1992 edition of *The Lord of the Rings*). The *melée* on the battlements is regular movie action: Gimli and Aragorn both dispatch the 'berserker' orcs, giants with white helmets. All of the main characters are seen doing their stuff (though Théoden remains somewhat removed, above the gatehouse).

A loud finish to the Isengard music helps to propel the narrative to the Entmoot. When the film cuts back to the Treebeard and the Entmoot, it's always with Treebeard acting far too slowly for the hobbits (for Merry in particular). The Fangorn scenes are also much shorter than the Helm's Deep scenes here, but offer a respite from the action. Notice that the filmmakers have adopted a narrative and editing pattern that only allows them, really, to cut to the Treebeard and the Entmoot for a relief from the intensity of the battle, because they've chosen to leave Gandalf and Éomer as a last minute arrival. Cutting to Arwen, Elrond and Rivendell wouldn't work (the wrong mood and pace, and no obvious narrative link). Cutting to the Frodo and Sam story was possible, but Shelob was shifted to the third film, which left out that action beat. The last time the audience saw Frodo and Sam was in the confrontation with Faramir in Henneth Annûn, when the captain announced that the ring would be going to Gondor. So the battle for Helm's Deep focusses on two narrative strands:

(1) Aragorn, Gimli, Legolas and Théoden fighting the orcs, and
(2) Merry and Pippin with Treebeard.

The old ent approaches the hobbits in Derndingle to inform them that the ents have agreed that the hobbits are not orcs. That's not good enough for our Merry, who tells Treebeard that there isn't much time. Each of the subsequent visits to Fangorn have the same narrative pattern. It gets quite tiresome, really, but it does hammer home the point to the audience that the ents must act. (There is also the problem of the pace of the ent scenes, which are far slower than the battle. Editor Michael Horton said he didn't like Treebeard's s-l-o-w delivery, and thought the film might risk boring viewers. Director Peter Jackson liked Treebeard, calling him a ponderous committee kind of guy, where everything has to be decided slowly and methodically. So Treebeard was sometimes deliberately slow, and even appears to fall asleep in mid-sentence at one point, like Grandpa in *The Simpsons*, while Merry and Pippin wait on his words).

Merry uses familiar modern arguments to persuade Fangorn that the ents must act: the ents can't carry on in isolation, like a neutral nation that pretends that war isn't on its doorstep. If the War of the Ring is a WW1 or WW2 scenario, then the ents are an independent country that is reluctant to be drawn into conflict. Again, very different from the book, in which Treebeard decides with the other ents what they're going to do, and the hobbits are observers.

Back to Helm's Deep yet again. Gimli on the battlements, hewing down orcs climbing the ladders with his axe. Orcs edge up the causeway in a Roman turtle formation (shields above their heads). Théoden mocks Saruman – 'is this all you can conjure, Saruman?' As soon as that moment of hubris's depicted, two hidden weapons of the wizard's forces are revealed: the first is the bombs, hauled into the culvert by orc sappers. An orc runs in slow motion towards the wall, holding an Olympic torch which emits white sparks (accompanied by the orc chants heard in the Nuremberg scene).

The explosion is shown twice (a rare break with continuity editing in the *Lord of the Rings* films), from different angles. It's a big moment, and hence the editors Michael Horton and Jabez Olssen reckoned that it deserved a variety of angles (it's often tempting, when using multiple cameras or tons of coverage, to put in some additional shots). Our heroes are flattened; plenty of debris falls about them. Cut to the second secret weapon, the battering ram concealed by the orc on the causeway. Cut back to orcs pouring through the fissure, into the water of the stream. Aragorn, knocked out, comes round, in time to see orcs approaching him. Gimli rushes to his rescue, performing an impossibly enormous leap (and landing on an orc). Gimli sets about the orcs, but in turn has to be rescued by Aragorn from the water. Aragorn orders up a volley of arrows to help the dwarf from the elven warriors behind him (which's depicted with an arrow p.o.v. shot). He then leads a charge (cue slow motion and the elf theme).

The next gag in the saga of the battle of Helm's Deep involves the biggest 'Leggy moment' in the 2002 *The Two Towers:* the elf skateboarding down the steps, while loosing arrows, accompanied by the heroic fellowship theme (the shield he rides on even hurtles into an orc). The skateboarding elf sequence is stretched out by the editors as much as possible: there are *seven* shots of Legolas skating down the stairs (not including the ones to set up the action, and to finish it off with some crazy elf combat), and Leggy sets about demolishing the enemy single-handed.

It was crucial, J.R.R. Tolkien stated, to maintain the sense of enchantment in the creation of the Secondary World of fiction and fairy tale. The spell mustn't be broken. When it is, the reader is dragged back into the primary (or real) world. That was where 'willing suspension of disbelief' came in:

> The moment disbelief arises, the spell is broken; the magic, or rather art, has failed... If you are obliged, by kindliness or circumstance, to stay, then disbelief must be suspended (or stifled), otherwise listening and looking would become intolerable. (MC, 132)

The filmmakers of the two thousand one-three *Lord of the Rings* films thought, fuck it, let's have Orlando Bloom skateboarding! It'll be so cool! The audience'll love it! But this's just one of numerous moments in the early 2000s Tolkien films that lifts the viewers out of the fiction, like the quips 'nobody tosses a dwarf!' and 'let's hunt some orc'.

Cut to oldest ent of them all in M.C.U., talking to the hobbits. This scene closes the conflict between the hobbits and Fangorn, as the ent tells them to go home. The Shire theme accompanies a small scene with Merry and Pippin alone, apparently preparing to leave. The scene, where they agree they can't seem to do much, is important because it shows the turning point for Pippin: when Merry tells his friend that there might not be a Shire to go back to, the camera lingers on Pippin in C.U., hinting that he might be musing over this piece of information (which foreshadows the scene where Pippin, not Merry, asks Treebeard to walk towards Isengard).

Having the hobbits influence Treebeard and the ents makes sense dramatically, because the hobbits are simply observers or 'luggage' otherwise, and don't affect the narrative (the film didn't show or hint at Gandalf's influence on the ents' decision to join the War of the Ring). But it makes Treebeard and the ents look stupid; now, in the film, they gather for an entmoot (which's a big deal for ents), and talk and talk, but decide to do absolutely fuck all! Now these wonderful, ancient tree-like creatures simply disband, it was all a complete waste of time, all that build-up is for nothing, and Treebeard carries the hobbits to the borders of Fangorn, so they can go home. If you see the alteration from the book from the scriptwriters' and the hobbits' point-of-view, the switch makes sense, but from Tolkien's and the ents' point-of-view, it sucks.

In the Rohan stronghold, the fighting continues (introduced with an aerial shot that is a continuation of the end of the previous scene but one). The three heroes are shown in rapid succession (Aragorn, Gimli and Legolas). But now the combat has moved into a montage mode of slight slow motion, muted and reverbed sound effects, and slow, elegiac music. It does this partly, perhaps, to offer a different way of showing fighting but also to suggest the costs of war. It also serves as lead-in to Haldir's death, which is played out in slow motion, muted sound, and melancholy music.

Théoden calls for the retreat to the keep, which Aragorn passes on to Haldir (Haldir's still up on the battlements; Aragorn's on the lower level). After acknowledging Aragorn, Haldir is hit a couple of times by orcs. Vocals by the wonderful Liz Fraser (reprising Gandalf's lament in *Fellowship*) express not only Haldir's death (the only substantial character to die at the end of *The Two Towers*), but also his puzzled recognition of death and mortality. Notice how the film switches into a subjective, point-of-view shot here, with the camera tilting as Haldir falls (his vision is filled with slain elves). Intercut with Haldir's death are images of Aragorn is struggling up the stairs to aid him, fighting orcs along the way (those stairs saw quite a bit of action in *The Two Towers*). This was a scene originally intended for Arwen and Aragorn (which puts Haldir in the feminine position – in fact, Haldir does stand in for Arwen, or elves in general, in some respects).

Aragorn turns into Errol Flynn again here in a surge of vengeance and noise, leaping onto a ladder and hurling himself into the fray below (the audience has already seen Aragorn take on 150 orcs by himself at the end of *The Fellowship of the Ring*, so they know he'll be OK, although the Aragorn of the book would never be that stupid). Colin Wilson, writing in 1974, found Gondor and its brave warriors 'like an Errol Flynn movie', and the 2001-03 films duly supplied some Errol Flynn moments.

Things seem to be going badly now for our heroes: the gate is breached; orcs with crossbows down a few Rohirrim; Théoden finally moves. Aragorn races up the stairs, pursued by orcs (one of the best wide miniature and CG shots of Helm's Deep occurs here), and joins Théoden at the gate. The king has been wounded by a spear but manages to dispatch his opponent (the extended cut adds some more limb-hacking and gore here, as in the rest of Helm's Deep). Most of the shots in the gate scenes are handheld – for obvious practical as well as æsthetic reasons.

Aragorn and Gimli creep out to the side door. A brief revival of the dwarf-tossing joke prior to two leaps, the big, heroic fellowship theme, and a high angle shot of the man and dwarf slaying the enemy. Next: the orcs bring out the catapults, *de rigeur* in any Middle Ages siege scene. Wide ladders festooned with orcs are hauled up to the castle walls (shown in long shots, like the previous ladders scene). Legolas shoots down one of the ladders with his magic bow (apparently, this idea wasn't in the script, but suggested itself during editing, as so many of the best ideas do).

Down in the outer court, Théoden calls the retreat. Cue one of the biggest Helm's Deep shots, a crane shot over the stronghold from just outside the walls. Hordes of orcs (mostly digital characters), as well as retreating Rohirrim soldiers, are glimpsed running through the lower levels, and beyond the walls; the heroes fall back (the film doesn't return to Helm's Deep now for four further scenes).

Back in Fangorn, the hobbits are on the move in Treebeard's branches (with Pippin now in the crow's nest, so to speak). Treebeard talks about them going home. Merry appears gloomily resigned to their fate. This is Pippin's great moment, when he makes his first really important decision and act in the movies: he tells Treebeard to go South. It perplexes the ent for a moment, but he swiftly complies, turning about.

It's all different from the novel, of course: in J.R.R. Tolkien's beloved book, Treebeard and the ents decide for themselves at the Entmoot to march on Isengard and send the huorns to Helm's Deep. The film gives the hobbits more to do in these decisions, otherwise it appears as if they are just along for the ride and have no effect on anything. Thus, Merry gets to go head-to-head with Treebeard, urging him to action in a series of short arguments. When that fails, it's up to Pippin to make the critical decision of asking Fangorn to take them South (helped again by Merry putting the idea in Pippin's crop that the Shire might not exist if things keep going as they are). Gandalf does suggest (TT, 126) that the arrival of the hobbits in Fangorn forest has helped to persuade Treebeard to act.

Finally, the film of *The Two Towers* cuts to Frodo and the ring. Frodo, Sam and the Gondorians are seen in late afternoon on the lower slopes of North Ithilien overlooking Osgiliath and the Great River. The first close-up in this scene (the second shot) is quite rightly a C.U. of Frodo, looking tired and forlorn. A wide shot from the reverse angle reveals Osgiliath in the distance, with Minas Tirith far away, below the mountains (according to producer Mark Ordesky, the white city was removed from theatrical prints, because audiences might get it confused with Helm's Deep).

Straight away the ring quest is addressed: Frodo tells Faramir that 'the ring will not save Gondor'. Frodo continues to implore the captain to let him go, but Faramir ignores him, and the party moves on. A distinct departure from the novel has Frodo speaking openly of the ring, in the midst of Faramir's men. Sam does the same later on in the middle of a huddle of soldiers, and Faramir tells Madril he's sending a 'mighty gift' and weapon to his father. (Maybe he's so desperate he hasn't any choice; but it's also because of the pressure of time in a movie; having Frodo and Faramir going to one side to converse would add another scene).

With the re-introduction of the Frodo story at this point, the editing pattern shifts – now it will cut between Helm's Deep and Fangorn, as before, but will also include Frodo's journey to Osgiliath.

Back to Pippin, Merry and Treebeard (note how Pippin is more prominent in this scene that Merry, in the C.U.s and reaction shots). The travellers arrive at the decimated edge of Fangorn forest, a gentle slope now reduced to tree stumps and branches. To Treebeard, it looks like devastation of his friends, but to viewers it might recall coppicing, regular wood management which humans do the world over. The sight also suggests deforestation and blighted rain forests – picking up the ecological undercurrent in J.R.R. Tolkien's writing. In that sense, Saruman is portrayed as an evil capitalist, embodiment of the machine, The Man. As Treebeard, says, 'a wizard should know better' (the words are from the book).

An over-the-shoulder shot reveals Isengard in the distance and Treebeard's voice intoning '*Saruman*'. Treebeard's bellow echoes over an aerial shot of the forest (the sound appears to be, as so often in contemporary Hollywood movies, a combination of manipulated animal noises). One of the best music cues in the three films is inserted here – Howard Shore's choral cue for the 'last march of the ents'. In the extended cut, there's a very long shot of the huorns starting to move off (compared to the book, the huorns react very quickly to Fangorn's call to arms, as do the ents). The miniature and digital shots of the ents marching on the Wizard's Vale are some of the most memorable in the *Lord of the Rings* films, but it's the music that does a lot of the work here.

Osgiliath again: Gollum (absent from the previous Frodo scene) is shown on a leash, held by a Gondorian. A wide shot booms up to reveal the war-torn city, a fairy book version of a familiar 20th century landscape: gutted and ruined buildings, empty streets, debris everywhere. All of the Osgiliath scenes are shown in drained colour, greys, whites, pale blues and blacks, with no warm colours at all. Another establishing shot shows boulders hurled by the enemy landing in water near the Gondorians, like shelling in a WW1 or 2 movie. Arrows whizz by, which the Gondorians dodge like bullets. It's all a very 20th century rendition of mediæval fanfare.

In rewriting Faramir's character, Fran Walsh acknowledged that, given more time, the writers might've developed a different way of approaching his character. Part of the problem with *The Two Towers* was that the writers were locked into footage that had already been shot, so their new conceptions for characters had to fall into line with what had already been filmed. So rewriting Faramir's character once more would have meant reshoots that would be too extensive (i.e., too expensive).

The next scene takes off in two different directions: Faramir handing Frodo over to another commander, and Frodo having a 'ring moment'. Incredibly, Faramir does not take Frodo and the ring – the most important matter in Middle-earth at that time – to Minas Tirith himself, but hands him over. The earlier scene in the extended cut, which established the uneasy relationship between Denethor and Faramir, only partly explains Faramir's reluctance to take the 'mighty gift' to daddy. But in either cut, it seems utterly bizarre for the captain to let go of Frodo and the ring in the midst of a city overrun with enemies. The Faramir of the book, whom Denethor calls Gandalf's pupil (thus deemed somewhat wiser than Boromir in these worldly affairs of rings and Dark Lords) wouldn't have done that. He's got the One Ring, but doesn't bother to travel the 15 or 20 extra miles to take it to Minas Tirith! Er, yeah, right...

The second element of the Osgiliath scene is Frodo's 'ring moment'. Maybe the adaptors reckoned that now we're back with Frodo and the ring again, it was time for another 'ring moment' – to remind the audience of the danger of the ring, to show that it's effect has intensified with proximity to Mordor, and to show that Frodo is becoming more susceptible to its power. The 'ring moment' employs the methods elaborated in film one – local sound dips out, high-pitched warbling and the ring's 'heartbeat' come in, and Frodo looks drugged. The film also shifts into subjective camera – a point-of-view shot of Sam talking to Frodo, his voice fading away. Notice too that there aren't any reaction shots of Gollum during Frodo's ring experience – and Gollum is the one person who really knows what it's like. Gollum is seen moments later cowering from the nazgûl beside a wall.

When Faramir turns away to leave, Sam pipes up in an attempt to sway the captain of the rangers, telling him that the ring sent Boromir mad and he tried to kill Frodo (that's another totally unconvincing moment – that Sam would speak up like that, not only to Faramir, not only about the ring, but in front of Faramir's men, too. He does in the book, but in a different context and manner). But there's no time for Faramir to digest this information; a rock demolishing a nearby tower breaks up this confrontation (a shot which Alex Funke said was achieve practically on the model). Then the nazgûl appear. Before they do, Frodo slips into a 'ring trance' again, but now the beating sound of the ring is the beat of the wings of the fell-beast, a subtle piece of sound design. Close-up, wide angle shots of Frodo muttering 'they're here' (with his ring-sense, Frodo is aware of the nazgûl before the others, including Gollum). Faramir yells 'nazgûl!' and people duck as if they're avoiding another burst of shelling or a low-flying aircraft.

An aerial view over Osgiliath follows, with the fell-beast and ring-wraith flying into frame. There's an important cut from a M.C.U. of the wizard king up in the air to a C.U. of Frodo, establishing the hidden connection between Sauron's chief of police and Frodo and the ring. Faramir grabs the small-scale double of Frodo (Kiran Shah) and takes him to cover, ordering him to stay put. Sam spots them and follows on their heels.

Back to Helm's Deep with another panorama. The orcs are now in the inner court, right up to the doors of the Burg, which they are duly ramming. Inside, Théoden seems to have given up, and speaks fatalistically (in Tolkien's novel, Théoden does begin to doubt the wisdom, and Gandalf's advice, to go to Helm's Deep, but he certainly hasn't given up. Pretty soon, he's leading his troops in a last ride out). Aragorn tries to rally him. A cut to the women and children in the caves, including Éowyn (the first glimpse of her for most of the Helm's Deep battle). Legolas is in the background, but doesn't take part in the conversation (as so often in the films).

Aragorn suggests riding out to meet the enemy face-on while a female choir sings the march of the ents theme, forging a link between the ents marching on Isengard to their possible doom, as Treebeard said, with the last charge of the Eorlingas at Helm's Deep. Théoden interprets this final act as if he – they – are definitely going to their death. A cut to a window with low level light shining through it is accompanied by Gandalf's words in the stables at Edoras. Théoden announces that the horn of Helm

Hammerhand will sound once more, and Gimli (why Gimli?!) dutifully scurries off to blow it (the horn is enormous, like a single organ pipe the size of a factory chimney). The sound of the horn doesn't have any effect on the enemy, however, as horns do in Tolkien's fiction (Tolkien likes to have foes quaking at the sound of heroic horns, but that's difficult to carry off in a contemporary movie, where you need something as bit more impressive than someone blowing a musical instrument to be fearsome).

It's all very different from the book, where Théoden isn't about to give up – he suggests riding out to meet the enemy, not Aragorn. Transferring the decision to Aragorn is part of the over-arching shift from the book towards Aragorn taking control at Helm's Deep, and Théoden being much more unsure and unheroic. In the book, Théoden is more of a blustery war-mongering type, a character very familiar in literature and cinema. In the films, he is riven with doubts and dark moments, and isn't the strong leader that the Rohirrim want him to be. Aragorn, too, remembers Gandalf's words about returning on the fifth day at dawn, and looks up to see the sun shining through a high window.

These scenes – like most of the other indoor political or courtly scenes in the *Lord of the Rings* films – are indifferently directed. (This scene is also awkwardly edited – there are odd ellipses in the dialogue between Théoden, Aragorn and Gamling). These critical scenes, which call for some big drama at this point in the film, seem anti-climactic. Don't expect Peter Jackson to mount some of William Shakespeare's plays any time soon. Where is Orson Welles when you need him?

Théoden gives the 'now for wrath' speech in close-up, which's a momentary tease, because he and the others are already on horseback. Orcs break through the doors; the cavalry charge them on Théoden's signal of 'forth Eorlingas!' They cut their way through the orcs in the inner court, down to the lower level and the causeway.

The big wide shot of the cavalry riding down the ramp and running down orcs before them, so they fall off the causeway, is a combination of miniature, matte and digital elements (with digital doubles for the horses and riders; it looks phony to me). The camera tracks behind and above them. Brief low angle handheld shots of hand-to-hand combat follow (the shots of Aragorn that follow are ropey green screen). A M.C.U of Aragorn looking up to see (from his point-of-view) an image of Gandalf on Shadowfax up on a high ridge, silhouetted against the sky, the horse rearing. With the huge choral music, it's a clichéd surge of sentiment and action-adventure film dynamics. It could be an image from a Western in Hollywood's heyday – the Lone Ranger or Billy the Kid, say. If Gandalf yelped 'hi ho, Silver!' it would fit nicely.

It's quite right, too, that it's Aragorn who sees Gandalf first – Aragorn has dominated Helm's Deep, and it was to Aragorn that Gandalf foretold his return. A C.U. of the white wizard, and back to Aragorn, who says 'Gandalf' (movie characters have stated the name of a character when they encounter them since the early days of sound, just so the audience really gets it, and the *Lord of the Rings* flicks are no exception – why break with a solid gold movie tradition?).

An over-the-shoulder view of Helm's Deep and the battle below shifts the narrative to Gandalf's point-of-view. Éomer comes up into medium close-up, and calls 'Rohirrim!' Horsemen gather around and charge down the steep slope into the line of orcs. The enemy has lined up with long staffs. The riders crash through the orcs, hacking away at them. (In the film, it's the arrival of the Rohirrim that saves the day; in Tolkien's novel, the battle at Helm's Deep was already won before Erkenbrand and the wizard arrived; the orcs are driven into the line of huorns [TT, 180]).

The picture moves into its tried and tested epic slow motion mode, with a big choral cue from Howard Shore. Some very wide shots (using models, digital characters and matte paintings) depict the clash of Rohirrim and Uruks from the side, from above the orcs, and from above the cavalry. Sunlight breaks over the ridge into the orcs' eyes; God-rays hover over the *melée*. (It's as if the gods are shining on the goodies, and the orcs, although they're Uruk-hai who can travel by day, are dismayed).

It's the first time that viewers have seen Gandalf in action like this on a horse (a kind of swishing, clubbing fighting style was developed style that relied on physicality rather than magic. He uses his staff to beat the orcs, not his sword). C.U.s on Éomer fighting too.

An abrupt cut on action takes the film to one of the most impressive sequences in the *Lord of the Rings* films, the ents' assault on Isengard. It's almost exclusively a visual effects show, this part of the film, with practically everything on screen being a miniature, a digital character, a matte painting, or digital set extensions, plus a few kitchen sinks. The live action elements of the actors – of Saruman, Merry and Pippin – are completely dwarfed by the scale of the visual fx. (It's all the more impressive because most of it was apparently put together in the final weeks of post-production).

The animators went to town on coming up with cool ways for the ents to destroy Isengard. The sequence opens with a wide shot of the ents standing on the outer wall and hurling large chunks of rock at the orcs, who are downed like ninepins. A series of gags shows the ents in action: they kick the orcs into the air; they stomp on them; they use an orc like a club, swinging it to hit other orcs; they smash orcs together in each tree hand; they pull scaffolding and machinery into the pits.

The sequence is very busy and intense; each shot is fairly short, with plenty of action in the fore- and mid-ground. The action is big, generalized destruction. These are some of the densest visuals in the *Lord of the Rings* films (made more complex in terms of visual effects by the water). A strident choral cue pulses throughout the sequence.

The orcs fight back by firing arrows at the ents, or stones. They set fire to an ent with arrows (it emits a high-pitched squeal – what does an imaginary creature like a walking tree-like beast make when it's set on fire?). They pull one ent down with a rope and climb onto it, hacking at it. Treebeard comes to the rescue with a well-aimed boulder hurled from a distance. Merry and Pippin join in by throwing stones at the orcs. They are enjoying themselves.

Saruman rushes out onto his balcony (for his last significant appearance in the theatrical version of the films) to watch the devastation below. A L.S. reveals Saruman on the balcony in the left of the frame, and the mountains in the distance; the shot is reprised a moment later, this time with the water flooding down the hills.

Models and CG ents and orcs depict the release of the dam (the extent of Treebeard's tactical warfare is revealed. Flooding Isengard was a clever move by the ents). As in the rest of the *Lord of the Rings* films, verticality is highly exaggerated, so the dam holding back the Isen is way, way above the Wizard's Vale below (it could have been further up a much gentler slope from Isengard, for instance. And it's much bigger than it is in the book). Standard vfx model shots of water pouring through the dam and down the mountains follow, with one or two minor details added (like the orcs on top of the dam falling into the water in a God's-eye-view shot, or the debris churned up in the waves cascading down the slopes. What the orcs were doing up there is unclear – particularly during a battle).

Very long shots of Nan Curunír depict the ents bracing themselves against the rush of water (and the ent that was on fire douses the flames – added to assuage the kids in the audience who might've been upset by the sight of a burning ent. I know I was. I wept for days afterwards).

The film follows the water pouring through Isengard, and into the mines, a Biblical cleansing of the machinery and industry seen in the first film. (The storming of Isengard follows the book in essence, but leaves out plenty of elements, too – such as the fires sent up by Saruman from the mines to burn the ents, or the ents trying and failing to pull Orthanc apart).

Cut to Frodo in Osgiliath in what appears to be a trance (he stares straight ahead, ignores Sam, and the ring 'heartbeats' are heard). He walks away from cover to the steps. Sam calls after him. A close-up of Frodo is followed by a reverse angle L.S., which shows Frodo to be standing on a second storey landing, with Osgiliath and the mountains beyond. The Witch-king riding on the fell-beast rises from behind the wall (unexpectedly – rather than hurtling down from above, like the mothership rising up behind Devil's Tower in *Close Encounters*). Reaction shots of Sam and Faramir (but not Gollum) watching this scene unfold.

Cut back to Frodo in C.U., and the Witch-king. Nothing is said, but Frodo is pulling out the ring and seems about to put it on. The audience guesses, from the construction of the scene, that with Sauron's first-in-command right in front of him, when Frodo puts on the ring he will be a goner. Cue Sam to the rescue, rushing up the stairs (in slow motion, of course). But it's not Sam alone who saves Frodo – Faramir helps enormously by firing an arrow at the fell-beast, causing it to lurch forward then back up into the air (it's a kind of replay of the moment when both Merry and Éowyn take on the Witch-king at Pelennor, as well as the moment when Faramir shot down the soldier on the *mûmakil*, demonstrating his pinpoint Robin Hood accuracy with a bow and arrow). Note than when Sam and Faramir help Frodo, Gollum is absent, and Faramir is separate from his men (this dramatic moment needs the concentration of just a few characters). It's also a variant on the Amon Hen scene in the book (which was never filmed for *The Fellowship of the Ring*). But in Morgul Vale, Frodo *resists* the Witch-king, without needing Sam's help.

Sam and Frodo tumble down the stairs. The music stops suddenly, as well as the ring heartbeats, the flapping of the fell-beast's wings, and the other sounds; just wind (atmos) and breathing remain. Big close-ups on Frodo and Sam which deliberately echo the introduction of Gollum scene in the Emyn Muil, as Frodo draws his sword on Sam (there was more fighting shot between Frodo and Sam but, as editor Michael Horton commented, this was all you needed).

Frodo throws Sting away. Gollum is now shown, crouched nearby. Frodo, leaning against a wall, confesses that he can't do it. Sam begins one of the worst sections of the films (no matter how many times I've seen it, it still stinks) with his speech about not giving up. The monologue is given at a window overlooking Osgiliath (an over-the-shoulder shot reveals the fell-beast flying away); Frodo and Gollum are on the ground, listening. The speech's a statement of intent, a summary of what the picture, and the struggle of the characters, is about. And (for Philippa Boyens), it's about the value of stories and storytelling. (It took Sean Astin 25 takes to nail it).

As Sam continues to speak (with the music moving into a suitably elegiac mode), the film cuts to Helm's Deep, and the final moments of the battle. Medium close-ups of Théoden, Aragorn and Gandalf, fighting. Théoden is crying 'victory!' Another cut, to Merry and Pippin still riding in Treebeard's branches, in the last acts of the battle at Isengard, and Saruman on his balcony. An extreme long shot of Isengard shows the pizza model flooded, with plumes of smoke rising, and a sullen sky beyond.

Back to Sam and Frodo in Osgiliath. In the pause, where Frodo asks Sam what they are fighting for, Sam helps Frodo up and delivers the stinger to his tiresome monologue: 'that there's some good in this world, and it's worth fighting for'. *Bleeeeccgh*. Frodo has tears in his eyes (understandably – who wouldn't be – let me out of here!). Gollum looks duly downcast, with a puppy dog look out of Disney or Chuck Jones. Faramir is nearby (but not, notice, his men at this moment – they appear a beat later).

Faramir approaches Frodo and kneels before him (that gesture demonstrates as much as his dialogue his intentions). He tells Frodo that they now understand each other (i.e., he has finally realized how dangerous the ring is. To be picky, the scene with Frodo, the ring and the Witch-king could be interpreted in different ways. For instance, the captain of Gondor, who has stuck by his decision to send it to Minas Tirith, might be convinced that, yes, the ring is powerful, and the enemy really wants it, but that could make him even more resolved to deliver it to his father).

Faramir's no. 2, Madril, protests. But Faramir orders the release of the prisoners. For Cynthia McNew, the alterations in Faramir's weren't convincing; the audience might have believed that Faramir could resist the ring if they'd seen the temptation and his resistance.

Cut to the huorn scene at Helm's Deep (Howard Shore and his orchestrators and music editors are still earning for every cent of their fee with a busy, strident score). A L.S. reveals the line of huorn trees in the

Coomb below (basically, it looks like Fangorn has been transplanted to Helm's Deep, like 'Great Birnam wood to high Dunsinane' come [*Macbeth*, 4.1.92]). Orcs rush down to the forest. C.U.s of Gandalf, Aragorn, Théoden and Legolas (our heroes are ranged in a row, looking down on the huorns. Éomer yells at his men to keep away from the trees. Noisy cries and rumbles as the huorns dispatch the uruks – the filmmakers wisely leave the orcs' death up the audience's imagination, and suggest it with waving trees and sounds, seen from a distance. (Tolkien's narrator was also vague about exactly *how* the huorns killed the orcs.) Showing the walking trees killing the orcs was considered at one point, but it's much better to let the reactions of the heroes do the talking.

With the battle over the climax of *The Two Towers* film has been reached. The enemy has been routed or destroyed, the heroes are victorious, so there's time now for a couple of lighter moments. The first comes with a brief scene of Legolas and Gimli in the midst of the aftermath of the battle, with corpses everywhere. The running gag of comparing body counts is revived here. Gimli squats on a twitching orc, unhelmeted and smoking his pipe.

The second light scene is next: Merry and Pippin at Isengard. They stand waist deep in the water near the outer wall. Debris floats in the water. Merry compares his height with Pippin. Saruman and Wormtongue on the balcony survey the wreckage of the wizard's realm (they are shown from a distance, from the hobbits' point-of-view, and there's no dialogue. Indeed, this is the last time Saruman will be seen in the theatrical cuts of the films. The Saruman-Gandalf scene was not in *The Return of the King* script; it was shot for *The Two Towers*, but was left out of the theatrical then the extended cut. Really, it should have gone into the theatrical cut if anywhere.)

After some brief comments about Saruman, and the brief reprise of the comparing height gag, the hobbits follow a trail of floating apples to a nearby storeroom. A pullback reveals a generously stocked storehouse, including small barrels of the hobbits' beloved tobacco. Pretty soon the hobbits are smoking; Treebeard approaches the doorway, sniffs the smoke, and crouches down to peer inside. The hobbits scene brings Merry and Pippin back to what hobbits love most: eating and smoking. As Merry says, all's right with the world.

The following scene sends Frodo and Sam on their way, in preparation for the third film in the set. Again it is Faramir alone with the hobbits, rather surrounded by his soldiers. The ranger leads Frodo, Sam and Gollum to a tunnel, which's revealed to be part of a sewer which leads out of the city. The farewells; a reconciliation between Faramir and Sam which kinda follows the book (though why Sam thanks Faramir, who's taken them miles out of their way and in the process endangered the whole of Middle-earth, seems odd). And discussions about the route. Faramir pins Gollum against the wall with his fingers around his neck (rather like the way Gollum prefers to dispatch his foes), and interrogates him about the route to Cirith Ungol.

Gollum is re-introduced as a major character now the hobbits are setting off into the wilderness with the one-time Stoor hobbit. When Frodo and Sam have departed along the sewer, Faramir lunges for Gollum again, wishing him a sudden death should any harm come to the hobbits (this's partly to explain why Faramir should allow Gollum to go with Frodo and Sam).

Gollum skitters after the hobbits (on all fours, in pain). A brief scene between Sam and Gollum follows (Frodo is walking on ahead) which establishes the uneasy, bickering relationship between Sam and Gollum (this will culminate with the break-up on the mountains above Minas Morgul). Sam mentions having 'no hard feelings' about what happened to Gollum at the hands of the rangers, but the subtext sows the seeds for the way Gollum manipulates Frodo against Sam in the 2003 film of *The Return of the King*.

Back to Helm's Deep, for the penultimate scene; the heroes have ridden on horseback to a ridge overlooking Rohan. By the miracle of movie-making, the characters can see all the way towards Mordor, with fires and lightning glimpsed behind the mountains, and the sound of thunder (even though it's about 450 miles from Helm's Deep to Mount Doom and Barad-dûr).

Gandalf, Aragorn, Théoden, Legolas, Gimli and Éomer are present (with Gamling behind, but, curiously, no Éowyn). Gandalf leads the scene, by stating that the battle of Helm's Deep is over but the battle of Middle-earth has begun (a scene tailor-made for the trailer; the phrase 'the battle for Middle-earth has begun' was employed in the advertizing). In this scene the action and characters look forward physically and literally, as well as imaginatively and psychologically, towards the battlegrounds of the third film – Mordor and Gondor.

Peter Jackson pointed out that the action climax of *The Two Towers* was kept separate from the psychological climax, involving Sam and Frodo; that was one reason for putting Shelob into the third film. The final scenes of the 2002 adaption of *The Two Towers* are with Frodo, Sam and Gollum. The three scenes begin with a short dialogue between Frodo and Sam, then feature Gollum in the middle in an extended monologue, and the finally unite the three characters and send them on their way to Mordor. The duologue between Frodo and Sam is important because it re-establishes the affectionate bond of trust and friendship between them, now that they are away from the big geo-political affairs of Middle-earth (and those bullying Gondorian soldiers); they are now shown as just humble hobbits who talk about hobbit things.

One of the few self-conscious moments in the text of *The Lord of the Rings* – where J.R.R. Tolkien's narrator talks about the value of storytelling – is inserted here (transplanted from another spot in the book), where Sam talks about whether they will be put into stories. Steadicam shots cover the hobbits walking in a sunlit pine forest (notice how it is daytime and sunny, as opposed to the gloom and night of the previous section). In the final section of the scene, Frodo and Sam move closer, into close-up (and with a reprise of the Shire theme, of course).

The next scene is Gollum's monologue, very much drawing on the book: '"Must have it. We wants it, we wants it, we wants it!"' (TT, 299). Technically, this was a tricky scene to pull off, for a number of reasons: it was a lengthy take (always difficult in any visual effects shot); all of the focus was on one character, in medium close-up; dramatically, the scene moved through a number of phases, which had to be rendered in animation; finally, the shot was a moving camera take (a locked off camera is best; and it wasn't filmed using a motion control rig, or even a track, but a loose Steadicam shot, which had to hit many marks and points). Needless to say, it took all day to shoot.

Narratively, the Gollum monologue has one overriding goal: to show that Gollum is still a principal player, and is planning something catastrophic for the hobbits. Dramatically, the scene is basically the Gollum-Sméagol schizophrenia scene from earlier in the film (when the hobbits were in Ithilien), but staged this time with continuous movement (Gollum halts by a tree halfway through, and hides behind a tree at the end). The dialogue reprises the love-hate relationship in Gollum's split personality, the bullying, scheming Gollum and the cowed but just as devious Sméagol. Both sides of Gollum, though, are desperate for the ring. The previous scene, between Frodo and Sam, had avoided discussion of the primary narrative of *The Lord of the Rings* – the ring and the quest to destroy it. That had been depicted in the climax of the Frodo-Sam story, the encounter with the Witch-king. The Gollum monologue brings the ring back into focus again, reminding viewers that even those very close to Frodo, like Gollum, are after it.

At the end of the complex Gollum shot, Frodo and Sam can be glimpsed in the background, out of focus, calling for Gollum, and looking for him. After Gollum has finished his gloating scheming about Shelob (not named as Shelob, or a giant spider or monster, just a 'she' and 'her' – an unusual tease, because there are precious few 'shes' or 'hers' in *The Lord of the Rings*), he comes out of hiding. Reunited, the three travellers continue to walk on, towards Mordor, their route leading away from the camera towards the hills, and their motion leading the audience towards the final installment.

The final shot of the 2002 *Two Towers* adaption is a big crane up and away from the hobbits and the wood, up and up, maybe two thousand feet, past trees and mountains, until it reaches over the mountain range to reveal Mordor beyond: Mount Doom and the Dark Tower are prominent; nazgûl on fell-beasts fly about; lightning crackles in the distance, and the volcano pours out smoke and fire. (It's a complex visual effects shot, which combines live action, models, matte paintings and digital components – Sauron, the nazgûl, the lightning, the fire and lava on Mount Doom, and so on. Using the Vale of Morgul instead was contemplated, but altered, because the ultimate goal is Mount Doom). The shot reveals the final destination for Frodo and Sam, and the landscape of the third film, but it also reminds the audience of the obstacles the heroes still face – not only to traverse Mordor undetected, but also to encounter the baddest baddie of them all in Middle-earth, Sauron. The Dark Power has been curiously absent from much of *The Two Towers* (although it is one of the two towers, as far as the title is concerned); it's been shown once or twice, but not as much as in *The Fellowship of the Ring* (Saruman having usurped Sauron in his role as chief villain in many respects (the battle of Helm's Deep wasn't really Sauron's doing).) So the last shot of *The Two Towers* reminds viewers that the heroes are still to face up against one more villain; it is also quite an elegiac close to the film, with a melancholy cue from Howard Shore (and another fade to black, of course). It's another version of the ending of *The Fellowship of the Ring* (which also closed with Frodo and Sam near the mountains of Mordor).

CHAPTER 17

THE RETURN OF THE KING FILM (2003)

> *Still round the corner there may wait*
> *A new road or a secret gate;*
> *And though I oft have passed them by,*
> *A day will come at last when I*
> *Shall take the hidden paths that run*
> *West of the Moon, East of the Sun.*

J.R.R. Tolkien, *The Return of the King* (375)

The Lord of the Rings: The Return of the King (2003), released globally on December 17, 2003 (after its premiere in New Zealand on December 1, 2003), was not the end of the story as far as the *Lord of the Rings* movies were concerned: the home entertainment releases (in video cassette and DVD video formats) of the film in August, 2004, and December, 2004 (for the *Extra Special Oh-So Special Extended Gold Platinum Diamond Collector's Edition*), would be the final installments (there would no doubt be further editions: anniversary editions, perhaps. The filmmakers joked that there might be anniversary editions which would add extra material. Another edition was released in 2006). Or versions in which all three films were edited together as a continuous film. Or turned into a twelve-hour TV series. A number of series of films have been re-edited for transmission on TV – one of the more celebrated was the *Godfather* series which Francis Coppola and Barry Malkin reworked for television, putting the material of *Godfathers I* and *II* into chronological order.[1]

Further material could be shot and included in the *Lord of the Rings* films. These films were never really 'finished' – the filmmakers were re-shooting many scenes way after principal photography had wrapped. And scenes were filmed for the home entertainment releases of *The Return of the King* after the theatrical version had been and gone in cinemas. Filmmakers have occasionally been tempted to go back and tweak their earlier movies, and the *Lord of the Rings* films may be well be the same.

For the global movie audience, *The Return of the King* was the final installment in a trilogy which had begun with the release of *The Fellowship of the Ring* in December, 2001. The film would have many functions (and expectations) to fulfil, but one of the main ones would be to pay off and resolve all of the storylines. Tom Shippey said he'd been struck at the end of *The Two Towers* how much narrative the filmmakers still had to get through – not only all of *The Return of the King*, but also plenty of *The Two Towers* which hadn't made it into the adaption of *The Two Towers*.

For director Peter Jackson, *The Lord of the Rings* was all about the third film. The two previous flicks are there because you want to get to the third film, Jackson explained. Doing *The Lord of the Rings* at all was 'all about the third film really'. You've had a beginning and a middle, but *The Return of the King* makes sense of it all, and offers closure.

There were five narrative strands in *The Return of the King*: (1) Aragorn, Gimli and Legolas; (2) Gandalf, Pippin, Faramir and Denethor; (3) Théoden, Éowyn and Merry; (4) Elrond and Arwen; and (5) Frodo and Sam. These of course crossed over, too: the Aragorn, Legolas and Gimli story mixed with the Rohirrim for a while, before splitting off for the Paths of the Dead. And there were smaller plots, like Faramir and Denethor; Faramir and Éowyn; Gandalf and the hobbits in the final reel, and so on.

For the J.R.R. Tolkien fan, there was much to admire in *The Return of the King*. As one would expect from the previous two films, and from any number of contemporary Hollywood blockbusters, the battles in *The Return of the King* would prove astonishing (*Alexander, Kingdom of Heaven, King Arthur, Sword of Xanten* and *Troy* were other epics of the same time which took advantage of the new digital animation technology to stage enormous battles). The main conflict in *The Return of the King* – the siege of Minas Tirith and the Battle of Pelennor Fields – did not disappoint: dive-bombing nazgûl, vertiginous aerial fly-bys over the city, trolls storming the gates and fighting in the courtyards, the giant battering ram Grond, with its flaming wolf's head, pushed by trolls, pulled by giant beasts and operated with ropes, Grond battering down the gates, enormous wooden siege towers (some blown apart by the Gondorian catapults), catapults firing the heads of Gondorian soldiers, rocks and flaming missiles over the ramparts of the first level, trolls and orcs streaming through the gates and clashing with Gondorians, the arrival of the Rohirrim, the rousing speech by Théoden, the charge of the Rohirrim, the Rohirrim fighting a line of marauding *mûmakil*, horses and soldiers riding between the mûmakil's legs, the *mûmakil* swinging giant tusks to bat away opponents, Legolas's athletic, single-handed demolition of a *mûmakil* and its crew, Gandalf and Pippin exchanging a few words about death, the face-off between Éowyn and the Witch-king, Éowyn dispatching the fell-beast, then (with Merry) the Witch-king himself, the arrival of the Army of the Dead, and so on and on.

The Battle of Pelennor Fields was pure boys' stuff, *Boy's Own* adventure, boys being boys, the kind of battle that kids would enact on blankets on the floor with plastic soldiers, or in sand hills with wooden sticks. Like so many cinematic battles, Pelennor Fields in *The Return of the King* was the filmic equivalent of a fantasy battle played out in a million boys' heads. It appeared as if the filmmakers had said, well, we've got a few million dollars to put a big battle on the screen, what would we really like to see if we were sitting in the audience?' That was how, for instance, David Koepp, writer of the second *Jurassic Park* film, *The Lost World* (1997), said he went about writing the script: if I were in the audience of a dinosaur movie, what would be cool to see?

Clearly, quite a few of the film production team on *The Lord of the Rings* (and not only in the visual fx departments) were like big kids playing around with battles, monsters and heroes, keen to put up on screen stuff they thought would look cool. So if the Battle of Pelennor (and the other sequences in *The Lord of the Rings*) looks familiar, that's because they're amalgams of the production team's favourite battles and action scenes. In the Pelennor battle, there's bits of *Spartacus, El Cid, Braveheart, Gladiator*, Errol Flynn and Burt Lancaster swashbucklers, World War Two combat films, and plenty of Westerns. (There's also some of the more visceral Vietnam and combat movies in the *Rings* battles – *Full Metal Jacket, Platoon* and *Saving Private Ryan*, for example).

The first battle in a film with a number of battles was Osgiliath, the orcs crossing the Anduin on World War 2-style landing craft, while Faramir and his men defend the Western bank. This conflict, which turned into a rout, was intercut with other scenes, and was employed as a taster or prelude for later scenes, and a way of quickening the blood for the audience.

The enormous size of the Fields of Pelennor was captured in the big wide shots: one was of Denethor's view of the hordes from the Citadel; another of the Rohirrim's first sight of their opponents from a distant hill; another, a pull-back shot (so fast it must have been the equivalent of 500 m.p.h.) from Denethor plunging to his death from the Citadel, to a long shot revealing the battle below; aerial views of the dive-bombing nazgûl; and other clarifying long shots which depicted the stages of the battle.

The new digital technology was able to mount battles with thousands of participants, but the problem was swiftly apparent that when one has above, say, a couple of hundred people in a shot: they mostly become tiny dots in the distance, and have little impact on the viewer. And when the numbers reach tens of thousands, it looks impressive in the big wide shots (only wide shots can capture that many soldiers), but they also become just another mass of people. The 'Massive' software becomes self-defeating. What makes a battle scene really effective is basics like staging, editing, movement, sound, lighting, camera angles, etc. Keeping the principal characters close to the camera helps. It's also crucial for the audience to really care about the characters. That's why the battle that Orson Welles staged in *Chimes At Midnight* (1966) was so effective, even though he used only a few extras and horses (and it was shot in a guerrilla manner over many days, whenever extras, costumes or horses were available. Mud and smoke disguised the fact that Welles had only a few soldiers and weapons. The budget of $800,000 for *Chimes At Midnight* was tiny for a historical film).

There's an added problem in the battles in *The Lord of the Rings* (in the book and in the films), in that ultimately the reader/ viewer knows that the heroes will win out, and that nothing seems to be really at stake. Another problem is the lack of significant deaths (hence the addition in *The Two Towers* of Haldir at Helm's Deep). The Pelennor Fields at least has two significant deaths: Théoden and his nemesis, the Witch-king (the filmmakers added a third in the *Extended Edition* – Gothmog, the Witch-king's lieutenant). There are others in the book. Another drawback is the length of the battle: in the extended edition, Pelennor goes on far too long, even for fans of big battles like me.

In the last battle at the Black Gate, it was business as usual for the 2001-03 *Lord of the Rings* films (though this time it was intercut with Frodo and Sam at Sammath Naur): a vast army streaming out of Mordor surrounded and encircled our heroes (in a near circle). In the 1955 book there are said to be some 'seven thousands' in the Host of the West (RK, 188). In the film, it looked like less than a couple of thousand. The Dark Lord, meanwhile, seemed to have two or three hundred thousand troops at his command (the army stretched right into Mordor). As at Helm's Deep in *The Two Towers,* the 2003 film of *The Return of the King* highly exaggerated the odds stacked against the good guys. In this last battle, great eagles arrived to attack the fell-beasts (the film followed the book closely when it had Pippin crying 'the eagles are coming!').

The film departed from the 1955 book at key points in the battle before the Black Gate, however:

(1) there was no Mouth of Sauron, for a start (perhaps that would mean yet more talky scenes; he appeared in the *Extended Edition*).

(2) The Captains of the West were all together, rather than on separate hills.

(3) It was Aragorn, not Pippin, who was attacked by a troll (with Legolas saving him).

(4) Aragorn has a strange moment when he's addressed by Sauron (the remnant of an earlier idea that was ditched).

(5) The battle's recounted mainly from Pippin's point-of-view in the book (but not in the film).

(6) Aragorn leads a charge, crying 'for Frodo!', which was part of the re-shoots.

(7) When the Dark Tower's fallen and Mount Doom explodes, the chief characters look crestfallen, thinking Frodo is dead.

(8) Various 'Captains of the West' are absent: the sons of Elrond, the Dúnedain, Prince Imrahil, and the knights of Dol Amroth (RK, 189).

Probably the most rousing sequence in *The Return of the King* (of the big battle scenes) was the much-anticipated arrival of the Rohirrim: King Théoden gives a stirring speech to his cavalry (yelling 'ride now! Ride now! Ride to Gondor! Death! Death! Forth Eorlingas!'), and the 6,000-strong army of men on horseback gallops into the orc lines (with Merry perched in front of Éowyn, the only woman there). This was a clichéd moment: a king encouraging his men to fight. It was already a cliché in movies by the 1930s. In literature, it was already a cliché by the time William Shakespeare wrote the battle speeches for Henry V, and was probably already a cliché in ancient Greek drama, two and a half thousand years ago. But if the formula of a king leading his soldiers into battle works, why not use it again? *The Lord of the Rings* films were very much 'old-fashioned' filmmaking in that respect, with old-style battles, sword fights, encounters with monsters, beautiful princesses, powerful wizards and magical objects. (Bernard Hill did OK in his speech to his soldiers, but Viggo Mortensen was less than a firebrand when exhorting the Army of the Dead to join him, or encouraging the Host of the West in front of the Black Gate. Mortensen could do the fighting and the stunts, and he could look the part of Aragorn, but he couldn't do a bit of *Henry V*. His speech at his coronation, and the subsequent song, was also underwhelming). (Tolkien might have objected to Théoden crying 'Death!' to rouse his troops, which completely misunderstands the Anglo-Saxon cultures that Tolkien was drawing on. It's Éomer who goes all fatalistic, but only when he's found his sister on the battlefield. It recalls the moment in the *Iliad* when Achilles finds that Patroklos is dead. *Only then* is the moment for defying the gods and crying for 'death!').

The filmmakers (particularly Fran Walsh) worried about the slow start to *The Return of the King*, how for a long time not a lot seems to be happening. In the *Daily Telegraph*, Sukhdev Sandhu complained about *The Return of the King*'s slow first hour, Viggo Mortensen's 'over-seriousness' and uninspiring battlefield speech, the 'oddity' of Sam, the gay subtext between Sam and Frodo, and the long ending.

Fran Walsh recalled that early cuts of *The Return of the King* hadn't been satisfying, with an hour going by without much of a story emerging. Lots of scenes, but only vague rumours of a threat. Pippin and the *palantír* is where Sauron is introduced, and the story starts to get moving.

Sections of *The Return of the King* (theatrical) seemed awkwardly and jumpily edited. Not internally, within scenes (in general), but how the scenes played together, in sequences or acts. If the viewer's already read Tolkien's tome, they're aware that numerous scenes have been omitted or added or altered. But one can always ignore the omissions, additions or alterations. Despite that, the film still ought to flow on its own anyway, and should work for audiences who haven't read the professor's book. But for the viewers who'd only seen the theatrical versions of the films, and came to *The Return of the King* hoping for more of the same, might have noticed some glaring omissions (such as Saruman). There were also many characters who had featured prominently in film one or film two who hardly made an impact on film three, such as Treebeard, or Éomer, Elrond, Galadriel or Celeborn. Gimli and Legolas also disappeared for long chunks of *The Return of the King* (and the only bit of characterization or plot they carried for themselves was their running competition over who had the most kills).

And then the *dénouement* had a peculiar, dream-like quality to it, following the drawn-out climax and intercutting between Sammath Naur and the Morannon. The non-Tolkien fan might have been perplexed by the coronation scene, with Faramir, Merry and Éowyn suddenly seeming shiny and happy and healthy (and no explanation of their healing, which is a significant incident in the book). Aragorn's coronation speech is but a single line in length, something about peace (before he starts singing). And there's no mention of Denethor, or Théoden, or much of the Army of the Dead, and, most extraordinary of all, no big farewell scene between the hobbits and Legolas, or Gimli, or Aragorn, or Faramir, or Éowyn, or Arwen or Elrond. Some of those characters were the hobbits' companions for much of the three films: Aragorn, Gimli, Legolas and Éowyn, and the viewer might've expected some kind of acknowledgement. Maybe there isn't time for 22 major characters to say farewell to each other, and the big farewell scene was saved for the penultimate scene. So, after the scene where the Gondorians kneel before the hobbits, the film cuts to the map and the hobbits back in the Shire. (Peter Jackson remarked that *The Return of the King* had been very difficult to edit, and the theatrical version reveals those difficulties).

In none of the *dénouement* scenes were there (m)any questions or explanations. Gandalf laughs and Frodo laughs when he wakes up in bed alive and well in Minas Tirith; there's a big reunion scene for the main members of the fellowship, but no mention of Faramir or Éowyn or Éomer or Théoden or Arwen or Elrond. It's as if Frances Walsh and Philippa Boyens thought, well, it's enough to have our main characters happily reunited, and the danger and jeopardy over, and Middle-earth saved from Sauron, and hoped that questions about the many other characters would simply dissolve under the smiles, laughs, affectionate looks, freshly scrubb-ed faces, soothing music and high key cinematography.

In this reunion scene and the following coronation scene, Walsh and Boyens seemed to have hoped that viewers won't be asking tricky questions. Such as: what about Théoden? he gave his son a decent burial, doesn't he get one? How come no one mentions the dead from the battle? Or Denethor? What about the aftermath of the battles? Is Éomer now king of Rohan? How come Faramir, Merry and Éowyn are so suddenly rejuvenated? And is Saruman still stuck in Orthanc? Is Wormtongue still with him? And what about the Fourth Age?

Apart from the coronation itself, Aragorn's song, the romantic reunion with Arwen, and the cast of characters bowing to the new king, kneeling before the hobbits, there were other scenes one might have expected in this final section of the film: one between Elrond and Gandalf; one between the four hobbits talking on their own; a scene between the hobbits and the surviving members of the fellowship about what had happened to them (including the hobbits saying goodbye to the fellowship); a scene with Gandalf, Aragorn and an assembly of captains and lords about the new reign of the king and the Fourth Age; a scene offering a resolution to Éowyn's unhappy life (hankering after Aragorn through two movies, Éowyn isn't shown finding her man, Faramir), and so on. (Some of these were resolved in the *Extended Edition* of *The Return of the King*).

The encounter with Saruman and Wormtongue on the return journey would've been interesting: here, not only Gandalf but also Galadriel and Celeborn come face to face with the down-on-his-luck, spiteful Saruman.

The film hasn't got time to show the rest of the War of the Ring – how Sauron's forces attack the woodland elves in Mirkwood, and Lórien, and the Lonely Mountain and Laketown, and the Dúnadan. (In the audio commentary, Peter Jackson remarked that it would have been nice to show some of those conflicts).

Some J.R.R. Tolkien fans would find much to disappoint them in *The Return of the King*, as with the previous two movies. Again, it wasn't just a case of numerous omissions (which would be expected in a film adaption of a lengthy, dense book), or the alterations (which would be required for reasons such as clarification, simplification, budget, scheduling, time, etc). While Tolkien fans might acknowledge that omissions and alterations were inevitable for a film to fit into a less-than-three-hour slot for cinema release, it was the *additions* to the film which would offer the most grimaces or howls of pain.

Among the additions in *The Return of the King* was Gandalf beating Denethor with his staff to stop him from ordering the retreat of his troops. This was an obscene addition to Tolkien's fiction and completely out of character for Gandalf, and a desperate acknowledgement by Walsh and Boyens that they couldn't find a better or quicker or simpler way of having Gandalf deal with Denethor (Denethor going mad and shouting from the battlements of the Citadel was another addition. Boyens remarks on the DVD commentary that Gandalf hitting Denethor was a Peter Jackson moment).

Another significant addition had Gollum suggesting to Frodo that Sam wanted the ring and would try to take it. Using the McGuffin of lembas bread (which Gollum uses to frame Sam), Walsh and Boyens wrote a highly charged argument above Minas Morgul in which Frodo breaks with Sam and tells him to go home. Sam withers and weeps, after complaining that Gollum has poisoned Frodo against him. It was another example of the screenwriters racheting up the dramatic tension by forcing the characters into confrontations. Injecting a nervous tension between Frodo and Sam was one of the scriptwriters' favourite ways of intensifying the drama of the Frodo-Sam-Gollum scenes.

The thinking seemed to be that, without the added tensions between Frodo and Sam, the Frodo-Sam scenes would largely consist of two hobbits making their way slowly and doggedly towards and across Mordor. In other words, not 'dramatic' enough, and lacking a character 'arc'. Thus, the writers found new ways of stirring up the tension between Frodo and Sam (so they could make up again, or so that Sam could rescue Frodo again) and used the device in many scenes: (1) after Frodo encounters the nazgûl (Sam saves Frodo, Frodo nearly stabs Sam, then they make up); (2) in Ithilien, when Sam calls Gollum 'Slinker' (and Frodo defends Gollum and tells Sam he doesn't understand what it means to be a ringbearer); (3) when Frodo follows Gollum's advice at the Black Gate to try another way into Mordor (while Sam protests '"No, Mr Frodo, no"'), and so on. Walsh and Boyens were fond of reversals, of forcing characters apart to strengthen the bond when they were reunited. In the 2003 film, as in the 1955 book, Sam rescues Frodo a further time, in Cirith Ungol. And there's one more rescue: at Sammath Naur (two, actually: Sam carries Frodo, and later saves him from falling into the lava).

The conversation between Gollum and his reflection in the pool, early on in *The Return of the King*, while entertaining, was seemed to be a case of the filmmakers finding a place in the film to develop the schizophrenic scene in *The Two Towers* which had become a favourite with audiences (this scene came first, though). However, the scene commits one of the cardinal sins of scriptwriting: it *tells* the audience what's going to happen, rather than *showing* it. And it tells the audience what will happen next. It's the Villain Plotting and Scheming Scene, but Gollum goes on for far too long about what he intends to do.

The lighting of the beacons sequence goes on for ages, too: endless 2nd unit shots of mountains with tiny flames on their summits, lasting far longer than necessary. The mountainscapes are all very pretty, and the sequence appears like an ad for the New Zealand tourist board. (Fittingly, it's Aragorn who spots the beacon and rushes into Meduseld to tell the king).

What came across very strongly in *The Return of the King* (theatrical) was the bond between Frodo and Sam. The strongest and most powerful relationship in *The Return of the King* was between Frodo and Sam. Only the Aragorn-Arwen romance rivalled it in emotional depth; in the films as a whole, the Frodo-Gandalf relationship was central. The lingering affectionate looks between characters, usually the province of the romance between the hero and heroine in a typical entertainment film, were here between two young men (or hobbits). The first *dénouement* scene in *The Return of the King*, a replay of the Rivendell scene, has Frodo waking up in bed to find Gandalf at his bedside. The main characters file in to greet Frodo, one by one (Merry, Pippin, Gimli, Legolas, Aragorn), but the final one (i.e., the most one given most dramatic significance, and value), is Samwise Gamgee. The looks between the two hobbits (in glowing slo-mo) are long and deeply-felt.

Towards the end of *The Return of the King* (both versions), the scenes are exaggerated and squeezed until every ounce of emotion has been wrung out of them. Many of the scenes are dominated by Howard Shore's music, rather than dialogue, and play a little longer than they might do had they appeared earlier in each of the films. The filmmakers were clearly aiming to make the last 30 minutes of *The Return of the King* as emotional as possible. There was also a hint that the screenwriters were running out of steam, or maybe they were unable to come up with suitably grand dialogue to go with the visuals, or perhaps they felt the film would have more emotional impact if the dialogue was trimmed.

The writers, Frances Walsh, Philippa Boyens and Peter Jackson, didn't really find a fully satisfying shape to the story of Denethor in *The Return of the King* (theatrical). It's a tricky one to pull off: a major character has to be introduced a quarter of the way into the final film in a three-film set, has to slowly (or, rather, *quickly*) turn from haughty and stern to desperate and finally suicidal, and then dies two-thirds into the film. Thus, in the theatrical version, out went the *palantír*, Citadel guard Beregond, and the back-story about Minas Tirith (some this found its way into the *Extended Edition* of *The Return of the King*, in a short sequence where Gandalf and Pippin discuss the city on the stone prow).

The *palantír*, though, would have been a useful dramatic device to show how Denethor had been corrupted and weakened by the Enemy. It would have helped explain his descent into madness. Plus, the films had already shown the way the *palantíri* were used to communicate with Sauron, and, earlier in *The Return of the King* (theatrical) itself, the effect of the *palantír* on Pippin – and Aragorn – had been dramatic (if a little over-the-top). (The seeing stone is referred to in Denethor's line to Gandalf.) As Gandalf says, '"the vision of the great might of Mordor that was shown to him fed the despair of his heart until it overthrew his mind"' (RK, 156).

Taking away the *palantír*'s influence on Denethor makes the steward's descent into madness not Sauron's doing, but grief at losing his sons and the fear of Gondor falling to Sauron's army.

The visualization of Sauron took on a slight refinement in *The Return of the King*: now, when the hobbits were actually inside the borders of Mordor, the Eye became a searchlight, with a beam flicking to and fro from the summit of Barad-dûr. It might have sounded like quite a good idea on paper, but on screen it was a hopelessly literal and ineffectual embodiment of Sauron's power. In J.R.R. Tolkien's book, when Sauron searches out Frodo like a giant finger, or Frodo cringes out of sight of the Eye, it works. In a film, to turn the Eye into a searchlight, with Frodo and Sam cowering from it like prisoners escaping from the watchtower of a prison camp *à la* Colditz or Alcatraz, was feeble. The Eye also wobbled and quivered in its horns, becoming more expressive, like a human eye. (The alteration in the visualization of the Eye came about when the filmmakers realized the Eye would need to move).

One of the most outrageous omissions from *The Return of the King* was Saruman. The white wizard had played such a crucial role in the first two films. The writers had bumped up Saruman's role to that of chief villain in both *The Fellowship of the Ring* and *The Two Towers*, so he was on screen far, far longer (and seemed to have more influence in *The Fellowship of the Ring*) than Sauron. To drop Saruman completely from the theatrical version of *The Return of the King* was extraordinary, when one considers that Saruman had been shown in so many scenes in *The Fellowship of the Ring* and *The Two Towers*: conversing with Gandalf; fighting and imprisoning Gandalf; overseeing the birth of his Uruk-hai; commanding the Wild Men to rape and pillage Rohan; ordering the leader of the Wild Men to swear allegiance; conjuring the spell on Caradhras; overseeing the industrial revolution of Isengard; ordering the destruction of Fangorn; sending out his warg riders; communing with Sauron via the *palantír*; conversing with Wormtongue; directing Lurtz to kill the halflings and find the ring; and addressing his 10,000 troops.

Much of this material had been added to Tolkien's book in order to have Saruman play the role of chief villain in the movies (an easier thing to sell than a giant flaming eyeball). But in *The Return of the King* it seemed as if, because the story had finally reached Mordor, the screenwriters simply rejected Saruman: he wasn't needed anymore as a movie villain. With Sauron now visible atop Barad-dûr in many scenes featuring Frodo and Sam (and the Host of the West when it reached the Black Gate), Saruman was simply dropped. (He wasn't seen at all, and barely noted in the dialogue, other than in the short scenes at Isengard).

The lack of pay-off or resolution as far as Saruman was concerned was a massive hole in the theatrical version of *The Return of the King* (and *The Two Towers*). Even more so when one considers that *The Lord of the Rings* films employed an old-fashioned, conservative kind of filmmaking, and a very conventional sense of morality and ethics. And one of the things that mainstream Hollywood movies like *Star Wars* or *James Bond* or *Indiana Jones* or other action-adventure yarns absolutely *have* to do is to punish the villain. Saruman's forces were shown in the films killing hundreds of people, including minor characters such as Háma and Haldir, but he went unpunished (and unseen). In contemporary movie terms, Saruman simply *has* to be seen dying or banished to eternal hell. Amazing that he was completely absent (from the theatrical release).

Originally, a scene with Saruman at Orthanc was going to have closed *The Two Towers,* but was dropped during editing, when it was decided that after the big battle and the scenes with Frodo and Sam at Osgiliath, it would have made the movie drag on too much with a talky seven minute scene. A few months after *The Two Towers* opened, Peter Jackson explained that the Gandalf-Saruman scene would now be placed at the front of *The Return of the King*. In the event, it didn't appear in *The Return of the King* (theatrical), either: a different scene, a flashback to Sméagol and Déagol, now opened *The Return of the King*. That particular scene is a 555-year flashback (to 2463 of the Third Age in fact, though the time-scale isn't noted in the film).

Another reason was the scene was difficult to write and edit. Christopher Lee said he had shot it twice and looped it four times, and editor Jamie Selkirk said they had edited it at least 20 times, but couldn't make it fit in *The Return of the King*. Film editor Annie Collins said when a scene's so difficult to get right, it's sometimes better to drop it altogether. (Jackson acknowledged that *Return* had been significantly reworked in the editing, and departed from the script [Sib, 507]).

In the film of *The Return of the King*, it's Éowyn, not Merry, who's beside King Théoden when he dies. The dialogue here (as everywhere) was altered from the book, and given a contemporary touchy-feely spin. For instance, Théoden tells Éowyn: 'you must let me go' (i.e., let him die), a very New Age, modern psychotherapy idea. He also says something about being reformed (it wouldn't be surprising if he murmured 'I have issues' or 'I've moved on'. Yeeuck). In the 1955 book, though, just before Théoden dies, Éomer rides up to him, and Théoden hails him as the new king of the Mark (RK, 140). This was dropped from the film (neither version really indicates that Éomer's new king of Rohan).

When Gollum falls into the fire at Mount Doom, he takes Frodo with him. For a moment, it's a tease: has Frodo died? But no: the next shot has Gollum falling backwards into the lava, a pathetic smile on his face (he has his 'precious' at last), which withers as he lands in the lava, and realizes that the ring had betrayed him. Then the old, old dramatic device of one character hanging onto a cliff was employed, with Sam again saving the day, pulling Frodo to safety. This was another example of the screenwriters pushing situations much further than they were in the book (and though they always wanted to avoid silliness and cheese, this was it in spades – triple cheese on rye on extra cheese on a double cheese pizza base).

Another tease was Elrond bringing the reforged sword Narsil to Dunharrow: his arrival was covered with visual teases – images of his horse's legs and long shots of Elrond on horseback cloaked and hooded. Right up to the moment when Aragorn enters Théoden's tent Elrond's identity was withheld. Who is this hooded person? Is it Arwen? Having Elrond bring the sword would no doubt irritate some diehard Tolkienites, for whom Elrond is a crucial elven character who remains at Imladris throughout *The Lord of the Rings* until the final pages when he travels with the elves and other lords to the Grey Havens. But it had to be someone of some magnitude to deliver the magical sword, not just some lackey. It would be, in this movie adaption's terms, Elrond or Arwen (it had to be, because the story of the sword was tied in with Arwen, Elrond and Rivendell in this version, and it's Arwen who persuades daddy to reforge the sword).

Elrond's appearance at Dunharrow thus takes on the form of Merlin to Aragorn's Arthur: i.e., Elrond is the magical helper character of mythology, a facilitator who encourages or advises the hero in classical stories and folk tales, and gives him magical objects. Elrond unveiling the sword to Aragorn was given the full filmic treatment for a heroic moment (slow motion, an overhead shot, big music). Like Merlin with Arthur, Elrond reminds Aragorn of his destiny and responsibilities, and also suggests that Aragorn take the Paths of the Dead. (Questions like: why didn't Narsil get remade during the two months at Rivendell, or why Elrond travels alone in war-time, or what happens to Elrond after he's delivered his message and the sword are quietly forgotten).

One of the more curious additions to the 1955 book in *The Return of the King* was Sauron directly addressing Aragorn when the Dúnadan stands before the Host of the West. It's a hallucinatory moment, possibly included to depict Aragorn as one of the people Sauron fears, and the ascension of Aragorn to kingship. The composition, lighting and staging suggest a relationship between Aragorn and Sauron on his Dark Tower at this moment as something Biblical, like God talking to Moses or Jesus. But it turns out that this was a remnant of an abandoned concept (of which more later).

Ghân-buri-Ghân and his band of Wild Men in the Druadan Forest were also dropped from the films (there were the other Wild Men, of course, the ones appropriated for Saruman and his cause). The reasons for losing Ghân-buri-Ghân and the Woses were probably time restrictions, and budget, and having to introduce yet another people and culture. Plus the Wild Men function in the book really to speed the Rohirrim on their way, and weren't absolutely essential to the plot. There is also a political correctness aspect: Ghân-buri-Ghân and the Woses are a little like the stereotypical tribespeople of the fiction of Rudyard Kipling or Edgar Rice Burroughs.

After the ring has been destroyed, there are still many plotlines to tie up – but there wasn't time, in either the theatrical or the DVD versions of the film, to do so. Sequences were shot – of Legolas wandering in a forest (presumably Fangorn) and Gimli eyeing up some jewels (presumably in the Glittering Caves), but the screenwriters decided to stick pretty much to Frodo's fate, and followed him back to the Shire and then to the Grey Havens. The reunion of Arwen and Aragorn was an important subplot, and was dealt with straight after Aragorn's coronation. Sam's marriage to Rosie occurred after the *Green Dragon* scene, but that was about the only other subplot in the *dénouement*. In the book, of course, there is a further major section of the story after the ring is destroyed – principally concerning the hobbits return to the Shire, and the battle with Saruman and his 'ruffians', but also dealing with storypoints such as Galadriel, Celeborn and Elrond, Faramir and Éowyn, the Field of Cormallen, Théoden's funeral, Frodo and Sam both being mayor, and Merry and Pippin.

The first rough cut of *The Return of the King* was four and a half hours long. Jamie Selkirk and assistant Annie Collins hacked, slashed and burnt the film, as they put it, until they cut it down as much as possible.

NOTES: *THE RETURN OF THE KING* FILM

1. The television version of the first two *Godfather* films became a TV saga, with scenes not in the theatrically-released films included. *Mario Puzo's The Godfather: The Complete Novel For Television* was broadcast on NBC in November, 1977, with an extra hour of footage, making 7 hours 14 minutes, shown over 4 days (NBC paid $15 million for the omnibus edition). NBC reckoned that 100 million people watched the mini-series.

CHAPTER 18

THE RETURN OF THE KING, SCENE BY SCENE

ACT ONE AND PROLOGUE

The Lord of the Rings: The Return of the King: The Motion Picture (2003) opens, like the previous two *Lord of the Rings* films, with a prologue. While the opening of *The Two Towers* offered a flashback to a critical moment towards the end of *The Fellowship of the Ring* (Gandalf's fall), and *The Fellowship of the Ring* began with a history of the ring (from Sauron forging it to Bilbo finding it), the prologue of *The Return of the King* concentrated on one character alone: Gollum, and how he obtained the ring (it's taken from *The Fellowship of the Ring*). The prologue wasn't just about Gollum, though: it also introduced the ring again, in a film set entitled *The Lord of the Rings* (the ring had been lost from view a little in *The Two Towers*). That is, the prologue outlined crucial plot points such as: the ring's powerful hold over people (to the point where Gollum slays his brother within minutes of catching sight of it), and the ring's effect on Gollum's body as well as his soul, and foreshadowing what might happen (or is happening) to Frodo. The prologue thus took the outward form of showing how Gollum obtained the ring from his brother and crawled away into the mountains, but the inner theme or subtext was the ring's power. The prologue reminded viewers that the ring was thoroughly bad news, and had to be destroyed.

Originally, this scene of Gollum's back-story was going to be placed in the middle of *The Two Towers*, the set-up for it being the scene where Frodo approaches Gollum at night in the Dead Marshes. Gollum thinking back to when he was called Sméagol would have been the cue for the flashback. (As editor Jamie Selkirk remarked, the opening of *The Return of the King* was the only place the scene could go, really, because once the story got started, there wasn't a place for it. Assistant editor Annie Collins commented that it was an unusual way to open the film; the audience would be expecting something else).

The other scene that was carried over from *The Two Towers* was Saruman at Isengard. Another way of opening *The Return of the King*, which was planned, was to begin with the reforging of the sword Narsil in Rivendell, which would've introduced the return of the king theme (and the magical sword he'll be wielding to achieve kingship). Another opening was a nightmare of Aragorn's, as he sleeps in Edoras, with the camera flying from the Paths of the Dead. Then he would have woken, and entered the Golden Hall, finding Éowyn asleep (and also having a nightmare).

The opening shot of *The Return of the King* was a big close-up of a worm and Sméagol/ Gollum (Andy Serkis) smiling (though, in the age of political correctness, and not harming animals in making movies, the hook going into the worm occurred just off-camera – even worms have feelings). These scenes, and Gollum's deterioration which followed, were directed by writer Fran Walsh (as with so many of the Gollum scenes). A pastoral, summery, sunny scene showed Gollum and Déagol (Thomas Robins) in a coracle on what looked like a lake (though it's meant to be the Great River – but a lake is more practical for shooting).

It's the most peaceful, sunlit image in the film until the hobbits return to the Shire. As Gollum and his brother are hobbits too (Stoors of the Gladden Fields), it's fitting that this scene should look back to the rural sunniness of the Shire scenes in *The Fellowship of the Ring* (the music – light-hearted, with the flute prominent, enhances this). Sméagol's costume is dark, but also slightly aristocratic (Sméagol also sports a neckerchief, hinting at his vanity, costume designer Ngila Dickson said). A few of the filmmakers saw Gollum as something of a diva, given to melodrama; all of the Gollums on screen and radio have been over-acted to the max).

Fairly rapidly, the action begins, with Déagol hooking a fish on his line (with Gollum encouraging him). Déagol's pulled into the water; underwater images (shot dry for wet) follow of the hobbit trailing the fish (not the best visual fx work in the films – the fish, for instance, doesn't look big enough to pull even a puppy along). Déagol, just about to return to the surface, spots the ring. The shot of the hand grasping the ring on the bottom of the river is taken from the prologue of *The Fellowship of the Ring*. The only time the ring theme music is heard in a humorous mode occurs here.

Wider shots depict Déagol climbing out onto the bank (alone). Quiet amos; bird-song. Déagol studies the ring in his palm. The ring's high-pitched calls and a slower version of the ring's heartbeat are heard (the film is thus still in Déagol's mindscape, and these sounds describe the ring taking effect on Déagol, which isn't mentioned in the book). The audience is way ahead of Déagol here – he doesn't really know what it is apart from a pretty golden ring. (The ring's sounds are sweet when Déagol's holding it, but turn more evil when Gollum's sees it, as the sound designers explained: the ring reacts according to person holding it or near it, and the ring recognizes that Gollum is a corruptible soul. The scene plays through without music, the ring's sounds predominating. None of these weird sounds and the ring's 'heartbeat' are heard at many other times, though, such as at Bag End).

Gollum approaches his brother from behind (as if he's already taken to lurking about unseen). As soon as Gollum catches sight of the ring he stares at it intently, and his jokiness dissolves (but Gollum, pre-ring, was also creepy). The elvish music cue is revived from film one. Gollum demands the ring; they start fighting. No swinging fists from Westerns, or martial arts moves here – it's a grappling, rough tussle. The high-pitched calls of the ring increase; as does the ring's heavy heartbeat. Gollum bites Déagol's wrist. In return, Déagol strangles Gollum, and Gollum does the same. Now they're on the ground, with Gollum kneeling above his brother. The ring's heartbeats diminish as the life drains out of Déagol (the extended cut adds some more shots of strangulation – which were requested by the MPAA in the U.S.A. to be cut. And quite right, too: extra images of people being strangled in fantasy films always leads to outbreaks of mass strangulation. 200 people died after seeing Darth Vader strangle someone at the start of 1977's *Star Wars*).

Gollum takes up the ring, for the first time. The low sound of Sauron's voice is heard now, as well as the high-pitched calls (notice how much music and sound effects are doing the narrative work in this largely wordless scene). The sequence closes with Gollum's catchphrase – 'my precious', and when he puts on the ring, he disappears (originally, Gollum wasn't going to put the ring on, but the filmmakers decided to include the moment, as it hadn't happened since film one).

The next scene in *The Return of the King* is a montage sequence detailing Gollum's decline – from hobbit to emaciated wretch and 'ring junkie' (it was directed by Fran Walsh). The montage is narrated, aptly, by Gollum himself (though the dialogue is spare); however the account of Gollum comes from Gandalf at Rivendell, at the Council of Elrond. There are individual shots describing the stages of Gollum's transformation and, as in the prologue of *The Fellowship of the Ring,* fades to black in and out of each segment. An image of Gollum, still in hobbit clothes, among some rocks and dead trees; he makes the *gollum* noise in his throat; he is dishevelled, with straggly hair. Another brief section has Gollum catching fish, his hands now with long finger nails, and his body further degenerated (Fran Walsh explained that the gully set was dressed in various ways to suggest the passage of time). The following segment shows Gollum crawling into a cave in the Misty Mountains, in daylight. He is now extremely frog-like – crawling on all-fours, and his face is made up a little like one of Dr Seuss's things from *The Cat In the Hat.*

There is a hand-over in the next section of the Gollum montage from Andy Serkis in complex make-up as Gollum to the digital Gollum (the *Lord of the Rings* films will revel in on-screen visual effects hand-overs, using them on Sam and Legolas, among others). It's a big close-up of the Gollum familiar from the previous two films (Serkis's eyes were enlarged digitally, to blend with the CG Gollum's). And he whispers his catchphrase once more at the end of this montage: 'my preciousss'.

Ithilien. Stark lighting; grey clouds; a wintry treescape (the visuals in this scene are the basic combination of the films as a whole: live action in a brightly lit foreground, from the New Zealand sun, or studio lamps, combined with darker, brooding matte paintings or models in the middle and far distance). Most of the scene was shot in 2000, but some close-ups were part of the reshoots in 2003.

Frodo's awake; Sam's asleep; Frodo takes out the ring, the link to the previous scene, his little secret which he contemplates when he's alone (the film links together the two ringbearers). Gollum disturbs Frodo's ring reverie, appearing overhead, upside-down (a call-back to his first appearance in *The Two Towers*: upside-down above the sleeping hobbits). Sam wakes. Frodo says the days are getting darker. The ring music is heard. The setting is a disused trapezoid culvert (presumably made by the Gondorians).

An earthquake occurs (presumably from Mount Doom, though it's still far away, on the other side of the Ephel Dúath). Next is the lembas bread, which a piece of plot information which foreshadows the break-up between Frodo and Sam. Gollum appears again, and the hobbits move off. The landscape comprises blasted trees; grey and monochrome vistas (they are far from the greener forests of Ithilien now. A burnt section of woodland was used as the location). A long shot tilts up from live action of the figures in the landscape to a matte painting of the Mountains of Shadow.

Fangorn: Aragorn, Gandalf, Legolas, Gimli and Éomer riding through the trees (on the Fangorn interior set, shot with the background out of focus, to disguise the cyclorama). Most of the major characters are introduced early on, as with the previous two films (and most Hollywood movies). The title of the film comes over a crane up from the horseriders to reveal Isengard flooded beyond in sunshine, ringed by snowy peaks.

Merry and Pippin are encountered next, joking, eating and smoking on a wall on the edge of Isengard (the extended cut adds a little more banter). The riders stop near them. Gimli is the chief speaker in the reunion with the hobbits, and the conversation is light-hearted (the meeting pays off the long chase the Three Hunters gave in *The Two Towers*). The dwarf is a little disgruntled that the hobbits have been eating, drinking and smoking, and seem to be oblivious to the chaos around them.

The company ride on, to meet Treebeard, who stands near (but not underneath) Orthanc. Saruman is dispensed with in the dialogue (in the theatrical edit). This's Treebeard's only appearance in *The Return of the King*; at least he *was* included; Christopher Lee complained about being cut from the film, Luckily, digital characters don't moan – though their animators might). Isengard is being cleansed by water, which is waist-deep, as at the end of *The Two Towers*. The hobbits are riding behind the men.

The howling mistake of not showing Saruman or what happens to Saruman, occurs here (in the theatrical release of *The Return of the King*). Such a glaring omission, which perhaps the filmmakers hope will slip by unnoticed by the audience. It breaks a cardinal rule in Hollywood movies, from the early silent days onwards: a major villain *must* be dealt with. Saruman's forces have slaughtered hundreds, maybe thousands of people on screen, including secondary characters such as Edoras doorward Háma or Lórien elf Haldir. But Saruman's escapes judgement and sentence. (Christopher Lee was 'crestfallen and offended and pissed off', recalled Sean Astin. It hadn't helped that the decision to axe Saruman had been taken quite late in the process, and Lee had already been supporting the film publicly [S. Astin, 2004, 293]).

In the *Extended Edition* of *The Return of the King*, Saruman is introduced, and killed. He appears not on the stairs (as in the 1955 book), nor on the balcony but, improbably, on the roof of Orthanc (where it would be pretty difficult to have a conversation, even one shouted at the top of one's voice – Orthanc being 500 feet high). He's up there partly 'cos it looks good, partly because of the way he dies – a knife in the back from Wormtongue, and then toppling over the edge (and winding up impaled on a spike on a wooden wheel, part of some machine, so he's killed by his own industrial devices (which then – oddly – rolls over into the water, with the wizard attached to it). The *palantír* slips out of his sleeve, which explains how it gets into the water for Pippin to spot it). Chris Lee joked that he'd been in this situation before – lying down impaled and looking up at Peter Cushing (Sib, 459). The impaled by a stake demise has been used countless times, not least in the many Hammer films; Lee and Cushing were the grand masters of Hammer horror. (The *Lord of the Rings* films are a compendium of horror film clichés – giant spiders, monsters, strangulation, demonic possession, magic duels, decapitation, haunted castles, beastly transformation, hooded villains, etc).

Before Saruman is dispatched, there is a shortened version of the dialogue in "The Voice of Saruman" chapter (many of the phrases are straight out of the novel). Gandalf rides forward a few yards to parley wizard to wizard. One of the biggest alterations from text to celluloid here is the virtual elimination of the magical, persuasive power of Saruman's voice (there are hints of it, but it's much more to the fore in the book). But Chris Lee's white wizard does get to run through 2 or 3 pages of dialogue, while the others listen far below. Saruman brandishes the *palantír*. Wormtongue appears lurking behind the sorcerer.

Saruman accuses Gandalf of wanting power for himself, as he does in the book. Saruman also refers to Aragorn as the would-be king of Gondor (there's a cut to a reaction shot of Aragorn looking uncomfortable). When Saruman appeals to Théoden (which he does first), in the book Théoden surprises his men when he breaks Saruman's verbal spell and answers the wizard harshly ('Harsh as an old raven's their master's voice sounded in their ears after the music of Saruman. But Saruman for a while was beside himself with wrath' [TT, 231]). In the film, he shouts loudly up at Saruman (and also addresses Wormtongue, who was a man of Rohan once).

When things don't go well for Saruman, he sends a bolt of fire down at his rival; the flames seem to engulf Gandalf for a moment, but he emerges unharmed from the fireball. Gandalf then breaks Saruman's staff, to Saruman's astonishment. Théoden calls to Wormtongue to come down, but Saruman launches into an attack on his servant, which spurs Wormtongue on to kill him. Part of Saruman's death follows the book – Wormtongue is behind the wizard, and pulls out a knife and stabs the wizard (but he doesn't cut Saruman's throat – perhaps that would be to gory for a 'PG-13' movie, although some 'PG-13' flicks have shown that). Legolas looses an arrow which hits Wormtongue in the chest, and kills him.

So the manner of Saruman's death does evoke "The Scouring of The Shire", with Wormtongue attacking Saruman, then being killed with an arrow. But in terms of context, location, meaning and narrative placement, Saruman's demise is quite different from the 1955 book. In the movie, he has a spectacular movie fall (like Denethor), with the camera flying closely behind him as he tumbles over and over to the ground (in a way, it's a mirror image of the shot where Gandalf spins upwards to the roof of Orthanc in the first film). For many reasons, already outlined, this scene should have been in the theatrical cuts of *The Two Towers* or *The Return of the King*. In movie terms, it's one of the biggest mistakes of the film series.

The scene was shot a number of times (at least three – partly in the parking lot on the wet set, on a very windy day, and partly in the studio). Originally intended to close *The Two Towers*, the scene was rewritten for the beginning of *The Return of the King*, with Saruman now announcing that he has some information which Gandalf wants. The information the screenwriters wanted to include here was about the Enemy corrupting Denethor. Something 'festers in the heart of Middle-earth', Saruman tells Gandalf (though how Saruman knows that isn't explained).

The *palantír* sub-plot is introduced here, though in a slightly different way from the book. In the theatrical cut, it's still Pippin who handles the seeing stone before Gandalf can hide it, but it's not Wormtongue throwing it down from Orthanc in a bid to kill Saruman or Gandalf. In the film, the *palantír* is glimpsed under the water by Pippin (note how Pippin is riding behind Aragorn, one of the other characters who looks into the seeing stone). Gandalf swiftly takes it from the hobbit and wraps it up (with a brief, sly glance from Pippin). (The extended cut adds a few more images of the *palantír*, and also links it to Saruman when he shows it to Gandalf and the others below).

The scriptwriters remarked that the only reason for going to Isengard was to get the *palantír*, which was needed so that Gandalf and the allies could find out where Sauron planned to strike first. Too much was made of that: in the book, Gandalf knows that Sauron will go for Minas Tirith first. Also, in the map scene in *The Two Towers* movie, Faramir had explained what Big One-Eye will do. In movie terms, a far more pressing reason for returning to Isengard was to deal with Saruman.

To Edoras next, and more major characters are re-introduced: Théoden and Éowyn. The riders head for Edoras, accompanied by the Rohan theme played on a fiddle. A helicopter shot of Éowyn in white standing outside the Golden Hall (that kinda gives Éowyn something to do – she's still waiting, but not forlornly slumped over a mug of wine by the fire). Ranks of soldiers in battle dress are gathered in the hall; Théoden stands before his throne, and hails the victorious dead (meaning the Rohirrim who died in the battle of Helm's Deep). As they drink, there's a reaction shot of Aragorn (perhaps he's thinking about his friends lost at Helm's Deep, such as Haldir, or the responsibilities of future kingship).

Cut to a feast in Meduseld, some time later (part of the reshoots). This scene logically fits in with the close of *The Two Towers*, but it's here partly because the filmmakers opted to tie up the end of the second film fairly promptly, and not to have too many scenes which resolved other sub-plots or slowed down the *dénouement*. The Edoras feast is another 'watering hole' scene: it offers an opportunity for exposition about the primary plot (which occurs between Gandalf and Aragorn), and a little more development of sub-plots (such as the will-they-won't-they? sub-plot romance between Éowyn and Aragorn). There is also time for some light-hearted moments (much of the rest of the film is intense and not a bundle of laughs).

So Éowyn approaches Aragorn (note it's not the other way around – it's usually Éowyn who approaches Aragorn in the movies), and offers him a drink, inspired, Mirando Otto remarked, by an Alan Lee painting (she also speaks in Rohirric, Tolkien's version of Anglo-Saxon and pre-mediæval English). Aragorn drinks. They exchange a look (the extended cut adds a little more here, but nothing significant). Aragorn moves away, and Théoden turns up at his niece's side, and says he's happy for her and her choice of intended. In the book, Théoden never recognizes like this that Éowyn hopes to be the ranger's beloved or wife. Éowyn doesn't say anything, but smiles and acknowledges Théoden's statement (again, something the Éowyn of the book doesn't do). Théoden also admits to her that he wasn't responsible for the victory at Helm's Deep.

Cut to the same scene, later: Merry and Pippin are dancing on a table, in front of a laughing crowd (Philippa Boyens and Fran Walsh were keen to have the hobbits sing and dance in the films, and it's nice to have scenes which reminds viewers of the hobbits' true nature, when they can forget about the serious political issues of Middle-earth). The *Green Dragon* song is a light-hearted moment before the more sombre dialogue between Aragorn and Gandalf. It's also one of the few times in the picture when things do lighten up – for long stretches after this *The Return of the King* is fairly grim (to use one of Tolkien's favourite words – Aragorn is often 'grim', so is Gandalf, Gimli, Elrond, and Boromir, Minas Morgul is 'grim', and Mordor is mega-grim, etc). (The extended cut adds a meaningful look from Pippin to Gandalf – clearly about the seeing stone – as Pippin dances with Merry on the table).

The sound dips right down during the next scene, the low-voiced dialogue between Gandalf and Aragorn, as they discuss the primary narrative: Frodo and the ring (Aragorn and Gandalf often speak close to whispers – a nightmare for the sound editors and designers in a loud, busy action-adventure movie, the kind of films where actors are often yelling their lines over hundreds of sound effects and music). Their conversation reminds viewers of the main spine of the film again (destroy that friggin' ring!), and the film duly cuts to a shot of the hobbits asleep in Ithilien at night. The setting comprises rocks, stunted trees, and a pool (one of countless studio sets of rocks, trees and bushes).

The next scene reprises the schizophrenic Gollum dialogue from *The Two Towers*. It begins with Gollum dreaming and talking in his sleep in a big close-up (this was going to begin the Frodo-Sam-Gollum scenes, tying in with Aragorn and Éowyn having nightmares in Edoras, when everyone in Middle-earth seems to be having nightmares). In the colloquy with his darker side, Sméagol is framed against the sky, while his reflection in the pool is the nasty Gollum. A flashback to Déagol's murder is inserted here (viewers can't have forgotten already, it wasn't that long ago). The duologue between Gollum and Sméagol foreshadow the Shelob scenes at length – too long, I think: all the audience really needs to know is that Gollum is still scheming, still hoping to win back the ring, and the dark Gollum side is still bossing the nicer Sméagol side about.

As Gollum talks to himself about Shelob, there's a cut to Sam in C.U. waking up and listening. In an over-the-shoulder of Gollum leaning over the pool, Sam appears behind him, in the water (i.e., it's the dark, Gollum side that Sam wants to deal with). Sam strikes Gollum with one of his pots, then goes for the creature again. Frodo intervenes. Gollum crouches behind a tree. Frodo reminds Sam that they need Gollum as a guide. Like a child or a monkey, Gollum takes Frodo's hand, and gives Sam a mean backward glance as he walks off with his master, a nice touch from the animators.

Back to Edoras, a day-for-night scene between Aragorn and Legolas. The ranger joins Leggy standing outside the Golden Hall, in starlight. The elf can sense that 'the Eye of the Enemy is on the move' – presumably the elf means that the Eye moves by rolling about in its spiky socket on the tower of Barad-dûr, because it never leaves the tower in the films (sometimes Sauron must curse himself for transforming into a Big Eye – wouldn't a giant hand be a lot more useful? He could scuttle about like the one in the *Addams Family* movies). Anyway, Legolas reminds the audience of Sauron.

The *Extended Edition* of *The Return of the King* adds a wonderful scene just before Aragorn joins the elf outside, one that would've enhanced the theatrical cut: Aragorn rises from his bed and enters the Golden Hall, to find Éowyn sleeping on a couch. After putting the covers around her gently, she wakes (no suggestion of Aragorn taking advantage of Éowyn, though here's the opportunity for a love scene), and says she had a dream of a giant green wave engulfing the countryside (it's Faramir who has the dream in *The Lord of the Rings*). This's a marvellous addition by the screenwriters to the novel, because it's one of the major recurring themes in all Tolkien's writing: the myth of Atlantis, which lies behind Tolkien's creation of the island of Númenor, and also the vision the writer had of a tidal wave of green water sweeping across the land.

Next, Pippin lies in his bed, awake (as is Merry nearby). The room at Edoras is crowded with sleeping bodies. Why is everyone, including dignitaries such as Gandalf and Aragorn, packed into one small room? Is it just a lack of studio sets in Wellington? Or is it a quick way of getting all of the characters together? But hasn't the king of Rohan got anything better to offer his guests? The audience knows, for instance, that Edoras wasn't exactly over-populated in the first place, and many died at Helm's Deep. Surely there must be a few more decent rooms? After all, Edoras is the capital of one of the key cultures in Middle-earth.

Despite Merry's protests, Pippin creeps closer to Gandalf (who's asleep, like Smaug, with his eyes half-open), and takes the *palantír* (substituting a jug in Gandalf's arms that's roughly the same size). (The extended cut adds some more images here). The hobbit kneels on the floor and looks into it. Pretty rapidly the Eye of Sauron appears. The Dark Lord's voice is heard (at this point, presumably in Pippin's subjective experience of the seeing stone, but not heard by anyone else in the room). The Barad-dûr theme music is reprised as Pippin falls to the floor, writhing. Stepped slow motion captures the grimacing hobbit clutching the glowing stone. Merry looks on in horror.

A brief cut back to Aragorn and Legolas outside and the elf saying 'he's here!' (but how can he know that?) brings them rushing into the room. Aptly, it's Aragorn who takes up the *palantír* from Pippin, but he can't control it, it's too powerful (the elf supports him by the shoulders). It rolls away along the floor, making fiery sounds (it's wreathed in flames). Gandalf chucks a cloth over it, and its magic disappears (it's fairly easy to switch the *palantír's* power on and off, then). Pippin lies on the floor, in a frozen, catatonic state, staring upwards. Gandalf kneels over him, taking Pippin's hands, and putting his hands to his face. Gandalf mutters some magical healing words. As Pippin comes around and tells what he saw, staring upwards and trembling, there are cuts to what Sauron wanted Pippin to see: the White Tree of Gondor – dead, with Minas Tirith behind it on fire.

The Golden Hall, presumably the morning after the night before. A gathering of the major characters – Théoden, Aragorn, Gimli, Gandalf, Legolas, and the hobbits (the gathering turns into a war council). It's a dully directed scene. Gandalf explains about the *palantír* (if Gandalf's around, it's always Gandalf who delivers exposition in the *Lord of the Rings* movies). The enemy now knows that the heir of Elendil has come forth (although the battle of Helm's Deep scenes didn't show that). Maybe Sauron knows about Isildur's heir from Aragorn's brief grasp of the seeing stone last night (but the audience wouldn't know, without knowledge of the 1955 book). And they now know that Sauron will attack the City of the Kings first (this is the pay-off of the *palantír* scene, as far the scriptwriters were concerned. It's a little pointless – might as well have Gandalf telling them he'll attack Minas Tirith first, which Faramir, Gandalf's pupil, already knows).

Anyhoo, after explaining that no great harm was done by Pippin, Gandalf tells Aragorn (unheard by the others) to look to the river and the black ships: this's the first foreshadowing of the different route that Aragorn will take to Minas Tirith and the big battle that climaxes the *Lord of the Rings* movies (again, it is quite different from the book). Only Gandalf and Elrond (and also Arwen, though in a different manner) tell Aragorn about the other route he must take, through the Paths of the Dead and the Great River. At the end of the Meduseld scene (the last in the films), Théoden expresses Rohan's reluctance to come to Gondor's aid (again, a different characterization of Théoden, and the plot from the book). Gandalf says that Rohan must answer Gondor's call.

A brief scene has Gandalf with Merry and Pippin walking down from the Golden Hall to the stables in daytime (it's one of the few times that the Rohan capital is seen in an everyday mode). Gandalf soon hurries on ahead, and Merry tells Pippin (i.e., the audience) what the *palantír* episode really meant: the Enemy thinks Pippin has the ring. In the book, Gandalf interprets the outcome of Pippin looking into the *palantír* thus: Sauron thinks that Pippin is in Saruman's keeping, in Isengard (and will send a nazgûl to Isengard to fetch him the hobbit to Mordor). It bides the allies a little time, a bit of doubt in the Enemy's mind: '"That dark mind will be filled now with the voice and face of the hobbit and with expectation: it may take some time before he learns his error. We must snatch that time"' Gandie explains (TT, 251). Merry telling Pippin that the Dark Lord now thinks that Pippin has the ring is a way of simplifying a lot of explanations (even though the ring wasn't mentioned by Pippin in the film or in the book).

The stables scene that follows is continuous with the previous scene: the following two scenes are essentially about the two hobbits, on an emotional level, because they are parted for the first time in the films. Gandalf puts Pippin on Shadowfax. Merry stands below; they say farewell, after Merry's given Pippin the last of the pipeweed. Gandalf and Pippin gallop out of the stables; a big romantic string theme wells up, as Merry (in the extended version of *The Return of the King*) hurries up a wooden tower on Edoras's curtain wall, in order to watch the wizard and the hobbit riding away. Aragorn joins him (appearing from nowhere).

It's as if Merry is desperate to catch the last glimpse of a lover, rather than a friend. If this scene isn't a *hommage*, it certainly looks like the famous scene in *Doctor Zhivago* (1965) when Zhivago rushes upstairs in the snowbound *dacha* in the Russian countryside to see Lara for the very last time, while Maurice Jarre's beautiful music fades to a murmur. Somehow, Dominic Monaghan pining after Billy Boyd riding away isn't quite the same as Omar Sharif in *Doctor Zhivago* watching the luscious Julie Christie disappear over the horizon. (The extended cut adds a little dialogue between Merry and the ranger, mainly about Merry's relationship with Pip, how they've been together since childhood, and never been separated. *Ahh, bless! Soooo cute*).

The last group of major characters – Arwen and Elrond – are introduced next, as the film makes a dramatic change of pace, setting (and time frame – Arwen, in terms of the movie's chronology, would presumably have left for the Grey Havens by now). The scene was one of a number inherited from *The Two Towers*. Elves are travelling through a small valley of trees and ferns, some on horseback, some walking. A white light (from the side) bathes the scene in pale colours (greys and blues in the costumes. It's suitably elvish weather, fey and wispy – not the rains of Bree or the snowstorm of Caradhras). Arwen is soon singled out as the focus of attention, riding a horse.

In slow motion, a boy (with dark curly hair and a white shirt), about 5 or 6 years old, runs in front of Arwen's horse. Only she sees him (presumably it is Eldarion (Sadwyn Brophy, son of Jed Brophy, one of the actors in the films), the only son of Arwen and Aragorn. In the novel, Arwen and Aragorn also have some daughters).

Elrond is now heard in voiceover explaining about the last journey of Arwen Undómiel (Elrond has yet to be seen in person). Local sound drops out and a solo voice (Renée Fleming) sings. (Originally, Arwen was going to be singing on the track, in her mindscape, while she stared at the vision. Instead, the song, sung by Liv Tyler, was placed over the Houses of Healing scene in the extended cut).

The boy runs from the sunlit forest to a large white room (a gradual blend within the shot, though the boy's movement is a little awkward in the animated hand-over between the different scenes; apparently, it was a bitch of a shot to complete for the vfx people). It must be Minas Tirith. Aragorn greets Eldarion and lifts him up – the proud, smiling father of the child. Aragorn's been aged up 10 or 15 years (grey beard, wrinkles). Cut to a big, expressive close-up of Liv Tyler's Arwen as she watches what is a vision of the future: the husband she hasn't married, and the child she hasn't had. When the film cuts back to the boy in Aragorn's arms, he looks into the camera (a point-of-view shot for Arwen. And *of course* Eldarion's wearing that bloody pendant).

Elrond now appears, briefly, talking to her (he's back in Rivendell, so this's a flashback). And when she looks again, the forest is empty of the boy, Aragorn or Minas Tirith. (The scene is narratively complex, combining the cinematic present with a vision of the future, and a flashback).

It's a male child in Arwen's vision, as are many of the prominent children in the films: the elder of the children sent by Morwen to Edoras was male, as was Haleth, Háma's offspring. Théoden mourns his dead son Théodred. Denethor has two sons. And even Aragorn is a son, which comes out in the graveside scene in the extended cut of *The Fellowship of the Ring*. Daughters and female children are much less common (Arwen and Éowyn (poor thing, an orphan) being the most significant in the films).

The flashforward scene serves as a motive for Arwen to turn back from the caravan of elves, and rejoin the story (well, the bit of the story that's been left behind with Elrond in Rivendell). It offers an emotional reason for her returning to Imladris – a child, a family, a future she might share with Aragorn. It offers a picture of a more maternal Arwen than the virginal elf bride of the book (at 2805 years old, Arwen must be one of the oldest virgins in film history and literature).

Here it's about children and families and living with Aragorn as wife and mother, rather than as an ethereal and aloof elf-maiden, who seems somewhat removed from life. Certainly the Arwen of the books isn't portrayed as a devoted mother. But Fran Walsh and Philippa Boyens have introduced mothers (and fathers) with children a number of times: Morwen and her two kids in Rohan; Elrond and Arwen; Denethor, Faramir and Boromir; and the women and children in Helm's Deep and Minas Tirith.

(Even though the romantic sub-plot concerns Arwen and Aragorn, there are plenty of scenes between father and daughter too. Partly out of necessity, of course, because Aragorn is away fighting wars in Rohan and

Gondor, so scenes depicting Arwen talking a lot to daddy are necessary to keep the narrative ticking over. Another character could have been invented – an elf friend for Arwen to talk to, for instance. That might've given the Arwen-Elrond scenes a different dramatic tone, but Arwen and Elrond are not only always portrayed *alone*, there aren't any handmaidens for Arwen, or companions or friends at all. She must know some people in Rivendell – she's lived there for many years. And she's an important elf, being Elrond's daughter, and has no less than Eärendil, Elwing, Galadriel and Celeborn as grandparents. But no, Arwen's all alone or with daddy. Elrond, too, as top elf in Rivendell, is curiously never surrounded by companions or aides. In the Rivendell scenes in *The Return of the King*, it appears as if every elf has already gone to the West, and Elrond is the only elf left. And when he travels to Rohan, it's all alone – a little dangerous in war-time).

So Arwen turns up at a deserted Rivendell, to confront daddy about her vision of the future. One of the most beautiful wide shots in the films of the valley hideaway occurs here, and the elven realm now looks very Autumnal, with dry, yellow leaves everywhere. Elrond's sitting (alone) in another open-air bower. Arwen approaches him rapidly, complains that she wasn't told about the child, and tells him she won't leave Aragorn. (Elrond seems surprised and saddened to see her there).

The scriptwriters gave Arwen a little more to do here, by having her being instrumental in the reforging of the sword Narsil. Arwen's shown persuading her father to have the sword re-made. She and he talk in a different room, presumably at a different time (a day or so later, perhaps). Arwen's now clad in a natty scarlet and dark blue dress (the kind of outfit a Goth girl would kill for. The wardrobe department called it Arwen's 'dying dress').

Another motive for Elrond agreeing to reforge Isildur's sword to aid the free peoples is because he sees that his daughter is also being directly affected by the spread of Sauron's evil over Middle-earth, which's reaching even into Rivendell: Arwen, sitting on a couch, drops a book (in slow motion, of course). Elrond takes her hands and finds her cold (plaintive choir music enhances the melancholy). So the adaptors add a personal, emotional reason for Elrond reforging the sword, and also tie it into the central quest to destroy Sauron and his ring.

The Narsil montage which follows is narrated by Arwen – not the first choice, perhaps, for the minor sub-plot, but, given the elevation of Arwen's function in the film adaption, it's understandable. The montage comprises images of Arwen in a dark hood and cloak wafting through the hall in Rivendell in slow motion; flashbacks to the prologue of *The Fellowship of the Ring*, and the Lord of the Rings being divested of his One Ring (to remind viewers of the significance of this sword – those oft-repeated images have certainly done a lot of narrative work). At one time, the reforging of Narsil was going to open *The Return of the King*.

The reforging itself occurs at night (the better to show off the sparks and the flames of the forge) by two elven smiths (this's very Tolkienesque imagery – the forge, the sword and the starlight – which the professor would probably love). Cut to C.U.s of Elrond – he's overseeing the forging, not Arwen.

ACT TWO

The music keeps up the pace from the Narsil montage (using a reprisal of the Rivendell theme) running over into about ten second unit shots of Gandalf and Pippin riding on Shadowfax to Minas Tirith. They ride through woods, rivers, beneath mountains, and the sequence culminates in the first big reveal of Minas Tirith in daytime (a crane up behind the horse over a grassy ridge).

The gallop of Gandalf and Pippin from the bottom to the top of Minas Tirith serves to establish firmly the city for the viewer, because this's where a lot of the action will take place for the rest of the film. It also shows off the production values, the sets, the decoration, the props, the extras, the costumes and make-up, the miniatures, and so on (one key area is saved for later – the Great Gates and main square of the first level which Shadowfax must have ridden through). Live action shots are mingled with long (model) shots of Minas Tirith and digital doubles of the horse, riders and extras. The first, second and third gates are some of the key areas in the film.

Minas Tirith in the 2003 film is pale white stone, green of a few trees, banners with the White Tree, a catapult on a wall (looking forward to the battle), and rather subdued inhabitants (all clad in dark hues, to stand out against the white stone. Costume-wise, Gondor is black and silver). Architecturally, Minas Tirith is a mixture of European secular, royal and sacred buildings: gatehouses, archways, battlements, buttresses. Some of it recalls a French château, as well as cathedrals and churches, and of course many castles and fortifications. It looks ancient, but in pretty good repair (which's right for the capital of humanity in Middle-earth, even if it's long past its glory days). At the top is the Place of the Fountain (built on the car lot wet set), the withered White Tree in the centre of the courtyard, guards, two statues in armour, a cropped lawn, paths, and the imposing entrance to the Citadel.

Denethor waits alone for the wizard and the halfling in the throne room, sitting on a chair below the dais and the throne itself (on a black, more modest throne; maybe drawing again from an Alan Lee painting). He sports a gorgeous black robe with grey fur lining, shoulder-length grey hair, stubble and a stern, grim visage (the costume suggests ostentatious luxury, but also vanity). It's all pretty much as it is in the novel, down to Denethor holding Boromir's cleft horn in his lap (however, Denethor's cast much younger than the late seventies of the 1955 book, and he doesn't have any aides). To remind viewers of the significance of this particular object, five or so shots are inserted from Boromir's death in flashback, as seen from Pippin's point-of-view. (The *Extended Edition* includes a little more of Pippin talking about Boromir, and a line or two from Gandalf at the end of the scene as they leave the hall, about Denethor using his grief as a shield).

When Denethor reveals that he knows about Aragorn and won't give up the rule of Gondor to the ranger from the North, that would be the moment to reveal the *palantír*. But the filmmakers perhaps decided that one seeing stone was enough, or it would take too much time to explain it, or that it would complicate things too much (maybe they thought viewers might think it was the same *palantír*). Without the *palantír*, however, Denethor's descent into madness is far harder to explain. It's true that in the book Denethor's corruption via the *palantír* does pretty much repeat what happened with Saruman. The picture thus uses the steward's grief at the death of his favourite son Boromir as a key factor in his decision to commit suicide, as well as giving up in the face of Sauron's overwhelming force.

The *Extended Edition* of *The Return of the King* includes some further scenes of Minas Tirith here, which largely consist of Gandalf explaining to Pippin about the history of the city (really Tolkienesque scenes). After the meeting with Denethor, Gandalf and Pippin walk out onto the tongue of rock of the seventh level, in hard, unforgiving light, passing the white tree with its guards with their over-the-top winged helmets (courtesy of Alan Lee). Gandalf tells Pippin they guard it because they hope the king will one day return, hope the tree will flower again, and the city and state will be renewed (the pay-off comes with the shot of the white flower on the tree). They walk out further, Gandalf continuing to deliver more Gondorian backstory, about the decline of the kings of Gondor, and he also indicates Mordor in the distance. As he talks, there are more shots of the city and its inhabitants. Gandalf also tells Pippin that they won't be going any further: any help will have to come to them. Clouds move out from the Mountains of Shadow; Gandalf says when they reach the city, the battle will begin. The brown murk, so important in the book, is introduced but then pretty much ignored in the movie.

An additional scene in the *Extended Edition* is inserted here, of Frodo and Sam in Ithilien, with Frodo wondering if he'll return from the journey. Sam reassures him. Another deleted scene, of the Crossroads of the Fallen King, was cut because it although adds some background (and it's a lighter moment), it has no important narrative information (but it's a poignant moment in the book). Frodo, Sam and Gollum are in another part of Ithilien (maybe the same day as the previous additional scene): the crossroads with the statue of the king, which has been vandalized by orcs. Frodo and Sam spot the statue's head nearby, on the ground, with flowers growing over it. A ray of sunshine (low and from the West – i.e. the Blessed Realm) glows for a moment on the head, and Sam says the king is crowned again (another instance of the return of the king). Then the sun flare fades and it's overcast again.

The Crossroads scene has more resonance when it comes after the scene on the prow of Minas Tirith where Gandalf explains about the cloud cover Sauron sends from Mordor to aid his orc army. It shows that there is still hope (literally, a ray of hope), that the gods (the Valar) haven't forgotten our heroes.

Cut to Gandalf and Pippin at night, in their quarters: a room high up in Minas Tirith (better then being crammed into one rom at Edoras). A more peaceful scene: Gandalf has time for a drink and a smoke (the extended edit has Gandalf coughing quite a bit from his pipe, which explains Pippin handing him the cup. In the strange world of commercial movies, someone coughing a lot usually means they'll be dropping dead fairly soon. Or maybe it's a bit of politically correct anti-smoking). After a brief reference to Pippin becoming a Guard of the Citadel, Gandalf and Pippin look out over Minas Tirith and Pelennor, towards the Mountains of Shadow. The volcano of Mordor can be seen lighting up the clouds beyond – in fact, it's so bright, it even lights up the actors' faces, impossible because it's many miles away (that glowing volcano has been used as often in the films as the Eye to suggest the menace of Mordor and the inhospitable realm to which all roads seem to lead). The white wizard and the hobbit could be anywhere as they talk of Frodo and Sam, but they're placed on a balcony for a specific reason, which isn't revealed until after the next couple of scenes.

Gandalf narrates a brief montage showing the gathering forces: Haradrim; *mûmakil*; fleets of boats on the Great River (all pointy metal armament; soldiers manning giant crossbows. Why do villains always have hard, spiky stuff in movies, and the heroes soft, curvy stuff?). Gandalf is setting up the central battle in *The Return of the King*. Gandalf points out Osgiliath in the distance, where the blow will first fall. Finally, the Witch-king of Angmar is introduced as the chief enemy in the forthcoming battle: over Gandalf's voiceover, the film cuts to a stone room in Minas Morgul, and his primary opponent suiting up. There's a wooden rack of weapons, and a lackey placing a big, spiky shaped helmet onto the Witch-king. (But in the theatrical version, the Witch-king as Gandalf's chief foe doesn't pay off – the confrontation between the two wizards at the third gate was cut).

Minas Morgul is the Witch-king's lair, remarks Gandalf, and the film duly cuts to Frodo, Sam and Gollum right there, outside the Dead City. The Minas Morgul sequence is one of the best in *The Return of the King*, in terms of visual design, visual fx, sound design, spectacle and execution. The filmmakers have departed from the book in various ways, but the sequence is so good, it really doesn't matter. The fortress itself is lit with livid green, with high, implacable, windowless walls and buttresses sharpened into spikes and points (four different lighting schemes, including ultra-violet, contributed towards the look of Minas Morgul). An enormous tower, and the gatehouse glimpsed in the first film, when the Black Riders rode out from it.

Ronald Tolkien called the light of the 'city of the Ringwraiths': 'wavering and blowing like a noisome exhalation of decay, a corpse-light, a light that illuminated nothing' (TT, 392). Tolkien's writing in this part of *The Lord of the Rings* is absolutely stunning, so the filmmakers had plenty to inspire them:

> Wide flats lay on either bank, shadowy meads filled with pale white

flowers. Luminous these were too, beautiful and yet horrible of shape, like the demented forms in an uneasy dream; and they gave forth a faint sickening charnel-smell; an odour of rottenness filled the air. From mead to mead the bridge sprang. Figures stood there at its head, carven with cunning in forms human and bestial, but all corrupt and loathsome. The water flowing beneath was silent, and it steamed, but the vapour that rose from it, curling and twisting about the bridge, was deadly cold. Frodo felt his senses reeling and his mind darkening. Then suddenly, as if some force were at work other than his own will, he began to hurry, tottering forward, his groping hands held out, his head lolling from side to side. Both Sam and Gollum ran after him. (392)

Minas Morgul looks a bit like a Las Vegas casino of the Underworld, or Dracula's castle decked out for Hallowe'en. Minas Morgul, of course, was not built by Sauron's forces, but Gondorians. However, in the film, its Gondorian origin is lost under the nazgûls' influence (the Dark Lord's special forces have been in Minas Ithiel for about a thousand years).

At the other end of the causeway (which is not across water, but what appears to be vague wreathes of fog and rock – in the book it's vapours and meads), two demonic gargoyles grimace atop pillars (horns, tongues sticking out – familiar Christianized versions of pagan demons. Similarly bestial carvings can be seen on many European churches). The Stairs of Cirith Ungol are handily built right next to the road (for dramatic purposes – in the 1955 book they're miles further up the valley).

The colours of this part of the film, and the subsequent Frodo scenes, are desaturated greys, greens, blacks, with nary a warm hue in sight. As in the book, Frodo is drawn to the stronghold; he clutches the ring (which he usually does to indicate the lure of Sauron or some other evil). Point-of-view shots follow next, of Frodo's view of the causeway. It's similar to a ring moment. Low rumbles and roars erupt, and the camera starts shaking about. Something like an earthquake. A sheet of green flame shoots up from the fortress and spirals around the tower, up into the clouds (after a moment when the sound drops out with a judder). It's called the 'Great Signal' in the book.

Cut to Gandalf and Pippin in Minas Tirith – this's why they're on the balcony: they embody the heroes' view of events, because the army that issues from Minas Morgul is on its way to its companion stronghold across the Anduin. There's a long shot of the point-of-view of the heroes in Minas Tirith of the light pouring up into the clouds (the visual effect is reminiscent of the climax of *Raiders of the Lost Ark*, when the ark is opened).

The Witch-king is riding the fell-beast up on the battlements above the main gate, a marvellous image out of John Howe's art. The beast screams. But the high-pitched screech, which's in the book, might come from the fell-beast, or the Witch-king, or Minas Morgul itself – the book also doesn't say exactly (it's very high up the scale, and piercing, a more extreme version of the Black Riders' screams in the first film). There's a cut from a C.U. of the Witch-king to a C.U. of Frodo, who's cowering with Sam with his hands over his ears. There's a reference to the ring, of course, and also to Weathertop, which still haunts Frodo.

The hordes of Mordor pour out of the gate and along the causeway, their marching feet loud on the track. The Witch-king flies down from the battlements and soars close to Frodo and Sam. It's a fearsome ring moment for Frodo, when they might be discovered, but in movie terms it's superb spectacle, driven by some inspired visuals, sounds, and effects. And though the vfx and visuals are terrific, it is the sound editors and designers who steal the scene, yet again. In Tolkien's 1955 book, it is a more complex moment, with Frodo resisting putting on the ring, and the Witch-king 'sensing some other power within his valley' (TT, 395-6):

> There was a pause, a dead silence. Maybe it was the Ring that called to the Wraith-lord, and for a moment he was troubled, sensing some other power within his valley... as [Frodo] waited, he felt, more urgent than ever before, the command that he should put on the Ring. But great as the pressure was, he felt no inclination now to yield to it. (RK, 396)

The perspective of the unleashing of Sauron's army is reinforced by the film cutting back to Gandalf and Pippin a couple more times, as well as some of the soldiers on the battlements of Minas Tirith. The sequence closes with Frodo, Sam and Gollum starting to climb the secret stair, and the introduction of the vertiginous mobile God's-eye-view shots which characterize the master shots of this part of the film. (The winding stairs were a combination of miniatures and full-size sets, with some of the steps being very steep. When the camera looks down on the actors from above, Minas Morgul looms green and black below – a model was specially constructed for these bird's-eye-view shots).

Cut back to Gandalf and Pippin in a side street in Minas Tirith during the day, presumably the morning after the Great Signal. Gandalf sends Pippin scurrying off. Now to Osgiliath at night, and the first big fight of *The Return of the King*. The chronology of the film is a little confusing from this point onward, for the next couple of scenes, because the Osgiliath battle takes place at night and carries on into a morning, so perhaps it's meant to be the night before; but if it's the same host which issued from Minas Morgul, then it must be the following night (the army having travelled from Minas Morgul to Osgiliath. It's 15 miles from Minas Tirith to Osgiliath in the 1955 book, but only 3 or 4 miles in the movie, with absolutely nothing but grass in between). Either way, cutting from Gandalf and Pippin in the white city during the day and the attack on Osgiliath at night is confusing. (A result of many re-edits of the film).

Fleets of boats with boarding planks at the front (consciously recalling World War Two landing craft) move stealthily over the Anduin towards the West bank (though why the orcs have flaming torches on their boats, when they're aiming for secrecy, is a mystery. Oh yeah, it's so the boats can be seen in long shots). Gothmog (played by Lawrence Makoare), the Witch-king's commander in the field, is introduced here: an elaborate (and grotesque) Elephant Man-style make-up hides the fact that Gothmog is nothing more than a narrative device, to personalize the countless orc forces. (His role is bumped up from the novel, but it's still wholly mechanical. In the extended cut he has a little more to do – most significantly, menacing Éowyn before she can reach a sword).

A late introduction in *The Return of the King* of a major character – Faramir – also occurs at this point. He is easily the most prominent character amongst the Gondorian soldiers, who are ready in waiting for the orcs. (Faramir's second-in-command (Madril) has one or two lines, and he does get a death scene, too – at the hands of Gothmog, of course. Gothmog's a standard movie baddie, because fairly soon after he's been introduced, he's killed someone). The fighting that ensues between the Gondorians and Mordor's orcs is routine stuff, and on the loose and rough side (again, the camera lingers on Faramir above all of the other characters). Gothmog doesn't do much fighting, but he does appear when the Gondorians have been routed to stick a spear in a victim.

The extended cut of *The Return of the King* adds a brief scene just before the orcs attack, between Faramir and his second-in-command; they discuss where and when the attack will come. they stand near or above the Anduin, in the ruins. Gondorian soldiers are glimpsed resting or eating or talking. A big crane shot down from the Gondorians in the ruins to the river and the fleet of orc boats. A Gondorian guard spots them through a window; Gothmog orders an orc to kill him. Hit by an arrow, the soldier tumbles down some steps and alerts the soldiers (and Faramir) that the attack will come from the river (the *Lord of the Rings* films have a penchant for using corpses to alert others: a skeleton falls down the well in Moria – it's a stone in the book; an orc falls out of the tower of Cirith Ungol which helps to start the mass fight). Faramir orders his men to the river. A busy scene ensues of soldiers running and preparing for battle (the score adds to the anticipation by rising one note after a bar or two). There are more images of fighting in the *Extended Edition*.

A vfx shot reveals the orcs above Osgiliath, traversing the remains of the bridge (a wooden bridge had been laid across a gap). It's still night, but when the film cuts back to Pippin and Gandalf, it's daytime. Pippin climbs the watchtower, at the wizard's bidding, covered with further aerial imagery of Minas Tirith. Pippin handily happens to be an expert mountain climber, 'cos the beacon's high up on a pinnacle. If the Witch-king can send out signals, so can Gandalf. Pippin lights the beacon on a partial set built, like the rest of Minas Tirith, in the quarry at Lower Hutt near Wellington (storyboard artist Christian Rivers has a cameo as a guard). Barrie Osborne directed the scene.

Gandalf watches from below, pleased when the job's done. He moves out to a balcony to wait to see if the next beacon will respond. There's muttering about Amon Dîn (an obscure reference to the beacon East of the Druadan Forest). There's also a brief reaction shot of Denethor looking over out a window somewhere above (in the book, Denethor calls upon Théoden's aid, by sending him the Red Arrow).

So the film moves into a heroic montage of second unit shots and model shots of the mountains. Beacons alight in the foreground and others in the distance being lit. Some of the beacons are situated on impossibly high and inaccessible peaks – very unlikely that they would (or could) be manned year-round. It's also appears as if the whole route from Gondor to Rohan is nothing but alpine mountains. Howard Shore delivers a busy heroic theme for this wordless segment of the film (and he hasn't got fifty channels of sound effects to compete with, either, so his music can really stand out. Gandie and Pip pass the beacons in the 1955 novel).

The beacons montage culminates with Aragorn (sitting and eating, on his own), in an area of Edoras set apart from the Golden Hall. As soon as he sees the beacon, he dashes over to Meduseld. Close-ups of Théoden, Legolas, Aragorn, Éowyn and Éomer and others (who, handily, are all gathered in Meduseld), as Aragorn brings the news that Gondor calls for aid. Théoden orders the muster of Rohan, and issues further orders to characters like Gamling. A martial version of the Rohan theme accompanies the images of characters busying about. (The *Extended* cut allows time for Merry to offer his services to Théoden, kneeling before him outside the Golden Hall; Théoden accepts). Another addition is a brief scene between Legolas and Gimli, discussing war, both sitting on a horse surrounded by Rohirrim. There's a blue screen shot of Merry trying to make his horse move, while horseriders pass him by in a convoy.

In less time than it takes to gather two hundred soldiers on horseback, Théoden is now depicted leading the Rohirrim away from Edoras, in the valley below the town (he also delivers a line in voiceover). There's also a very brief scene between Éowyn and Aragorn, though not a lot of any significance is said or shown (the shield maiden explains it's customary for the women in the royal house to accompany the men to Dunharrow).

As the writers explained, in movie terms, the Rohirrim should really ride straight to Gondor, in all haste. They don't: in Tolkien's schema, they have to gather at Dunharrow first, another tricky concept to explain to the audience. One of the chief reasons for going to Dunharrow at all, as far as the movie was concerned, was for Aragorn to go to the Paths of the Dead.

Cut to Osgiliath, now in daytime. The battle between orcs and Gondorians led by Faramir continues, but the goodies are being overrun and beaten (reshoots were made to include more of Faramir, showing him commanding his troops, and getting in some fighting gags). There's a cameo from Tolkien's grandson Adam, as a Gondorian soldier (he came to New Zealand keen to be visit the production). In a striking handheld 360° shot, the nazgûl appear to buzz the allies. It's the first time they've been seen in attack mode: they swoop down to pick soldiers off the walls and hurl them down (as well as using bits of masonry as ammunition). And they shriek, of course. Always with the shrieking.

Faramir orders the retreat (in modern movies, only wimps retreat), which the Gondorians do – on horseback. The action moves onto the grassy plain, the Gondorians galloping towards Minas Tirith, and the nazgûl (not orcs) pursuing them, attacking their horses, snatching up riders and dropping them. It's a terrific action sequence, and looks as if the

Gondorians will be devastated. Gandalf appears, galloping on Shadowfax out from Minas Tirith (though, bizarrely, and dangerously, he has Pippin riding before him – in the book, Pippin is part of a large crowd on the walls of the city watching Faramir's retreat and Gandalf zooming in from the North. Pippin's there because, originally, when Gandalf and the hobbit reached Minas Tirith, they would've turned to see the rout of Gondorians and ridden to the rescue).

The wizard holds up his white staff and beams of light issue from it, accompanied by a solo choiring voice. The nazgûl are scared off rather like crows: to cover over exactly how Gandalf's magic works at this point, the action is portrayed via extreme long shots. (There's also an impressive rapid trucking shot filming behind Gandalf on horseback, with Minas Tirith lurching into frame as the camera pans right).

Next: into the main square of Minas Tirith behind the Great Gates (accompanied by the heroic Gondorian theme). A few of the shots here show off the art department's labours: images of the tall wooden gates and the locking mechanisms (designed by Alan Lee), and a crane shot of the main square, one of the biggest builds in the *Lord of the Rings* movie project. Again, a distinctly Northern European flavour to the setting, which has an equestrian statue in the centre. The wooden gates are adorned with bronze statues (recalling the Baptistery in Florence with its famous reliefs by Lorenzo Ghiberti).

A brief dialogue between Faramir and Gandalf (who's often called 'Mithrandir' by the Gondorians), which moves quickly to Frodo and Sam, after Faramir catches sight of Pippin sitting in front of Gandalf (Pippin's handily next to Gandalf). The dialogue about Frodo leads yet again to a cut to Frodo himself: close-ups of Frodo climbing the near-vertical stairs of the Cirith Ungol pass (the *Rings* films exaggerate verticality in many scenes, like the follow-up film that Jackson, Walsh & co. made next, *King Kong*).

For most of the rest of *The Return of the King*, Frodo, Sam and Gollum will be traversing endless amounts of rocks and stones, with the odd stunted tree to relieve the monotony but, even though most of the scenes from Minas Morgul to Mount Doom are outdoors, most were shot in the studio. The active volcano of Mount Ruapehu was used for many of the Gorgoroth plateau shots (such as the ones near Mount Doom), but most of the Frodo and Sam scenes were filmed in the studio. All of the journey to Cirith Ungol and through Shelob's lair are studio scenes (as are the Cirith Ungol scenes, and most of the ones in Mordor and the Sammath Naur).

A short addition in the extended edit of *The Return of the King* has Sam grabbing Gollum by the throat (Gollum seems doomed to be strangled, or to strangle others) and warning him not to harm Frodo. Dark green-grey hues predominate in the trek to Cirith Ungol scenes, giving the film a near-monochrome quality. Each character has a filthy face (including the CGI Gollum) and all look tired and shabby. Gollum leads the way, Frodo's in the middle, and Sam's in the rear. God's-eye-view shots reveal the Dead City far below the climbers.

The ledge they halt at is a humble setting for a critical scene, which occurs after the hobbits wake in the dark morning (it was shot early in principal photography, the first of the major *The Return of the King* scenes for Astin and Wood, with another actor standing in for Gollum, as Serkis hadn't been cast). First, Gollum turns to help Frodo up onto the ledge, which inaugurates another ring moment, when Gollum catches sight of the ring dangling from Frodo's neck on its chain as the hobbit struggles to climb up (the clink sound of the ring on its chain is prominent in many of the Frodo scenes – often in situations where it would be impossible to hear even an air raid siren: it's a not-so-subtle way of reminding viewers of the importance of the ring. It's such a tiny object, it can easily get lost in the busy visuals of a scene. Pushing the clinks high up in the mix is a means of telling the audience that it's all about the ring). The ring's sounds and the ring theme music wells up. As Gollum appears to be reaching to grasp it, Sam draws his sword. Instead, Gollum takes Frodo's hand and pulls him onto the ledge (the close-up on Gollum's hand is another tease for the audience, who know that once Gollum gets hold of the One Ring, he'll never let go).

Then, as the exhausted Frodo lies on the rock, Gollum bends down to whisper in his ear that 'the fat one' (as he often calls Sam) wants the ring, and will ask for it soon (the shot frames Frodo and Gollum in the foreground in close-up, and Sam behind them, between them). But just as significant as Gollum dropping devilish ideas into Frodo's crop is Frodo's apparent acceptance of them: he doesn't negate Gollum's notions once. Maybe he's too tired. Maybe the ring means more to him than ever, even though it's destroying him. Maybe he's forgotten how desperately Gollum wants the ring. Needles to say, Sam hasn't shown any interest so far in having the ring.

Before the film returns to Minas Tirith (it has been jockeying back and forth between Minas Morgul and Minas Tirith for some time, as well as Osgiliath), it returns to Osgiliath for a brief invented exchange between the Lord of the Nazgûl and his lieutenant, Gothmog (both, incidentally, played by the same actor, Lawrence Makoare, who said he loved playing the Witch-king, because it meant only 20 minutes in make-up, while Gothmog was a four-and-a-half hour job. Other actors also played Angmar). They are depicted up on a roof or wall above Osgiliath; the Witch-king still on his flying steed and Gothmog standing nearby. When the orc mentions 'the wizard', Angmar replies 'I will break him'. A cut follows that train of thought to Gandalf himself, on the battlements of the first wall of Minas Tirith, surrounded by soldiers. When will Rohan answer the call? they want to know.

An intriguing addition to the theatrical cut on the longer DVD and video cassette (entitled "The Wizard's Pupil") has Denethor and Faramir alone together, in the White Tower, discussing the ring. It's rare to see the ring being talked about outside of scenes with Frodo or Sam, or one or two others (such as Gandalf and Elrond). Denethor tells Faramir that Boromir would have brought him 'a kingly gift'. Faramir quietly disagrees. Denethor whispers that it should have been hidden, but used only in direst need (clearly intending to wield it himself). It's a pity this scene wasn't in the theatrical cut, because it makes explicit Denethor's desire for the ring.

Apart from the ring, the other chief topic (as in other scenes involving Denethor and Faramir) is the uneasy relationship between father and second son, and the patriarch's preference for Boromir. Sean Bean gets to appear in the *Extended Edition* of *The Return of the King* when Denethor stumbles back to the dais, and sees Boromir behind Faramir's shoulder in a vision. His firstborn walks towards him in slow motion, smiling. The vision fades; in big close-ups, John Noble over-acts plenty here in suggesting Denethor's obsession with his elder son and his descent into madness.

After the scene where Gondorians ask Mithrandir 'will Rohan come?', Pippin is shown alone in an ante-chamber or hall of the Citadel, next to the Tower Hall (another new scene in the *Extended Edition*). He's in his tower guard costume (black, with the White Tree embroidered in silver on the chest). He talks to himself about being a guard. Faramir approaches, and they discuss the uniform (which used to be Faramir's). But that banter soon moves into something more serious, about Boromir and Denethor. Pippin reassures Faramir that he has a different kind of strength. The scene's partly there is suggest the relationship between Pippin and Faramir, to explain why Pippin should feel motivated to rescue Faramir. There's also a hint of a character dropped from the film, the young Gondorian Beregrond.

Now to the Tower Hall, with Denethor, Faramir and Pippin present, and one or two attendants. Pippin, kneeling, swears fealty, awkwardly reciting. Denethor smiles indulgently (one of the few times he lightens up). Denethor's subsequent references to fealty, valour, honour and other chivalrous concepts are aimed ironically at Faramir who watches Pippin. The hobbit then becomes an observer himself in the uneasy dialogue between father and son. The lines are pretty much out of the 1955 book: '"fealty with love, valour with honour, oath-breaking with vengeance"' (RK, 27), but they are given a different meaning when they are directed not at Pippin, but at Faramir. Tears well up in the second son's eyes as the stern patriarch tells him bluntly that he had rather Faramir had died than Boromir. As Denethor continues to eat at a small table, Faramir leaves, resolving to do what he can (he comes up with a cavalry charge on Osgiliath).

Now back to the crucial scene between Frodo, Sam and Gollum (a more striking contrast between the lofty, elegant halls of Minas Tirith and the tiny rocky ledge above Minas Morgul would be hard to find in Middle-earth. We have to forget that the characters haven't learnt shit about climbing mountains, and haven't roped themselves together). The seeds of the break-up are sown by Gollum with lembas crumbs. In the first scene, it's night (though, as in all movies, it's never completely black: rather, there's always a brooding, sullen sky at night. In this film, as in many flicks, night means a weird half-light, a perpetual twilight). Frodo's already asleep; Gollum appears to be asleep; Sam tries to stay awake but eventually succumbs. When he does drop off, Gollum's making mischief with the lembas, dropping crumbs on Sam and throwing the rest of the food over the cliff.

In the next scene (nearly continuous with the previous one), Sam wakes up, angry at himself for falling asleep, and troubled by what Gollum seemed to be up to. Frodo's also waking up; Sam discovers fairly rapidly (perhaps a little too quickly) that the lembas has gone. There are some big close-ups of eyes and mouths in this scene, recalling those in the first film. The argument between Frodo and Sam is when all of the scheming of Gollum comes to fruition. It isn't in the book: the Sam of the novel never leaves Frodo willingly, or has this kind of confrontation with him. In the movie, aided by Gollum's encouragement, Frodo comes round to believing that Sam is endangering the mission, and perhaps wants the ring.

It's not very convincing, for Frodo to doubt Sam in this manner so late in their journey, after all they've been through. Gollum has to be the one to drive a wedge between them but it doesn't ring true to what the audience knows of their characters. At the end of it, Frodo tells Sam to go home!!!, then leaves with Gollum behind him. Sam crumples against a wall and weeps. (Some much fiercer takes of Frodo telling Sam to go home were shot, with Frodo fairly yelling at his friend, but it was decided later that it was too out of character for Frodo. Elijah Wood remarked that he requested some less intense takes of the scene, and during ADR the dialogue could be played more moderately. The scene had been filmed with a year gap between Astin's side and the reverse angles on Wood, as a wet set cover shoot in a squash court at the Coronet Plaza Hotel. The Cirith Ungol set stayed in the hotel for a year before the production returned to it).

Really, the split needs more setting up and narrative work; it requires at least one or perhaps more scenes to make it convincing. And the argument scene itself is too short. The lembas, too, doesn't work as an element of contention. And the way Gollum calls Sam the 'fat hobbit' isn't believable – that Sam would accept it (or Frodo). I don't like the way the scene is written, or directed, or performed. Some more rehearsal might have helped, but on a big movie like this, it's unlikely to have that luxury (although multiple takes were allowed). And why would Sam wait until Mordor to take the ring? And the way that Sam dutifully goes home – all the way from Mordor. Soooo dumb.

But perhaps it was simply the pressures of time that forced the screenwriters to play it fairly quickly. It's more exciting, though, for Frodo to enter Shelob's lair alone, and to push the Frodo-Sam relationship to the point of breakdown. The addition of the split alters Frodo's character more than Sam's, because Sam still comes out of it as the ever-loyal companion, while Frodo has been swayed by Gollum and has doubted Sam. Viewers who don't know the book could assume that it's the ring which has affected Frodo so much that he can doubt Sam's loyalty. (Reasons given by the writers for the break-up was to introduce dramatic tensions in the Frodo-Sam relationship, to make real the threat that Gollum could break the friends apart, to show that Sam was still loyal, to have Frodo enter Shelob's lair alone, and to have that rescue moment when Sam returns. Critics have noted that the argument 'has all the air of lovers' tiff', hinting at the gay undercurrent in the Frodo-Sam friendship).[1]

For Roger Kaufman, Gollum is Frodo's homosexual other.[2] And Sam may be Frodo's soul-mate and guide, akin to a gay man's 'inner lover', a "soul figure' and guide who loves us just as Sam loves Frodo' (ibid.). For some critics, adding Frodo's alienation from Sam and finally his rejection of him adds to the corrupting power of the ring, as well as complexities to the hobbits' relationship. It also adds to the sense of jeopardy – that Frodo might be in more danger if he carries on with Gollum, without the stalwart Sam to protect him.

The traces of the portrayal of Frodo as a gay, effeminate man can be discerned in the films if one wants to find them: the way that Frodo looks at Sam at times; how he nearly kisses Sam on the lips at the Grey Havens; how Frodo is protected and cared for by the fellowship like a woman; and Frodo's appearance with androgynous, elfin hair, ears and make-up.

Minas Tirith. Day. A company of Gondorian soldiers on horseback in full armour processes down the steep streets lined with people (the extras are mostly women, and they're all very solemn. No cheering – or jeering – here – it's as if the soldiers are already dead. They're going to war, folks!). Flowers are thrown in the road; the horses trot in stately slow motion. Gandalf appears, telling Faramir not to throw away his life needlessly (a wonderful Tolkienesque moment in the *Extended Edition* has Faramir mentioning that he is defending the city built by the men of Númenor – one of the many examples where the screenwriters slip in references to the vast history of Middle-earth. It's appropriate for Faramir to speak thus, too, because in the book he has the most affinities with the era and people of Númenor – more than his brother or father, anyway).

In the next scene, the horsemen are ranged in a row on the plain below the City of the Kings, preparing for a charge to Osgiliath (this scene was directed by Geoff Murphy). The hero shot is an aerial image of the riders in a line, with Osgiliath beyond. Most every shot is slow motion; Faramir leads the charge (shot close to the camera, on a fake horse mounted on a truck). It's a good job that Alan Lee shortened the distance between Minas Tirith and Osgiliath for the film, to something like 3 or 4 miles, because it's about 14 or 15 miles (according to the maps of Karen Fonstad and Barbara Strachey), quite a long way for a gallop. The lines and trenches of fire were left out of the movie (expensive to do in live action of with effects). And, oddly, there are no major roads in the movie, between Gondor's two principal cities. And no settlements. No great wall. No fields of crops; what do the people of Minas Tirith live on?

Back at the Citadel, Denethor is *still* at his table set at the side of the hall, eating (although it must have taken Faramir at least two hours to get into armour and muster his men). Pippin is commanded to sing a song, and reluctantly does so (this idea grew during production, and wasn't scripted, when Philippa Boyens and others discovered that Billy Boyd had a good singing voice; Boyd was asked to write the song, the lyrics coming from *The Fellowship of the Ring;* Howard Shore layered delicate strings underneath).

The song turns the cavalry charge into an ironic montage, a

commentary on the waste and loss of warfare, as it cuts back and forth from Pippin and Denethor to Faramir and his soldiers. Pippin's melancholy song is heard throughout (with some reverb added), while the charge to Osgiliath is largely muted, with one or two spot sound effects. It's going to be a massacre, a noble but ultimately pointless endeavour: the orcs are ready for the Gondorians, and launch arrows. Instead of showing the carnage, the montage and the song do the work.

A big shot of Osgiliath shows the bridge, with trolls pushing huge wooden siege towers. Drumbeats and cries; Minas Tirith glows white in the distance. Gandalf sits on his own in a back alley of the white city, looking dejected. Aren't there are bars in Mins Tirith? He looks like he could use a drink.

The whole sequence seems to have a conscious link to the First World War in books and movies (in which Tolkien fought of course, and lost his friends): Denethor is the general, living in luxury in his French chateau, as he sends the sons of the land out to fight (in this case, led by his own son). Sauron too is a general who never comes out to fight himself (the incident shown in the prologue of *The Fellowship of the Ring* was a rare instance of Sauron coming forth, and only when it seemed that it was the only way to win). A contrast's evoked between eating and killing, life and death. And Faramir is leading his men 'over the top' in a charge, literally, and aware that he is possibly going to his death (that might be true in any armed conflict, but here Faramir, like Denethor and Gandalf, knows that the odds are stacked heavily against him). It's *Paths of Glory*.

Extending the comparison further, that puts the orcs as the Germans, the enemies of the British, the Commonwealth and the Allies in the First World War. That's the kind of link (which can lead to accusations of racism) which the filmmakers and many Tolkien fans claim can't be applied to *The Lord of the Rings*. Sure, the 2003 movie isn't consciously racist, was an international production, and didn't set out to offend anyone on that level. But notice how, for instance, the cast was drawn from Australian, New Zealand, British and American actors (nearly all white), nations which have fought together in world wars, Vietnam, the Gulf War, Iraq, and others. That gives the *Lord of the Rings* films a particular cultural and ethnic mix, which is deliberate. There are plenty of fantastic actors in France, Italy, Germany, Russia or China who could have been cast, say.

The 2003-04 film of *The Return of the King* then alters pace and mood when it cuts to the muster of the Rohirrim at Harrowdale and Dunharrow (with an upbeat version of the Rohan theme on the track). This's a large field backed by trees. Bright sunlight; tents and camps; fires; smoke; extras bustling about; horses. It looks like an encampment of mediæval re-enactment performers, the kind that meet at mediæval castles, palaces and abbeys to give combat displays (indeed, re-enactment teams are often employed by film productions. The *Lord of the Rings* production itself was like a professional mediæval re-enactment group with enormous financial backing).

King Théoden rides at the head of the column of horses moving through camp, with Aragorn beside him, and Éomer and Legolas behind him. A tilt up shot from a reverse angle (behind the convoy) reveals Dunharrow above the valley, with its winding track, and the White Mountains above. The King of the Mark acknowledges the different groups of soldiers who've come to the muster. In the following scene, Aragorn and Théoden stand on the edge of the cliff overlooking Harrowdale. They contemplate the troops assembled below. There are 6,000 spears, but Aragorn says that will not be enough to break the lines of Mordor. The overriding narrative line in these scenes is the build-up to the Pelennor Fields battle.

In the next scene, Sauron is sitting at a Miami hotel poolside with a beautiful, giggling woman on either side of him clad only in silver thongs. It's quite a sight, a twenty foot flaming eyeball trying to sip a cocktail. His buddy, Lieutenant 'Witch' King, played by Will Smith, swaggers up and yells 'Hey, motherfucker, the boss wants to see us down the precinct.' Sauron sighs, 'Shi-it', and struggles to put on his holster (not easy for a giant eye). 'Fer Chrissakes, doesn't that fucker Morgovsky ever sleep?' he moans. 'Witch' laughs, 'hell, no.' Oh, sorry, wrong film.

Éomer, Legolas and Gimli meet in the centre of the encampment and discuss the Dimholt Road. A bit of exposition, delivered in a dark, grim mood (Karl Urban's Éomer seems to be perpetually 'grim' in the Tolkien manner – does he smile even once in the theatrical releases?). Cut to Aragorn, who approaches the narrow, grey gap in the cliff face. A horse rears up, unsettled, with a soldier trying to calm it down, right in front of the Dimholt Road. A p.o.v shot shows Aragorn seeing a ghostly green shape at the end of the track, the first hint of the dead Dunlendings.

Part of the Dunharrow set was a disused quarry in Wellington. It was considerably smaller than the Hold of Dunharrow in the 1955 book, which was an alpine field that could accommodate several thousand soldiers. What was required for the film was a grassy area backed by a rocky wall. The Dimholt Road was added in post-production, like the cliff overlooking Harrowdale, and the switchback road up the mountain. The art department did add some standing stones, however, and one of the Pûkel-men statues (about the only reference to them in the films). Much of the rest of the Dunharrow, like all of the *Lord of the Rings* films, was a studio set. (In all about five different locations made up Dunharrow).

Next up is a more lighthearted scene, between Éowyn and Merry, in a tent (still on the same night). The shield-maiden is helping the halfling with his war gear. It's played in a jokey manner, when Merry brandishes his sword, which turns out to be blunt (the screenwriters seem oblivious of the Freudian subtext of a scene between a man and a woman in a tent at night and the man complaining that his sword is blunt.)

The filmmakers were aware of the sexual undertones of Tolkien's text, it seems, and at times they appear to have acknowledged it. Most of the time, they chose to ignore it, hoping it would go away. For instance, a recurring scenario in *The Lord of the Rings,* book and film, has hapless men entering dangerous caves, clefts, tunnels and doorways.[3] All very uterine and feminine. The filmmakers seem to hope that the audience will be too distracted by the pretty visuals, the effects, or the story to notice the blatant phallic, vaginal, anal, oral, gay and lesbian subtexts and tropes.

So Éowyn packs Meriadoc off to the smithy (presumably meaning a long walk down the mountain for the hobbit). That leads in to a short scene between Éowyn and her brother, who sits by a fire with Gamling, eating (the *Lord of the Rings* films have lots of scenes of people eating. When the filmmakers need to give an actor something to do, it's often eating. However, Gandalf, Elrond, Galadriel and the Witch-king, characters in the upper echelons, aren't shown stuffing their faces).

Éowyn tells Éomer that one should be allowed to fight for those one loves. The *Extended Edition* adds a little more conversation here, with Éomer reminding his sister of the horrors of warfare. War, Éomer says, 'is the province of men'. That rejoinder plays into the fact that Éowyn dresses up as a man (Dernhelm) to join the warriors in Gondor. (Not much – well, nothing – is made of Éowyn crossdressing in the film. And in one scene in the extended cut, she stands in the midst of the Rohirrim without her helmet, fairly easy to spot. It might have been tempting to add a quip about Éowyn dressing up as a guy. But, although there are belching, farting, eating and drinking gags in the films, Éowyn is kept noble and untouched by mockery). The writers decided to drop the idea that Éowyn was 'Dernhelm', and that Merry was too stupid to realize that he was a she.

A God's-eye-view shot introduces Elrond on horseback coming up the Stair of the Hold. There's a brief glimpse of a statue carved by the Men of the Mountains. The filmmakers tease the audience, withholding the identity of the rider until the scene in Théoden's tent. The arrival of Elrond seems to cause Aragorn to have a nightmare (or he just happens to dreaming about the same issue), which's cast in the form of a montage, like so many dream sequences in cinema: first, an image of Aragorn asleep and dreaming; then an overhead shot of Arwen in her 'dying dress', lying on her back on a couch in Rivendell (she could be asleep, or dead); then a rapid push-in to the Dark Door below the Dwimorberg; Arwen whispers, in voiceover – 'I choose a mortal life'; a different angle of Arwen, in glowing white light, and washing out, whispering: 'I wish I could have seen him one last time', a shot of Aragorn looking down at the falling Evenstar, which shatters on the floor in slow motion, accompanied by its high-pitched sound (symbolizing Arwen's death, presumably, or the destruction of their love). The nightmare concludes in the most clichéd manner: Aragorn lurching up in bed, and drawing his dagger (does anybody really wake up from bad dreams like that, except in movies? It seems to be a convention that nobody bothers to break). A guard in the doorway of Aragorn's tent informs him that Théoden awaits him. (Something like this montage might've opened the film at one time).

Théoden's tent is a large circular canvas structure familiar from hundreds of Middle Ages movies (tapestries, blankets and cushions, heraldic and horsey motifs, reds, browns, greens and yellows). A hooded figure sits with their head concealed. Théoden takes his leave (with a dark, unexplained look at Aragorn. So much for the ritual greetings among the great and the good that J.R.R. Tolkien liked – he just walks out!). Elrond reveals himself; Aragorn bows. Then follows a lengthy two-hander, the bulk of which comprises Elrond encouraging the ranger to take up his responsibilities, and become 'who he was born to be'.

First, Elrond appeals to Aragorn emotionally, and tells him that Arwen is dying, that her fate is tied to the fate of the ring. That gets Aragorn's attention (in choosing to become mortal, the writers had Arwen literally dying, so that Aragorn – or Frodo – had to destroy the ring and Sauron to save her). Elrond offers some exposition – about the Corsair ships sailing up the Anduin in secret (cut to a brief extreme long vfx shot of the boats). Next, Elrond outlines the army that might come to aid Gondor, the thieves and renegades who deserted eons ago. A flash cut to a C.U. of the King of the Dead (a p.o.v shot, he leers into the camera). Wind momentarily blows around the tent, a nice touch – the wind blowing at night being one of the primal manifestations of otherness and strangeness.

Then the reveal of the reforged sword, which Elrond holds up for Aragorn to take. That's the climax of the scene, in terms of action (the entire scene is just two people talking), but not the end of it: after Elrond has belted out a line about Aragorn becoming the leader of men, the two talk much quieter, in Elvish (Aragorn's reluctance continues to be an obstacle).

Next up is the farewell scene between Aragorn and Éowyn, with the culmination of their on-off, will-they-won't-they? storyline. This's the only place the romantic subplot can be concluded. It wouldn't work on the battlefield of Pelennor, of course, nor in the Houses of Healing (when Éowyn begins her romance with Faramir).

The scene is set at night beside Aragorn's horse Brego. (Miranda Otto explained that the scene was originally shot in a tent, which didn't look as good, and Éowyn was played much harsher and angrier, which didn't fit.) When Aragorn quietly rejects her, she steps away from him, eyes filling with tears. He leaves. And that's that. That's what Éowyn gets after desiring the guy for a film and a half, a quiet but firm rebuttal. (She might've known it was headed that way: after all, she does ask Aragorn about the woman who gave him the Evenstar).

Éowyn's response could've been played many different ways (angry, shouty, pained, shocked), but what really counts, as far as the film's concerned, is that this storyline is resolved (Éowyn has two more vital roles to perform, however: to take Merry with her to Gondor, and to kill the Witch-king. Aragorn's rejection of her love can also be seen as a motivation for throwing herself into battle so wholeheartedly, as she rebounds from being rejected).

But what a let-down to this sub-plot. It literally goes nowhere. Oh well. In the 1955 book of *The Return of the King*, Tolkien plays the scene like this:

> "No, he is gone," said Éowyn turning away and looking at the mountains dark against the East and South.
> "Whither did he go?" asked Éomer.
> "I do not know," she answered. "He came at night, and rode away yestermorn, ere the Sun had climbed over the mountain-tops. He is gone."

"You are grieved, daughter," said Théoden. "What has happened? Tell me, did he speak of that road?" He pointed away along the darkening lines of stones towards the Dwimorberg. "Of the Paths of the Dead?"

"Yes, lord," said Éowyn. "And he passed into the shadows from which none have returned. I could not dissuade him. He is gone." (RK, 77)

Cut to Aragorn encountering Gimli and Legolas: the three team up again (though Aragorn is reluctant). But the elf and the dwarf are already ready to leave, with Legolas leading his horse. (All of these scenes are pretty much continuous.) Next: Théoden and his soldiers gather outside the tents, watching Aragorn leave (the Dúnedan and his companions ride away *without explanation* or *even a farewell*, not quite how it happens in the book, and *utterly stupid* when you think about it. That Aragorn would leave like that without any explanation is *so dumb*). There is some muttered dialogue among Gamling and the men about why Aragorn is leaving. Théoden encourages Gamling and his men with some words about going to battle knowing they are outnumbered. For f◊$!¢'s sake, write the scene properly!

(There's a silent elision here: what happens to Elrond? Does he go all the way back to Rivendell? On his own? Wouldn't he go with the Rohirrim to Gondor? Or Lórien, perhaps? After all, the viewer's seen that Elrond is an important commander in wartime, in the prologue to the *Fellowship* film. Instead, the movie quietly hopes the audience will forget about Elrond. He's done his bit in the movie, so it's: *so long, Elrond!*).

The next scene is the Paths of the Dead. It's one of the sequences which had some substantial additions in it in the extended version of *The Return of the King*. (The additions are lengthy, but do not add a single significant plot point, and were not necessary to tell the story in the theatrical edit.) As the three ride through the Ered Nimrais below the Dwimorberg, Legolas takes up the exposition about the Army of the Dead (someone has to do the explanations, and it should logically be Aragorn who does it – he'd know more than Legolas, presumably. But it's more dramatic if Legolas outlines the backstory and the viewer sees the impact of the information on Aragorn. Indeed, it's one of the most significant acts, cinematically, that Legolas performs in *The Return of the King*). In the book, of course, Aragorn has a company of rangers of the North with him, led by Halbarad, but the films dispensed completely with the Dúnadain, along with Elrond's sons. In an early draft of *The Lord of the Rings*, it was Éomer who led a force over the mountains to come upon the enemy from behind (HME, 8, 253).

Long lens shots cover the actors riding through the grey, stony, rocky canyons and hills (filmed at Putangirua Pinnacles). Legolas continues to speak in voiceover. The *Extended Edition* adds a montage of rapid, tilted, low angle tracking shots circling Legolas, combining them with shots of the other two.

The Dead Door is set in a narrow, muddy gully, with dead trees on either side, and plenty of smoke effects. The door itself is squat and prehistoric (like the entrance of a European Neolithic long barrow), with carvings like hieroglyphics over it, and human skulls cemented on either side. A breath or gasp issues from it, over rapid Steadicam shots, which frightens the horses (that's the last sight of Aragorn's wonder horse Brego, which bolts). Aragorn enters the Dark Door first, followed by Legolas, then Gimli (a brief beat has Gimli hesitating, but not wanting to be outdone by an elf. From the first time they meet in the first film, at the Council of Elrond, the screenwriters locked Gimli and Leggy into an uneasy, competitive companionship, part-serious, part-joky, and it continues throughout *The Return of the King*).

NOTES: ACT TWO

1. In C. Wrigley, 55.
2. R. Kaufman, "*The Lord of the Rings* Taps a Gay Archetype", *Gay and Lesbian Review Worldwide*, July, 2003.
3. G. Fuller, "Kingdom Come", *Film Comment*, 40, 1, 2004.

ACT THREE

Now in *The Return of the King* we cut to King Théoden at Dunharrow. Horses; busy people getting ready to leave. Little Merry wants to fight, but Théoden forbids it. Merry stands alone, watching the riders depart. The film gets Merry on his way as swiftly as possible, in cowboy movie-style: Éowyn gallops up behind him and grabs him by the scruff of his neck, plonking him in front of her (no mean feat for Éowyn – Merry can't be that light). Rather than being winded, or strangled, or bruised, or terrified, Merry beams: he's pleased (and he knows instantly, without looking round, who's lifted him up).

The horse convoy moves out. Two big visual effects shots follow this: first, an aerial shot of Harrowdale, and hundreds of riders streaming over the field. Second, the first big reveal of Minas Tirith under attack by the armies of Mordor. A crane up portrays ranks of orcs (in squares, like Roman legions – a Roman army set-up is employed a few times in the visualizaion of Sauron's forces – the scene's a bit like a Roman army assaulting a mediæval castle); standards held aloft; and trolls pushing siege towers.

The colours of the orc army are predominantly grey and black, with some brown and white (the Gondorians are also depicted in white, black and grey – but the shiny silver of their armour distinguishes them from the grubby orcs). On the track, drumbeats (trolls beating large drums, and other drumbeats), marching feet, and the orc chant (of Black Speech) from the Isengard 'Nuremberg' scene.

The shots of Minas Tirith from the battlefield introduce the big conflict that's been foreshadowed throughout this and the other two films. It depicts the arena where the action of this part of the War of the Ring will take place – the scale and look of it, and how Minas Tirith is completely surrounded. And it shows the sheer numbers Sauron has unleashed. It sure appears hopeless for our heroes!

The Paths of the Dead. Additional scenes in the extended DVD and video cut of New Line's *The Return of the King* include images of the man, elf and dwarf walking through tunnels, carrying torches (Peter Jackson said they had even considered showing how Aragorn makes the fire and the torch, but thought that was going too far. It is. Even an ardent Tolkien fan wouldn't care a jot about the fire. Characters in tunnels or caves in mediæval films always have flaming torches. It's part of the genre that nobody questions, and no one cares how they lit the bloody things).

The Ranger leads the way through the Paths, past low rocks. Legolas talks about the dead being summoned. The next scene is another addition to the theatrical version: ghostly computer animated arms reaching up from below the camera towards our heroes. The dry ice machines are humming away, providing the ubiquitous smoke (another mandatory element of every dark tunnel scene in any movie. This part of *The Return of the King* is very *Dungeons and Dragons*, and also not much different from countless action-adventure movies). Gimli puffs at the spectral hands and they blow away. Howard Shore adds a soft string score, while the sound designers add plenty of ghostly whooshing noises and echoey sounds.

Aragorn, Legolas and Gimli are walking on human skulls. There are no long shots of the scene, or feet on skulls, and only one (p.o.v.) shot of the skulls. Rather, the filmmakers suggest the action through an over-cooked sound effect of cracking skulls which's like eggs cracking. (Gimli was filmed on a blue screen stage, miming it all – like so many of the scenes in the *Lord of the Rings* films).

They emerge into a vast cavern (which's predominantly model work). There's an open space, a long ledge, and an abyss. Behind them is an imposing stone necropolis – a city of the dead (with an angular Mayan or Aztec look, with some dwarvish influence). Dark colours; green and white light. The King of the Dead (Paul Norrell) appears first, in voiceover. He laughs menacingly (slowed-down, and echoey, *of course*), and a slow pan to the left reveals the rest of the city of the dead, the sepulchres and tombs which loom out of the cliff face above the abyss. The dead seem to float in the air.

The look of the Dead Men of Dunharrow has their skeleton visible underneath rags and decayed skin; it becomes more discernible at times – when the King of the Dead gets angry, his skull can be seen underneath. The visual effects team were pipped to the post here by the 2003 Summer blockbuster *Pirates of the Caribbean*, which had a ghostly pirate army with a similar (and far superior) special effect. The device of the King's scary stretching lower jaw was a big element in the design of the fabulous villain in *The Mummy* (1999). (*The Mummy* also got there first with many other visual effects, such as the villain's henchmen who can climb walls and ceilings.)

The dead appear behind the King, then all around our heroes. Whispers and chants accompany their appearance. The King approaches

Aragorn, Legolas and Gimli. A brief duel of swords; Aragorn grips the King by the throat (presumably, these are not disembodied ghosts, or maybe Aragorn can touch the King because he's the future king of Gondor).

But the screenwriters don't make it so easy or quick for Aragorn to get the Shadow Host on his side: in fact, they want to keep it in doubt for as long as possible: so, the King laughs once more, and the army of the dead retreats then disappears, accompanied by low rumbles. The *Extended Edition* of *The Return of the King* added another beat here: a cascade of millions of human skulls. First, a few skulls roll on the ground (these were apparently the last ever shots for the *Lord of the Rings* movie; they were filmed in Spring, 2004, after the Oscar ceremony, and in preparation of the DVD extended cut. That demonstrates the impact of the home entertainment market on contemporary filmmaking, because in the old days few filmmakers would consider shooting material for their films *after* they'd been out in cinemas and earning Academy Awards). The skulls then pour from two sides of the necropolis, forming a vast bank of skulls which, in a long shot, cascades over the ledge into the abyss. The heroes somehow manage to wade through the stream to the other side of the cave, with Aragorn leading the way. Rocks and dust fall from the roof, with earthquake rumbles and camera shakes.

The next scene is another addition to the theatrical cut of *The Return of the King*: our heroes emerge from a fissure in a rock face into daylight on a hillside. Below them, lies the River Anduin in a wide valley, at the bottom of grassy slopes. Fires and smoke rising from the attacks of the enemy on dwellings can be seen in the distance. Corsair ships on the river. Aragorn, taking in the extent of the opposition, kneels in despair (unusually close to weeping). At that moment, the King of the Dead pops out of the rock behind him and states 'we fight'.

Bringing the army of the dead to Pelennor helps to make the victory of the free peoples more convincing, perhaps. Peter Jackson admitted being uninspired in directing by the Paths of the Dead sequence, and it really shows (the whole sequence is lacklustre). Part of the problem was a narrative one: the army of the dead are invincible, can't be killed, and are great warriors. So, with them on the heroes' side, the goodies can't really lose: the Grey Host can (help to) win the day at Pelennor (which they do), and sweep on to Mordor, overcoming the orcs at the Black Gate. (The Shadow-men are shown in the film routing orcs, trolls and *mûmakil*, so not much in Sauron's arsenal could stop them – presumably only the nazgûl and the Dark Lord himself).

So, obstacles are put in the way of Aragorn's quest to secure the use of this army of Dead Men, and whether he is successful is left to the last possible moment. Also, an important line from Gimli was inserted on the Pelennor battlefield, expressing for Jackson the audience's obvious question: why don't the heroes hang onto this invincible army? Tolkien faced the same problem, and had them fulfilling their oath after Pelennor (even though, the next battle, at Morannon, is still part of the same battle, the same war against Sauron). The Shadows of Men are thus exposed as a narrative device: to help to good guys win at Pelennor when they are faced with overwhelming odds. After they've fulfilled their plot function, they are discarded, in both book and film.

Back to Pelennor Fields in the midst of battle: C.U.s of siege towers, and lines of orcs spread out rather like Roman legions. Next: Faramir being dragged by his leg along the ground behind his horse through the main gate (actor David Wenham held a release device in case anything went wrong with this stunt). He's the sole survivor of the Gondorian cavalry charge on Osgiliath. Very different from the book, where Denethor releases aid – and so silly that nobody even bothers to rush out to help Faramir.

Setting the catapults comes next, with Gothmog on the back of a warg, riding between lines of orc troops. He stumbles as he gets off (which Peter Jackson put in as a little bit of character business for the orc leader, like something out of a Western, when a guy gets off a horse and tries to look cool. There are more allusions to Western movies in the *Lord of the Rings* films than one might think at first for the fantasy genre – take the large number of horse scenes for a start).

Faramir is carried on a stretcher in the Place of the Fountain. Denethor appears at the steps and hurries to his son, distraught. Denethor seems to think Faramir is dead, but Pippin, examining Faramir, declares him still alive. Back to Gothmog, now in place on the field to begin the assault. He has a sergeant with him who sports a helmet that incorporates a skull. It's quite silly (the filmmakers joked that this particular orc was a mother's boy, and it was his mother on his head, a Norman Bates touch). As well as Gothmog, a number of other orcs were carefully individualized at Pelennor, through costumes, props, gestures and other attributes, to give more of a personal face to the enemy, who could simply fuse into a single, blank mass of orcs and Haradrim.

Gothmog orders the catapults to hurl the heads of the Gondorians who charged on Osgiliath over the walls. The battle begins. The heads rain down on Gondor's soldiers behind the walls, who hold up shields to protect themselves. Back to Denethor (all of these scenes are intercut, to enhance the dramatic tension): Denethor wanders away from Faramir in bewilderment, muttering 'the line has ended' (meaning the line of stewards), and ends up by the wall (you'd think Boromir and perhaps Faramir would have a few kids by now). A big crane up shot behind Denethor reveals the vast array of Mordor's forces in the fields below, which Denethor seems to see for the first time. The sight hastens his madness.

Trolls lug rocks into the catapults. A series of shots depict the impacts of the rocks on the city (some of the missiles hit people). Debris and dust flies about (the *Extended Edition* adds more shots here, such as a balcony of civilians being demolished. Up at the Citadel, Denethor calls out 'flee the city!' Gandalf pops up from nowhere and clouts the steward twice with his staff. Denethor collapses. In the DVD commentary, the writers call it a typical 'Peter Jackson moment', very over-the-top. Maybe, but f-u-c-k, it still stinks.

Gandalf is next seen galloping through the streets of the city (that wizard sure gets around); he's now taken command of the Gondorian forces (the issue of how the soldiers suddenly follow Gandalf is not addressed – which's odd, because Denethor and his underlings regarded the wizard with suspicion; only Faramir seems to really admire Gandalf among the Gondorians). Mithrandir rides up some steep steps onto the battlements, which're lined with soldiers (it's one of the classic images in the film) He orders the retaliation. Slingshots open fire, hurling masonry, walls and bits of buildings into the orc horde. The orcs return fire. (Trebuchets like the ones used in the film are certainly very powerful, but they're not strong enough to project missiles of that mass. The abysmal Crusades film of 2005, *Kingdom of Heaven* – which starred Orlando Bloom – had catapults and trebuchets acting unbelievably like rockets and missiles).

A '*Pearl Harbor* shot' follows (the camera, suspended in mid-air between Minas Tirith and the orcs, catches part of a building hurtling towards it, pans and follows on behind the projectile, all the way into the ground). Peter Jackson recalled how he had that particular shot in mind from early on in pre-production, but when *Pearl Harbor* was released in 2001, he saw that Michael Bay and Jerry Bruckheimer had got there first (with a shot that follows a bomb being dropped. Actually, a much better example than either *The Return of the King* or *Pearl Harbor* occurred at the famous climax of *Dr Strangelove* [1963]).

The 2003 film of *The Return of the King* cuts back and forth between catapults and trebuchets firing from each force, and missile impacts. One of them nearly hits Gothmog, who steps aside at the last moment, and spits on it. Next up is the arrival of the nazgûl, *en masse*, on their fell-beasts: it's one of the most spectacular moments in the film, accompanied by a marvellous bold choral cue from Howard Shore. Rapid aerial shots follow the nazgûl dive-bombing the city (World War Two movies are an obvious reference point here, in particular German Stukas from films like *The Battle of Britain* [1969], a favourite with war film fans. A few critics have likened the ringwraiths to the Nazi SS. Minas Tirith can evoke England – or London – as an island under attack from the German forces).

There are some extra shots in the *Extended Edition* here, in particular more of the Gondorians running in fear from the nazgûl, clutching their ears against their piercing cries. It's something that works in the 1955 book, but Peter Jackson said it was tricky dramatizing that kind of dread. Pippin is spotted in amongst the fleeing soldiers and crowds. Gandalf rallies the men against the attack. An orc siege tower explodes. Plenty more additional shots are included here in the longer version of *The Return of the King*, of Gondorian soldiers firing arrows (these and other battle shots are the sorts of images that can be added or taken away without altering the conflict too much, other than in terms of pace, duration, and odd details. In trimming the battle for the theatrical cut, these images of anonymous soldiers on both sides fighting and dying are interchangeable to a certain degree, and were probably some of the first things to go).

On the battlements, Gandalf orders the archers to bring down the trolls pushing the siege towers (and the trolls seem to be able to continue with their work even when pricked with many arrows). Additional scenes of Pippin lost amongst the crowds come next (these were directed by Fran

Walsh). These scenes, like the one of Gandalf and Pippin talking about death on the second level, were added during the pick-ups and reshoots, because it was felt that our heroes were lost a little in the chaos of the battle.)

A complete scene is added here to the longer version, of the first battering ram assaulting the main gates of Minas Tirith (as happens in Tolkien's book). It doesn't have much effect. On the tower above, Gondorians rain down arrows. Orc corpses pile up on the ground. Gothmog berates his sergeant. Pippin meets Mithrandir on the battlements, in a bewildered state.

A major stunt scene has the siege towers dispensing orcs on the wall (with some more gags added for the extended cut). When even more orcs rush towards Gandalf and Pippin, the wizard leaps into action; it's Gandalf's big fight scene in *The Return of the King*. He whirls around, clubbing with sword and staff, rather than hacking, slashing or stabbing. It's a curious fighting style, probably conceived to give Gandalf a style of combat more elegant and less gory and brutal than the others seen in the films (even though killing people is automatically brutal), and to make it distinctive to Gandalf (and to wizards). As with the other fights with orcs in the films, there's hardly any resistance at all from the orcs: they fall down at the first blow (Sam, Pippin, Merry, Éowyn, Aragorn, Legolas, Gimli, Éomer, Théoden and others all dispatch orcs with one stroke like this).

When an orc lumbers towards Pippin, the hobbit manages to stab it. Gandalf looks on admiringly, then orders the halfling back up to the Citadel (and off Pippin duly scurries). Back down to the main gates again, and the battering ram. Gothmog announces Grond. The battering ram is an extravagant prop (it was also a pretty big model): it's a vast metal-clad behemoth, hung on ropes from a wooden frame, with trolls pushing it from behind, and pulled at the front by dinosaurish, horned beasts (these latter were designed by Alan Lee, and appeared in the film largely due to Lee. The Hildebrandts got there before this, I think). The head of Grond is a grimacing wolf, with a prominent snout and teeth, claws thrust forward under its skull, and flames in its mouth. The orcs leave a wide corridor for it, and chant 'Grond! Grond!' The Grond scene is pure Tolkien, really, and even the perfectionist professor would have to admire it.

Aragorn, Legolas and Gimli stand on a pebbly shore with a vertical cliff-face behind them, in an additional scene in the *Extended Cut* (opening disc two of the DVD). Aragorn hails a passing galleon, populated by pirate cameos from the senior members of the production team (Porras, Taylor, Jackson, etc, all dressed in black, with piercings, dreadlocks, and chunky leather). Legolas looses an arrow; Gimli nudges the bow and it hits and kills a pirate (played by Peter Jackson, fulfilling a dream of many a film crew – to shoot and kill the director).

Aragorn warns the Corsairs they'll be boarded; the retort – 'by you and whose army?' – is classic Hollywood (the screenwriters probably couldn't resist it). The army duly appears: the Army of the Dead streaming from behind the elf, dwarf and man, weapons raised (the King of the Dead passes right through Aragorn). But the devastation the Dead Men bring about isn't shown – it's saved for later, when the ships land at Harlond.

In the next scene, Frodo and Sam emerge onto Fifth Avenue in the rain from a cinema showing *Duck Soup*. Frodo, now clad in a check shirt, glasses and a tweedy jacket, gesticulates wildly as he rants neurotically: 'I can't believe it, Gollum left us again, two minutes into the film, he's gone. I swear to God, next time I see him I'm gonna kill him. I want my popcorn back! My analyst told me this would happen...'

No, no, wrong film. Cut to the beginning of the impressive and exciting Shelob's lair sequence. Two Hollywood films were released a year earlier which took a lead on depicting giant spiders on the big screen: *Harry Potter and the Chamber of Secrets* (2002) and *Eight-Legged Freaks* (2002). Boyens and Walsh joked about identifying with Shelob – she's overweight, has hairy legs, can't get around like she used to, and has trouble finding decent men – she prefers to eat or kill any guys who venture near.

Director Peter Jackson explained how inspired he was in this sequence to exploit well-known phobias – of spiders, of the dark, of unseen foes, of enclosed spaces, of a chase. The inspiration shows: compare it with the decidedly lacklustre Paths of the Dead sequence.

And the Shelob episode in the book is Tolkien writing at his best. Tolkien is the king of cave and tunnel scenes, and night, and evoking a sense of dread:

> There age-long she had dwelt, an evil thing in spider-form, even such as once of old had lived in the Land of the Elves of the West that is now under the Sea, such as Beren fought in the Mountains of Terror in Doriath... she served none but herself, drinking the blood of Elves and Men, bloated and grown fat with endless brooding on her feasts, weaving webs of shadow, for all living things were her food, and her vomit darkness. (TT, 417-8)

Frodo and Gollum stand outside Shelob's lair in the perpetual dusk around Mordor, a ways further up the stairs of Cirith Ungol. Frodo notices the smell; a point-of-view track-zoom shot recalls the moment in *The Fellowship of the Ring* on the path, when Frodo sensed the Black Riders. The tunnels are roughly semi-circular, pockmarked with holes, with uneven floors (to move away from the usual studio tunnel or cave sets in movies). Cobwebs hang down, water drips, colours are strictly black, dark browns and greys. Gollum soon disappears, his echoey calls to Frodo come from off-screen. Handheld point-of-view shots of Frodo walking through the tunnels are augmented by a different p.o.v shot, behind cobwebs, presumably of the monster watching its prey.

Frodo encounters sticky cobwebs as the music swells to a crescendo. He draws Sting. He looks down, and sees skeletons, and bodies of animals hanging in cocoons from the ceiling. One of the best things about the Shelob's lair sequence is the music: the filmmakers encouraged Howard Shore to go to town with it, to do something different from the rest of the

Lord of the Rings score, and to go back to the scores he produced for David Cronenberg. Shore turned in a nervy, Hitchcockian score that recalls the guru of New Hollywood composers – Bernard Herrmann.

Back to poor old Samwise Gamgee, going back down the stairs – did audiences really believe that Sam would hike all the way back to the Shire, after coming all this way to Mordor, over two-and-a-half films? No, of course not. A clichéd piece of business has Sam tripping and falling, slipping down the stairs, landing on his front and finding the discarded lembas bread. Sam's mounting anger (played deliberately slowly by Sean Astin) has the hobbit girding his loins for revenge on Gollum.

Frodo also trips and falls – but into a killing zone in the spider's lair. Classic horror movie imagery of skeletons, bones and cobwebs. Frodo's fear intensifies; he crawls on his back, fighting off the cobwebs (the filmmakers played up the ancient phobias of nasty things touching the body). The music also intensifies.

In voiceover, Galadriel makes the first of her three very brief appearances in *The Return of the King*: she reminds our three-foot-six-inch hero of the star glass, paying off the prop planted two-thirds into *The Fellowship of the Ring*. Frodo finds the phial and holds it up. He cries out in Elvish. The first reveal of the spawn of Ungoliant comes from a photograph that Peter Jackson saw in *National Geographic* (or a similar publication or documentary), in which a spider's legs were bunched up together in a hole. The reveal is a 'behind you!' pantomime moment, the monster emerging from a narrow crevice in the rock behind Frodo. Shelob raises herself up, revealing her size and fearsome appearance.

Like many other creatures in the *Lord of the Rings* films, Shelob underwent a lengthy design process. The spider chosen for the basis of Shelob was the tunnel web spider found in New Zealand (which had frightened the young Jackson), but there was plenty of movie monster design work done on the face, mouth, scale, colour, and of course the performance. Again, it's that balance between something that's grounded in reality, and something for the movies (the clusters of eyes, though, so prominent in the book, didn't really make it into the final design. And the sounds that Shelob makes, like other monster spiders in movies, are pure hokum).

Confronting the monstrosity, Frodo brandishes the phial, which halts Shelob for a moment. Frodo falls to the ground, and slashes at a leg with Sting. The spider chases him; Frodo dives through a narrow hole, and the spider, unable to reach him, retreats and goes another way. Frodo runs into a thick wall of spider webs, so dense and strong he's held up, off the ground, and can't slash them away with his sword. The betrayer, Gollum, is reintroduced at this point, watching from a safe distance behind a rock. He appears to be gloating at first (he sings and taunts Frodo), but then is terrified when the monster looms behind Frodo (Gollum's not so much afraid for the ringbearer, as running to save his own skin). The monster crawls closer; Frodo hacks at the web. But the filmmakers delay the moment of capture further when Frodo manages to escape (but leaving behind Sting hanging in the cobweb. Somehow Sam manages to retrieve it). Good fun, but not a patch on Tolkien's book:

> Slowly the eyes crept nearer.
> "Galadriel!" he called, and gathering his courage he lifted up the Phial once more. The eyes halted. For a moment their regard relaxed, as if some hint of doubt troubled them. Then Frodo's heart flamed within him, and without thinking what he did, whether it was folly or despair or courage, he took the Phial in his left hand, and with his right hand drew his sword. Sting flashed out, and the sharp elven-blade sparkled in the silver light, but at its edges a blue flame flicked. Then holding the star aloft, and the bright sword advanced, Frodo, hobbit of the Shire, walked steadily down to meet the eyes. (TT, 414-5)

Frodo escapes into a narrow gully, the chief purpose of which (apart from delaying the end of the chase), is to encounter Gollum. The wretched creature leaps on Frodo, and they throw each other about. Frodo is at his most savage with Gollum here, but still doesn't kill him. He does hit him hard, though, and strangles him (some of the action concerning Sam in the Shelob's lair episode was transferred to Frodo). Gollum pleads for his life, maintaining that it was the precious that drove him to do it. That's about the only thing that could stop Frodo at this point – it's something that Frodo can readily identify with: the ring's effect increases the closer it gets to Mordor.

Frodo relaxes his grip, stands, and tells Gollum he has to destroy the ring, for both their sakes. Gollum seems to realize this for the first time. This was inserted to ram home the point for audiences, although it must have been obvious even to Gollum, and had been mentioned before (Andy Serkis performed the additions to this scene in the London house of the filmmakers, who were working on post-production and music for *The Return of the King*. Peter Jackson shot Serkis with a video camera – before Serkis had even had a cup of tea, he complained – and sent the footage back to Weta in New Zealand to be animated).

Gollum lunges at Frodo, and, as they grapple each other, Frodo hurls Gollum over an abyss, handily nearby (note how Gollum manages to fall feet first, with his front to the rock wall, so we know he'll be back). Frodo staggers along the rockface, away from the crevasse, but he's in a bad way. He stumbles and falls. Frodo in particular falls down a lot in the *Lord of the Rings* films (he's almost like a toddler learning to walk at times). Later on in *The Return of the King*, when Sauron's buzzing him, he performs a showy slow motion fall. Frodo falls in the *Prancing Pony*, on Weathertop, in Moria, at Parth Galen (in slow motion), the Dead Marshes (again in slo mo), etc etc. Frodo's also often lying on the ground (always when he puts on the ring, and enters the wraithworld. Significantly, when he puts on the ring at the Crack of Doom, he is standing – and Gollum is on two legs, too, a gesture that Andy Serkis was saving for precisely that moment of triumph). Stumbling and falling are rather hackneyed dramatic conventions for expressing doubt, confusion, vulnerability, or weakness.

In the scene on the edge of the tunnel maze of Shelob's lair, the editors perform a match cut of Frodo's fall, to Frodo on a forest floor (in daylight, in Summer or Spring, with birdsong, grass, leaves and smoke drifting), which might be an unidentified part of the Shire, or could be Lothlórien. It's somewhere much nicer, anyway, than the Mordor borderlands. Frodo has wisps of cobwebs in his hair (suggesting he's just been transported from Mordor, or he's still really back in Mordor). Frodo looks up, to see Galadriel looking down at him and smiling. It's a wish-fulfilment dream, with Galadriel appearing in person to inspire Frodo to get up and carry on (she speaks in voiceover on top of her shots, as in the Lórien scenes). She pulls him up by the hand, and another match cut puts the hobbit back outside Shelob's lair. He walks on, alone.

A scene follows that was never considered for the theatrical cut depicts a bit of characterization between Éowyn and Merry (included so they can bond a little before the battle, and to remind the audience that they're fighting for their friends). They're resting on the journey to Gondor in daytime (the location looks suspiciously like a reverse angle of the grassy, rocky lakeside used in the trek through Rohan scene in *The Two Towers* – and it is: Deer Park Heights outside Queenstown). Not bothered about being recognized in a throng of Rohirrim (although Miranda Otto's Éowyn is very boyish anyway), Éowyn has her helmet off as she talks to Merry (helmets have often been a problem for actors, but Otto looking uncomfortable in her helmet aids her character and her situation in some respects. Éowyn, though, should seem quite at home in warrior garb). The hobbit muses on seeing his friends again (why is Merry allowed to eat throughout the scene?). Théoden announces the departure: to battle!

That leads in to a cut to Minas Tirith, but now it's at night (let's ignore the time gap here): trolls and orcs and catapults (which are now hurling flaming boulders). Grond is in place. Trolls haul on chains, to pull the enormous battering ram back, so it can swing against the gates. On the other side, Gondorian soldiers rush to the gates and form a defensive line (it's Grond vs. Gondor).

Up to the prow of the citadel next, and Pippin watching the battle. Muttering to himself, Denethor leads a group of his servants, all clad in black. Faramir, unconscious still, is carried on a bier on their shoulders. A crane shot lifts up the White Tree, to a small white flower, as if the tree senses the coming of the king; it's a signal of hope (and a smidgen of Tolkienania for fans of the details in Tolkien's mythos). A big aerial shot reveals the far side of the city, where Alan Lee imagined a causeway leading to the Houses of the Dead (entirely a model and CG shot, as is the next one, showing Pippin following behind the solemn procession).

The scene introduces the tombs: four arched corridors lead off a central area, which has a dais in the middle. Flickering torchlight; figures in grey marble lie on the tombs; Denethor continues to speak in voiceover. Back to the gates; Grond breaks through, wood splintering and flames boiling. Gandalf, on horseback, rallies the troops, reminding them that they're soldiers of Gondor. Trolls lurch through the gap first; the extended version of *The Return of the King* adds plenty more fighting gags here; sword fighting, arrows firing; there are orcs and wargs causing havoc;

Gandalf downs a troll; the Gondorians put up a fierce resistance, but are out-numbered. Peter Jackson had suggested throwing everything they had in the enemy's arsenal against the city – hence the digital animated additions of trolls and wargs to the original plates, which mainly consisted of soldiers fighting orcs (the shots weren't filmed with additional visual effects in mind).

To Frodo alone now, some way from Shelob's lair. He enters a circular space surrounded by rocks twenty or thirty feet high (which just happens to be the height of a movie studio). Stone steps lead off the other side, with the tower of Cirith Ungol and torchlight visible at the end (Elijah Wood recalled that, unusually, the model of the tower was brought to the studio so it could be included in the shot). The studio intentionally looks like an arena, and will be the setting for four key scenes: Shelob stinging Frodo, the Sam-Shelob fight, an emotional scene between Sam and Frodo, and Frodo's capture by orcs.

Shelob appears in an overhead shot, from the edge of the frame. A very low angle shot tilts as it captures the monster looming behind the halfling, creeping closer above him (keeping amazingly quiet for such a hulking beast), until she straddles the gully. The sound designers take the sound down very low, so that a stone falling is prominent. Frodo looks round, sensing something. Handheld p.o.v. shots of the area. But it's too late: the giant spider stabs him, stinging him in the belly. A big, lengthy close-up on Frodo shows the poison taking effect. And Frodo falls yet again – but this time, the monster takes up him in her claws just below her mouth, and cocoons him all over in white strings (cue gloopy sound effects over a C.U. of Shelob's maw for this gross moment. The animators of Shelob added those inserts after seeing sound man David Farmer's test run for the scene).

In the nick of time, Samwise Gamgee returns, sword in one hand, phial in the other (amazing how he found them in the dark tunnels, and without a torch too. Peter Jackson recalled that he had posed for Sam's arm and sword himself, to show the folk on the blue screen stage how he wanted Sam to appear. But the Shelob fight was shot mostly by John Mahaffie). The heroic fellowship theme plays as Sam opens the attack. He swings at the monster's legs; he's thrown onto his back, and loses the elven phial (the spider kicks it away – a neat detail). Poor Sam is thrust against the rock wall, then pushed up it fifteen feet (that's gotta hurt – but it's a CG Sam and a CG Shelob). Sam holds onto the spider's mandibles and kicks at her head in an O.T.S. shot. Sam turns and tries to climb up the cliff, but he's dragged back. He falls a long way, rolling over the creature's back, onto the ground (a hand-over shot between a digital double and the actor).

Samwise snatches up the sword; the monster approaches him; he manages to stab one of Shelob's eyes; she retreats, hurt; the sword is caught in her head; Shelob wrenches Sam from side to side, and the sword goes flying. In slow motion, Sam is pushed, and falls. Shelob stands on the sword. Her sting is uncoiled, and it looks as if Sam's going to get it; Sam rolls out of the way, yet again, to avoid the sting, which hits the dust. Sam grabs Sting and stabs Shelob in the belly. Now she's really hurt, and cowers back, making a high-pitched mewling noise (what sound does a wounded giant spider make? Probably nothing like this). The phial helps Sam drive the monster back into a hole.

The fight over (it has plenty of gags, but doesn't outstay its welcome, unlike the Moria troll fight), Sam rushes to Frodo, who's prone and face-up on the ground near the steps. He tears away the cocoon around his master's face, and weeps, thinking Frodo is dead (if only he'd checked for a pulse, like in other movies). A tearful farewell scene, as Sam hugs Frodo, who stares up unblinking. A C.U. of Sting turning blue, meaning orcs are nearby. A Sam p.o.v. shot of Cirith Ungol, and orcs are heard shouting offscreen.

A cut suggests a few minutes have passed, and orcs appear in the oval arena between the rockfaces. An orc leader (walking crouched, with a whip) examines the body. Sam watches from behind some rocks, nearby. He realizes that Frodo isn't dead (it's a good job the orcs speak in English – in the book, the ring gives the hobbit the power to understand orc speech). P.o.v. shots of the orcs with Frodo; they pick him up; the leader, Shagrat (Peter Tait), orders 'get him to the tower'.

The editing (and staging) of this section of the film was tricky – to show how much Sam knew, how the orcs managed to take Frodo without Sam putting up a fight (he's just seriously wounded a monster spider, for instance, to protect his great friend; in the mood he's in, wouldn't he feel inclined to take on four or so orcs? There are 30 or 40 in the book). But this whole section is also awkward in the 1955 book – how Frodo is captured, but not the ring; how Shelob attacks Frodo but doesn't kill him; how Frodo isn't sent to the Dark Tower immediately; how a hobbit defeats a giant spider; and, most unconvincing of all, how a hobbit manages to rescue Frodo from a garrison of 200 orcs who manage to destroy themselves just in time.

Tolkien knew he had written himself into a helluva fix here. Note how the filmmakers elide the moment when Sam takes the ring (saving it for a later revelation), and move straight on to the entry of the orcs into the arena. And they decided not to show any of the scenes in the book where Sam puts on the ring, in either version of *The Return of the King* (although the scene where Sam slips past the watchers at Cirith Ungol was shot, but dropped). Both book and film are unsatisfactory in the chain of complicated events in this part of the story, but the film simplifies the book a great deal.

Now back to the Houses of the Dead behind Minas Tirith: the film is now cutting between four main storylines: Gandalf and the battle down at the gates; Pippin, Denethor and the Houses of the Dead; Théoden and the ride of the Rohirrim; and Frodo and Sam with Shelob (there are many ways of inter-cutting four storylines).

The Houses of the Dead sequence is partly depicted from Pippin's point-of-view. Faramir is laid on the funeral pyre (a life-size dummy of actor David Wenham was employed for sections of the pyre scenes –

partly because of safety – the fire gags – but also because Wenham didn't have much to do in the scenes except lie as if dead. Dummies are used in movies more often than you might think, and not only for throwing off cliffs).

Pippin yells 'he's not dead!' and tries to take away the wood. Denethor grasps him by the collar, and drags him to the doors, throwing him out and releasing him from his service. He slams the door. (A simple in-camera gag had Billy Boyd's hobbit-size stand-in, 'Phon' Chansantor, and Boyd swapping over just beneath the camera. Another old cinematic trick was deployed in the tombs scene: a partial mirror was used to reflect flames onto the pyre from a safe distance).

A cut to Pippin calling for Gandalf amidst rushing soldiers suggests half-an-hour or so has passed. Wobbly handheld shots evoke Pippin's panic. Big model and CGI shots next, of the lower levels, soldiers fighting, and flaming missiles. Gandalf calls the retreat to the second level. Images of Gondorians hurrying up the streets; Gandalf on horseback; fires; flaming sphere missiles; and orcs pouring in (one or two wargs and trolls were added in post to beef up the shots).

On the battlefield, Gothmog orders orcs into the city; cut to women and children running scared in the streets, accompanied by the loud roars of trolls and the shrieks of orcs. And a bold choral cue. (Peter Jackson noted that shots of soldiers under attack weren't particularly moving, because that's what soldiers did anyway, but civilians in jeopardy upped the drama). Civilians are seen fleeing the orcs, but there are no scenes of the orcs raping and killing women (but sure as shit they would do).

Pippin fights his way though soldiers, trying to find the wizard. He tells Gandalf about Faramir; Gandalf pulls the hobbit onto his horse. At this point, an additional scene was inserted into the extended version of *The Return of the King*: the face-off between the two wizards on the third gate set. This scene was used as part of the pre-publicity for *The Return of the King*, but was dropped from the theatrical edit (odd, because it is foreshadowed earlier, in the scene where Gandalf tells Pippin, and the audience, about the Witch-king of Angmar; and the Witch-king informs Gothmog that he will break Gandalf).

One of the reasons that the scene was dropped is that **it doesn't work**. The Witch-king breaks Gandalf's staff, and has him fallen from his horse, cowering on the ground, at his mercy, but then *he flies off!* Sure, the horns of the Rohirrim pull him away, but he could have stayed five minutes longer to finish off the commander of the forces at Minas Tirith, and Sauron's chief opponent. But he doesn't. Very silly. It weakens the Witch-king as a villain: he promises to do something, then doesn't do it (Walsh and Boyens acknowledge the inadequacy of the scene in the DVD commentary).

What happens in the film is the Witch-king lands on his fell-beast on the far side of a square; Gandalf brandishes his staff; the Witch-king unsheathes a flaming sword; Pippin cowers; Gandalf's staff is broken, and he is flung from his horse, along with Pippin. The hobbit draws his sword and makes to help, but is scared off by the fell-beast roaring. Just then, the horse-lords arrive, and off goes the Witch-king. It's not the best moment in the 2001-03 *Rings* movies.

> The Black Rider flung back his hood, and behold! he had a kingly crown; and yet upon no head was it set. The red fires shone between it and the mantled shoulders vast and dark. From a mouth unseen there came a deadly laughter.
> "Old fool!", he said. "Old fool! This is my hour Do you not know Death when you see it? Die now and curse in vain!" And with that he lifted up his sword and flames ran down the blade. (RK, 120-1)

A big wide shot follows of the ridge of a hill, a mile or two from the main battlefield. Dawnlight behind the hill, above a line of horses. It's a classic movie image, as my son pointed out. It could be from any number of mediæval or cowboy flicks. Théoden, Éowyn, Éomer and the Rohirrim see the Battle of Pelennor for the first time, and the white city besieged. Éowyn comforts Merry (courage, she says, for our friends). But the hobbit isn't the only one seeing an enemy on this scale for the first time: no one else among the horse-lords will have seen anything this big before. But we movie-goers have, oh yes, my precious.

A brief cut to the orc forces, who've spotted the Rohirrim, and Gothmog issuing orders to form ranks. Back to Théoden, also giving out orders, to the leaders of the left and right flanks. Éowyn hides from Théoden as he rides a bit too close. Théoden is now working up his troops into a battle state, yelling at the top of his voice. Spears are lowered on both sides. Théoden gallops along the front row of the Rohirrim, clashing his sword on the spear tips. (This was actor Bernard Hill's idea, and proved tricky to accomplish, partly because Hill is left-handed, and the action was staged so Hill had to hold the sword in his right hand as he rode towards the camera).

Théoden's battle cries of 'Death!' and 'Forth Eorlingas!' are taken up by the hundreds of warriors behind him. Howard Shore provides a brassy, heroic cue (of the Rohan theme) for the shots of the horse riders charging down the slope, with Théoden leading the charge. Close-ups of Théoden, Éowyn and Éomer pick our heroes out of the six thousand-strong army hurtling down the hill. This is undoubtedly the best of the many heroic moments in *The Return of the King*, in terms of rousing spectacle. It's very old-fashioned, very formulaic, very clichéd (like most of the *Lord of the Rings* films). But there's nothing wrong with that, because those clichés and formulas really work, and there's no need to do anything self-conscious or flashy here.

The orcs prepare to meet the horse-lords, but they cower back as the riders close in. The music stops abruptly when the two forces clash, and the sound team take over with hundreds of sounds of impacts, horse neighs, galloping hooves, grunts, yells, sword clashes, and horns. A couple of long shots take in the vast scope of the battle.

The ride of the Rohirrim was staged on a grassy plain at the Ben Ohau Sheep Station at Twizel, near Canterbury (on the South Island – also used for other Pelennor Fields scenes). For this kind of dangerous sequence, each rider carefully checked the ground beforehand, and were organized into lanes. The camera angle was the standard one for a horse charge: from a camera truck at the side, so that the lanes were flattened, and the horse riders appeared as a mass. For the clash with the orcs, the visual effects team provided digital horses and riders who could perform tumbles and stunts which would be too dangerous at those speeds (and some of the methods for achieving horse stunts, such as tripping the animals with wires, are frowned upon in the contemporary Hollywood industry). So the stumbling horses and thrown riders (and the orcs who got in their way) were chiefly computer animated, and inserted into the empty lanes between the riders. (There was a budgetary reason for this, as well as the obvious one of not wanting to harm horses or riders: the *Lord of the Rings* films didn't have the many stunt riders of the older Hollywood epics, although animating horses and riders ain't cheap, and may cost more, but in different areas of the budget).

The 2003 adaption of *The Return of the King* cuts from that epic-scale drama to the smaller-scale but equally intense melodrama in the Tombs, opening on a C.U. of Denethor pouring oil over his head (a classic editing device, cutting from a big shot to a C.U., a dramatic change in scale). The twenty-sixth steward of Gondor is now standing on the pyre, arms raised, with Faramir unconscious at his feet. Servants bearing flaming torches approach the bier.

Cut to Gandalf and Pippin at the door, riding Shadowfax. Denethor takes up a torch. The wizard grabs a lance from a guard and rides closer. Pippin leaps onto the pyre from the horse's back. Somehow, the three foot six inch hobbit manages to drag and roll Faramir off the pyre, landing on the floor. Denethor sits up, and grasps Pippin. Shadowfax rears, knocking Denethor onto the pyre. Denethor is allowed a last look at Faramir, whom he now realizes is not dead; Faramir looks at him, but it's too late: he's already burning.

The scene involved one of filmmaking's trickiest stunts – a body burn. The horse and other stunts within a confined space also meant that this scene had to be shot carefully and piece by piece. At the end of the scene, another of the many unbelievable moments in the films occurs next, as Denethor runs the half-mile or three-quarters of a mile from the Hallows to the prow of Minas Tirith, leaping from it with a scream in extreme long shot – a rapid aerial shot which tilts down to the battlefield, leading into one of the stand-out action scenes in the three *Lord of the Rings* films: the Rohirrim versus the Mûmakil.

ACT FOUR

A good deal of the Rohirrim-Mûmakil battle was created in post-production, by the visual effects teams, the animators, the matte department, the miniatures crew, the sound effects team, and Howard Shore and his assistants. The live action for the scene comprised stunt people on horses riding about a grassy plain (at Twizel), swinging swords and firing arrows at invisible opponents (additional footage was shot by the visual effects crew, and directed by Jim Rygiel). There was plenty of empty space, and not a lot happening. But when the animators, visual effects supervisors, digital compositors, picture editors, sound editors and designers and all the rest had done their work, it became a marvellous chaotic battle between humans and forty or fifty foot tall elephantine monsters, and the Haradrim riding them.

A classic device introduces the *mûmakil* – which has been tried and tested in movies since the advent of sound in the late 1920s: offscreen sounds (the thumps of their enormous feet) suggest the approach of the *mûmakil* (accompanied by a choral cue). A C.U. on Théoden; it seemed as if the good guys were winning the Battle of Pelennor. The first reveal of the *mûmakil* has them marching in a line, seen from behind and above the Rohirrim. Sounds of horns blowing, and the Haradrim chanting, and the *mûmakil* bellowing. Their leader's introduced; clutching the reins: he's a fearsome figure with white war paint and a bulging-eyed glare. Large towers are mounted on the elephantine creatures' backs (with two storeys to them), and soldiers inside. The animals have giant tusks, with chains and metal spikes attached.

(There were many different groups of men fighting at Pelennor in the book: the Haradrim, the Easterlings, the Southrons, the Corsairs of Umbar, the 'black men' from Far Harad, and the Variags of Khand. The film simplified the groups of enemy men to the Haradrim and the Corsairs. There wasn't time to explain who the Easterlings or the Variags were).

Théoden orders 'reform the line!' and rapidly the horses are gathered in a row, and charging at the *mûmakil* (Sauron's orcs seem to have handily disappeared). Wide aerial shots cover the action as the good guys and bad guys clash. The *mûmakil* swing their heads, mowing down horses and riders, or batting them into the air. The Horse-lords launch arrows into the hides, and the Haradrim rain down arrows from their towers. Stunt falls and gags follow. The *mûmakil* stomp on horses and riders. There are many arrows in the animals' skin, particularly in their legs. (Peter Jackson remarked that the production team was conscious of not wanting to portray the *mûmakil* as circus elephants who did tricks, and also not being too cruel in the depiction of the *mûmakil*. The *mûmakil* in the film are essentially exaggerated elephants, with elongated tusks).

Éomer's big action moment at Pelennor occurs now, as he stops, turns his horse and waits to throw his spear at the Haradrim leader. Of course it hits and kills the leader, who falls, causing the reins to make the creature stagger to the left. It crashes into another oliphaunt, and they fall in a spectacular wipe-out (Gamling was also shown underneath the beast, firing arrows at it). The vfx team recalled how this particular shot had involved months of work, but was re-done in a couple of days to get back to the impact of the original concept, with the beasts slamming together, seen from ground level.

Now to Éowyn and Merry (and with them, the music returns). Éowyn weaves her horse in and out of a *mûmakil*'s legs in a few shots. Merry takes the reins (he doesn't seem to have got the hang of controlling a horse, although he's been on horseback for a number of days). Éowyn employs swords in each hand to cut the beast's legs; it collapses. Another oliphaunt totters on its back legs and crashes to the ground (the filmmakers have clearly storyboarded this section of the film so that each *mûmakil* would be dispatched in a different fashion). Éowyn and Merry are thrown from their horse. Confusion reigns.

The battle is consuming the visual effects budget by thousands of dollars with each shot, each frame, each pixel (but, by 2003, when much of the fx work on the movie was being produced, New Line Cinema knew that these movies would make lots of $$$$$). The Rohirrim-*mûmakil* sequence presented a number of dramatic problems: how do the *mûmakil* attack? what weapons do they have? what scale are they? how fast do they charge? how are they controlled? what do they carry? how do they interact with humans and horses on the ground? and, crucially, how do the Rohirrim bring them down? The solutions the filmmakers came up with were varied: two of the *mûmakil* crash into each other; Éowyn downs another by slashing at the inside of the creature's legs; Éomer spears a driver; they're pin cushions with arrows; Legolas single-handedly demolishes an oliphaunt after slaughtering everyone on board it; finally, the Army of the Dead are seen swarming over a *mûmakil*. (Note how each of the major characters in the Battle of Pelennor are depicted bringing the creatures down. But not Théoden – because he has the face-off with the Witch-king).

Images of Théoden, Éowyn and Merry fighting follows. The *Extended Edition* adds footage of Éowyn killing some orcs. Merry emerges from the wreck of the *mûmakil*, coughing. In the extended cut, he stabs some orcs and Haradrim (appearing as an accomplished warrior). Éowyn tussles with Gothmog, and cuts him on the leg. The longer version now follows the theatrical cut: a shot of the Witch-king flying above the second level introduces Gandalf and Pippin behind the gate, which's being pounded by a troll (note how the Witch-king shot reminds viewers of this particular villain, who's going to kill Théoden shortly).

The quiet moment between the wizard and the hobbit is one of the most moving sections in the 3 films; it was added after principal photography, when it was thought that some quieter scenes were needed to break up the incessant din and chaos of the battle scenes (and also because Gandalf and Pippin were lost from the film for some time). The dialogue is about death – Tolkien's grand theme – and comes from the scene in *The Fellowship of the Ring* when Frodo is dreaming in Tom Bombadil's house:

But either in his dreams or out of them, Frodo heard a sweet singing running in his mind: a song that seemed to come like a pale light behind a grey rain-curtain, and growing stronger to turn the veil all to glass and silver, until at last it was rolled back, and a far green country opened before him under a swift sunrise.

The vision melted into waking; and there was Tom whistling like a tree-full of birds; and the sun was already slanting down the hill and through the open window. Outside everything was green and gold. (FR, 185)

Tolkien reprised that moment on the last page of *Lord of the Rings*, when Frodo is voyaging into the West:

And the ship went out into the High Sea and passed on into the West, until at last on a night of rain Frodo smelled a sweet fragrance on the air and heard the sound of singing that came over the water. And then it seemed to him that as in his dream in the house of Bombadil, the grey rain-curtain turned all to silver glass and was rolled back, and he beheld white shores and beyond them a far green country under a swift sunrise. (RK, 378)

Both moments, which have the sweet poetry of Will Shakespeare's *The Tempest,* are Ronald Tolkien at his best. It was Fran Walsh and Philippa Boyens who thought of introducing these two moments from *The Lord of the Rings* at this point in the film of *The Return of the King*, and it was an inspired choice. Ian McKellen and Billy Boyd are terrific in this scene, but what really adds the kicker is the first introduction of Howard Shore's *Into the West* cue, which plays over the Grey Havens, and the end titles. Thus, without following Frodo and Bilbo sailing into towards Valinor, the film suggests it through dialogue (and it's fitting that it's Gandalf who delivers the lines. The only other two characters who could do so would be Elrond or Galadriel).

Back to Pelennor Fields, and Théoden rallying his troops. Oliphaunts are destroying Rohirrim left and right. From Théoden's point-of-view the fell-beast is seen flying towards him, snatching the king in its mouth and hurling him savagely from side to side. Éowyn looks on horrified. Théoden and Snowmane roll away, with the king trapped under his horse but still alive. The nazgûl and fell-beast trot closer, but Éowyn stands between them. The 2003 film of *The Return of the King* follows the book closely here, but shuffles the order of the action (for instance, in the movie, Éowyn dispatches the fell-beast first, and the dialogue between her and the Witch-king follows). It's no mean feat to hack off the head of the fell-beast (it must be at least three feet thick of muscle and sinew), but Éowyn manages it in the film with a couple of strokes, and it dies, flailing its neck and shuddering.

Angmar rises from between the creature's wings, and looms over Éowyn. The fight begins (the Witch-king has a giant spiky, metal mace, which the prop department rebuilt much bigger, because the director wanted the weapon to be huge). At first, Éowyn dodges the blows from the oversize mace, accompanied by a fierce choral cue. Lines of Rohirrim and *mûmakil* can be seen in the background (but there's no fighting going on nearby, and no one apart from Merry to help Éowyn).

The warrior-maiden collapses against a horse, and her shield's shattered, when the Witch-king lands a blow. (The extended cut adds some beats to the fight). There's a pull-back to the docks now, with the battle and the white city glimpsed in the distance (the arrival of Aragorn and his chums is thus occurring in parallel with the fighting on Pelennor). The black ships roll up (fairly rapidly), and an orc band gathers on the quayside. In slow motion our heroes leap off the boat, led by Aragorn of course (Orlando Bloom is a cartoon character here, because he wasn't available on the day). The heroic theme from *The Fellowship of the Ring* is reprised as the good guys rush forward to the orcs, flanked by the dead. A long shot depicts the stream of the host of the dead as a solid green sweep of ghosts from the river (the dead in action are always shown in long shot, and exactly how they kill the living is kept mysterious).

Back to Éowyn and the Witch-king: she's gripped by the throat, and it seems to be the end for her, when Merry stabs the nazgûl in the back of the knee. Wounded, he falls to his knees; Éowyn delivers her *Macbeth* line, after pulling off her helmet. She rams her sword into the Witch-king's helmet. (The extended version adds some other shots in this and the following scene.) There's a cut to Aragorn and Gimli hacking and fighting orcs.

The nazgûl's death recalls the Wicked Witch in *The Wizard of Oz*, which is probably the most famous death of a witch in Hollywood history ('I'm melting!'): Angmar writhes and crumples into the ground (the film is speeded-up). High-pitched cries and hissing sounds accompany the demise, and his helmet collapses and implodes. The filmmakers worried that the Witch-king's death wasn't big enough (I don't think it is, and something more spectacular is required here), but it received a big cheer from audiences, so it seems to have worked. (Earlier drafts of *The Lord of the Rings* book had the Haradrim fleeing when the Witch-king is dispatched by Éowyn, and the Witch-king becomes a 'headless thing' crawling on the ground, 'snivelling' until it dies 'and a long thin wail rent the air and vanished in the distance' [HME 8, 366]). It's a famous scene in the published book:

> "Éowyn! Éowyn!" cried Merry. Then tottering, struggling up, with her last strength she drove her sword between crown and mantle, as the great shoulder bowed before her. The sword broke sparkling into many shards. The crown rolled away with a clang. Éowyn fell forward upon her fallen foe. But lo! the mantle and hauberk were empty. Shapeless they lay now on the ground, torn and tumbled; and a cry went up into the shuddering air, and faded to a shrill wailing, passing with the wind, a voice bodiless and thin that died, and was swallowed up, and was never heard again in that age of this world. (RK, 138)

The *Extended Edition* adds images of Gothmog lurching around nearby, and Éowyn amidst corpses and battle detritus. An additional scene to the theatrical cut has Éowyn, wounded and crawling, alerted to Gothmog's presence and searching for a sword. The film now intercuts three people: Éowyn looking for a weapon, Gothmog getting closer to her, and Aragorn also nearby, fighting orcs. So of course it's Éowyn's beloved man who rescues her (even though he doesn't realize it): he chops off Gothmog's arm, and he and Gimli finish him off. That winds up Gothmog's story (the theatrical cut hadn't resolved that, but I doubt if anyone cared, although villains *must* be dispatched in movies).

But where's Legolas? What's he up to on the battlefield? The audience finds out in the next scene, created to capitalize on the 'Legolas moments' which viewers had loved in the first two films. Legolas single-handedly takes down a *mûmakil*, after slaying the whole crew. For Orlando Bloom it meant a day of shooting on a blue screen stage, but most of the sequence comprises computer animation, mattes and models. It's Legolas's big scene in *The Return of the King*: he leaps onto an oliphaunt's tusk, then a leg, then a back leg; he climbs up the animal (ghosts are glimpsed below, streaming across Pelennor). Legolas fires arrows, swings onto the front leg of the *mûmakil*, and cuts some ropes. The tower slides off, taking Haradrim with it (and pulling the elf up). It's just Legolas and the *mûmakil* now. Legolas shoots arrows into the back of the beast's head, and it collapses. To top it all, Legolas rides down the creature's trunk (like Batman in *Batman and Robin*), landing up in front of Gimli, ready to take the applause. (And the dwarf mutters gruffly that all that only counts as one in their Kill The Enemy competition).

A brief cut to Aragorn on the battlefield, with the dead swarming up and over a *mûmakil* some way behind him, emitting high-pitched squeals. A L.S. of Minas Tirith, wreathed in smoke, depicts the dead streaming through the streets incredibly rapidly (an explanation shot).

Next is Théoden's death scene (which was directed by Fran Walsh). The scene had been shot during principal photography, but was re-shot as part of the pick-ups for *The Return of the King* (in early 2003). It was Bernard Hill's very last day on *Lord of the Rings*. Walsh and Boyens wanted to rewrite the scene, in order to have Éowyn less weepy, to get across how Éowyn has 'saved' Théodeon, and has fought for him, and how she doesn't break down and cry until the king is dead. The intimate scene plays in standard movie style, with tight close-ups, and slow strings and choral music. (The scene has affinities with the end of *Return of the Jedi*, and the death scene of Darth Vader: Luke: 'I'm going to save you'; Vader: 'you already have'. Yes, even sick mass murderers can be redeemed. They might have slaughtered entire planets, but if they say 'sorry', they are forgiven!).

Théoden's passing signals the end of the battle of Pelennor Fields in the 2003 film. All of the material in the 1955 book about the Rohirrim and their dead king, and Éomer, and the Rohirrim's song, was dropped (so Éomer's story arc isn't resolved). Instead, the film shifts to Aragorn letting the dead go, after an aerial long shot of the battle arena, with sunlight breaking through the clouds. Gandalf picks his way through a field littered with corpses, spears and lances. Smoke drifts. Gandalf and Pippin look on as Aragorn releases the King of the Dead. The ghosts turn to dust on the wind with a sigh. (Gimli provides the audience's question here, about keeping the Army of the Dead for future battles).

After helping Aragorn and his small army to take the ships, the Shadow Host disappears back into the Paths of the Dead in an early outline (HME, 8, 398). The account of the journey through the Paths of the Dead was to have followed Pelennor, told by Gimli and Legolas to Merry and Pippin (HME, 8, 399).

Gandalf and Aragorn meet again; in the *Extended Edition*, Éomer discovers his sister unconscious on the battlefield and, in slow motion, weeps as he holds her and cries out (accompanied by a choral cue). Another scene dropped from the cinema cut occurs here: the Houses of the Healing, high up in Minas Tirith. It's night; a stone room, with windows overlooking the city. Aragorn tends Éowyn, lying on her back on a couch, while Éomer looks on. Liv Tyler (or is it Renée Fleming?) gets to sing here, a slow, plaintive song over slow motion images, lap dissolves and echoey sounds.

Éowyn is next shown alone, a little later (or maybe a day or two later): now she's up and about. A bandaged Faramir watches her from a distance (no one else seems to be about, even though the biggest battle for centuries has just ended, when the city would be in turmoil). The Houses of the Healing scenes have to show a romance blossoming in a very short space of time (in fact, the extended version of *The Return of the King* only has two romantic scenes between Éowyn and Faramir).

Thus, when the film now cuts to Peregrin Took searching for and finding Meriadoc Brandybuck on the battlefield, it is going back in time a few days. It's the evening of the last day of the battle (though the scene was originally shot as a daytime scene, and was switched about from day to night, and was put back into the film on the last day of editing [Sib, 510]). Merry is found near the *mûmakil* corpse (a giant prop built in five sections, and slotted together on the Pelennor location in Twizel, on the South Island. The Merry and Pippin scene in the final film was a reshoot, however, in the studio).

An elaborate miniature shot (which combines models, matte paintings and CG embellishments) introduces Cirith Ungol at night, with a red glow beyond the mountains. The camera flies up to the uppermost room in the tower and through a narrow stone window, where Frodo lies on the other side. He's dirty, topless (he's naked in the book), lying on the floor facing the camera with his hands tied. A few strands of the cocoon cling to him. Sound designer Ethan van der Ryn explained that for this scene he wanted the sense of Frodo waking up and feeling disoriented: he can hear the distant sounds of the orcs partying. (Van der Ryn recalled that he had woken up once as a child in the middle of the night, and heard people having a party. So the sound team gathered a bunch of people and had them acting out partying hard).

Behind Frodo are Gorbag (Stephen Ure) and Shagrat, the orcs who captured Frodo earlier, sorting through his belongings, and fighting over the mithril shirt. Frodo suddenly remembers the ring, and searches for it: it's gone. The orcs continue to argue, and Gorbag is pushed through the trapdoor in the floor, and falls down some stairs. A fight breaks out among the orcs down below (yet another aerial descending shot – a favourite device in the *Lord of the Rings* movies – follows an orc out of a window and down the tower, to his death in the courtyard below). The *Extended Edition* adds footage of the stunt people clobbering each other, swinging, falling, taking hits and leaping at each other. It's all very silly and over-the-top, a little like a schoolyard romp.

The narrative switches now to Sam's point-of-view of the Cirith Ungol tower and the fight. The famousest gardener of the Shire approaches the gateway. The psychic barrier of the Watchers was shot, but wasn't included in either version of *The Return of the King* (it was thought to slow down the film). And it's another of Tolkien's invisible obstacles or threats that's difficult to get across on film. There is a nice medium shot of the art department's Watchers, though. (The scene worked quite well in the BBC radio version of 1981, with Sam narrating the action in the first person, as it was happening to him, which's how Tolkien wrote parts of the Cirith Ungol sequence):

> "Come on, you miserable sluggard!" Sam cried to himself. "Now for it!" He drew Sting and ran towards the open gate. But just as he was about to pass under its great arch he felt a shock: as if he had run into some web like Shelob's, only invisible. He could see no obstacle, but something too strong for his will to overcome barred the way. He looked about, and then within the shadow of the gate he saw the Two Watchers. (TT, 212)

Sam, brandishing two swords (all of a sudden he's Jet Li), moves cautiously through the Cirith Ungol complex (this was chiefly a miniature, but still required quite a bit of set building – the courtyard area, the staircase, and the tower room). It was also a busy and costly scene in terms of costumes, props, make-up, stunts, extras, and so on.

The whole Shelob's lair/ Cirith Ungol sequence in J.R.R. Tolkien's book contains some of the most memorable moments in the novel – Sam and Frodo versus the monster spider, Sam wearing the ring, and Sam rescuing Frodo from a heavily populated orc stronghold. But it also has some unsatisfactory decisions and unbelievable events (which Tolkien recognized): Sam thinking Frodo's dead; Sam leaving Frodo's body; Frodo being captured while Sam's nearby; Sam taking the ring (and putting it on briefly); 200 orcs helpfully killing themselves before Sam arrives, and so on. The 2003 film rightly streamlined a lot of the events: it quietly elided the key plot point of Sam taking the ring, and putting on the ring, for instance.

Sam as the superhero elf follows next, suggested with the very familiar cinematic device (at least as old as Expressionism) of big shadows on the wall of the castle (plus some aggressive grunts from Sean Astin). He climbs the stairs, while three orcs descend them higher up. One hobbit versus three orcs is tricky to pull off, and the film isn't wholly convincing here: Sam fights the orcs, and pushes one of them off the stairs. (Astin said it was fun to do the Errol Flynn bit – the *Lord of the Rings* movies contain quite a few Errol Flynn/ Douglas Fairbanks moments). In the book, one orc flees from Sam, but Shagrat does confront him – though, conveniently, Shagrat's wounded, and manages to get past Sam and escape (with the bundle of Frodo's things [RK, 218f]). So Sam doesn't kill any orcs in the book, and certainly doesn't dispatch four in a row as he does in the film.

The viewpoint shifts to Frodo now, with Shagrat alone with Frodo and deciding he's going to kill the hobbit (going against Sauron's orders – he boss's only 60 miles away). So when Sam runs him through with a sword from behind, it's a (mild) surprise to the audience that Sam's rescued Frodo, as well as to Frodo. The next scene has two important plot points to convey: the first is Frodo apologizing to Sam (he says 'sorry'), and Sam forgiving him. That is dealt with in a cursory fashion (no big hugs or shows of emotion here, for instance. Instead, the hobbits stay apart: Frodo is sitting up, and Sam stands before him). It's quite different in the 1955 book, which's much more emotional:

> "Frodo! Mr Frodo, my dear!" cried Sam, tears almost blinding him. "It's Sam, I've come!" He half lifted his master and hugged him to his breast.
>
> "Am I still dreaming?" he muttered. "But the other dreams were horrible."
>
> "You're not dreaming at all, Master," said Sam. "It's real. It's me. I've come."
>
> "I can hardly believe it," said Frodo, clutching him. "There was an orc with a whip, and then it turns into Sam! Then I wasn't dreaming after all when I heard that singing down below, and I tried to answer! Was it you?"
>
> "It was indeed, Mr Frodo. I'd given up hope, almost I couldn't find you."
>
> "Well, you have now Sam, dear Sam," said Frodo, and he lay back in Sam's gentle arms, closing his eyes, like a child at rest when night-fears are driven away by some loved voice or hand. (RK, 222)

The reunion is critical in the story, because both hobbits have been very close to death, and their survival is pretty much miraculous, but the film plays it much cooler. However, the scriptwriters had already altered the reasons for Frodo and Sam going their different ways, so maybe the more restrained reunion makes sense. Alternatively, the fact, in the film's version of events, that Frodo had doubted Sam, and had been influenced by Gollum, and told Sam to go home, might have been a good reason for a much more emotional meeting.

The second plot point in this scene is of course the ring. Originally, the scene was conceived by the screenwriters with Frodo being much more aggressive and nasty, and virtually yelling at Sam (in the book he cries at Sam to give him the ring). But the intense and grasping characterization of Frodo as a ring junkie was altered chiefly in the editing suite. The filmmakers opted to use the quieter takes of Elijah Wood, and then they extended the moment by adding the empty spaces in Sean Astin's reaction shots. So the scene was largely rejigged in the editing, with many cuts back to Sam waiting.

In the book, Frodo demands the ring from Sam, and Sam is reluctant to hand it over, offering reasons such as the ring's effect on Frodo, and the danger of carrying it (RK, 224). But Frodo snatches the ring, calls Sam a thief, and sees Sam as a leering, pawing orc, 'a foul little creature with greedy eyes and slobbering mouth' (RK, 224). So the 2001-03 film of *The Lord of the Rings* as often tones down the drama of Tolkien's 1955 book as it intensifies it. While the picture expands on Tolkien's vision at many points, and increases the spectacle and the tensions (to the point where Frodo and Sam split up, for instance), it also holds back on many occasions, and scenes are often underplayed (as here, in this critical reunion). That fits in with the mood and culture of the contemporary audience, which maybe finds huge outbursts of emotion difficult to take. (The big hug between Frodo and Sam doesn't occur in Minas Tirith, either, the reunion after it's all over and the ring's destroyed – instead, it's saved for the parting at Grey Havens).

The hobbit reunion scene in Cirith Ungol in the film is also a ring moment: the ring's voice and its 'heartbeat' is heard, and the clink of the ring on its chain is loud in the mix. By concentrating now on Sam's reaction shots, the viewpoint in the scene shifts to Sam, and hints of Sam's reluctance to give up the ring (which's in the book, but played in a different fashion). 'It will destroy you, Sam,' Frodo tells him.

Sam, ever the down-to-earth hobbit, swiftly moves the mood onto practicalities like clothes (and away from the ring, which will be Frodo's until the climax). A cut pushes the film on to the hobbits marching over a bridge (a miniature), with Cirith Ungol some way behind them. They're clad in out-size orc gear. The next scene takes place at the pass in the Morgai, with the first big reveal of the interior landscape of Mordor: the tower of Barad-dûr, the Eye, the volcano, the black country, the fires of orc camps dotted everywhere, and grey skies overhead. Now the Eye moves around in its rooftop socket, and sends out a white spotlight beam which moves restlessly and nervously, as if searching for something (for the spotlight beam over the Mordor model shots, a mirror with a lamp was used to provide interactive lighting on the miniatures. The Rankin/ Bass *Return of the King* cartoon had introduced a spotlight for Sauron, though theirs was red). Frodo mentions the Eye, and they move into the Black Land (reminding audiences of their chief obstacle in this part of the film – Sauron – although a band of orcs provide a fearsome complication in the extended cut of *The Return of the King.*)

Once the Frodo and Sam storyline has been resolved to the point where they are on their way again, *The Return of the King* cuts back to Gandalf, Aragorn, Gimli and our other heroes. Of the other characters: well,

Denethor is dead, as is the Witch-king, Gothmog and Théoden, but no one has a funeral scene (much is made of Théoden's journey back to Rohan in the book, for instance. I wonder how they kept the corpse intact, though, as the procession takes place some months after Pelennor). The theatrical cut has Faramir and Éowyn disappear from the film until the coronation scene (where their only act is to smile at the crowned Aragorn), but in the *Extended Edition* their romance in the Houses of Healing is briefly suggested.

In the next scene, Pippin is wandering through the devastation of Pelennor Fields, wearing a long black gown and a pretty bonnet, looking like Vivien Leigh for some reason. The camera begins on Pip in medium close-up, then cranes up and back, revealing first a few bodies and wounded soldiers, then as it goes higher and higher, showing hundreds and hundreds... No, wrong film.

A war council in the Tower Hall of the Citadel in daytime, around the throne: Gandalf and Aragorn are the principal characters in this scene (which's really a two-hander, apart from Gimli's ad-libbed line which closes the scene, and the reaction shots of Legolas and Éomer). The film departs from the book at this point in the narrative in some key respects: in the film, Gandalf is feeling much more hopeless, and admits that he's sent Frodo to his death. Gandalf gloomily states that they have only bought a respite from Sauron with the victory at Pelennor.

The scriptwriters give Aragorn more to do in this scene by having the ranger offer the suggestion of riding out to meet Sauron's forces at the Black Gate (in the book, it's Gandalf who proposes this; Roger Sale calls the war council 'Gandalf's finest hour').[1] There's also a lot more talk in the novel before a course of action is decided upon, and there are many more characters present (such as Elrond's sons).

> "We must march out to meet him at once. We must make ourselves the bait, though his jaws should close on us. He will take that bait, in hope and in greed, for he will think that in such rashness he sees the pride of the new Ringlord..." (RK, 186)

The war council in the film has – amazingly – only about five people present (why do so many of the Minas Tirith interiors look deserted? The white city's the capital of Gondor, and everyone from roundabout has come there for sanctuary from the enemy. In the movies, it seems as if the plague's already swept through it). The war council should really have been a little more formal; Gimli lounging in the steward's throne is humorous but out of place here. Where all the representatives of the city – have they given over rule to wizards and others, just like that? The direction and performances are too low key. This is shit, on so many levels.

NOTES: ACT FOUR

1. In N. Isaacs, 270.

ACT FIVE

The cinema release of *The Return of the King* now cuts to the Army of the West leaving Minas Tirith led by Aragorn. It seems as if one big battle is over and already an army is marching to another one. It's much more useful thinking of the *Lord of the Rings* films *in toto* as a *war movie* than a *fantasy movie*, just as the 1955 book is a war book as much as a fantasy or heroic adventure book. The *Extended Edition* of *The Return of the King* adds, before the exodus, a scene at the same location, at night, with Aragorn consulting the *palantír* alone (in the book, this scene takes place earlier, in Rohan). Flames and roaring noises reprise the *palantír* effects, and the Eye appears, as before. In close-up, Aragorn shows Sauron the sword; there's a brief image of Sauron from the prologue of *The Fellowship of the Ring* inside the ball, reminding viewers that the sword had cut the ring from the Dark Lord's finger. And then there's an impossible image: Arwen asleep in Rivendell, an image from Aragorn's dream. Sauron would have no way of knowing that image: he doesn't have access to Rivendell or Arwen or, even more improbably, Aragorn's own dreams. In that case, the seeing stone must have switched halfway through the session from being a communication between Sauron and Aragorn (though why would Sauron show an image of himself at Dagorlad?) to a psychic mirror, reflecting back Aragorn's dreams, and the object of his secret desires, Arwen.

Thus, although the *palantír* scene works fine on a movie-movie level (it demonstrates Aragorn having the confidence and strength to withstand the encounter with Sauron, and shows him becoming kingly, as well as offering a serious threat to Sauron), the images in the seeing stone don't really make sense. As in the other dream sequences of Aragorn's, the scene moves into slow motion and dream sounds, as the Evenstar – symbolizing Arwen and their future life together – falls and shatters on the floor. The extended cut of the film then washes out to the close-up of Aragorn on his horse, at the head of the Host of the West. Gandalf, Legolas, Éomer and co. are behind him, and Merry and Pippin ride, as before, in the saddle in front of their companions.

The longer DVD and video cut of *The Return of the King* adds a brief scene of Éowyn and Faramir in the Houses of Healing here, looking out of the window towards the East. They hold hands, and embrace (but gently, not erotically or passionately). Quiet flute music, a muted interpretation of the heroic Gondor theme, plays.

Aragorn donning special armour in the Great Hall of Minas Tirith was a scene that didn't make it into either version of *The Return of the King* (two of the Weta team who'd built the armour played the aides). We probably don't need to see *another* scene of someone putting on armour at this point in the 3 movies.

Now comes an involved and detailed sequence which was dropped entirely from the theatrical cut of *The Return of the King*: Frodo and Sam are captured by a band of orcs, and escape them. A favourite sequence with director Peter Jackson (partly because it includes plenty of down-and-dirty orc shenanigans), it offers a not inconsiderable obstacle for

Frodo and Sam (Jackson remarked that critics had said it was relatively easy for Frodo and Sam to traverse Mordor, so this scene explains that the halflings did run into obstacles. There are further set-backs in the book, though why Sauron kept the road to Mount Doom clear but neglected to station orcs to guard it is never explained by Tolkien. Sean Astin said that many additional scenes of Frodo and Sam suffering and walking through the Black Land were shot but not used).

The exteriors for many of the Sam and Frodo Mordor scenes were staged on a real volcano, Mount Ruapehu and the Whakapapa Ski Field, in the middle of the North Island of New Zealand (also used for the prologue of *The Fellowship of the Ring*, the Ephel Dúath, and other scenes). There are three active volcanos here (Ruapehu, Tongariro, and Ngauruhoe), in the Tongariro National Park (the production wasn't allowed to use the summits of these sacred Maori mountains in the film, so the tops were generated on paper and in the computer).

The orc band scene opens with Frodo and Sam descending a bank to a stony track, and trying to look inconspicuous against a rockface as an orc army (extras from the New Zealand Army) troop by. One of the orc drivers spots them, and whips them into line. Soon the hobbits are in the midst of the column of orcs. The sound department added plenty of orc grunts and voices, and Howard Shore composed a suitably grim cue. Part of the impressive long shot of thousands of orcs streaming Northwards to the Black Gate, with Barad-dûr behind, appeared in the theatrical cut. It might have been useful for viewers to have some kind of a map here, like the map moment in *The Two Towers* with Faramir. It would have shown how the Army of the West was riding to the Black Gate, while Frodo and Sam were (ironically) being dragged in the same direction. But shots with the scale of a Biblical epic, during the Morannon battle, did depict the topography clearly – showing the Host of the West, the Black Gate, Sauron's forces, with Barad-dûr and Mount Doom beyond.

Back to the Gondorians, Rohirrim and our heroes now – establishing that the film's moved into a parallel action narrative mode (only the most pitifully pedantic Tolkien fan would complain about the timelines, which Tolkien slaved over, not matching here. In every other respect, it makes perfect dramatic sense). *The Return of the King* will now cut back and forth between the big battle scenes at the Black Gate and the smaller, more intimate (but ultimately far more important) struggle of the two hobbits. It's all down to two storylines now. The editing pattern will usually keep each scene self-contained, but will sometimes also cut back after a one or two shots (such as during the fight with Gollum on the steps leading to the Sammath Naur, which's tightly intercut towards the end with the battle at the Morannon). The scenes will also vary in terms of sound: the rousing music and din of battle and quieter sounds (the wind, or breathing).

Back inside Mordor, a burly, thick-set orc (with prosthetic make-up comprising an eaten-away nose and a white contact lens), inspects the orc grunts. Frodo is wilting under the weight of the ring (as well as hunger, thirst, exhaustion, etc), and it seems as if our heroes are going to be discovered. So Sam starts a fight (at Frodo's instigation) with the other orcs pressing in around them, as a distraction. The orc officer loses them before he can reach them and, in the confusion, the hobbits manage to slip out of the column, off the track, through a tent, and out onto the rocks beyond.

Cut to some time later, the hobbits now alone in a different part of Mordor: the visuals comprise the black rocks of the Dark Country (there's virtually no colour); isolated flames; smoke drifting; and Orodruin looming above them. Frodo collapses – the ring's too heavy as they near its place of origin. To lighten the load, the halflings throw away their orc clothes (Peter Jackson said he wished he'd made more of Sam jettisoning his beloved pack and pots and pans, which he'd carted around since the beginning of the quest. In the film, it's just one shot, really, of the items falling towards the camera (it's enough, though). Dominic Monaghan commented that it was ironic – Sean Astin had finally gotten rid of his pack, but was given it back at his leaving party).

The next scene, directed by Fran Walsh, has the hobbits huddled against the cold. An additional moment in the extended version has Sam looking up to see a star (presumably it's Elrond's dad, Eärendil), unveiled by clouds rose-pink in the afterglow of sunset. Frodo sleeps fitfully. (This scene was reshot, like so many scenes in the whole *Lord of the Rings* project, in the pick-up sessions, but the filmmakers opted, unusually, to go back to the original production photography – partly because the actors gave the impression of being cold, because they really were). The actors were disappointed that the scene had been axed from the theatrical version of *The Return of the King*; Sean Astin said that some of the crew were crying during the filming – hopefully because of the performances (2004, 290).

A travelling shot reveals the Black Gate, emerging behind some rocks, by day. Alex Funke, head of the *Rings* miniatures unit, speaks lovingly of this and other shots of Black Gate. Funke enjoyed this model of the Black Gates, with its rusty lead panels giving off a silvery sheen, and its spiky design by John Howe. Howe saw the Black Gates as Sauron's perverse, misconceived version of grandiose Númenórean architecture. The Black Gates are very important in the *Lord of the Rings* films, though: they are nothing less than the setting for the climactic battle, and required the model team to photograph them every which way.

A small Frodo-Sam scene is next, with the hobbits sitting against some rocks again (always with the rocks), and Frodo trying to squeeze out the last of the water (this was shot the day after the scene with the lembas in *The Two Towers*, and was the first time actors Elijah Wood and Sean Astin had the make-up of scarred skin and chapped lips applied). Now back to Aragorn and the Army of the West getting into position in front of the Morannon. Lances; spears; banners; shields. (Later, the Host of the West form a single, defensive circle; in the 1955 book, the Host of the West is located on two hills). The filmmakers also simplified the terrain in front of the Black Gate: in the novel, there's a 'a great mire of reeking mud and foul-smelling pools' lying before the Morannon like a moat (RK, 196); in the film, the area is a relatively flat, stony landscape (it was shot on part of the

New Zealand Army's firing range).

Now back to Frodo: he's warding off invisible assailants in slow motion like swatting flies, in a slightly different landscape (filmed on the other side of Mount Ruapehu). The slow motion indicates another ring moment, and ring sounds are heard (now, as sound designer Mike Hopkins commented, more like a migraine throb than a heartbeat). The rest of the scene is studio-bound, with Barad-dûr and the Eye prominent in the background. Sam ducks to the ground and yells at Frodo to follow suit. Frodo falls in slow motion as the beam of Sauron hits him. (Peter Jackson wanted it to appear as if the light was pinning Frodo to the ground, but it doesn't come across like that. It's more like prisoners being caught in a searchlight on the other side of the fence.)

The scene is unsatisfactory, but it is a crucial dramatic moment, because it seems as if Sauron might realize that the ring is right there, thirty or forty miles away, in his own land. To emphasize the significance of the moment, the filmmakers intercut it with the Black Gate scene tighter and tighter. Aragorn, Gandalf, Éomer, Legolas, Gimli, and the hobbits ride out towards the Black Gate.

Aragorn calls out for Sauron to come forth. The *Extended Edition* adds a new scene here: the gates open and the Mouth of Sauron rides out, on a horse fitted out with barbed armour rather like the ringwraiths' steeds. Actor Bruce Spence (from *Mad Max 2* and *3*) is overwhelmed by a huge helmet which only reveals his mouth and yellowy teeth. But he still manages to deliver a strange, gloating performance (with a slightly slowed-down American voice, which also, curiously, retains the *thees* and *thous* of Tolkien's dialogue). The strangest aspect of this scene, apart from Spence's odd grunts and leers (his performance belongs to wholly different movie), is his too-large mouth (the filmmakers wanted something weird about the Mouth of Sauron, and tried a number of variants, including having the mouth vertical. In the end, the actor's heavily made-up mouth was enlarged and placed on top of his real mouth in the computer. The effect recalls Samuel Beckett's play *Not I* which focussed solely on Billie Whitelaw's mouth floating above a blacked-out stage).

Plot points like the mithril shirt are paid off, and there's an emphasis on Frodo's death, and reactions from the members of the fellowship. Aragorn rides up beside the Mouth of Sauron and beheads him (Aragorn decapitates people in every *Rings* film). Sauron's attention is suddenly drawn to the Morannon (with a loud tiger snarl), saving Frodo and Sam from discovery. It's a bold but not terribly convincing staging of how Sauron's attention might be snatched away from Frodo and the ring. The Mouth of Sauron scene was dropped from the theatrical cut partly because the information it offered was somewhat redundant: the Dark Lord's lieutenant uses the suggestion of Frodo's death to frighten the allies, but the audience knows that Frodo is alive.

The gates open, and orcs march forward; beyond, Barad-dûr and the Eye can be seen, putting together the lay-out of this part of Mordor for the viewer. This's the first of some spectacular extreme long shots in the Black Gate battle, which are some of the most memorable in the 2001-03 series.

Back to Frodo, still in slight slow motion, being helped up by Sam (note how the sound team keep the sound of the chink of the ring on its chain prominent in these and subsequent scenes, as a psychological reminder of the significance of the ring, even though that sound would be inaudible in the wind and volcano rumbles and roars, and because even in a M.C.U. a little thing like a ring get lost).

Aragorn's speech to rouse his troops is delivered on horseback as he rides up and down the front row of the Army of the West, with reaction shots of the Gondorian and Rohirrim soldiers. A very familiar scene in movies (the model is the 'we happy few' speech in *Henry V*, 4:3). Although the original production dialogue of actor Viggo Mortensen was employed here, it still isn't the best example of this kind of scene in movies (Bernard Hill was far better, for instance, earlier in the film). Wide reverse angles reveal the spotlight of Sauron's Eye trained on the Host of the West.

At the end of the speech, the soldiers draw their weapons; Aragorn turns to face the enemy. Our heroes are now surrounded on all sides by thousands of orcs and trolls and enemies (the film doesn't have time to differentiate between the various forces making up Sauron's army, as the book does).

The Return of the King shifts back to Frodo and Sam, now climbing the lower stony slopes of Orodruin (the actors had safety wires attached to them. The incline was much steeper than it looked on screen, which's often the case. To make a hill look really forbidding, you need inclines sharper than 45°). Smoke drifts over tight shots of the hobbits; they end up on all fours, crawling across the stones and dust. One of the most moving sequences in the film occurs here, with big close-ups of Frodo crawling, accompanied by a terrific music cue, of poignant whistle and strings, from Howard Shore (an example where film music doesn't have to be bombastic and full-throated to achieve an emotional impact, but it does need a bit of space and quiet to work its magic).

The editing between the Black Gate and Mount Doom accelerates now. A vast aerial shot (entirely CG and models) reveals our heroes at the Black Gate surrounded by enemies on all sides. Orodruin and the Dark Tower are visible beyond. Cut to close-ups of the goodies, looking suitably grim, afraid, or resolved to die (the heroes in both book and film know they are likely to die against such overwhelming odds, but the reader and the viewer know that there's no way major characters will be dispatched by mere orcs or trolls – no hero ever has been in any movie ever. The only casualties will be minor characters, if any). There's a brief exchange between Legolas and Gimli (their last in the *Lord of the Rings* films): a farewell and a statement of friendship. Theirs will be one of many fates left unresolved by the 2003 adaption.

As film editor Jamie Selkirk recounted, the filmmakers realized during editing *The Return of the King* that the Black Gate battle had to be reduced, and the emphasis had to be on Frodo and Sam at the Crack of Doom. Apart from the troll fighting Aragorn, there's not a lot of dramatic development in the battle at the Gate. The nazgûl arrive, followed by the eagles, but that's about it. And we've just sat through a battle that's lasted 320 hours.

Back to Frodo and Sam: Frodo lies in Sam's arms, on his lap. They are lodged on the rocky side of the volcano, with lava streaming down in the distance, and the mountain spewing out balls of lava which land like meteorites. Both hobbits are exhausted, filthy, scarred, hot, sweaty. Sam paints a picture of Spring in the Shire, with a lyrical whistle soloing underneath (the Shire is what the filmmakers have reckoned that Frodo and Sam are fighting for). Frodo, meanwhile, seems farther gone than Sam, and is haunted by Sauron and the ring. The lyrical whistle changes to a bold choral cue when Sam, summoning a last gasp of strength, resolves that if he can't carry the ring, then he can carry Frodo, staggering to his feet and hauling Frodo onto his shoulders. The audience has to be cheering at this point. It's a heroic moment when Sam comes across as the true hero of the piece (Tolkien often thought so – and increasingly as time went on).

Sean Astin recounted how important that scene was for him and Elijah Wood (he returns to it repeatedly in his account of making the films), and how they had managed to move their director to tears ('the single greatest acting experience of my life' [2004, 234]). As Peter Jackson recalled, the dialogue part of the scene had been pushed to the end of the day, because he had concentrated too much on shots of the hobbits crawling up the hill. So two cameras were run simultaneously on the actors, to save time. Apart from the close-ups, there was time for a wide shot and not much else. (The scene was looped, because of the noise of wind machines and the like).

A ring-like moment occurs next between Aragorn and Sauron, when the Dark Lord appears to be addressing Aragorn directly from the summit of Barad-dûr. Aragorn is standing in front of the Army of the West, sword in hand. Eerie sounds and slow motion are used, as before, to suggest an internal communication. But Aragorn snaps out of the reverie (perhaps aided by Gandalf, who seems to be making a magical gesture with his hand). Aragorn turns to his companions and says 'for Frodo' (showing how he was never seduced by Sauron), and starts running (this was apparently Viggo Mortensen's idea). A nice touch has the hobbits (Merry and Pippin) following next, with swords raised and battle cries, before being overtaken by the whole army. It's akin to 'going over the top' of the trenches in World War One movies, and is rightly accorded a heroic choral cue.

The suggestion of a strange communication between the Dark Lord and Aragorn is the remnant of an idea that was storyboarded and shot (though the visual effects of the angelic presence weren't finalized), in which Sauron would appear as an avatar, an angelic vision. Reaction shots were filmed of a bright light shining on our heroes. Then Sauron, changing into his Sauron the Warrior guise from the prologue of *The Fellowship of the Ring*) would do battle with Aragorn. It was a way of getting Sauron off that bloody tower. As Philippa Boyens explained, the adaptors were thinking in scriptwriting rulebook terms – staging a showdown between the hero and villain. Thankfully, although the idea had some merits, and made sense in movie terms, the sequence was dropped (and Aragorn fought a troll instead). Peter Jackson added that it was difficult to make fourteen foot figures look convincing (the *Lord of the Rings* films already had giants like Treebeard and trolls), and the fight would give too much emphasis to Aragorn and Sauron, whereas the centre of the story was Frodo (and a similar fight had been seen in the prologue, which would've been anti-climactic. The true heroism of Aragorn is really about him and his friends giving up their lives so Frodo can achieve his task). So Aragorn's act of charging with a 'for Frodo' cry was about buying time for Frodo. (Mortensen had the idea of using the footage shot of the light shining on the actors in the Army range location, by suggesting that it was the moment when Sauron's spotlight would turn from Frodo to the Black Gate). Thus, yet again, editing saved the day, and turned the sequence about.

Sam and Frodo are next up, with the return of Gollum. They are on the stone steps leading up to the Sammath Naur, an immense doorway into Mount Doom, below a towering cliff-face. It was a model designed by John Howe, with a dark, grim, barbed verticality reminiscent of Barad-dûr (which Howe had also created). A tilt-up model shot (combined with CG fire and smoke) a little later on shows off this miniature well.

The audience knows that Gollum will return – he was last seen falling down a cliff outside Shelob's lair (but he was still very much alive, managing to fall feet first, with his head facing the rock). So the question is *how* he'll come back: the filmmakers opted to reprise his first appearance to the hobbits, way back in *The Two Towers:* he's hiding on a rock, above the hobbits. Just like that time, the wretched creature leaps onto the hobbits and a fight begins. He aims for Frodo first, in order to grab the ring. Gollum and Frodo roll over and over, down the steps (which were built from rubber, for the falls). Frodo's on his back, being throttled by Gollum, but it's not the last battle of the ringbearers. Mustn't hurt the precious, Gollum hisses (the *Extended Edition* adds more lines here, about Gollum lying). Sam, recovering, manages to knock Gollum off Frodo by lobbing a stone, then launches himself at Gollum before he can reach Frodo.

(The fight was shot early on in principal photography, Peter Jackson explained, when they didn't know quite what they were doing with Gollum; when it was re-shot during the pick-up period, in June, 2003, motion capture was employed on set at the same time the scene was being filmed. This was something that producer Barrie Osborne had been proposing for a long time. He said it was very inefficient to have the scenes shot again for days in the motion capture studio, tying up valuable resources and the directors).

The moment when Frodo slips away from Sam and Gollum fighting is elided, because the narrative cuts back to the Black Gate now – thereby quietly stepping over the reasons why Frodo doesn't stick around to help his friend beat off Gollum. He just runs off, and Sam's fighting for his life! (maybe Frodo's so far gone with ring-induced madness, or scared, or exhausted, or something, but he doesn't help his friend). The film plays other parts of this crucial scene differently from the 1955 book: textually, Frodo manages to overcome and then dominate Gollum, ordering him to:

"Begone, and trouble me no more! If you touch me ever again, you shall be cast yourself into the Fire of Doom."

The crouching shape backed away, terror in its blinking eyes, and yet at the same time insatiable desire. (RK, 266)

Sam moves to save Frodo, and tells Frodo to go quickly, while he will deal with Gollum. Sam then has a moment when he can kill Gollum, which the 2003 film doesn't show at all: although it seems just, and deserved, and safe to kill Gollum, Sam can't do it (RK, 267). So he tells Gollum to leave, then remembers Frodo and hurries after his friend (267).

Instead, the film cuts to the battle at the Black Gate, and the chief heroes, with the choir belting out on the soundtrack (Howard Shore dredges up echoes of Giuseppe Verdi, Ludwig van Beethoven, Johann Sebastian Bach, Wolfgang Amadeus Mozart and of course Carl Orff's *Carmina Burana* here. Odd, isn't it, in these totally *un*religious times in the late capitalist West that cynical, hard-bitten Western filmmakers should look to *sacred* choral music of 1600-1900 to accompany their big action scenes? The same bold choral music's heard in *Spider-man, Star Wars, Planet of the Apes, Men In Black,* and every superhero movie).

The nazgûl appear on their fell-beasts (a similar appearance, caught in an aerial shot, flying from behind the camera, to their introduction at the Battle of Pelennor – coming from *behind* the camera gives them that horror movie *frisson*, like pantomime villains – 'they're behind you!'). Back to Frodo, with the scenes noted above elided: he's on his own, away from Sam and Gollum, scrambling up the slopes. Meanwhile, Sam is still tussling with Gollum: Sam manages to wound Gollum with his sword; they both slam each other's heads against a rock; and Gollum bites Sam on the neck, as before.

Now to the battle again, this time to the white wizard (blue-screened, not very convincingly, against the battle behind him). His little friend from *The Fellowship of the Ring,* the moth, appears flying before his eyes (very silly – it's a long way from Isengard for a moth, or maybe there's a secret network of moths that aid Gandalf), heralding the arrival of the eagles. An iconic moment in the book, the coming of the eagles, and it's done full justice here, complete with Pippin yelling "the Eagles are coming!" (RK, 203. The eagles were a late addition to the show. John Howe said he'd forgotten about this moment, and nearly fell off his seat when he saw the whole film). The birds attack the fell-beasts, attaching themselves to their necks, biting them (in earlier drafts of *The Lord of the Rings,* the fell-beasts were much more like birds, with beaks and claws [HME 8, 366], rather than the flying reptiles they became in both book and film).

The first introduction to the interior of Mount Doom in *The Return of the King,* the Chambers of Fire, the setting of the movie's climax (it was seen in Elrond's story at Rivendell, of course, and the images of Sauron forging the One Ring in the prologue of *The Fellowship of the Ring*). The studio set comprised the surface of the rocky prow and the door (in forced perspective), but not much else (the scene was filmed in an apple storage shed next to Wellington airport). Interactive lighting flashes around the actors, on each side, throughout the scene, and there's plenty of smoke of course (always with the smoke in adventure movies, especially during the climax). The colours – hot oranges, yellows and reds – contrast vividly with the gloomy monochrome greys and blacks of Mordor and the Black Gate. The Crack of Doom seems much angrier and livelier than before, as if it can sense the ring has returned.

Aerial shots, from above the stone prow, reveal the extent of the interior of Orodruin, the smoke moving in a vortex, the lava splashing up and back. Loud earthquake rumbles and growls are accompanied by camera shake to evoke the power of the forces inside the volcano. A high angle shot above and behind Frodo reveals the river of lava flowing some two hundred feet below (the lava was achieved with a gummy chemical flowing along glass on a 20 foot table, and lit from above and below.) David Hardberger and Chuck Shuman helped to shoot different lighting passes for the lava-filled Sammath Naur, with light reaching the set from below, above, the side, and so on.

In all, the Sammath Naur sequence is a complex combination of miniatures, CG, sound effects, music, lighting, make-up, hair, costumes, and live action. The setting of lava and a volcano and a high path or ledge is a familiar one, though: it's been a staple of action-adventure films for years (like the Irving Allen *Lost World* of 1960, or *The Land That Time Forget* movies of the 1970s, or *Journey To the Centre of the Earth* of 1959, or *Star Wars: Revenge of the Sith* in 2005, or the two volcano flicks of 1997).

Frodo's already at the end of the prow when Sam arrives, halting a little way off from Frodo, who's standing near the tip of the prow, looking more composed and focussed now. To a suspenseful music cue, Sam urges Frodo to destroy the ring. Frodo holds it up: in close-up, Frodo is transfigured. He's still filthy, scarred and exhausted, but now he has a defiant, scary expression as he fixes Sam with a glare.

Frodo's dilemma, and another ring moment. The high-pitched calls and heartbeats return (for the last time): this part of the film is a series of close-ups of Frodo, Sam, and very big close-ups of the ring. Frodo holds up the ring on its chain in front of his face, and stares at it. Note how he has his back to Sam, facing towards the abyss, indicating how he's contemplating life without the ring, but how good now it would be to hang on to it, to become a ring lord. In the book as in the film, when Frodo claims the ring it's a refrain of Isildur claiming the ring as his *weregild*.

> "I have come," he said. "But I do not choose now to do what I came to do. I will not do this deed. The Ring is mine!" (RK, 269)

Finally, Frodo turns, yanks the ring off its chain, and smiles at Sam as he puts on the ring and disappears (he says 'the ring is mine' in a quiet voice, but in the 1955 book Frodo speaks 'with a clear voice, indeed with a voice clearer and more powerful than Sam had ever heard him use' [RK, 268-9]. But the film plays it much more restrained, partly because the scene's played in tight close-ups. Elijah Wood said they tried many ways of delivering the lines).

The film rapidly cuts to Sam's shocked reaction, then to a medium shot of Sauron's Eye, which swivels round, towards Mount Doom, then a L.S. of the exterior of Sammath Naur, with the Eye's white beam on it, and finally an aerial shot above the Black Gate, and the nazgûl swerving and flying off towards Orodruin at their master's beckoning (a moment I've always loved in the book, when Sauron quakes and realizes his stupidity, and the film does full justice to it):

> And far away, as Frodo put on the Ring and claimed it for his own, even in Sammath Naur the very heart of his realm, the Power in Barad-dûr was shaken, and the Tower trembled from its foundations to its proud and bitter crown. The Dark Lord was suddenly aware of him, and his Eye piercing all shadows looked across the plain to the door that he had made; and the magnitude of his own folly was revealed to him in a blinding flash, and all the devices of his enemies were at last laid bare. (RK, 269)

A C.U. of Frodo's footprints on the rock. Gollum rises behind Sam and knocks the hobbit out with a rock (editor Jamie Selkirk remarked how the editors pondered exactly *when* to re-introduce Gollum, because Gollum could have been watching for some time; they chose the significant moment when Frodo has already put on the ring). The film switches to Gollum's point-of-view as he spots Frodo's footprints, and leaps onto Frodo.

One of the lengthy discussions in pre-production of *The Lord of the Rings* was how to sell the idea of Gollum clinging to an invisible Frodo without it looking silly. In the end, the filmmakers rightly opted to minimize the number of shots (there are three): a medium close-up of Gollum attacking Frodo, an aerial long shot high above the prow (drifting to the right), where Gollum is a small dancing figure against the fiery glows, and lastly one where Gollum bites off Frodo's finger.

Notice how the filmmakers keep the viewer *outside* Frodo's ring experience for the first time in the films: at Bree, and Weathertop, and Amon Hen, when Frodo put on the ring, the audience was taken into Frodo's subjective experience of the 'wraithworld'. But that doesn't happen at Orodruin: instead, the viewpoint seems to be aligned with a more objective observer (and perhaps Sam). There could be all sorts of reasons for dropping the wraithworld here, but one must be that it would confuse and complicate the scene, which's partly about the tussle between Frodo and Gollum for possession of the ring. There's also plenty going on, in terms of drama and noise and music (as well as cutting back to the battle at the Black Gate), without needing to use the wraithworld. (The climax to the 2003 movie is trying to depict a bunch of things happening simultaneously, as so often in movies at the resolution: if there was a way of showing it all at once, filmmakers would. As Tolkien's narrator notes: 'at that moment many things happened at once' [RK. 269]).

A cut back to the Morannon battle, now in full swing, and tight, handheld shots depicting Aragorn fighting a troll. The choir are singing their hearts out to help sell this climax. Back to Sammath Naur, and the aerial shot of Gollum fighting the invisible Frodo. After he's bitten off Frodo's finger, Frodo becomes visible again; he collapses, clutching his bleeding finger; Sam comes round. (Andy Serkis recalled that he was biting a carrot for the mo-cap reference for the scene. Peter Jackson wanted the wound to be bloody, not to soften its effect).

The music signals a dramatic shift into a different emotion: Gollum finally has his precious. To indicate the joy of Gollum-Sméagol at this moment, there's an audacious shot which begins on a close-up of Gollum holding the ring up above his head, *through* the ring, pulling back higher (it's an impossible shot, and breaks the fourth wall, but works well here. Well, it's not impossible for miniature cameras to pass through a finger-sized ring, but it is for a 35mm movie camera). A solo male voice accompanies the shot, with the rest of the sound dipping to nothing (the realistic sounds inside Mount Doom would drown anything less than bellowing out). Gollum is now standing upright for the first time in the film (Andy Serkis was adamant about saving Gollum standing on two legs for this final triumphant moment. He has often been kind of standing upright, though).

Gollum's dancing upright, joyous. Frodo, eyes full of revenge, clutching his wounded hand, approaches him. The choir's singing even louder. Sauron can be heard, too, as if trying to persuade these ring junkies to stop fighting. The film now rapidly intercuts between Frodo and Gollum's tussle for the ring with the Black Gate battle, and the troll getting the better of Aragorn, with Legolas struggling to come to his rescue. Slow motion is used extensively here, to emphasize that this is the moment of crisis. Aragorn is trapped under the troll's foot, and manages to stab it with a knife.

Back to Frodo and Gollum fighting for the ring in slow motion, right at the edge of the stone prow. Peter Jackson wanted to rewrite the way John Ronald Reuel Tolkien had depicted the scene: in the novel, Gollum totters over the edge as he dances 'like a mad thing' (RK, 270): '

> "Precious, precious, precious!" Gollum cried. "My Precious! O my Precious!" And with that, even as his eyes were uplifted to gloat on his prize, he stepped too far, toppled, wavered for a moment on the brink, and then with a shriek he fell. (ibid.)

In the film, both Frodo and Gollum go over the edge together (and seen from further back, as if from Sam's point-of-view), making Frodo instrumental in Gollum falling. The scene had been shot originally with Frodo seeming to push Gollum, which would have made him a murderer. Another variation had Gollum falling by accident, as in the book, but that seemed too anti-climactic.

A slow motion shot follows of Gollum's demise, the camera following Gollum all the way as he falls backwards into the lava below. The animation of Gollum had to be complex here: lead animator Randy Cook, one of the best commentators on the making of the *Lord of the Rings* films, explained that the animation had to express Gollum's joy at finally gaining the ring, his desperate sorrow when he loses it again, and his agony when he realizes that the ring has betrayed him again. The immense pain of falling into molten lava, which would realistically overcome any other feelings, had to be suspended, so that a psychological, emotional moment could take over. Gollum also dies in an extended fashion: he doesn't dissolve into nothingness, but floats briefly on the lava, holding up his hand and staring at the ring before disappearing. (Andy Serkis said they shot about 25 takes of this moment, in a special harness, on the motion capture stage).

The ring stays afloat on the river of lava in giant close-ups, accompanied by the ring's high calls and loud, low drones. When the scene was first edited, the ring was dispatched fairly quickly, but the filmmakers decided to draw out the ring's destruction, as well as Frodo hanging off the prow, and also intercut that scene with the battle at the Morannon. Again, it makes dramatic sense, even if it stretches plausibility.

Philippa Boyens explained that the scriptwriters wanted to have Frodo fall off the cliff too because they wanted him to make the decision to live or die. It's a classic cinematic device, found in many, many movies. And Sam, like thousands of actors before him, somehow manages to hang onto Frodo by one sweaty hand, and not fall himself. The problem is, there's no sense of suspense or jeopardy for the audience. Sure, Frodo is dangling by one arm two hundred feet above a fiery abyss, but the audience knows there's no way the filmmakers are going to kill the hero just as he's achieved his quest, just as the ring is being destroyed. The audience also knows from seeing countless other renditions of the same scenario that good guys *never* fall, and villains *always* do. In the cliff-hanger, the villains always fall to their deaths (*Batman, GoldenEye, Sabotage*), and the good guys are always saved (*North By Northwest*, the *Indiana Jones* films, *Blade Runner, Star Wars*).

So Frodo decides to live (he looks down, then back up at Sam who's urging him 'don't you let go'). The two scenes – the ring melting and Frodo being saved (or deciding to save himself) – are intercut. In a big C.U., the ring slips under the lava after the lettering shines out. Then a cut to a big close-up of Sauron, accompanied by loud roars, scrapes, hisses, and drones (it's absolutely fitting that the film should cut to *Sauron* first when the ring's finally destroyed). Then a series of rapid (and silent) reaction shots of our heroes at the Black Gate, in slow motion (and, also fittingly, Gandalf has the first reaction shot, teary-eyed, as he realizes that something momentous is happening, and at last his mission in Middle-earth is at its crisis).

Trolls and orcs lose heart and run away. Then follows a series of expansive (and expensive), complex visual effects shots:

(1) An impressive shot looking up at Barad-dûr from right next to it shows the tower crumbling into pieces as well as toppling (the computer model of the Dark Tower was constructed by Gray Horsfield over the Christmas vacation of 2002; the collapsing structure couldn't be achieved by miniature photography. 2-D particle systems were used to drive the

breakdown of 250 million polygons in the digital model, overseen by Tweak Films). The filmmakers were concerned that the tower collapsing shouldn't be reminiscent of the destruction of New York's Twin Towers in September, 2001. Peter Jackson suggested that the Dark Tower should be brittle, like glass, exploding into many pieces.

(2) The Eye dwindles down to a dot, flaming erratically, then explodes (the sound designers pull out some of their best work to sell the destruction). The Eye had exploded in the 1980 *Return of the King*.

(3) The Eye and the summit of the Dark Tower topple over into space. A blast wave of smoke and debris shoots outwards from the Eye, in a shot down on the Plain of Gorgoroth (a familiar bomb blast image from movies such as *Independence Day, Attack of the Clones, Dinosaur* and *The Mummy Returns*. All derive, I think, from Japanese *animé*, such as *Akira*).

(4) Another extreme long shot follows the path of the explosion into the orc multitudes, seen from high above the battle (accompanied by a low rumble), directly evoking the Last Alliance images in the prologue (as then, the good guys are somehow magically immune to this atomic blast wave).

Orcs and trolls flee, and wide shots depict the Black Gate and the towers on either side crumbling, and tumbling into crevasses which are opening up around the Army of the West. The choir is still earning its fee by belting out at full volume suitably epic music for these Biblical-sized images. The nazgûl fry in the explosion of the summit of Mount Doom.

Having Sauron expire in an explosion is a tried and tested way for the villain to die in movies: *Jaws, Waterworld, The Mummy 2, Die Hard*, and every *James Bond* movie (indeed, in its spectacular images of the wholesale destruction of the villain's strongholds, *The Lord of the Rings* is *exactly like* a *James Bond* or Arnold Schwarzenegger movie).

Inside the erupting volcano, all is chaos as lava boils and rises. Frodo and Sam flee as the prow crumbles. In true movie form, they escape *just as* the prow's demolished, and *just as* a tidal wave of lava gushes out of the Sammath Naur doorway. They manage to leap onto a safe lump of rock (the heroes always escape unscathed from the destruction of the villain's compound, and always in the nick of time). Now come another series of reaction shots of the Host of the West, as they see Mount Doom exploding and their jubilation swiftly turns to thoughts of Frodo (some of the characters, such as Pippin, are seen mouthing 'Frodo!').

The hobbits are revealed to be on an island of rock in an ocean of red lava pouring down the slopes on all sides. Frodo's response to events comes first: 'it's gone, it's gone' he tells Sam. His relief at finally being rid of the ring echoes Bilbo's near the beginning of *The Fellowship of the Ring*. Finally, the Biblical epic music gives way to soft choral sounds behind Frodo's reawakening, indicated by his recall of images from the Shire. His nostalgic evocations of the Shire show that Frodo has come back from being possessed by the ring (and wanting to possess it and not destroy it). Sam adds the rider of Rosie Cotton dancing, and weeps. Frodo comforts him. There's a slow fade to black, which stays dark for a long time – this really might be the end for our heroes. That was Peter Jackson's idea, and it doesn't fool the audience for a moment. They know there's *no way* the heroes of the three flicks can die now, like this (they've already seen the eagles arrive, for instance, and how Gandalf was rescued from Orthanc).

The fade to black does act as a link to a different mood for the narrative, though, because when the fade in comes, it shows Gwaihir and his eagles flying out of the sun (in slo mo), with sunbeams playing around their wings. Gandalf rides one of the eagles. A solo male voice sings as the eagles pick up the hobbits in their claws (note how the eagles do so gently, because when enormous birds do this in fantasy movies, like those of films of the incomparable Ray Harryhausen, they're usually snatching people off to eat. The BBC radio version of 1981 also used a solo choirboy voice for this part of the book).

> "Well, this is the end, Sam Gamgee," said a voice by his side. And there was Frodo, pale and worn, and yet himself, and in his eyes there was peace now, neither strain of will, nor madness, nor any fear. His burden was taken away. There was the dear master of the sweet days of the Shire. (RK, 271)

ACT SIX

An overhead view of Frodo lying on his back in an eagle's claw flying above lava washes out to white, and match dissolves into a shot of Frodo on his back in bed in a sunny room in Minas Tirith (recalling the similar moment in Rivendell, when it was also Gandalf who was there when Frodo woke up in a bed, with a similar fade to white). Now Frodo's clean, washed, renewed and dressed in white. Philippa Boyens remarked that some viewers hated this reunion scene (too sentimental, too cheesy), but Peter Jackson said if he'd watched a film of *The Lord of the Rings,* he'd want to see this sort of scene. It is played entirely without dialogue (apart from muted dialogue in the background, which fades). It is dreadful on many levels.

Gandalf, like every other character here, looks fresh and restored, and neatly dressed. All the battle fatigue, the scars, the blood, the dirt has gone. Sunlight bathes each character. Gandalf looks at Frodo and laughs (Ian McKellen commented that this was what he thought Gandalf would do – in the 1955 book, it's actually Sam who wakes to find Gandalf standing before him in Ithilien, and Sam's viewpoint is used to re-introduce the other characters: 'Full memory flooded back, and Sam cried aloud: "It wasn't a dream! Then where are we?" And a voice spoke softly behind him: "In the land of Ithilien, and in the keeping of the King; and he awaits you." With that Gandalf stood before him, robed in white, his beard now gleaming like pure snow in the twinkling of the leafy sunlight.' [RK, 276]). In the 2003 adaption, in slow motion the rest of the fellowship arrives: Pippin and Merry first, joyously leaping onto Frodo's bed, like children; then Legolas, and Gimli, and Aragorn, and finally dear old Sam. Sam remains at the door, and he and Frodo stare at each other in big close-ups, smiling affectionately.

When the film now cuts to the coronation of Aragorn, it is flying over many passages in the latter part of the *Return of the King* book. The pay-off of the Aragorn-Arwen romance was the only other climax to the film for Peter Jackson, which he would consider showing – because the real story was still Frodo's. Thus, the long *dénouement* of *The Return of the King* movie chiefly concerns Frodo (the narrative is the same in both versions of the films): his journey back to Hobbiton, his reactions to his experiences, and his decision to hand over the *Red Book* to Sam, then travel to the Grey Havens. (*The Return of the King* does tie up some other subplots, though, such as the Sam-Rosie romance). It's Frodo, for instance, not Gandalf or Galadriel or whoever, providing the voiceover at the end of *The Return of the King*. A lot more voiceover from Frodo was recorded but not used.

Other material was shot for the *dénouement*, but not included in either version of *The Return of the King*: for instance, images of Legolas in some woods (presumably Fangorn, which he promises to visit after the War of the Ring), and Gimli examining jewels – presumably in the Glittering Caves). Faramir and Éowyn were also filmed but not included.

From the coronation at Minas Tirith to the end of the film, the two main versions of *The Return of the King* are virtually identical, with no substantial additions in the *Extended Edition*. The coronation is introduced via a (simulated) helicopter shot up to the prow and Citadel, which's packed with people from the doors of the White Tower to the tip of the prow. An expansive, sweeping, romantic cue goes with the aerial shot. It's a pleasant, sunny day (of course: the gloom of Pelennor, the Black Gate, Mount Doom, Mordor and all the other grim landscapes of the second half of the *Lord of the Rings* films has been dispersed).

Echoing many illustrations of the event by Tolkien artists, Aragorn is crowned by Gandalf, with Gimli attending (the Hildebrandts produced an appealing painting of the scene). Aragorn is clad in full armour and ceremonial dress. Guards and banners flank him. Aragorn rises, turns to the throng, says some words about peace and then – incredibly – he *sings*. That was Viggo Mortensen's idea, and it's unexpected and unusual enough to work (although Aragorn has displayed a penchant for song from time to time). It's not a triumphant song of victory he sings (in Elvish), though, but a soft, lyrical piece (with Howard Shore providing a bed of sustained strings).

Confetti flutters down, and the scene segues into Aragorn walking amongst his subjects, who line each side of the prow, applauding and smiling. *The Return of the King* nods to some of the supporting players, for their final appearance and bow: Éomer, Éowyn and Faramir, Legolas, Gimli and lastly Elrond. Arwen hides coyly behind a banner, in a striking dress of white, silver and pale green. (This was another re-shoot; one of the reasons for doing so was the odd hairstyle of ringlets that had been devised by the hair and wig department for Hugo Weaving's Elrond. Another was the rushed way the scene had been shot at the end of principal photography first time round. And Aragorn and Arwen's embrace hadn't been passionate enough for director Peter Jackson).

Arwen and Aragorn hug – she's a little shy at first, as if unsure of his response, but he kisses her passionately. (Director Jackson reckoned a big kiss was required here). It works fine. The crowd bows to the king, and now we see the four hobbits for the first time, standing in a row (back in their hobbit clothes). It's a moving moment when Aragorn tells them that they kneel to no one, and duly kneels before them (ironically, the actors weren't even there to receive their adulation – they were blue-screened in later). This scene depicts the much lengthier passages in book of *The Lord of the Rings* where the hobbits are celebrated. The host at the Field of Cormallen, for instance, cry out 'with many voices and tongues':

> Long live the Halflings! Praise them with great praise!
> Cuio i Pheriain anann! Aglar' ni Pheriannath!
> Praise them with great praise, Frodo and Samwise! Daur a Berhael, Conin en Annûn! Eglerio!
> Praise them!
> Eglerio!
> A laita te, laita te, Andave laituvalmet! (RK, 279)

The camera trucks in to a close-up of Frodo, who looks bemused at the kneeling crowds, then cuts to an extreme long shot of Minas Tirith, pulling back with the rapidity of a space rocket, followed by a match dissolve to the white city on a map of Middle-earth. Now Frodo is on the voiceover, and he will be narrating the final sections of *The Return of the King*.

First, Frodo describes the journey back to the Shire, while the camera follows on the map, neatly excising 60 or 70 pages of *The Lord of the Rings*, and the bulk of the three chapters "Many Partings", "Homeward Bound" and "The Scouring of The Shire".

For Peter Jackson, it was a 'no brainer' to drop the scouring of the Shire, a decision made early on in writing the script and never seriously questioned. It would be simply impossible, he reckoned, to start the story up again with a whole new sequence, when the climax of the film had already occurred, and the ring and the enemy had been destroyed. (And even without the scouring of the Shire, some viewers and critics said the film went on for too long after the climax, and had too many endings. In an interview, Elijah Wood related how he'd met Jack Nicholson, who asked him if Frodo had died, because he'd walked out of the theatre way before the ending).

It is a let-down, though, that when the hobbits return to Hobbiton in the film of *The Return of the King* all they encounter is the old coot hobbit (Proudoot) from *The Fellowship of the Ring* sweeping his front yard, who frowns at them and shakes his head. In losing "The Scouring of The Shire", you lose a major sequence and a major theme of Tolkien's 1955 book: that the evil of Mordor, Sauron and the ring has spread all over Middle-earth, even to somewhere as homely and apparently safe as the Shire. As Tolkien explained in his *Rings* foreword: 'it is an essential part of the plot, foreseen from the outset' (FR, 12). Tolkien maintained that the scouring of the Shire had been part of his overall conception from the beginning, and was a vital part of *The Lord of the Rings*.

But to put the scouring of the Shire in the picture would mean another 15 or 20 minute section, as well as a bunch of new characters (plus explanations of Saruman's presence there). But the abrupt shift from the coronation at Minas Tirith to the hobbits returning to the Shire also elides a vital scene which should've been there, in *movie terms*: the hobbits saying farewell to Aragorn, Gimli, Legolas, Faramir and Éowyn, among others. There is no farewell to the fellowship in the 2003 film. But there wasn't time for that in an already over-long movie. The filmmakers already had their big farewell scene – at the Grey Havens (and that did include Gandalf, Galadriel, Bilbo and Elrond, some of the principal players). But proper goodbyes to Leggy, the dwarf, Aragorn *et al* are missed.

Instead, the film cuts to the map then to a scene of the hobbits returning on horseback, and the *Green Dragon* scene. Here, the four hobbits sit around a table, drinking, looking at each other, but saying nothing (there's a lyrical violin cue). Around them hobbits talk and laugh happily (acting as if nothing has happened, as if they've been unaffected by the War of the Ring; the hobbits have saved the Shire, and life goes on). The scene is about everything they've been through and seen, and the solidarity of their companionship. They really are different people now. Notice how they don't really react to anyone else in the pub (Frodo, getting the drinks in, nods to another hobbit), and also no one seems to take notice of them (as if they've never been away). For some critics, *The Return of the King* would have benefitted from giving screentime to, say, the fates of Faramir and Éowyn, than this apparently eventless and pointless scene (I'd say it was a deliberately *non*-dramatic scene). It was intended to be like soldiers returning from a war, changed beyond the understanding of the people they've left behind, with an unbridgeable gulf between them.

The tail end of the *Green Dragon* scene has Sam resolving to approach Rosie, who's behind the bar, and glances over to Sam (the filmmakers squeezed out a lot more mileage from Rosie's character than there is in the book, as they did with all of the female characters bar Galadriel). The scene closes with a grin from Pippin, and a cut over a few weeks or even months of film time, as Sam and Rosie marry (in the book, Sam marries Rosie on Mayday, 3020 of the Third Age, i.e., some five months after the hobbits return to the Shire). The wedding's staged as a recognizably Western – Christian – wedding ceremony – but there's no priest or official in sight. No altar or ceremonial building, either: the wedding takes place out of doors, in what seems to be the party field. It's a sunny, happy scene, of course, with flowers and decorations. In another comic moment, it's Pippin who receives the bouquet.

Now the film leaps ahead some time. The timeline in the film departs from the book again: in the movie, Frodo tells Sam it's been four years since he was wounded at Weathertop. In the book, it's two years since Weathertop when Sam discovers Frodo ill in his study in 1420 (the anniversary of October 6th). No matter: what counts is Frodo's psychological state: that he is the only one among the hobbits who can't re-enter his former life, that he has been permanently marked by his experiences, and will never be fully healed. He is shown on his own wandering around Bag End during the day, and in voiceover talking about picking up the pieces of a former life (the format echoes Bilbo at the start of the extended edition of *The Fellowship of the Ring*). There's no going back for Frodo, no happy ending: he is forever wounded.

The following scene is some time later, days, weeks or months: Frodo is writing in his study, at the writing desk where Bilbo narrated the section "Concerning Hobbits". Sam appears (carrying a book that he seems to have borrowed from Frodo). Both Frodo and Sam are smartly dressed in hobbit suits, vests (waistcoats) and shirts, both recalling Ronald Tolkien in his elder days. Sam notices something wrong with Frodo, and Frodo tells Sam it is four years since Weathertop, and the wound's never healed.

> One evening Sam came into the study and found his master looking very strange. He was very pale and his eyes seemed to see things far away.
> "What's the matter, Mr Frodo?" said Sam.
> "I am wounded," he answered, "wounded, it will never really heal." (RK, 372)

The second part of this modest scene between the two lead hobbits in Bag End concerns the book that Frodo's been working on: the *Red Book of Westmarch*, a fabled, leatherbound tome which was much copied and handed down over the years (part of Tolkien's mythology was that such a book could eventually find its way into modern times). Indeed, the *Red Book* is *the* magical book in the world of *The Lord of the Rings:* it's the War of the Ring according to the hobbits Bilbo, Frodo and Sam (and, later, other authors). It's part of the Tolkien mythos that the professor simply translated from the *Red Book* into English, and that became *The Lord of the Rings*.

It's a nice touch to include something as apparently innocuous as a book at this point in the three films, after all the sensational scenes the audience has witnessed. The *Red Book* also ties in with the early scene of Bilbo writing about hobbits in the same book, and with the sourcebook of the films themselves, of course – *The Lord of the Rings*. It's cool too that Frodo is shown in the *act of writing in it*, emphasizing that he is that most wondrous and most extraordinary of all people… a *writer*! Yes, folks, even multi-million dollar cinematic extravaganzas involving hundreds of technicians and talented types start with words written by the humble scribe. (Or you could say: someone's got to write something, and sign it, so 64 lawyers and banks will release the money).

Gandalf arrives at the yard in front of the *Green Dragon* next, at the magic hour, driving a covered cart. Now he's the regular, cloaked wizard of the first scenes in *The Fellowship of the Ring*. (And a smiling, genial Gandalf, too). A slither of voiceover (from Frodo) introduces Bilbo and the journey to the Grey Havens. A brief scene in the cart (no Sam, Pippin, Merry or anyone else is present) has Frodo and Bilbo talking quietly together, with Bilbo even more wizened and white than Yoda. It's Ian Holm's only appearance in *The Return of the King*. Bilbo appears as he does in the book, when the hobbits hurry to find him alone in his room at Rivendell in the chapter "Many Partings": 'he looked very old, but peaceful and sleepy' (RK, 320). In the movie, Bilbo brings up the subject of the ring, and Frodo confesses that he lost it.

The quiet, elegiac and somewhat dreamy tone of the last scenes of *The Return of the King* continue with the introduction of the Grey Havens, the last of the big vistas. Alan Lee's rendition of the elven harbour doesn't disappoint: it's a group of Classical and Italian Renaissance buildings (domes, towers, colonnades) ranged around low hills, with two prongs forming the mouth of the harbour in the distance. The sun shining bright from the West, low in the sky, over the harbour mouth, evoking the Classical reveries of Claude Lorrain, and one of Lorraine's biggest admirers, J.M.W. Turner. It's amazing to see Turner crop up in this kind of Hollywood blockbuster, but his oil paintings of ancient Roman and Greek architecture imagery combined with Mediterranean seascapes and radiant sunsets have a wistful melancholy which fits the mood of the final scenes of the *Lord of the Rings* films perfectly.

A quayside; seagulls; an elven boat; and three of the top elves in Middle-earth standing in a row beside the boat: Elrond, Celeborn and Galadriel (another elderly elf, presumably Círdan the shipwright, is in the background. In the 1955 book Celeborn remains in Lórien, before going to Imladris to live with Elrond's sons). Curiously, there are no other elves about, and no one's on the ship. Little is said by the elves: instead, they smile enigmatically. Gandalf and the five hobbits halt nearby; Bilbo moves forward, and greets the elf-gentry with a nod. He walks onto the boat; Elrond and Galadriel speak briefly, then leave Gandalf alone with the four hobbits.

Over a soft choral cue, Gandalf says farewell, and also adds his last line in Tolkien's book: 'I will not say: do not weep; for not all tears are an evil' (RK, 378):

> "Well, here at last, dear friends, on the shores of the Sea comes the end of our fellowship in Middle-earth. Go in peace! I will not say: do not weep, for not all tears are an evil."
> Then Frodo kissed Merry and Pippin, and last of all Sam, and went aboard; and the sails were drawn up, and the wind blew, and slowly the ship slipped away down the long grey firth... (RK, 378)

By now the hobbits are weeping – except for Frodo – but they don't say anything (Billy Boyd and Dominic Monaghan don't have any lines in this scene, but they're doing a lot of acting, as are Elijah Wood and Sean Astin). It's the long goodbye for the characters, but also for the viewers who've stuck with the three two-and-a-half hour movies to the bitter end (and who haven't walked out, like Jack Nicholson).

Gandalf moves away, to allow Frodo to say farewell to his friends: the camera trucks in from a four-shot to a close-up of Frodo. Sam now realizes that Frodo intends to leave Middle-earth. They exchange short lines; Frodo hands over the *Red Book*. All three hobbits are weeping openly now. Frodo hugs each of them in turn – Sam last, of course. It's all very emotional, very weepy, like the end of *E.T.* or a Disney cartoon.

Frodo kisses Sam on the forehead, then moves onto the boat (this was a model, like so much else in the Grey Havens scene. The scene might've benefitted from real water and a real ship, rather than models and mattes). Frodo has one last lingering, smiling look back at his companions (note how he looks into the camera – it's a farewell to the audience, the equivalent of taking an actor taking a bow and thanking everyone for coming).

Philippa Boyens said she thought of Frodo as going to his death. There's always been a debate about the fate of Frodo (and Bilbo) going to Valinor, and exactly what happened to them. It is ambiguous in the book, and in the picture. Cinematically, Frodo and the boat sailing into bright light which washes out to white could suggest a character going to heaven or some other realm.

The scene was reshot initially because Sean Astin had forgotten to put on his waistcoat (vest) for the scenes shot after lunch, so they didn't match for continuity. Much of the second day of the weeping scene was out of focus. So it was done a third time (or at least a second, maybe the vest (waistcoat) error was the same day as the out-of-focus stuff).

Merry and Pippin turn and leave, but Sam stays to watch. When the film cuts to a wide shot of the harbour, the elven craft is already out near the edge of it, sailing directly towards the sun, into the West (eliding a few minutes, or perhaps the ship has some special elven magic to drive it). A shot just of the boat now washes out to white, accompanied by Howard Shore's beautiful music.

That's where the film should end for me: Frodo on the boat, the music, a fade to white, then black, then the credits (the 1980 cartoon has a better final image – it ends with the sea and the sky). But the filmmakers wanted to honour the very ending of Tolkien's book (which wasn't Tolkien's original intention: the epilogue published in the *History of Middle-earth* volumes is much more satisfying, though Tolkien cut it close to publication). So there's the scene of Sam returning (alone) to Hobbiton (on a sunny day, of course), to his own home, and being met in his little front garden by his wife Rosie and two children (one of them is presumably Elanor). Smiles and cute kids. Frodo is heard in voiceover (is he speaking from the grave? From the Undying Lands? From the boat?). Sam, in medium close-up, holding one child while Rosie holds another, speaks the last line of *The Lord of the Rings*: 'well I'm back'. The camera follows this perfect hobbit family into their home, holding on the front door. The caption comes up: 'The End'. (The end credits, to Annie Lennox singing 'Into the West', feature Alan Lee drawings of each character).

CHAPTER 19

FURTHER CRITICISMS OF THE *LORD OF THE RINGS* MOVIES

One of the laudable aspects of the *Lord of the Rings* films is how they have (on the whole) successfully navigated the treacherous waters of fantasy movies, where it's so easy to sink into ponderous idiocy (*Legend*, *Hawk the Slayer*, *Krull*. The case of *Legend* is a warning to every fantasy filmmaker. Was there ever a fall so great as that of director Ridley Scott: from *Blade Runner* in 1982 to *Legend* in 1985? Wow, that's incredible: from *Blade Runner*, the movie probably discussed more than any other in film studies of the past 20 years, to *Legend*, one of the most abysmal crocks of dreck ever put on celluloid. Actually, it's not really a 'fall' for Ridley Scott, because most film directors' contributions are overrated, and the success of *Blade Runner* owes a huge amount to writers Hampton Fancher and David Peoples – not forgetting Philip K. Dick's fiction – and the lush music of Vangelis, the visual effects of Doug Trumbull and Richard Yuricich, the production design of Lawrence G. Paul, the cinematography of Jordan Cronenweth, the cast, and many others.)

As to the critics: for German critics such as Thomas Binotto and E. Krekeler, viewers who didn't know the 1955 book or who hadn't seen *The Fellowship of the Ring* would be 'hopelessly lost' in trying to work out what's going on in *The Two Towers*.[1] 'Nobody explains anything', Krekeler complained, and 'several laws of gravity are broken'.

For Cynthia McNew, the 2001-03 *Rings* movies relied too much on action and missed much of the richness of the story. The contrivances that films have to use unbalanced the book. 'Tolkien's story flows more naturally than any other book I have ever read', McNew asserted.[2] Although the characters went where they were supposed to go and did all that they were supposed to do in *The Fellowship of the Ring*, Cynthia McNew still found that 'much of it felt hollow and lacking to me'.[3]

For Alexander Walker (writing in the London *Evening Standard*), *The Fellowship of the Ring* only remotely touched *Harry Potter*'s pitch of precise and prolific invention in its visuals. Walker really didn't like the movie: it was a road movie with more of the same thing every reel: 'the trouble is, much the same sort of battle-scene repeats itself every 20 minutes or so; only the environments and the monsters inhabiting them are changed'.

As Greg Harvey pointed out, the lack of romance, love and sex in *The*

Lord of the Rings makes it 'really a stretch to turn this novel into date-night movie material'. The filmmakers of the 2001-03 films tried: they had cute Orlando Bloom, they had Tyler and Mortensen's chivalrous romance, they had pretty frocks for Otto, Blanchett and Tyler, they had comic asides from Rhys-Davies, Boyd and Monaghan, but with all that war carnage, the orcs, the old wizards and a flaming eyeball for a baddie, they didn't succeed for everyone.

For M. Wolf, writing in *Der Spiegel*, the world of *The Lord of the Rings* comprised 'petty bourgeois', under-written hobbits, 'a confused battle', 'various unappetising monsters', and a 'hermetic fantasy world called Middle Earth which is packed with myths, monsters and loads of infantile botch-up'.[4]

Head web geek Harry Knowles (at Ain't It Cool News) couldn't contain his orgasmic pleasure at *The Two Towers*. Knowles adored the films, which revived the action-adventure genre. For some critics, *The Lord of the Rings* adaptions seem to have made good the crushing disappointments of the two *Star Wars* films (*Phantom* and *Clones*).

DIALOGUE. The dialogue had to be rewritten, Philippa Boyens said, partly because it had to be immediate, and couldn't be long-winded; it had to be clear; and it had to feel real (i.e., it had to be contemporary). So Tolkien's archaic constructions went out the window. Some of the classic lines were retained, but most of the exchanges were rewritten.

The result was that some of the dialogue was dreck, really terrible writing. But in a film like *Lord of the Rings*, and in most movies, the dialogue doesn't matter too much. Critics fasten onto dialogue, as if the whole of a film can be contained within the exchanges between actors, but there are so many other things going on in a truly cinematic piece, from music and sound to movement and camera to light and colour to visual effects and design and settings and editing and so on.

William Goldman rightly says that real film scriptwriting isn't about writing clever, witty dialogue, it's about the structure, about creating scenes and situations, about inventing characters. But film critics, who deal in words, always concentrate on the words in movies. They'll say, oh the dialogue in *Star Wars* or *James Bond* is awful. Maybe so, but if you're thinking that you've completely missed the point.

If some of the performances in the *Lord of the Rings* films aren't so wonderful, that's partly an outcome of the movies being large-scale productions. John Boorman, who made two abandoned attempts at filming *The Lord of the Rings*, had some sympathy: on a big film, Boorman said, the director spends 90% of their time preparing shots, rather than directing actors. So there's much less time for the smaller, intimate scenes. 'That's why, in so many epics, the performances are inadequate. The fact is, quite simply, that the director hasn't had time to concentrate on them' (245).

NOTES: FURTHER CRITICISMS OF THE 2001-2003 *LORD OF THE RINGS* FILMS

1. E. Krekeler, "Kantersieg des Kinos über die Literatur", *Die Welt*, Dec 16, 2002; T.

Binotto, 2002.
2. In E. Challis, 308.
3. In E. Challis, 309.
4. M. Wolf, "Murks In Mittelerde", *Der Spiegel*, Dec 17, 2001.

THE *LORD OF THE RINGS* FILMS AND CONTEMPORARY POLITICS

The *Lord of the Rings* films might've been about a mythical realm of seven thousand years ago, whose tales were lost in the mists of time and were miraculously found by an Oxford professor (in the *Red Book of Westmarch*) who brilliantly transcribed them... which were then put on celluloid by a bunch of filmmakers who congregated in New Zealand with four hundred million dollars of someone else's money and magically distributed their efforts to ten thousand cinema screens with the aid of a helper with Zeus-like powers (alias mega corporation Time Warner), but they were also very much about the contemporary world. And the contemporary world includes contemporary ideology and politics. Don't let the olde worlde leathery costumes, pointy ears and *faux* Englishe accents fool you: the *Lord of the Rings* movies were very much to do with the contemporary Western world, and critics picked up on the ideological elements in the 2001, 2002 and 2003 films.

Some critics drew attention to the *Lord of the Rings* films' uncomfortable proximity to pro-military ideology and even fascism. It's been remarked of J.R.R. Tolkien's fiction many times before, but the pictures reminded everyone again of Tolkien's right-wing politics. For Thomas Binotto, the psychologically flat characters, the black and white portrayal of good vs. evil, brought the *Lord of the Rings* films 'dangerously close to what can be considered a "proto-fascist" æsthetics' (2002). Not only Adolf Hitler, George Bush probably loved the *Lord of the Rings* movies, some critics thought.[1]

Some film reviewers found the preponderance of war-mongering scenes ideologically dubious. For Dietmar Kanthak, the *Lord of the Rings* films came across as '*Apocalypse Now* in Middle Earth': any poetry was drowned in the noise of battle, and the emotional scenes were mere spots of colour in amongst the *tableaux* of war. Gunnar Decker found that the 'massacre scenes' had doubled in *The Two Towers* from the first movie, so that *The Two Towers* resembled 'a giant military mobilization movie' (2002).

For Thomas Kniebe, if the *Lord of the Rings* films had come from America or from a former superpower in Europe, the movies, with their images of war and calls for military idealism, would have been unbearable.[2] That prolongs the view that the *Lord of the Rings* films were somehow Kiwi movies, coming from New Zealand, not Hollywood or America.

Some critics linked the 2001-03 films to the current state of world politics – to the 'war on terror', for instance, or America's war in Iraq. The

War of the Ring certainly had numerous links to the political climate of the 2001-2003 period, including the events of September 11, 2001 and their aftermath.

Philippa Boyens and Frances Walsh rewrote some of Tolkien's concepts, such as the line 'war is kindled'. Boyens said that idea was changed to 'hope is kindled' but that wasn't in response to the current political climate (the war in Iraq, or the war on terrorism). That didn't soften the *Rings* adaptions for some film critics, who still found them aggressively pro-military and pro-war.

Katja Nicodemus in *Die Zeit* said that the *Lord of the Rings* films reflected the contemporary situation of the 'war on terror' and the war in Iraq: don't the

> horizon-filling armies of the black spotty Uruk-hai not look like the Al-Qaida nightmare of every American citizen looking onto the world from his suburban home? Indeed, the axis of evil runs through Tolkien's Middle-earth as dead straight as it runs through the rhetoric of a George W. Bush.[3]

Gunnar Decker likened the political situation of war in Middle-earth to contemporary anxieties over Palestine and Israel, or North and South Korea. And for European audiences, it suggested the fortress of Europe 'being invaded by the onslaught of poverty from outside' (2002).

Among the war movie tropes that *The Two Towers* employed were male bonding, pathos, the ringwraiths as a bomber attack and the catapults as shelling. FX supervisor Jim Rygiel thought of *The Return of the King* as a 'World War Zero' movie. The filmmakers referred to war films (Peter Jackson alluded to movies like *Zulu* and *Pearl Harbor*). Indeed, the *Lord of the Rings* films can be seen as part of the recent cycle of World War pictures which Paramount's *Saving Private Ryan* (1998) helped to instigate: *U-571, Pearl Harbor, Hart's War, Enemy At the Gates, The Windtalkers, A Very Long Engagement* and *We Were Soldiers.*

However, some critics pointed out that the *Lord of the Rings* films lacked some important elements of the war film, such as empathy for the enemy. For Claudius Seidl, the *Rings* films propounded a 'synthetic racism': the films turns the warriors into butchers: the orcs are to Aragorn and his people what a herd of buffalo is to Buffalo Bill'.[4]

Ultimately, on the whole, in the final analysis, the *Lord of the Rings* films were excellent – as movies. Just think how bad they could have been! By being the equal of other product in the same arena (*Harry Potter, Star Wars, Spiderman*), the movies have been very important for the Tolkien industry, and for the cultural status of J.R.R. Tolkien. Ultimately, they are just another addition to the vast Tolkien industry – which was doing fine without the Time Warner/ New Line Cinema films, but is now doing even bigger business because of them. Thousands of people in hundreds of companies benefited directly – publishers, licensees, toy manufacturers, Kiwi tourism, hotels, airlines, etc. New Line, Warners,

HarperCollins and Scholastic and Saul Zaentz must have been very happy indeed. For a little admin time and signing a contract or two, associated companies will have seen their ancillary product lines climb and climb, with AOL TW and New Line footing much of the advertizing spend.

The *Lord of the Rings* movies will have done a lot of good for Tolkien, culturally. If the films had tanked, it would have been ammunition for opponents of Tolkien (and of fantasy). Detractors could've pointed to the films and said, 'yep, this crap about elves and dwarves and hobbits is even worse than we thought!' By being as good as other blockbuster flicks in the marketplace they have enhanced Tolkien's reputation.

There's got to be some positive knock-on effect, too: the movies must've encouraged people to explore J.R.R. Tolkien's world further (the sales of Tolkien's books since 2001 have demonstrated that). After all, even the director of the *Lord of the Rings* pictures, Peter Jackson, got into Tolkien as a result of seeing the 1978 film (and that was a problematic adaption, to put it politely). So, although the 2001-03 *Lord of the Rings* may not be a wholly satisfactory literary adaption of a classic text (it's a heart-breaking misinterpretation for some Tolkien fans), it must do some good, on the whole.

And not only Tolkien's sales, but also other fantasy writers, such as the three Terrys (Brooks, Pratchett and Goodkind), Tanith Lee, C.S. Lewis, Robert E. Howard, and the queen of them all, Ursula Le Guin.

NOTES: THE *LORD OF THE RINGS* FILMS AND CONTEMPORARY POLITICS

1. S. Eichner *et al*, in E. Mathijs, 2006, 147; D. Kanthak, 2002; S. Hermanski, "Mit der Heimat Verwurzelt", *Süddeutsche Zeitung*, Dec 13, 2001 and "Lichtgestalten Im Kampf Mit der Finsternis", *Süddeutsche Zeitung*, Dec 20, 2001.
2. T. Kniebe, "Heil den Neuseeländern", *Süddeutsche Zeitung*, Dec 11, 2003.
3. K. Nicodemus, "Der Bush der Ringe", *Die Zeit*, Dec 17, 2003.
4. C. Seidl, "Hinter tausend Kriegern keine Welt", *Frankfurter Allgemeine Zeitung*, Dec 17, 2003.

FIFTEEN BEST MOMENTS IN THE *LORD OF THE RINGS* MOVIES

1. The prologue to *The Fellowship of the Ring*.
2. Gandalf and Frodo in the kitchen at Bag End.
3. Gandalf vs. the Balrog in *The Fellowship of the Ring*.
4. Frodo in the 'wraith-world' in *The Fellowship of the Ring*.
5. The shift from Frodo wounded to Gandalf at Orthanc in *Fellowship*.
5. The laments for Gandalf outside Moria in *Fellowship*.
6. Frodo: 'I will take the ring' in *The Fellowship of the Ring*.
7. Gandalf battling the Balrog in *The Two Towers*.
8. The Gollum schizophrenia scene in *The Two Towers*.
9. The build-up to the battle of Helm's Deep in *The Two Towers*.
10. The march of the ents in *The Two Towers*.
11. The Ride of the Rohirrim at Pelennor Fields in *The Return of the King*.
12. The nazgûl and the eagles appearing at the Black Gate in *The Return of the King*.
13. The Minas Morgul sequence in *The Return of the King*.
14. Arwen's future life without Aragorn.
15. Gandalf and Pippin talking about death in *The Return of the King*.

SEVENTEEN WORST MOMENTS IN THE *LORD OF THE RINGS* FLICKS

1. The endless and psychotic emphasis on violence in each movie.
2. The wizard duel in *The Fellowship of the Ring*.
3. The troll fight in Moria in *The Fellowship of the Ring*.
4. Frodo cast as an 18 year-old kid.
5. Aragorn tempted by the ring in *The Fellowship of the Ring*.
6. Saruman taking over many of Sauron's functions.
7. Gimli, Leggy and Strider beating up Théoden's guards in *The Two Towers*.
8. Aragorn's death and resurrection in *The Two Towers*. Come on!
9. Faramir: 'the ring will go to Gondor!' in *The Two Towers*. Oh baby!
10. Faramir's characterization drastically altered.

11. Sam's speech at the end of *The Two Towers*. Beyond horrible.
12. The Frodo-Sam split in *The Return of the King*.
13. Gandalf clubbing Denethor in *The Return of the King*.
14. Gandalf giving up all hope at the war council in *The Return of the King*.
15. The Witch-King vs. Gandalf encounter in *The Return of the King*.
16. Saruman's death being left out of the theatrical cuts.
17. Wretched dialogue – numerous examples – take you pick.

AVAILABILITY

There are two main versions of each film on video and DVD, readily available: the theatrical versions and the extended edition versions. These have been released in single disc, two-disc and four-disc sets on DVD. There have also been boxed sets. The *Limited Editions* of 2006 were yet another repackaging (with a new 'making of' documentary). There are further versions for television and airlines, etc.

The main distributors for the *Lord of the Rings* films are:

U.S.A.: New Line Home Entertainment.
U.K.: New Line, and Entertainment In Video.

BIBLIOGRAPHY

J.R.R. TOLKIEN

The Adventures of Tom Bombadil and Other Verses From the Red Book, Allen & Unwin, London, 1962
Ancrene Wisse: The English Text of the Ancrene Riwle, Early English Text Society, Original Series no. 249, Oxford University Press, London, 1962
Smith of Wootton Major, Allen & Unwin, London, 1967
The Road Goes Ever On: A Song Cycle, Allen & Unwin, London, 1968
Farmer Giles of Ham, Allen & Unwin, London, 1949
Tree and Leaf, Unwin Books, London, 1975
The Father Christmas Letters, ed. B. Tolkien, Allen & Unwin, London, 1976
The Silmarllion, ed. C. Tolkien, Allen & Unwin, London, 1977
The Hobbit, Allen & Unwin, London, 1978
The Lord of the Rings, Allen & Unwin, London, 1966, 1979
Pictures of J.R.R. Tolkien, Allen & Unwin, London, 1979/ HarperCollins, London, 1992
Sir Gawain and the Green Knight, The Pearl, Sir Orfeo, ed. C. Tolkien, Unwin Paperbacks, London, 1979
Unfinished Tales, ed. C. Tolkien, Allen & Unwin, London, 1980
Poems and Stories, Allen & Unwin, London, 1980
The Letters of J.R.R. Tolkien, ed. H. Carpenter & C. Tolkien, Allen & Unwin, London, 1981/ HarperCollins, London, 1999
The Letters of J.R.R. Tolkien, HarperCollins, London, 1995
Mr. Bliss, Allen & Unwin, London, 1982
The Monster and the Critics and Other Essays, ed. C. Tolkien, Allen & Unwin, London, 1983
The History of Middle Earth 1: The Book of Lost Tales, vol. 1. ed. C. Tolkien, Allen & Unwin, London, 1983
The History of Middle Earth 2: The Book of Lost Tales, vol. 2. ed. C. Tolkien, Allen & Unwin, London, 1984
The History of Middle Earth 3: The Lays of Beleriand, ed. C. Tolkien, Allen & Unwin, London, 1985
The History of Middle Earth 4: The Shaping of Middle-Earth, ed. C. Tolkien, Allen & Unwin, London, 1986
The History of Middle Earth 5: The Lost Road and Other Writings, ed. C. Tolkien, Unwin Hyman, London, 1987
The History of Middle Earth 6: The Return of the Shadow: The History of The Lord of the Rings, Part 1, ed. C. Tolkien, HarperCollins, London, 1994
The History of Middle Earth 7: The Treason of Isengard, The History of The Lord of the Rings, Part 2, ed. C. Tolkien, Unwin Hyman, London, 1989
The History of Middle Earth 8: The War of the Ring: The History of The Lord of the Rings, Part 3, ed. C. Tolkien, Unwin Hyman, 1990
The History of Middle Earth 9: Sauron Defeated: The History of The Lord of the Rings, Part 4, HarperCollins, London, 1992
The History of Middle Earth 10: Morgoth's Ring, ed. C. Tolkien, HarperCollins, London, 1993
The History of Middle Earth 11: The War of the Jewels, ed. C. Tolkien, Harper-Collins, London, 1994
The History of Middle Earth 12: The Peoples of Middle-earth, ed. C. Tolkien, HarperCollins, London, 1996
The Children of Hurin, HarperCollins, London, 2007
The Legend of Sigurd and Gudrún, HarperCollins, London, 2009
Bilbo's Last Song, Unwin Hyman, London, 1990
The Annotated Hobbit, ed. D. Anderson, Allen & Unwin, London, 1988

The Tolkien Reader, Ballantine, New York, NY, 1989
Roverandom, HarperCollins, London, 1998
Tales From the Perilous Realm, HarperCollins, London, 1998
Farmer Giles of Ham, 50th Anniversary Edition, HarperCollins, London, 1999
Letters From Father Christmas, HarperCollins, London, 1999

OTHERS

M. Barker & E. Mathijs, eds. *Watching Lord of the Rings*, Peter Lang, New York, NY, 2006
T. Binotto. "Der herr der Ringe", *Film-Dienst*, 26, 2002
P. Biskind. *Down and Dirty Pictures: Miramax, Sundance and the Rise of Independent Film*, Bloomsbury, London, 2004
J. Boorman. *Adventures of a Suburban Boy*, Faber, London, 2003
I. Brodie. *The Lord of the Rings Location Guidebook*, HarperCollins, Auckland, 2004
G. Campbell. "Lord of the Tax Deal", *NZ Listener*, Oct 21, 2000
J. Campbell. *The Hero With a Thousand Faces*, Paladin, London, 1978
H. Carpenter. *J.R.R. Tolkien: A Biography*, Allen & Unwin, London, 1977/ 1995
E. Challis, ed. *The People's Guide to J.R.R. Tolkien*, TheOneRing.net/ Cold Spring Press, Cold Spring Harbor, NY, 2003
—. *More People's Guide to J.R.R. Tolkien*, TheOneRing.net/ Cold Spring Press, Cold Spring Harbor, NY, 2004
T. Christie. *Liv Tyler*, Crescent Moon, 2007
H.G.P. Colebatch. *Return of the Heroes: The Lord of the Rings, Star Wars, Harry Potter and Social Conflict*, Cybereditions Corporation, 2003
J.C. Cooper. *Fairy Tales: Allegories of the Inner Life*, Aquarian Press, London, 1983
M. Coren. *J.R.R. Tolkien*, Boxtree, London, 2001
P. Curry. *Defending Middle-earth*, HarperCollins, London, 1998
D. Day. *The Tolkien Companion*, Mandarin, London, 1993
—. *Tolkien's Ring*, Pavilion, London, 2001
G. Decker. "Nach der Schlacht ist vor der Schlacht", *Neues Deutschland*, Dec, 18, 2002
J. Donald, ed. *Fantasy and the Cinema*, British Film Institute, London, 1989
K. Fonstad. *The Atlas of Middle-earth*, HarperCollins, London, 1992
R. Foster. *The Complete Guide to Middle-earth: From The Hobbit to The Silmarillion*, Allen & Unwin, London, 1978
G. Fuller. "Trimming Tolkien", *Sight & Sound*, 2, 2001
D. Grotta. *The Biography of J.R.R. Tolkien*, Courage Books, Philadelphia, PA, 1992
R. Harryhausen & T. Dalton. *The Art of Ray Harryhausen*, Aurum Press, London, 2005
A. Hitchcock, *Hitchcock On Hitchcock,* Faber, London, 1997
D. Kanthank. "Peter Jackson Ausflug In Die Hobbit-Welt", *EPD Film*, 1, 2002
S. Kim. "Beyond Black and White: Race and Postmodernism in the *Lord of the Rings* Films", *Modern Fiction Studies*, 50, 4, 2004
A. Lee. *Tolkien's Ring*, Pavilion, London, 1999
W. Lee, ed. *Reference Guide to Fantastic Films*, 3 vols, Chelsea-Lee, 1972-74
U. Le Guin. *The Earthsea Quartet*, Penguin Books, London, 1993
C. Manlove. *Modern Fantasy*, Cambridge University Press, Cambridge, 1975
—. *From Alice to Harry Potter: Children's Fantasy in England*, Cybereditions Corporation, 2003
E. Mathijs, ed. *Lord of the Rings: Popular Culture In Global Context*, Wallflower Press, London, 2006
—. & M. Pomerance, eds. *From Hobbits To Hollywood: Essays on Lord of the Rings*, Editions Rodopi, New York, NY, 2006
C. McNew, in E. Challis, 2003
I. Nathan. "Battlefield Middle-earth", *Empire*, 151, Jan, 2002
—. "Peter Jackson", *Empire*, 175, Jan, 2004
A. Owen, ed. *Story and Character*, Bloomsbury, London, 2003
I. Pryor. *Peter Jackson*, St Martin's Press, New York, NY, 2004
T. Reeves. *The Worldwide Guide To Movie Locations*, Titan Books, London, 2003
Scoping the Lasting Effects of The Lord of the Rings, New Zealand Institute of Economic Research,

Wellington, NZ, 2002
T. Shippey. *The Road to Middle-earth*, Allen & Unwin, 1982
—. et al, eds. *Leaves From the Tree: J.R.R. Tolkien's Shorter Fiction*, 4th Tolkien Society Workshop, The Tolkien Society, London, 1991
—. ed. *Essays and Studies 1990: Fictional Space: Essays On Contemporary Science Fiction*, Oxford University Press, Oxford, 1991
—. *J.R.R. Tolkien: Author of the Century*, HarperCollins, London, 2000
T. Shone. *Blockbuster: How the Jaws and Jedi Generation Turned Hollywood Into a Boom-Town*, Scribner, London, 2005
R. Shorto. *J.R.R. Tolkien: Man of Fantasy*, Kipling Press, New York, NY, 1988
B. Sibley. *The Lord of the Rings: Official Movie Guide*, HarperCollins, London, 2001
A. Smol. ""Oh… Oh… Frodo!": Readings of Male Intimacy in *The Lord of the Rings*", *Modern Fiction Studies*, 50, 4, 2004
M. Stanton. *Hobbits, Elves and Wizards: Exploring the Wonders and Worlds of J.R.R. Tolkien's The Lord of the Rings*, Palgrave Macmillan, New York, NY, 2001
B. Strachey. *Journeys of Frodo: An Atlas of J.R.R. Tolkien's The Lord of the Rings*, Unwin Paperbacks, Allen & Unwin, London, 1981
K. Thompson. *Storytelling in the New Hollywood*, Harvard University Press, Cambridge, MA, 1999
—. "Fantasy, Franchises, and Frodo Baggins: *The Lord of the Rings* and Modern Hollywood", *Velvet Light Trap*, 52, Fall, 2003
J.E.A. Tyler. *The Tolkien Companion*, Gramercy, New York NY, 2000
M. White. *Tolkien: A Biography*, Abacus, London, 2002
G. Wright. *Peter Jackson In Perspective*, Hollywood Jesus Books, Washington, 2004
J. Zipes. *Breaking the Spell: Radical Theories of Folk and Fairy Tales*, Heinemann, London, 1978
—. *The Brothers Grimm: From Enchanted Forests to the Modern World*, Routledge, New York, NY, 1989
—. *Sticks and Stones: The Troublesome Success of Children's Literature From Slovenly Peter to Harry Potter*, Routledge, London, 2002

FILMOGRAPHY

This is a selective cast and credits list, with only some of the key supervisors and managers noted in each department (for instance, only the supervisors among the many visual effects houses). Some of the main doubles and scale doubles are included in *The Return of the King* credits. The lists include the theatrical and extended editions of the movies. Full lists are available elsewhere.

The Lord of the Rings: The Fellowship of the Ring (2001)

Release dates: U.S.A.: Dec 19, 2001. U.K.: Dec 10, 2001.

Length: Theatrical version: 178 min. Extended Edition: 208 min.

Directed by Peter Jackson
Written by Fran Walsh, Philippa Boyens and Peter Jackson
Barrie M. Osborne – producer
Peter Jackson – producer
Michael Lynne – executive producer: New Line Cinema
Robert Shaye – executive producer: New Line Cinema
Mark Ordesky – executive producer: New Line Cinema
Rick Porras – co-producer: WingNut Films
Tim Sanders – producer
Jamie Selkirk – co-producer: WingNut Films
Ellen Somers – associate producer
Fran Walsh – producer
Bob Weinstein – executive producer
Harvey Weinstein – executive producer

CAST

Alan Howard — The Ring (voice)
Elijah Wood – Frodo Baggins
Noel Appleby – Everard Proudfoot
Sean Astin – Samwise 'Sam' Gamgee
Sala Baker – Sauron
Sean Bean – Boromir
Orlando Bloom – Legolas Greenleaf
Billy Boyd – Peregrin 'Pippin' Took
Marton Csokas – Celeborn
Megan Edwards – Mrs. Proudfoot
Michael Elsworth – Gondorian Archivist
Mark Ferguson – Gil-Galad
Ian Holm – Bilbo Baggins
Christopher Lee – Saruman
Lawrence Makoare – Lurtz
Andy Serkis – Gollum/ Witch-King (voice)
Brent McIntyre – Witch-King
Ian McKellen – Gandalf the Grey
Peter McKenzie – Elendil
Sarah McLeod – Rose 'Rosie' Cotton
Dominic Monaghan – Meriadoc 'Merry' Brandybuck
Viggo Mortensen – Aragorn
Ian Mune – Bounder
Craig Parker – Haldir
Cameron Rhodes – Farmer Maggot
John Rhys-Davies – Gimli
Martyn Sanderson – Gate Keeper
Harry Sinclair – Isildur
Liv Tyler – Arwen
David Weatherley – Barliman Butterbur
Hugo Weaving – Elrond
Victoria Beynon-Cole – Hero Orcs/ Goblins/ Uruks/ Ringwraiths
Lee Hartley – Hero Orcs/ Goblins/ Uruks/

Ringwraiths
Sam La Hood – Hero Orcs/ Goblins/ Uruks/ Ringwraiths
Chris Streeter – Hero Orcs/ Goblins/ Uruks/ Ringwraiths
Philip Grieve – Hero Orcs/ Goblins/ Uruks/ Ringwraiths
Jonathan Jordan – Hero Orcs/ Goblins/ Uruks/ Ringwraiths
Semi Kuresa – Hero Orcs/ Goblins/ Uruks/ Ringwraiths
Clinton Ulyatt – Hero Orcs/ Goblins/ Uruks/ Ringwraiths
Paul Bryson – Hero Orcs/ Goblins/ Uruks/ Ringwraiths
Lance Fabian Kemp – Hero Orcs/ Goblins/ Uruks/ Ringwraiths
Jono Manks – Hero Orcs/ Goblins/ Uruks/ Ringwraiths
Ben Price – Hero Orcs/ Goblins/ Uruks/ Ringwraiths
Thomas McGinty – Hero Orcs/ Goblins/ Uruks/ Ringwraiths
Kate O'Rourke – Hero Orcs/ Goblins/ Uruks/ Ringwraiths
Billy Jackson – Cute Hobbit Child
Katie Jackson – Cute Hobbit Child
Peter Corrigan – Otho
Lori Dungey – Mrs. Bracegirdle
Norman Forsey – Gaffer Gamgee
Bill Johnson – Old Noakes
Elizabeth Moody – Lobelia Sackville-Baggins
Brian Sergent – Ted Sandyman
Timothy Bartlett – Hobbit
Jarl Benzon – Elf
Jørn Benzon – Rumil
Rachel Clentworth – Goblin
Sabine Crossen – Rivendell Elf
Taea Hartwell – Cute Hobbit Child
Peter Jackson – Albert Dreary
Alan Lee – King of Men – Prologue Sequence
Bret McKenzie – Elf at Council of Elrond
Leo McKern – Man smiling
Miranda Otto – Eowyn
Shane Rangi – Witch-King of Angmar

CREW

Original Music by Howard Shore
Cinematography by Andrew Lesnie
Film Editing by John Gilbert
Production Design by Grant Major
Art Direction by Joe Bleakley, Dan Hennah, Philip Ivey, Rob Outter-side, Mark Robins
Set Decoration by Dan Hennah, Alan Lee
Costume Design by Ngila Dickson, Richard Taylor
Peter King – hair designer/ makeup designer
Angela Mooar – coordinator: makeup assistants
Peter Owen – hair designer/ makeup designer
José Luis Pérez – key hair stylist
Richard Taylor – special makeup, creatures, armour and miniatures
Caroline Turner – wig technician
Gail Wilson – hair coordinator/ makeup coordinator
Carolyn M. Fenton – wardrobe supervisor
Bridget Bourke – production manager: 2nd unit
Rosemary Dority – post-production supervisor
Carla Fry – executive in charge of production
Carol Kim – production manager: 2nd unit
Nikolas Korda – unit production manager
Zane Weiner – unit production manager
Jonas Thaler – post-production supervisor
Marc Ashton – 2nd assistant director
Richard A. Barker – 1st assistant director: 2nd unit
Guy Campbell – key 2nd assistant director
Emma Cross – 2nd assistant director: 2nd unit
Carolynne Cunningham – 1st assistant director
Louise Harness – key 2nd assistant director: 2nd unit
John Mahaffie – 2nd unit director
Richard Matthews – 3rd assistant director
Ian Mune – additional 2nd unit director
Dave Norris – 1st assistant director: 2nd unit
Guy Norris – additional 2nd unit director
Liz Tan – 1st assistant director: 2nd unit
Simon Warnock – 1st assistant director: 2nd unit
Barrie M. Osborne – additional 2nd unit director
Rick Porras – additional 2nd unit director
Edith Thompson – additional 2nd assistant director: 2nd unit
Fran Walsh – additional 2nd unit director
Stephanie Weststrate – additional 2nd assistant director: 2nd unit
Tim Abbot – props maker

Gareth Jensen – props designer
Brian Massey – greensmaster
Ed Mulholand – construction supervisor
Brent Burge – sound effects editor
David Farmer – sound designer
Mike Hopkins – supervising sound editor
John McKay – sound effects editor
Timothy Nielsen – sound effects editor
Ethan Van der Ryn – supervising sound co-designer
Ray Beentjes – sound editor
Gino Acevedo – prosthetics supervisor: Weta Workshop
Sue Hardy – production manager: Weta Workshop
Peter Lyon – sword smith: Weta Workshop
Richard Taylor – supervisor: special makeup, creatures, armour and miniatures
Matt Aitken – digital models supervisor: Weta Digital
Nancy Bernstein – visual effects executive producer: Digital Domain
Andrew Calder – senior animator: Weta Digital
Randall William Cook – animation designer: Weta Digital
Steve Demers – look supervisor: Weta Digital
Geoff Dixon – visual effects supervisor: Oktobor
Peter Doyle – supervising digital colourist: The PostHoust AG
Yannick 'Botex' Dusseault – senior matte painter: Weta Digital
Mark O. Forker – visual effects supervisor: Digital Domain
Chris Godfrey – digital effects supervisor: Animal Logic
Wayne John Haag – senior matte painter: Weta Digital
Matt Holmes – visual effects editor: Weta Digital
Steven Hornby – senior animator: Weta Digital
Gray Horsfield – conceptual digital visualization: Weta Digital
François Laroche – motion capture supervisor: Weta Digital
Paul Lasaine – visual effects art director
Kelly L'Estrange – visual effects producer: Digital Domain
Matt Logue – senior animator: Weta Digital
Dean Lyon – visual effects supervisor: Oktobor
Richard Mahon – matte painter: Weta Digital
Charlie McClellan – visual effects producer
Sarah McLauchlan – visual effects coordinator
Chad Moffitt – senior animator: Weta Digital
Eileen Moran – visual effects producer: Weta Digital
Gerard Benjamin Pierre – on-set digital effects supervisor: Weta Digital
Darren Poe – compositing supervisor: Digital Domain
Murray Pope – visual effects executive producer: Animal Logic
Kelly Port – digital effects supervisor: Digital Domain
Christian Rivers – visual effects art director: Weta Digital
Carlos M. Rosas – senior animator: Weta Digital
Jim Rygiel – visual effects supervisor
Eric Saindon – creatures supervisor: Weta Digital
John Sheils – digital effects supervisor: preproduction, Weta Digital
Mike Stevens – senior animator: Weta Digital
Adam Valdez – animation supervisor: Weta Digital
Brian Van't Hul – visual effects cinematographer: Weta Digital
Alice Capper-Starr – stunt coordinator: sword master
Casey O'Neill – stunt coordinator: horse
George Marshall Ruge – stunt coordinator
Greg Powell – stunt coordinator
Brian Bansgrove – supervising chief lighting technician
Nigel Bluck – director of photography: 2nd unit
Richard Bluck – director of photography: 2nd unit
John Cavill – director of photography: 2nd unit
Alun Bollinger – director of photography: 2nd unit
Allen Guilford – director of photography: 2nd unit
Phil Pastuhov – director of photography: aerial unit
Simon Raby – director of photography: 2nd unit
Nicola Benton – casting assistant
Victoria Burrows – casting: USA
Sian Clement – casting coordinator: New Zealand
Amanda Duncan – casting office manager
Amy Hubbard – casting: UK
John Hubbard – casting: UK
Cynthia Morahan – casting coordinator: New Zealand
Liz Mullane – casting: New Zealand
Ann Robinson – casting: Australia
Jody Levin – executive in charge of post-production
Jabez Olssen – assistant editor
Jo Priest – assistant editor
Jamie Selkirk – supervising editor
Peter Skarratt – 1st assistant editor

Heather Small – assistant editor
Nancy Allen – music editor
Paul Broucek – executive in charge of music
Peter Cobbin – scoring mixer
Ruth Cornes – music contractor
Terry Edwards – choir master
Igelese Ete – choir master
Mabel Faletolu – featured vocalist
Isobel Griffiths – music contractor
The London Oratory School Schola – musicians: boys choir
Howard Shore – conductor/ orchestrator
Michael Tremante – associate music producer
Ravi Dube – transportation manager
Jane Abbott – riding double
Bob Anderson – sword master
Melissa Booth – assistant publicist
Kristie Breslin – production coordinator
Roisin Carty – dialect coach
Praphaphorn 'Fon' Chansantor – stand-in
David Comer – location scout
Matthew Dravitzki – travel and accommodation coordinator
Carla Gammons – horse wrangler
Andrew Jack – supervising dialect coach
Dave Johnson – head animal wrangler
Bhoja 'BK' Kannada – double
Shona McCullagh – choreographer
Dianne Moffatt – script supervisor
David Nuku – physical trainer
Steve Old – horse coordinator
Pat Robins – script supervisor
Christopher Rutten – horse wrangler
David Salo – translator: Tolkien language
Kiran Shah – double
Oksana Sokol – script supervisor
Victoria Sullivan – script supervisor
Peter Tonks – location manager
Aubrey Tredget – production coordinator
Helen Young – riding instructor
Brett Beattie – scale double: Gimli
Paula Jack – dialogue advisor
Bhoja 'BK' Kannada – scale double: Frodo and Sam
Paul Randall – scale double

The Lord of the Rings: The Two Towers (2002)

Release dates: U.S.A.: Dec 18, 2002. U.K.: Dec 18, 2002.

Length: Theatrical version: 179 min. Extended Edition: 223 min.

Directed by Peter Jackson
Written by Fran Walsh, Philippa Boyens, Stephen Sinclair and Peter Jackson
Barrie M. Osborne – producer
Michael Lynne – executive producer
Mark Ordesky – executive producer
Peter Jackson – producer
Rick Porras – co-producer
Jamie Selkirk – co-producer
Robert Shaye – executive producer
Fran Walsh – producer
Bob Weinstein – executive producer
Harvey Weinstein – executive producer

CAST

Bruce Allpress – Aldor
Sean Astin – Samwise 'Sam' Gamgee
John Bach – Madril
Sala Baker – Man Flesh Uruk
Cate Blanchett – Galadriel
Orlando Bloom – Legolas Greenleaf
Billy Boyd – Peregrin 'Pippin' Took
Jed Brophy – Sharku / Snaga
Sam Comery – Éothain
Brad Dourif – Grima Wormtongue
Calum Gittins – Haleth
Bernard Hill – Theoden
Bruce Hopkins – Gamling
Paris Howe Strewe – Théodred – Prince of Rohan
Christopher Lee – Saruman the White
Nathaniel Lees – Uglúk
John Leigh – Háma
Robbie Magasiva – Mauhur
Robyn Malcolm – Morwen
Ian McKellen – Gandalf
Dominic Monaghan – Meriadoc 'Merry' Brandybuck
Viggo Mortensen – Aragorn
Miranda Otto – Eowyn
Craig Parker – Haldir
Bruce Phillips – Rohan Soldier
Robert Pollock – Mordor Orc
John Rhys-Davies – Gimli / Voice of Treebeard

Andy Serkis – Gollum
Olivia Tennet – Freda
Ray Trickett – Bereg
Liv Tyler – Arwen
Karl Urban – Eomer
Stephen Ure – Grishnákh
Hugo Weaving – Elrond
David Wenham – Faramir
Elijah Wood – Frodo Baggins
Victoria Beynon-Cole – Hero Orc
Lee Hartley – Hero Orc
Philip Grieve – Hero Orc
Billy Jackson – Cute Rohan Refugee Child
Katie Jackson – Cute Rohan Refugee Child
Sean Bean – Boromir
John Noble – Denethor
Jarl Benzon – Elf
Jørn Benzon – Elf Archer
Karlos Drinkwater – Easterling Warrior
Daniel Falconer – Elvin Warrior
Phillip Spencer Harris – Ranger 1
Dan Hennah – Man of Rohan
Paul Holmes – Orc
Peter Jackson – Rohirrim Warrior
Sandro Kopp – Elf
Alan Lee – Man of Rohan
Timothy Lee – Wildman
Joseph Mika-Hunt – Uruk-Hai
Henry Mortensen – Reluctant Rohan Child Warrior
Paul Norell – Easterling
Barrie M. Osborne – Rohirrim Soldier
Marcus Thorne – Featured Orc
Piripi Waretini – Uruk-Hai Soldier
Hannah Wood – Woman in Cave

CREW

Original Music by Howard Shore
Cinematography by Andrew Lesnie
Film Editing by Michael Horton
Production Design by Grant Major
Art Direction by Joe Bleakley, Dan Hennah, Philip Ivey, Rob Outterside, Mark Robins
Set Decoration by Dan Hennah, Alan Lee
Costume Design by Ngila Dickson, Richard Taylor
Peter King – hair designer
Peter Owen – hair designer
Peter Owen – makeup designer
José Luis Pérez – key hair stylist/ key makeup artist
Richard Taylor – special makeup effects artist
Bridget Bourke – production manager: 2nd unit
Rosemary Dority – post-production supervisor
Carla Fry – executive in charge of production
Fiona Fry – post-production supervisor
Erik Holmberg – executive in charge of production
Carol Kim – production manager: 2nd unit
Nikolas Korda – unit production manager
Kevin Magill – unit manager
Peta Sinclair – unit manager
Fridtjof Stechmann – production manager
Jonas Thaler – post-production supervisor
Mike Turner – unit manager
Zane Weiner – unit production manager
Marc Ashton – 2nd assistant director
Richard A. Barker – 1st assistant director: 2nd unit
Guy Campbell – key 2nd assistant director
Carolynne Cunningham – 1st assistant director
Zo Hartley – 3rd assistant director
Belindalee Hope – 2nd assistant director
Eric Houghton – 3rd assistant director
Chris Husson – 3rd assistant director
John Mahaffie – 2nd unit director
Geoff Murphy – 2nd unit director
Rick Porras – additional unit director
Liz Tan – 1st assistant director: 2nd unit
Guy Norris – 2nd unit director
Ed Mulholand – construction supervisor
Richard Taylor – supervisor: Weta Workshop
Brent Burge – sound effects editor
Jason Canovas – dialogue editor
Hayden Collow – sound effects editor
Kyrsten Mate Comoglio – sound effects editor
David Farmer – sound designer
Mark Franken – dialogue editor
Mike Hopkins – supervising sound editor
Craig Tomlinson – sound effects editor
Dave Whitehead – sound effects editor
Fabian Sanjurjo – sound effects editor
Gino Acevedo – prosthetics supervisor: Weta Workshop
Jason Docherty – workshop supervisor: Weta Workshop
Marjory Hamlin – prosthetics supervisor: Weta Workshop
Steve Ingram – physical effects supervisor
Kym Sainsbury – prosthetics supervisor: Weta Workshop
Dominie Till – prosthetics supervisor: Weta Workshop
Matt Aitken – digital models supervisor: Weta Digital
Jon Allitt – massive crowd supervisor: Weta Digital
Richard Baneham – animation supervisor: Weta Digital
Jim Berney – visual effects supervisor: SPI
Brad Booker – senior animator: Weta Digital
Nick Booth – scanning and recording

supervisor: Weta Digital
Randall William Cook – animation supervisor/designer: Weta Digital
Peter Doyle – supervising digital colourist
Nika Dunne – digital paint/roto supervisor: Weta Digital
Joe Letteri – visual effects supervisor: Weta Digital
Dean Lyon – visual effects supervisor: Oktobor Films
John P. Nugent – 2D supervisor: Weta Digital
Christian Rivers – pre-visualization supervisor
Jim Rygiel – visual effects supervisor
Eric Saindon – creatures supervisor: Weta Digital
Remington Scott – motion capture supervisor: Weta Digital
John Sheils – digital effects supervisor research and development: preproduction, Weta Digital
Kevin L. Sherwood – post-production coordinator: Weta Digital
Daniel W. Barringer – assistant stunt coordinator
Casey O'Neill – horse stunt coordinator
George Marshall Ruge – stunt coordinator
Brian Bansgrove – supervising chief lighting technician
Nigel Bluck – director of photography: 2nd unit
Richard Bluck – director of photography: 2nd unit
Alun Bollinger – director of photography: 2nd unit
John Cavill – director of photography: 2nd unit
Victoria Burrows – casting: USA
Amanda Duncan – casting office manager
Amy Hubbard – casting: UK
John Hubbard – casting: UK
Cynthia Morahan – casting coordinator: New Zealand
Liz Mullane – casting: New Zealand
Ann Robinson – casting: Australia
Carolyn M. Fenton – wardrobe supervisor
Liz McGregor – wardrobe coordinator
Matt Diezel – assistant editor
Megan Doneman – assistant editor
Mark Hawthorne – assistant editor
Jody Levin – executive in charge of post-production
Jabez Olssen – additional editor
Michelle Robertson – editorial production assistant
Jamie Selkirk – supervising editor
Peter Skarratt – 1st assistant editor
Brett Skinner – assistant editor
Loren Squires – assistant editor
Paul Broucek – executive in charge of music

Peter Cobbin – score mixer
David Donaldson – music designer
Andrew Dudman – music editor
Terry Edwards – choir master
Karen Elliott – music production coordinator: London
Malcolm Fife – music editor
Rebecca Gatrell – music editor
The London Oratory School Schola – musicians: boys choir
David Long – music designer
Michael McCarthy – choir master
Raphaël Mouterde – music editor
Michael Price – music editor
Steven Price – music editor (as Steve Price)
James Rhodes – additional music crew
Steve Roche – music designer
Janet Roddick – music designer
Jonathan Schultz – music editor
Nigel Scott – music editor
Howard Shore – conductor/ orchestrator
Mark Willsher – music editor
Toby Wood – additional music crew
Ravi Dube – transportation manager
Jane Abbott – riding double
Bob Anderson – sword master
Melissa Booth – assistant publicist
Praphaphorn 'Fon' Chansantor – double
Matthew Dravitzki – travel and accommodation coordinator
Carla Gammons – horse wrangler
Vance Hartwell – puppeteer
Dave Johnson – head animal wrangler
Mark Kinaston-Smith – wrangler
Andrew Matthews – executive in charge of film investment
Dianne Moffatt – script supervisor
Robin Murphy – supervising location manager
Steve Old – horse wrangler
Leslie Oliver – publicist: Weta Digital
Pat Robins – script supervisor
Merrin Ruck – script supervisor: miniature unit
David Salo – translator: Tolkien language
Kiran Shah – double
Victoria Sullivan – script supervisor
Harry Whitehurst – location manager
Tony Woolf – consultant: cultural fighting styles
Paula Jack – dialogue advisor

The Lord of the Rings: The Return of the King (2003)

Release dates: U.S.A.: Dec 17, 2003. U.K.: Dec 17, 2003.

Length: Theatrical version: 200 min. Extended Edition: 250 min.

Directed by Peter Jackson
Written by Fran Walsh, Philippa Boyens and Peter Jackson
Barrie M. Osborne – producer
Michael Lynne – executive producer
Mark Ordesky – executive producer
Peter Jackson – producer
Rick Porras – co-producer
Jamie Selkirk – co-producer
Robert Shaye – executive producer
Fran Walsh – producer
Bob Weinstein – executive producer
Harvey Weinstein – executive producer

CAST

Noel Appleby – Everard Proudfoot
Alexandra Astin – Elanor Gamgee
Sean Astin – Sam
David Aston – Gondorian Soldier 3
John Bach – Madril
Sean Bean – Boromir
Cate Blanchett – Galadriel
Orlando Bloom – Legolas
Billy Boyd – Pippin
Sadwyn Brophy – Eldarion
Alistair Browning – Damrod
Marton Csokas – Celeborn
Richard Edge – Gondorian Soldier 1
Jason Fitch – Uruk 2
Bernard Hill – Theoden
Ian Holm – Bilbo
Bruce Hopkins – Gamling
Ian Hughes – Irolas
Lawrence Makoare – Witchking / Gothmog
Ian McKellen – Gandalf
Bret McKenzie – Elf Escort
Sarah McLeod – Rosie Cotton
Maisy McLeod-Riera – Baby Gamgee
Dominic Monaghan – Merry
Viggo Mortensen – Aragorn
John Noble – Denethor
Paul Norell – King of the Dead
Miranda Otto – Eowyn
Bruce Phillips – Grimbold
Shane Rangi – Harad Leader 2
John Rhys-Davies – Gimli
Todd Rippon – Harad Leader 1
Thomas Robins – Deagol
Andy Serkis – Gollum / Smeagol
Harry Sinclair – Isildur
Peter Tait – Shagrat
Joel Tobeck – Orc Lieutenant 1
Liv Tyler – Arwen
Karl Urban – Eomer
Stephen Ure – Gorbag
Hugo Weaving – Elrond
David Wenham – Faramir
Elijah Wood – Frodo
Alan Howard – The Ring (voice)
Sala Baker – Orc / Sauron
Robert Pollock – Orc
Ross Duncan – Orc
Pete Smith – Orc
Jed Brophy – Orc
Lee Hartley – Orc
Billy Jackson – Child
Brad Dourif – Grima Wormtongue
Christopher Lee – Saruman
Bruce Spence – The Mouth of Sauron
Jørn Benzon – Traveling Elf / Various
Peter Jackson – Mercenary On Boat
Royd Tolkien – Ranger

CREW

Original Music by Howard Shore
Cinematography by Andrew Lesnie
Film Editing by Jamie Selkirk
Production Design by Grant Major
Art Direction by Joe Bleakley, Simon Bright, Dan Hennah, Philip Ivey, Mark Robins
Set Decoration by Dan Hennah, Alan Lee
Costume Design by Ngila Dickson, Richard Taylor
Vance Hartwell – special makeup effects artist
Peter King – hair designer
Peter Owen – hair designer
José Luis Pérez – key hair stylist/ key makeup artist
Richard Taylor – special makeup effects artist
Carolyn M. Fenton – wardrobe supervisor
Bridget Bourke – production manager
Rosemary Dority – post-production supervisor
Carla Fry – executive in charge of production
Erik Holmberg – executive in charge of production
Nikolas Korda – unit production manager
Jonas Thaler – post-production supervisor
John Mahaffie – 2nd unit director
Geoff Murphy – 2nd unit director

Rick Porras – additional unit director
Dean Wright – 2nd unit director
Guy Norris – 2nd unit director
Jim Rygiel – 2nd unit director
Richard Taylor – supervisor: Weta Workshop
Mike Hopkins – supervising sound editor
Ethan Van der Ryn – supervising sound co-designer
Gino Acevedo – prosthetics supervisor: Weta Workshop
Jason Docherty – workshop supervisor: Weta Workshop
Marjory Hamlin – prosthetics supervisor: Weta Workshop
John Harvey – armour weapons supervisor: Weta Workshop
Steve Ingram – physical effects supervisor
Gary Mackay – armour weapons supervisor: Weta Workshop
Kym Sainsbury – prosthetics supervisor: Weta Workshop
Dominie Till – prosthetics supervisor: Weta Workshop
Richard Taylor – workshop supervisor: Weta Workshop
Matt Aitken – models supervisor: Weta Digital
Jon Allitt – Massive supervisor: Weta Digital
Richard Baneham – animation supervisor: Weta Digital
David Bawel – motion capture supervisor: Weta Digital
Nick Booth – scan/ record supervisor: Weta Digital
Greg Butler – 3D sequence supervisor: Weta Digital
Hannah Clarke – publicity coordinator: Weta Digital
Randy Cook – animation designer and supervisor: Weta Digital
Tim Crosbie – digital effects supervisor: Rising Sun Pictures
Marion Davey – visual effects coordinator
Peter Doyle – supervising digital colourist
Theresa Ellis – 3D supervisor: Weta Digital
Jim Hourihan – C4 coding supervisor: Tweak Films
Sandy Houston – paint/ roto supervisor: Weta Digital
Bret Hughes – pipeline engineer supervisor: Weta Digital
Alex Lemke – 2D sequence supervisor: Weta Digital
Dan Lemmon – 3D sequence supervisor: Weta Digital
Joe Letteri – visual effects supervisor: Weta Digital
Mark Tait Lewis – 2D sequence supervisor: Weta Digital
Dean Lyon – visual effects supervisor: Oktobor Films
John P. Nugent – visual effects supervisor: Sandbox Pictures
Dana Peters – creature supervisor: Weta Digital
Jim Rygiel – visual effects supervisor
Eric Saindon – 3D sequence supervisor: Weta Digital
Nelson Sepulveda – 2D supervisor: Weta Digital
John Sheils – digital effects supervisor research and development: preproduction, Weta Digital
Nicholas Titmarsh – digital effects supervisor: Rhythm & Hues
Guy Williams – 3D sequence supervisor: Weta Digital
Pete Williams – digital imaging supervisor: Weta Digital
Daniel W. Barringer – assistant stunt coordinator
Augie Davis – assistant stunt coordinator: New Zealand
Kirk Maxwell – stunt coordinator: New Zealand
George Marshall Ruge – stunt coordinator
Brian Bansgrove – supervising chief lighting technician
David Brown – supervising chief lighting technician
John Cavill – director of photography: 2nd unit
Victoria Burrows – casting: USA
Amanda Duncan – casting office manager
Amy Hubbard – casting: UK
John Hubbard – casting: UK
Cynthia Morahan – casting coordinator: New Zealand
Liz Mullane – casting: New Zealand
Carolyn M. Fenton – wardrobe supervisor
Liz McGregor – wardrobe coordinator
Silvana Sacco – costume breakdown supervisor/ costume illustrator
David Birrell – assistant editor
Annie Collins – additional editor
Megan Doneman – assistant editor
Mark Hawthorne – assistant editor
Jody Levin – executive in charge of post-production
Steve Pang – assistant editor
Lynne Reed – color timer
Peter Skarratt – first assistant editor
Brett Skinner – assistant editor
Jonathan Woodford-Robinson – assistant editor
Paul Broucek – executive in charge of music
Peter Cobbin – score mixer
David Donaldson – music designer
Andrew Dudman – music editor
Marie Ebbing – music editor

Terry Edwards – choir master
Karen Elliott – music production coordinator
Malcolm Fife – music editor
Rebecca Gatrell – music editor
Simon Kiln – music editor
The London Oratory School Schola – musicians: boys choir
David Long – music designer
Michael McCarthy – choir master
Charles Portney – music production coordinator
Michael Price – music editor
Steven Price – music editor
Steve Roche – music designer
Janet Roddick – music designer
Jonathan Schultz – music editor
Nigel Scott – music editor
Howard Shore – conductor and orchestrator
Paul Kegg – musician: cello
Renée Fleming – featured soloist
Sissel Kyrkjebø – featured soloist
Frank Welker – special vocal effects
Ravi Dube – transportation manager
Jane Abbott – riding double
Bob Anderson – sword master
Dave Andrews – wrangler
Jarl Benzon – double
Mark Bowden – character voices
Tom George – character voices
Linda Cartwright – dialect coach
Roisin Carty – key dialect coach
Suzanne Celeste – dialect coach
Kristie Breslin – production coordinator
Jenny Carter – wrangler
Praphaphorn 'Fon' Chansantor – double
David Comer – location scout
Jared Connon – location manager
Robyn Dunmore – wrangler
Deborah Fox – legal counsel: New Zealand
Jo Friesan – coordinator (as Jo Friesen)
Dominique Fromont – accounting assistant
Jason Frost-Evans – riding double (as Jay Frost Evans)
James Galway – featured soloist (as Sir James Galway)
Carla Gammons – rider
Carla Gammons – wrangler
Richard Gardner – riding double
Narretta Gascoigne – unit assistant
Marcus Gaylor – rider
Marcus Gaylor – wrangler
Jenny Gibbons – wrangler
Vance Hartwell – puppeteer
Veronique Lawrence – script supervisor
Rochelle Mabey – wrangler
Hamish Matheson – double
Brian Hotter – double
Andrew Matthews – executive in charge of film investment
Ann McCaw – rider
Kerrie Morgan – rider
Robbie Miller – riding instructor
Robin Murphy – supervising location manager
Steve Old – horse coordinator
Joel Tobeck – character voices
4Con O'Neill – character voices
Craig Parker – character voices
Brian Sergent – character voices
Anthony May – character voices
David Salo – linguist: Tolkien
Sam Orbell – rider
John Osborne – rider
Paul Randall – double
Paul 'Sled' Reynolds – animal coordinator
Paulina Saxton – rider
John Scott – horse wrangler
Kiran Shah – double
Christopher Rutten – rider
Richard Sharkey – supervising unit location manager
Peter Tonks – location manager
Oksana Sokol – script supervisor
Catarina Strom – rider
Patrick Thomas – rider
Cowan Wards – rider
Jenny Wards – rider
Graham Ware Jr. – horse trainer
Jasmine Watson – jeweller
Gary Wells – rider
Harry Whitehurst – location manager
Alicia Williams – location coordinator
Tony Woolf – consultant: cultural fighting styles
Helen Young – riding instructor
Paula Jack – dialogue advisor

THE *LORD OF THE RINGS* MOVIES   437

ARTS, PAINTING, SCULPTURE

The Art of Andy Goldsworthy: Complete Works
Andy Goldsworthy: Touching Nature
Andy Goldsworthy in Close-Up
Andy Goldsworthy: Pocket Guide
Andy Goldsworthy In America
Land Art: A Complete Guide
Richard Long: The Art of Walking
The Art of Richard Long: Complete Works
Richard Long in Close-Up
Richard Long: Pocket Guide
Land Art In the UK
Land Art in Close-Up
Land Art In the U.S.A.
Land Art: Pocket Guide
Installation Art in Close-Up
Minimal Art and Artists In the 1960s and After
Colourfield Painting
Land Art DVD, TV documentary
Andy Goldsworthy DVD, TV documentary
The Erotic Object: Sexuality in Sculpture From Prehistory to the Present Day
Sex in Art: Pornography and Pleasure in Painting and Sculpture
Postwar Art
Sacred Gardens: The Garden in Myth, Religion and Art
Glorification: Religious Abstraction in Renaissance and 20th Century Art
Early Netherlandish Painting
Leonardo da Vinci
Piero della Francesca
Giovanni Bellini
Fra Angelico: Art and Religion in the Renaissance
Mark Rothko: The Art of Transcendence
Frank Stella: American Abstract Artist
Jasper Johns
Brice Marden
Alison Wilding: The Embrace of Sculpture
Vincent van Gogh: Visionary Landscapes
Eric Gill: Nuptials of God
Constantin Brancusi: Sculpting the Essence of Things
Max Beckmann
Gustave Moreau
Caravaggio
Egon Schiele: Sex and Death In Purple Stockings
Delizioso Fotografico Fervore: Works In Process 1
Sacro Cuore: Works In Process 2
The Light Eternal: J.M.W. Turner
The Madonna Glorified: Karen Arthurs

LITERATURE

J.R.R. Tolkien: The Books, The Films, The Whole Cultural Phenomenon
J.R.R. Tolkien: Pocket Guide
Beauties, Beasts and Enchantment: Classic French Fairy Tales
Tolkien's Heroic Quest
Sexing Hardy: Thomas Hardy and Feminism
Thomas Hardy's *Tess of the d'Urbervilles*
Thomas Hardy's *Jude the Obscure*
Thomas Hardy: The Tragic Novels
Love and Tragedy: Thomas Hardy
The Poetry of Landscape in Hardy
Wessex Revisited: Thomas Hardy and John Cowper Powys
Wolfgang Iser: Essays and Interviews
Petrarch, Dante and the Troubadours
Maurice Sendak and the Art of Children's Book Illustration
Andrea Dworkin
Cixous, Irigaray, Kristeva: The *Jouissance* of French Feminism
Julia Kristeva: Art, Love, Melancholy, Philosophy, Semiotics and Psychoanalysis
Hélene Cixous I Love You: The *Jouissance* of Writing
Luce Irigaray: Lips, Kissing, and the Politics of Sexual Difference
Peter Redgrove: Here Comes the Flood
Peter Redgrove: Sex-Magic-Poetry-Cornwall
Lawrence Durrell: Between Love and Death, East and West
Love, Culture & Poetry: Lawrence Durrell
Cavafy: Anatomy of a Soul
German Romantic Poetry: Goethe, Novalis, Heine, Hölderlin
Novalis: *Hymns To the Night*
Feminism and Shakespeare
Shakespeare: *The Sonnets*
Shakespeare: Love, Poetry & Magic
The Passion of D.H. Lawrence
D.H. Lawrence: Symbolic Landscapes
D.H. Lawrence: Infinite Sensual Violence
Rimbaud: Arthur Rimbaud and the Magic of Poetry
The Ecstasies of John Cowper Powys
Sensualism and Mythology: The Wessex Novels of John Cowper Powys
Amorous Life: John Cowper Powys and the Manifestation of Affectivity (H.W. Fawkner
Postmodern Powys: New Essays on John Cowper Powys (Joe Boulter)
Rethinking Powys: Critical Essays on John Cowper Powys
Paul Bowles & Bernardo Bertolucci
Rainer Maria Rilke
Joseph Conrad: *Heart of Darkness*
In the Dim Void: Samuel Beckett
Samuel Beckett Goes into the Silence
André Gide: Fiction and Fervour
Jackie Collins and the Blockbuster Novel
Blinded By Her Light: The Love-Poetry of Robert Graves
The Passion of Colours: Travels In Mediterranean Lands
Poetic Forms

MEDIA, CINEMA, FEMINISM and CULTURAL STUDIES

J.R.R. Tolkien: The Books, The Films, The Whole Cultural Phenomenon
J.R.R. Tolkien: Pocket Guide
The *Lord of the Rings* Movies: Pocket Guide
The Ghost Dance: The Origins of Religion
Cixous, Irigaray, Kristeva: The *Jouissance* of French Feminism
Julia Kristeva: Art, Love, Melancholy, Philosophy, Semiotics and Psychoanalysis
Luce Irigaray: Lips, Kissing, and the Politics of Sexual Difference
Hélene Cixous I Love You: The *Jouissance* of Writing
Andrea Dworkin
'Cosmo Woman': The World of Women's Magazines
Women in Pop Music
Discovering the Goddess (Geoffrey Ashe)
The Poetry of Cinema
The Sacred Cinema of Andrei Tarkovsky
Andrei Tarkovsky: Pocket Guide
Andrei Tarkovsky: *Mirror*: Pocket Movie Guide
Andrei Tarkovsky: *The Sacrifice*: Pocket Movie Guide
Walerian Borowczyk: Cinema of Erotic Dreams
Jean-Luc Godard: The Passion of Cinema
Jean-Luc Godard: Pocket Guide
John Hughes and Eighties Cinema
Ferris Buller's Day Off: Pocket Movie Guide
The Cinema of Richard Linklater
Liv Tyler: Star In Ascendance
Blade Runner and the Films of Philip K. Dick
Paul Bowles and Bernardo Bertolucci
Media Hell: Radio, TV and the Press
An Open Letter to the BBC
Detonation Britain: Nuclear War in the UK
Feminism and Shakespeare
Wild Zones: Pornography, Art and Feminism
Sex in Art: Pornography and Pleasure in Painting and Sculpture
Sexing Hardy: Thomas Hardy and Feminism

In my view *The Light Eternal* is among the very best of all the material I read on Turner. (Douglas Graham, director of the Turner Museum, Denver, Colorado)

The Light Eternal is a model monograph, an exemplary job. The subject matter of the book is beautifully organised and dead on beam. (Lawrence Durrell)

It is amazing for me to see my work treated with such passion and respect. (Andrea Dworkin)

Sex-Magic-Poetry-Cornwall is a very rich essay... It is like a brightly-lighted box. (Peter Redgrove)

CRESCENT MOON PUBLISHING P.O. Box 393, Maidstone, Kent, ME14 5XU, England
0044-1622-729593   cresmopub@yahoo.co.uk   www.crescentmoon.org.uk

Lightning Source UK Ltd.
Milton Keynes UK
UKOW051914120612

194307UK00001B/1/P

9 781861 712790